THE OLD
HOMESTEAD

THE OLD HOMESTEAD

STEELE RUDD

University of Queensland Press

Published 1984 by University of Queensland Press
Box 42, St Lucia, Queensland, Australia
Reprinted 1993, 1994, 1995.

Compilation © University of Queensland Press 1984

Printed in Australia by McPherson's Printing Group, Victoria

Cataloguing in Publication Data
National Library of Australia

Rudd, Steele, 1868-1935.
  The old homestead.

  I. Title.

A823'.2

ISBN 0 7022 1806 5

Contents

Foreword

Steele Rudd's pictures of farming life, certainly his best-known creations, contain a robust, even defiant humour, which has preserved them to this day. Both country folk and townsfolk enjoyed these sketches, and they sold enormously well. But underneath the humour there was, as well as a gritty determination, something else that is generally not so evident and has not been much noticed. And that is a sort of unpleasantness.

In the book *The Old Homestead*, which provides the title for this volume, is a family as clumsy, ignorant, and inept as could be imagined. Nobody can perform a simple multiplication — perhaps not even an addition. They cannot tell the time from a watch, and often quarrel furiously. As in earlier tales, one small accident can lead to an escalating sequence, so that fire and destruction ensue. They are jealous, deceitful, and callous; the cripple, for instance, is nicknamed Limpy.

Almost as if emphasizing this oafishness by contrast, Rudd wrote *The Romance of Runnibede*, a novel in which the family are well-to-do — they are squatters with a cattle station of 100,000 acres. They are literate, tolerant (they treat the Aborigines humanely, for instance), they help others (or rather other squatters), and they pursue some of the time-honoured practices of the great open spaces such as rounding up wild horses and breaking them in. They do not refer to their father as Dad but as the Governor. The title itself is relevant, for it is unthinkable that any of Rudd's farm volumes should be thought "romantic" in any sense. But in these spacious acres some of the old themes of early Australian fiction recur.

The last book Rudd wrote is a return to his beginnings, a farm novel, *Green Grey Homestead*. With a rather blander background, a more sober style, fewer bursts of accidents, less explosive laughter, it is nevertheless an extreme — the reverse of the mirror. Here the family is prosperous — polo players, no less, make an appearance. The farmers herd wild cattle, they hunt wild pigs. There is even a bush picnic.

These last two books, *The Romance of Runnibede* and *Green Grey Homestead*, give Rudd's most benign accounts of the outback, of squatters and selectors. They are reversals of a trend. And they are novels, not collections of short stories. Perhaps like Lawson he felt that a writer of fiction was expected to produce a novel or two. He need not have worried; for Rudd remains perhaps our best-known verbal caricaturist.

CECIL HADGRAFT
UNIVERSITY OF QUEENSLAND

In Australia

Introduction to *The University of Queensland Press Edition*

In 1907 Steele Rudd took his family to Sydney to extend the activities of *Steele Rudd's Magazine*; but, although it had become one of the leading monthlies of its day,.the venture was not as successful as anticipated and the *Magazine* went out of publication.

In 1908 the Rudds returned to Greenmount on the Darling Downs. Greenmount was a small township, only six miles from Emu Creek, the place where Steele Rudd's father, Thomas Davis, had settled in the 1870's; here he had built "Shingle Hut", which figures prominently in Rudd's first famous book, *On Our Selection*.

Pleased to be back in his native area, Rudd wrote *In Australia* that same year and, living first at Greenmount and then at "The Firs" at Nobbey, only seven miles away, wrote many books and two plays between 1908 and 1917.

ERIC DAVIS
BRISBANE
NOVEMBER 1968

1. *Past and Present*

It was the last days of the great land monopolists of South Queensland. The squatters and their vast sheep herds were raipdly disappearing. The great rolling, grassy plains of the Darling Downs, which, from the earliest days of the colony's history, had been conserved as sheep walks, were gradually being acquired by progressive and democratic Governments, and sold in small holdings to the farmer.

A hundred homesteads in full swing, their green wheat-fields, their hay-sheds, their dairy herds, dotted over the verdant expanses of plain and timberlands, where before a set of dusty drafting yards, and a few barren salt camps, were the only symbols of industry or civilisation. The solitary railway-sidings, the "gates" and the "crossings" that had marked the distant settlements were now converted into lively townships, consisting of stores, hotels, bakers', butchers', and blacksmiths' shops. Co-operative and private cheese and butter factories sprang up in every district. The London market, as fast as ships could convey it, absorbed to the last pound the produce turned out, and cabled demands for more.

An earth hunger set in. Land values went up, till even waste selections that a few years before "went begging" at 30 *s.* per acre, could not now be purchased at £8. And many of the one-time struggling cockies who had but too often known the pangs of nursing their hunger, till the pinch of flour that was to provide a few scones to go on with for the mid-day meal arrived from the store; and who year after year were forced to leave their holdings, and seek work at the shearing sheds, in order to meet the interest accruing on the mortgage, and keep the wolf from the door—were now rising to comparative wealth.

2. A Terrible Drought

It was the middle of summer. And such a summer! There had been no rain for months—not as much as would wet a pocket handkerchief; and the relentless, pitiless sun, day after day, blazed steadily down from a clear, cloudless sky, and set in the west like a ball of fire. The intense heat was almost unendurable. Workmen, at intervals throughout the day, left the field and sought the shade beneath the trees. The women abandoned their housework, and with their gowns opened at the throat, sat in the passages of their homes, fanning themselves for a breath of air. The grass and herbage withered away. The corn crops drooped and died. The dairy herds went back in their milk, gallon by gallon. Every day saw a serious shrinkage. Anxiety began to fill the hearts of the people. In vain they studied the heavens, from dawn till dusk. God! would it never rain! How long was it to last! The new moon, that was a fortnight off, would surely bring a change! In its coming there was hope—hope that was soon to give way to despair and discouragement. For the new moon came, and—Oh, God!—it was the same, same, old moon! A moon that shed its pallid, ghostly glow over the baked and barren earth—that mockingly led the thirsty, famishing stock to holes that were dry and bare, and went its way.

A few more maddening weeks dragged on, and—still no rain! One by one, the tanks and dams gave out; then, what a drag! What trudging! Hauling and drawing water every hour of the day, for man and beast. Bush fires licked up the dry grass, till the earth became a veritable flame of fire; then sank to a mass of dust—dust, and dead leaves!

The milk supply fell to nothing; the cows wasted away to shadows, to walking skeletons. What fodder the stacks and hay-sheds contained was doled out with a sparing hand; the stock were placed on a daily allowance, that life might be kept in them till rain came. The rain didn't come, and the fodder exhausted itself. People were on the verge of insanity. The money they had been saving—the first few hundred pounds they had been able to bank, to call their own, since they first began their life struggle on the land, was withdrawn, to purchase fodder to save the herds. Ah, it was hard! And produce at such prices—prices never before heard of in the history of the colony. The starving stock were literally eating money—money that amounted to more than they were worth. But there was no alternative; the people could not let them go; it might rain any moment, and how, with the money used up, was another herd to be purchased? Where would they raise the means? And if they did raise it, what a price they would have to pay for cows when the drought was over!

But the drought queen continued to hold sway, and the day came when the people could no longer afford to purchase fodder. Banks were forced to turn their ledgers down upon them. And the storekeepers, in turn, to press for payment of long accounts. God! What a year it was!

Then, as a last resource, the axe rang out, and its ring was heard all through the land; and everywhere that a tree swept the ground it was surrounded eagerly by hungry, moaning, maddened cattle, with just sufficient strength left to munch the bitter leaves. But that was the last straw. The wretched stock began to drop out and die—to die in twos and threes—to die in the yards, and on the roads, and in the people's very doorways! Ah, it was heart-breaking! Then, one night, when no one was even hoping for it, it came on to rain. It rained for several days—rained, till there was a flood. And when it was over the stock for several weeks died faster than before. But the drought was ended. Ended!

Then the reckoning, the pain and suffering. Crushed and broken, many left their holdings to the banks, and walked out penniless. Others saw nothing but years and years of struggle and stint before them, ere they could regain their feet, and were broken-hearted. One man alone, in the district of Longer-Linger, came through it almost scathless. The cringing, ill-disposed Piggy Potthouse, seemed to have the luck of the very devil. To assign to the uncharitable old sinner's fortune any special favour of Providence would be blasphemy. Not a hoof did he lose! Numerous stacks of ill-cared for hay that had lain on his land for many years, and was looked upon as so much rubbish by Piggy himself, saved most of his stock, and even kept them in a low percentage of milk. And with the devil, still inspiring him to fortune, Piggy, only three days before the drought broke, took a sporting risk, and, riding round the district, purchased some hundreds of cows—cows, that a few months before couldn't be bought for ten or twelve pounds— at fifteen shillings and one pound per head, and made a pile of money out of the misfortune of his neighbours.

"H'm! h'm! h'm!" Piggy said, when he walked in to deal with Mrs. Ryle. "An' you've not even wan left?" '

"Not one—nothing in the wide, wide world, except one horse!" the heart-broken woman said, without lifting her head from the pillow of the sofa on which she lay. "The remains of the cows I suppose you saw about the yard as you came in?"

"H'm! h'm! h'm! 'Tis bad; 'tis bad!" Piggy grunted, glancing with his sphinx-like eyes round the little room.

"If you could have kept them alive, I do believe I would have bought them from you, and taken the risks ov them dyin'. And you would have made sure ov a few pounds, anyway; for 'tis a terrible drooth, a terrible drooth. And I do be thinkin' to myself in bed, at night, that none of us can stand to see through to the end of it all. Not wan ov us. Only for a little haay, I'd been keepin' and keepin' for years and years past, and would never sell it—would never sell—thinkin' 'twud be wanted for the cows some day, in a dry time, I would have been ruined— ruined a month and more ago. Johnny West have lost a hun-dred head, poor man! And Dan Wilks, they tell me, have gone to the mad-house only this vera morning. Lord have mercy upon his poor wife. 'Tis, indeed, a terrible, terrible drooth!"

Mrs. Ryle, crushed into the recesses of her own mind, was silent and uncommunicative.

The lean head of a horse, with sad, but intelligent-looking eyes, and wide open nostrils, poked itself in through the open back-door of the cottage, and winnied feebly and plaintively.

"Poor old Newchum!" Mrs. Ryle murmured, compassion-ately, turning her head to greet the staring animal. "Get the pieces of bread from the pantry that I put by from the break-fast, and give them to him, Eric; he must be very, very hungry to-day," she said to her son.

And, as Eric appeared from the pantry with the bread-dish

in his hand, the dumb animal winnied his gratitude, and feebly pawed the ground with his lean limbs, as he started to eat ravenously.

"Poor old Newchum!" Mrs. Ryle said again; "he's all that's left, and he can hardly carry his hide. But I hope he doesn't get down on us."

For a moment or two, Piggy seemed to be thinking hard, and raking his memory.

"Newchum, did you say?" he said, stepping to the door, and eyeing the frame closely. Then, while Eric patted and fondled the animal's head, Piggy walked round it several times.

"Newchum!" he murmured, as though there was something familiar about the name. And, stepping inside again, he asked aloud:

"Is that the horse that—that——"

He turned and looked anxiously at the animal again, "that——"

"That my husband thought so much of," Mrs. Ryle put in gently.

"No; that—that——" Piggy was gasping with excitement, or surprise, or fear, or something, and couldn't get out what he wanted. "That all the trouble—all the—the——. But didn't he go to New South Wales after the—the——"

"What do you mean—what trouble?" Mrs. Ryle asked, rising, with flashing eyes, from the sofa, and fixing them full upon Piggy. "What trouble do you mean, Mr. Potthouse?" she demanded. "My husband was never in trouble!"

Piggy realised in a flash that Mrs. Ryle had not been in the full confidence of her husband, and felt he was "putting his foot in it."

"Oh, may be I do be forgettin', an' mixin' wan thing up wid the other, like I do since my memory have been goin'," Piggy answered, to escape the quandary. "What was in my mind, I suppose, if I ain't dreamin', was the trouble he had to get paid for a horse he sold to a chap that wasn't the clean goer, in New South Wales, and when I heard Newchum, I wondered to myself if it could be the same, because that one he called Newchum, too, if I remember right, but it couldn't be; it's too long ago. H'm! h'm! h'm!"

Piggy was an artful and hardened old liar.

"Ah, no!" and Mrs. Ryle sank back, with a sigh. "Harry would never think of selling Newchum. The last thing he said to me, the morning he went away, was to keep Newchum always about the place, and never to let anyone ride him till he returned. But Eric used to ride him a little."

"H'm! h'm! h'm!" Piggy grunted, thoughtfully.

Another sigh escaped Mrs. Ryle, and she added, pathetically, "The last letter of Harry's, posted at Camooweal, just a month before his death——"

Piggie's eyes and mouth opened wide, and he voluntarily muttered "Death!"——

"Was full of questions about Newchum, and gave all his pedigree. And I was never to part with him—if anything happened to himself—unless I was very hard up, and then only through ——"

Mrs. Ryle broke off abruptly. She was ill.

"And then through?" Piggy, with a clumsy attempt to conceal his anxiety, asked.

The woman sighed wearily, and said:

"I'm too unwell to talk any more to-day, Mr. Potthouse."

"H'm! h'm! h'm!" disappointedly, from Piggy, who again cast his eye at the starving horse; then turned his attention to Eric.

"He reminds me of his father," he said, looking at the boy.

Memories of his mother's description of the father he had never seen, flooded Eric's mind, and his young heart beat fast and pumped the blood in crimson flushes to his handsome face.

Mrs. Ryle turned her eyes affectionately upon her son, and shared his feelings of pride.

"What's your age, boy?" Piggy asked of Eric.

"Eight on nineteenth of next June, sir," was the answer; "and I'm just two years older than Newchum. But he's grown more than me, hasn't he?"

"H'm! h'm! h'm!" Piggy grunted, ignoring the question. Then, addressing the mother: "I'm in want of a boy about his size for the yaard, so I am. He'd just do me, I think; and I'll give him half-a-crown a week and his keep, if you send him over?"

Mrs. Ryle shook her head, and replied:

"Eric has been doing well the little while he has been at

school, Mr. Potthouse, and the teacher has been so impressed with him that he has great hopes he will rise to something one day. So, if I have to work my hands off in order to do it, I will give him the opportunity, at all events, of becoming something better than a cow boy."

"Then—then——" Piggy snorted, angrily—"he might be something a damn lot worse, so he might," and took his leave abruptly.

All the way across the yard, to where his horse was fastened, Piggy talked to himself.

"H'm! h'm! h'm!. That's the horse; and she do think that Harry Ryle is dead—that he is dead! dead! when he isn't, when he isn't!" he said. "H'm! h'm! h'm! 'twould be better, 'twould be better if he were—if he were; and if the cub of a boy were dead, too! were dead, too! H'm! h'm! h'm! The son of Piggy Potthouse might then be a Lorrd! A Lorrd, a real Lorrd he would be. Lorrd Henry Pigford Potthouse. H'm! h'm! h'm!"

And the birds chirped and whistled cheerfully, as Piggy rode away across the paddock.

3. By the Death Bed

A glorious Queensland day; the air clear and crisp, and the sky all purple and blue. The blazing, blistering sun no longer baked and parched the earth. The drought had relaxed its death grip. The leafless trees had already started into foliage again. A cool, fresh breeze flirted with the boughs. A mild and temperate heat rested on the land, coaxing new life into grass and vegetation. The hand of the Great Painter was at work, and a gorgeous curtain of green and gold was falling over the last act of the awful tragedy.

Outside fires were burning, and the washing flapping and ballooning on the lines in every yard round Longer-Linger—in every yard but Mrs. Ryle's. The one solitary horse grazed near the house, upon the green, tender shoots of the returning grass, his fleshless ribs still showing, like two washboards.

The front door of the house was closed, and, an unusual circumstance, Eric was at home from school. At intervals his little figure could be seen hurrying in and out the kitchen— sometimes with a steaming basin in his hand; sometimes a plate, or a cup and saucer.

A gloom hung over the humble homestead, contrasting sadly with the spirit of rejoicing invited by the buoyant day without. It seemed as if something was going to happen.

"Und how is modder to-day?" old Hartmann inquired, appearing at the door, for the second time that morning.

"She isn't no better, Mr. Hartmann," Eric answered, allowing the tears to trickle over his cheeks without restraint. "She says she will never be better any more," and leaning against the door-post, he wept copiously.

"You must not dake no notice of dot, leetle fellow," the old man said, kindly, patting the boy encouragingly on the head with his horny hand. "She vill get better for you soon again; don't be frighten for dot. Und mine vife says she vill coom again in a few meenits, so soon as she haf done a leetle vork that cannot could stand a vile, and vill stay mit her to-day some more."

The boy's heart was full, and he cried harder.

"Don't let modder see you cry like dot, leetle man; you must keep cheerful, and talk mit her to keep her bright," Hartmann went on, consolingly. "Dot is a good leetle shap, be a prave poy." Then the old German turned sadly away, and went home again.

Ah, yes! Mrs. Ryle was ill. How ill Eric could not realise. But the wife of the old German realised it to the full. "Ven dot voman," she told her husband, "dake to her bed she is vera, vera bad—vera bad!" And so it was. The physical strain and anxiety put upon her in the struggle for subsistence, had been telling on the woman fast enough; but when the merciless drought came, and rested like a curse on her homestead, till everything was gone—till every vestige of that hope she had long clung to was blasted, her heart broke; despair entered her soul, and the weary, over-wrought soul-case was crushed and prostrated.

Poor little Eric! How he watched. How he sobbed by the sick bedside, and in boyish efforts appealed to that mother to "look at him!" How pitifully he beseeched her "not to turn her eyes like that!" How he pleaded in vain to her to take the cup of tea from his hand that he had made! And then:

"No! No! don't say that, mother! Oh, mother, don't!" he cried, in a frantic scream of anguish. And when the sinking voice counselled him to be honest and truthful in all his dealings, when she was gone, and to put his trust in God, it was more than the young heart could hold.

"Oh, no! mother! You are not going to die!" he shrieked in sobs, and clutched at the bedclothes.

"Don't say it, mother! Don't say it!"

And when the glassy eyes of the sick woman settled in their sockets again, and a ray of light returned to them for just a moment, Eric threw his arms about her neck, and nestling and crooning beside her on the pillow, assured her "she was better now, and would be all right soon." In that attitude he remained on the bed till Mrs. Hartmann came in.

Ah, yes! there's an end to all things. "A season to every man!" And, next morning, the clear, silent air round the little homestead was suddenly pierced with cries of sorrow and distress! And such cries!

"Mother! Mother! Mother!" rang out in the stillness; and rang out again, and again.

Something had happened.

"Poor leetle shap!" old Hartmann murmured—the big tears filling his aged and sunken eyes—"Poor leetle man! By Got, I am zorry for you!"

And next day, when the last shovelful of earth was heaped on the new-made mound, in the little country graveyard, by the range; and Piggy Potthouse, by the wretched privileges of relationship, installed himself as guardian to the bereaved and homeless boy, and hurried him, sobbing and reluctant, into his dog-cart, the old German, standing bare-headed by, shook his head sadly, and said again:

"By Got, I am zorry for you, my leetle man!"

4. Eric Makes an Acquaintance

"It's no use yer whimperin' all night about it!" Piggy grumbled, when Eric, his eyes red as hot coals, from the scalding tears, took his seat at the kitchen table, of what, in future, he was to regard as home. "She's gone—an'—an'—no one can bring her back!"

The boy smothered a sob, and hung his head over the table board.

"Hand the end of it will be," Mrs. Potthouse, a wrinkled-faced hag of fifty, said, in a shrill voice, as she shoved a plate of cold meat in front of him, "the end of it will be, yer'll be makin' yerself hill. Hand then who's goin' ter look after yer, I'd like ter know? People wot comes here doesn't come to be waited on, remember!"

"Oh, hold yer jaw!" Piggy growled across the table at his wife.

Mrs. Potthouse held her jaw.

Without raising his eyes, Eric nervously ate some of the meat, and sipped some black tea. Then he sat back, and thoughts of home—thoughts of that mother who was gone, rushed to his unhappy mind, and a chain of broken sobs burst from him.

"I want home!" he cried. "I want mother! . . . I want my mother!"

"Can yer not stop yer blubbering?" Piggy snapped. "Stop it, will yez!"

"Hand get off to th' barn ter bed," the woman put in. "Hand don't think yer can alwuz eat in the 'ouse; because yer can't, it gives too much work. Yeh'll have ter take yer meals with Snowy Wing. But wot uset yer goin' to be to this place is more than I can tell!" And she wiped the butcher's knife across the bread, preparatory to cutting it.

"P'shaw! Stop yer cacklin!" Piggy growled again.

There was an interruption.

A bare-footed, coatless boy, about ten years of age, with a wild shock of dusty, white hair, rushed in at the open door, and snatching up all the meat that was on the table with one hand,

and a billet of bread with the other, dashed out again with lightning rapidity.

"Luk! luk at there, th' dog of a thief!" Piggy burst out, like a volcano, as the provender vanished from under his eyes. And the hag, having no time to stay the theft, turned and flung the butcher's knife with full force at the head of the absconder. The point of the long blade buried itself deep in the pine door, and remained there, shivering, in its grip.

"Ther vagaboan of a boi!" Piggy said, turning his eyes toward the door.

"It's a terin' lot yer gained be stoppin' his dinner," his wife jibed. "Hinstead o' stoppin' 'is gallop with ther end o' ther leg-rope, yer——"

"Shah! dry up!" Piggy grunted, and began stirring his tea with the handle of a fork.

"Well, if yer finished," Mrs. Potthouse said, turning to Eric, "yer better come an' see where yer bed is."

The little chap rose to obey, and the case on which he was seated fell over.

"Hare yer goin' ter leave it layin' there?" she cried. "Who do yer think is goin' ter foller you round pickin' heverything up hafter yer?"

Mumbling a nervous apology, Eric turned and adjusted the furniture, then followed his foster mother out the back-door, and across the yard to the barn.

A family of pigs prospecting at the door gave a chorus of grunts at their approach, and scurried through the darkness.

"In there," Mrs. Potthouse said, pressing open the large wooden door. "There'll be lots o' room for you with Snowy Wing. If there haint enough blankets, you'll find lots o' empty bags about, if yer look, but mind yer don't take any of ther new ones, an' don't frighten ther fowls at ther other end."

A dim light was burning in one corner of the barn, behind a medley of old harness, that flapped from a beam like vines dangling in a scrub, and a husky voice drawled lazily:

"Are y' puttin' ahn anoother hahnd, moother?"

"Oh, you're there, are you, White Ants?" Mrs. Potthouse answered; then added: "A 'and one as won't hearn very much, I'm thinkin' . . . Is Snowy Wing there, White Ants?"

"Ah think he be aboot, moother." And White Ants, the

eccentric one of the farm, stirred up the slush-lamp, that frizzled beside his bunk, with an old table-knife. "Ah think ah heerd him a-nibblin' th' sooper yer sent on of 'im, moother."

"Snowy Wing! Yer thievin' 'ound," the woman squealed; "if yer don't soon come 'ere and take this chicken ter bed with yer, yer'll get it termorrer—yer'll get a hextra length o' th' leg-rope around yer, 'instead o' a short ration!"

A heap of lifeless-looking baggage began to move in the corner opposite White Ants, followed by a rustling and grating of dry, crispy corn-husks, and Snowy Wing, in the same old rags, the same old dirty face he had worn all that day, and the day before, glided silently forth into the dim light.

"Where's he. Is this 'im?" he said, reaching cautiously for Eric.

"Yer young dingo!" And Snowy's foster mother struck viciously at him with her sharp, bony knuckles. But she had often attempted to assault Snowy in a like manner. He ducked skilfully, and danced away, and the blow belaboured the air.

"Yer young dog! Wait till Pott'ouse deals it out to yer hin th' mornin'!" And, mumbling further threats, she returned to the house.

Snowy Wing approached Eric, and for a while eyed him closely and curiously in the dim light.

"Stow me!" he said, "you're on'y a tibby little bloke. Yer won't be hable ter milk cows fer 'im. Yer ain't ten, is yer?"

Eric, too nervous to speak, shook his head, feebly.

"How did 'e git yer out o' the Orph'?—yer muster did a bunk, did yer, blokey?"

Eric made no reply. Then Snowy looked him over again, and seeming satisfied, invited him to his quarters at the other end of the dim, dusty barn.

"You an' me 'll be cobbers," he said. "You can doss at the foot o' my crib; theer's lots o' room in it, fer two."

In the distressed little stranger, the uncouth, ill-used, orphan boy saw a silver lining to his own cloud of woe and hardship.

But those eerie surroundings chilled the very soul of Eric. The thoughts of sleeping there with strangers struck terror into his heart, and memories of his home, and fresh thoughts of his mother filled his mind again.

"I only want my mother," he sobbed, "my mother!"

At the child's outburst of grief, Snowy remained thoughtful and silent. The bereaved one's earnest appeals recalled sad memories of his own. He knew the feeling, and his heart went out to this latest little orphan.

"Where is she?" he asked.

"They b-b-buried her, to-day," Eric said, between his sobs. "But I want her—I want her back."

"Hoh, Crikey!" Snowy murmured. "An' 'es took yer! So yer niver got a chancet ter be sent to the Orph'? Hoh, Crikey!" And for a moment he became silent and reflective again.

After a while he advanced and took Eric by the hand.

"Don't get scared, little blokey," he said kindly. "There ain't nothink ter be frightent fer in here. There's on'y me an' White Ants sleeps 'ere, an' y' know I wouldn't hurt yer. And White Ants wouldn't either. He never says anythink 'ardly, except when he gets the giblets, and then he's on'y queerish, y'know, and does things that makes yer larf. And you'll soon get used to everythink, same as I did when I comed first. But y' won't stay longer'n yer can help, little blokey, if yer listens ter me. An' I means to do a bunk soon as I gets a little stuff. It ain't no good of a place yer've come ter, but yer isn't ter blame. An' he won't give yer any stuff fer workin' when he didn't get yer out o' the Orph'. He'll give you nuffing, cuz the law can't make him. He'll give yer th' leg-rope, though, often enough, the old Dago, just as he gives it to me, when he does things wrong his-self. Oh, I tell y' I can't stand much more of his beltin' and bruisin' of me, and gettin' starved by her for it too! But don't be scared, blokey; there's nothink like that goin' on to-night. I'll see no one 'urts y'."

And Eric, yielding submissively, allowed his new found friend to lead him to his rudely-made up "doss."

The bed of husks rasped and crackled beneath their weight, as they sank, together, on the bag mattress, and by the flickering glow of White Ants' slush lamp, spluttering from its place on a box opposite, Snowy was able to observe closely the face of his companion, and to note the neatness and cleanliness of his clothes.

"Yer a orlright little toff, blokey," he said, with a glow of admiration in his sharp eye. "And you's have real swell breedin' in yer. It's in yer face, an' the way yer hold yer head. But I hain't asked yer yer name, has I, little 'un?"

Eric gulped down a lump that was in his throat, and made an effort to pronounce his name; but his voice only came in a thin, muffled whisper.

"What did yer say, blokey?" And Snowy held his ear low to him.

"Eric Ryle."

"Eddy Rye?"

"Eric Ryle," with vague emphasis.

"Oh, Herric Ryle!" Snowy repeated, pleasantly. "Herric! . . . I knows a chap called Herric, he was at the Orph. He's a lot bigger'n you . . . Mine's 'Arry—but they all calls me Snowy."

Here White Ants left his bunk, and moved silently about the barn, in search of more fat to replenish the lamp. On noticing his massive figure upend itself, Eric's heart started to flutter, and his staring eye-balls to project, and his whole frame to quiver like a young hare held in captivity. He crouched involuntarily into Snowy for protection. To allay his fears, Snowy forced a short laugh, then said, softly:

"He ain't goin' ter touch yer, Herrick. He's a good old chap, is White Ants. He never says anythink, or does anythink to anyone. He on'y works and sleeps, and wakes up, and works again, except when he's havin' them giblets, and then he's all fun."

Then, addressing White Ants, himself:

"Yer ain't seen this little covey yet, has yer, White Ants? He's come ter live here. What do yer thinks of him?"

"Ah heerd moother bringint of him in," was the slow, dull response; then White Ants, having discovered some fat, returned to his bunk again.

"I gets fine sport outer him, sometimes, an' so'll you, Herrick, drekeley," Snowy said, breaking into a playful mood. And in practical demonstration of White Ants' harmlessness, he threw an empty sack at him, and giggled when it covered the man's face, and extinguished his lamp.

Eric gave a jump, and clung in terror to Snowy. But White Ants merely removed the sack from his face, and dropped it on the floor. Then, in a quiet, unruffled voice, he said: "Ah doont kno' where the matches be." And while he groped patiently about the floor for them, Snowy, who had possession of the box, struck one, and applied it to the slush-lamp.

"That took a start outer yer, White Ants, didn't it?" Snowy said, taking a fistful of the man's long, silvery beard in his hands, and dragging at it playfully.

White Ants lay back, and smiled up at him.

"Oh, no," Snowy said, turning with further assurance to Eric, "he wouldn't 'urt yer."

Then Eric ceased to tremble, and became calm again.

Letting fall a tear at intervals, however, he leaned on his elbow, and rested on the bed. And as the desire to sleep crept over him, his head drooped and nodded, his eyes closed and opened. And there, while Snowy hunted round, and ransacked in search for more bed-clothes, he reclined, forlorn and for-saken-looking,—a tender object of the deepest commiseration and pity.

5. Solving the Mystery

While Eric Ryle lay on his bed of husks, sobbing himself to sleep on the lean arm of Snowy Wing, Piggy, and his jade of a wife, by the light of the kitchen fire, were going through the tin trunk which contained the little fellow's few articles of clothing, and his mother's private papers and effects.

"Receipts for the instalments she has been paying on the selection. H'm! h'm! h'm!" Piggy grunted, looking hard at a scroll of paper that had been carefully folded, and placed in a corner of the box. "I'll take th'm; I'll take th'm. They wud only get losht to the cub in the barrun, so they wud. H'm! h'm! h'm!'

Mrs. Potthouse made no remark. She was making discoveries on her own account. For quite a long interval she sat back, flat on the floor, pouring laboriously over a faded letter that she held in her hand, till at last her shrill, rasping voice broke in on the silence, and she started to spell the document out.

"My dearest Nellie. There—was—no—let—letter when Hi reached Cam-Camoo-Camooweal, hand Hi was very—dis—dis—disappointed——"

Piggy gave a jump.

"Show it ter me!" he cried, snatching the document from his wife's hand, and upsetting the tin trunk by his action. " 'Tis from Harry Ryle. It is, it is." And while his small, evil eye glistened, Piggy turned the letter over and over, and upside down, scanning it endways and sideways, and from top to bottom. "There y' are!" he exclaimed, " 'tis there, at the bottom. 'Tis he! luk! luk! 'tis his signature! Your lovin' hoosband, Harry Royle."

"Well, hit's like yer hill-bred manners, Pott'ouse, not ter wait till Hi gived hit ter yer," the hag snarled.

"My dearest Nellie," Piggy muttered, ignoring her and proceeding to read for his own benefit, "My dearest Nellie! H'm! h'm! h'm!" And he lifted his eyes in astonishment, and said:

"But her name—her name—it were never Nellie. Were it ever?"

"Well," Mrs. Potthouse sneered, "Hi was never 'er god-mother, Pott'ouse, thank the Lord, so 'ow could I tell yer?"

" 'Twas Sarah," Piggy cried; "Sarah (thinking hard, and wrinkling his brow), Sarah . . . Sarah . . . (thinking some more) Sarah . . . Sarah Smith. It's on them paapers he left wid me . . . But why ever do he be writin' it Nellie?"

"Well, an' dersent hall men," Mrs. Potthouse answered, "chrisern ther woman they breaks their 'eart on, theirselves? Didn't you, Pott'ouse? Hif Hi remembers correctly yer never called me be me name. Hoh, no! It wasn't 'Mrs. Pott'ouse' them days; hand, blarst yer! hit was 'little Tick', hand 'Pretty Tick'. Huh! yer fergets it, no doubt!" And she chuckled, maliciously.

Piggy lost his temper. "Yer'e like a clucken hen, y'are, wid yer dang noise, an'—an'—yer pretty Tick! . . . Pretty luna-tic!" he roared.

Mrs. Potthouse's susceptibilities were offended.

"Hif yer dare calls me a lunatic, Pott'ouse"—she squealed, "I'll tear th' heyes hout o' yer! Who are you Hi'd like ter know?"

Piggy was glaring ferociously at her when a noise was heard at the door. The expression on both their faces changed in a flash.

"What 'n th' deuce wer' that?" Piggy whispered. Then step-ping to the door he opened it cautiously and peered into the darkness.

Mrs. Potthouse started quickly to fold the articles of clothing strewn about the floor, at the same time humming in a cracked voice.

"Is there any wan there?" Piggy called tremulously.

"Well, that's finished markin' hall his little things," from Mrs. Potthouse in a high pitched key of sympathy that might have been heard in any part of the yard—"hand 'e houghtn't ter lose hany o' them when they goes ter th' wash, th' poor 'omeless little chick."

Piggy closed the door quickly, and for a while, stood with his ear to it, listening. But no further sound came.

"Maybe it were only th' wind or th' pigs," he said. "But I thought—I thought—I—I——"

"Yer thought hit were' 'Arry Ryle comin' ter th' funeral of his wife, Pott'ouse," the hag said leeringly.

"Well, he were in me mind, so he were, but I dunno why I wud expect it were him."

"Well, isn't it halwez them wot yer least wants ter see that are halwez in yer mind?" Mrs. Potthouse put in, as she lifted another letter to spell over. "But," she added, glancing over the top of the paper, "I don't see why you should hexpect a man what's dead an' buried ter frighten yer!"

"What's dead an' buried!" Piggy snorted. "What's more alive than—than yez are yerself!"

"Well, I tell yer 'e his dead," his wife answered, shaking the letter she held in her hand, "an' 'ere's evidence in writin' of it."

Piggy sat back, and cogitated deeply. When he had finished cudgelling his brain, he turned again to the letter, commencing, "My dear Nellie," and read it through.

"Newchum," he continued, turning back and repeating portion of it aloud, "should turn out a splendid horse. I wish I could induce William to take him to Melbourne, and look after him till we go back to live there."

"To live there?" Piggy soliloquised. "What did he mean at all? 'Tis more villainy, Harry Royle! and she must have known ud, though 'tis dead and gone she is!

"His sire was Leopold, the horse that was planted, and his dam, French Lady, mother of a cup winner, and one of the stolen mares. It was luck to get him from William"—(who would William be, Piggy asked of himself, as he put aside the letter. "I'm sure I don't know who he mean, an' I dunno if ud were 'luck'. It were bad luck fer yer Harry Ryle, the daay yer stole Leopold from Clifton. And I know all that you have been writin' to her is forgery.")

Taking a light, he glided through a side door into the house, and returned with a packet of letters, which he carefully examined.

"Here's wan," he muttered, straightening out a portion of a letter, written on foolscap, with "Boggo Road Gaol" printed at the top of it. He placed it beside the one written to Eric's mother, to compare the handwriting.

"No more like it than—than—it is—like mine," Piggy chuckled. " 'Tis a forgery, as I knew, and someone have been doin' it forrim."

6. "Are Yez Stirrin' Y'self?"

It wanted an hour to daylight. The door of the barn grated and groaned on its solitary hinge. A cracked bullock bell rang with great violence, and the voice of Piggy Potthouse growled, aggressively:

"Now then, out yez turn to it, Snowy Wing. Shake yerself up, an' get them cows rounded up."

Then he tossed the bell into a corner, and the row it made when it struck and rolled on the floor, was itself sufficient to disturb the slumbers of the dead.

Snowy, half-dazed, sat up in the bag-bed, and rubbed his weary eyes. He closed them again, and for a moment allowed his head to hang over on one shoulder. Ah, it was cruel to break his sleep, just when he was in the middle of it! Poor Snowy, he longed to fall back on those bags again, and go off for a week into a deep, deep slumber.

"Are yez stirrin' yerself?" Piggy called from the door again, "or do yez want to be livened up wid somethin'?"

" 'Im coming'," Snowy answered, bounding from the bed.

"Yer just saved yer skin, me shaver, so yez did!" And Piggy went off, and turned into his warm bed again.

There was no necessity for Snowy to dress himself.

The law of self-preservation dictated the wisdom of sleeping in his clothes—though his scant raiment was, after all, but poor protection against the leg-rope!

"It's mornin', White Ants," he said; "ain't yer goin' ter turn out?" But White Ants slept on.

Then striking a match, Snowy held it close to the pale, tear-stained face of little Eric, who lay with his head off the roll of bags that served as a pillow, sleeping as sound as the dead.

"Ain't 'e a hangel!" he said, speaking to himself. "It ud be a sin ter wake yer, little covey; hand they hasn't sed if yer has ter come or not. I'll fix yer up, anyway (lifting the little sleeper's head back to the pillow), hand they can wakes yer theirselves—there 'y are."

Then at that unearthly hour of the morning, with a lantern in his hand, to distinguish the milkers by when he would stumble across them in their respective haunts and camping grounds, Snowy Wing, in thin calico shirt sleeves, cut off at the elbow, torn, dilapidated pants, grease and dirt bespattered, and narrowly kept from departing from him for ever by a quaint pair of braces, designed and constructed by himself out of strips of moleskin and a quantity of string, and no boots, issued from that beautiful elysium, and limped tenderly across the yard—a yard where Bathurst burr and bull-head grew thick and rank, to tramp and search the grass paddock for two hours at least. And Piggy's grass paddock contained over a thousand acres. There were other paddocks around Longer-Linger, however, that also contained a thousand acres, and some of them adjoined Piggy's. And on the lightly timbered flats and ridges at that same, merciless hour, eerily flashed distant lanterns, like so many will-o'-the-wisps, each lantern accounting for a child missing from its bed—perhaps a girl of tender years, sleepy, hungry, weary, and thinly clad! Had they been tutored in some form of flashlight telegraphy the mites might, at least, have spent the first hour of their morning's misery pleasantly enough in communicating their sufferings and conveying messages of sympathy to each other across the dark and silent valleys, which Nature, in her wisdom, had not yet deemed fit to awaken from a healthy slumber.

7.   A Cow-yard Scene

It was broad daylight, and the sun rising in all its splendour, when Snowy, trailing along behind fifty cows, arrived at the milking yard. Calves were bellowing in the pens, half-starved "poddies" moaning in the barn; some more wagging their stumps of tails and poking their nose into the row of empty milk cans that White Ants had placed in readiness on a rough stand beside the yard rails. Draught horses, kicking and squealing, were taking possession of each other's feed-boxes, placed all about the yard, and returning greedily to their own when they saw the contents being devoured by the one whose claim they usurped.

Piggy emerged from the kitchen with several buckets hanging on each of his arms. Mrs. Potthouse, yapping at the top of her shrill voice, appeared with some more buckets; and work for the day commenced in real earnest on "Daisy Vale."

"An'—An'—what have been keepin' yez to this late?" Piggy growled as he entered the yard. "If I thought yez wud be skylarkin' in the paddicks me boy, I'd—I'd—" and approaching Snowy he shook his fist at him.

"Nothink has been keepin' me," Snowy answered sullenly, backing into the yard among the restless cows. "They wuz all over the place, so they wuz; some of 'em wuz away up at th' top o' the mountain, an' old Spot an' Madam Melba was away down——"

"Get on—get on—an'—an' don't be standin' there talkin' all the day," Piggy snorted. "Put them in—an'—an' get yez a bucket. Where're th' leg-ropes?"

The cows, meanwhile, had been poking and hustling each other till they worked all round the yard, and Piggy was left reproving Snowy in the middle of it, like a ring-master. Suddenly, a heifer that found herself hoisted on the horns of a huge slabsided old warrior with a head on her like a stag, gave an appalling bellow, and in a blind effort to escape further punishment struck Piggy in the rear with the full force of her shoulder and knocked him into the dust.

"Help! help!" Piggy yelled thinking the attack was premeditated.

The absurdity of the situation was too much for Snowy. He started to titter.

Mrs. Potthouse put down a bucket and responded to her husband's cries. She commenced by calling Snowy a "whelp" and chasing him with the leg-rope.

" 'Twas th' cow—'twas th' cow," Piggy shouted in explanation—"she charrged me wid her horun."

"Hand that's hall yer 'ad ter roar about?" Mrs. Potthouse said, eyeing him disgustedly. "Huh! yer as 'elpless as a baby!" and she returned to her bail.

Snowy, with a broad grin on his face, shuffled through the yard and bailed up several of the cows.

Then for quite a while nothing but the sound of milk squirting into the foaming buckets could be heard.

Mrs. Potthouse, whose mind had been active, suddenly remembered something.

"Where hon hearth his the hother himp?" she called out, rising suddenly from beneath the cow, and staring over the top of the yard towards the barn.

"Oh, be gob, the cub!" Piggy exclaimed. "I—I—never guv him a thort—not a thort, and he cud be here bailin'-up, he cud, so he cud!"

"Hand 'ave yer left 'im lyin' in 'is bed ter this blessed hour?" Mrs. Potthouse shrieked across the cow's back to Snowy.

"I wasn't told that I wuz ter wake him!" Snowy answered.

"Yer wasn't told!" Mrs. Potthouse sneered, "What did yer think—thet he's ter stick hin bed hactin' th' gentlem'n and wearin' hout ther bed-clothes till someone brings him coffee hand cake! Here, hundo this leg-rope, hand bail hup Lady Hogan. Hi'll soon teach 'im wot his work is ter be." And leaving the yard she strutted to the barn.

"Here!" she cried, approaching the bed and taking a firm grip of the bagging with both hands. "Yer've had about enough o' this. Out yer come!" And with a lunge she brought Eric on to the floor.

"Oh! Oh! Mother!" he gasped, unconscious for the moment of his surroundings.

"M-Mother!" Mrs. Potthouse snapped. "Wot are yer

dreamin' about? Do yer think there's nothink to be done but sleep hall day. Get hout with yer!"

Poor Eric, dazed and confused, didn't know which way to turn.

"Here!" and grabbing him by the coat collar, Mrs. Potthouse propelled him, at arm's length, out the door and across the yard. "Get in under there!" she said on reaching the yard-rails, "an' bail hup ther cows when ther're wanted."

Eric crawled under the rails and stood staring from bail to bail.

Mrs. Potthouse, keeping up a running fire of "language," took her seat beneath the flank of Lady Hogan and began milking her.

Receiving a smile of encouragement from Snowy, Eric gained confidence, and moved about the yard.

"Now then, hunt Spot along," Piggy said, as he finished milking Violet, and slipped the leg-rope off her.

Eric, not knowing the cows by their names, stared in bewilderment at them all, then murmured timidly, "This one, sir?" indicating one nearest him.

"Spot, I said," Piggy shouted angrily. "Wud yer call a—a— red cow 'Spot'? There she is lukin' at yez, in th' corner. An'— an'—wonderin' wuz there ever such a eedgit!"

Eric succeeded in fixing his eyes on the right beast, and bailing her up.

"Bring Bawley," Mrs. Potthouse squeaked, releasing Lady Hogan, and giving her the double of the leg-rope as she departed, for having kicked mud into the bucket.

Snowy caught Eric's eye, and quickly pointed to Bally. Eric, without hesitation, separated his cow from the others, and slipped her into Mrs. Potthouse's bail.

"Hoh," she said, looking surprised, "Yer 'ave got some intelligence, then? Yer do know a balley cow from a black one or a red one?"

Snowy peeped round the hind-quarters of the animal he was engaged on and winked at Eric. Eric's pale little face never changed.

"Coome on wi' y', Beauty," White Ants drawled, mooching round the yard with his hand on the back of a beast.

"Yer lazy young 'ound, yer—" Mrs. Potthouse shrieked at Eric, "Are yer goin' ter stan' there starin' erbout yer hall day, hand letting White Hants waste time bailin' hup for hisself, hand doin' yer work for yer?"

Eric bounded to White Ants' assistance; but that silent irresponsible paid no more attention to his presence than if he were a butterfly fluttering through the yard.

Snowy let go, and bailed up for himself.

"The Duchess," Piggy shouted.

Eric unconsciously glanced to Snowy.

Snowy gave him the "tip."

"H'm! h'm! h'm! Yez are comin' on," Piggy said, when Eric, without a word, headed the Duchess for the bail. "Yez'll be worth ye're tucker, y' will, some day, if yez keep on."

The color mounted to Eric's cheeks. He felt he was being praised (Praised! the Lord forbid!) and his conscience seemed to tell him that in accepting such words of encouragement without offering an explanation or refusing credit for them he was doing something wrong—something very dishonest. But the desire to offer the explanation was soon dominated by the fear of what its effects might be.

Snowy leaned round and again winked knowingly at Eric, and pulled a satirical face in the direction of Piggy.

There were not more than four or five beasts now remaining in the yard.

"Blossom! hand 'urry up," Mrs. Potthouse cried sharply; and again Eric's watchful eyes sought assistance from Snowy.

Snowy gave his head several shakes, and pointed to the cow he was himself milking.

Eric understood.

"Snowy has that one, mum," he murmured.

"Hoh! 'as 'e! Hit wouldn't be 'im hif 'e 'adn't th' heasiest hin th' yard. Yer take them has they come, Mister Snowy Wing (lifting her voice for Snowy's benefit), hand don't be halwez leavin' th' tough ones to hother people, hor yer'll find th' leg rope'll be a bit tougher 'n hany o' them."

"Roany," Piggy shouted.

Snowy glanced at Eric and pointed again. Eric saw a roan beast handy, and rushed it. He succeeded in separating it from the others. The roan beast refused to face the bail. It dodged. It refused a second time. It was a bull.

"Th'—th'—Lord save me!" Piggy burst out, "is ut Digby

Denham yez ud have me milkin'? Let Digby alone afore he gore yez, yer cub!"

Eric looked puzzled, then coloured to the roots of his hair, when he saw the absurd mistake.

Snowy, screwing and twisting about on his milking block like a snake taking a hot breakfast, finally broke into an irrepressible burst of mirth.

"Hare yer goin' ter stand this sort o' thing, Pott'ouse?" Mrs. Potthouse squeaked in a fresh fit of temper, "hand sit listenin' ter yerself made fun hof, hand ridiculed hin yer own yard—hare yer?"

A low mumbling noise came from the vicinity of White Ants' bail. Snowy immediately stood up, and elevating himself on the milking block, stared expectantly over the cow's back. Piggy and Mrs. Potthouse also rose, but their faces bore looks of deep concern.

White Ants, with a finger in each ear, was standing a few paces from Mary Ellen, laughing idiotically at her.

"Devil take hit, 'es goin' ter 'ave hanother o' 'es mad fits," Mrs. Potthouse whined.

"H'm! h'm! h'm!" Piggy grunted gravely. "H'm! h'm! h'm!"

"The giblets!" Snowy with a sparkling eye, whispered exultingly across the yard to Eric. "The giblets!" Eric gulped down a lump that had settled in his throat and moved to higher vantage-ground.

Becoming impatient, Mary Ellen started to kick.

"There be devils int her," White Ants said, raising his hollow voice. "Devils! devils! devils!" And he sprang back and rolled the whites of his eyes about like the lion in the magic lantern.

Snowy tittered, and tossed a mud pebble across at Eric.

"Yer hold fool," Mrs. Potthouse called out in a conciliatory tone. "There haint no devils hin Mary Helen; she hon'y wants ter be let go. Take the leg-rope hoff 'er."

White Ants sprang back a further pace or two, still keeping his wild eyes roaming over the cow.

The beast kicked with increased energy.

White Ants emptied a bucket of milk over her and sprang away again to watch results.

Mrs. Potthouse shrieked and wrung her hands. Piggy thought of his loss and groaned.

White Ants lifted a heavy stick lying at his feet, and rushing in at Mary Ellen, smote her hip and thigh.

"They're all on her, they're sittin' on her. There's one!—there's one!—there's one!" And to every one he dealt a fierce blow, which the unfortunate beast received.

Mary Ellen plunged, struggled, and bellowed till her tongue touched the ground.

" 'E'll kill th' poor thing; he'll kill her right hunder hour two very heyes!" Mrs. Potthouse screamed, taking shelter behind the rails of her own bail.

"He will, then; he will, then; th' damn madman!" Piggy groaned, also seeking shelter.

White Ants broke ground again, and belaboured the air with the waddy to beat off some imaginary foes that were attacking him.

A burst of facetious joy came from Snowy, which escaped the attention of Piggy and Mrs. Potthouse. They were now only concerned about the safety of themselves and the cow.

Eric seemed riveted to the ground. He didn't know whether to laugh with joy or to cry with fear.

White Ants threw the waddy at the devils and struck Mary Ellen hard on the ribs, then with a yell of terror he turned and started to run. He encountered the form of Snowy, and stopped short, jumped back, and baring his teeth to the gums, craned his neck and hissed at him like a serpent.

Snowy grinned.

White Ants crept down low to the ground, still hissing, as though preparing to spring upon him like a tiger. But he didn't spring. Slowly he drew himself to his full height; then pointing a long, thick, hard forefinger straight at Snowy, edged closer and closer to him.

Snowy stood his ground, and broadened his grin.

The rigid finger approached and approached till it was almost touching Snowy's face.

"Be careful ov him when—when he is like that," Piggy cried warningly, pressing closer into the rails himself.

Then Snowy calmly opened his mouth and closed his teeth like a steel trap on that finger. The rapidity with which it was withdrawn nearly decapitated Snowy. There was a loud demoniacal yell from White Ants. He mounted the highest part of the yard like a great ourang-outang, and fell over on the other side with a loud crash. Regaining his feet he ran. Three of Piggy's mongrel dogs ran after him, barking at his heels, bounding at his head, and falling across his path. White Ants turned on them. They surrounded him, and kept him at bay. They kept him at bay till the "giblets" wore off him, then he strolled calmly back to the milking yard.

The row of milk cans standing outside the rails were full to the brim, and the work of milking for that morning was over at "Daisy Vale."

8. *Orders for the Day*

"Well, now," Piggy said, looking round from his seat on the milk waggon, when the full cans had been lifted in. "Wan ov yez young devils have ther gate open fer me; an'—an'—when yez have put th' horses that won't be usin' back intil th' th' grass-paddock, an'—an'—chops some o' th' pumpkins up intil small pieces fer th' peegs; an'—an'—drags th' harry lyin' bey-ont there (pointing with the handle of his whip to where it lay) over 'ere, an'—an'—stands it up agen th' hole in ther fence where th' poddies got intil th' lucen; an'—an'—chops up a heap o' wood fer th' misses, an'—an'—feeds Brindle (his favorite dog, that was chained up), yez can then be havin' yez break-fast." And tugging at the reins like the unskilled driver he was, Piggy drove off through the gate and along the broad, black soil lane to deposit the morning's milk at the factory.

Slicing pumpkins for the pigs and feeding Brindle were light enough tasks, but ah! it was a hard struggle the two boys went through to drag that heavy wooden harrow on its back over the rough, uneven ground! Stones and sticks would accumulate beneath it and clog its progress; and every now and again they were compelled to exert themselves to greater efforts to upend it and relieve the debris. Then hitching themselves to a rope they had fastened to it would haul and haul again, pausing, panting and breathless, every ten or twelve yards or so, to re-cruit their strength. After a while they succeeded in dragging it to its destination and stood it up against the damaged fence. Then they directed their steps to the horses. The animals had long since finished feeding, but their passion for biting and kicking had in no way become mollified. One brute in partic-ular seemed to incur the displeasure of all the others, and one after another they viciously resented his presence. A pair of heels narrowly missed the head of the outcast when the boys came up.

"It's Newchum! Oh, old Newchum," Eric exclaimed, a look of genuine joy lighting up his sad little face. On hearing his name, and the sound of a familiar voice, the horse pricked its ears and turned round, holding its head high in the air. "Old Newchum! Newchum, it is!" Eric said again. And giving a low, pleased whinney in recognition, the horse trotted feebly forward and rubbed his head fondly against the boy. Eric in return stroked the white stripe down his forehead and put his arm around his lean, lengthy neck, and caressed him as though he were a long lost brother.

Snowy, surprised, stood for a while, an amused spectator of the affectionate meeting.

"I see the old Dodger," he said, "bringing that cove inter th' paddock yes'd'y. Ders 'e belongst ter you, Herrick?"

"Yes, he's ours," Eric murmured, the large tears that had been stirred to his eyes by the sad memories the unexpected presence of his dumb friend, awakened within him, rolling down his cheeks. "He was always mother's old pet, and mine. He was father's horse before, and he left him when he went away, for mother to mind till he came back. But he never came back. He said he was too valuable to take on the roads; and that no one was ever to ride him. And no one ever did, but me. Did they, Newchum?"

"Crikey! but ain't he a scarecrow, Herrick?" Snowy observed, walking round the horse and eyeing him critically. "He muster been close up a gonner. Yer'd think his 'ide was jest 'angin' over a lot o' brambles. He's a chestnut, heh?"

"Ah, poor old Newchum!" Eric said, placing his cheek caressingly against the animal's nose. "You nearly went in the drought, didn't y'? But we managed to save you, mumma and me, with little bits of bread, didn't we?"

Again the horse whinnied fondly and rubbed his head against the boy.

"Fetch 'im over ter th' barn, Herrick," Snowy counselled, with boyish enthusiasm. "An we'll give him a feed o' punkkins; them's th' things ter make 'im fat an' put a shine on his coat. We can give 'im some every mornin', an' when 'e gets round a bit, an' puts up condition, we'll ride on 'im after th' cows, you an' me, instead o' walkin'. Yer haint got a saddle too, has yer, Herrick?"

Eric mildly shook his head, and wiped away a tear.

"It don't matter, there's a hold one in the barn that th' hens roosts on; we'll mend thet up some night when they reckons we'll be sleepin', an' 'ide it in ther corn, so's th' old Dago wont know . . . Fetch him on, Herrick. Hi'll cut 'im up a punkkin; then we'll shut 'im in the yard so as them other 'ungry dorgs of his can't get at 'im while we're choppin' wood. Then we'll put the whole lot in th' padduk tergether."

Eric, with his hand resting on Newchum's mane, as he walked along, followed Snowy to the barn.

"That'll fatten 'im, I bet," Snowy said, cheerfully, struggling with a large box laden with sliced pumpkin, which he dumped down in the yard.

Closing the gate behind Newchum, the two boys stood for a moment contemplating him with pride, through the rails, as he waded into the pumpkin, then went off to the woodheap.

9. Assertive Mrs. Potthouse

A blunt, cranky old axe it was that did service at the wood-heap, and every moment or two the head of it left the rough-hewn ironbark handle, for the shaping of which White Ants was responsible, and lost itself in the thick weeds, or amongst the wood. And while Eric held the lantern in position, and stacked the small pieces, Snowy wielded the implement, till the perspiration coursed down his face and down his heated body in miniature rivulets. At intervals Eric would essay to "give him a spell," and, gripping the rough handle, would struggle in the undertaking, until he hadn't strength enough remaining to raise the axe above his head. Finally, both would give in from sheer exhaustion, and sitting on the ground, limp and languid, would puff and fan themselves with their hats.

"His that 'ow yer cuttin' th' wood!" the voice of Mrs. Potthouse rang out, suddenly, from the kitchen window. "An' me waitin' 'ere hall mornin' fer it! Hoh! Hi'll warm th' skins o' th' two of yer, hif there hain't soon some fetched hin 'ere!"

Eric loaded himself up to the chin with an armful, while Snowy went on chopping feebly.

"His that hall yer've cut hin hall that time?" the hag exclaimed, glaring disparagingly at the load Eric dropped in a corner of the kitchen.

"No, Mum; there's a big heap outside yet."

"Well, then, just—you—bring—it—hin!" giving the ear a squeeze, "and don't be sittin' down—loafin'."—and she gave his ear a parting pinch at the door.

Eric, holding his hand to the wounded part, returned to the woodheap.

"Never mind 'er, Herrick!" Snowy said, consolingly. "She's done that ter me orften!"

Then the two of them carried in as much wood as their arms could hold, and dumped it down.

"Do y' want ter fill ther kitchen hup, an' leave no room fer to turn in?" Mrs. Potthouse screeched. "Take it hout again, an' leave it till its hasked fer." And she reached for Snowy's ear. But Snowy, having been "there before," ducked, and shouldering his way along the wall, escaped.

Two minutes later, Mrs. Potthouse's voice was heard in conversation with the magpie. She was asking Maggie its private opinion of Potthouse. And when the bird defamed Piggy, in an eloquent string of profane adjectives the woman chuckled in approval, and added a few choice touches of blasphemy in the interests of the bird's vocabulary.

10. *Mrs. Potthouse Plays the Devil*

"She's a—a bad, wicked woman, and—and I don't want to stay here no—no longer," Eric sobbed beside the woodheap.

"But there ain't no one yer could go ter, is theer, Herrick?" Snowy answered, "lest yer got inter the Orph'. But 'e (meaning Piggy) 'ld keep yer all 'e knew from gettin' there, be tellin' lies ter them about 'ow kind they is ter yer 'ere, an' all th' rest, jist as they stuffed th' Inspector about me. An' 'e's a bloke what swallers all theer lies and skite about ther hacts o' kindness, an' their good nater, an' about my playin' up on them, an' me hingratitune or somefing. He takes it all has th' straight hout gorspels truth; Oh, no; there's no chancet for yer, Herrick, yet a while; but waits till I gets a bit o' panum! I've five peg hid away in me tin now, what Mr. Ray McKay gived ter me fer tellin' 'im where ter find a horst 'e lost. Yer 'aven't saw Mister Ray McKay yet, has yer, Herrick? Oh, 'e's a shiney torf; han' so is Miss Beatrice, who 'e rides hout with every day. Oh, she's a hangel! han' ain't she a beauty on 'er new side-saddle 'orse? Not a bit stuck hup neither, like some o' them what passes yer by with their blokes. She'll hask yer ter th' Sunday School treat, Herrick, same as she ders me; an' if 'e won't let yer go, as 'e won't, o' course, not 'im, 'e ain't likely ter, she'll send over what cakes she keeps fer yer next day, an' ther prize that yer ould 'ave won if yer 'ad gone——"

Just here, Snowy's rambling discourse was interrupted by the voice of Mrs. Potthouse calling upon the magpie to give a rendering of "How Snowy Wing squeals when Mother 'ides 'im."

Snowy stared, suddenly, at Eric, and Eric stared at Snowy.

The bird opened its beak, and after the manner of Snowy, squealed tragically. Then, resting several semi-breves, it broke out in a dramatic voice: "Oh, yer killin' me! Yer killin' me!" Resting a second or two, for effect, it wound up, melodramatically, with: "Never! Never! Never! Mother! I'll never do it again! never do it again! oh, never! never! never!"

Snowy's fists clenched, his teeth set, and his eyes flashed like the villain's in the play. Only on one solitary occasion, and then in a weak moment, when he first came to Piggy's inferno, had he given in under the bruises of the leg-rope, and pleaded for mercy. And for the screams on that far-off occasion, and his futile requests for mercy and forgiveness, to be now reproduced like words spoken into a gramophone, and used in ridicule against himself was worse than ten floggings—worse than death! His pride was insulted; his spirit of taking his gruel like a man trampled upon; his heart stabbed to the very core.

Lifting the axe high above his head, where it poised for a second, he said:

"The first chancet I ever get, I'll chop that magpie's damned head (down came the axe) right hoff!"

"It's not the poor magpie's fault, Snowy," Eric said, holding a brief for the bird. "It doesn't know its doing any wrong, y' know."

"Hi don't care, Herrick (lifting the axe again), Hi'll chop—"

Once more Mrs. Potthouse's voice intruded.

"Now, hif yer're finished yer work," she cried, "hand yer want hany breakfast, yer'd better look sharp hand 'ave it, 'cause Hi'm not agoin' ter keep ther things awaitin' on ther table hall day fer yous."

"The horses?" Eric said, looking up, interrogatingly, at his friend.

Snowy turned his eyes in the direction of the animals, then to the kitchen.

"Well, Herrick," he replied, philosophically, "a breakfust in yer hinside is better'n two locked in ther hoven." And tossing the axe aside, Snowy slunk off, leading the way to the kitchen.

Eric, feeling abashed, removed his hat, and looking about him, hesitated in the door-way. To sit to a meal with soiled face and hands, and without arranging his hair, was repugnant to his nature.

"What hare yer glarint erbout hat?" Mrs. Potthouse shouted to him. "There's yer breakfust hon th' table, starint hat yer; hain't yer got heyes ter see it? Hif yer don't want it, git hoff hout, there's plenty o' work waitin' ter be done."

"I was looking for a dish to wash in, Mum," Eric faltered.

"A dish to wash hin! hoh!" she sneered, placing both hands on her ill-shaped hips, and fixing him steadily with her glaring eyes. "That's hall what's wrong with yer, his it? Wouldn't yer like a warm plunge hin a marble bath? hand a pair o' hivory brushes hand lookint glass ter do yer 'air up be? Hand, may be, yer'd like yer carpet slippers fetched, hand put down beside yer for yer to put yer feet into—wouldn't yer?" lifting her voice fairly into the rafters, and approaching the shivering boy. "Wouldn't yer?"

"N—n—no, Mum," was the nervous response.

"Well, 'ere!" And grabbing poor Eric roughly by the shoulders, she ran him to the table, and squashing him down hard on a stool, yelled. "There!" shoving a pint pot under his nose, "hand there!" bashing a cocoa tin, containing dripping, hard on the board, "hand 'ere!" dumping the full tea-pot down heavily beside his elbow. "Hand can yer see that?" banging a burnt damper, the shape of a cartwheel, down in front of him, with so much force that it shook half the tea out of the pint that Snowy had filled for himself. "Hand hare yer satisfied—or d'yer want someone t' heat it fer yer?"

Snowy, munching ravenously, looked over the edge of his pint of black tea, and grinned at the tigress, as she left the kitchen to tidy the "parlor."

"Never mind, Herric," he said, between gulps; "don't lose any time, tho'. Heat hall yer can afore she comes ter whip heverythink away from year!"

And, forgetting his soiled hands, in the moment of hunger, Eric, acting on Snowy's advice, hurriedly devoured as much damper and dripping, and swilled as much black tea as he had appetite and capacity for—and a little more.

"Hit's th' only innings we gets," Snowy added, after a long interval. "'S' keep yer wicket up as long as yer can."

Then, having finished to his satisfaction, he leaned across, and whispered, confidentially:

"Now, while theer's a chancet, I wanter show yer somefing." Then keeping one eye closely fixed on the open door, Snowy noiselessly slipped from the table, and tip-toeing across the room, bent down, and, raising the end of a short, broad slab, which served as a floor-board, disclosed to the astonished gaze of Eric a large hole beneath, containing several tins, a jug, and a tin-plate. Cautiously replacing the slab, he tip-toed back to the table again.

"That's me cold storage," he whispered, with a grin. "Hit's horiginal, Herrick. I thought it hall out, and made it meself harfter workin' hours. Yer gets to it from under th' front o' th' house. An' when they sends me ter bed without supper, thinkin' they've did something smart for theirselves, I comes up theer," pointing to the floor, "an' inter th' cubbard. It comes awkward but, when they sits 'ere fer long, same as they did larst night, when yer comed."

11. Mr. Mullett

Eric was sitting, staring at his friend, with wide open eyes and mouth, when Piggy's voice was heard roaring in the yard, and confusion set in.

Mrs. Potthouse rushed in from the parlor.

"Hain't yer finished yet?" she cried. "Hand yer master back from ther fact'ry with th' waging! Hoh, yer'll catch hit, yer young whelps, fer not bein' hout ter hopen th' gate . . . Go hon hout till him!"

The two boys snatched up their hats, and hastened to answer the howls that every moment were growing more and more in volume, and violence. As they filed past Mrs. Potthouse, recoiling instinctively from her, she delivered them, in turn, a blow with the broom that she held in her hand, yelling, as she did so:

"Hand take thet ter go hon with!"

A flash, stylish-looking man in breeches and boots, who had arrived with Piggy, to inspect some of the pigs that were for sale, dismounted from his horse, and awaited the latter's pleasure.

"An'—an'——" Piggy foamed, jumping from the waggon, "didn' I tell yez ter put the horses that wouldn't be usin' back intil the grass paddock—didn' I?" approaching Snowy, with blood in his eye.

"We wuz jest goin' to do it," Snowy answered, dropping his head humbly.

"Jest goin' to do ud!" Piggy raved. "Yer whelps! yez wud never do ud if yer cud—cud—help ud! . . . An'—an'—who tell yez to put that—that skeleton of a horse in the ya-ard an'—an'—give ud th' good pumpkin to stuff itself wid—the pumpkin, bought in the drooth—who telt yez?"

"The others kept 'untin'' im," Snowy said, "an' we put 'im there till he finished."

"I'll—I'll put yez somewhere, some day, fer something, me young cock-o'-th'-walk, where yez won't get any pumpkin to—to thrun away, if ye're not careful wid yourself . . . Here," pointing peremptorily to the cans on the waggon, "get that whey out, an'—an'—guv it to the pigs, an'—an'—be th' tare o' war if yez don't clean th' cans better'n yez cleaned them yesterday, I'll—I'll break your baacks for you, I will."

Then, turning sulkily to the visitor:

"Th' d——n young devils! alls they thinks erbout is sky-larkin' round the place from—from morning till noight, an'—an'—comin' up fer their meals, like wild wolves, when ever they are ready fer them."

The other smiled cynically; and casting his eyes in the direction of the yard, where Newchum was moving restlessly about, and whinneying, said:

"What's this you've got, Piggy? Something new?"

"P'shaw!" Piggy answered, affecting indifference. "Some trash that even th'—th'—drought cudn't kill."

The man in the boots approached the rails of the yard, and eyed Newchum closely.

"He certainly got a gruelling from the drought," he said, "but he's a d—— good frame, all the same, Piggy . . . What's his age?"

"Th' Lord only cud tell!" Piggy answered, impatiently.

"Oh, there's more than the Lord can tell that!" And breeches and boots crept through the rails, and entered the yard.

"What ders 'e wants pokin' about Newchum fer?" Snowy growled, jealously watching the man from the milk waggon.

"What's th' gentleman's name?" Eric inquired.

"Him!" Snowy snarled, contemptuously, " 'e's only Tom Mullett; 'e ain't no gentle'un; 'e comes 'ere sometimes in ther night, yer'll see 'im often drekely, an' they talks with theer 'eads tergether like thieves, as don't want ter let on. I heerd 'im once, when I was in th' cold storage, 'er talkin' erbout, Mr. Ray McKay, an' hittin' th' table, an' a-swearin' to th' Dago that he'd beat th' parson's son fer Miss Beatrice yet, or bust 'isself. I thinks he'll bust 'isself."

To his great surprise, Mr. Tom Mullett failed to place his hands on Newchum. The horse gave an unexpected display of temper. He ran at the intruder with wide open mouth; and low condition, and all that he was in, tried to impress Mullett with his heels, as the former took refuge on the rails.

Snowy, gazing across, was delighted. "I 'opes 'e heats 'im, Herrick!" he said, chuckling.

Eric looked concerned, and murmured, apprehensively, "He'll bite, or do anything to strangers if they go near him."

"Where the deuce did yer get him from, Piggy—out of a circus?" Mullett said, looking down on Newchum from the top of the yard.

"He's—he's—in a circus now, I'm thinkin'," was Piggy's surly reply. "Just look at them—them two clowns, there," indicating Snowy and Eric, "starin' their eyes out ter see what's goin' on here, in—in—instead o' lukin' after th' wheay (yelling at the boys) go on there, yer young vagabones, an'—an'—does yer work."

The boys went on.

Then, throwing open the yard gate:

"We'll—we'll let this scarecrow out, an'—an'—go round an' see th' pigs when they be feedin'."

"I'll give you fifty bob for him, as he stands, Piggy," Mullett remarked, as Newchum strode through the gate.

"Go 'long, go 'long!" Piggy answered. "I—I—don't wants ter be takin' yer money, Tom. 'Tis bad enough ter be takin' me 'inemies in. Come on, an'—an'—luk if any o' the pigs 'ill sood."

But Mullett's eye followed the movements of the horse. Newchum stood, looked around; whinneyed.

"Hello, Newchum," Eric couldn't resist calling out.

In recognition, Newchum whinneyed again, and trotted to the waggon. He switched his tail, stamped his feet, shook his head, and went through various forms of horse-play, to mark his delight. Then he poked his nose under Eric's arm, and remained motionless.

"By Heavens! look at that," Mullett exclaimed. "I've seen horses take to dogs and cats; but I never saw a horse make so much fuss over a kiddy before."

Piggy lifted his eyes.

"Oh! he do be givin' th' damn thing bits o' bread, an'—an'—stuffin' 'im every day," he grunted disparagingly. "Come round wid me this wa-ay"—directing his steps to the rear of the barn where the styes were located.

"Who is the kid?" Mullett asked casually, as they turned away.

" 'Tis a wise child what knows its own father," Piggy answered. "An'—an'—'twud be a wise orphan what cud tell y' who he is, or who he isn't, when he haven't no one to tell him his pethigree."

Tom Mullett dealt with Piggy for several "porkers"; and when he had gone, and the gate closed behind him, Piggy shouted lustily to Snowy and Eric, who with cloths in their hands, their sleeves tucked up to their shoulders, were employed rubbing and scrubbing and scalding a dozen milk-cans:

"Put that—that skeleton intil th' little windmill paddock; am'—an'—leave 'um there. An'—an'—don't yez ever bring 'im intil this ya-ard again!"

"A good job, Herrick," Snowy chuckled. "It'll suit uz hall ter pieces."

12.   Twelve Months After

More than twelve months had passed. The first call of the jackass had gone, and the grey dawn was beginning to break over the verdant valleys, and still lagoons. Two shadowy forms flitted round the dim outline of a horse in the Windmill paddock of Daisy Vale. Snowy Wing and Eric Ryle were saddling New-chum, as they had been doing every morning at that hour for several months.

"We'll fold th' cloth up double, this mornin', Herrick," Snowy said, " 'Cause th' stuffin's sinking down a lot an' th' saddle might touch 'e's wither."

"Do you think the circingle is strong enough to hold?" Eric said, carefully testing the gear. "We don't want to come off again, like we did yesterday morning."

Memories of the double catastrophe set Snowy chuckling as he strained on tip-toe to tighten the greenhide girth to the last pole. "I mended it to-day," he answered, "when 'e was away and she" (grunting in his efforts to tighten the circingle) "talkin' to them lydies. I put two ribbits in it—two (grunt) that 'e was keepin' fer th' (grunt) harnish. It's strongerer than ever now."

Then the reins were thrown over the animal's head.

"Now, on yer get, Herrick," Snowy advised, "an' ride 'im over to ther stump, an' I'll get on theer."

When Eric took hold of the reins and climbed into the saddle, the horse, answering to the touch, moved off proudly at a swinging walk, as though he was built on springs; his head carried high, and his long tail, held well out, flowing gracefully behind him. And this was "old Newchum"; this the "frame"; the "bag o' bones," the "skeleton," the "dying object," the relic of the awful drought; this animal that now was all life, all action, sleek-skinned, and rolling fat! Ah! yes! The times had indeed changed.

"Now, we'll jes' see 'ow 'ard 'e can cut this mornin' afore we goes after ther cows," Snowy said, scrambling on behind Eric, "and send im twicet round th' course, Herrick, an' let 'im go all

'e knows—but I wisht (sorrowfully) he'd go with me on in
front. Curioust 'ow 'e won't!"

The next moment Newchum's head was turned, and, prancing and champing the bit, he faced the "course" (a rude circle
indicated within the 50-acre paddock by certain trees and
objects familiar to the two boys). He felt the gentle pressure;
the nervous touch of a pair of heels. He reefed; carried the full
rein with him; was away, stretching to it, doubling to it, bending to it, thundering down the stretch of grim, grey plain.
Around the curve he swept like a demon, the riders crouching
low on his back. A shirt ballooned violently in the wind for
just a second, then burst from its moorings, and flip-flapped
like a whirling flag. Furiously they swept round the second
curve. A tree flashed, and the first "mile" was circled. Down
the plain again. The speed was too much for Eric. He gasped,
gulped, dropped his head, recovered. "Fer th' finish! Give it
'im"—in muffled jerks from Snowy. Then two pairs of heels
worked like wings. The grass whistled beneath. Muscles,
strained and stretched. The old saddle creaked like a ship. The
earth rocked, lifted. Then the tree flashed again and the "spin"
was over.

"Oh, 'eavens!" Snowy gasped, rolling from the saddle to the
ground. "Hif 'e 'adn't stopped, Herrick, I'd a-tumbled hoff—
right hoff on me 'ead; fer th' breatht wuz blowed right outer me
stomick, an' I couldn't git any more hinto it. Oh! bless me!
wuz hever theer sich a racet 'orse?"

Eric dropped forward on the arched and heated neck of
Newchum till his full breath returned. Then, taking Snowy up
behind again, cantered leisurely off into the grass-paddock;
and rounding the cows up, started them for the yard. Returning
to the Windmill paddock, they dismounted and concealed
their riding gear. Then, after rubbing the animal dry, they let
him go, where he remained for the rest of the day, out of
everyone's sight, and knee-deep in clover and wild lucerne. And
this exciting ride on the back of Newchum every morning was
the one bright circumstance in the long, dull rounds of their
sordid existence—'twas the oasis in the desert of their hard,
wretched lives.

13. Trouble on the Lucerne

"Breakfast" was over, and Snowy and Eric were engaged in scrubbing and cleaning the milk cans.

Piggy came along clearing his throat.

"When yez be finished them cans," he said, "if—if—yez 'll ever be finished, drive th'—th' cows down an'—an'—put them on th' lucen; an'—an'—shepherd them there till yez see me wave th' flag from th' randy; then—then taake them off ud at oncet, right at oncet, or they'll be bustin 'in ud. An'—an'—be th' dogs of war, if yez let any o' them bust, I'll—I'll shoot yez in th' paddick like rats, so I will. D' yez hear me?"

The boys hastened to assure the old tyrant that they heard him.

"Hand don't ferget," Mrs. Potthouse squaled, adding her injunction, "don't ferget who's ter be 'ere fer dinner, hand that yer is ter heat hin th' parlor. Hand don't come hin without yer manners, hand sit down has dirty has two blacks; cleant yerselves fer oncet in yer lives, hand put hon ther coats that's been washed hand hironed fer yer, hand don't try ter give ther place a bad name. Hand when yer are hasked hany hofficial questions, Snowy Wing, as yer will be, Hi've no doubt, erbout 'ow yer are fed, an' 'oused, hand waited hon, mind yer don't tell no lies."

Snowy ground his teeth and bit his lip.

"Yer needn't pull no faces erbout it," the hag went on. "We knows yer quite capable o' doin' it."

"Be—be cripes, then," Piggy broke in, "if—if there's any mis'renting th'—th' treatment that—that any ov yez get under me roof, I'll—I'll strangle yez in yer sleep, I will, yez pair o' tieves."

And with various imprecations and warnings, and threats of after-vengeance if they failed to be well-behaved, and loyal, and truthful, and clean, in the presence of the inspector, Piggy and his wife left the boys to their cheerful reflections.

"It's on'y one of two things, Herrick," Snowy mused feelingly, as they sauntered into the lucerne paddock at the tails of the straggling milkers. "Heither I must make up me mind ter tell the 'onest truth, an' say it straight hout, thet they ain't fit ter 'ave dorgs under them; an' run away drekeley arter. Gord knows where to, Herrick! an' p'raps ter be brought back be Constable 'Enery to 'im ter-morrer! Hor, Herrick, ter put me tongue hin me cheek, an' tell hall th' lies I can think o' erbout th' nice, kind, generous people they are; an' 'ow self-dernyin'; an' ow' good they's ter me, and 'ow it'd break me very heart ter be took away from me happy 'ome."

"But you mustn't tell a lie, Snowy; it's wicked," Eric said. "It would be worse than everything. You must—you must—"

He paused. He was in a quandary.

"Yer thinks Hi should stick ter th' truth, an' then do a bunk?" Snowy said, helping him out.

"Oh, no! no! not that either; that would only make every-thing blacker against you; and they would perhaps get Mr. Ray McKay and Miss Beatrice, and everyone on their side. But maybe the Inspector is a good man, and would believe what you tell him, Snowy; and perhaps he would take you from here, and get you a better place."

"No chancet, Herrick!" Snowy answered gravely. "He ain't th' sort; I knows 'im. 'Sides, if 'e did believe me, an' took me away, I'd be clearin' out an' leavin' you ter go through a nice picernic on yer own. No, Herrick, you an' me's pals, an' I never deeserts a pal. Leave it hall ter me, Herrick. I'll go through with it; an' if I ders tell a fib or two, it's on'y because I 'as ter, an' it'll be them as 'll 'ave to answer."

Leg-weary and bodily tired, the two boys sat beside the fence while the cows spread out and fed on the lucerne.

The day was promising warm. After a while, there was a silence. First Eric, then Snowy dozed and dropped to sleep. Friendly soldier birds came and perched on the fence, and "tweeked" above their heads. Hares disturbed in their formes darted from the shelter of the thick lucerne and raced in pur-suit of each other to cover in the grass-paddock.

The time arrived to remove the cows. The flag waved from the verandah of the house. It waved violently for ten minutes, and roars interspersed with angry oaths were borne vaguely upon the wind.

An aggressive bull-dog ant disturbed the slumbers of Snowy.

He awoke with a jump, danced about and rubbed his bare leg.

"Herrick!" he shouted, with alarm. "Th' flag's wavin'. I don't know how long. Come on!"

They both ran as fast as their legs could carry them to round up the milkers.

"Oh, look!" Eric cried with fearful apprehension. "There's one bursting, I do believe!"

"Oh! 'eavens!" from Snowy, as he ran faster. "Get them hout! Get them hout, Herrick! Quick! quick! Oh-h, we're hin for it."

Rushing the cows out through the barb-wire gate, the boys turned and raced frantically back to the beast that was down and swollen like a balloon.

With the aid of a pair of field glasses, Piggy, from his seat on the verandah, saw by the commotion going on that something was amiss, and swearing at the top of his voice, hobbled off to the scene.

Eric and Snowy were nearly out of their minds. Both were shedding tears.

"I'll go an' tell 'im ter come," Snowy said in desperation, and started off. But seeing the form of Piggy already on the way, Snowy bounded back; and with increased fear and alarm, endeavored in all manner of ways to persuade the cow to rise and save the situation.

"Oh! if we could only let the wind out of her, and get her up before he comes!" Eric whined. Like a flash Snowy remembered he had a pocket-knife. Opening it hurriedly he stabbed the cow in the flank with the blade. She didn't budge. Piggy came nearer and nearer. The moments were flying. Snowy kicked her with his bare foot. Eric kicked her. Snowy jumped astride her barrel-like carcase and bumped her with all his weight to force the gas out. Eric got astride behind him to add his power. Piggy arrived, puffing, perspiring, and with fire and fury in his eye.

"Oh, megod, it's Lady Morgan! Lady Morgan!" he yelled pathetically. "Have she busht? Have she busht?" One glance convinced him that she was dead as a door-nail. Then his voice changed.

"Yez ——! ——! ——! ——!" he yelled; while Snowy skidaddled one way, and Eric another.

14. Stibbening, the Inspector

"Good day, Mr. Potthouse," the Inspector said, riding into the yard on a horse that he hired at the railway station.

"Hello, Mr. Brown," Piggy responded, lifting his whiskered face from a dish of water that he was sluicing himself in, and reaching for a towel. "Yez are just in time for yer dinner."

Snowy promptly appeared, and took possession of the horse.

"Guv it a derink, an'—an' a good feed ov oats," Piggy shouted after him.

Then, tossing the towel on the ground:

"Come 'long, an'—an'—sit yez down, Mr. Brown. 'Tis fine weather we're havin'."

The Inspector followed Piggy into the parlor, where Mrs. Potthouse, busy setting the table, received him with a smirk which answered for a smile, and ducked her head like Judy bowing to Punch in the show.

"Yer lookin' well hon it sincet yer wuz here last," she said, complimenting him upon his well-fed appearance.

"Well, you see, I haven't much to worry me, Mrs. Potthouse," the easy-going official replied. "So long as I find the youngsters are doing all right on the farms, and I get three meals a day, and somewhere to sleep at night, I'm happy."

"Then yer hain't got much ter trouble yer 'ead erbout," she rejoined. "Hit's hother people, Mr. Brown, who gets hall th' worry o' th' youngsters; they're more trouble than they're worth, Hi'm thinkin'; hand they do more 'arm hon a place than they'll hever be able ter make good. Leastaways, that's hour experience."

"Why, what has been going wrong, Mrs. Potthouse?" the Inspector asked.

"Well"—and fire flashed from the eyes of the hag as she straightened up and pointed through the front window. "Yer can't even trust th' one we have 'ere ter watch th' cows fer ten minets on that bit o' lucen without he clears hoff somewhere hafter birds hand lets th' hanimals bust."

"I'm sorry to hear that of him," gravely from the official

"Yes, yes!" Piggy chimed in, as he produced a whisky bottle and two glasses. "Me—me very besht cow, Lady Morgan—that—that I refused twenty sovereigns fer from Johnny Grogan —he let busht on th' lucen this vera morning, th—th' d—— young whelp! If ud had been my own son who's awaay ad th'—th' Grammar Schule, I'd—I'd have half killed him forrid, I wud."

"Oh, that's too bad of the young vagabond," the other murmured. "Too bad, altogether! It's a thing he should have been severely chastised for—not the slightest doubt of it."

"Well, yez know, Mister Brown," Piggy said in a low, humble, sympathetic voice, "one never likes to—to put hand till a child what ain't his own. An'—an' when yez know a boy has never father or—or mother, th' feelin' that it puts until your heart prevents yez from ud, an' yez can't do ud."

"Well, you know," the Inspector replied, with an air of wisdom mingled with justice, "it is worse for the boy—it's against his interests—if it isn't done in cases where he richly deserves it, such as this one."

"Oh, dersen't I know ud—know ud well," Piggy mumbled, affecting indifference. "But we'll let it go, let it go . . . What will yez take wid id, Mr. Brown? A little well-water, or a drop o' ginger-beer?"

Mr. Brown said he always took water with his. Ginger-beer or soda water, he reckoned, was injurious to the system when taken with whisky; it wouldn't assimilate in the stomach.

"Well, well! I—I never knew that now," said Piggy, smacking his lips after tossing his down.

"Oh, yes, that's well known to whisky drinkers in town," the visitor added, planking his empty glass beside Piggy's, and taking out his pocket handkerchief. "Water with whisky every time."

"See that now! An'—an' it's cheaper," Piggy put in, this view of it recurring to him after an interval of reflection. Then bending over the table once more:

"Fill up again, Mister Brown, an'—an' then we'll hab a moutful to eat."

The official filled his glass again, and having emptied it like winking sat down to dinner.

"Now I wonder where is them boys?" Mrs. Potthouse remarked, leaving the room and going to the back door.

The boys, with a look of fear and uncertainty on their polished faces, were waiting about outside.

"D' yer want ter be carried hin?" the old fiend raved. "Hor d' yer want yer dinner fetched hout ter y'?" Then, hissing into Snowy's ear as he stepped past her:

"Hand yer 'ad better heat yer skin full, me sparrow 'awk, fer yer'll go to yer bed pretty 'ungry han' sore ter night, Hi know."

Snowy and Eric slouched in with awkward, uneasy step, looking more like lambs going to the slaughter than youths promoted to a place at the best table.

The Inspector condescended to pause in his conversation, and nod stiffly to the waifs, as they took their seats, then continued his observations on the joys and excellence of good whisky.

"Some of the stuff you get in hotels," he told Piggy, "is deadly; it's not fit to give to travellers. But with 'Wild Cat' you can't go wrong; it's the best in the market, and you can drink bottles of it without feeling the least effect."

"What 'ave Hi halwez told yer erbout usin' yer knife han' fork, Master Snowy?" Mrs. Potthouse remarked, when Snowy, who had not been used to cutlery in the kitchen, took the roast beef in his hands to devour it. "Yer soon forgets th' manners that's taught yer!"

Poor Snowy took up the knife and fork, but how to manipulate them he hadn't the slightest idea. Stealing a glance at the Inspector, next him, to learn his methods, he made an heroic effort to imitate his dexterity. His display was feeble. He reversed arms, and taking a firm grip of the handles with full fists, set to work in his own way. He leaned forward and put all his strength into the operation. It became a tug-of-war between the knife and the fork. The knife severed its hold, and the fork, having nothing to resist, flew from the plate, taking the meat and the gravy with it, which it propelled with a splash into the lap of the loquacious Inspector. That gentleman shoved his chair back with a great noise and heaved the roast beef to the floor as though it were a live thing.

Piggy, from his place at the head of the table, poured a torrent of language over the head of the surprised and disappointed-looking Snowy. Mrs. Potthouse walloped him vigorously with her hands—walloped him till he found his feet, and scrambling from the chair, rushed outside.

Meanwhile, the Inspector had risen from the table, and was standing in the middle of the floor rubbing and scrubbing the gravy out of his pants with his handkerchief.

"That's hon'y some o' ther things we 'as ter put up with from 'im," Mrs. Potthouse said apologetically, "Hoh, 'e's a hin-corriable scamp! hand gets worst hevery day!"

"An'—an'—I do believes he did it o' purpose," Piggy groaned, reaching for the whisky bottle. "Howsomever, 'tis done, 'tis done. But take yez another little drop, Mister Brown, an'—an' —wash ud down—wash ud down."

Mr. Brown half filled his glass, and promptly washed it down.

"Well, now," Piggy said, when the meal was over, "I suppose yez wud like to have a word with Snowy Wing afore yez go?"

"May be-sh I'd (hic) better," was the answer. "Theresh (hic) just time. Sen' him (hic) in."

Snowy, battered and dishevelled, and in his shirt sleeves, entered the parlor again, looking like an escapee going up for sentence.

"Havesh you (hic) any plaints to makesh to me about (hic) treatment, boy? Are yoush er—er (hic) satisfied?" Mr. Brown asked.

"Oh, it's a lovely placet ter be in, sir, when yer gits used to it," Snowy answered, with a twinkle in his eye. "It's simply divine; an' I'm satisfied about it orlright."

"Well, then, yoush (hic) can thinkshelf luck (hic) lucky. My horsh (hic) ready?"

With a grin on his face, Snowy withdrew. And when Mr. Brown's horse was saddled and brought to the door, Piggy helped him into the saddle, and saw him safely through the gate.

15.   Ray McKay and Beatrice Appleby

Amid the green lucerne squares, and golden cornfields sur-rounded with hills and scenes of peace and quietude, nestled "Todmorden," the home of Beatrice Appleby.

The slowly sinking sun was shedding fantastic rays upon the tinted pines and the garden that was ablaze with bloom and bud.

Beatrice plucked a red carnation, and pinning it in Ray McKay's button-hole, said with a smile:

"I've a great favor to ask of you, Ray?"

"The deuce you have," he said. "Well, sit over here and break it gently."

He led her to a seat beneath one of the murmuring pines. It was a lovely spot. The sweet-smelling air filled the garden with fragrance. The rose and honeysuckle clung about in profusion. The ivy climbed over the walls of the bush house beside them. Beneath rippled the limpid waters of the winding creek; and away beyond, as far as the eye could see, stretched the great rolling downs.

"Now you won't think me dreadfully silly, will you, Ray?" Beatrice commenced.

Ray replied with a gentle squeeze of her slender waist.

"I know what I'm going to tell you will sound awfully funny, but——"

"Then it's a joke, is it, Beatrice?"

"I am afraid you will think it is."

"When are you going to come to it, Beatrice?" with another squeeze.

"Now listen. I saw my two little friends this afternoon—the poor little orphan boys, and we had such a long interesting chat under the willows."

"And how is the lively White Ants?" Ray asked. "Has he had the 'giblets' this week? And is My Lady Morgan in the best of spirits?"

"Oh! I knew I had something to tell you," and Beatrice broke into a short, silvery laugh. "She's dead; poor thing! She 'hover et 'erself an' busted on th' loosum'."

Ray thought of Snowy, and laughed.

"It's a fatality that will never overtake the poor kids themselves while they're at Potthouse's," he said.

"Ah! poor little chaps!" and Beatrice changed suddenly. "It's a shame to laugh at them. But that's not what I was going to tell you, Ray. The little fellows have got a horse——"

"A horse?" Ray laughed, "the deuce! Something will break at Daisy Vale, now, Beatrice. The last time I saw them they were going full split, bare-headed, on two calves, a red one and a white one; and the further they went the further apart they drifted."

"Oh! that would be 'Carbine' and 'Fair Ellen'," and Beatrice broke into a fresh ripple of laughter. " 'Th' Dago 'e ain't tumbled yet erbout them bein' broket ter saddle, but when 'e do won't 'e go crook'."

"Ha! ha! ha!" loudly from Ray. "Ha! ha! ha! He's a quaint cus, Snowy. Do you know, I enjoy a chat with the little beggar, Beatrice."

"Ah! but it's a shame the treatment they get, Ray! It's really cruel. And that little Eric is such a quiet, gentle boy, and so well mannered. They're kept so ragged and dirty too, that really someone should speak to that old Potthouse about them!"

"I am afraid, though, Beatrice," Ray said, seriously, "that it wouldn't do any good to meddle in the affairs of a neighbour. It might be a matter, perhaps, that my old pater, as the clergyman of the district, might take——"

"Yes; but that's not what I wanted to ask you just now," Beatrice interrupted. "This horse——"

"Oh, yes; I forgot; they have a horse."

"And it's a racehorse, Ray—a real racehorse."

"Go easy, Beatrice."

"I'm really serious, Ray. They gave me all its history, and I believe everything the little chaps told me. It belonged to Eric's father, and all its pedigree is in a letter written to his mother, that the little chap has in his box amongst his mother's papers. Newchum is the horse's name, and they told me so much about him—how fond the poor mother was of him, and how she kept him alive all through the drought with pieces of bread—how he waits with his head over the fence watching for Eric; and how he calls to him and rubs his head against him when he comes— that I'm just dying to see him. I'm sure he must be a lovely horse, Ray!"

"Yes; he must be, Beatrice," Ray drawled.

"And do you know how they train him?—but you mustn't tell anyone a word about it, especially Mr. Mullett; it's a great secret."

"All the brumbies in the bush wouldn't drag it out of me, Beatrice."

"They keep him in a small paddock where no one ever sees him, and every morning at break of day they gallop him round it."

"Which of them rides him, Beatrice?" placing his cheek against hers.

"They both ride him, Ray, and ——"

"Ha! ha! ha! If ever old Potthouse catches them you won't hear any more about your lovely chestnut."

"Oh! I'd love to go up some morning, early, just to see the little chaps galloping him."

"Yes; and take an eight-day clock with you, Beatrice, and get Snowy to time him."

"Snowy says when Newchum is going at his top the trees fly past so quick, Ray, that ' 'hif hever they hits 'im they'll only be a wet spot left hon th' bark'."

A loud "Ha! ha! ha!" came from Ray, and he said: "And if ever they get as far as racing him, Beatrice, there might only be a wet spot left on the course."

"Now that's just what I've got to ask you about. Do you know what it is, Ray?"

"I don't, indeed."

"Well, I want you, for my sake, to enter Newchum in the Toowoomba Cup in your own name for the little fellows."

Ray held her from him and looked into her face.

"Well, this is a joke," he said.

"I'm so earnest about it, Ray" (putting her arms around his neck). "Now, won't you?"

"Beatrice, I can hear the laugh that would ring on the lawn, now! Ha! ha! Fancy those two ragged young beggars coming out on some mule of a horse, perhaps walloping it with a hoe, that was entered and blazed about as 'Ray McKay's New-chum.' Ha! ha! ha!"

"But you will, Ray; you'll do it for me, won't you?" And Beatrice snuggled close to him.

Ray laughed harder; then, after reflecting, held Beatrice from him again and said: "Well, after all, a little ridicule from my friends in town won't kill me; and there's nothing that I wouldn't make of myself over to please you, Beatrice (pause). I'm blowed if I don't do it."

"I knew you would, Ray," and in compensation she planted a kiss somewhere about his tanned cheeks.

"Ha! ha! ha!" involuntarily burst again from Ray McKay as arm in arm together they strolled inside for tea.

16. Piggy Uses the Leg-Rope

While Ray McKay and Beatrice joined round the full and merry board in the large and well-lighted dining-room at "Todmorden," poor Eric and Snowy, after having fed the pigs for the night, and distributed hay to the draught horses, were sitting together irresolutely thinking and brooding beside the barn at "Daisy Vale."

Silent, bitter forebodings of plaited greenhide being the only item on their bill of fare filled their unhappy minds. They feared to show up at the kitchen door. Their eyes, dimmed with gathering tears, met, and each read the mental anguish of the other.

"I can't go in if he means to hammer me," Eric said in a broken voice.

"An' 'es fit fer anything ter-night," Snowy murmured gloomily. "'E's been 'avin' drink, yer know!"

Just then Piggy called in a loud voice to his wife, as he passed from the kitchen to the "parlor":

"Guv them they're supper," he said. "So they can go over to Fegan to—to—borry me a pair o' whinkers fer th' black mare, afore ud gets bed-time."

"It's orlright, Herrick," Snowy said, brightening up, and rising promptly to his feet, " 'E's fergottent erbout it. Come on. Don't let them see we wuz expectint a hidin' or they might think as it might be a shame ter disserpoint two poor blokes like hus."

With lighter hearts they hovered round the kitchen door. Snowy, to announce their presence, instructed one of the dogs to "go and bark at itself." And all doubt and distrust vanished completely when Mrs. Potthouse contented herself with warning them to "sling theirselves erbout hif they wanted hany tea"; and that they could "thank their lucky stars they wuz goin' ter get hany at all."

With a twinkle in their eyes, the waifs "threw themselves about," and in a trice Snowy was slicing bread, and Eric pouring out tea.

Suddenly the doorway was darkened, and Piggy, carrying a leg-rope in one hand, and a heavy greenhide slogger in the other, glided in and calmly fastened the latch behind him.

A thrill of terror shot through the boys. In a flash they realised they had been trapped like rats! The tea-pot and the bread loaf fell from their hands to the table. A cry escaped Eric, as he shrank shivering into a corner. Snowy, bewildered completely, rose to his feet, and standing with back to the table, clutched the edge of it with both hands. Pale and dogged-looking, he waited like a condemned prisoner.

Potthouse grinned in malevolent triumph at the foiled and helpless victims.

"An'—an' yez young cubs," he roared, by way of preliminary introduction, "yez have th—th cheek to come an'—an' get ye'er fill of grub, after all th'—th' ruination yez did this daay!"

"Don't, oh! don't touch us! Please don't! Oh! don't!" Eric screamed distractedly, flying to another corner.

The woman leered at the frantic boy.

Piggy advanced to Snowy.

"Put this on yez," he said, looping the leg-rope round the boy's neck, and drawing it tight. Snowy's eyes flashed and bulged; his teeth set like a vyce; his hands gripped the table till his finger-nails sunk into the very pine.

"Oh-h! He's going to hang him!" Eric screamed, springing to the door and trying to unfasten it. "He's going to ——"

He stopped suddenly. There was an interruption.

A tall, well-built, clean-shaven man of athletic appearance walked into the room.

17. Harry Ryle Appears

"Stop!" he cried. "Isn't the life of one sufficient to have on your conscience, Mr. Pigford Potthouse?"

Piggy's eyes and mouth opened wide. The greenhide fell from his hand.

"Lor-d! Lor-d 'tis Harry ——"

"Mention that name and I'll strangle you as I would a rat."

Mrs. Potthouse gave a sharp cry of recognition.

"You know me, do you?" the stranger said, turning quickly upon her. "Well, my name now is Don Fitzrobertson, and don't you forget it."

Then to Piggy:

"Send these boys about their business—mine is more important. I'm in a hurry."

Snowy and Eric stood staring.

"Get a move on!" the stranger commanded, "the lot of you."

Shrieking like a lost soul, Mrs. Potthouse rushed into the house, while the two boys, feeling like reprieved prisoners, went off and ran excitedly across the yard towards the barn.

"A sad mistake, wasn't it, Piggy?" said Fitzrobertson, "for a clever old dog like you, after successfully stealing a will that you thought was made in my favour, to postpone burning it. Ha! ha! As Harry Ryle I impersonated my relationship heroically, you must admit—but what a defamation it was on my glorious English pedigree! Sit down, man, and make yourself comfortable."

Piggy dropped down on a gin case, which creaked mockingly beneath him.

Closing the door, and placing a chair beside it to keep it fast, Ryle sat down at the table.

"It's a long while since we saw each other, Piggy," he began, "and, with me, the intervals have been pretty long between the drinks."

Piggy sat staring into vacancy. He was dumb-founded.

The stranger smiled maliciously; then, rising and taking the chair that was under him in his two hands and lifting it high above his head, brought it down upon the table, smashing what crockery there was upon it into small pieces of china.

Piggy jumped as if he had been shot, and glared at his visitor.

"Some whisky," the man said, "and hurry up."

Piggy came to his senses, and hobbling off, returned with a bottle.

"Well, here's short life to you, if ever you again betray me," and lifting a glass he swallowed the contents of it.

"I—I—I wuz alwez sorry for ud," Piggy stammered, when at last he found his voice.

"You sorry!" replied Ryle sardonically. Then added: "Well, you can now show your repentance by opening your bulging purse strings."

Piggy shuddered and shook from head to foot.

"It was a thoughtful omission of your worthy relative, old Hungry Potthouse, to die without making a Will, when you were his nearest next of kin, wasn't it? More especially when he wouldn't trust you inside his gate when you came here to hover round him like a crow nine years ago."

Piggy's whole frame quivered, and his fingers worked involuntarily.

"There—there never was a Will! Me uncle wud—wud never make one," he burst out. "Yez—yez sed yez had ud; but yez never showed ud! Ah-h-h, yez never!"

"No, I never showed it—but it's quite safe; though it isn't made in my favour. And I suppose it wouldn't be any use to me, now, even if it was. But it's in your Victorian cousin's favour, who died conveniently, and you know it, Piggy!"

"Then guv ud to me!" Piggy choked, rising and shaking in his agitation like one seized of delirium tremens. "Guv ud to me!"

Ryle laughed mockingly. Piggy sat down again and groaned hopelessly.

"I—I—have done a lot for yez, Harry Royle," he murmured.

"Yes, you have! You were instrumental five years ago in getting me fifteen years at Roma, you disloyal old hypocrite!"

"I—I—I fed your—your wife in the drooth, an' guv her cattle; an'—an'—your ——"

"You confounded old fraud, my wife, as you call her, left the shores of this accursed land seven or eight years ago, thank God!"

"Whaht!" and Piggy bounced up again, and glared, and trembled more than ever.

"Yez told people ——"

"That my wife was here on a selection," Ryle interrupted, coolly. "It suited me to, when her husband died at Camooweal, and I still had the Will that you didn't burn, Piggy, in my pocket."

Consternation and perplexity filled the features of Piggy.

"An'—an'—how comes yez here?" he stammered dreamily.

"Ah! how?" Ryle answered, jauntily. "It would bring fame and fortune to a novelist, I seized time by the forelock, my friend, and scaled the gaol wall when Brisbane was under flood and the city, like Gommorror, in total darkness. Then, while the hounds were in full blast upon the tracks of escaped prisoner Blackburn, I—that is, he—Mr. Potthouse, became a useful citizen, and a public benefactor. He—I got into a boat along with the police, and helped rescue the distressed and house-wrecked from watery graves. Tiring of that, the cheerful life of the lame, and the halt seduced me, and I became maimed. I had string-halt bad for six months, and at your hands was refused a feed, you miserable old hound." Piggy started as he suddenly recollected. "The string-halt left me," Ryle continued, "and I rose in the world till now Don Fitzrobertson is a welcome guest at even the parson's house at Longer-Linger. He is inspecting large mobs of horses just now for shipment to Manchuria; besides having placed before the Government a stupendous timber scheme. Mr. Don Fitzrobertson had the honour only the other day of riding side by side with the wealthy Piggy Potthouse (fixing an eye-glass to his eye and changing his manner and voice to suit an English dude's). And, ah, gathered from him quite a fund of—th—maost valuable information about his yearly profits and—ah—the amount of monaey he made out of the—ah—losses of other poor devils. He's an awfully faine fellah, though, and a jollay old dog is—ah—Potthouse, devilish faine."

Piggy was thunderstruck. He tried to speak. He could only gasp.

"And now," said the other, removing the eye-glass, and resuming his natural voice; "to get down to business. I want five hundred pounds to go on with."

Piggy clasped his hand over his forehead, and sat silent, and dazed-looking.

"I'll give you twenty-four hours to think it over and to get the money," Fitzrobertson said, rising. "This time to-morrow night, I'll be here, and I'll bring the Will with me. Good-bye, Mr. Potthouse—for the present."

A few moments later the rattle of horse hoofs were heard along the black soil road.

18. *In the Cold Storage*

With a groan Piggy rose and left the kitchen. His footsteps had scarcely died away when the short slab in the floor rose up, and the hatless head of Snowy Wing appeared and for a moment peered cautiously through the gloom. Satisfied that the coast was clear, the slim body followed; and Snowy silently and stealthily stole his way across the room to the pantry. Loading himself with all the food supplies within reach, he glided back and disappeared into the "cold storage." Then for quite a long interval, a quick, sensitive ear might have detected an exchange of whispers, accompanied with a noise that sounded like rats in a ceiling knawing at bones.

"Five 'undered quids, Herrick," Snowy whispered, "th' Dago's got ter part hup termorrer night. Hoh crikey, 'ow 'e must be enjyin' 'isself! Hi couldn't understan', though, wot he said about ther Will—could you, Herrick?"

"There's something been done that's not right, I think," was the hushed response.

"Hi couldn't catch everythink he said, but did yer 'ear 'im say as 'e's name were 'Arry Rylle? You ain't got any relatints knockin' about, 'as yer, Herrick?"

"No—none."

"It was curioust 'ow 'e put ther fear o' the perleece inter th' two o' them! Hoh crikey, didn't theer 'earts drop whin they tumbled ter who 'e were!"

"How lucky it was that he came!" feelingly from Eric.

"Hi thought he fell houter th' clouds, it wuz so suddent," Snowy answered. "But 'e's got a game on, Herrick, like them blokes in your story books. 'E's playint fer stakes, Hi'm thinkin'; an' we'll be in 'ere termorrer night when ther money's bein' paid over. Hoh, crikey, the Dago must be enjyin' 'isself!"

The voices and footsteps of Piggy and his wife returning to the kitchen became audible, and the waifs nudged each other to silence.

"If I—I—I dersn't get the Will from his hands be—be some

means," Piggy said, "then that—that cub in th' barrun 'll have ter be got out o' th road, he will—he will."

Snowy nudged Eric, and the latter's heart started thumping hard.

"Well, there might be some chancet o' snatching th' Will when 'e takes it hout of 'is pocket, hand chuckin' hit inter th' fire," the woman answered; "but there's no uset trying' ter get th' boy haway while Snowy Wing his halwez habout 'im. Yer'd get th' rope, Potthouse, if anything happened him; hand so would Hi. And wot would be th' use then?"

With fresh fear at their hearts the boys held their breath, and listened intently.

"Snowy Wing cud—cud be away on a nerrand," Piggy replied, lowering his voice so that the eager listeners were forced to strain their ears at the crack to hear, "An'—an' if yez could—could——"

But the voice lowered again, and the boys heard no more.

"Don't be frightn't, Herrick," Snowy said when they lay on the bag bed an hour later, "Hi'll stick close to yer, an' if they means any 'arm ter you we'll both clear hoff."

19. In the Fire Wid 'Ud

Next morning there was a change in manner of Piggy and Mrs. Potthouse—a change which became more marked as the day wore on. They were moody, and silent, and displayed no inclination to ill-treat or abuse Snowy and Eric.

"It's a-weighin' on 'es chest," Snowy chuckled to Eric, when, after being allowed to take their tea without a growl or grumble, they were retiring to the barn. "Theer both a cuttin' up rough hon' th' five 'undred. Hoh! But theer hain't no time ter waste, Herrick. We won't go hinto the barn jist yet; we'll cut round hand take our seats hin 'th' cold storage afore the bloke comes."

And scarcely had they carried out this resolution when their ears detected a commotion above that warned them of the arrival of Mr. Fitzrobertson. Footsteps, and the sound of chairs being moved hurriedly about, were plainly audible in the "cold storage"; then words that could scarcely be heard were interchanged at the door.

The footsteps crossed the room; the legs of the old rickety chairs scraped the floor just above the heads of the two boys, and voices fell clear and distinct upon their ears.

"Well," Fitzrobertson said, "have you got the five hundred, Piggy?"

"I—I—have," Piggy replied, in a trembling voice; "but before I—I—give ud to yez, Harry Ryle——"

"Fitzrobertson, if you please," the other interrupted.

"Before I—I—gives ud to yez," Piggy went on, "jest yez han'—hand th' will to th' old woman."

"I've got it here, all right."

A pause, and a crackling of paper followed.

"That looks like it; now, where's the boodle?"

There was a pause on the part of Piggy, accompanied by the rustling of something.

"Is—is ud witnessed be—be anyone?" in a nervous, shaky voice.

"That's William Brown's signature, isn't it?" (another rustle) "and that's John——"

A loud shriek from Mrs. Potthouse suddenly filled the kitchen, and penetrated to the "cold storage." A curse from Fitzrobertson followed, then nothing but the noise of falling furniture and hisses and oaths could be heard. A fierce struggle was being waged.

Snowy and Eric clutched each other in their dark hole, and gasped and shook with excitement.

"Curse you! Let go, you she devil! or I'll—strangle you!" fell from Fitzrobertson.

Several thuds came, and a series of shrieks from Mrs. Potthouse.

"In the fire wid ud! In the fire! In th' fire!" Piggy cried, wildly.

This was instantly followed by the sound of a heavy blow, and the voice of Piggy groaned, "I'm kilt! I'm kilt!" Someone fell heavily on the floor, and Fitzrobertson cried: "You old dog, where is it! Hand out the money, or I'll do for the two of you!"

A roar like the bellow of an enraged bull came from Piggy, and again he cried: "In the fire wid ud!"

The combatants shifted ground. The struggle was going on near the door.

"Inti th' house—th' house!" excitedly, from Piggy.

"I'll tear you to pieces, but I'll have every fraction of it!" Fitzrobertson hissed. Several blows in succession, sounded clearly; then an enraged howl from Piggy, and yells of "Bite th' dog! Bite th' dog!"

The parties fell through the door, and the struggle was renewed without. Only the loud shrieks of Mrs. Potthouse now reached the "cold storage." Cold beads of perspiration were rolling off Snowy and Eric. Their little hearts were rattling like kettledrums. Snowy's eagerness to know how the fight was going was uncontrollable. "I'll 'ave a look," he whispered. Eric clutched him, but didn't speak. Snowy shoved the slab up cautiously. A scroll of paper lying lightly across the crack in the floor, tumbled through on to Eric's lap. At the feel of the document, his fingers grasped it, and he nudged Snowy.

"Theer goin' hin hat it 'amer and tongs houtside," he said, "like wild haneemals . . . But wot were thet fell hin, Herrick?"

"Don't know," Eric whispered back. "Paper o' some kind,"

pushing the scroll into the groping hand of Snowy.

"Hoh, Crikey!" he said. "It might be what hall th' 'moosh' is erbout."

Slipping and sliding of boots, and more oaths became audible again.

"I've got the money out of you," the voice of Fitzrobertson exclaimed, in angry triumph, "so you can do what you d—— well like now with the will!"

"But I—I—haven't ud!" Piggy cried furiously.

"Well, if you haven't, she has!" was the answer.

"Have yez ud?" was yelled by Piggy to his wife.

" 'E took it, th' lyin' robbin' gaol-bird!" Mrs. Potthouse squealed. "Don't let 'im hout; don't let 'im!" And another scuffle commenced.

"Back!" in a stern voice from Fitzrobertson. "Back! or I'll scatter your brains on the fire! You pair of toothless tigers. Were I free to act the part of the honest man, I would take it from you, even now, and put the son of Harry Ryle in possession of every stick of property you have. But I'll leave you, as it suits me, to enjoy your ill-gotten gains." Then steps were heard crossing the floor, and the kitchen door opened and closed with a loud bang.

"Dang me, Herrick!" Snowy whispered, with fresh excitement. "Hi believes 'e means you."

Eric made no answer, but his heart beat faster. The man's words had sent a strange thrill through him. The warm blood coursed and tingled through his veins, and his crowded brain reeled.

A hasty nudge from Snowy, in warning of what was going on above ground, however, dispelled the thoughts that had flashed into his mind.

"Tell me if yez have—have got ud, woman!" Piggy groaned despairingly.

"Hit's God's trutht that Hi 'aven't!" the hag answered. "Hi tried ter throw hit hinter th' fire, but 'e kitched me wrist."

"Then—then he have ud still, th' th' damn robber! Oh, lorrd! oh, lorrd! an', an', he will blackmail me all my life!"

"Well, hit's a pity," Mrs. Potthouse said, "that yer didn't stab 'im when yer had theh chancet, yer chicken 'earted fool, yer; who would 'a know'd?"

"Oh, it is; it is; it is!" Piggy sighed, heavily, and proceeded to tramp restlessly about.

"Hand yer let 'im tear th' money hout o' yer pocket?" came in angry censure from the hag. "Hoh, yer wuz halwez a 'elpless coward! Hi hain't a man meself (lifting her voice to the highest key), but Hi would 'ave fought 'im hup ter me knees in blood afore I would a give hin!"

"May be it—it were dropped outside," Piggy suggested humbly, and hopelessly.

"Well, for th' love o' 'eaven, let's 'ave a look then!" Mrs. Potthouse answered. Next moment they both left the kitchen to search for the lost will.

"Hi believe we've got what theer harfter, Herrick," Snowy chuckled. "Hi thinks this merst be it," touching his companion with the document. "Hoh, Crikey! they've a nice chancet o' gettin' it hout o' hus. We'll see hif theer's any writint on it when we gets ter ther barn."

Leaving the "cold storage," and stealing quietly out from under the house, Snowy and Eric ran through the darkness, like frightened emus, and entered the barn, where nought but the loud snores of White Ants disturbed the eerie silence. Lighting the slush lamp, they prepared to turn in for the night.

"We'll jest see hif there's any writint hon it," Snowy said, unfolding the will, and crouching close to the light with it in his hand.

"Hoh, Crikey!" he exclaimed, when his eyes rested on the hieroglyphics; "hit's full o' it."

Eric drew close, and peered curiously over his shoulder.

Snowy proceeded to read:

"This his th' lost will hand—hand er tes——"

There was a noise at the door of the barn. They both started up and listened.

"Are yez asleep in, in there, Snowy Wing?" Piggy growled.

Snowy hurriedly concealed the document in the folds of his shirt, and feeling as guilty as a thief, answered, with a stammer:

"N—no—no, Sir."

"Well, when yez get up in th' mornin'," Piggy said, "keep yez eyes about yez, an', an', if yez see a, a paaper wid writin' on ud bring ud ter me; I'm lukin' for ud."

Snowy gained confidence.

"Hoh, horlright, Sir," he replied, "Hi'll 'ave a good look, Sir; an' if Hi seez it——"

"Bring it ter me at wonst," Piggy said, cutting him short, "d'yer hear?"

"Yes, Sir; Hi'll be sure ter, Sir."

"Then don't forget ud!" And Piggy went away.

"Hoh, Crikey, Herric!" Snowy said, throwing himself on the bed. "The Dago nearly copt us red 'anded! Hoh, it won't do ter chancet it any more ter night, Hi'll put it away in me tin, halong with me Savings' Bank, an' me privet papers, lest 'e comes sneakint back again. Hoh, gee wiz, what a bonser joke ter go lookin' fer it in th' mornin'. Crikey, hain't 'e a soft un, Herric!"

"But it's not ours, you know, Snowy," Eric said, after reflection. "Do you think we should keep it when it isn't?"

"Think we should keep it?" Snowy repeated, with surprise. "Yer don't think we should give it ter 'im, do yer? Why, 'e wouldn't be arter it if it wern't waluable ter some one. Hoh, no; we don't give it ter 'im. We might shows it ter Ray McKay when we reads whats hin it. Howsomever, hits goin' ter be kept safe fer ter night, an' we'll 'unt 'igh an' low fer it, termorrer."

And chuckling to himself, Snowy arranged his 'doss," and jumped into bed.

After lying, thinking' in the dark for sometime, he said:

"Ray McKay sez th' weights 'll be out soon. He 'opes we wins th' Cup, an' th' five 'undred pound with Newchum . . . Don't you, Herrick?"

But Eric, worn out with the strain and excitement of the evening, was already fast asleep.

20. At the Parson's

The Winter months had passed, and it was Summer again.

Mrs. McKay, the wife of the parson at Longer-Linger, was knitting at the window in the sitting-room of the manse. Looking out, she saw old Mrs. McSturt and Beatrice Appleby coming through the garden gate, and, throwing aside her work, ran to the verandah to welcome them.

"An' how are you the day?" Mrs. McSturt said, as they entered the room. "We've been thinking we must have offended you at 'Dunalkie,' it's so long sin' you were there."

"Well, it has been my loss, Mrs. McSturt," Mrs. McKay answered. "But my hands have been so very full, you know. I've been helping the girls with the sewing for the bazaar, and I don't know if you have heard, but both Mrs. McNeil and her husband are down with influenza, poor bodies, and I've been doing what I could for them."

"She never has any time for herself," Beatrice put in. "Always helping and thinking of someone else. That would never do for me; I'm afraid I'm too selfish."

"Well, may be then," Mrs. McSturt said, with a knowing look, "there'll come a day, and perhaps it's no' so far off, when you'll find little time or inclination to gang oot yoursel', my lassie. Eh, see her blush, Mrs. McKay?"

Beatrice laughed.

"Well," Mrs. McSturt continued, turning to her hostess. "A' this week I've had my own hands quite fu' too. I spent a' day Tuesday sortin' and cleanin' three bags o' faithers that I were four years accumulatin'."

"Feathers!" from Mrs. McKay, with a look of surprise. "What on earth kind of feathers, dear?"

"Why, hen's faithers, of course. It's what I make a' my pillows out o'. McSturt wouldn't gi' you thankyer for any other kind. An' on Wednesda' Jeaney an' mysel' were washin' oot th' blankets (breaking into a cheerful chuckle, and lowering her

voice). But ye mus'na tell I told you this: (the others smilingly
nodded their heads) Well, she didna want to wet her skirts
when she would be trampin' th' blankets, so what did she do,
think yer? (the others smiled expectantly) She pulled on a pair
o' her brothers' pants, an' stepped into the tub on top o' the
blankets wi' her bare feet. (Screams of laughter from her
audience.) An' who should walk into the corner o' th' wash-
house, quite unexpec'ed, but auld Piggy Potthouse! (more
laughter) Eh! an' he's been tellin' it a' roon th' country; an'
she's awfu' wild aboot it. But you musna' say I telt you."

The others cheerfully pledged themselves to secrecy; then
Mrs. McKay left the room to prepare her visitors a cup of tea.

"As I was sayin', Beatrice," Mrs. McSturt took the opportunity of remarking in a hoarse whisper, "I don't at all approve
o' the way this wi' body's son is going aboot wi' that good for
naething, Fitzrobertson."

Beatrice smiled good naturedly, and said:

"Oh, I don't think there's any harm in Mr. Fitzrobertson,
Mrs. McSturt. He's cynical and all that, but he appears to be a
gentleman; and I'm sure a gentleman would not do anything
dishonorable."

"Maybe he's a gentleman in appearance," Mrs. McSturt
replied, "but ye canna always go by appearances; and there's
something about this gentleman's appearance that I distrust."

Beatrice laughed lightly.

"Anyway," Mrs. McSturt continued, "you have some influence with the lad, so strive my lass to keep him away from
Fitzrobertson, if you care anything for him."

Beatrice shrugged her shoulders.

"Ah, you may shrug, you may pout an' pu' faces, but you
canna deceive Vi McSturt."

Mrs. McKay returned with a loaded tea-tray, and a plate of
home-made scones, and the party sat and supped, and talked
about fancy work and the bazaar for an hour and more.

"You'll show me how the plants are doing that I sent you
ower wi' John," Mrs. McSturt said; and leaving Beatrice
absorbed in the family album they rose and went into the little
garden.

Ray McKay flushed and heated after a sharp ride across the
plains with Fitzrobertson arrived at the manse on a blood horse

"You're wanted most particular in the hoose," Mrs. McSturt said to him as he raised his hat and dismounted, "so dinna lose no time."

Ray, in riding boots and breeches, entered the sitting room, and with a face beaming with smiles joined Beatrice.

"Well, little one," he said, taking a seat close beside her and winding his arm around her waist, "how's the racing stable and the world-beater, Newchum, getting along? Is he thoroughly wound up yet, or does his trainer advise a few days in the plough to top him off? Raymond McKay's chestnut gelding, Newchum, seven stone six," he went on breaking into a laugh, "looked well, in the paper, didn't it? Fitzrobertson wanted to know this morning what horse it was, and I could only tell him it was a dark horse, Beatrice."

Beatrice laughed.

"Oh, the poor little chaps," she said, "they're both awfully excited about it, and they think the world of you, Ray. I have made a red silk jacket for Eric to ride the race in, and you should have seen how proud he looked when the tried it on. Snowy said it was a 'bonser'."

They both laughed.

"A red silk jacket," Ray repeated, maliciously, "and a pair of bran-bag riding pants, with 28lbs. overweight down the legs of them, will look attractive on the lawn, Beatrice."

They laughed together again.

"Oh, it's a shame to poke fun," Beatrice said; "but I told them, Ray, that you would be able to fix them on the course with anything else they wanted."

"The devil, you did, Bea——"

They were disturbed.

Mrs. McKay and Mrs. McSturt were mounting the steps, and Ray and Beatrice suddenly separated, and became interested in the pictures on the wall.

"Sosh! Raymond," Mrs. McSturt said, "you're most absorbed. Permeet me to introduce you to Mr. Raymond McKay, Miss Appleby."

"Oh, we've met before," Ray said, with a smile.

"Well, by your looks, I would have thocht you were strangers."

Beatrice blushed, while the others smiled.

When it was time to leave, and Ray McKay was escorting the visitors to the gate, Beatrice said:

"If we don't see you at 'Todmorden' before we leave for town, Ray; you know where to find us in race week? And don't forget (with a laugh) the Cup is run on Friday."

"I'm hardly likely to, Beatrice," Ray answered, opening the gate, "not when I have a chestnut gelding, called Newchum, entered for it."

21. At the Circus

It was only three days to the Toowoomba races—only three days, till Eric would ride Newchum for the Clifford Cup, and a stake of five hundred guineas.

The boys hurriedly finished their tea, and were in the barn, preparing to go out, unknown to Piggy, for the evening. A travelling circus had struck the township, and Snowy and Eric had made up their minds to see the performance. Apart from putting in a pleasant evening, they saw possibilities of doing business.

"I see th' tent an' all th' 'orses when I were at th' store, ter day, Herrick," Snowy said, enthusiastically. "They's a lot o' donkeys, too, Herrick; and a buckin' mule, an' they gives a prize o' ten shillin's ter any bloke as can stick ther mule. Ten bob is jist wot we wants ter feed Newchum, an' pay our way inter th' races with . . . If Hi can't stick ter 'im, I reckons you hought ter, Herrick, an' pretty heasy. Hi'll lift er bob from me savins bank, ter pay fer th' two of us."

Then, procuring the shilling from the tin which was hidden under the flooring, he added: "Now, where's me coat, Herrick?"

Disturbing the foot of his "doss," he dragged a long, swallow tail coat, that was left him as a legacy by an Irish immigrant, who had worked a week or two for Piggy, into the light, and slipped into the ill-fitting garment with as much satisfaction and confidence as another person would a coat he had been fitted for. The tails of it reached to his bare calfs, and to give his hands full fling the sleeves were turned well back, displaying two broad bands of lining that resembled elaborate silk cuffs. And with hair standing on end, his bootless feet showing beneath the coat, Snowy looked a prehistoric prince in fancy costume. It was the first time Eric had seen his friend in full dress, and with a smile of amusement lighting his face, stood contemplating his figure as he moved about.

"Hoh, me coat?" Snowy said, in reply to a remark from Eric. And locking his two hands under the tails of it, he walked round like a pea-cock, and tossed his head from side to side in self-admiration. "Hi got it from Paddy Moriarty, a jimmygrant what comed 'ere ter work. Hoh, Crikey," memories of his benefactor causing him to chuckle, "yer should 'a seen what Paddy called 'es swag! 'E 'ad 'es bed in it, an' a lot o' sheets, hand ernough hother things ter open a shop with. 'E wuz all clothes, an' when 'e wuz leavin' 'e thought 'e would lighten th' swag a bit, an' gave this bit o' material ter me" (looking down at the fall of the coat). "It suits me a lot better'n it did 'im though. 'E uset ter wear stockin's with it, like a woman, an' looked a real trick."

Then, clapping a slouch hat on his head, and feeling his pocket, to make sure the shilling was there, Snowy was ready to make a start.

"We'll cut through the lucerne," he said, leading the way to the door, "an' acrost Fegan's paddock; it's the shortest."

Then, when out in the yard, he added, in a whisper, "Walk heasy, Herrick, or ther mongrels 'll start barkin' if they don't know who we are, an' fetch 'im hout ter see wot's up."

"I don't think they'll know it's you then, Snowy," Eric answered, the humorous figure his friend and mentor had cut in the light still occupying his thoughts, and tickling his risible faculties.

"Damn them! Hi thought they would!" Snowy ejaculated, angrily, as the canines suddenly started up and rushed noisily across the yard. "We'll 'ave ter cut fer it, Herrick." And setting the pace, Snowy went full speed ahead, with Eric panting at his heels. Like a pack of wolves the dogs pursued, and serenaded them all the way to the lucerne paddock. At the fence they stopped for breath, and groping about for missiles, pelted the brutes in the dark.

Away behind, at the house, the voice of Piggy was wafted on the night:

"Pincher! Pincher! Caesar! Stumpy!" he called; "come 'ere, boys, come here."

"The Dago 'll find hus hout fer certint," Snowy murmured, leading the way again; "but it dersn't matter. We are payin' hour own way, an' it's worth a tannin' if we gets ther ten bob."

The flaring torchlights that showed the entrance to the circus, and illuminated the tall, adjacent pine trees, ornamenting the storekeeper's residence, and revealing the dim forms of the storekeeper himself, and the local banker, and the baker, and the commission agent ascending to the limbs of them to secure a vice-regal view of the show, came full in sight. Then the blare of a broken-winded cornet and the thump! thump! of the big drum broke upon their ears. The music was heaven to the waifs. Its effect upon them was electrical. Snowy nearly jumped out of his coat.

"Hoh! 'ear th' band!" he exclaimed. "Come hon, Herrick!" And on he bounded, like a deer, never pausing again till he stood in the full glow of the torchlights.

"Fer two," he gasped, pushing several females aside, and delivering up the shilling to the painted, pallid faced doorkeeper. "This little bloke an' me," grabbing Eric by the sleeve, and dragging him after him. A remark passed on his personal appearance and the giggling it provoked among those in the rear were lost on Snowy.

Inside the tent, he tilted his slouch hat back over his forehead, and locking his hands under his coat-tails again, Snowy sauntered around, surveying the interior like a captain taking observations from a ship's deck. Eric, with a shy, self-conscious look, kept close to his side.

The eyes of those who had taken their seats were turned on the two boys, each inviting the other to "look at Potthouse's orphan boys."

The boss storekeeper from his exalted perch in the pine trees, discovered their presence, and in an amused tone, called the banker's and the baker's and the commission agent's attention to them. The banker, in his hurry to obtain a clearer view, broke several branches, and incurred the storekeeper's wrath.

"Mind what you're doing!" he growled. "If you're going to watch the circus from here, you needn't break all my shade trees down."

"Wot hoh! Snowy!" came in greeting across the ring, from the boy who worked at Regan's. "Is yer goin' ter ride 'im?"

"In arf a tick, Stinker," Snowy shouted, cheerfully, back.

There was a loud laugh, and all eyes were turned to locate the individual who answered to the odorous appellation.

"Are you going to ride him in that coat?" a gruff voice bellowed from the back.

"Arst yer ol' man!" Snowy replied; and a burst of mirth rang out at the expense of the man with the gruff voice.

The storekeeper and the banker, in the boughs of the pines, joined in the merriment. The banker's foot slipped off the limb in the exertion, and the heel of his boot made a dint in the baker's head. The baker was moved to bad language, and asked the banker if he had a mortgage on the whole (unprintable) tree!

"Heigh, Mister!" Snowy said, button-holing one of the officials, who, at the moment, was hurrying through the ring with a hammer and a wooden peg in his hand. "Is ther buckin' mule ter be fust?"

"In five minutes," the man said, and hurried on.

"Hoh, Crikey! Woh!" Snowy exclaimed, in a sudden fit of jubilation; and tucking his head under his chest, and contorting his body to the shape of a horse bucking, commenced "rooting" in rare style through the ring.

The audience yelled, and cheered him.

Snowy squealed, like an outlaw, and threw up the dust, while the tails of his coat fell over his head and flapped like sails. The storekeeper, in the excitement of the moment, lost his grip of the pine-tree, and slipped on the banker's neck. The banker shifted his footing, and stood heavily on the baker's fingers, that were clasping a limb. The baker took revenge in profanity and useless argument, and annoyed the commission agent, who threatened to stick a knife in him if he didn't keep silent.

The yells of the audience attracted the officials. They rushed in. The clown took in the situation at a glance. "Woh! woh!" he cried. "The mule's broke loose after takin' his feed o' ginger. Woh!" and he threw sawdust over Snowy. The crowd howled their delight. Snowy bucked on. "Woh!" the clown called again; then kicked Snowy hard on his coat end. Snowy stopped suddenly, and ran out of the ring, feeling the part that was kicked, while the spectators roared their appreciation of his performance.

"He's a quiet mule, though you wouldn't think it," the clown explained. "It's the rug they put on him that made him buck."

Snowy met the round of mirth that followed the clown's remarks, with a broad, cheerful grin.

The bell tingled, and a rake of a horse trotted into the ring and plunged, and kicked and jumped in amongst the spectators, and disorganised them, when the ring-master cracked his whip at him, and commanded him to lie down, and go to sleep. The ringmaster stared disappointedly at the fractious brute, then consulted a brother official. While they had their heads together, one of the audience made a discovery.

"That's the publican's old chestnut," he bellowed. Then a score of voices echoed: "The publican's old moke! Take him out!" Some more started hooting, while others laughed boisterously at the presence of the impostor.

The ring-master held up his hand, to appeal for silence. Then, in indignant tones, he complained of a practical joke having been played on his show. "Some person," he said, pointing the finger of scorn at the publican's horse, "has substituted that thing for our own trick horse, which, in appearance, is his double."

This announcement was received with a burst of hilarity from the merry assemblage. The publican's chestnut was ignominiously pelted out of the ring with sawdust, and felt hats, and the bucking mule brought in.

"A sum of 10s.," the ring-master said, "will be given to any boy under sixteen who can sit this mule for half a minute."

Snowy looked the enemy over calmly, then taking off his coat, which he handed to Eric, strode into the ring. His advance was encouraged with several rounds of laughter from the audience, and a dozen watches were taken out to check the time for him.

The agent's view of the entertainment became obscured, and he threatened the baker's life, if he didn't push himself further into the pine-tree. The baker appealed to the banker for more accommodation; but the banker was too excited to hear him.

The rign-master held the mule firmly by the head, and said: "Are you right?"

"Right! lettim went! Woh!" Snowy shouted. The mule went. So did Snowy—but in a different direction. And while he was spitting, and gathering himself up out of the dust, the crowd enjoyed him.

Three, four, five more boys, and one with whiskers, rushed into the ring to try their skill. In due course, the mule put them all down and trampled on their chests.

" 'Ere!" Snowy cried, dragging Eric forward, "this little bloke 'll ride 'im!"

"A whole sovereign if he does," the ring-master answered, boastfully.

"Wait till 'e's hon right!" Snowy appealed, angrily; "give th' littel bloke a proper chancet."

The crowd sided with Snowy, and cheered him, and barracked for "a fair deal."

Eric settled himself firmly on the mule's back.

The circus man cried "Right!" Then jabbed the animal in the ribs with a spur.

The mule went off like a blast of dynamite, rising and twirling as though he were caught in a mighty whirlwind.

"Stick ter 'im! Stick ter 'im, Herrick!" Snowy shouted, bounding frantically about the ring, with his hat in one hand and his coat in the other.

The spectators rose and cheered, and crowded the space. The storekeeper in the tree slipped back on the banker, and the banker, a man of mild and gentle disposition, broke several of the Commandments.

"Hoh! Herrick! Hoh! Stick—stick—stick ter 'm!" came anxiously from Snowy.

Around the ring, and across the ring, and up and down the ring, the mule bucked, his hoofs walloping the earth every time he landed on it, like so many flails. But, like a piece of beeswax, Eric stuck fast to his back.

Snowy threw away his coat, and with bent back and both hands on his knees, watched every motion of the mule, muttering to himself.

"Hoh, Herrick! Hoh! hoh! hoh!"

"Time!" burst loudly from a spectator. Then, "Time!" "Time!" "Time!" was echoed all around the ring.

The mule, as though he understood the meaning of the cries, made a final effort. But it was useless.

" 'Ooray! 'Ooray!" Snowy shouted, and falling upon Eric, dragged him, amid deafening cheers, to the ring-master, and cried into that official's ear:

"Come hon, hout with yer quid; 'e rode 'im."

"Take your time; anyone would think it was you who rode him," the circus man snapped.

The audience took a hand in the argument. It feared repudiation, and howled, "Pay! Pay! Pay!"

Then the showman's hand went to his pocket, and he handed Eric the stake.

Snowy nearly bounded over the open tent, as he shouted:

"We'se got ther bloomin' quid; our fortens made. 'Ooray!"

Then, seizing Eric by the hand:

"Come hon! we won't stay no longer 'ere, Herrick; we'll cut hoff, an' see if ther nose bag's hon Newchum, so's 'e can't be heatin grass. Han' we'll rub' im down ergain. Hoh, come hit, Herrick."

Ten minutes later they were streaking through Fegan's paddock.

22. On the Road to the Races

It was the night before the races. Snowy and Eric had returned to the barn, after treating Newchum to his final rub
down, and fastening the nose-bag on him, with a good supply
of Piggy's oats in it, and were in bed, plotting and planning
their departure in the morning.

"Everythink's ready, an' we'll 'ave ter be hup be three
o'clock, Herrick," Snowy said, "an' git away with 'im before
there's hanyone erbout. Hit's twenty mile ter Toowoomba, an'
it'll take hus five hours or more ter lead 'im in. Hoh! Crikey!
won't ther Dago an' 'er go ter market when they'se finds we'se
missin'; ther circus night won't be hennerthin' ter it! But wot
his ter be his ter be, Herrick! An' we'll give ther cows a start
ter ther yard fer 'im as we goes hup ther paddick, if we comes
acrost hany o' them, so's 'e won't 'ave so fer ter look fer them.
Han' when we comes back, termorrer night, Herrick, we might
be hable ter settle 'im be sayin', ' 'Ere, 'ere's twenty quid fer yer,
which is more'n yer lost be givin' hus 'er 'oliday.' Hoh, Crikey!
Herrick! Hi 'opes we wins it."

"I don't think there's any horse can race Newchum," Eric
replied, with boyish confidence.

Then, settling themselves, with their minds fixed on an early
start, the boys relaxed into silence, and closed their eyes to a
light sleep. Had they the faintest knowledge, however, that
Tom Mullett, in taking a short cut that day through Piggy's
property, came across Newchum in the windmill paddock, and
was so startled and tempted by his change of appearance that
at that very moment, when they had closed their eyes, he was
making preparations to steal him at daylight next morning,
they would have started for the races right away, instead of
going off to sleep.

It could not have been more than half-past three when the
two waifs, cautiously leading Newchum through the dark,
emerged from the thick box-tree timber, and came out on to the
main Toowoomba road, and an hour later the outline of a

horseman might have been seen riding round and round Piggy's windmill paddock, with a look of disappointment in his face, and a halter hanging loosely round his horse's neck.

With light, hopeful spirits, the boys stepped briskly along the broad, well-beaten road, one leading the horse by the bridle-rein, the other holding the stirrup-iron.

A sudden peal of laughter from a family of jackasses on the ridge, rang out the first herald of the coming day, and, passing the venerable, crumbling yards at Eton Vale, that had held untold mobs of surging, ringing cattle, "spear-horned and cur-ly, red, spotted and starred" from the pioneering days of Arthur Hodgson, to the passing of that great landed estate, the dawn was breaking on the ridge-lands that skirted the range, and flushing down the never-ending plain.

Removing his coat, for the sake of comfort, Snowy carried it across his arm.

Crossing the wooden bridge that spanned the creek at the station homestead, and afforded shelter to a slumbering swag-man beneath, they crossed the flat and started up the long hill, and reached the top, with the rising of the sun. Halting for half-an-hour by the roadside, they fed Newchum from the nose-bag that hung from the saddle dee, and broke their own fast on some bread and meat that Snowy had thoughtfully procured from the "cold storage." On slowly again, past the ancient station hut, and Smith's Gate, where the aged and solitary Moreton Bay fig reared its massive green foliage; past Rosevale, the famous stud farm, the early home and nurse of Nemo, of Goldfinder, of Bendigo, of Greygown, Megaphone, and many other champion performers on the Australian turf, and the stable and training ground of My Love, the unbeaten black mare, and first favorite for the Cup. A string of horses, in their gaudy colored "clothes" was returning from their morning work; sweet-smelling hay tumbling in rolls and bundles from the stable lofts; windmills spinning and throbbing on the morning breeze, and all seemed life and activity at the farm. A neat, slightly-built horseman rode out of the big white gates, on a flighty hack, and, for the first time since leaving Daisy Vale, Snowy and Eric heard the sound of a voice, other than their own.

"What's that?" the horseman said, steadying his hack, as he

came up in the rear, and running a critical eye over the form
of Newchum.

"A racer," Snowy answered, proudly.

"What's his name?"

"Newchum."

The horseman looked closer at Newchum, and knitted his
brow, as if something was puzzling his brain.

"Newchum!" he soliloquised, aloud. Then, as if remembering what he had been trying to recall: "Oh, that's the horse
McKay has running in the Cup."

" 'E's hours, but ——" Snowy answered, with the pride of
ownership in his eyes.

"Yours!" the horseman said, with a grin. "What would you
be doing with a horse like that?"

" 'E berlongs ter this little bloke's father," came from Snowy.

"And are you his trainer?" the other asked. And when
Snowy, with an old-fashioned shake of the head answered in
the affirmative, the horseman grinned, and asked further:

"And who's going to ride him?"

"This little bloke," and Snowy indicated Eric, with his
thumb.

"All right," the horseman added, with another grin. "I'll see
him there—I'm riding, too." And he quickened his pace.

"High, Mister!" Snowy called after him. "Heigh!"

He pulled up short, and leaning back over the saddle, put
his hand to the back of his ear.

"Wot orst 'll yeou be hon?" Snowy inquired.

"Oh! a little black mare," was the answer; "but don't be
afraid of her, she's not much good." And the horseman rode on
again.

"Yer wouldn't 'ave much chancet, anyway," Snowy yelled
after him, at the top of his voice; but the other showed no signs
of having heard him.

On they went, through the deserted streets of old Drayton,
where a number of boys, about their own size, greeted them as
strange curiosities.

"We'll take that 'orse from you!" one called out, Snowy
turned his head, and shouted back:

"Yer'd take a pretty photergrapht hafter yer tried hit hon!"

And a couple of loungers on a pub verandah hailed them:

"Where are y' takin' th' horse to, Jack?" one asked, with a glint of admiration in his eye.

"Takin' 'im ter win the Cup," Snowy replied.

"Is he one of Finney's?" the other inquired.

"No; 'e berlongs ter hus," was the curt answer. And the loungers laughed, and watched the waifs till they were out of sight.

The last few miles were slowly covered, and with Newchum looking fresh and fit, they rounded the hospital corner, and entered the main street of Toowoomba at nine o'clock.

Remembering Ray McKay's advice, given to them a few days before, the boys inquired the way to Smith's Hotel. And being safely directed there by a man in an apron, they were received with an amused smile, and a kindly word by the genial proprietor.

23. At Smith's Hotel

The hotel proprietor took a fatherly interest in Snowy and Eric. He invited them to a good breakfast, and directed a groom to give Newchum special care and attention. At regular intervals he accompanied his numerous custom from the bar to the stable to "show them a starter for the Cup," and asked their opinion of him. He introduced them, too, to the "trainer and rider," both of whom the whole time sat in the dirt near the open stall guarding Newchum like two faithful watch-dogs. The "custom" stared in admiration at the dark chestnut, who, with his coat now shining like a new shilling and his long tail combed out, looked a work of art; then they turned with wondering eyes to the careless, neglected looking waifs. One and another carried the news into the streets, till the stable-yard was filled with men and boys eager to see the "two queer-looking country kids who had a horse running in the Cup."

Eric, shy and reserved, shrank from their curious gaze and evaded their interrogations; but Snowy met them all with an air of supreme confidence and unmistakable superiority.

"Well, yer don't think we's walked hall ther way hinter 'ere fer nothink, d' yer?" he said to one who satirically inquired if he was going to win.

"I suppose you'll get a new coat, then, Joe?" another added with a wink at his companions, causing them all to chuckle.

" 'Ere," Snowy said, elevating his big bare foot with a load of dust on it, " 'Ave a pull at this." And the laugh went against the shrewd city man.

"He's out of the Ark, all right," a third remarked in a loud voice, as he turned away.

"Yes," Snowy shouted, rising to his feet. "Hi wuz Norah's Harc hangel; an' these," lifting the tails of his long coat and flapping them about his body, "wuz me wings."

Then, turning and speaking in a serious tone to Eric, he said:

"Hi thinks hit's time we wuz gettin' hout with 'im, Herrick. Three erclock th' race starts, han' it's hafter twelve, now."

In silence Eric rose and took possession of the horse.

The racecourse lay about a mile and a half from the town; and the road to it, as Snowy and Eric led Newchum along, followed frantically by a galaxy of city urchins, was thronged with pedestrians and people on horseback. All manners of cabs, carriages, sulkies, dog-carts, and vehicles of every description, heavily laden with passengers, were whirled furiously along in thick clouds of red dust. Mounted police, military men in gorgeous uniforms, bushmen of every degree arrayed in spurs and their Sunday clothes, all pressed eagerly forward.

The man on the gate, with a broad grin, admitted Snowy and Eric amidst clamours and cries of "Here y' are, race-cards one shilling," from a band of energetic boys. And a steward directed them to a stall provided for Newchum, and volunteered other useful information, and delivered a message from Mr. Ray McKay to them.

The eyes of the bewildered-looking country waifs danced and sparkled as they beheld the scene within the grounds. To paint their feelings of surprise, of wonder, of delight, what a genius one would need to be! A great concourse of people were moving about the grounds, and promenading on the green, closely-shaven lawns. Crowds of elegant women, dressed in all the colours of the rainbow, tripped leisurely about, their silk ribbons streaming from them, their coloured shades and petticoats, their hose and furbelow showing in the sun. Longcoated, bell-toppered men with umbrellas twirling in their hands, and field-glasses slung over their shoulders, hob-nobbed with each other and paid visits to the stalls to inspect and discuss the form of the various horses. Jockeys boys in their silken jackets, carrying their saddles on their arms, hurried briskly from saddling-paddock to weighing-room, and from weighing-room to saddling-paddock. The Premier was there. Essex Evans was there. Jack M'Quade was there. A Cabinet Minister, who regulated his eye-glass at intervals and said "Haw!" was there. There were refreshment rooms there, where corks were popping and flying, and waiters rushing up and down, rattling glasses and breaking glasses, in their hurry to keep pace with the demands of the crowds that breasted the bars. The military band was playing; racehorses rearing and plunging in the hands of the grooms. A race was coming on. A jargon of voices adjacent to the lawn were lustily calling the odds: "Two to one bar one!" "Any money Laurel!" "Five to one Lady Lee!" "Twenty to one, Lord Clifton!" And a crowd of eager speculators surrounded the bookmakers. On the other side of the white palings rang out the voices of half a hundred spielers, all catering strenuously for the custom of the simple and the unwary; and above them all the husky, familiar roars of "Daylight," the dark "sport," as he hung over his improvised table and with his big white eyes glared threateningly at those who were slow to come forward and be relieved of their silver: "Now den, gen'lm'n, dis is der wery game dat'll make you smile arter you're dead! Dree timbles and dis little pea—wid a one, two, tree, an' a two, tree, one—pick it when yer can, look on culose, keep yah eyes wide open, an' never say die. Don't mind der change, all fair wid dis coon an' above board. Dem wot don't play, can't win; an' yah liuck attend that royal sportsman. Bet yah any sum of yah own money," and so on. Such a scene Snowy and Eric never even dreamed of ever seeing. And for a long interval they stood contemplating it all with a fixed gaze of strange and silent wonder. While they were thus engaged, Ray McKay, accompanied by Fitzrobertson and Beatrice, and several fashionable ladies, came along, and surprised them.

"Hoh!" Snowy ejaculated with a grin of pleased recognition. "We's got 'ere horlright."

"Hullo!" Ray McKay said, with a smile, as his eyes rested on Snowy's coat. "You've got them all on to-day, Snowy. Where's this racehorse we've heard so much about?"

And while Beatrice extended her daintily gloved hand to our ragged little heroes, and displayed more genuine joy at meeting them than she would have shown to an English prince, and introduced them to her smiling, amused-looking friends, Ray and Fitzrobertson turned their attention to Newchum. They were both taken aback, and with amazement depicted in their faces stood staring at the animal.

"This is not the horse, surely?" in a tone of inexpressible surprise, from Ray.

"That's 'im," Snowy said proudly. "Why, hain't yer seen 'im before?"

"Oh! what a lovely creature!" Beatrice exclaimed. "And such a beautiful dark chestnut!"

McKay and Fitzrobertson exchanged several silent looks·

"By George, Beatrice!" Ray, in a burst of enthusiasm, remarked, "you were right in calling him a real racehorse." Then he turned and eyed the boys for a moment, as if drawing a mental comparison between them and their horse.

Fitzrobertson, speaking kindly to the animal, passed into the stall, but Newchum, putting back his ears and displaying his teeth, resented the intrusion.

Beatrice laughed and said:

"Didn't I tell you he wouldn't allow anyone to put hands on him but themselves."

"Fetch him out and let us have a look at him," Fitzrobertson suggested.

Eric entered and led Newchum into the light of the bright, glorious summer day. The presence of the crowd perambulating round, the strange hubhub of the surroundings, and the strains of the brass band, had an exciting influence on Newchum. He elevated his head, his staring eye-balls flashed; he neighed, extended his massive, sweeping tail, and as he stamped restlessly round Eric, he looked a king of racehorses.

Beatrice went frantic about him, and attracted the attention of the passing crowds.

With the light of admiration sparkling in his eyes, Ray McKay stared, fidgeted, dragged at his moustache, and "cracked" all his fingers.

"Gad!" Fitzrobertson said, "what sort of a game is this you have on, McKay?"

"Upon my soul," Ray replied, with a remorseful kind of laugh, "I never knew till now that he was the kind of horse he is."

Fitzrobertson referred to the race-book that he held between his fingers.

"Good heavens!" he burst out, going ashy pale. "Leopold! French Lady!" Then he looked hard and long at Newchum; walked round him; bit his lip. His mysterious manner was not lost on Ray McKay. A sudden suspicion that something "crooked" might be associated with the horse, entered the mind of the latter, and in turn he went pale. Out of hearing of the ladies, who couldn't command sufficient superlatives to express their admiration of the animal, he asked:

"What's the matter, Fitz? Is there anything wrong about him?"

"No—Oh, no!" the other answered, "except that I fancy I knew him as a yearling, when I first visited Australia, and might have bought him for a song. But," he added thoughtfully, "which of these boys do you say owns him?"

"Young Ryle—the little chap," Ray McKay answered.

"Good God!" slipped from Fitzrobertson; then, looking at Eric, he asked:

"Was your father Harry Ryle, sonny?"

" 'E were, yes," Snowy answered, rushing the question before Eric had scarcely heard it. "Hit wer' 'im what left Herric th' 'orset afore 'e went hout West an' died fer want o' warter."

With a visible effort Fitzrobertson concealed the effect Snowy's words had upon him, and addressing Ray, said with assumed indifference: "Yes; it's the same horse; Ryle bought him as a yearling from his friend, William McKenzie, who owned French Lady and won the Caulfield with her some years before."

The cries of the betting ring had now become a Bedlam. The bell rang, and the crowds flocked like sheep to the white palings and ascended in droves to the stands.

"They're coming out for the Welter," Ray said eagerly. Then, addressing the waifs as he joined Beatrice and her friends: "I'll be back as soon as this is over."

"Well, I've no interest in this race," Fitzrobertson said, raising his hat, "and if you don't mind my absenting myself a little while, I'll remain here and keep these young gentlemen company."

"I think Hi knows you, some'ow," Snowy said to him, when the others had hurried away. "Hi've seed you somewhere?"

"I don't think so," Fitzrobertson answered, looking him fair between the two eyes, and speaking in a resolute voice. "But even if you have, my boy, a wise man keepeth a still tongue in his head. Now, which of you is to ride the horse?"

"This bloke," Snowy answered, referring to Eric.

"Can he ride?"

"Hoh! can't 'e! Ride hanythink! Yer should 'ave seed 'im on ther buckint mule! An' 'e's a registered jock, now."

"Have you been on this course, at all?" addressing Eric.

Eric shook his head in the negative.

"H'm! that's a pity."

"Well, look here. Cut over and watch this race closely, and see how they do things, and how it lies. It might help you a little."

Eric, pleased at the opportunity, strolled off and took up a position at the palings, where he remained till the Welter was finished.

"What work has the horse been given?" Fitzrobertson inquired of Snowy.

Snowy told him of the morning gallops.

"And what sort of feed have you been putting into him?"

"Corn, han' chaff, han' hoats."

"How does he seem to gallop?"

Motor cars, railway engines, the wind, or chainlightning, were all fools to him, according to Snowy.

"The boy'll want a decent saddle and proper togs to ride in!"

"We 'as a saddle," Snowy said, pointing with pride to the one they had made themselves, "An' 'ere"—producing a paper parcel—"his ther red jackit han' blue cap Miss Beatrice made fer 'im."

"That saddle would never do!" Fitzrobertson answered with a smile. "I'll fix him up." And disappearing into the saddling rooms, returned in a minute or two, carrying a complete set of racing gear.

"Hoh! crikey!" Snowy ejaculated, as his eyes rested on the polished tackling. "Herric won't know hisself hin them! Hoh, don't Hi wisht Hi wuz hup hinstead o' 'im!"

24.   The Race for the Cup

The moment had nearly come. The great and gaudy assemblage was flocking to the white palings again, and crowding on to every available inch of ground on the grassy elevations of the lawn. A sea of faces beamed from the stands where the multitudes were struggling for positions. The band played its best. The recording bell of the "totes" tinkled rapidly. Above the hum and babel of tongues the voices of the bookmakers, in their final appeal, rose in confusion: "Even money, My Love!" "Even money, My Love!" "Two to one Projectile!" "Two to one, Projectile!" "Two to one B.Y.!" "Two to one B.Y.!" "Five to one Yabba, Trance, and Tornado!" "Ten to one Coronella!" "Ten to one Coronella!" "Fifty to one Newchum!" "Fifty to one Newchum!" "Fifty to one Newchum!" "Even money My Love!" And the excitement rapidly increased.

Inside the smaller enclosure, Eric, arrayed beyond all recognition, in boots and breeches, red silk jacket and blue cap, came off the weighing scales and was lifted lightly on to Newchum by Ray McKay.

"Hoh, crikey, yer hought ter win, Herrick!" Snowy said, with tears of delight in his eyes.

"Now, don't forget what I told you," Fitzrobertson quietly counselled. "It's two miles—twice round. Take no notice of what the other boys say to you. Don't let him go to the front at the start. Keep about fourth if you can, all the way, till you're turning into the straight; then, if there's anything left in him, come! Ride like the devil—as if it was for your life—and use this"—handing him a whip. Eric, pale and solemn, nodded in silence, as he took the whip and adjusted his reins.

The crowds were waiting anxiously.

Lenniger, on the Sydney champion, Projectile, appeared on the course.

"They're out!" a multitude of voices exclaimed. "They're out. Number 17."

Then quickly followed Tornado, Trance, Miribeau, Coronella, B.Y., Melbourne, The Rake, and all the rest, with the favourite, Feeney's bonny black mare, and Newchum quietly bringing up the rear. A ripple of laughter greeted Snowy as he tripped past the stand, the ill-fitting coat flogging him along, leading Newchum by the bridle-ring. And a running fire of jeers and "chyack" assailed him as he came abreast of the mass of faces extending all down the "outer" fence. But Snowy, now, was deaf to everything.

Next moment, the horses were trotting, cantering, and flashing past in their preliminaries.

Carrying out Fitzrobertson's injunctions, Eric extended Newchum down the length of the straight, and in a sweeping, powerful stride, he whizzed past. Before he had pulled up every race-book was hurriedly opened in search of his number and name. And every voice was murmuring "McKay's Newchum."

Fitzrobertson left his place on the stand and approached the betting ring, where at the moment "Fifty to one Newchum" was being hoarsely shouted. Pausing a second, he soliloquised aloud: "The last hundred! I'll risk it. Win or lose it all, for Auld Lang Syne." Then, with set teeth, he made the wager, receiving a signed official slip with "Newchum, £5,100" marked on it, he placed it in his pocket, and returned to the stand. The veteran owner of My Love took up a modest position beside the white palings, and with hard-set, unemotional countenance waited, silent and motionless.

The field drew into line, and fifteen horses faced the barrier. The silken jackets gleamed in the slanting sunlight. The black mare showed on the rails; Newchum right on the outside. The light breath of a wind was blowing. There was a lull in the babel of tongues. All eyes were riveted on the start. The hearts of the silent multitude beat with suppresed excitement. The suspense was awful. Every second seemed an hour. You could hear a pin drop. Then: "They're off!" burst like a clap of thunder upon the air, and all became a hum of commotion. It was a magnificent start. On they came past the gate-way like the roar of the rushing surf. "Coronella leading! Trance second! My Love lying third!" was murmured by a thousand tongues. As the field, pulling hard, swept past, Beatrice couldn't restrain herself. "Oh! look at Newchum! Look at him!" she cried exultantly. Ray, filled with mixed feelings, was speechless. Fitzrobertson, gazing through his field glasses, remarked calmly:

"He's in a fine position, right on My Love's flanks; and the boy is sitting like a rock." Down the long slope, the gold spangling the green, they flew like a vision; over the flat; and past the three-quarter mile post. "The mare is falling back," was lustily shouted. They came over the "hill," and entering the straight thundered past in two divisions. "Go hin, Herrick!" Snowy shouted from his place beside the fence. Maintaining his position on the outside, Newchum, fighting and pulling with wide-open mouth, was galloping like a demon. "Gad, the boy is a Freddy Archer," Fitzrobertson murmured, never for a moment taking the glasses off the red jacket. Beatrice clutched at the arm of Ray McKay, and despite her efforts to control herself gave vent to excited exclamations. But the gaze and interest of the vast gathering were centred on the yellow jacket. The bonny black mare was the idol of the public, and notwithstanding her top-weight, carried the bulk of their money. At the foot of the slope the positions changed with lightning rapidity, and a cry of "Projectile to the front!" rang out, as the brown horse seemed to cut them all down in a dash for the lead. But Blacklock, a champion amongst champions, riding with all the skill and judgment of his craft, gradually lessened his distance. And then, "My Love holds him safe!" was murmured all around. In a moment Trance shot out and challenged the leader, immediately followed by the famous "all blue." Then for the first time, Newchum's place in the race attracted notice, and a number of tongues vociferated: "By heavens! the red jacket is running a great horse!"

Ray McKay shook all over with suppressed emotion, but Beatrice screamed out her delight. The race now commenced in earnest. The field began to string out. The strength of several was spent. The whip was already at work on them. Taking the running at the back of the course Trance set the pace a cracker. It was awful. Projectile and B.Y. clung to her quarters. Lying handy to all three was the flying form of My Love. With his head at her girths thundered Newchum, the gleams of the red silk jacket preponderating in the sun. One and three-quarter miles were flung behind. The anxious moment of victory was rapidly approaching. A dead hush came over the multitude. Snowy wildly mounted the palings. A sea of hands reached for him and pulled him down. Numbers left the fence and rushed to higher vantage ground. The horses were verging over the "hill." Whips were hard at work in the rear. The crowds on the stands rose as one person to their feet. The horses' heads were turning for home. For the first time throughout the tussle the rigid owner of the favourite opened his lips.

"Now then, Watty," he murmured, "come away!" And as though by some form of magic the words had reached him, the rider of the favourite responded. His yellow jacket instantly shot into the straight by a lead of a couple of lengths. Then the pent-up emotion of the multitude exploded, and a mighty roar of "My Love! My Love!" filled the air. Snowy's heart nearly sank into his boots. "Hoh, Herrick!" he groaned. And a sickly lump rose to the throat of Beatrice. Then, from the outer lawn, went up: "Projectile! Miribeau! Projectile! B.Y.! My Love wins! My Love!" Whips were at the flog; rowels bleeding as on they came. On! nearer and nearer! They were half way up the straight. Like a volley of field artillery, a tremendous shout of "The red jacket! The red jacket!" belched forth as Newchum, almost unobserved in the clamour and struggle between the champions, came with a terrific run on the outside. All became confusion. Snowy mounted the palings again, and was promptly torn off them. Beatrice mounted a form and screamed "Newchum! Newchum! Newchum!" and wrung her hands. "By Allah! he wins!" came from Fitzrobertson. The multitude was nearly off its head. Their peals were deafening as the chestnut drew level with the mare. "Newchum! Newchum!" "My Love wins! My Love!" they yelled frantically. Blacklock shot an anxious glance at the horse thundering beside him; then with set teeth rode with double energy and determination. Both were under the whip. Stride for stride they raced. The ground shook. The multitude cheered. Weight was telling on the favourite. The chestnut was the stronger. The mare swerved; collected herself; made a final, gallant effort. "My Love! My Love!" rang again. Then, in a long, decisive roar, as the horse by a few feet drew away in the last couple of strides: "Newchum! Newchum! Newchum wins!" And "Newchum" the judge said, too.

25. After the Event

The excited crowds were suddenly reduced to silence. The public were "struck all of a heap," while the ringmen, with one exception, rejoiced loudly.

"Look at this!" Fitzrobertson said with calm indifference, thrusting his "bet" under the eyes of Ray McKay.

"Wha-at!" the other exclaimed in a voice of terrible surprise. "Five thousand! Fool that I was! I hadn't a shilling on him. My luck! Though I took a ticket on the tote for Beatrice."

"Then she has made a scoop, too," Fitzrobertson answered, "for there was only one ticket on him."

With the steam flying from his flaming nostrils, and flakes of foam falling from him, Newchum, carrying himself majestically, returned to the paddock. He was the idol of the hour. Cheers went up for him. What a moment it was for Eric! The "weight" flag was hoisted. Ray McKay and Fitzrobertson pressed forward, and warmly congratulated Eric. Beatrice could scarcely refrain from hugging him. The surging spectators wondered if she was his sister. Snowy danced and jumped his coat about, and shouted: "Hoh, Herrick! five 'undered bloomin' quid! Hi knowed he'd put 'em all down! Good hold Newchum!" patting the champion fondly.

A crowd of admirers followed the winner to his stall, but the great majority mooned about the grounds, gazing abstractedly at the toes of their boots. Many reproached themselves, and blamed someone else for having "put them off" the winner. Some groaned that they had "fancied the horse the moment he came on the course, and would have backed him right away but for listening to some fool," whom they referred to in language much too picturesque for print. "Only one ticket on him, too!" some one whined. "The chance of me (unprintable) life-time thrown away!" While others unselfishly passed sentence on themselves, and silently desired someone to come along and kick them for their own folly. "Why any kid with eyes at all in its head," they argued grievously, "should have seen through

McKay's bit o' bluff! Just imagine the simple lot of fools people were to think that the horse belonged to those kids, and that that umchah in the coat trained him! We're satisfied!"

"We're goin' 'ome dre'k'ely, Mister Ray," Snowy said. "What erbout ther five 'undered—does we get it now?"

"Oh, you can't get in just yet. I'll see to that for you. You had better stay in town to-night (putting his hand in his pocket and handing him a fistful of sovereigns), and go home in the morning; you might as well be killed for a sheep as a lamb. But as soon as you get home to-morrow," he went on earnestly, "I want you to be sure and do this for me, boys: bring me any papers, or writing of any kind whatever, that you have about Newchum! There might be some trouble raised over him."

"Hoh, they can't take 'im from hus!" Snowy said, his eyes flashing defiance. "We's th' receipt fer 'im hin Herrick's box, han' hall erbout 'im in letters, when 'e wer a foal. Haint hus, Herrick?"

Eric nodded in the affirmative.

"Oh, well, that's all right," Ray said. "I don't expect much difficulty; but bring all the papers along and let me see them."

The waifs said they would; then, leading Newchum from his stall, they both mounted him, and with joy in their hearts, rode from the course amidst rounds of cheers as they passed out the big gate.

The final race of the day was run, and the crowds were flocking from the course.

"Well, if I don't see you again before I leave," Fitzrobertson said, shaking hands with Ray McKay, "you won't forget to look after those horses well for me. The brown mare is well worth a bit of attention; and I don't expect to return before another six months, anyway. Good-bye."

Then they parted—to meet again another day, in another way!

26. Constable 'Enery Engaged

What a fishmonger's morning it was at Daisy Vale when
Piggy and Mrs. Potthouse sauntered forth, as usual, with the
buckets slung all around them, and only two or three of the
cows were in sight! And how their wrath and imprecations increased when breakfast-time approached, and there was no
sign of the waifs!

" 'Tis, 'tis terrible! 'tis terrible!" Piggy raved, hobbling up
and down. "An'—an' th' damn milk 'll be sour on me afore 'tis
in th' cans, 'twill, it will!"

White Ants was interrogated as to the whereabouts of the
boys, but nothing intelligible could be extracted from the
eccentric one.

Eventually Piggy was compelled to meander through the
paddocks and collect the cows himself, an undertaking which
occupied him till ten o'clock or thereabouts.

"Be—be th' heavens above!" he stormed, as he set out, "if
I does come across them, I'll—I'll smash every bone in—in
their bodies agen a tree!"

"Yer hain't likely ter get ther chancet," his wife jeered
savagely. "They're gone hoff! That's my idea, and you'll find
your hoily-tongued 'Arry Ryle, hor Fitzrobertson, hor what-
somever 'e calls 'isself, his hat ther bottom hof it. Hand yer'll
find, too, thet 'e 'as ther Will yer think he's burnt." She fairly
screamed with passion as she added: "Hand ther hend hof hit'll
be that kid whose throat yer should 'a' cut longer 'nough ago,
'll be put hinto th' proputty, hand th' both hof hus, hah! my
heyes! 'll be kicked hout on ter ther road ter camp like 'unted
dogs in poverty han' starvation hunder th' bridges hand th'
gum trees. Oh, yer wuz halwez a fool with no 'ead, Potthouse,
hand yer halwez messed hup heverythink yer hever touched."

Piggy shivered and shuddered, and went green at the thoughts
of the prospects painted by his wretched partner, and with
blood in his eye, answered:

"Then if I—I lay me hands on—on him agin there'll be an end till him, if I—I hang for ud."

"Then go hand send ter ther perleece erbout 'im, hand get ther kids fetched back, hand don't lose hany more time," Mrs. Potthouse shouted.

"I—I will, then," Piggy said, "so soon as I—I reach th' facthry."

When the milking was just about finished, Tom Mullett rode up to the rails of the yard, and under pretence of buying some horses, embarked in a conversation with Piggy about the stock in the grass paddock. After a while he drifted on to Newchum, referring to him as "the poor horse he saw in the yard one day after the drought."

"Be heavens!" Piggy broke out, turning to his wife, with a look of consternation, "That horrse he weren't in th' windmill paddock when I—I wer' down fer th' cows, though I—I luked ter see cud I see 'im. Ye're right, ye're right! th' young dogs have, have slithered, an'—an' taken 'im with them."

"Hoh, Hi knowed it longer 'nough ergo!" Mrs. Potthouse answered. "Hand fer Gord's sake 'urry hup hand tell th' perleece."

"What, don't you know where the horse is?" Mullett asked, becoming curious.

"Oh, them d—— young devils ov boys that I—I do be keepin' erbout me," Piggy explained, "have cleared awaay, an' —an' taken him wid them."

"And don't you know where they have gone to?" Mullett inquired.

"I doan't, then," Piggy snapped, "an'—an' if I did, wudn't I have them brought back quick enough be the ear?"

"Well, then," Mullett said with a vindictive leer, "As far as the horse is concerned, I dare say Mr. Ray McKay, the parson's angelic son, could tell you something about him."

"Wha-a-t!" Piggy cried, opening his eyes and mouth wide in surprise.

"He's getting a nice string of blood horses about him with the aid of his imported friend, Mr. Fitzrobertson——"

"Fitzrobertson!" and Piggy's eyes opened wider.

"Why do you look like that? Do you know him?"

Piggy made no reply, and the other continued: "I have some

particulars of horses here missing from Noovindah"—taking a slip of paper from his pocket and reading, "Brown mare, 15½ hands, star on forehead, off fore fetlock white. Three-year-old bay gelding, 15 hands, white blaze. Both branded with station brand." And if I haven't seen the pious McKay riding those horses at various times, well, I'll eat my hat."

"Do yez tell me that, Tom Mullett?" Piggy said, with treachery in his eye.

"I do," the other replied calmly, "and I'll tell you a good deal more by the end of the week." And having, as he thought, set enough poison for Ray McKay, of whom he was violently jealous on account of Beatrice, Mullett, leaving the Potthouses staring hard at each other, rode away.

An hour after, Piggy arrived at the factory, and the "morning's" milk failed in the test.

"You can take it all back with you," the manager said, squirting a stream of it from his mouth. "It's sour!"

The factory verandah wasn't nearly large enough for Piggy to swear on. He grabbed, in desperation, at the few remaining hairs he had in his head, and mounting the waggon again, whipped up the horses, and didn't stop till he reached the telegraph office.

Having communicated with Constable 'Enery, of the Plain-land Police Station, some eight miles distant, he returned to Daisy Vale in a terrible temper, and throwing himself on the couch in the parlour, lay there for an hour and more, raving and groaning like a miser who had received word that his bank had failed.

In the course of the afternoon, and just about the time the Cup was being run, Constable 'Encry, mounted on a bike, and armed with pencil and paper, arrived in a state of perspiration at Daisy Vale. After receiving a full description of the missing boys, and other information regarding them from Piggy, he left to institute inquiries round the district. But Constable 'Enery didn't look upon the case as important; and when the storekeeper at Longer Linger, in no uncertain voice, said it was "a good job they had cleared out," and expressed surprise that "they hadn't bolted from the old dog long ago," he attached less importance to it, and went cold on his investigations.

Next morning, however, the Law abandoned proceedings

completely. The morning newspaper arrived on the "eight train," with a full and startling account of the race meeting. In sensational headlines was printed:

"THE CUP WON BY NEWCHUM."
"AN EXCITING FINISH WITH THE FAVOURITE."
"The Winner Owned by Two Orphans, well known at Longer Linger."
"Trained by Orphan Wing."
"Ridden by Orphan Ryle."

The surprise the township received amounted to a shock. In less than no time the news travelled far and wide, and for days nothing but Newchum and the orphan boys was talked of. And no one was more surprised than Piggy Potthouse and his wife.

"Good lorrd!" Piggy said, " 'tis—'tis five hundered pounds they have won for me." And like the Jew in "Oliver Twist," he rubbed his hard, wrinkled hands, and chuckled with hideous glee. The prospects of appropriating the prize were too much for him.

"As fer has ther money part hof it goes hit's horlright," the hateful hag said, "but yer needs ter get ther imp outer ther way hall ther same, Potthouse, hand ter be pretty quick erbout hit."

27. The Return

The departing sun was darting its last rays across the golden
valleys and over the timbered hollows, when Snowy Wing and
Eric, their hearts palpitating with feelings of uncertainty
mingled with hope cherished on their victory, rode into the
yard at Daisy Vale, and dismounted from the back of Newchum.

They were not kept long in suspense.

Piggy came out and welcomed them with excessive joy—a
joy that in their wildest dreams they had hardly dared expect.

"I—I knowed all about ud, yez vagabonds," he said, with an
unusual attempt at pleasantry. " 'Tis all in th' paper. But why
th' divil did'n' yez tell me ov ud—that, that it wuz racin' 'im
yez was; an'—an' I wud have baacked him, an'—an' med a
fortun' for us all. Guv 'im a feed ov th' good oats, an'—an' a
derrink. 'Tis to Melbin we'll take him, an'—an' run 'im in the
Melbin Cup. But hurry up an'—an' attend till him, an come
yerselves into th' parlor, yez young divils, an'—an' I'll derrink
yez helth.' I—I never thought it wer' in yez."

Poor Snowy and Eric were carried right off their feet!

"Gee wingo, Herrick!" Snowy gushed, as they procured a
feed for Newchum. "Hain't th' hold buck pleased erbout hus.
Hoh, crikey, we'll be hable ter do hanythink with 'im now. 'E's
hours, Herrick! We'll heat with hour feet hon ther parlor table;
hand horder th' hold woman erbout. Hoh! come hon! 'e's
agoin' ter shout!"

And skipping lightly across the yard, they entered the house
with all the confidence and relish of pauper politicians proceeding to a banquet provided out of purses other than their own.

"There's ginger ale, an'—an' ginger beer, an'—an' port
wine," Piggy said, producing a number of bottles, with an
alarming display of hospitality. "An'—an' just taake whichever
yez like."

"Blowed hif Hi dersent think Hi'll 'ave a toothful o' ther port
on this 'ere ercasion," Snowy said, winking at the black bottle.

"Will yez hab some ov ud, too?" Piggy asked invitingly of Eric.

But Eric shook his head, and reached for gingerbeer.

"Good luck to yez bote," Piggy said, raising his glass.

"Ther skin hoff yer nose," Snowy responded, raising his.

"An'—an'—it were th' divil's own race th' horse run?" Piggy remarked, putting down the empty.

"Broke hall th' preevious reckhords o' th' world," Snowy replied, smacking his lips. "Hoh, crikey, hit wer' wuth bein' 'anged ter see."

"Be gobs, then, 'tis Melbin' fer ther three ov us," Piggy exclaimed. "An'—an' ten tousan' apiece. 'Tis millionaires yez 'll bote be."

Then, rubbing his hands, and lowering his voice to confident, fatherly tones, he said:

"But did, did they guv yez th' prize ter bring home wid yer?"

"Some of it!" from Snowy, as he drew the money from inside his shirt and flashed the gold proudly on the table. "Catch hus comin' away without a draw."

"But did yez count it?" rising to his feet and approaching the money. "Are yez sure they didn't cheat yez?"

"Hit's hall there, wot we got," Snowy said with pride and port in his eye.

Piggy eagerly counted it—and then pocketed it.

"Ten there," he said. "I'll—I'll keep ud for yez till th' rest comes." Then, changing his tone and manner: "Now yez had better take th' horrse to th' paddock, and put a padlock on th' gate, an'—an' lock ud, an' bring me ther key."

"But yer ain't goin' ter keep ther stuff, is yer?" Snowy said, a feeling of suspicion and distrust creeping over him, as they rose to go.

"Oh, no!" Piggy replied, with an ugly chuckle. "I'm goin' ter give ud to th' poor!"

Snowy's countenance suddenly dropped. He knew he had been duped. He turned at the door to protest, but had hardly opened his mouth when Mrs. Potthouse flew at him like a wild cat.

"Go hon, yer pup," she squealed, helping Snowy through the door with a shove, "han' do wot yer told ter do. Hit's drawn an' quartered yer ought ter be fer runnin' away. Go hon!" following him up, "hit'll take hall thet yer've won ter make hup fer th' milk that wuz lost hover yer!"

Poor Snowy! he was beside himself with anger, remorse, and vain regrets.

"Hit's hall my fault, Herric!" he cried bitterly, "hall my fault! Hi shouldn't a' told 'im hanythink erbout it. But he won't see no more!"

But Eric endeavoured to soothe his friend by saying, "it didn't matter, and perhaps he won't keep it, after all!"

28.   The Stolen Will

With all the letters and documents they could rake out of Eric's tin box concealed in their shirts, and with a bitter grievance in their hearts against Piggy for retaining the sovereigns, the two waifs stole away one day and sought an interview with Ray McKay.

"I was afraid of that," Ray said, when they spoke of the money. "The old dog! I thought he would! However, I'll see to the rest for you, and bank it."

Then, after casually examining some of the private papers: "Ah! here's the receipt," and muttering as he scanned portions of it, hurriedly, "Sold to Harry Ryle, one chestnut yearling, out of French Lady. . . . Oh! that's all right. . . . You can leave the others with me, and I'll go through them presently."

With fresh hopes in their hearts, Snowy and Eric scampered back through the paddocks to Daisy Vale in time to feed the pigs.

They could hardly have been out of sight when Ray McKay suddenly jumped from his chair and exclaimed:

"Why, this is old Hungry Potthouse's Will!" his hand trembling as he held the document that had fallen through Piggy's kitchen floor into the "cold storage." Seating himself again, he began mumbling to himself as he hurriedly read: "This is the last will and testament of Henry Potthouse . . . will and bequeath all my real and personal estate whatso . . . to Harry Ryle . . . his heirs, executors——"

Breaking off abruptly, he struck himself on the knee with his open hand, exclaiming:

"Bless my soul, it's young Eric's father!"

Then he rushed from the room.

"Pater! Pater!" he cried, hurrying along the verandah to the venerable clergyman's modest little study.

"You remember 'Hungry' Potthouse?" he said.

"Well," his father replied, looking up wonderingly.

"Look at that!" and Ray thrust the documents into his hand, and seated himself opposite him.

"A Will!" the clergyman murmured, proceeding to read. Reaching the end of the codicil, he looked closely at the signatures; then turned the document over. Lifting his eyes to Ray's, he said, gravely:

"This is the lost Will there was so much talk about, after Mr. Potthouse's death. I remember the circumstances well."

"You see what it means, Pater?" Ray said with a tremor in his voice.

"That the present Mr. Potthouse is in possession of an estate which really isn't his."

"That he is in possession of an estate," Ray added, "that belongs to the little orphan, Eric Ryle, Harry Ryle, his father, being dead."

"That is so, and this must be handed to a solicitor. Then, after reflection: "But how come you by the Will, Ray?"

"It was this way, Pater," the son answered, settling himself to explain. But he had not proceeded far when it was announced that his presence was required outside.

"What can I do for you? Ray said cheerfully to the man waiting on the verandah.

"Is your name Ray McKay?" the other asked.

"It is."

"I'm sorry, young man, but it's no pleasant errand I've come on. I've a warrant for your arrest (producing it). I'm afraid you must consider yourself my prisoner."

"Arrest! Your prisoner!" Ray said, bewildered looking.

"And let me assure you," the officer said kindly, "that my duty is the more painful since I am convinced that you will be able to give a satisfactory explanation."

"But what are you talking about—what is it for."

"For aiding and abetting a man named Arthur Blackburn," the constable replied, reading the warrant, "and illegally using stolen horses received from him."

"I never heard of the man," Ray stammered, more bewildered looking than ever.

The constable went into details about the horses.

"Good God!" Ray said, staggering back. "Fitzrobertson's?"

"That's his latest name, I believe," the officer replied, calmly.

"Great heavens! What—what! My God. I—I must tell my father!"

But the old clergyman, becoming impatient within, came to the verandah himself.

The constable explained.

Recovering from the shock, the venerable parent took his son by the hand, and in a broken voice, said:

"I know how absurd this is, Ray. I am sure you will be able to explain it away. Go, Ray!"

And that evening as Ray McKay rode silently off in company with the police officer, only two persons other than his father knew why or whither he went. The two others were Tom Mullett and Piggy Potthouse!

Those were anxious weeks that followed in the homes of the old clergyman and the Applebys! What took place at the trial need not be traversed. It was much like other trials. But on the lying evidence of Tom Mullett and Piggy Potthouse, poor Ray McKay was found guilty, and sentenced to three years' hard labor!

"Hi know'd there was some 'arm goin' ter come ter Mr. Ray!" Snowy said sorrowfully, "when Hi heerd Tom Mullett that night talkin' ter ther Dago, han' tellin' 'im that 'e know'd Ray McKay had got ther Will, han' wuz goin' ter turn 'im hout!"

29. His Majesty's Gaol

Six months had passed. It was Sunday evening in His Majesty's Gaol, Bogga Road, and prisoner Ray McKay was sitting thinking, thinking in his cold, lonely cell. Warder McGinty was doing his rounds, a bunch of keys jingling at his belt.

"I know not whether laws be right, or whether laws be wrong," came weirdly from the prisoner, as he quoted to himself the lines from "Reading Gaol." "All that we know who lie in gaol is that the wall is strong; and that each day is like a year, a year whose days are long!"

"Silence, Number 999!" the warder called. "Don't yez know that talkin' in the cells is against the regulashuns of th' Gaol?"

Then to himself, as he fumbled with the bunch of keys: "An' so is a lot more damn nonsense!"

"Would it be against the regulations, Warder," Ray McKay said, slowly lifting his blood-shot eyes, "if you handed in a cigarette or something to pass the time with?"

The rough, but kindly warder cautiously took a fragment of tobacco from his pocket, and handing it through the bars shouted:

"Silence, Number 999! Rule 6,458a of the Prison Act says: 'All prisoners shall be carefully searched, an' any bits of tobaccy, or matches, or anything wotiver found on their persons shall be taken from them,' lowering his voice, and mumbling to himself, "and detained by th' warders."

"I suppose the regulations don't contain a rule that would enable a man to escape from a place like this?" indifferently, from the prisoner.

"Silence, Number 999!" then, lowering his voice again, and chuckling to himself: "Well, perhaps there is, if he only knew it; but it's embodied in the unwritten regulashuns, and was only extended once that Oi know of—once!" raising his voice a little, "when Warder John Terence McGinty" (tapping himself proudly on the chest) "was th' 'look-out' sinthry, standin' on th' battlemints wid a loaded roifle in his hands, and th' promise of a hundered pound in his eye; and th' horrse thaif, Blackburrun—who they niver heerd of since—wint up th' big wall on a rope and over the other side like a toiger-cat." chuckling again. 'Oh, lorrd! It wer uttherly impossible,' said the Super., and th' Cumtroller, and th' Sheriff, an' th' polaice, and th' Govermint, 'fer a prisoner in th' first plaice to cloimb such a wall; and in th' second to do it widout bein' seen b th' wardher on sinthry. Oh, dear! oh, dear! oh, dear!" breaking off into a low, rumbling laugh. "Oh, th' wooden heads! And there was th' horrse thaif," raising his voice slightly again, "every mornin' fer six munce, runnin' round and round the yaard, as if th' divil wer' thrainin' fer th' Melbin Cup, till he showed th' mussles of a kangaroo deviloped all over him, and divil th' wan but John Terence McGinty ever suspected phwat was in his moind. 'Is there a lidge on the other soide of that wall?' sez he to me wan mornin'. 'Ther is, and there's a loaded roifle on th' prisoner that ever raiches it,' sez Oi. 'And there's a hundered pound,' sez he, 'waitin' at Piggy Potthouse's, of Longer-Linger, for the wardher who——'."

Hearing a noise in a distant cell, Warder McGinty broke off his soliloquy, and patrolling the gaol, cried, "All's well!"

Sounds of the evening church bells tolling, followed by the strains of a choir, found their way into the gloomy prison.

"The church bells!" prisoner McKay murmured, coming to a listening attitude. Then, in a voice husky, and full of feeling: "Tolling their summons to the innocent and the faithful! The innocent! Ah, yes! But not for the outcasts—not for the convicted felon entombed here in a lonely dungeon, behind these prison bars—not for you, Raymond McKay! Your time will come when you have paid the penalty of another's crime—when the precious ties of blood and love have been sundered—when you leave this iron-bound hell disowned, disgraced, the creaking of bolts and hinges ringing in your ears, and the stain of the gaol for ever and for ever upon you! God!" And, breaking down, he buried his face in his hands.

The faint, distant voices of children reached him. He raised his head slowly, and listened again.

"But God watches over the poor prisoners, too, even though they are all bad, bad men," a simple voice seemed to call out.

"All bad, bad men!" the prisoner moaned, turning his eyes to the cold stone floor. "And I, then, am a bad, bad man! What hope is there now in life for me?" Turning his eyes in the direction from which the voice seemed to come: "Ah! little one, in your innocence you have stabbed like a knife-thrust one who is as innocent as you—one who, in the eyes of a dear old Dad, in the eyes of a good, kind, and noble mother, in the eyes of the Almighty God, whom you, maybe, are on your way to worship, is as innocent as you!" He dropped his head. "And Beatrice! Poor, sweet Beatrice, I wonder if she believes in me still—Ah! dare I wonder?" He broke off, hysterically: "Believe in me— a bad, bad man!"

At the far end of the yard the warder cried: "All's well!" And "All's well!" in a grim voice, was echoed by the prisoner McKay. "Ah! I wonder if she still believes in me?" he went on, looking around his cell, then down at his prison clothes, while the light died out of his face. "But what use is her belief— now? It is impossible!"

He rose; paced the cell, restlessly; sat down again.

"Ah!" he hissed. "Why do I think of him! Tom Mullett, my dear friend! The nests we robbed together—the football we played together—the fences we took together! And he acted the liar, and slandered me!! And, my God!" suddenly working himself into a fury, "he will have her, too—what chance have I? He will have her. No!" He rushed to the bars, bearing and dragging at them in his madness. "If these bars were his throat!" he raged. Then pausing, and relaxing his grasp: "Oh, horrible! horrible! Three years!!"

"Hush, Number 999!" the warder said, appearing before the cell. "Phwat th' divil's the matther wid you? Do yez want to rouse the super?"

At the same moment a window opened in the super's quarters, and his head appeared:

"What the blazes is that row about down there?" he called angrily.

"Number 999 having a night-mare, sorr," Warder McGinty answered.

"If there's any more noise in the gaol," the Super. growled,

"I'll give him a night-mare in a solitary cell."

"Get off to sleep wid yez," the warder counselled his prisoner: "and don't be a fool!"

Then, sinking down on his grey, thread-worn blanket, the prisoner remained quiet, and dropped off to sleep.

30.   His Majesty's Gaol

Ray McKay, along with a number of other convicts, with sullen, dog-like looks on their faces, was engaged in the "big" yard, making ropes. A number of warders, on duty, were moving to and fro.

"Order prisoner McKay forward," came from the Superintendent, "for interview with the Reverend Mr. McKay."

A warder saluted the Super.; then crossing the yard, commanded, in loud, authoritative tones:

"Prisoner McKay this way, for interview with the Reverend McKay. Attention! Quick march!"

With a lump rising in his throat big enough to choke him, Ray silently advanced before the warder to the "interviewing" cage. The warder deferentially stood off a few paces, out of hearing, a mark of respect not always shown to prisoners or their friends.

"Raymond!"

"Father!" There was an impressive silence.

"Oh, Ray! to see you here!" the grey-haired old clergyman broke out. "To see you suffering like this! Innocently suffering the disgrace and tortures of another's wrong-doing. It is the heaviest of all my afflictions, that you, our only child—the pride of your mother's life and mine, should have been condemned on the false witness of enemies, and sent here!"

He broke down.

"Yes, on the lying evidence of a pack of crawling, cadging, ill-starred reprobates, father," the son said, bitterly. "I was sent here—sent to the infernal shades of this gaol to associate with fiends—sent where the very air I have to breathe sears and scorches my soul, like a brand of flame. And this is called Justice! Justice! Father, there is no justice, and there can be no just God, or He would never see an innocent man suffer like this."

The clergyman held up his hands, and cried:

"Ray! Silence! Do you know what you say? Such words deal

me a greater blow than if I heard you say you were guilty. Ray, do not allow bitterness to enter your heart, and rebellion to destroy faith and belief in the justice of the Almighty. Be courageous, my son, and patient, and trust in Him. My prayers for you He will surely answer, and the wrong that has been done you and us will be righted."

"I have had faith," the prisoner answered; "and I have believed, father; and yet, while that belief was strong within me—while night after night I was praying on my bended knees to Him to protect me from evil, my hopes and happiness were wrecked, and I was doomed for ever to be branded as you see me now—a wretched gaol-bird!"

"Oh, listen to me, Ray!" the father pleaded. "Would you have me return home to your mother, who, if it were not for the unshakable faith she has in the mercy and justice of the Almighty God, would this moment be broken-hearted. Would you have me send her in disappointment and sorrow to the grave, by telling her that her only son had lost hope and faith in the mercy and power of that Being to Whom, night and day, her earnest prayers are directed in your behalf? That Being, by Whose Will alone she feels and knows your innocence will be established, and you delivered. Oh, Ray! would you shame and kill that mother—the mother at whose knee you learnt to lisp His name?" He paused a moment. "Lord, God, surely the trial put upon my strength is even greater than that of Abraham's."

He was overcome again.

"Father, forgive me!" the prisoner broke out, the tears rushing from his eyes. "Tell my mother that I trust in God to right the wrong, and to restore her son to her arms."

"There spoke my son—Heaven bless you, Ray!"

"The time is up, your Reverence," the warder in attendance said quietly.

"Good-bye, Ray. I will come again."

"Good-bye, dear, old Dad!" the prisoner responded firmly, as the aged parent bowed and turned away.

Looking after him, as he was escorted to the gate, the Superintendent remarked, sympathisingly:

"Poor old chap! I'd like to offer him some whiskey—it wouldn't do him any harm just now; but I don't suppose he would take it."

31.   His Majesty's Gaol

A dapper-looking, well-dressed man of middle-age, approached the large gate of the gaol, and rapped it with his cane. Receiving no immediate answer, he paced up and down before it, with a confident, careless air, and a slight, decided swagger.

"Seems a devilish, ah stoopid and ah reckless sort of idea," he said to himself, "to come strolling back heah, like this, to renew acquaintance with the jollay old dogs I left behind the walls of this homely-looking establishment, when I went out of it, without telling any one where I, ah, was going to. Bai Jove! and when Ai think of it, it was a devil of a claimb, even with a rope." He wiped his eyeglass with his handkerchief. "But people, ah, do get seized with these peculiarly irresistible, ah, confounded notions. Some jollay beggars gratify their curiosity on occasions—very, ah, rare occasions—by jumping, ah, like toads over cliffs. Others, and, ah, more humorous dogs, suddenly bellow out 'Murdah!' in the middle of a solemn church service. Devilish funny! It's that Divinity, I suppose, ah, that shapes our ends, as the ah, poets say; just as it influences other beggahs' horses when they, ah, get out of your hands to, ah, make back to their own runs. It's, ah, water finding its own level. Ha! Ha!" rapping the gate again. "Must be out visiting, or, ah, having four o'clock tea with their, ah, wives and friends. Ha! ha!. . . Bai Jove, though——" suddenly feeling his breast pocket, and taking out a fistful of papers— "I hope I haven't lost my visiting card."

Commencing to read: "The bearer, Captain Hayes-Courtney, just arrived from Western Australia, is a friend of mine, and desires to look over the Gaol. I'll be glad if you'll show him round, and pay him every attention.—P.B., Home Secretary." He laughed to himself, and repeated: " 'Captain Hayes-Courtney is a friend of mine'. Awfully droll! Hope none of these jollay beggahs inside, recognise his 'friend' as escapee Blackburn, for whose capture there is a nice reward."

The small door in the large gate opened, and Warder John Terence McGinty's red face, looked out.

"Who is there?" he asked.

"How do, Wardah McGinty? What sort of, ah, day is it inside?"

"Who are you; and how do you know that Oi'm Wardher McGinty?" the official growled.

"Oh! ah!" with a smile, "Everyone knows you, McGinty."

"Everyone, perhaps, who have been in here for some toime, at any toime at all! But phwhat is your business at th' gaol?"

"I, ah, merely wish to come in. I'm, ah, doocid lonely, doncher know; and, ah, homeless." And he handed the letter to the warder, with another smile, and dropped a coin in his palm.

"Oi beg your parrdon, ye'er honour," McGinty said, in a grovelling tone, when he saw it was from the Home Secretary, and immediately drew the grating bolts to admit "Captain Hayes-Courtney." Then he nearly fell over himself in his hurry to acquaint the Superintendent of the presence of the distinguished visitor.

"I'll be delighted to take you in hand, Captain," the Super. said, "and to show you over our establishment. It's the first time you've been in gaol, I suppose?" attempting one of his stock jokes.

"Well—ah—yes," the Captain answered. "It's—ah—my first offence."

"You've struck rather a field day, Captain," laughing patronisingly. "The Sheriff is round in No. 1 yard, just now, manipulating the gallows. I'll escort you there, first, and you'll be able to see how a hanging is conducted; which will be something; though it doesn't interest me very much. I'm rather used to that sort of thing!"

"Oh, bai Jove; he's going to hang someone! how awfully jollay. I shall be delighted." Then, adjusting his eye-glass, and looking hard at Warder McGinty, who was standing at "attention," his head up, and holding a carbine by his side, the "Captain" added:

"Is—ah—this the lucky beggah who's to be scragged?"

Warder McGinty turned his head slightly, and glared at him out of the corner of his eye.

"Oh, there's no hanging, exactly, to-day," the Super. explained; "the Sheriff is here merely to test the gallows, with a bag of sand—a dummy, you understand—just to make sure everything will work smoothly, and that there'll be no hitch when he's despatching the chap that's condemned, to-morrow morning."

The Captain looked suggestively at the motionless form of Warder McGinty, and said:

"I would—ah—rather see something that's alive, operated on, doncher know; it's so doocid funnay. But let's see how the sand goes down, old f'lah."

"This way, then, Captain. And after we've seen the gallows, I'll show you the dark cells—they're rather interesting."

The Captain turned his head away, and murmured to himself: "I know all about them; they're awfully damned interesting!"

"Then I'll bring you round through the big yard, where the prisoners are rope-making."

"And where a lot of my dear old pals," the Captain thought, "will be waiting to salute me. How awfully droll and funnay!"

The Super. led the way, leaving Warder McGinty on duty at the gate.

"Now, how in the name of the devil," said the warder to himself, as he paced up and down, "and all th' pretty girrls, could his Honour know me name was McGinty? It's not a common name, an' there isn't another like it in the gaol, and" (with an effort to mimic the "Captain"), "there's—ah—half-a-crown fer ye—ah, McGinty,' sez he; 'go an' bought yerself ah—ah—communion in the Arrmy'." McGinty broke into a low, stifled laugh. He was laughing, when a sudden, heavy thud came from the dropping of the sand-bag, and shook the building. He sprang several feet in the air, and dropped the rifle. "Good Lorrd!" he exclaimed; "but I thought the whole caboodle wer' down on top o' me, and I'd losht me paay an' position. Shure if they give his gills in the cell there a dhrop like that in the mornin' he'll go right through the earth, and get drowned in the ice round at Canady or some plaace."

There was another groaning of bolts, and a heavy, reverberating thump. McGinty sprang up again.

"Shure, I think the Sheriff, himself, have gone down wid th' throp!" he said.

One more bump.

"Well! all that," said McGinty, "must be the swatest of swate music to the ears of the poor devil, in whose honor 'tis all bein' got up! Oi think Oi would enjoy it meself."

Having seen enough of the "hanging," the Captain was conducted to the big yard, where the prisoners were rope-making.

"Attention!" the burly, chief warder roared, in a voice like a drill inspector's, as he announced: "Captain Hayes-Court-ney."

The convicts fell into line, and saluted the distinguished visitor. The visitor raised his eye-glass, and scanned them long and curiously.

"A fine—ah—intellectual-looking regiment," he said.

The Super. could scarcely control the workings of his features, while the chief warder suddenly saw something to interest him at the other end of the yard.

"Is this the—ah—kind of rope" (lifting a rope end as thick as his leg), "that you—ah—use, Superintendent, when—ah—" The Captain paused, and drew his finger across his throat, to indicate a hanging.

"Oh, no; that's a ship's rope, Captain," the Super. answered, with a smile. And proceeded to add, as he moved away a pace or two, and stooped down, "this is some of the hemp——"

But the "Captain" was more interested in the convicts. He raised his eye-glass, and looked at them again, and, recognising Ray McKay, dropped it suddenly, and murmured:

"The devil! McKay, the old Parson's son of Longer-Linger. Reallay, it is a field day. Bless my soul! Am I—ah—inside or outside this confounded gaol, or where, ah, the devil am Ai?"

Then addressing prisoner, Ray McKay:

"Well—ah, 'pon mai soul, McKay, I—ah—positively wouldn't have known you; but what—ah—the devil fetches you heah?"

"Silence!" the chief warder thundered, exercising his author-ity. "Visitors are not allowed to speak to prisoners."

"Bai Jove!" the Captain thought to himself: "I might have remembered that."

"If you wish to speak to a prisoner, Captain," the Super. said, coming to the rescue, "I'll have him brought round to the cage for you."

"That's reallay fine of you," the Captain answered, "really. It'll be awfullay jollay."

Returning to the general yard, the Superintendent despatched a warder to order prisoner McKay forward for interview with Captain Hayes-Courtney.

"Well—ah—pon mai soul, McKay," the Captain said, when the prisoner, with set teeth and a scowl on his face, appeared at the cage. "Ai never got such a beastly shock in all mai life. What, in the devil's name, brings you heah?"

"The stolen horses which you, my friend, were so careful to leave in my possession; and the lying tongues of your worthy confederates!" the prisoner replied, scornfully.

The Captain seemed to be taken aback.

"I—I—I'm reallay awfullay sorray, old chap—awfullay damn sorray!" he said. "Of course, there are two courses open —ah—to me. I reallay hate to see you heah for what I've done. But—ah—confound it, old chappie, you can't expect me to— ah—take ten years heah to oblige you—now, ah, can you?"

"No!" the prisoner replied. "I begin to see that honour among thieves is a pleasing fiction—among horse-thieves, at any rate."

"Now, deah boy, don't rub it in. I suppose—ah—you haven't got more than two or three years? You—ah—are still young—with the world—ah—all before you, you know; and— ah——"

The prisoner abruptly turned his back on him.

"How dreadfully rude of you!"

The Superintendent stepped forward.

"What the devil do you mean, prisoner McKay?" he said, "by insulting a visitor and friend of the Home Secretary? I've a good mind to give you 'solitary'," Turning to Warder McGinty, "Take him away!"

Then, 'to the Captain: "I'm very sorry, Captain Courtney, that the fellow had not better manners. I suppose you knew him before he came in?"

"Well—ah—slightly. His—ah—mothah was a—ah—house-maid at Courtney Hall. A rather jollay and—ah—decent fellah he was. I'm awfullay sorray for him, bai Jove, awfullay sorray, awfullay! awfullay!" Then, turning to take his departure, the Captain added: "Well, Ai've been terriblay interested; rather sad, doncher know; but—ah—awfullay jollay place, all the same. And the—ah—hanging was delightful. Now—ah—Ai will really have to go."

"Well, before you leave Captain," the Super. said, hospitably, "come into my office and have a drink."

The Captain's eyes twinkled.

"Well, how awfullay kind. Lead ah—on, Macduff," he said, "I—ah—never refuse to drink with any good fellah, bai Jove, nevah!"

The Super led the way to the office, and pressed a button.

"Two glasses and some water," he said to the warder, who appeared at the door and saluted; then took a bottle from a private recess and placed it on the table.

"Bai the way," the Captain said, helping himself from the bottle, "what's that—ah—poor devil, McKay in for?"

"Horse-stealing—and a bad case." And the Super. took up the bottle.

"For—ah—how long?" the Captain asked.

"Three years," was the answer.

"A doocid—ah—long time, bai Jove! And—ah—talking about horse-thieves—didn't Ai heah something about a fellah named—ah—Blackstone, or something, escaping from this— ah—mansion sometaime ago?"

"Yes," the Super, replied, nursing his glass. "The papers here, especially the labour rags, made a great fuss over it. See that wall there" (pointing through the window), "well, he must have flown over that. They gave us the devil over the affair. Headlines, you know: 'Official Ineptitude'—'Culpable Carelessness.' You know the sort of thing. It was damned unjust— for how could we know the man had wings?"

"Quite so, deah boy—quite so," the Captain answered, in sympathetic tones. "And has this—ah—Blackthorn, evah been traced?"

"Blackburn, Captain," the other said, putting him right, then adding: "No, he's believed to have got away to South America."

"A low, brutal fellah, Ai dare say, he would be?"

"No—not at all," the Super. answered. "A smart-looking fellow, well set up, and clean shaved." (The Captain twirled his moustache.) "About your height and build, Captain."

He touched the button again.

"Here, Casey," he said to the clerk, who responded, "bring me the gaol album, volume 17, I think it is—the one with Blackburn in it."

The album was brought in. Then, turning over the pages, the Super. said:

"Here's the photograph, Captain," displaying the picture.

"Reallay," the Captain said, looking at it; "how awfullay interesting. Valuable curiosity."

They drank up half their whisky.

Turning to the photograph again, the Captain said: "Ai—ah—ah, am very interested in this fellah. Er—had he, er—any marks about him you could—er—identify him by?"

"Oh, yes—but—but why do you ask?" from the Super.

"Oh—ah—meah curiosity," the other replied. "I—ah—know I'm verray rude, but—er—what were they?"

"Well," the Super. replied, "you can see one of them—that white mark just under the hair-line, is a scar he got when he was a boy. Besides, he wears a horse's head tattooed just below his elbow, on the inside of his forearm. Here" (taking the album) "this is the photo of his forearm."

There was a short silence.

"Is the—ah—scar anything like this, old chap?" the Captain asked, pushing back his hair.

The Super. leaned forward, and stared at him; then he leaned back, changed colour, and seemed bewildered.

"And is the forearm anything like this?" drawing up his sleeve, and dropping into his natural voice.

The Super. stood in silence.

"Just as big an ass as ever, Jones-Smith, old chap," the other said, firmly. "And you would never have got me, only twelve fools like yourself sent an innocent man here!"

The Super. sprang back, gasped, and stared at Blackburn, whom he now recognised. Then he stretched his hand towards the bell.

"One moment, Jones-Smith," the other said, pushing the hand away, and seizing his glass, and raising it: "Let me finish my drink. Your very good health, and vastly increased intelligence."

Then, taking the paralysed Super.'s hand, he placed it on the bell button.

When Warder McGinty appeared, they were both staring across the table at each other.

The warder waited, with look of wonder.

"A pair of handcuffs," the one said, calmly.

"Escaped prisoner, Blackburn!" the Super. roared, recovering himself. "Seize him! into leg-irons with him, warder!"

McGinty dropped all over the floor. "Oh, lorrd! oh, lorrd! I'm losht!" he groaned. "Me peesition and me paay have gone!"

Conclusion

In the midst of the wonder and sensation that followed the "arrest" of Blackburn, alias Fitzrobertson, Ray McKay was released from gaol, an innocent, though injured and prematurely aged man. The gloom and sorrow that had darkened the homes of the old clergyman and the Appleby's speedily passed away, and all was sunshine and rejoicing again. The rest must be conceived.

Meanwhile, at the instigation of the Reverend Mr. McKay, the legal machinery had been put in motion with regard to the Potthouse estate, worth fifteen thousand pounds; and six weeks or so after Ray McKay's release, the will was proved in favour of Eric Ryle, an orphan, to whom the Court decided, all the real and personal estate of the late "Hungry" Potthouse, should revert at the age of 21.

Little Eric received the news of his inheritance almost in silence; but Snowy danced hysterically round his friend, and cried:

"Hoh, Crikey! Then Hi'm yer manager. His that a bargint, Herric?"

Eric smiled, and nodded in the affirmative.

"Hoh, where's me coat?" Snowy exclaimed, excitedly, "till Hi goes, dressed hup, an' gives ther Dago his fust horders!"

Jumping into the roomy garment, and throwing out his chest, Snowy marched across the yard, direct to Piggy's parlour.

Piggy and his wife were brooding miserably over the turn things had taken, when he entered. Holding the collar flaps of his coat with fingers and thumb, and striking a lordly attitude, he said:

"Yer sees before yer a gentle'n whose been permoted. Hi'm happointed ther manager hof this 'ere placet, wot now berlongs ter my cobber, Herric Ryle, Hesquire. Hi 'opes both hov yer'll like yer new boss. Hif ther two hof yez does yer work well, hand gets hup hin ther mornin' hat four an' runs hin th' cows, an' does ther milkin', an' dersent let hany hof it git sour, han' cleans th' cans well, han' looks arter me dorg, an' hother things yer'll be spoke ter erbout, later in th' day, yer won't get ther leg-rope, but can stay hon th' farm at' arf a quid a week hand yer grub, with yer washin' throwed hin hif yer does it yerself. Hotherwise yer can come round ter me hoffice an' Hi'll pay yer hoff.''

With heads bent forward, their chins touching their chests, the Potthouses received the jibe in silence.

Let us leave them.

For Life
and other stories

(with illustrations by H.J. Weston)

Introduction to *The University of Queensland Press Edition*

At Christmas time in 1898 a man and his three sisters were murdered on their way to a dance in Gatton; a suspect was eventually caught and charged with the murder and, to establish his alibi, offered to retrace his tracks about southern Queensland, to prove that he was not in the Gatton area at the time of the murder.

Shorthand being a rare accomplishment in those days, Steele Rudd was seconded from his clerical position in the Sheriff's Office in the Supreme Court to accompany Inspector White and the troop of mounted police who would go with the suspected murderer; Rudd was to take notes of all that occurred.

This is only one of the numerous occasions on which Rudd's ability to take shorthand gave him the opportunity to observe Government enquiries in a secretarial capacity, and he put it to good use. He does not dwell on the rather grim aspects of this unusual trip, but lets the story tell itself in his own style of natural humour. The book was published in 1905, two years after he had left the Queensland Public Service and had established his own *Steele Rudd's Magazine*.

ERIC DAVIS
BRISBANE
NOVEMBER 1968

Acknowledgment

A few of the stories in this volume have appeared in the columns of *Steele Rudd's Magazine*, *The Australian*, and *The Worker* (Q.), and I have to thank the editors of these papers for permission to republish in book form.

For Life and others are here published for the first time.

A. H. D.

For Life

1. Murder!

Murder! It *was* murder! When the wires flashed the news that the Kellys had shot the police at the head of the King River, in Victoria—when word reached civilisation that the Kenniffs had "done for" Constable Doyle and young Dalke on the Maranva River in Queensland, and had burnt their bodies to a cinder to hide their crime, the excitement in Australia was indescribable. But when one December morning in the midst of all the Christmas festivities, the inhabitants of the small, peaceful, country township of Trackson awoke out of their sleep and learned that the three Maguire girls and their brother, all of whom had only the evening before left for their selection in a dog-cart at 8 o'clock, were lying dead in a paddock not a quarter of a mile out, the unfortunate girls brutally outraged and strangled with pocket handkerchiefs, the brother shot in the back with a rifle, the dog-cart, all blood-bespattered, tilted near the bodies, and the horse lying with its throat cut—Australia was staggered!

Fear and alarm filled the hearts of the people in the country, and from one end of the land to the other, the cry went up for protection and vengeance. Then the Police and the Press commenced their work—especially the Press. "Specials" were hurried to the scene of the tragedy on board police trains, and column after column of grim, gruesome details were wired to the cities, and sought and jostled for by the eager, horror-stricken citizens.

Unfortunately, said the specials, the Sergeant in charge of the district, though recognised as a most capable officer, lost his head, and instead of roping off the scene of the outrage, unwittingly permitted the spectators to gather about the bodies and obliterate the tracks of the perpetrators of the deed. This unfortunate mistake has made the task of the black-trackers much more difficult than it would otherwise have been. When interviewed this morning, however, Chief-Inspector Banks, who has full charge of the case, intimated that the police have already a very strong clue, and an arrest may be expected at any moment.

In one column of the various prints appeared exhaustive pedigrees and descriptions of the whole of the Maguire family, from the father, an inoffensive, struggling, old selector, to the baby at the mother's breast, and illustrated with their alleged photographs. In another, just to balance the interest, was a long, vainglorious history of the uneventful career of Chief Inspector Banks, with loud and exaggerated accounts of deeds of daring he never did; of the long, hard rides he had ridden through drought-stricken country in the West; of the skill he possessed in the art of tracking; of his ability to go without food and water for weeks and carry home the corpses of several prisoners on his back before breaking his fast; of his marvellous analytical mind, and of his genius for weighing and sifting evidence.

And when the excited people had ravenously read all these things, their hearts went out to Chief Inspector Banks, and they cheered silently for him. Then they went home and read the account of his life over, and decided amongst themselves how the murder was committed, who committed it, how many were concerned in it, what sort of murderers they were, and what tale they told their victims to lure them from the main road into the paddock. And finally they agreed that Banks was a clever officer. Then, expressing sympathy for their brothers and sisters of the bush who were without police protection, they retired to bed, and dreamt the dream of tragedies.

In the morning they would seek the newspapers for news of the expected arrest, and in bunches would gather round the one sheet and peer over each other's shoulders. "There you are"—from the outside one of the group; and the centre man, in a voice full of emotion, would proceed to read for the benefit of the others.

THE TRACKSON TRAGEDY
POLICE ON THE TRAIL
SENSATIONAL DEVELOPMENTS EXPECTED
A BLOOD-STAINED SADDLE-CLOTH
AN EX-PRISONER SUSPECTED
POLICE RETICENT
MORE HORSES REQUIRED

And after repeating all the ghastly details printed on the previous day, the "Special" would proceed to tell how the blood-

In the Morning They Would Seek the Newspapers

stained saddle-cloth had been picked up in the mountains, some twenty or thirty miles from the scene of the murder, but about the finding of which Chief Inspector Banks would permit no information to leak out.

A man named Burke was to-day brought before the visiting magistrate, Mr. P. J. M. Smith, and Messrs. J. O. Jones and T. Brown, Js.P., and formally charged with vagrancy. The Courtroom was thronged with people anxious to catch a glimpse of the prisoner, many of whom had come twenty and thirty miles to see him. Burke, who is a notorious character, has already served several sentences for horse-stealing and criminal assaults, and was only liberated from gaol six or eight weeks before the Maguires were murdered. A remand was granted.

For a while there was a lull in the proceedings, and no more dead horses having been found, no more blood-stained saddle-cloths picked up, people began to get restive, and wondered what the police were doing and what had become of Burke, and if, after all, he was only a vagrant.

2. *The Fight for Life Begins*

A few days after, the writer of these pages received the following letter from an Under-Secretary:

I have the honour to inform you that prisoner Burke, at present serving sentence for vagrancy in H.M. prison, Muddy-road, is to be escorted by the police over the route which he travelled when discharged from gaol in November last, and to request that you will make the necessary preparation to join the party which is to leave on Monday next in charge of Inspector Black, and take full shorthand notes of all the evidence and forward same along with your report to the Commissioner of Police as soon as the journey is completed.

The sun was just rising when I picked the Police up outside the city on the following Monday morning. They were waiting for me on the main road. At first glance one would have thought they were a travelling show just breaking camp. The party consisted of one inspector, four mounted troopers, two black-trackers (each leading a pack-horse burdened with blankets, hobbles, quart-pots, etc.), while the police van, driven by two constables, in which Burke had travelled from the gaol, was wheeling round in the act of returning. Burke himself was standing handcuffed between two constables. As I approached he eyed me curiously. He seemed to wonder what part *I* was to play in the expedition. I made no speculations as to his part.

"You're a bit late," the Inspector said. And looking over the "show" I asked him what sort of a house he had had last night. The rest of the Force smiled, and Burke, who was watching me from under the rim of a soft felt hat that had once been white—white until he started sleeping in it and using it for a bellows—broke into a rasping, grating laugh and said:

"He thinks we're a bloomin' circus!"

The troopers smiled and fumbled with their saddle gear, and gathered up their bridle reins; the two trackers grinned hard and showed their white teeth, and the Inspector said cynically:

"Yes; and unless you prove all you say you can, the last item of it will be Richard Burke performing on the end of a tight rope."

"I know bloomin' well," Burke snapped back, "that that's what you would like to bill me for, but by——"

"Come along"—sharply to Senior-Constable Adam Jackson —"Put him on his horse and let us make a start."

Jackson saluted his Inspector, and, ordering the prisoner to mount, said: "Can you get on?" (wondering if the gaol bird could climb into the saddle handcuffed). But Burke, with several oaths, despised assistance, and gripping the pommel with both hands started to mount. The burly constable stood holding the horse by the head. The rest of us sat on our horses looking on. The animal Burke was mounting, a long-limbed chestnut with a game, clean-cut head, was just off the grass after six months' spell in the police paddocks, and was fresh and touchy as an unbroken colt.

"Are you right?" Jackson gasped, struggling with the horse to prevent him rearing, in the same breath calling the animal names for not taking things quietly.

"Right," Burke answered as he landed in the saddle. Then, in spite of Jackson, down went the chestnut's head, and, with a snort, it put in one—two—three bucks, all in the same place. Jackson hung on like grim death to the reins. Powerless to balance himself without the use of his hands, the prisoner rose about three feet out of the saddle.

"Hold him, Jackson! Hold him!" the Inspector cried apprehensively, and the other constables scrambled from their horses to try and save the situation. But the chestnut got in some more good work, and the next moment Burke left the saddle, and, flying through the air, fell into the arms of two policemen, who fell on the top of each other under the weight of him.

"Are you hurt?" the Inspector asked when Burke rose spitting out dirt and cursing.

"Hurt be damned!" was the answer.

Then turning to me the Inspector explained, alluding to the horse:

"I picked that old dog as the quietest and slowest we could put him on."

"Yes," Burke gasped savagely. "I know all about the brute being quiet! And do you think I don't tumble to your capers?

Here"—struggling violently with the handcuffs—"take these blamed things off and give me a fair show and I'll ride the beggar bare-backed."

The Inspector wasn't to be caught napping so easily, however, but jumping across the chestnut himself he dug his heels into him, and laying the whip on his ribs put him through a lively ten minutes. Then, throwing the reins to the constable again as he dismounted, he said:

"Put him on again, Jackson; he's all right now," and once more Burke climbed on to the chestnut, but this time was allowed to remain in the saddle. Then, when his legs were manacled by passing a chain under the horse's belly, the escort started in double file on its three-hundred-mile journey.

3. A Dash for Liberty

It was an imposing-looking cavalcade. Constable Jackson in cabbage-tree hat, shirt sleeves, riding tweeds, a revolver clinging to his belt, went first, leading the prisoner's horse by a well-polished dog chain. Behind him Constables Edmunds and Taay with more revolvers. Then Inspector Black and the writer. Behind us a junior constable on probation with another revolver, the possession of which distressed and hampered him visibly; and bringing up the rear the two trackers leading the packs and filling the morning air with the sound of jingling hobble chains and pint pots. And the milkmen coming along, making townward with their supplies, drew off the road and glowered as we trooped past, then sat staring after us till we were out of sight.

"It'll be all over town in a couple of hours that we've left," Black murmured, casting a sullen, unfriendly eye on the milk vendors. "Damn them!" and he hit his boot with his riding whip. I was unable to see that it could make any difference to the long arm of the Law, anyway, but suggested that we raid their carts and drink the milk, and deprive them of an excuse to go to town.

"Talk sense," he answered shortly. I was trying to think of some, when one milkman, more curious than the others, shouted out in an anxious tone, "Is that the cove who did the murder you've got there?"

"You blasted cow!" Burke yelled back furiously. "I'd like to murder *you*!"

"No doubt but you would," the other answered. "It's your business." Then he whipped up his horse and drove on.

"Now there you are," Burke explained, turning his head and shaking it frantically at the Inspector. "What rotten chance has a chap got of clearing himself when every darned cove in the country already reckons he's guilty?"

The Inspector made no reply.

"I think every chap ought to get a fair show," Burke added sullenly.

Then, after riding along for about five minutes: "Now, if I get tried for this murder that darned cove might be put on my jury."

Still there was no reply. The hoof-beats of the escort rattled on the hard road, and the chains on the legs of the prisoner jingled an eerie refrain.

Constable Taay's horse, a raw, handsome colt not long broken, stumbled badly, and the long, supple Australian in khaki, who had served a long apprenticeship horse-breaking in the West before joining the force, drove the spurs into the animal's ribs to rebuke him. The colt began to buck. And how he did buck!

"Stick to him, Taay!" his brother constables called, pulling out of the way to make room for the performance. Taay began with the whip, and next moment the colt bucked in between Constable Jackson and his prisoner and separated them. Burke glanced quickly round; then, driving his heels into the chestnut's ribs, yelled, "Come on!" and off he went full gallop. Then there was excitement! Dick Turpin's ride to York was a fool to what followed.

"Look out for him, Jackson!" the Inspector shouted, realising the position a moment too late, and, putting whip and spurs to his own horse, raced furiously in pursuit. Whip and spurs were applied to every horse there, and Taay and his bucking colt were left standing. Even the trackers in their excitement walloped the packs along, at the risk of strewing the road with blankets and provender. Constable Jackson, drawing up on the near side of the fugitive, let fly a revolver shot, which fortunately missed. "Don't shoot, Adam! Damn it, don't shoot! Get hold of his reins!" came wildly from the Inspector, who was racing on the off and overtaking Burke every stride. Burke, with a fiendish grin on his face, threw a glance back over his shoulder at his pursuers, then used his heels harder than ever. But the chestnut was all out and outpaced, and the Inspector and Jackson, closing in on either side, leaned out of their saddles and grabbed his reins.

"You damned scoundrel!" Black gasped when they came to a standstill, the steam flying from the nostrils of the horses.

Off He Went Full Gallop

"Think yourself lucky you didn't get your brains blown out."

Burke seemed to regard it all as a good joke, and grinning amusedly at the excited constables around him, remarked: "Well, some of you *did* have a shot, but you couldn't hit a haystack. It didn't go within a mile of me."

"Within a mile of you!" Jackson snapped, inserting his finger into a newly-made hole in the side of Burke's shirt. "You didn't want it to go any nearer than that, did you?" Burke glanced quickly at the bullet hole in the garment and went a little pale.

"You meant it all right," he mumbled, looking Jackson in the face.

"Meant it!" from the Inspector. "I rather think he did, and meant a second one, too, if I hadn't stopped him."

"And I would have brought you out of that saddle," Jackson snarled, "much quicker than the old chestnut did."

Burke said nothing, but regarded Jackson steadily till the black boys came up, when the Inspector gave the order and the procession shifted ground again.

"Heavens!" said the Inspector, leaning forward and stroking his horse's neck. "We had to ride like the devil for a while to get near the old chestnut! If it had been in rough country anything might have happened. But nothing must be said about this."

I nodded.

Behind me the two simple-minded trackers were discussing the incident.

Garrione said, "By crites, that cobe Burkes he been go it that time."

"Nudding like how he been go when I catch him over der border, long fellow time ago," Norman answered, seriously.

"Yaas?" in surprised tones from Garrione. "You been 'rest him one time?"

"Oh, yaas," Norman answered proudly. "I been arrest him two times twice."

"Yaas? How—what he been do dem times?"

"Oh, shootit a cobe in a arm and plant in it big scrub, and trabel in a dark night. I catch him sittin' alonga log New Sout Wales."

The Inspector, catching the words, turned in the saddle and said:

"What's that, Norman? You been arrest Burke? You mean it Sergeant Walker, don't you?"

"I been *trackit* him, though," Norman claimed, "trackit him all three day."

"Oh yes, but you didn't arrest him. You remember you been two three hundred yards away when the sergeant shoot Burke in the leg?"

Norman remembered.

"Oh! that been right," he answered, showing his teeth; "but I been watch it all."

We smiled, and for some moments there was a silence. Then Garrione, who had been turning the matter over in his mind, said in low, disappointed sort of tones to his brother tracker:

"I tink it you been blow it a damn good lot, Norman."

We smiled.

"All right," the other answered indignantly, "you tink it dat!" and he flicked the pack-horse and shook an extra rattle out of the pint pots and hobble chains. Then added, "When we stoppit fo' breakfast you askit Burke. He tell it you all about me."

4. *An Anxious Moment*

It was about nine o'clock when we came to a tributary of the great river that glided calmly through the capital. The Inspector called a halt and suggested breakfasting. The trackers and the cadet relieved the packs and attended to the horses. Constable Edmonds, the boss cook and caterer in the force, saw to the fire and looked after the breakfast. Jackson and Taay attended to Burke, relieved him of his handcuffs and sat down beside him on the grass, and engaged him in friendly conversation about crime and criminals, and the security and insecurity of the various gaols in Australia. Inspector Black and I reclined in the shade on our elbows and nibbled blades of grass and thought a good deal.

The cadet went off to a neighbouring farm-house, and returned with a billy-can of milk. The Inspector sat up, and glanced carelessly across at the prisoner. An oath escaped him, which made me sit up and stare. He beckoned the cadet and muttered angrily, "Who the devil left that rifle there? Get it away at once." The cadet looked about him, and seeing a rifle leaning against a tree within arm's length of Burke, glided stealthily across and secured it quietly. Burke's quick eyes noticed the movement.

"Are you afraid?" he said cheekily to the Inspector.

"Oh, no." Black replied calmly, "but I fancy I see a bear on a tree down the creek."

He took aim from where he sat, and fired. The bear, which was a hundred yards off, reeled out of the tree and thumped the ground hard.

"Knocked him, blowed if you didn't!" Burke said; then in admiration added, "By gums! You can use a rifle all right!"

"I thought it just as well to let him know I could," the Inspector said in an undertone to me, "in case he tries on some of his games with us, if he gets another chance."

Constable Edmonds called "Breakfast," and all of us except the Inspector rose and approached the spread that was prepared beneath a tree, a short distance off, and crouched round it. The Inspector remained awhile silently examining the rifle.

"Here's one for you, Burke," Edmonds said, tossing the prisoner a pannikin. "You'd better scratch your name on it— any one of them will do; I know you have a good few."

The rest of us remembered Burke's numerous aliases and smiled. Burke scowled and looked about for something to scratch "his mark" on the pint with. His eye rested on Constable Edmonds' belt and revolver lying on the grass at his elbow. He lifted the weapon, and, while the others were reaching for tea and digging into the bread and beef, toyed with it. Then he said, grinning, "Wonder could I write my name with this at a couple of hundred yards?"

The others looked up. Dismay suddenly filled their faces. The Force looked as if it had been struck by lightning. Crouched on my haunches just opposite Burke I sat heavily back and tried to conceal my head behind a large pannikin of tea. I spilt a lot of that tea into my lap and didn't feel it burn me.

Burke toyed more with the weapon. Still the Force remained dumb. Some of it had lifted large wedges of bread and beef to its mouth, and there the provender was suspended. It was a terrible moment—for me.

But the suspense broke suddenly.

"*Burke*," in a sharp, ringing voice, "*put that revolver down or I'll blow a hole through you!*"

Burke glanced across quickly and saw himself covered by the Inspector's rifle. With a cynical chuckle he put the revolver down and said, "You fellows are easily frightened."

I believed him.

Four pairs of hands instantly went out and reached for that weapon. Then the Inspector with fire in his eye came forward and said:

"The next man who lets his revolver get out of his hands returns to head-quarters under suspension." There was a silence; then Burke looked across at me and said:

"Chuck us across a slice of that beef, boss."

I chucked him across a slice, and the breakfast proceeded again calmly.

Advancing to our horses when we were prepared to start again the Inspector said:

"Wonder Could I Write My Name with This?"

"I don't know how the deuce you would have got on if I had
had to fire at him. A bit of your ear just covered the sight of
my rifle."

My hand went voluntarily to the side of my head, but my
ear was still there, and I was glad.

5. Proving His Alibi

On a good breakfast, and with tobacco clouds blowing from half a dozen pipes, we moved along at a brisk walking pace. The hard, made roads gradually gave way to soft grass and herbage under foot, and the bushland commenced to open out. Over the brow of a sand ridge the prisoner led the cavalcade; on past a deserted orchard, where a few ragged orange trees and the broken walls and sapling rafters of a humpy reared themselves like grim sentinels of the dead; past an old pumping station long since disused; then down on to the river and into a lane that led by the door of a dairyman's home.

Constable Jackson, with the prisoner, reined up, and their horses breasted the fence until the last of the escort drew up.

"What is it, Jackson?" from the Inspector.

"Burke says this is the first place he called at, sir."

"Very well; get off and we'll see what he remembers about it."

All of us, glad to ease our limbs, dismounted—all except the trackers. They were sent on ahead to wait at a certain spot till we came up.

I seated myself comfortably on the ground with my arm in the bridle reins, and took out my note book.

"What day, and what time of the day was it," the Inspector asked of Burke, "when you reached here? And tell us whom you saw, and what the people are like who live here, and what conversation you had with them?" The prisoner leaned on the fence, and ran his fingers up under his slouch hat and thought hard for several moments.

"I got here," he said, "on the tenth of November; that was a Saturday; and it was just about sundown when I reached these rails. There were some cows inside this little paddock—I don't think they belonged to this cove here—and a red bull with one horn was with them. I noticed the bull particularly, because he had just been staked in the barb-wire, and his near hind leg was nearly cut off. This cove who lives here is a bloomin' old Irishman, and he has finger-nails as long as——"

He stopped short, after waiting a while for his next words, and glared at me with blood in his eye.

"Oh!" he rasped out. "Is this the caper? This is what *you're* here for? You're not a blamed trap at all, then?"

I said "I was sorry I wasn't, and that I was merely there to take a note of everything that was said."

"I know that fancy caper!" he stormed. "You've been sent here by the dirty Government to put the rope round my bloomin' neck!"

"Perhaps," I answered, "to keep the rope from going round your neck. Everything said in your favour will go down in my notes."

"But how am I to tell," he protested furiously, "what you put down?"

"I'll read the notes over to you," I suggested, "whenever you wish me to."

"Yes," he insisted sullenly, "and afterwards you can knock out anything that doesn't suit the police. I know these little tricks."

I endeavoured to assure him I had a conscience and that I would sooner forfeit my billet and go cracking stones than take a hand in anything that wasn't strictly honourable. The Inspector reasoned with him; and finally in a sour, dogged sort of way he consented to proceed.

When he began to think again the whites of his eyes rolled suspiciously in the direction of my notebook, and I became conscious that a constable had placed himself between us. I felt shaky. The feeling somehow interfered with my pencil, and the notes I made were illegible. I was not happy.

"Well," Burke said, leaning on the fence again, "this chap who lives here has got finger nails as long and as hard as a cockatoo's beak, and he peels potatoes with them. His name is Ryan. He's a bad-tempered old dog, and I gave him a hiding for calling me a loafer."

The Inspector said, "That will do," and led the way into Ryan's residence.

Ryan was sitting in a poky back room, with a dish of potatoes in his lap, peeling them with his finger nails, with which he sliced them as you would with a knife. All of us stood and stared.

Ryan looked up in surprise.

"It's the polis!" he stammered, recognising the khaki.

"Did you ever see this man before?" motioning Burke forward.

"I never. Oi don't know him at all."

"What! you never saw me before?" in surprised tones from Burke.

"How cud Oi? *Oi* have never been in gaol."

"You old crawler!" savagely from Burke. "Do you remember me giving you a hiding out there in the yard for calling me a loafer?"

"An'—an'—if me gun had been at home," the old man squealed, springing at him like a cat, "Oi—Oi wud have shot ye that same evenin', ye dhirty gaol bird!"

Burke smiled.

"Then you remember him now?" the Inspector asked for final assurance.

"I doan't!" howled the old man indignantly.

The Inspector turned away.

"You —— old dog! You would see a man hang right enough!" Burke hissed as he was bundled off by the constable. And Ryan sat down and went on peeling potatoes with his finger nails.

Overtaking the trackers, the cavalcade headed towards the river and travelled without incident for a couple of miles.

"Hello!" the Inspector remarked in tones of surprise; "he's making for the ferry. Aha! This is interesting. If he crossed the river here that evening, he's done. We've got him beat! He'll fix himself up for the Pixley affair as sure as the Lord made little apples. He hasn't the faintest idea, either, that he's suspected of it."

The "Pixley affair" was the murder of a boy who was riding on a pony along a lonely part of the road on the eastern side of the river the evening of the day that Burke was released from the city gaol, and the solution of which hopelessly baffled the police.

When about fifty yards from the ferry Constable Jackson reined up again and waited. A hopeful look was in the Inspector's face as he came up.

"What happened here?" he asked of Burke.

"When I left Ryan's I took the road we just came, and got to the ferry here a little after dark, and spoke to the ferryman."

"Of course you crossed over, I suppose," the Inspector said, assuming indifference.

"No; I had no money on me, and this miserable hog down here (meaning the ferryman)—I think it's him—he wears a cabbagetree hat and a red beard—wouldn't take me across, and I told him to go to hell. Then I turned back and went along the river bank and camped in some thick shrubs."

"And you didn't cross the river at all, then?" the Inspector repeated.

"No; I hadn't the luck."

The Inspector exchanged a meaning look with Jackson, and the escort advanced to the ferry.

"No," the ferryman said, shaking his head, "I don't remember refusing to take anyone across in my life. In fact, I'm sure I never."

Then, after looking Burke all over at the Inspector's request:

"No, I never had a conversation with that man; never saw him before that I remember." Then, exhibiting a desire to be just: "Of course, I don't say that I didn't take him over. I might any time do that without recollecting his face again."

"Don't you remember," Burke asked, "that I had no money, and we had a bit of a barney over it, and I told you to go to hell?"

The ferryman, a big, hard-looking man, smiled and said quietly: "It isn't likely I'd forget that if it happened, because I would have thrown you into the river if it had."

"You would have to be a lot better with your hands than you are at remembering things, old chap," Burke said with flashing eyes. Then to the Inspector: "It's no use wasting time here; this fellow doesn't remember anything or doesn't want to."

"Well, you're a cheeky gentleman, anyway," said the ferryman, "and those handcuffs, I think, just suit you."

Burke scowled at him as we rode away.

A new interest now seemed to enter into the proceedings. Constable Jackson was allowed to get well ahead, and the Inspector rode close to the other constables, and asked them "what they thought of it."

About a mile or so along the bank of the river Burke pointed

to a clump of thick undergrowth no higher than a man's head
as the spot where he slept that night.

"Did you make a fire?" the Inspector asked, scrutinising the
place.

"No, I did not bother making one. I had a bit of tucker with
me, and when I finished it just crept in amongst these bushes
and went to sleep."

"A curious place for a bushman to select a camp, wasn't it?"

"Oh, I dunno" (sullenly); "just as good as any other; and I
didn't want the whole country to see me, anyway."

The Inspector smiled meaningly; then, directing the escort
to a waterhole, decided to halt for lunch.

6.   The Way of the Transgressor is Hard

When the meal was over we were lounging in the shade of the trees, smoking and watching the horses with their bridles on cropping the grass round about.

Burke lay on the broad of his back, staring silently into the green foliage that waved above his head, thinking of days and dates, raking his memory to recall the tracks he had trodden—the faces he had met, the things he had seen and said and heard said during those unlucky weeks he had been a free man. Failure to account for one single link in the chain of evidence that was to establish his alibi he knew was to miss the life line. Sympathy he had none; assistance he could not command or expect; conscience told him he was a criminal; experience warned him that the police regarded him as a useless and dangerous member of society, and that if he were even innocently hanged for the crime they were anxious to sheet home to him to save themselves, they would plead that his life was no loss anyway. In short, he saw plainly that it was to be a fight with himself on the one side and the whole police force on the other, and the trophy—his own miserable, misspent life!

With a calm, determined expression on his face he turned over on his elbow and looked around.

Locating me, he crawled across and asked to have the notes I had taken at the ferry read over to him.

"H'm!" he muttered, nipping the end of a blade of grass, "that cove should have remembered me."

Then he reflected again.

Criminal and all that I knew the man to be, I couldn't withhold all compassion from him, and, with an effort, made up my mind to take a risk.

"It's well for you, Burke," I said, "that you didn't cross the ferry that evening."

He opened his eyes and stared tragically.

"There was a boy murdered on the other side about the time you would have crossed," I added.

"Gord blast and burn them!" he exclaimed, bounding to his feet and glaring round on the Law. They instantly came to the perpendicular with their hands on their revolvers. "And you're trying to saddle me with that blanky crime as well! You ——! ——! ——!"

The very leaves on the gum trees, overhead, trembled at his outburst of profanity.

The Inspector warned him to be careful.

"Curs! Cadgers!" Burke muttered bitterly, and threw himself on the grass again, and writhed like a wild animal.

I felt guilty of having disturbed the harmony of the expedition, and remained silent.

"Doing all they can to hang me!" he muttered again, tearing fistfuls of grass out of the earth and throwing them violently from him. Some of it scattered over the tea bucket and landed in the tea.

"Damn it!" in reproval from Constable Edmonds. "Don't do that! We'll want another drink of tea before we start."

Burke tore out more grass, but this time didn't cast it from him; he crunched it viciously in his fists instead.

Then he stretched himself out on his back again and reflected as before.

"You thought you had me beat at the ferry," Burke with a savage chuckle said to the Inspector, as we moved along again, "but you hadn't. I've thought of something now which I'd forgotten then. Come back to the bushes where I camped, and we should find a pickle bottle that I left there. I got it full of jam from a woman whose house we passed a little way back, and whom I told that the ferryman would not take me across. Now that I know what you are after I'm damned glad he didn't."

Returning to the clump of shrubs, one of the constables dismounted and, searching the spot, found the pickle bottle. It was labelled in a woman's handwriting, "Melon and lemon."

"That's it," Burke said. "Now bring it down and see if the woman remembers it."

The woman did remember it. She also remembered giving it to Burke, and supported his statement in respect to the ferryman.

"There you are, me shavers," Burke, with a malignant smile, said to the force. Then to the woman, as they hurried him away:

"They would like to make out that I crossed the ferry that evening, missus, so as to fix me with the murder of that boy."

"Hold your tongue and be civil!" the burly senior-constable growled, "or I'll give you a lick on the jaw."

Burke held his tongue, and the cavalcade once more proceeded along the banks of the river. For miles we travelled over barren, unproductive patches of clay country; at intervals hugging picturesque pockets on the river: through gaps in the broken fences of the abandoned sugar fields we rode, and not a sound all the while except the jangling of bridle bits, the ring of stirrup irons, and the incessant rattle of the packs. Crossing the river where the broad expanse of water divided itself into several limpid streams, trickling calmly over shallow, sandy beds, the rude habitation of a timber-getter rose before us.

"I came to this place," Burke said, "about dinnertime on my second day out, and seeing no one about called out, 'Is anyone at home?' A man answered me from inside. He didn't show himself. I told him I wanted a bit of tucker. He said 'Go to the devil and buy tucker the same as I have to!'

"I went further on to a place about a mile from here, and got a feed from a Danish woman."

The timber-getter, a big, hairy, sunburnt man, had just drawn his team up alongside a fence to unyoke; and, as the escort approached, dropped his long whip and stared in surprise.

"Do you know this man?" the Inspector asked, indicating Burke with his hunting-crop. The bullock-puncher walked all round the prisoner as he sat on the horse and looked hard and long at him.

"I have not had that pleasure."

To the next question he answered: "That's right; I did tell a cove one day to go to the devil and buy some tucker, but I did not see the chap. If I was to hear this man speak, though, I could tell you if he is the same, because the cove that spoke to me had a voice that no one in this world would ever forget."

The Inspector asked Burke to say something. Burke lifted his voice and said: "Can you let us have a bit of tucker in there?"

"That's the cove!" the bullock-puncher exclaimed, with an

amused look on his face. "I'll stake my blanky life on it."

The Inspector was satisfied, and, directing the party to an adjacent box-tree ridge as a suitable spot to pitch camp for the night, followed in the rear with a thoughtful look on his face.

"I'm afraid that gets the dog out of the Pixley affair," he said sorrowfully to me, after covering a hundred yards or so.

"I'm afraid he was never in it," I answered heroically.

"Perhaps," he muttered. "But if he doesn't get nailed for the Trackson murder before we're done with him, then my name isn't James Morcum Black."

"If he's guilty," I replied, "I hope he swings for it—and promptly."

"It's darned little odds whether he is or not; for he's bad enough for anything," he answered.

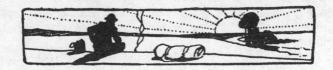

7. A Devil of a Fright

We rode along together, and reached the spot where the boys were unpacking, in silence.

Then, as the sun went down, a white calico tent pitched to a sapling, to which the prisoner was to be chained over night, was flying on the ridge: and all around saddles, bridles, packs, blankets, and baggage were strewn. A great fire blazed a few yards off, and the sweat-marked horses clanked their hobble-chains and waded knee-deep into the long bluegrass.

It had been a long, hot day, and when tea was over we lay in the cool and smoked, listening in silence to the dismal hoots of the night birds. The prisoner sat on his haunches, the reflection of the fire shedding a pallid, hunted look over his drawn features, thinking and thinking. From a log, a short distance off, the two black boys chanted weird dirges in their native tongue. In the middle of their song Norman suddenly stopped, and yelling to the other to "Lookit out—death adder!"— bounded up and peered cautiously down beside the log. Sure enough a death adder was there. Charlie stunned the reptile with a short stick, then, yabbering excitedly, conveyed it to the light for inspection.

"Chuck it on the fire," the Inspector cried. The tracker threw it on the fire, where, for a moment or two, it wriggled in its agony. But Burke never shifted his eyes; he hardly seemed to notice the incident.

There was a rustle in the long grass, and the forms of several shy sons of a neighbouring selector cautiously appeared in the light. They nervously murmured "Good-night," and for some time stood surveying the camp with wonder in their eyes. Finding their presence not resented, they gained courage, and seating themselves beside each other on the grass, settled down to enjoy the grotesque duets of the gorgeously-uniformed trackers. Occasionally they would steal sly glances at the prisoner, then shift their gaze to the constables lounging around.

Constable Edmunds, with a sense of humour, rose suddenly.

"You are the very coves we want," he said, striding towards them. The next moment they had vanished like a vision into the night, and the sharp sound of dead sticks breaking under their bare feet as they skedaddled down the ridge, was all that proclaimed their whereabouts. The other constables chuckled amusedly, and Norman, with a loud, cheerful laugh, said, "By cripes, you been frightenit dem coves that time."

Edmunds, lifting an empty bucket that stood near the fire, said: "Here! go down the gully and fill this for the night." The cheerful expression on Norman's face changed instantly. His white eyes rolled in their sockets like a pair of billiard balls, and with a look of alarm he murmured:

"Oh, I not been go down dere when it dark."

"What the deuce you frightened of?" the constable growled. "Charley, he go with you."

It was Charlie's turn then to feel alarmed. With a sulky look in his eyes, he shook his head firmly in the negative.

The Inspector's voice rang out: "Go on, you pair of fools, and bring the water; and a darned good job if some devil devil does get hold of you!"

The rest of the force chuckled again.

"Well, we not go without plenty fire stick," Norman muttered, and the two of them, arming themselves with most of the fire, trudged off reluctantly, swinging the flaring torches round their heads as they went.

An idea struck Constable Edmunds.

"I'll give them both a devil of a fright," he said, and, hurrying into the darkness, made a detour, and arrived on the opposite bank of the waterhole before the superstitious ones reached the spot; then, crouching down, waited for them.

They approached the hole cautiously, swinging their fire sticks with increased energy.

"You dippit up water," Norman whispered timidly to his dusky companion.

"Oh, no, you been do dat," Charlie answered. "You takit bucket; I been wavit fire stick."

After some more yabbering in undertones, Norman took the bucket, and, as he stealthily hung down over the bank of the hole, which was a couple of feet high, to fill the vessel, *bang*!

Bang Went the Constable's Revolver

went the constable's revolver. Norman with a yell and a heavy splash fell into the water: Charlie abandoned the fire stick and ran like an emu for the camp. With a shout he bounded over the fire, and, landing breathless among the members of the force, vociferated excitedly:

"Murderer been camp alonga water and shootit Norman! Lookit out! Lookit out!" (peering wildly into the darkness). "Getit rifle quick; he been come dis way pretty soon!"

The words had hardly left his lips when Norman, breathing like a colt choking, and wet from head to foot, rushed into the light and threw himself into the arms of the Inspector.

"Get out!" Black shouted indignantly, and jumped to his feet to escape a bath. "What the devil have you been doing?"

Norman had only wind enough left to roll his eyes about, and gesticulate, and point in the direction of the waterhole.

The constables rolled over and over on the grass and held their sides, and kicked the earth hard with delight.

After a while Constable Edmunds returned into camp from an opposite quarter.

"Did you bring the water?" he asked in an unconcerned sort of tone of the excited blacks.

The two trackers looked at each other, and Charlie rose and said wildly:

"Norman, he been reachit down" (suiting the action to the word), "and big pfella rifle fire, and him fallit in water."

"And did you leave the bucket in the hole?" the constable yelled at Norman. Norman, his eyes still bursting from his head, nodded in the affirmative.

"Well, back you go and get it, the two of you," Edmunds commanded. "No one fired a rifle at you; that's only a yarn. You were too frightened to go near the hole."

The thought of having to return to that waterhole was too much for Charlie, and, seizing a long stick, he waved it defiantly at the constable, and yelled, "I been go there no more; you been go your plurry self!"

Then for the first time since tea Burke spoke.

"Good man, Charlie," he said, turning his head; "I'm glad to see you've got some courage, anyway."

"Oh, well," Edmunds chuckled, "*I'm* not afraid to go," and went off to fish the bucket out of the hole.

When he had gone, Charlie said apprehensively to the Inspector:

"You waitit a while, Mr. Black: he come back here pretty quick."

Then the form of the constable, bending to the weight of the water, appeared, and the simple trackers stared at him in amazement.

"You no been see no one?" Charlie asked, wonderingly.

"Oh, yes," Edmunds growled. "I saw a cove down there— big, wild-looking cove with long whiskers."

"Yair" (excitedly). "What he been do?"

"Oh, he been runnit like the devil, all the same as you."

Charlie looked at Norman, and in an analytical sort of way, murmured, "He been habit only one cartridge that cove, Norman, by cripes! I been trackit him, though, alonga daybreak."

When we had finished smoking and it was time to turn in, we spread our blankets on the ground and lay with our heads in the saddles. Burke was placed in the tent between two constables, his feet chained to the sapling, and one of his wrists handcuffed to the senior-constable's. Word had been previously passed round to all hands not to sleep too soundly, in case of emergency. The warning, however, was scarcely necessary, for to sleep at all the first night out on the hard, uneven ground, with two blackfellows snoring at your ears like a thousand bears, was a difficult proposition.

The Inspector himself slept least of any; whether the responsibility of the charge weighed too heavily upon his mind or whether he apprehended an effort might be made during the night to rescue the prisoner, I do not know; but the least sound or the slightest movement would bring him to a sitting position with his eye fixed on the slumbering form of Burke and his hand on a revolver. Nothing extraordinary happened, however, and at daybreak the horses were rounded up and breakfast got ready.

"Where the devil is Charlie?" the Inspector asked, missing the tracker. No one seemed to know.

"Fooling round somewhere," Constable Taay answered, rising and looking round the ridge to locate him.

In a while the missing one appeared. He came over the back of the ridge with a large grin on his face, and approaching

Edmunds, who was seated on the grass, lifted his foot and examined his boot.

"*You* been him," he said. "You been shootit Norman last night; I been trackit you all a down a this way" (pointing over the back of the ridge).

The camp smiled.

"I thoughtit been him," Norman said in tones of forgiveness. Norman was a transparent sort of liar.

Then the camp laughed at his expense, and gathering the baggage together, prepared to make a fresh start.

8.   A Tale of a Tub

Before Burke was placed on the horse the Inspector asked him if anything important happened at the Danish woman's house.

"No," he answered. "I merely asked her for some tucker, which she gave me, and then I went on."

The Danish woman was just out of bed when the escort surrounded her door.

"I don't know noddings," she answered stiffly, in reply to the Inspector. "I don't get mixed up in novon's peesness. You mosht find oud dem dings for youselluf."

"Did you ever see this man before?" the Inspector asked in a firm voice, pointing to the prisoner. "You had better say so if you did."

"I saw noddings" (dropping her head sulkily).

The question was repeated.

"Ask himselluf," the woman replied stubbornly. "He can tole you so well as me."

"I know all about that, but I want you to tell me. Did you see him before?"

No answer.

"Don't you remember a man calling here about dinner-time, missus," Burke chipped in quietly, "and you gave him some dinner: a piece of bread and some stewed rat, I think it was?"

"Vell, I do noddings wrong by dat, and it is not a shame to givf rat ven I am only a poor woman, do you think?"

"I don't mean that" (from the Inspector). "I'd eat rat myself if I could not get anything else. But you saw this man before—that's all I want to know?"

"Vell, I did see him, if you vill make me say so; and he asked me vare vas my husban', and I say he vas inside, ven he vas dead ten, twelf year. But I vas vrightent, for dat man, he haf a bad face."

Burke smiled. So did we.

"Well, why did you not tell us that before?" the Inspector replied shortly, and we rode on.

We rode on till noon, when the iron-roofed houses of two humble homesteads, standing about two hundred yards from each other, came into view.

"I called at this near house," Burke began before we approached the place, "about five o'clock the second day I was out. I couldn't see anyone about for a while, but the front door, which you'll find is made of split timber, was slightly opened, and I saw a woman having a bath in a tub. I sang out, 'Is there anyone at home?' and when she saw me standing outside she rushed out holding her dress round her, and ran over to this house here" (pointing to the other habitation).

The force smiled, and moved toward the place. A tall, old-maidish-looking woman appeared in the doorway, and over her shoulders two young girls peered at us. The woman coloured up and shook her head when questioned by the Inspector, and was sure she had never seen Burke before. In fact, no man of any description had called at her place about the date mentioned. She was positive of that. She would have remembered if there had, because hers being such an out-of-the-way place she had very few callers of any kind.

The Inspector remained silent for a few moments. The situation was a delicate one, and he was considering how to frame his next question, when his eyes wandered unconsciously to Burke's. Burke immediately jumped into the breach.

"Don't you recollect a man coming to the door one evening when you were having a bath," he said, "and when he called out you got a fright and ran over to that house there?"

The old maid scowled and went scarlet.

"Oh, yes, aunt," one of the girls said. "That was when you ran over to mother's, and that is the man" (looking at Burke) "who opened our window the same night."

The old maid silenced the girl with her elbow, but made no remark.

"What did you say?" the Inspector said coaxingly to the girl. "That this man opened your window the same night?"

"She's talking through her neck," Burke growled, shifting restlessly in the saddle. And the girl received another dig in the ribs from her aunt.

The Inspector dismounted, and exerted all his powers of persuasion, and applied all the intimidating tactics he could invent, but his efforts to extract any further information were futile.

"Did you put down what the girl said about her aunt running over to the other place?" Burke said to me as we rode along again.

"Yes; and about the window, too," I answered maliciously. Burke scowled.

With unerring direction the prisoner conducted the escort to a secluded spot at the bottom of a deep gully where he had camped the same night, and pointed to the ashes of the fire he had kindled.

"If he keeps this up," the Inspector murmured to me as he turned from the place, "he's a wonder."

And a wonder Burke was. Day after day he ran his own tracks through the broad, silent bush; over mountains and through scrub; avoiding stock routes and roads; veering off townships that contained police stations; mistaking no spot that he camped at; passing no place where he had called; forgetting no face he had seen; recalling and verifying every word he had spoken to strangers and every word they had spoken to him; describing their build; detailing their peculiarities in manner, gait, and speech; giving their nationalities, and frequently their relationship one to the other. And all this he gathered during his hurried peregrinations of eight weeks! His bush instincts, his memory and his observation, might well have been the envy of any Australian story-writer.

A fortnight went by—a fortnight of slow, sleepy rides often extending long into the night, often through rain and slush, and in the face of storm and hail—and the escort found itself dragging along about thirty miles to the eastward of the scene of the Trackson murder. The prisoner was trespassing on dangerous ground. Was he going to run his tracks into Trackson and seal his fate, or would he shy off and steer a different course were questions that silently engaged every mind. We were not left long in suspense, however. He turned his back completely on the fated township, and led the cavalcade to the foot of the great mountain range.

"I don't believe the cunning dog came this way," the Inspector murmured disappointedly, casting his eye on the form of

Burke jogging leisurely along beside the senior-constable, "I'm darned if I do!"

A depression seemed to set in all round, and weighed heavily upon the police; and miles and miles of the way were covered without a word being exchanged between any of them.

Striking a bridle track that wound up the steep sides of the range and led through a historical gap to the broad expanse of tableland beyond, Burke halted and pointed to a bark humpy hidden away in a deep gorge.

"An old man and his three sons live here," he said, "and when I called about four o'clock on the second day of December, the two big boys were wrestling on the grass, in front of the hut, and the old man was cutting the other one's hair with a pair of shears. I sat down for a while and watched the boys wrestling. They weren't much good at it, and I offered to show them some points. One of them had a 'go' at me, and I threw him over my head. The old man, thinking there was a row on, rushed out and woodened me behind the ear with a lump of stick while my back was turned. It knocked me silly for a while, but when the boys explained that it was all in fun the old man apologised and made me stay the night with them."

We found the old man and the three boys sitting down to their evening meal together, and on hearing the tramp of our horses they came to the door.

"Ai," the parent said, on being interrogated, "that's quaht correct; and from what Ah've heerd o' him since Ah'm dev'lish sorry Ah didn't give him a hardey yun in the year."

"Then he did stay with you that night?" the Inspector said with a smile.

"That he did, and from all Ah hear abaht him it waint no angel we were 'arbouring unawares," the old man replied.

"Well, I'm pretty sure," Burke put in, "that you don't follow the occupation of an angel yourself, or you wouldn't be hiding yourself away in these ranges."

"Well, Ah'm certain, m' shaver, from the looks o' you, that y' never followed e'er a occupation at all—not on yer own choosin'. I baint have any doubts tho' but what you could crahk stones or pick oakum wi' any yun i' the land."

Burke winced, but before he could make a reply he was hustled away.

The Two Big Boys Were Wrestling on the Grass

We went into camp along with two drovers, and shared with them the comforts and discomforts of a deserted hut. The drovers were in charge of a mob of cattle, and it was their third day on the road. They were short-handed, and had taken watch the whole of the first two nights.

A large fire burned, and illuminated the trees around. Two emus approached cautiously, then turned and fled into the gloom.

Tea was over; the camp still and quiet. Showers of sparks wreathed up through the tracery of branches—up, up, and out into the silent void.

The Inspector was kindly disposed.

"You know how to watch cattle?" he said to Charlie.

Charlie did.

"Well, get a horse and watch the mob for Mr. Jones till middle of night; then you turn in."

Charlie rose reluctantly to secure a horse.

The drover was grateful, but wanted assurance that the darkie wouldn't go to sleep on watch and lose the cattle.

"Now, don't you go to sleep," the Inspector said. "If you do, the devil devil catch you sure as your name is Charlie."

"Oh, me not been go to sleep," Charlie answered, "not while him been about." And mounting the horse, he rode quietly round the resting mob.

"He'll watch them all right," the Inspector assured the drovers; "he'll be too frightened to go to sleep." And the "camp" turned in for the night.

For a couple of hours Charlie rode round the mob. It was tedious work, and more than once he found himself and horse nodding to sleep. Finally they both went to sleep; and dreamed. Suddenly a startled emu came streaking through the timber, as emus will at night, and collided heavily with the slumbering horse. The old horse bounded out of its dream without giving Charlie any warning. Charlie left the saddle and fell on his head. He yelled and jumped up hurriedly. He didn't wait to find out things. He ran. He came to earth again in a stump hole, and yelled some more. He ran faster and fell over a fence. Then the door of the hut burst open, and he fell inside on top of the slumbering Inspector. The Inspector bounded up and reached for his revolver.

"What the devil's the matter?" he said.

"By cripes, HIM been come, boss!" Charlie gasped, glaring at the door.

"My God! they're off!" And the drovers bounded from their blankets.

Then a thousand devils seemed to be thundering and crashing through timber. The hoof beats of galloping horses rang on the night, and cries of "Werp! Werp! Woa, there! Woa!" grew fainter and fainter till they died away.

9. *Divers Diversions*

Next morning the cavalcade in single file climbed the mountain sides, and reached the great plateau.

Descending from the plateau we struck the head of one of the largest of Australian rivers. A magnificent waterhole and abundance of grass were there, and the Inspector decided to camp for a couple of days to spell the horses. It was a weary, monotonous time. With little to converse about and nothing whatever to read, those two days dragged tediously by. A big scrub was there, however, and the rifles supplied us with turkeys and pigeons without number, and we fed in style equal to Paris House.

On the afternoon of the second day the prisoner expressed a wish to indulge in a swim. He said he wanted "a good wash badly." We believed him. We knew he did. We had to sleep near him; and his wardrobe was not an extensive one. The shirt and trousers he was wearing were those he had worn during the eight weeks he was out. He had no others with him, and he never borrowed ours.

"Let him have a dip," the Inspector said to the senior-constable, "but leave the leg-irons on one of his ankles." Then, while Burke was undressing, he whispered in an undertone to Constable Taay to "slip round to the other side of the hole, in case he might try something on."

Taay, taking up the rifle and pretending to be looking for game, sauntered round and took up a position on the other bank.

Burke, with the leg-irons jingling like hobble chains as he faced the water, plunged head first into the hole and dived. All eyes were immediately fixed on the surface to locate the spot where he would likely appear again. He didn't appear. The circles he left behind on the face of the water grew larger and larger. The Inspector became concerned. "Look out for him!" he cried, standing up revolver in hand. "Get to the bottom end, some of you, quick!" The next moment all hands were gathered round that hole watching every motion of the water, and listening intently for the faintest sound. None came.

Ten, fifteen minutes went past; yet not a sign of the prisoner! The Inspector became frantic. He called loudly to him by name —called a dozen times.

Still no response.

"He has either come up close to the bank with his head behind them reeds there," the senior said, "or the leg-irons have him caught in a bramble at the bottom of the hole, and he's done for."

"But surely there'd be bubbles come on the water if he was caught at the bottom," the Inspector said despairingly; then tore at his hair and called for the prisoner again.

"By ——!" he cried desperately at last, "if he's behind those reeds and won't come out, I'll riddle him with bullets!"

Burke *was* behind the reeds; but only his nose was above water, and as the Inspector raised the revolver to fire in his direction he disappeared like a turtle; and when the shooting was over rose noiselessly again to the surface.

An hour—two hours passed; still no trace of the prisoner.

"He's stuck by the leg-iron, all right," the senior repeated in hopeless tones; and the Inspector murmured, "There'll be a hell of a row" and ran wildly about the banks peering over the edges of them.

At last an idea suddenly struck him, and he cried, "Can any of you dive?"

"Charlie, he been a great diver," Norman said proudly.

The Inspector turned hopefully to Charlie. Charlie demurred. The darkie had no wish to emulate the bad example of Burke.

"Not in dare," he said stubbornly. "I been get stuck, too. By cripes!"

The next moment Constable Taay had stripped off, and, facing the spot where Burke disappeared, took a header. The rest of the force waited breathlessly.

"By cripes, boss," Charlie said with enthusiasm, "if him been get stuck, too, I ridit in his saddle."

The Inspector scowled at Charlie and fixed his eyes on the water again.

In a few seconds Constable Taay, spouting water with the noise of a whale, came to the surface.

"I felt the head of a tree or something," he gasped, "but nothing else."

"He's under it all right," the senior murmured again, "and out of it he'll never come."

After a few minutes' rest Constable Taay dived a second time. As he disappeared again, Burke left his hiding place and swam under water towards him.

Taay in groping about embraced the form of the latter, and seizing him by the hair rose triumphantly with him. Burke came to the surface as limp and lifeless as a dead man.

"I've got him!" Taay cried. "He was under a log," and swam to the bank with the corpse.

"Dead, by G—!" the Inspector muttered, as the body was dragged out and stretched on the grass.

"Wait a bit—wait a bit!" the senior cried excitedly. "Turn him over; put his head down hill and let the water run out of him, and rub him—rub him, every one of ye."

All of us set to work, and rubbed and scrubbed and patted and spanked the body of Burke. Then we held him up by the heels, but no water ran out of him.

"By gobs!" the senior exclaimed, making a discovery, "I believe he's breathing."

Burke was breathing, but slightly.

"Run to my valise," the Inspector said, "and bring a flask of brandy that's there."

Norman ran and brought the brandy flask, and the neck of it was inserted in the drowned man's mouth. He began to drink feebly.

"By heavens, he's coming round!" the Inspector cried, putting the neck of the flask into Burke's mouth again. Burke closed his teeth upon it and drank greedily.

He drank it all before relaxing his grip.

"By cripes!" Charlie moaned as the brandy disappeared, "I don't think he been drowned very much, somehow."

Burke groaned, and opening his eyes murmured, "Wheresh [hic] are we?"

"How do you feel?" the Inspector asked sympathetically.

Burke lifted his voice and in a cracked, drunken key began to sing; "We wonsh go home [hic] till mornin'; we won'sh go home [hic] till mornin'."

Burke Suddenly Aimed Several Kicks at Charlie

A cheerful chuckle came from the force, and Charlie said:
"Brandy putit life into him. By cripes!"

Burke suddenly staggered to his feet, and yelling, "You were too d—— frightened to go in after me, anyway, you black scrubber!" and aimed several kicks with his bare foot at Charlie.

The Inspector stared, and said to Taay, "*Was* he under the log?"

Then, swinging his arms about like flails, Burke cried, "Come on! I'll (hic) fight the wholsh dam lot yoush!"

They came on, and three heavy policemen fell on him, and bore him to the ground again. Then they handcuffed him and secured him in the tent, where he struggled and howled like a wild animal till long into the night.

10.   A Forlorn Hope

At daybreak the escort, with feelings of thankfulness, left camp, and for several miles ran the river down in a southerly direction. Steering a westerly course, we travelled inland, and, crossing the border again, were once more moving along the heights of the plateau.

Our faces were now turned in the direction of the scene of the murder, and fresh hopes filled the hearts of the police. A tramp of four days and a drop over the ranges by a well-known mountain pass would land a footman in Trackson. The Inspector mentally calculated distances, and with feelings mingled with joy and anxiety reckoned up the dates supplied by the prisoner. The prisoner himself seemed the least concerned of the party.

Two more days passed. Then the rolling plains, fringed with ridge and timber-land, dotted here and there with farm-houses and miscellaneous habitations, spread themselves out before us.

"Rather a good class of people live here," Burke said as we came to a gate leading to a comfortable-looking homestead; "and when I struck it about sundown on the ninth of December all the men were at the killing-yard killing a bullock. There were two very good-looking girls sitting sewing on the verandah. One of them had very dark hair, and the other was fair. The fair one's name was Stella. I asked them over the fence for something to eat. They gave me a loaf of bread, a bit o' tea, about half a pound of butter, and a big slice of cheese."

The escort then advanced to the house, and found the two pretty girls still sitting on the verandah. With looks of surprise and confusion they tripped down the steps and came to the garden fence. When questioned by the Inspector they looked hard at each other, and thought hard. The dark one shook her head dubiously, but the fair one suddenly remembered that a traveller had called about the date mentioned, and that she and her sister had given him something to eat. She remembered it because they happened to have more bread in the house that day than they knew what to do with, and were glad to give it to someone rather than waste it.

"Don't you recollect," she added, turning to her sister, "that pa was in a great scot, and said we were only encouraging 'sundowners' to make the house a place of call?"

Then the other remembered also.

"Is your name Stella?" the Inspector asked, addressing the fair one.

She stared in surprise, then laughed and said: "It is; but I'm sure I don't know how you know."

"Would you know the man again if you saw him?" the Inspector further interrogated.

The fair girl seemed doubtful, but her sister was sure *she* would.

"Do you see him here, then?" was the next question.

The dark girl ran her eye over the line of dusty faces fronting her across the fence. She ran her eye over us several times.

At last she made up her mind.

"That's the man," she said, pointing to me.

A broad official grin stole over the features of the police, and the two trackers broke into a variety of giggles, and made jokes in their own language at my expense.

"Are you quite sure?" I asked, straightening myself up, and endeavouring to look attractive and innocent. It was a difficult proposition.

She hesitated a moment.

"N-n-no," she said, "not when you speak." And then she smiled and showed an enviable set of teeth and how nice she was. I longed to pull the palings down and hug her.

"Would you think *I* was the man?" Burke broke out in his harsh, grating voice.

"Oh! that's the man!" both girls exclaimed. "And you were carrying a small calico swag, and wearing the same hat you have on now," one of them added. Then turning apologetically to me, the brunette said with a smile, "But you're *awfully* alike, you know."

The desire to pull the palings out and hug her melted suddenly from me. She didn't strike me as being a nice girl.

Like explorers of the past, the escort slowly crossed the plains. The homes of a dozen selectors were visited; the rich pastoral lands of various stations, where the great sheep-walks mocked the small and struggling landholders, were traversed; another of the prisoner's camping-places identified; another night under the trees by the bank of a creek; and then the day of all days—the day that would either set the prisoner free or see him hanged by the neck in the city gaol—was entered upon.

Burke had now accounted for his every movement, and proved his whereabouts right up to the morning of the tragedy; and not more than thirty miles of country lay between the escort and Trackson. Could the prisoner have made a quick day's march, taking a direct course through the mountain ranges, and reached Trackson in time to intercept the Maguires when returning from the ball they had never attended? The police scarcely dare ask themselves that question; but silently and with a look of anxious expectation they moved from camp, watching their prisoner closely as they rode along. When some three miles had been covered, Burke directed the way to a clump of grasstrees.

"I reached those trees about ten o'clock, and camped under them till one or two, then went on to a township about four miles from here."

"You camped under them till one!" the Inspector murmured incredulously. And: "I don't believe it!" in an undertone from one of the constables.

"All right!" the Inspector sighed, touching his horse with the riding whip. "We'll soon see all about it, I suppose."

Those grass-trees were a wet blanket on the hopes and prospects of the police.

Presently the township came into view. So did a crowd of excited-looking people—a galaxy of men, women, and youths, some mounted on horseback, some driving in sulkies and traps. News of the escort's advance was brought in the evening before, and the inhabitants, anxious to see the notorious suspect, turned out to meet us. They lined up on both sides of the black-soil lane, and, like a guard of honour, awaited us. As we drew near we felt like conquering heroes. The prisoner felt like a wild animal being exhibited. He disliked admiration. He was displeased. He began to show his displeasure. At range of a hundred yards he opened a slow preliminary fire of profanity on them. We smiled. We knew what was coming, and what a

shock the crowd would get. At seventy yards Burke's voice rose
to a shout, and he became violently profane. Several females
left the ranks and drove away. At fifty yards the prisoner went
off like a cannon, and belched forth such a volume of blasphemy that the two lines broke into disorder and fled down the
road to the township. But a square-shouldered man with a
slouch hat shading his eyes, a pointed, faded beard of no
particular variety or consequence, sleeves rolled up, grease on
his shirt, and blood splashes on his trouser legs, remained
sitting calmly on a yellow, shoulder-marked mare with a thick,
heavy tail and a strawberry neck. He was the butcher. Burke
gasped for breath, then attacked him. He called him a variety
of blood and birth stains; threw doubts on his pedigree and his
nationality; questioned his sex, and threatened when he was
free to return and murder him in his sleep. Then, in spite of the
senior-constable, he spurred the chestnut round in a half-circle
and tried to ride the butcher down.

"You're a queer card," the vendor of tuberculosis said, and,
putting spurs to the yellow mare with the strawberry neck,
raced in pursuit of the main body.

"The —— dog!" Burke murmured. "I'll look him up when
I come out!"

Before entering the township the escort left the main road
and turned down a lane leading to a primitive dairy farm.

"The man who lives here," Burke said, "is an Irishman, and
his name's Malone. He has only owned the farm about two
years, and he bought it from a chap called Regan. I got some
bread and tea from him about six o'clock in the evening and
made a fire and camped just in front of the house. That was the
night you fellows reckon I was in Trackson murdering the
Maguires."

The Inspector bit his lip and rode on in silence.

Malone was at dinner, and, with excitement in his eye, and
twirling a fork in his fingers with a lump of fresh meat impaled
on the prongs of it, came out to meet us.

"I do thin remimber him," he snapped with emphasis; "remimber him damn well. And what's more, ye're barkin' up the
wrong tree—ye haven't the right mahn."

"I don't want your opinion on that," the Inspector snarled.
"Is he the man who called here on the evening of the twenty-

sixth December, and can you swear to him? That's all I want
to know from you."

"Of courrse Oi can swear to him; and Oi cud swear *at* him.
And Oi cud swear he was just across the road under that tree
the very next morning. And Oi cud swear if it wasn't him it was
someone else who got awaay with me Christmas ham from out
me kitchen that same night."

"And you're certain it was the twenty-sixth December?" the
Inspector asked as a last hope.

"Just as certain as I am that ye are all wastin' ye're toime
draggin' him round the country, and lettin' them who did the
murther get awaay."

"I only want you to answer my question," came angrily from
the Inspector.

"I *huv* answered ye're question," Malone replied, still twirling the steak about. "Oi huv *more* than answered it. And sure
there's the Dalys and the O'Briens, and ahl thim, who cud
answer it too; fer ahl ov thim recognised him as the mahn who
wer' here whin they see his picter in the paipers."

"Is your name Malone?"

"It is—Martin Thomas Patrick Malone! And I'm not
ashamed of it, neither."

"Did you buy this place from a man called Regan?"

"I did—from Terence Regan, senior."

The Inspector mounted his horse again.

"I'm obliged to you," Burke said to Malone, as we turned
away.

"Thin yez needn't be," answered Malone; "fer I'd give yez
ten year if Oi were a judge."

The same evening the police lay in camp resting and reflecting on the dismal results of their investigations, and their hopeless chances of reward. A messenger arrived on horseback, and
handed the Inspector a note from the stationmaster of the
township. The Inspector read it and brightened up.

"The stationmaster's office was broken into here last night,"
he said, looking at his subordinates, "and the iron safe, with a
lot of cash in it, taken into a gully and burst open."

The rest of the Force cheered up. They thought they saw a
silver lining to the official cloud. Their minds travelled again to

the Trackson tragedy, and a fresh clue loomed large in their imaginations.

The Inspector ordered his horse to be saddled at once; then, accompanied by Charlie, the tracker, and Constable Taay, rode speedily to the railway station.

The exact spot in the gully where the safe had been taken was pointed out by the officials. The Inspector noted the place carefully. Then the work of the tracker commenced. The darkie had no difficulty in picking up the tracks of the robber. They were as clear as day to him.

"I follow dem galloping," he said beastfully.

"Never mind," the Inspector answered. "We'll run them on foot."

The tracks led off through the grass that covered a long, sloping ridge in a station paddock. For about a hundred yards Charlie bustled eagerly along, keeping a straight line. Suddenly he stopped.

"He been crouch down here a little while," he said, "all alonga himself, and look round to see if anyone follow."

On again he went.

"Now he been run; and run it all a time with one cove leg. Him have it tshort foot."

And the black trotted along, all the while working round the grass paddock in a half-circle.

"He been sit it on his knee alonga here," and Charlie paused again. "Then him been turn round, and run it this way."

Charlie followed "that way," and the tracks led him right to the front door of the local Justice of the Peace. The Inspector stared in at the doorway, and commenced to think hard. While he was thinking, and the tracker "jabbering", the J.P., with his boots off, came to the verandah and stared also.

The Inspector explained.

"Oh, yes," the Justice said with a grin. "I was down having a look at that safe this morning, with the stationmaster, and afterwards went round the paddock to see if I could shoot a hare."

"Well, I'm d——d!" the Inspector murmured.

"That pfellow I been trackit alonga here have it tshort foot," Charlie said.

"So have I," the J.P. answered cheerfully. "I've no toes on

that foot—they were shot off," and he elevated the wounded member for inspection.

Charlie was silenced.

At the Justice's invitation the Inspector stepped inside and took a whisky, then returned to the camp.

The commission was over. The farce had finished. There was nothing more to do, and on the following evening, weary and worn out, we arrived at Trackson, where the Chief Inspector, sitting like a huge chrysalis amidst piles of documentary evidence, and waste paper, awaited our verdict.

"No possible!" Inspector Black said gloomily, throwing himself into a chair. "He wasn't within thirty miles of this place that night, and could have had no more hand in it than I had, as you'll see by the evidence."

"I don't care a d—— what the evidence is!" the Chief replied. "I still stick to my conclusion—that Burke was the man."

A few weeks after, Burke was released. He came to my office in the city and said he was grateful to me for having made a truthful report.

"What is your private opinion about the murder, anyway, Burke?" I asked as he rose to go.

"I have no opinion about it," he said; "no more than the police have."

Other Stories

ON THE CONDAMINE

1. *Down on Their Luck*

Ferguson was an artist, and occupied an office in an old tumble-down rookery of a town hall, where some barristers, money-lenders, and a female barber or two kept company with multitudes of moths and bats; and where an army of noisy aldermen met to discuss loans and plague and fought over the right and wrong way of keeping the rate-payers poor and the city dirty and behind the times, and always adopted the right way. Ferguson spent a lot of time drawing pictures of people, and cartoons of politicians, and scraps of landscape and pieces of the river, and packing them up to send away to the newspapers. He spent a good deal of time, too, unpacking them when they came back, and swearing over editors for not having brains enough to appreciate good work.

Merton was not so fortunate as Ferguson. Merton had no office. Merton was a writer. Writers rarely have offices. He used a corner of Ferguson's. Merton had plenty to do, though; he was always writing. When he wasn't writing paragraphs or articles against the Government, he was turning out short stories or long poems. And he regularly threw them all into the office of the "Miser," "Daily Dividend," "Morning Mopoke," "Weekly Wage", and other wealthy publications, and, like well-directed boomerangs, they came right back to him.

A team of visiting footballers were being welcomed to the capital by the mayor and leading citizens, and people were hurrying up the stairs of the town hall. A meek bailiff entered the building and went into Ferguson's office and sat down. He was a shabby, homely sort of man, and told Ferguson that if he was his only brother he couldn't feel sorrier for him.

"Oh, that's all right," Ferguson said, just as if it didn't matter. Then he and Merton went out and silently tramped about the streets. They trudged the town for hours, just as they

Ferguson Spent a Lot of Time Drawing Pictures

had done for weeks and months past, in a hopeless search for work.

"There's little chance of anything," Merton said, as they emerged from one of the Government Departments.

"None," Ferguson replied sadly, "none."

And none was there. Brisbane was in a bad way. The country was in the throes of a long, ruinous drought. Capitalists had taken alarm; no public works were being carried on; no money was in circulation; no business of any kind was being done. All was stagnation, and, to make matters worse, there had been a change of Government.

Lunch hour. Ferguson and Merton wended their way up Edward Street to their boarding-house on the Terrace. Other people going to lunch, bank clerks, civil servants, and shop hands rushed along as though every moment meant a million of money to them. But Ferguson and Merton sauntered along with their heads down and their eyes on the ground. Time was nothing to them.

At the boarding-house they washed their hands and gave their hair a brush, and as they entered the dining-room to take their seats at the table, a nasty look was lurking in the eye of the landlady.

"Any luck?" an elderly boarder seated opposite asked kindly.

Ferguson and Merton shook their heads gravely.

"H'm," the other said, and dipped into his soup.

There were eight or ten boarders gathered at the table, some of whom were new arrivals, and to these and the good payers the landlady was especially attentive and polite.

"What'll you take, Mr. Ward? . . . . Mr. Jones, will you try some steak hand honions? . . . Hand you, Mr. Brown? . . . shall Hi 'elp you to some tomatoes has well, Mr. Smith? . . . Mary, get Mr. 'Artley a spoon." But she didn't say anything to Ferguson and Merton. Somehow she seemed to forget they were present. She served everyone else, then joined in an argument with Brown and Smith about the wisdom of girls looking out for rich husbands.

Ferguson and Merton fumbled their knives and forks about with the tips of their fingers, and tried to look pleasant. Once or twice they glanced timidly at the landlady, but she didn't catch their eye. The elderly boarder opposite seemed to take in the situation. He looked up at the landlady, but she didn't catch his eye either.

Merton made some clumsy efforts to appear cheerful. In a low, uncertain voice he tried to start a conversation with his companion about the weather. But Ferguson wasn't in a talkative mood. He gazed along the polished blade of a table knife, and muttered "H'm." He muttered "H'm" several times, and Merton gave up the idea.

The elderly boarder opposite frowned, and looked up at the landlady again; but she was addressing some remarks to Ward about the new post office clock which had stopped.

Mary, the servant girl, entered, and ran her eye over the table. Mary was an intelligent girl. In that respect she was different to other girls. She took in the situation, and moved slowly up to her mistress and spoke quietly to her.

"Hoh!" the landlady said, looking at Ferguson and Merton, "what will *yous* have?"

Merton said he would try a little steak and onions, and Ferguson, with whom steak and onions didn't agree, was helped from the same dish, but Ferguson didn't protest. He gratefully murmured, "Thank you."

Then they both brightened up, and Merton rattled the cruet about, and passed the mustard and pepper to Ferguson, and helped him to some sugar for his tea; then entered into an argument with the elderly one opposite on the subject of deporting Kanakas from the State. A good meal made a difference to Merton.

"No," the elderly boarder said, rising from the table, "there's nothing of the Christian in sending the poor devils back to the Islands."

"Well," Merton called out after him, "we can't have Queensland overrun with walk-about Kanakas."

"Huh!" the landlady sneered, proceeding to gather some of the dishes together. "Hit might has well have Kanakas walkin' habout it has hother people, hif you hask me."

Merton went crimson; so did Ferguson.

"Another cup of tea, Mr. Ferguson?" Mary asked.

Ferguson wouldn't; Ferguson *couldn't*. But Merton, after hesitating and glancing out of the corner of his eyes at the landlady, risked another one. Merton was always taking chances.

With the exception of Brown, who had no teeth and found it hard to chew his meat, the rest of the boarders finished and hurried away. Ferguson and Merton kept their eyes on Brown. They took their time from Brown. When he rose they finished abruptly and rose, too. Ferguson and Merton didn't regard it prudent to be left alone with the landlady.

They climbed the staircase and went into their room again, where they sat on the beds and grinned grimly at each other.

"Strong, isn't she?" Merton said, thinking of the landlady. Ferguson paced the room in silence.

"Ah, well!" he sighed, putting on his hat, "we can only go out and try again."

And they crept down the stairs without making any noise.

"Hoh, Mr. Ferguson hand Mr. Merton!" the landlady, hurrying from the kitchen, called to them, as they were half-way out the door. They paused and turned round with a heavy sinking feeling at their hearts.

"What habout the money you wuz to let me 'ave larst night?" she asked, with an ugly screw in her mouth, looking from one to the other.

Ferguson lowered his head.

"Well, we're very sorry, Mrs. Braddon," Merton began, acting as spokesman; "we've not been able to get anything yet, though we're trying all we can; but as soon——"

"Hoh!" the landlady said, "that wuz halways your yarn. Hi'm sick hon it."

"Well, we feel it very much, Mrs.——"

"Hi don't care; Hi want to be paid. Hit's ten weeks since Hi seen a sign o' hanything from heither o' you, hand both hon you hever since you bin with me as been going to get a job."

"Well, you know, Mrs. Braddon," Merton pleaded, "what terrible bad times these——"

"Hi don't care!" the landlady screeched: "hit's nothing to do with me. *Hare* you going to pay what you howe, or *hare* you not?"

"How can we?" Ferguson put in pleadingly. "You can't draw blood out of a stone, Mrs. Braddon."

"Hoh, that's hit! Then y' don't come hin 'ere hany more. Keepin' hout gentlemen who's willin' ter pay fer th' room hin advance!"

And, slamming the door leading to the foot of the staircase, she turned the key and looked defiantly into their dejected faces.

"It isn't that we wouldn't pay if we could, Mrs. Braddon," Ferguson said with emotion, "but you *will* be paid, every penny. And I'm grateful to you for all you've done, and——"

"Hoh, hit's very easy ter be perlite to a poor woman when you're runnin' hoff without payin' for hall you've heat hon 'er. But yer can go; yer hain't men, neither hon yer."

That's how Ferguson and Merton came to be cutting prickly pear on the banks of the Condamine for the Queensland Government.

2. Prickly Pear

Midwinter. A bitter cold day. A westerly wind sweeping the frost-bitten plains of southern Queensland, driving great balls of roly-poly grass before it, rolling it into creeks, filling every gully and opening in the ground with it, banking it up in great brown walls, miles in length, against the fences and railway line.

On the edge of the sparse and stunted timber nestled a miniature township of weird, weather-worn calico tents; down on the plain a hundred men engaged clearing prickly pear—belting and bruising the pest with long-handled hoes, and gathering it into heaps with forks. They might just as well have been bailing water out of the bay with billy-cans, for all the good they were doing. The terrible cactus had well-nigh taken possession of the land. In less than fifty years it had spread over thousands of miles of country, covering meadow and mountain, growing luxuriantly out of wood and brigalow, choking the few water-holes that remained, blocking every roadway, obliterating the land marks of the men who "blazed the track" and camping grounds of the first inhabitants, and holding in its grip tracts upon tracts of pasture land which once might easily have been saved and preserved for occupation by millions of prosperous people.

The hundred men were from the city—they were a portion of the unemployed—and a sad and sorry galaxy they were. Men of all classes and callings comprised their number; men retrenched from the ranks of the Civil Service to save the country from bleeding; men who had lost fortunes in the terrible drought; men who never had any fortunes to lose; and men whose fortunes, like their future, were all before them. Ferguson and Merton were among the latter.

Ah, but it was hard on those city men, slaving amongst that wretched pear! Hack! Hack! Slog! Slog! the whole day long. Slashing at the masses of thick leaves, tramping among the thorns, poking and delving round the great bunches of crimson-fruited rubbish to get at its roots. And such roots! Like a network of scrub vines they lay concealed under ground and running in every direction for forty yards and more. And tracing the tangled meshes and tearing them from the soil was the devil itself. Whenever the men's hands or their trouser legs or shirt sleeves came in contact with the accursed stuff, clusters of prickles clung tenaciously and worked their way through the clothing into the flesh, and sores and festers and general misery resulted. To touch the pest with bare hands was out of the question. It was alive with prickles. The men's very boots and leggings—when they had any of the latter—became smothered with and were penetrated by the prickles. And even the hoe handles from one end to the other were coated with the jags till the hardest and horniest hand there could hardly hold the implement. Ah, there was no joy working amongst that pear! It was not a privilege for an Australian to be proud of. There was neither sport nor poetry in it. It was fearful, heartbreaking employment; a painful and useless occupation, but it gave the Government an excuse to pay wages to the unfortunate men.

The pear, too, was the home of all the vermin on earth. At the sound of the hoes, numerous rats and bandicoots and hares would dart into the open and scamper for dear life. And at regular intervals great lurking reptiles would cause commotion among the men and fill their souls with fear and apprehension.

Cutting that pear made a great change in Ferguson and Merton. In slouch hats and torn shirts and soiled moleskin trousers, no one from the city would ever have recognised them.

"How are y' hands, Freddy?" Merton sometimes would ask, leaning on his hoe and looking at his friend.

And Ferguson would pause and hold up both palms, displaying blisters that looked like poached eggs. Then he'd glance furtively back over the half-mile or so of "cleared" land, dotted with numerous peaks of the gathered pear standing out like small lucerne stacks, and at the vast expanse of horror stretching before·them; and, lifting the hoe, would go on again. Of whatever "light" or "shade" or "perspective" there might have been in the picture presented about him, Ferguson never spoke.

"How Are y' Hands, Freddy?"

Ferguson never discoursed on art at all now; not even for sun-sets—and the sun went down every evening on the pear—had he any admiration. But Merton was different to Ferguson. Merton had more to say now than he had when he was in the city, and he had been a prominent member of a debating class there. He spoke in plainer terms, too, and with more force, and his vocabulary seemed to be greatly enlarged.

"It's a cruel —— thing, this," he would say, glaring at the pear, when the overseer wasn't present. "A cursed —— —— of a game, Freddy! —— —— it! I wouldn't ask a mangy Chow or a —— nigger to tackle it!"

Ferguson, though, would never encourage Merton to blas-pheme or rebel against his fate.

"Never mind, Magnus, old chap," he would answer con-solingly; "try and put up with it a while."

Ferguson was a good young man, with a heart full of hope and a lot of faith in Providence.

Sometimes a casual selector would happen along, and, sitting carelessly on his hairy cart-horse, would shake his head like an unbeliever and grin weirdly at the men "exterminating" the pear.

Old Kiley rode up one day and inspected the "cleared" patch, where young pear was growing again like a field of transplanted cabbage; then approached the nearest gang of men.

"It's fine fun yer havin' here," he said flippantly.

"It's —— fine fun," Merton answered, looking up savagely.

The other men chuckled in a grim, sore sort of way.

"When d' yiz expec' to complate th' job?" Kiley asked satirically, gazing across the expanse of thriving rubbish that lay hundreds of miles ahead.

"Maybe in a fortnight," Merton replied ironically, "maybe in a —— ——."

"Well, yiz had betther hurry up," Kiley broke out cheerfully; "fur 'tis comin' up like th' divvle beyant there, an' if it overtakes y' yiz'll nivver git out iv it." And the old selector rode away.

And when the men knocked off at night and went to their tents for supper, there was no conviviality or rejoicing of any kind amongst them. There was no music—no merriment around their camp-fire. It was then that the poison began to find them out and to work in. And until it was time to "turn in," the men mostly sat swearing and searching every stitch of clothing they had for prickles, and picking them out; and in turn they extracted them with tweezers from the arms and necks and backs of each other. But that wasn't the worst; for, exercise what care they would, the wretched prickles found their way into every blanket in the tent, and robbed the men of their sleep. And more groans and profanity were heard through the hours of the night than sounds of peaceful slumber.

"Ah, it was purgatory those days, Freddy," Merton often says now, when he thinks of the prickly pear.

3. *In the Seat of the Mighty*

A cold, cloudy morning on the Condamine. There was no intermingling of "light" and "shade" on the landscape; no agreeable odours in the air; no buds; no animals about; nothing to soothe the ear, nothing to gratify the sight. The surroundings were hopeless, vile, sorrowful—the land was an endless, unconquerable mass of accursed prickly pear, through which the waterless river lay gaping like a crack in a brick wall.

The overseer, the day before, had taken Merton to task for blaspheming the pear and "talking in the ranks."

"I wouldn't take any notice of him, Magnus," Ferguson said, referring to the incident, as they left the tents together with their hoes on their shoulders to begin again on the wretched pear.

"It's all very fine, Freddy," Merton answered, "but how can a fellow help himself? He's always cocking his slant eye round to see what I'm up to, and nagging about something or other. Damn him, I do as much work for my seven shillings a day as anyone in camp, and a good deal more than some of them."

"Still, I'd simply do it, and wouldn't argue with any of them," Ferguson replied kindly.

"I'd go balmy, Freddy," Merton said. "You might just as well put me in St. Helena straight away."

The men took their places; the hoes moved again; and scraps of leaf and pulp, and sprays of juice from the bruised pear, began to fly about in showers.

The overseer strolled here and there with watchful eyes, and for an hour nothing but the chop, chop, of the hoes, and a smothered oath from the men when the prickles pierced their skin, was to be heard.

Now and again Merton would glance round and catch the eye of·the overseer turned in his direction.

"Look at him! His lamps are on me again!" he would mutter to Ferguson; but Ferguson would treat the matter lightly.

"He's got to look somewhere, Magnus," he would say, "and his eye is on the rest of us as often as it's on you."

"I Wouldn't Take Any Notice of Him, Magnus"

"I'd like to hit him in it with this!" Merton growled viciously, uprooting a bunch of pear weighing about one hundredweight.

Ferguson smiled, and for a long while the work went on smoothly.

Merton began to get fidgety and irritable. Merton was never happy when he wasn't talking or arguing with somebody.

Suddenly a mangy-looking kangaroo-rat, with most of the hair missing from its back, sprang out of the pear right in the teeth of a useless old dog that had been discarded by some of the selectors on the River, and had taken up its quarters with the pearcutters.

"Woh-h! *Shoo-h!*" Merton shouted, pointing his hoe at the marsupial. "A piebald!"

All the men looked round. The overseer, standing fifty yards off, turned and moved towards Merton.

The old dog, acting on the impulse of the moment, started up, and, on three legs, feebly pursued the vermin, yelping hard and hopefully in its tracks.

"Go it, you cripple!" Merton yelled satirically to the humorous mongrel.

The other men laughed.

"Didn't I tell you Rover had some foot, Dinny?" Merton called to a sympathetic old Irishman with whom the dog had made friends.

"You did then, be gob!" Dinny answered, following the canine's lame efforts, with admiration in his eye.

The overseer approached, and Ferguson, in an undertone, counselled Merton to get on with his work.

Merton lifted his hoe and made several savage slashes at the pear. Merton was a determined worker when the fit came on him. It took a good while for the fit to come on him, though; and it always went off quickly.

"Merton!" the overseer said sharply.

Merton looked round.

"I've spoken to you two or——"

The piebald rat, pursued closely by a reinforcement of noisy canines that had mysteriously risen from some place or other, was racing back to the pear.

"Hoh-h! Look out for the piebald!" Merton yelled excitedly,

ignoring the overseer, and charging forward.

Every man in the pear "looked out." Being mostly British, a chase stirred their dull blood, and a desire to be in at the death took possession of them.

"Yooh-h!" they shouted, and brought their hoes and pitchforks to the "present."

The rat was making a straight line for Dinny.

Dinny lost control of himself. He jumped forward, and heaved his hoe at it. The vermin veered off and headed for the overseer. More hoes flew after it, and the dog pressing hardest suddenly stopped and howled and dropped out of the hunt, lame.

"Men!" the overseer called angrily. He didn't approve of their turn for sport. He didn't attempt to kick the vermin when it was right at his feet, either.

"Look out!" Merton shouted warningly, and swung his hoe at the rat, and hit the overseer on the shins with the handle.

"Oo-h-h! Damn it!" the overseer said, suddenly flopping into a sitting position on the ground. He suddenly rose again, and bounded about, clutching at the slack of his pants, as though the pain from his shins had suddenly shifted there.

"Aisy, sir, aisy!" Dinny said, coming to the overseer's rescue. "Tis the divvle's own piece of pear yiz have picked up!" And Dinny proceeded cautiously to remove a broad prickly leaf from behind the overseer.

The overseer trembled and twitched and flinched and whined: "E-ee!" And when Dinny cautiously fingered the leaf he yelled:

"Don't! Don't weigh down on it! . . . . Ee-e! . . . Pull straight, man!"

"By damn, sir!" Dinny exclaimed, when the leaf refused to come away at the first pull, "but it have a dog's grip iv you!"

A half-dozen other men gathered round to lend a hand, each of them suggesting a different method of operation.

"Let *one* do it!" the overseer cried, and twitched some more, and whined again.

"Come out of the way," Dinny said, and brushed the others aside.

With both hands inside his slouch hat he seized the prickly leaf firmly, and wrenched it away.

"But It Have a Dog's Grip iv You!"

The overseer jumped in the air like a kangaroo shot in the tail, and made ugly faces, and placed his hand on the part to make sure the operation had been performed.

" 'Tis off! 'tis off!" Dinny said with cheerful assurance. " 'Tis there, see!" and he pointed to the leaf now on the ground.

Then the pain in the wounded shins re-asserted itself, and the overseer swore and limped about, and sat carefully down where there was no pear, and nursed his limbs and groaned.

"What th' divvle did become iv th' varmint?" Dinny asked, thinking of the piebald rat.

The others started discussing him.

"Get on with th' *work* . . . th' whole damned lot of you!" the overseer broke out, recovering himself a little.

The men separated, and searched for their hoes, and disputed the ownership of them, and after swapping and changing about, commenced again.

The overseer crawled to his feet, and limped towards Merton. Merton was stabbing a pitch-fork into loose leaves lying about the ground, and throwing them on a heap.

"You're to blame for all this," the overseer began bitterly.

Merton leaned on the fork, and looked at the overseer with a clear, humorous eye.

The other men stopped working and stared.

"I'm not talking to any of *you*," the overseer said, snapping his hand at them. They took the hint and began working again.

"It's not the first time nor the fifth I have had to speak to you, Merton."

Merton gazed thoughtfully at a bunch of pear that Ferguson was slashing at.

"An' if there's any more——"

A large black snake glided silently from under Ferguson's hoe.

"Loo' out, Freddy!" Merton shouted; "near your feet!"

Ferguson sprang back—so did the overseer. And all the men stopped again and stared. Some of them laughed. They all thought there was another rat.

Ferguson aimed blows at the reptile with his hoe, and made holes in the earth.

"Hit him!" the overseer shouted, springing further out of reach.

Merton stabbed at the snake with his pitch-fork, and buried the prongs in the ground.

"Another one!" the man working next to Ferguson cried out excitedly, dancing about and raining blows all round himself.

The other men rushed over.

Merton stabbed at his snake again, and it wriggled across the prongs of the fork.

"Look out!" he shouted wildly, and tossed the reptile high in the air above their heads. The men swore, and dropped their hoes, and scattered. The overseer, who was directly under the falling serpent, jumped backwards, and fell across a bed of pear, and gasped "Hell!" He seemed to think the snake was falling on him, too, and lashed out with his feet and hands, and covered himself from top to bottom with prickles. But the snake didn't fall on the overseer. Merton dexterously caught it on the fork, and, with a cheerful shout, heaved it after the men, who scattered again, and swore more. Then one of them attacked it in the open with a hoe, and put an end to it.

"God bless my soul!" Merton said sympathetically, taking charge of the unhappy overseer, and becoming his benefactor, "you're covered with the d——things! They're in your eyes! All over you, man! Come down to the river."

"B-last *you!*" the overseer spluttered angrily. "Clear out! Get out of here!"

Merton retired, and started chopping.

Then, along with Dinny, the overseer limped off to the bed of the river, where he took off his clothes, and lay shivering, while Dinny greased him all over with fistfuls of wet sand and mud, and rubbed it into his skin to kill the prickles.

The overseer didn't dismiss Merton. He called the men together in the evening, and told them that pear-cutting was a black's game, and went away himself.

A Note from Mary

Our school is on the bank of the creek. A big building it is, and holds a great many people. It's made of stringy bark. There's a door in it and three calico windows. A piece of board with SCHOOL marked on it is fixed on the roof over the door. Father had the board put up; he thought perhaps someone might mistake it for a hotel. Father is on the committee. Rose Ann Crowe is the teacher; but she doesn't get anything for teaching. Her father gets it. She gets out of peeling the potatoes and cutting wood and work like that, at home.

We have dances in the school sometimes, and last week there was a play got up. Sandy McCallum got it up. It was his own composing. "In Australia" was the name of it, and it was splendid. They learned to act it in Crowe's barn at night. A big crowd rolled up to see it when it was staged. Some came from the Rocky, some from Prosperity, some from Gurney's—from everywhere they came.

Old Riley was on the door, and Jim Smith shifted the scenery and looked after the lights.

There were twelve lights—big, fat lamps that flared like fires. At eight o'clock the play commenced, and Jim blew all the lights out, except those wanted on the stage. The smell of burnt fat was terrible, and drove everyone out. But they came in again. It must have been very old fat. Rose Ann played an overture on the concertina, and the curtain was lifted. The curtain was not a picturesque one. It was made out of bags that were stained with brine and pricklypear juice, and did not look artistic. When it was up, though, after a lot of pulling, the bark humpy that was on the stage was quite real. And the people laughed at Patsy Riley lying on his stomach in front of it, poking his tongue out at a goanna; a live one tied to a peg. Sandy McCallum was dressed in old clothes, and he had to pretend to hammer Patsy, and when he rushed at Patsy with a hoe, Patsy ran into the humpy, and it all fell down on him, and somehow the goanna got away and went among the people. All the women sang out and jumped up on the seats, and the men aimed kicks at it. But there was no light, and the goanna crawled up on a window and dropped down the other side on Goostrey's dog, and bit it on the back; then climbed a tree before anyone could secure it. But the play went on without its goanna, and was a great success.

Villiam Brandt Relates His Queenslandic Experience

It vas in der year eighdeen hundhert und sigty four dot I landed in dis golony. Dere vas altergedder about tirty of us young Sherman poys. Fine powerful shaps ve all, too, vas at dat dime. Ve vas brought all from Shermany under engagement to vork in de golony for dree years at tventy pounds a year, and by shingo ve dought it vas a fine vage, too.

Vell ve vas taken along to a sugar plantation on de river bank shust bedween Brisbane and Ipswich, and dere ve vas stardet. Mine vord, dat plantation vas sholly hard vork; sveat ran down us like vater. It vas yacker like der teufel all day; and at night ve all vas lodged on a hulk dat vas anchored in der river vere ve stay till it vas mornin' again. Not von vas allowed to leave der ship; but dot overseer he vent avay efery night. Alvays he vent ashore by a voodden landing, vitch he pull after him to de bank, and dere ve vas all left like lions in dat cage.

Ve vas all sholly coves, full of fun and mischief, and de noise ve make on dat poat dem nights vas most deriffic. Ve cooee and yell on de vater like a quandidy of vild animals.

Von bright moonlight night, vile de overseer vas avay, I see a small poat tied to de pank shust aboud forty yards avay. It vould hold aboud six. "Mine vord," I tells myself, "here's a shoke. Who's on for a pull?" I says, and off goes aboud half a dozen shaps.

Ve must have vent a vast number of miles down dat river in no time. De tide vas vid us, yer know, and, by shimny, how ve did pull!

At last ve come to a gread pig island, and oud ve shumps. I don't know vat de place vas call, but it vas full of derrible long dry grass and drees. Ve stayed a vile to spell; den ve set it all on fire and cleared back. Lort, how dat fire go up! Ven ve look pack and see dem flames rise high and higher, it tought me of Napoleon ven he vas runnin' avay from Moscow. But pulling

Den Ve Set It All on Fire and Cleared Back

dot poat back vos most frightful. Der tide vas against us this time, und it vas shust all ve could do to get along. Ve tugged and tugged at dem oars, till ve tought dey must break, an' de sveat dot rub oud of us nearly fill her oop. Ve didn't know how glad ve vas to get back.

De overseer soon find oud our leetle game, tho'; und a veek afder dot ve vas removed about tirty miles through de bush on to de Logan, vere dere vas a contract to clear drees. Dis vas our first time in der bush, and by Shove it vas a vilderness. Here ve vas put in gangs of seven und eight und set to vork. De humpy vere ve sleep und had meals vas a comeecal place. It vas made ot two valls of large logs vide at der bottom and rolled up to-gedder till they meet at the top, und vas a very long place. Dere vas nodding only drees und scrub to be seen for miles. It vas a hell of coundry altergedder.

Der third night ve vas at de Logan I vas shust goin' out of that humpy ven I heard a shtrange noise dat I never heerd pe-fore. "Quark! quark!" it vent, und shust then I see someding run like de vind up a dree dat vas shtanding by.

"I must see vat kind of a vild animal dot is," I says. For a long time then I look up dat dree till my neck was tired, but I couldn't see him yet. Dere vas a couple of axes layin' dere, and two of us shtarted at dat dree. It was a regular yiant of a one, too. Ve couldn't put our arms roun' him. Vell, ve vired in and belted avay for a long vile. He vas an ironbark, and my vord a tough feller. Shop! shop! vent dem axes on each side of him so quick as ever ve could make dem go. At last he give a crack—den anudder—and down he vent wid one derrific grash righd across the end of dat humpy.

Mine golly, dere vas drouble den! Dem fellows leave that humpy in a most vonderful state. They didn't know vat had happened yet. They couldn't make it all oud for a vile.

"Look oud, shaps!" I says; "dere is a vild animal up this dree; I vant ter get him." Dey saw then vat vas the matter, and for some leetle considerable time vent demselves into vild beasts, and svear at me in Sherman till I could see that vild animal no more. Dot vas all right.

Afder vorkin' dem gangs for some veeks I vas gettin' on pretty smart. De boss of our gang he vas English, und ven he showed me anyding I vas like a parrot. Yer know, I vas angshus to learn everyding. Von day he said to me:

"Vell, you musd be a fool vorkin' here for twenty pound a year ven yer could make a pound a veek and tucker."

"Look here," I says, "I have been tinkin' like dot myself, and I am goin' to clear. Some night I will go righd avay, and von't be seen here some more."

"Don't you," he says.

I dells him I am determined, and nodding vill shtop me.

Ven he sees I mean vot I says, he tells me dot if I go not to take any more wid me.

A couple of more days go py, and I says to my mate, "Phil, I is goin' to run away. 'Tis all tam nonsense vorkin for twenty pound a year ven ve could make a pound a veek and tucker."

"Vell, denn," says Phil, "I'm off, too"; and anoder shap called Yack Lynch said he vould go, too, likewise.—

"Dot vill be enough, den," I says; "no more then dree, or the game vill get upsit."

Everyding vas soon ready, and von night at twelve o'clock, mid our svags 'pon our packs, ve all go avay.

By Yorge! more drouble shtarted dat ve had not yet thought about. Werry soon ve was in de tick of a big scrub. It vas a derrible time altergedder. I had von box all of matches dot I dake from the camp, and ve shtrike dem eferyone, but ve could make not some progress.

"Oh, vell, poys," I says, "dere is nodding for it; ve vill have to go pack and camp outside the fence." Pack we goes agen and camped at the edge of dot scrub, shust not so far avay from de humpy. In de mornin' ve vas off shust pefore ve could see. Dere vas enough tucker in de plankets to last for von day. Ve got py the scrub, and efery minet be keep lookin' back to see if dat overseer vas afder us. The tree of us vas yolly pig shtrong shaps, and ve made up our minds tergedder dat if he vould come afder us ve vould give him a yolly good hammering. So ve vould, too, mine vord!

All dat day ve valked like horses through dat bush, and hadn't found a road yet. At last it vas gettin' dark, and ve vas comin' to a creek. A most enormous gum dree vas growin' py the bank, so I dells my mates ve vill camp under him for dot night.

Ve was off agen by sun break, and py Shorge, ve valk agen

dat day mit them svags. Gracious! I taught me dere vas gold in mine, he vas getting so heavy.

All day ve followed dot creet; I dink ve must have crossed it a hundred dimes. I vas sure ve had tramped sigsty miles. Shust ven it vas gettin' sundown, and ve vas all of us dead beat, I looks ahead a bit. "Goot Lort, shaps!" I says, "dere is dot same werry dree ve sleep under last night. Vere have ve been?"

My mates dey all shtare mit dere mouths at that dree, and couldn't make him oud. It vas him all righd, tho'. So ve drows our svags down and shleep under him von more nights.

The tucker bag vas run short now, and ve vas begin to see some more drouble. There vas blenty of flour, tho', yet, and I dink I vould make a yonny cake. It vas an awful job, and the oberation vas derrible. De odder two shaps hold a handkerchief by the corners vile I mix up the flour in him. To get that dough off my fingers vas de teufel. It shtick like glue to eferyding, and vouldn't come off that handkerchief, so I put de lot in the billy and boils dem all. Mine vord, it went high!

The next day ve shogs along, and ven nearly two o'clock ve sees a house. By Shove, vasn't ve glad that dime! It done our eyes goot to see dot house.

"Come on," I says; "ve vill go over and ask for a feed."

Over ve goes and drows down our svags on the grass. A voman comes to the door, and I dells her as vell as I could that ve vant tucker. She soon understand, and give us a yolly good blow oud. Ve vas werry sorry to leave that place, but ve must get along. Yust then ve loose Yack Lynch. He vas a cute bloke, und didn't like valkin' them roads, so he stay pehind, and hired mit de farmer. Ve never see him since. Ven ve leave there vas a loosern paddock, and ve vas goin' to make a short cut. Ve vas yirst getting trew, ven a man mid a gun come runnin' like a deemun.

"Py doonder!" he says, "if you don't got oud of mine loosern paddick I vill plow your prains oud for you."

Ve sholly soon got back ven ve see dot gun.

Dot day ve come to Ipswich. At first ve didn't know vedder to vent in de town, cause ve tought, as ve run avay, all de peleecemen vould be afder us.

"Anyhow, poys," I says, "ve must shance it," and in ve goes. It vas alrighd; no one vas dere, und nopody take any nodice

A Voman Comes to the Door

of us at all. Ve vas dinkin' to ask for some vork in Ipswich, but shange our minds. I dink ve shange our minds dem times more ofen than ve shange our socks.

Two or dree days more and ve reach Fassifern—dat vas Mister Veinholt's station. Ve soon make our minds up, and ask for a yob. Veinholt, he vas in his office yust then, and he could speak Sherman vell. He ask us in Sherman, "Vot you vant?"

I ask him if there is any shance of a yob. He scratch his head for a long vile, and says:

"Vell, there is a lot of shaps lookin' for vork now. Vot can you do? Can you garden?"

"Yes; oh, yes!"

"Shepperd?"

"Yes."

My mate Phil vas a gardener, but neider of us vas a shepperd; but you know ve vasn't going to lose a yob because ve don' could do it.

"Oh, vell," Veinholt says, "I might take you on."

"How much vill you give?" I ask him.

Agen he scratch his head for a long biece. "Vell, you know," he says, "vages is very low shust now. I vill give you £28 a year."

"Golly! dat vas not enouf," I says to Phil. "Better ve had not run avay at all."

"No," I dells him; "dot is too leetle; ve von't take it."

Afder anodder vile he say he vill give tirty.

Ve vas nearly takin' tirty, but ve tought ve vould have one more dry.

"Vell, I vill tell you vat I will do mid you," he says. "I vill give you £38 for twelve munce, and not von penny more."

"All righd," ve dells him, "ve vill take dot."

"Vitch of you is the gardener?" he ask.

Phil say he is.

"All righd."

"And you" (dat vas me, Villiam Brandt) "is de shepperd?"

"Yah," I say.

Next mornin' I find mineself aboud twelve mile from that station mid two tousand sheep. It vas derrible vork. Dem days went by like years. I never see a vite man for munce. Efery day I let them sheep go from the yard, den lay mineself down under a dree and shleep all the time. How I never lose dem all efery-one I don't could never know. I dells mineself, if I stick to dis yob long I vill soon go mad.

Von day the overseer he come oud.

"Vell, Villiam," he says, "how are yer gettin' on?"

"Don't like dis yob at all," I dells him. "Can't you give me someding else—shopping down drees or anyding. Vy, I'm oud here in de bush shust like a sapige—dere is no von to talk mid. Already I forget me vot leetle English I know, and soon I von't talk some Sherman."

He only laugh.

Efery day vent by shust the same. I alvays had nodding but salt yunk and damper ter ead. Von day I thought me I vould have some fresh mead; so I vent me in de yard ven the sheep was all dere and caught a fine pig fat vedder—de best feller in dot flock. I soon had him dead and hangin' in the hut like it vas a butcher's shop. Dot night I had me a gerreat feed. Ven the overseer come oud agen, he count them sheep twice.

"All right, Villiam," he say; "but dere is von missing."

"Oh, I ead dat feller," I dells him.

"Vot?" he says.

"I ead him."

"By Shove!" he tells me, "don't ead any more."

Afder dat he says:

"Dere is anodder shap comin' to shepperd, Villiam; ve vant you at the station."

Mine geracious, I vas glad to hear dat news!

Next mornin' I had me up pefore it vas day, and vas sittin' on mine svag outside de hut vaitin' for dat shap ter come. Ven I see him a long vay off, I picks up mine planket und vas gone.

Dere vas no more shepperdin' for Villiam Brandt.

Charley's Yarn

We were camped on the Bogan—four of us. We had finished tea, and were lying on our blankets, yarning and smoking, and lazily watching the stars. The moon came slowly up over the gloomy timber, and blazed on the surface of the big water-hole.

Each of us, excepting Charley, had told a yarn, and a silence set in—a silence broken only by the steady puffing of pipes. Charley wasn't a smoker, nor a talker—he was the chump, the "green" one of the party, and, as a rule, we acted charitably towards him on that account.

Miller lazily raised himself upon his elbow and proposed that Charley tell a yarn. He never expected that Charley would. Neither did we. We grinned in silence, and smoked harder.

Charley, who had been sitting on his blanket all the while, shook his head and grinned, too.

"Might as well," Miller said playfully.

"Only know one," Charley said, "an' it's true."

The rest of us sat up to look at Charley.

"All the better," Miller said, kicking Smith on the leg; "that's the kind we like."

Charley grinned and shuffled about.

"Go on," Smith said encouragingly.

Charley began:

"I was only a young fellow at the time." Then he stopped.

"Well?" Miller said. "Well?"

"Quite a kid," Charley continued. "We was all workin' for Brown up north Queensland, and we were out on the station by ourselves. I can remember the humpy we lived in just as if it was only yesterday. And me father and mother, and me brothers and me sister, I can see them now!"

Tears came into Charley's eyes, and we stopped grinning.

"The blacks was terrible bad," he went on, mastering his emotion, "and used to kill the cattle and th' sheep. And we were very frightened of them. One morning early they came

and yelled round the house, an' I remember how father jumped
up; an' I remember, too, how they shoved the door down, and
rushed in with tomahawks. Poor Dad! They killed him first,
and he fell in the front room."

Charley paused again, and passed his hand across his eyes.
Our hearts went out to him.

He proceeded:

"The way mother screamed is always in me ears. It's in them
now! They killed her in the bed. An' me sister and me brother,
it was awful how they died! I was the only one that got away.
A black gin saw me in the bed, and she picked me up and ran
with me to the edge of a scrub, hugging me close to her all the
time. She meant to keep me for herself. But when the blacks
had burnt the house, they came to the scrub where we were.
They talked angrily to the old gin when they saw me, but she
held me tight. Then two of them took me from her, and, each
taking hold of a leg of me, swung me round and round to
throw me over the top of a tree. It was awful!"

He paused again, and we could see how pale he was. Poor
old Charley!

"But the others stopped them," he renewed, "and they threw
me on the ground same as they would a kangaroo rat. Then
they gathered up all the dead wood about, and stacked it in a
heap round the foot of a tree, and placed me on the top of it
and set fire to it. I'll never forget that fire. It burned up all
round and in blue flames, and forked tongues shot up at me."

He stopped again. We waited. Charley lay back and gazed
at the sky.

"But you haven't finished?" Miller said. "Didn't the fire
burn you, man?"

Charley raised himself slowly.

"No, it didn't," he said. "*I was too green to burn.*"

The Man and the Millionaire

He was unfolding some tucker from his swag, and making profane remarks to the carcase of a dead sheep which floated calmly in the waterhole from which he had filled his billy, when a stranger rode up.

"Good-day, mate," he said, and, after a pause, "Have a bit t' eat?"

"I'll take a pint of tea," said the stranger, and got off his horse. Then rolling a stone over to sit on, he asked the other, "Where are you bound?"

"Heard old Tyson wanted a fencer—goin' up t'see. This is his run we're on now, ain't it?"

"Yes" (blowing the hot tea).

"The miserable old hound! B'lieve he'd skin a crow for his hide and stew him for the drippin'. Wonder, if he came along here now, would he strip and rescue that monkey for the wool? And he's a native, too—that's the part that hurts me! They say he's ugly, too—got a face like a broken fire-brand. Have some more tea, mate?"

"No more, thanks." And the stranger mounted and left.

The fencer arrived at the station, and threw down his swag on the verandah of the store, in front of which his friend of the day before was standing.

"Hello!" he said. "What the devil are you doing here? In before me for the job, eh? Thought that was your game yesterday."

Not waiting for a reply, he tramped in.

"Storekeeper, I've come to see about a job o' fencin'."

"Yes."

"Any show?"

"Ask Mr. Tyson."

"Where is he?"

"There on the verandah."

"H——!" (whispers) "*yer don't say so!*"

Dinny Delaney's Industry

"Dinny" Delaney (*Daniel*, he was christened) was a long, lazy, useless individual after the style of Dan Rudd. Their ambitions, their tastes and talents were identical; but in dissimulation and "ways that were dark" Dinny could lose Dan easily. He had forgotten more roguery than ever Dan learned. Dinny was Dan's tutor. He taught him to "battle"—to lie profitably and interestingly, and to live and enjoy life without working.

Dinny was a philosopher. He studied human nature, and reckoned the world was mostly made up of mugs, and that the Lord created mugs for the use of the higher and more intelligent class, just as He did horses and sheep-dogs.

Dinny, himself, was of the intelligent class. People sometimes spoke well of Dinny; said there was a lot in him. They envied him his brains, and wondered why a fellow like him didn't make better use of his head.

Dinny *had* brains. He was brimful of natural gifts, but—as with a bad conscience—he concealed them.

When his wife's people turned him out of (their) house and home, though, and cast him penniless upon the world, and libelled and belittled him to the neighbours, *then* his ability shaped and showed itself. Lazy and useless no longer, he wore a watch and owned a horse and saddle the first week out.

"Can make stacks o' money," Dinny said to Dan, "if on'y I find th' right cove to work an idea o' mine I've been thinkin' o' for years. . . . Twenty thousand in it inside a year, if there's a bob." And he went into details. But Dan shook his head and whistled. (Dan respected the police. Dan was not a criminal.)

Then one day Dinny disappeared from Saddletop, and left Queensland, and was never thought of any more.

Four years passed.

Dinny returned to his native land, returned in a first-class railway carriage, smoking big cigars, his luggage in leather bags, and with all outward signs of a gentleman in prosperous circumstances upon him. Dinny had risen in the world. He was a new man. His name wasn't Dinny any longer. 'Twas James—James Richardson.

Dinny didn't call at Saddletop (his home); he went to Brisbane, where all the big business people go, and put up at an obscure hotel in a back street. Dinny was not proud; prosperity hadn't spoilt him. Like Tyson he avoided society; his mind was all on his business. A good business it was, too. He engaged a cab and drove to the Lands Office, and made loud inquiries about land—good agricultural land—land that he hadn't any idea of acquiring, or even looking at. The Lands officials fell over their stools and hustled each other finding good country for Dinny. A rich customer from Victoria didn't adorn the office every morning.

Dinny thought Goomburra or Mount Russell Estate *might* fill the bill—he wasn't sure; he would have a look at them; and, loaded with information and maps, he returned to his hotel, where, sprawling on a bed, his partner (an amiable person named Johnson) awaited him.

"Go on th' land, young man," Dinny said, with emphasis, to Johnson, throwing the roll of maps he carried in his hand hard at the brick wall; "Go on the land."

Johnson chuckled cheerfully, and reaching for his coat, took from the pocket of it a railway time-table. He was a calm-looking man, Johnson.

"Leaves Toogoom 7.30 p.m.," he read aloud; "arrives Greenbank 8.47."

"Sooner we get to work, then, now," Dinny rejoined, "th' better."

The partner nodded.

"Everything's serene," he added, closing a huge leather bag that contained clothes and things belonging to the hotel.

The evening following, Johnson in a casual way entered the train that left Toogoom for Stanthorpe, and joined Dinny—the sole occupant of a first-class carriage. They were strangers to each other till the train started; then they became fast friends again and talked trade.

"No letters or anything in your bag, 's there?" Johnson said.
Dinny shook his head and gave a smile.

"Not *me*," he answered

"Nor about you, anywhere?"

Dinny shook his head again.

Johnson sat back and admired Dinny.

Several small sidings were passed.

"This is her," Dinny said, as the train slackened speed to stop at Greenbank, the place where all the cheese comes from. A stationmaster swinging a red light, a forlorn-looking person in shirt sleeves, and some dogs, were on the platform. The rest of the inhabitants were away laying poison for 'possums.

A farmer's wife with two children alighted, and the train moved again.

"Now fer it!" Dinny said, straightening himself up.

He opened the carriage door, stood on the step a moment, said "Look after y'self," to Johnson, glanced along the train, then dropped lightly to the ground, and proceeded cautiously along the line.

Dinny had never been employed on a railway-line, but he understood trains. He had been dropping off trains for four years. Johnson, his head and shoulders protruding from a window, grinned contentedly; then remained in contemplation. Telegraph poles flashed by in grey streaks; farms, ridges, and belts of timber were dimly outlined in the night.

The engine whistled again. Johnson roused himself. He ran his fingers through his hair and became agitated. Johnson was a man with a lot of emotion. He took it all from his father. *He* was an undertaker. Johnson signalled and called wildly to the stationmaster.

"A man fell out o' here!" he cried; "fell out the carriage—tumbled clean through this damn door."

The guard, hearing the commotion, came along. Guards are not so cautious as policemen.

"He was standing just here," Johnson explained excitedly, indicating the position, "and was strapping that bag" (he delivered Dinny's abandoned property a kick). "The strap broke, and he overbalanced against the door, and it flew open, and out he went. . . . Don't know who he was. He was here when I got in. My Heavens!"

The train went on, and the stationmaster sat and worked hard at the telegraph instrument.

The officer at Greenbank perused his tape, looked at it again, made an exclamation, snapped up a lamp, rushed away to procure some spirits, then hurried along the line.

Quarter of a mile from the platform he came upon Dinny. Unfortunate Dinny! There he was coiled up for dead—with all his best clothes on, too. A few yards from the rails he lay prostrate, doubled up as though he had been rammed into a gun and fired at a tree.

"Are y' hurt, mister?" the S.M. asked in a subdued voice that trembled with apprehension.

No answer.

"*Poor* devil!" the S.M. moaned; then knelt down and placed his ear close to Dinny's mouth. Dinny emitted just enough breath to convince his benefactor that there was yet hope. Dinny was not a man to discourage a good cause.

The officer raised Dinny's head tenderly and poked the neck of the whisky flask between his teeth. Dinny didn't resist. He drank feebly. He drank some more. He would joyously have swilled the lot but for a resolution he made in the firm's interest never to overdo things during business hours. The stimulant seemed to revive him. He opened his eyes and closed them again. Dinny *was* bad.

"Are you a married man?" inquired the anxious attendant.

"N-no!" (faintly).

"Have you any friends?"

"N-no."

"Poor devil!"

A "special" with a doctor on board steamed into Greenbank, and Dinny, to all appearances a corpse, was lifted into the van and taken back to Toogoom and placed in the hospital. Next day the whole continent read of the accident.

"Isn't that saad?" sighed big Mrs. McSmith, a sympathetic old person, and mother-in-law to Dinny. Th' peoor maan to trevell a' th' waay from Waste Ustralle an' fall out o' a train like thet; . . . . an' dyin' in the hospital and ne'er a frien' by; . ʿ . . th' peoor maan . . . a gentlemun, too!"

"*That's* y'r beautiful Gov'ment, an' y'r Railway Department, for y'!" her long-legged son, Johnny, who studied politics, declaimed. "By th' Lord Harry it beats me how there isn't *more* accidents. There's never any of those blooming doors shut.

It's blanky well time there was a change in th' ministration of th' 'fairs of this country, *I* promise yer!"

And a hundred other such humorists in a hundred different places could understand, from narrow escapes they themselves had had, how the accident happened.

Dinny didn't die. He didn't get any better, either. He *couldn't* very well, because his spine was injured. Crippled for life, Dinny was paralysed completely in his lower limbs. The patella and planter reflexes (whatever they were) had disappeared from both his legs. He was in a state of extreme nervous prostration, and his lumbar vertebra was shot, or shattered or something—so the doctors said.

Poor old Dinny! For four long sweltering months Dinny lay helpless in a private ward, and was never once off his back—at least not in day-time—not when anyone was about to observe him. And it couldn't have been that Dinny was sensitive in the presence of nurses. Dinny was not modest. But there *were* occasions when, without leaving bed, he could take healthful exercise. Dinny was never a believer in absolute inactivity. Raising himself on his palms and shoulders till his feet pointed to the ceiling, he would vigorously work both legs with the speed of a fly-wheel, resembling the orange-coloured acrobat manipulating the big ball with his toes. For variety, Dinny would balance the furniture on them till he got tired or heard a footstep.

One evening, when he was doing this, the door suddenly opened without any noise, and a voice said, "Aha!"

Dinny *did* get a fright; it nearly choked him.

"M-*mighty!*" he gasped, picking himself off the floor where he had rolled.

But it was only Johnson to see him—the stranger who witnessed the accident.

"Take three thousand pounds?"

Dinny answered feebly in the negative.

"If the cove who was in the train with me can be got," he said to his solicitor, "go to law with it, Sir!" Then, after reflecting, "But it can't matter much t' me now."

Dinny was a despondent client.

The "cove" was easily found, but he was sorry on Richardson's account that he couldn't remain to give evidence unless the case was brought on at once (Johnson was getting short of cash), as business was calling him to California. But he would do his best to stretch a point.

He'd "see," anyway.

Johnson was a humane man.

"Action against the Railway Commissioner," the Brisbane newspapers said. "Fall from a train. £15,000 damages claimed."

Daniel had gone to judgment.

"Richardson v. Commissioner for Railways!" cried a court official.

'Twas the last case on the cause-list—the grand finale to a long winter session. Dinny was a big draw. A crowd of eager, interested faces filled the court. People left business to flock there. Unusual solemnity marked the proceedings. There was a strong bar.

"I appear for the plaintiff, your honour," said Dinny's counsel, an alert, distinguished pleader.

From the other end of the table an eloquent K.C., assisted by juniors and surrounded with Crown officials, books, photographs, piles of documents, and the Railway Department, bowed the formal intimation. His honour made a note.

A short silence, then commotion behind the bar. The Judge, grave, dignified, lifted his head and peered through his glittering, gold-rimmed glasses. The Sheriff, composed, played with a pen. All eyes turned to a side door opening from the jury-room. A constable cleared the way, and the plaintiff, in charge of the ambulance, was conveyed into court on a bed, his lengthy form concealed beneath a cover resembling a trough turned upside down.

Dinny caused a great sensation. The bed was elevated on chairs adjacent to the jurors, and there, in full gaze of everyone, reclined Richardson, Dinny, the eldest son of Delaney—calm, collected, innocent-looking as an infant in its first sleep. Dinny had a fine nerve. He was a fine actor, too. The stage had lost a star in him. The hearts of the audience went right out to Dinny. Never since his birth did he receive so much sympathy. *They* would give him full damages.

Australians are a just people.

But there was no affinity between Dinny and the Defence. *They* hadn't any commiseration; but made audible jests and jeers that jarred the sentiment of the moment. They seemed to think Dinny was a fraud. But Dinny only looked at them. He expressed *his* opinion of *them* with his eyes.

Dinny's advocate rose to his feet. A clear voice he had and suave. Conscious of a good cause, he was all sympathy and assurance. He believed his client's story.

"What is your name?" he said to Dinny.

Dinny quietly told him "James Richardson." He told him a host of other things, too, equally false. He said he was thirty-five years of age (Dinny was forty-five if he was a day), that he was born in New Zealand (Dinny was a native of Boondooroo), worked hard there with his father for years (Dinny never worked hard anywhere in his life), went to Tasmania, to Victoria, to W.A. Came to Queensland to take up land. Then in tones that would move a marble monument he described his fall from the train, and, with real tears in his sad-looking eyes, declared that he hadn't been able to move his legs or sit up since.

"I on'y wish ter heavens I *could*, mister!" he added. "It wouldn't be *'ere* I'd be."

Dinny was a touching liar when he was in the mood. The spectators felt sorry for Dinny.

"Call Samuel Johnson."

"*Sam'el Johnson! Sam'el Johnson! Sam'el Johnson!*" echoed in the corridors and died off down the double stairway.

No response.

For the first time in his life Dinny was discomposed.

The spectators watched for Johnson. If Dinny hadn't been a strong man he must have fainted or fallen out of bed. He stared at everyone who entered, but there was no sign of Johnson.

Dinny reflected. So did the court. Plaintiff's counsel made an explanation. He deplored the absence of Johnson, and informed the court that the evidence the missing witness was able to give was most material to his suffering client.

Dinny *was* a "bit off" just then, but he controlled himself. He closed his eyes and waited. Dinny was a patient plaintiff.

Counsel for the Defence took the floor. He adjusted his glasses, fixed his legal eyes on Dinny, and with the apathy that "mocks a man's distress," shouted at him to "*speak out.*" Quite different he was to Dinny's advocate; he didn't consider an invalid at all. And he indulged in personalities; asked Dinny questions about two men named McDonald and Robertson who had fallen out of trains in other States, and were paralysed in the lower limbs, too; who went out walking with their girls immediately they received a solatium in large sums of money from the Governments interested.

Dinny scowled. He didn't anticipate these things. He could understand, too, now why Johnson didn't turn up. So could the spectators. They didn't believe any more in Dinny.

Australians are an unreliable people.

Several witnesses from down-South entered the box and claimed Dinny as a friend of theirs. *McDonald*, they called him. Dinny lost heart. His temperature went up and a change came over his demeanour. The audience began to enjoy themselves. They were an impulsive congregation.

"You were found lying on the railway-line near Paddy's Pinch, in Victoria, last October, were you not?" King's Counsel, in a careless, friendly kind of way, asked of Dinny.

"N-no, I *wasn't!*" Dinny answered, showing his teeth. Dinny was an ugly opponent when he was roused.

"And you were taken to an hospital for dead?" (continuing, as though he hadn't heard Dinny's reply).

"*No, I wasn't* taken ter *any* horspital *fer dead!*" Dinny sneered, glaring aggressively at the enemy.

"And you a strong, able-bodied man, in the best of health" (Counsel suddenly waxed vehement), "remained on your back for *five months*" (he paused, and then in a deep, dramatic voice), "*pretending you were paralysed?*"

Dinny, to the amazement of the court and his own counsel, raised himself on his elbow.

"*N-no!*" he shouted. "*N-no; ner* fer *one* month" (finishing in the same key as his opponent).

"And for this heinous piece of shamming" (Counsel's voice cracked like a rifle), "you received from the Government of Victoria a sum of £1500, in settlement of an action you threatened it with?"

"Find Mister Johnson!" He Said

"A lie!" Dinny yelled back, suddenly sitting bolt upright and facing his antagonist. (Dinny was always a tiger to fight.) He gulped down a lump that rose in his throat. "It's a lie! . . But if yer *want* ter know" (Dinny jumped off the bed and stood in his pyjamas), "if yer *want* ter know who *did*" (Dinny swung his hand round contemptuously and pointed through a window), "*find Mister Johnson!*"

The court didn't try to find Mr. Johnson, and the jury didn't give Dinny any damages. The Judge gave him gaol instead.

Out Driving

We used to go out driving a lot once; we don't now. There's no horse since the drought. One Sunday we were driving through Dirranbandi, and the horse (Sam) took bad. Father took him out of the cart, and pulled him across to the chemist's shop; and the chemist came out and bled poor old Sam till he staggered.

"Look out!" Father shouted. "That's enough, man; that's enough!"

But the chemist reckoned that he knew more about it than Father, and took another pint of blood out of Sam. Then all at once Sam tried to rear, and fell down, and shivered, and threw out all his legs, and shoved the side of the shop in, and broke a lot of bottles, and died. It cost Father ten shillings to bury Sam; and the chemist sent a bill in. That's twelve months ago, and the bill is on the mantelpiece yet.

The road from our place to Gurney's Gully runs through a station paddock. Father was driving us there in Baker's dray last week, and a mob of station cattle followed us along. Father stopped the dray to look at them. They came up quite close to us.

"Hold the reins a minet," Father said, "an' I'll give the big brindle fellow a start," and he took up a long rope that was lying in the bottom of the dray. It had been lying in the dray since we had dragged Betsy out of the creek, and one end of it was tied to the axle. Father heaved the rope at the brindle bullock, and it stuck on his horn (there was a loop on it which Father didn't know of).

"Moses!" Father said, when he saw what he had done.

The bullock plunged and bellowed, and frightened all the others away. Father got excited.

"Weh! Weh!" he shouted, and snatched the reins from Mother to stop the horse from bolting.

"My gracious me, what have y' done?" Mother said, and tried to jump out, but Father pulled her back.

The bullock ran round and round the dray, and tied us all up in the rope, and reared and fell under the horse's legs and bellowed.

"Oh, dear, dear!" Mother said, and looked quite white. Then the bullock got on its feet again, and burrowed under the dray and turned it over, and we all fell out.

"My God!" Father said, and Mother screamed.

All of us screamed, and escaped behind trees. But before Father could stop the horse it got away, and bolted through the paddock with the shafts and body of the dray. The bullock kept possession of the axle and the wheels, and dragged them about till he got stuck round a stump. Then, when Father got a chance, he ran in and cut the rope, and the brute galloped away.

"Blarst 'im!" Father said, and went off to see what had become of the horse. But he only saw bits of the harness.

Now Baker thinks it was all Father's fault, and wants to make him pay for the dray. But Father is going to town to see about it.

Odds and Ends

"Talking about buck-jump riders," Williams said, "a darkey at Toompine was th' best ever I see. Saw him on a chestnut mare one mornin' that no one down th' river ever could ride; only a bit of a thing, too—a little bay. Buck? By Christmas! On 'er side, straight ahead, and backwards, an' round an' round, an' straight up, an' high as your bloomin' head every time. Y' couldn't see 'er or th' darkey for dust—just like a big whirlwind tearin' th' yard up. Excitin'? Ghost! We climbed th' yard out o' the road. Th' saddle-cloth went first; then th' darkey's boots and his belt left, and his shirt and trousers came flying out o' th' cloud o' dust. Crikey! We thought it wer' himself, for th' moment. Then we started cheerin', bein' mostly British, an' th' bloomin' mare starts squealin' an' gruntin', sort o' hootin' like. By gad! 'Stick to 'er! Stick to 'er!' th' boss was yellin' an' gettin' louder every time, when th' darkey's saddle hit him hard in the vestcut, an' knocked him clean off th' top rail an' silenced him. Cripes! We got down off the yard in quick time, 'fore gettin' one with the darkey. But he never come off—not 'im. Th' mare give in, an' when th' dust cleared away there he was, sittin' across her neck with a short hold of th' reins, an' his toes in th' bridle-rings fer stirrups—an' smilin'."

Yellow Charley, a half-caste, arrested for cattle-stealing, slipped the constable during the night, and, in handcuffs, struck Caffery's place just before dawn. Caffery's yard was full of cattle. Caffery was stooping at a fire beside the rails, dusting a "johnny-cake," raked from the ashes, with an empty tea-bag.

"Mornin'," Yellow Charley said cheerfully.

"Mornin'," answered Caffery, without looking up.

"Seen any 'traps' about?"

"Nuh," said Caffery, carelessly, flogging the "cake" harder with the bag.

The escaped one grinned.

"What d' y' think o' these?" he said, holding out his hands and displaying the handcuffs.

Caffery looked up casually. Then he dropped the johnny-cake as though it burnt him, jumped over the fire, threw down the rails of the yard, rushed the cattle out, sooled the dog on them, and watched till they had disappeared in the timber. Then he turned, stared at the handcuffs, and said: "I didn't think there was any cops about."

There was blood in the sundowner's eye. "Cursed lot o' scabs!" he said. "They stole me damper out o' th' fire when I wer' in th' crick breakin' a few sticks fer th' night. I wouldn't 'ave minded s' much, though, if th' mean, loafin' lot o' cadgers hadn't covered th' hole up an' kep' me scratchin' fer it, an' spoilin' th' fire, 'fore findin' it wer' gone!"

Jones, a tea man, "doing" the West per bike, flashed along a scrub road late one night, and passed old Schultz, returning to camp from the pub. Schultz dropped his meat-supply in the dirt and jumped behind a blue gum; then ran back, hard, to the pub. "Whatever it was," he said, "it didn't run; it flew; and was about five feet high, with one eye like a ball o' blanky fire. By cripes! Give us a drop o' brandy."

"When my old horse jibs," Brown said, "I never worries about it, an' I don't swear or 'ammer 'im. I just opens his mouth wide 's I can an' chucks in a handful o' dirt. Then, while he's sneezin' an' snortin' an' spittin' it out, I sez, 'Get erp, Billy!' an' he goes off without thinkin'."

"Dalton?" Gallagher exclaimed; "old Johnny Dalton? I wouldn't take him wid me to look fer goats!" And he laughed heartily. "Johnny oncet came out with us mustering bullocks,"

he said, "an' we were camped one night there on th' crick, 'way below Dirranbandi. About eight o'clock th' dingoes found us out, an' made a devil of a noise, an' frightened th' wits out o' poor Johnny. When we turned in I was there" (Gallagher scratched the position in the ground with a stick); "Connolly was here" (another scratch), "an' here was Johnny, on the outside o' Connolly. When we woke in th' mornin' where d' y' think me brave Johnny was?"

Daley said he didn't know.

"*He was in th' middle.*"

The Old Homestead

(with illustrations by Lionel Lindsay)

*To the memory of my friend Rodie Tolmie this
book is tenderly and gratefully dedicated.*

Introduction to the University of Queensland Press Edition

The Old Homestead first appeared in 1912 in the *Lone Hand,* a monthly magazine published by the *Bulletin.* In 1917 Steele Rudd offered it to Angus and Robertson and was told:

> We duly received your letter dated 21st ultimo, together with your story, "The Old Homestead". We were hopeful the story would prove suitable for a 3/6d. volume but we find it would only make a 1/- volume.

> We decided several years ago that there was nothing in publishing 1/- volumes owing to the increased cost of production, and we are clearing out the whole of our Commonwealth series in consequence. The copy is returned herewith and we thank you for having given us the opportunity of considering it . . ."

Later the book sold approximately 50,000 copies as a paperback, sold by the N.S.W. Bookstall Co., who bought the book rights for £80. My father also wrote a play called *The Old Homestead;* it was never produced and all trace of the manuscript seems to have disappeared.

As with most of his stories, *The Old Homestead* tells of the hardships of land pioneering on the Darling Downs—the crooked land deals, worked by unscrupulous agents and bank managers on uneducated and simple people, the exhausting physical work of clearing in days before tractors and bulldozers, the unending struggle to have enough money to buy the barest essentials of food and clothing. But his stories never dwell on the grim side of life for long; it is always the ridiculous which catches his attention—a terrorfied boy hiding from his first job in a cask, a kangaroo falling into a partly-dug well, two not-very-young maiden aunts squabbling for a husband. In one chapter, "She Wouldn't Take Them", the author pays tribute to his mother-in-law; Mrs. Brodie, my grandmother, ran a small store at Greenmount, and helped many settlers through the trials and adversities of their lives. In the story she is called "Mrs. Brayton" and my father's admiration of her is obvious . . . "a woman in a million".

The book is dedicated to Rodie Tolmie, a friend of my father and a member of a family my parents held in great affection and high esteem. The drawings for this story were done by another friend of my father, Lionel Lindsay.

ERIC DAVIS
BRISBANE
FEBRUARY 1971

1. Why We Left Magoola

After we had all hunted and searched and turned the house upside down, Father one day found the deeds behind the calico lining of Mother's bedroom. Then early next morning, with a coat over his arm, he started for town. We didn't go with him because town was a long way off: besides it was summer time and Father decided to walk. He decided to walk because the drought left us no horse to ride or drive. We accompanied him to the slip-rails, though, and waved to him till he was out of sight. Then for quite a while we sat on the fence and wondered if he would bring any money back with him. And at intervals throughout the day we gathered at the sick bed and tried to comfort Mother by urging her to get well. But our efforts to cheer her were futile. No notice would she take of us. And one by one we turned away from the room with sad sinking hearts, and looked for something to do. Next day Father returned from town and brought £50 with him, besides a bottle of medicine for Mother and a swag of miscellaneous articles for the rest of us.

Aunt Sue and Dora unrolled the bank notes and counted them, and gazed at them, and felt them again and again with their fingers. They got as much joy out of the fingering of these notes as they would from the nursing of a new baby. And while Father sat to the meal they prepared for him, he entertained us with details of the trip; told us how he met Charlie Carpenter, who had become a J.P., and how Charlie introduced him to a commission agent, who advanced him the money on the deeds.

"Charlie's got a lot older since I seen him last," he said, "a lot older." But Father didn't tell us that the "receipt" he signed for the money advanced on the Deeds, and witnessed by his old friend Charlie, was a carefully folded land transfer form and that our selection home on Old Magoola was now really the property of a pair of city scoundrels! He couldn't tell us these things because he didn't know, or even suspect them himself.

Mother got over her illness and flew round with more life and energy than ever. The presence of a number of strange cows at the yard surprised her and started her thinking. She questioned Father about them. Father smiled proudly and told her how he became possessed of them.

"The Deeds?" she gasped. "Where did you get them?"

Father explained.

Then Mother walked about excitedly. Mother didn't believe in mortgages, nor in Father's ways of doing business.

"I'll go and see all about it at once," she said. "I could never rest till I know what you've done."

And she didn't rest. But she didn't go to town. The Commission Agent saved her the trouble. He came along in a buggy and wanted to know when we were going to leave the place and give him possession?

"What!" Mother said; "give you *possession?*"

"Surely you know that I bought the place?" the Commission Agent answered. "Anyhow your husband does."

"Bought it!" Mother gasped. "Are you mad?" And a cold, sickly feeling came over her.

"It was only a mortgage," Aunt Sue put in.

"Only a mortgage!" And the swindler laughed.

"What in the name of heaven does this mean?" And seizing hold of Father, who seemed to be in a trance, Mother nearly shook the life out of him.

"Only a mortgage!" Father stammered.

"Now, now, Pettigrew," the Commission Agent protested. "When Carpenter brought you to me didn't I say I would buy the place for £50?"

"For *fifty pounds!*" And Mother threw up her hands.

"And didn't I give you the money in notes," the Agent went on brazenly. "And didn't you sign a transfer of the land? And didn't your friend Charlie Carpenter witness your signature for you?"

"No!" Father shouted at the top of his voice—"*No!*"

Then Mother, who lost control of herself, sprang at the man and, taking him by the neck, shoved him out and showed him the slip-rails.

"You'll be sorry for this!" he shouted, getting into his buggy. "I'll show you whose property it is——I'll show you!"

Three months later. The Commission Agent, accompanied by the Sheriff's bailiff, a bum-bailiff and the township policeman, came into the yard.

All of us collected on the verandah, feeling sure that something terrible was pending.

"I've a Warrant of Possession here," the Sheriff's bailiff said to Father, "commanding me to hand over this selection to the plaintiff, James McGooley," And he pointed to the wretched Commission Agent.

Then he read a lot of highfalutin' stuff about "McGooley v. Pettigrew" and "whereas" and "I command you" and "hereof fail not"—until we all felt we were about to be hanged.

"And are we to be turned out of our home?" Mother asked.

The Sheriff's officer said he was afraid so.

"Well, I dare any of you to enter my house!" Mother cried, placing her back firmly against the door. Then addressing us. "Stand beside me children—everyone of you!"

We stood beside her, and Andy, reaching down an iron brand from the rafters, fixed his eyes on the Commission Agent.

Old Parson Bennie, on his rounds, rode in through the rails. He stared hard in surprise, then asked what was the matter.

Mother, bursting into tears, told him.

"I see—I see," he said sympathetically. "Now, keep calm, Mrs. Pettigrew, till I hear what they have to say on the other side."

The Sheriff's bailiff produced his warrant and waved it about.

"Mrs. Pettigrew is making matters worse for herself, sir," he said, "that's all she's doing."

The old parson thought hard. Then turning to Mother he placed a hand on her shoulder and said:

" 'Tis both foolish and useless to resist. Have courage and God will help you."

Mother gulped down a lump that was in her throat and silently led us all inside.

Then the bailiffs entered and carried all the furniture out.

And that was why we left Magoola and went to live on a homestead at Ironbark.

2. How Tom Got Lost

Ironbark was a wild, lonely, scrubby place. Besides the few struggling selectors scattered about, it boasted of an hotel. A fine, commodious hotel it was, too, built of bark and wool bales. The bark was taken from the tall, gaunt trees that stand there like skeletons to this day; and the wool-bales from a neighbouring station where Dunn, the proprietor, drove bullocks for 15s. a week before he went into business. A sign-board with "Dick Dunn—Travellers' Arms" printed on it with tar, stood above the front verandah, and before the bar-door a tree with the limbs lopped off supported a broken lamp that never gave any light. In the rear of the hotel a killing-yard and a number of rookeries were huddled together. And all the rest, as far as the eye could see, was boxtrees, gum trees, grass and ridges.

Dunn one day came to our homestead in search of a boy to do "light bits of jobs about the pub", and said the wages would be 2s. 6d. a week and keep.

Mother pointed to Tom, and said if Dunn thought he would be any use he could have him.

Dunn, a big, hairy, gravy-eyed, red-whiskered man, looked at Tom squatting under the wooden window on the ground floor of the verandah, and said:

"Stan' up till I have a squint at th' size o' y'."

Tom blushed and drew up his knees till they reached his ears, and hid his head and shoulders between them.

"He's fritent t'," Andy, a couple of years older than Tom, guffawed.

"Get up, you young wretch, when th' man asks you t', and let him see y'! Sittin' there like a porkapine!" Mother said, giving Tom a root with her big toe that protruded through her boot.

Mother was a strong, determined woman who wouldn't be

disobeyed, and who would always have her own way in everything.

"A porkapine!" Andy repeated in jeering tones, and pointed his finger at Tom.

Tom, pressing his chin hard against his chest, and turning up the whites of his eyes, slowly and laboriously shoved himself up along the slab wall.

"Just look at th' mopoke!" Mother said in disgust. "Hold your head up, can't you! You silly gork of a fellow! Wherever you got your manners from I'm sure I don't know!" And she shot an ugly, insinuating glance at Limpy, a nervous, stiff-legged, scraggy whiskered cousin of ours who lived with us, and who just then limped from the wood-heap with the axe in his hand.

Limpy shrunk back several paces, and starting thumping the axe-head on the face of a block to tighten the handle that already was wedged as tight as could be.

"How are y' on a horse—can y' ride?" Dunn asked of Tom. Tom didn't open his lips.

"*Him* ride! Crickey!" Andy said in derision—"why a calf slung 'im into th' dam this mornin', an' would a' smothercated 'im only I was there."

"Oh, indeed, 'e can ride every bit as well as yeou!" Martha, a year older than Andy, said in defence of Tom. "Who fell off Smith's pig? 'M, yah!"

Andy pulled a face at Martha behind Mother's back, and Martha pulled a series of faces at Andy.

"You can chop wood, I suppose—an' milk?" Dunn further asked of Tom.

Tom closed his eyes, and scratched the ground floor with his big toe, but made no reply.

"Why can't you answer when y'r asked a civil question— why *can't* y'?" And Mother seized Tom by his unkempt hair with both hands and shook him.

"Y-Y-Yes! YES, I *can*, Mother. I c-c-can, I *can!*" Tom bellowed.

"You can! You *can* what?" and Mother woolled him some more.

"C-C-Can *ride*," howled Tom.

"Oh, my word 'e can ride jolly well. Dom can d' so." Limpy affirmed, leaning calmly on the axe.

"Then he doesn't take after you, thank God!" Mother snapped at Limpy. Mother was always hard on her nephew.

Limpy staggered back another step or two, trailing the axe after him or before him.

"*You'll* be gettin' a woollin' next, Limpy," Andy with a grin, drawled in a low tone to his crippled cousin.

Limpy frowned at Andy.

Andy moved towards Tom, and asked him was he going to take the job or was he not?

"He's going to take it all right," Dunn put in. "An' I'll make a man of him in a couple o' months."

"He'll *have* to take it," Mother said firmly. "An' he's not going t' be asked about it, either. There's quite enough of them here without him—eating an' drinking what little's coming in, an' doing precious little for it. An' if there was situations for the lot o' them they could all go."

"Limpy, too, Mother?" chuckled Andy.

Limpy nearly dropped down at the mention of his name and, recovering, scowled at Andy.

"Oh! I didn't mean *him!*" Mother answered satirically. "The place couldn't get on without *him!*"

Andy guffawed; and Dunn looked at Limpy and laughed aloud.

Limpy shuffled back to the wood-heap, and in a feeble, useless way swung the axe several times at a log, then looked back over his shoulder at the rest of us.

Father, carrying a broken swingletree in one hand, and a piece of plough chain in the other, happened along.

Mother explained matters to him. Father gazed upon Tom in an amused kindly way, and expressed approval with his large, hairy eyes. Father mostly expressed himself with his eyes, and always laughed with them.

"All right, then," Dunn said, "send him over tomorrow, Mrs. Pettigrew."

Then, turning away he mounted his horse and rode off.

Next day.

Limpy drove Tom to Dunn's hotel in the old spring cart. There was a lot of commotion on the verandah as they drove up.

"Dere's a jolly row goin' on, I tink," Limpy murmured, steadying the old mare in her eternal jog, and staring hard with his dull little eyes.

Tom clutched Limpy's arm, and said he wasn't "goin' to stop there, not fer anything".

"Oh, dey won't touch you, Dom," Limpy assured him. "You're not big enough. It's me dey would like to hab a slab ad! . . . . . I don't tink I'll dribe right up to d' door . . . . I bedder stop d' jolly cart when we ged a bid closer an' let you jumb oud . . . . . . Den I can cut back."

Just then a drunk was thrown right off the hotel verandah on to his head, and a red swag flew after him.

"Cribes! *Woe! Woe!*" Limpy called to the old mare, and the cart stopped within half a chain of the hotel.

"Jump oud, Dom, quick! an' take y' clothes!" And lifting a bundle tied in a spotted handkerchief from the bottom of the cart, Limpy dropped it hurriedly over the wheel.

Tom cast a frantic look at the hotel, then at the drunk, and gripping the seat with both hands, blubbered:

"I won't get out! I won't go in there! I'm goin' back 'ome!"

The man who was thrown out rose from the dust and pulled his shirt off. Then, roaring like a bull, swung his arms wildly about, and challenged everyone in the hotel to come out and fight.

Limpy became agitated.

"Cribes, Dom, ged oud! Dere's a good chab!" he moaned. "If y' come bag y' know, y'r modder'll harp kill y'."

"I'd sooner be half-killed be 'er," Tom cried, eyeing the drunk, "th-th-than killed be *'im*."

Suddenly Limpy gave a start, and, dropping the reins, exclaimed:

"Oh, *cribes!* 'e's comin' dis way!"

Tom, seeing the man stagger towards them with a big stone in each hand, left the cart as though it were on fire. Limpy left it, too, but with a great struggle, and took shelter behind the mare. Tom bolted headlong for the rear of the hotel, and scrambled wildly into an empty cask that stood on its end in one of the rookeries. And as he scrambled into it a sitting hen flapped and fluttered out of it: then proceeded to make pandemonium in the yard.

Tom sank hurriedly down and sat crouched in that cask like a 'possum in a hollow tree. His eyes bulged in his head, and he started and trembled at every sound. For several minutes he sat there unconsciously on fourteen eggs. But when the contents of the shells began to soak through his double-seated pants, he realised everything. Poor Tom! The position filled him with a new terror. He deemed it prudent, however, not to make any effort to alter matters, and sat tight, and soaked and stared up in awe at the mouth of the cask.

The affrighted hen ceased her cackling and decided to return to her eggs. Determinedly she mounted the cask and looked down sideways at Tom. Tom shuddered at first sight of her; then he scrowled and shook his fist threateningly at her. The hen stretched her neck, and let out a loud *"kuk-kuk-kuk-a-kur-r-k!"* and emulating Blondin, she circumnavigated the cask, looking down all the while, and observing Tom from every point of the compass. Once she nearly fell in on top of him, and Tom shut his eyes and dropped his head. Finally he gathered enough courage to strike at her with his hat. The hen overbalanced, and, dropping to the ground, cackling and calling violently for assistance.

A pair of stately roosters and an aged, frowsy cockatoo came to her aid. The roosters yabbered incoherently, and clawed up the earth in a useless way. But the cockatoo started to inquire into the trouble.

"What th' hell's th' matter? What th' hell's th' matter?" he asked, strutting round the base of the cask.

Tom heard the strange voice, and thought his hour had come.

The cockatoo flew up, and, perching on the edge of the cask, gazed furtively down at Tom. Tom gazed wildly up at the bird.

"Who th' hell are you?" it asked in a deep bass voice.

Tom didn't say who he was. Tom couldn't.

"Who th' hell are you?" the cockatoo repeated.

Tom's heart jumped violently.

Then the cockatoo hopped round, and showing its tail to Tom, screamed at the top of its voice:

"Dick! Dick! Come and cut his head off!"

Out of that cask Tom plunged like a wild horse, and with egg shell and egg-flip dropping from him in flakes, raced furiously for the open. And in front of him all the way across the yard that cockatoo, flapping its wings, shrieked:

"Dick! Dick! Murder! They're killing cockie! They're killing poor cockie!"

Next moment the voice of Dunn thundered in Tom's ears as he reached the open, to "Come here! . . . . . . *Come here!"*

Tom ran harder.

Dunn shouted a volley of oaths after him.

Tom reached a clump of wattles, and like an emu disappeared in a flash.

"Th' d—d young fool!" Dunn growled, "he's cleared!"

And that was how Tom got lost for four days and four nights.

3. How Tom Was Found

Tom had been away two days, and Mother and Dora and Aunt Sue, busy at the washing, were talking about him, and wondering how he liked his new place. Aunt Sue always helped Mother and Dora with the washing because she lived in the some house as we did. In fact some of it belonged to her. The partition between her bedroom and our front room formed part of the line that marked the boundary between her homestead and father's. Father was a Socialist in some things, and reckoned it waste of time and labour building a separate house for his sister when she could fulfil conditions just as well by sharing the end of ours. And he considered it would be more comfortable for her, anyway; and said she would be company for Mother and the girls, and they would be company for her. And Mother and Dora became excited at the prospect of having Aunt Sue living so near, and one blazing hot day drove twenty-five miles in the old spring-cart to meet her and bring her to the homestead.

"I can only find one pair of Tom's trousers in the wash, Dora," Mother said, bending over a pile of dirty clothes, and tossing them and re-tossing them about. "There should be two—where's the new pair I made for him?"

"But he's got a pair on, hasn't he?" Dora answered carelessly, as she rubbed at a shirt of Father's.

"I suppose he has! I suppose everyone has! At least I hope they have!" Mother snapped angrily.

Dora wriggled silently over the tub for several seconds, then suddenly lifted her head and holding her sides with her wet hands, shrieked merrily into the overhanging boughs of the gum-tree that served as a wash-shed.

Mother, holding a pair of Andy's pants in her hand, straightened up and stared hard at her eldest daughter.

Aunt Sue looked up from the tub she was engaged over, and smiled in a cynical, wooden sort of way.

"It seems to amuse you very much!" Mother said to Dora.

"Goodness, Mother!" Dora gasped, getting her breath back, "was that meant for me or—or—for *Aunt Sue?*" And she let go another shriek.

"What was meant?" And Aunt Sue's long, serious face lengthened another inch or two. Aunt Sue was a sensitive, suspicious old maid.

"I don't know *what* she meant," and Dora bent over the tub and laughed more.

"I meant that your brother's trousers are not to be found! Is there anything funny in that?" Mother fumed,

"Oh, there's not—not in *that,*" and Dora tittered to herself.

"Did you ever see such a girl?" Mother cried, appealing to Aunt Sue.

"Don't make people think you're silly, Dora," Aunt Sue observed advisedly.

Dora's attitude changed suddenly.

"I wouldn't like to," she fired up, turning round. "If I did I might get left on the shelf all me blessed life—like some people I know."

It was Aunt Sue's turn to change her attitude. And she changed it like a moving picture.

"You're a cheeky girl—a bold, cheeky hussy, so you are!" She screamed at Dora; and covering her face with her apron, burst into loud, hysterical sobs.

Mother let fall Andy's trousers, and threw her arms round Aunt Sue.

Father's cattle-pup pounced on the trousers, and raced off with them in his teeth.

"Don't mind her! Don't take any notice, Sue!" Mother said, consolingly.

"It's not en-en-enough to be s-s-s-*slaving* an-an-and *working* one's hands off tr-tr-trying to please evryone!" sobbed Aunt Sue, "but to be in-in-insulted to me (sob) very face— and be a chit of a g-g-g-*girl,* too! (several violent sobs). Oh, I can't stand it any longer!"

"Well, if I am a chit of a girl," retorted Dora, "it doesn't hurt me if anyone says so. And it won't hurt me, neither, if they say I'm an old maid when I got to be one—if ever I do!"

Aunt Sue dropped her apron and squealed: "I'm *not* an old maid. You're lying, so you are! And your mother stands here listening to you!"

"Goodness me, what are you then?" retorted Dora. "You're forty, ain't y'?"

"I'm not forty—I am not; and that's where you're lying again!" shrieked Aunt Sue. "I'm only thirty-nine. And lots of girls have got married at thirty-nine. Better girls than you!"

"Lots of old women—lots of old wall-flowers have, y' mean!" Dora chuckled. And taking to her apron again, Aunt Sue wept loudly.

"Dora! go into the house and make up the beds, and leave the washing alone!" Mother commanded.

"Oh, very well, if that'll please her!" Dora answered, walking off. "But I won't make hers up for her!"

"Oh, I can't live here in this place any longer, Alice," Aunt Sue blubbered; "everyone hates me! I know they hate me! And you all want me to go! I know you all want me to go! I have felt it (sobs) ever since the first day I came . . . . Abe, as—as well as th' rest o' you is tired of me!"

Abe was Father.

"That's all rubbish and nonsense! Don't be stupid, Sue!" Mother said. "Why everyone of us would be real sorry if you were to go—Dora just as well as the rest. I'm sure of that."

"And I know I'm blamed for everything that goes wrong!" Aunt Sue, stubbornly. "Th' scones and th' cake (sobs) that were missed yest'day and th' day before I was blamed fer taking! Oh, it's too bad altogether!"

"Dear me, you must be going off your head, Sue!" Mother explained. "Who ever thought of blaming you for such things? Why, everyone knows the children took them."

At this stage Dora returned, and said Dunn, the hotelkeeper, was at the front door.

"Dunn, the hotelkeeper!" Mother repeated, in surprise; and, hurriedly wiping her hands, went off to see him.

Aunt Sue quickly dried her eyes in her apron; then, smoothing her hair over with the palms of her hands and adjusting the neck of her dress, returned to the tub and began washing again as though nothing had happened.

"Well, and how's Tom getting along?" Mother inquired pleasantly of Dunn.

Dunn thought Mother was jesting.

Mother assured him she was in earnest.

"Haven't you got the young beggar here?" Dunn said, looking puzzled.

Mother began to tremble.

"How—oh, how could we have him here?" she answered nervously.

Then, raising her voice almost to a shriek:

"Where *is* the boy? What have you done with him?"

"Done with him be d—d!" roared Dunn. "I never saw anything of him but his heels! He cleared out like a —— wallaby when he saw me! But (lowering his voice and looking sympathetic) are you serious—*isn't* he here?"

"Can't you see he isn't?" And Mother shook with excitement.

"Then be th' Lord, he's *lorst!*" Dunn concluded gravely.

"Oh, my God! and it's two days ago!" And Mother gazed in horror at the broad belt of grim, silent scrub that almost came to the very door of the homestead.

Aunt Sue, who had left the washing to see what was the matter, threw her arms round Mother's neck and whimpered:

"Oh-h, Alice, I am sorry for you! I have never been a mother myself, but"——

Mother shook herself free from Aunt Sue's embrace, and said scornfully:

"What need is there to be sorry for *me!* For heaven's sake have sense, and think of the child! For the love of mercy do something."

Then to Dora:

"Run, girl; run and tell your father!"

Dora ran to where Father and Andy and Martha and Limpy were burning off timber to clear a patch for the plough.

Presently Father and Andy and Martha, with Limpy far behind, arrived.

Father listened to what Mother and Dunn had to say, then smiled with his eyes, and said:

"Tom won't get lost. Tom's all right. Tom'll find his way."

"Lord o' mercy, haven't you any understanding, man?" Mother cried—"the boy is lost, and what are we going to do?"

"Yes, yes, Alice," chirped Aunt Sue. "You always did know what was best in everything."

Ignoring the latter, Mother waited for a suggestion from Father.

"No fear of it," Father answered cheerfully. "Tom knows th' country. Tom'll turn up directly all right."

"Good God!" Mother said in a voice that startled everyone but Father. Then she started walking about.

The cattle-pup, having finished with Andy's pants, sauntered round in search of a fresh toy. A tattered fragment dangling to the tail of Mother's skirt attracted the brute. It crept behind Mother and eyed that fragment suspiciously for several seconds, then struck at it with its paw. The fragment moved when Mother moved, and the pup sprang at it. Finally, it seized the tail-end of her skirt in its mouth, and raced round to the front of her with it. Mother felt her skirts raised behind, and kicked at the pup. The pup growled, and raced back behind her; then round the other way to the front of her again. Once more Mother felt her skirts lifting at the rear, and kicked out at the pup with both feet, and cried to Andy to "kill that wretch of a dog".

Andy shouted to the brute to "lie down", but Dunn, judging the distance like a footballer, kicked the pup into the air. And the pup took Mother's skirts up with him and spread them over her head.

Dora and Aunt Sue screamed, and rushed to Mother.

Dunn turned away and started grinning and talking to the yelping pup.

"I'm all right! Go 'way! Go 'way!" Mother said to Aunt Sue and Dora. And Mother turned very red in the face.

"What way did Tom go when he left yer place?" Andy inquired of Dunn.

Dunn told him.

"He'd never find e's road that way!" Andy judged. "He'd get into Devil's Gorge, where Grogan lost 'isself."

"Oh, wouldn't 'e!" Martha sneered at Andy. "He'd find th' road just as well as yer would."

Martha was a loyal sister to Tom.

"We must all go and look for him," Mother said—"every one of us."

Dunn agreed with Mother, and said he would ride round the district and inform the neighbours.

At that moment Limpy, with perspiration and charcoal on his face, and a look of wonder in his eyes, arrived.

"Wottid d' madder wid Dom?" he asked.

Mother flew at him.

"You wretch!" she cried, seizing him by the back of the neck. "You told us nothing about this when you came home with the cart. You said you left the boy all right at the hotel. *You liar!*" And she swung Limpy round and round as though he were made of straw, and contemptuously shoved him from her. Limpy toppled over backwards, and, falling into a sitting position, propped himself up with his hands and gazed bewilderedly at all of us.

For two days and two nights the whole countryside searched high and low for Tom, but not a trace of him could they find. One by one they gave up and abandoned hope. And, finally, everyone but Father was agreed that Tom's skeleton might one day be found, which was the most that could be hoped for. Father, though, couldn't see why Tom wouldn't turn up all right. Father never could see why anything wouldn't turn up or turn out all right. Nothing in the wide world could go wrong, according to Father. A confident, serene old soul was Father.

And as the sun went down on the third day Mother lost all hope. She separated herself from the rest of us, and went and sat on a large shell of a log that lay a short distance from the house, and with her head bowed down thought and thought about Tom. Aunt Sue went to her, and, taking the risk of annoying her again, sat silently beside her and put an arm around her waist. But Mother took it in the right way; and sadly shaking her head from side to side, murmured at intervals:

"Poor Tom! Poor, poor Tom! It was your Mother's doing! She should never have sent you away!"

And as Mother and Aunt Sue sat there on the end of the log Martha seemed to become demented. With her short, skimpy skirt flying above her knees she raced round the house and peeped at them first from one corner of it, then from another. Next she skedaddled across to a big ironbark tree and observed them closely from behind it.

Andy drew Father's attention to Martha, and for the first time in his life Father was puzzled and perturbed.

All at once a scream came from Aunt Sue that rang all round the ridges, and she and Mother sprang from the log and ran a distance from it. And curiously, Martha also screamed and fled to another tree.

"Oh, my heavens!" gasped Aunt Sue, "something's bit me! Something's bit me! Oh, mercy!" And, bending down she pulled up her skirts and shoved down her stocking.

Father and Andy and Dora ran to see what had happened.

"Something has bit your sister!" Mother said to Father. "Oh, Lord, I hope it wasn't a snake!"

Then, after examining the part:

"Oh, that's all right. It's nothing."

But it wasn't all right; and it *was* something. Aunt Sue felt it; and blood was oozing in three places from the calf of her leg. And when Aunt Sue saw the blood she started to faint.

Dora ran for water.

Andy, leaning forward, crept cautiously up to the mouth of the log, which, having been gutted by fire, resembled a hugh trough with no "ends" to it, turned upside down. Within a few feet of it he balanced himself lightly on his finger tips; and, craning his neck, stared into the dark recesses for quite a while. All at once Martha swooped down on him like a hawk, and kicked him with her bare foot. Andy got a start, and, jumping to his feet, turned upon Martha, and threatened her. Martha danced on to the roof of the log, and ran up and down it. Martha behaved like a plover when its nest is in danger. Andy got down on his hands again, and peered closer into the log. suddenly he sprang back and guffawed.

"Do you see anything, Andy?" Mother asked, pale and alarmed looking.

"By cripes, I do!" Andy shouted.

Aunt Sue swooned right off in Father's arms.

"By cripes, 'e ought to get a hidin'! By crimes, 'e is a bloke!"

"Who? What is it, Andy?" Mother asked excitedly.

"That dorg, *Tom!* That's who it is!" answered Andy. "And *she*," pointing to Martha—"knew 'e was 'ere all th' time; an' she's been feedin' 'im. There's plates and stuff in with 'im. By cripes!"

Martha bolted for the house; and Father and Dora left Aunt Sue to look after herself.

"Come out here!" Mother said, looking into the log. *"Come out here!"*

Tom crawled out in the new trousers that Mother had been looking for, and Mother pinned him by the back of the neck.

"Into the house you march!" she said, shoving Tom in front of her.

Tom marched into the house.

Dora raked several scones out of the log, and, holding them up, said:

"Look at that! That's where they went!"

Aunt Sue sighed; while Father humped his back and smiled on the provender.

Next day Andy asked Tom in confidence what he bit Aunt Sue for.

"I didn't!" Tom answered. "I was havin' me supper, an' she come an' sat on th' end o' th' log an' blocked out all th' light, an' I stuck th' table-fork in 'er leg."

4. A Bad Evening

We had eaten three scrub turkeys for supper, and all of us were in good humour.

"Well, there's one thing," Father said, pushing back his three-legged stool. "Whatever else goes wrong, we can't very well starve in a place like this, not while we have the gun and some powder and shot."

"Could lib jolly well," Limpy put in, "widdout eber buyin' a ting."

"*Some* people could, no doubt," Mother said, "and *do!*"

Limpy was always the weevil in Mother's wheat. But rarely did he take any notice of her. Limpy was a blind horse where hints and innuendoes were concerned.

"Turkey to-day; kangaroo-tail yes'-day; parrots th' day bufor' yes'-day—wonder what'll it be turmorrer?" joyfully from Martha.

"S'pose that 'possum we got in th' trap this mornin'," Tom said.

"Shut up, you vagabond," Mother cried. "Who do you think's going to eat 'possum!"

"Der blacks alwuz did, den," Limpy mentioned informatively.

"Did they!" snapped Mother. "Well, there's going to be no blacks here, if I know anything about it."

"And lived well on them," Father affirmed. "There were some fine men among the blacks." Father took a great interest in the history of the blacks, and used to read things out of the paper to us about them.

"Oh, it's not our stomachs, or what the blacks put in theirs, or what they didn't, that we've got to think of now," Mother said; "but it's getting some ground cleared and ploughed and put under wheat. Can it all be done in time for this season, that's the question?"

Mother was a pushing, practical woman.

"Oh, yes," Father answered, "can, easy." Father was the only one in the family who understood how to get land ready. Father worked in a cemetery when first he came to the country. And a good opening he reckoned it was for a new chum to drop into. All of us understood how to get land ready now, though.

"How many are dere ob us aldergedder?" and Limpy proceeded to count heads. *"Nine,"* he concluded. "Enub to plough twelve acres in no dime."

"And will the nine of us be ploughing?" Mother asked disdainfully of Limpy.

"It'd be a jolly lot quicker dan one; don't you tink so?" And Limpy appealed to Father.

Father smiled weirdly, and combed his hair with his fingers. Father's hair— excepting his whiskers—was all bunched at the back of his head and about his ears. And wonderful hair it was, too!

"What would we all have to do then?" Dora asked, smiling at Limpy—"pull along with the horses?"

The rest of us laughed.

"Dere ain't mudch to larf ad," Limpy protested.

"And is that what you mean?" sharply from Mother.

"Preddy well," Limpy answered.

"You *ass!*" And Mother rose from the table and carried away the teapot.

Limpy wheeled on his seat and blinked steadily into the fire, and didn't shift his eyes, or attempt to break the silence again till Tom, playing with a pair of rusty old pincers he had found while playing in the ashes of a surveyor's camp, took hold of his (Limpy's) ear with them. Limpy suddenly yelled, and hung backwards over the seat, and kicked Aunt Sue in the waist with his stiff leg, and nearly knocked her into the fire. Aunt Sue clutched at the mantelpiece—a dressed slab resting temporarily on two frail supports of Father's manufacture. The mantelpiece gave way, and came down end-ways on top of Martha and Andy and Limpy. And the alarm clock, and a quantity of shelled beans, and a tin of mustard, and a broken parcel of pepper, and a collection of "minerals" came down with it. The pepper lodged on Limpy, and went to pieces in his hair, and entered his eyes and mouth. Limpy snorted, and spat, and sneezed, and plunged round the room with his hands over his eyes.

Andy and Tom laughed. Martha broke in upon their mirth with cries of "Oh! oh! Aunt Sue's on fire! on fire!" Aunt Sue glanced quickly about herself, and discovering a flame mounting the back of her skirt, screamed and rushed for the door. Mother and Father intercepted her. "Hold her!" Mother cried. "Don't let her into the wind! Shut the door!" Dora slammed the door violently, and it flew open again. Limpy, staggering across the room, plunged blindly in his own interests. He collided with Aunt Sue and Father. Aunt Sue fell against the edge of the sofa. Limpy fell on her feet, and the flames raging in her skirt attacked his red hair and whiskers. "Cribes! FIRE!" Limpy shouted, slashing all round his head with both hands. Father, regardless of Limpy, seized hold of Aunt Sue and jerked, and bumped, and tugged at her till he emptied her out of her dress. Talk about screaming! We couldn't hear ourselves shouting for it! Aunt Sue screamed at Father, then at Mother, till her tongue came right out. "Stop it! stop it! stop it! Heavens, can't you see you've nearly pulled the clothes off me!" she cried at last.

All of us stood up, and gaped and gasped over the table at Aunt Sue.

"Sit down!" Mother shouted to us. "Sit down, you young

" Oh oh Aunt Sue's on Fire "

wretches!" We sat down and looked under the table at Aunt
Sue in her broken stays and red flannel petticoat. Just then
Dora rushed in at the back door with a bucket of water—good,
clean, drinking water, too, that Andy and Tom carried from
the rocks before tea—and as Aunt Sue opened her mouth to
scream again, Dora emptied it over her. Aunt Sue shut up,
and sank under the torrent as though the shock had killed her.
And as Dora saw the water go over Aunt Sue the humour of it
seemed to strike her. She squealed cheerfully. Then her eyes
rested on Limpy struggling on the floor, and she squealed
again, and threw the empty bucket at his head. Limpy called
out "Mercy!" and, rising to his feet, threw himself at the table
and broke some of the cups. And we hadn't enough to go
round as it was! But Mother didn't hear the smash. She was too
occupied with Aunt Sue.

"You can thank God, you can, you can, that you weren't
burnt to death!" Mother cried to her. "Oh, my! oh, my! oh,
my! Such an escape!" Then while Father, puffing like a draught
horse, stamped and danced heavily on the smouldering skirts
with his big boots, she hurried Aunt Sue into her room.

After that we thought the trouble and excitement were all
over, and started to grin at each other. We were grinning when
Father suddenly faced us and roared:

"I'll tear th' *liver* out o' th' one that did it! Who DID it?"

Never before had we known Father to take a turn like it,
and out of the door all of us scrambled—all except Dora and
Limpy.

"Who th' devil did it?" We heard him roar again as we
listened at the cracks. "I'm GOIN' to KNOW!"

Limpy started sneezing.

"Well, it wasn't ME!" Dora cried. "It was th' rotten mantelpiece that fell down, as we always said it would!" And she
burst into tears.

"Who *was* it, then?" Father bellowed stubbornly.

"Lizzen d' me"—and Limpy, raising his hands above his
head, essayed to make an explanation.

Father turned his hairy ear to him and listened.

Limpy contorted his features, and struggled inwardly with
himself. Then he opened his mouth wide and sneezed placidly.

"Atchew! Atchew! Atchew! Atchew!"

Father clutched himself by the hair and ran out the back-door.

We crept inside again, and looked wonderingly at Martha, and grinned at Limpy, and pinched him on the stiff leg.

Suddenly the back door burst open, and in walked Father again with a waddy in his hand, and a look of tremendous determination in his eye.

"Now then," he roared, covering the lot of us with the waddy, *"who did it?"*

Martha and Tom and Andy dived under the table. Dora rose from the box she was sitting on, and stood with her back to the wall.

"Who *did* it?" Father shouted again.

Mother, with her hair hanging down and disordered, and fire in her eyes, issued from the bedroom.

"Who DID it?" she echoed, flying at Father. "Who in the name of God do you think did it if you didn't do it yourself, man?"

Father dropped the waddy on the floor, and staggering against the wall, stood trembling beside Dora.

"Yourself! Yourself! YOURSELF!" And Mother stamped her foot, and shoved her face close to Father's. "The rubbishing way you do things!" she continued shouting. "Look at your work! Look at it! Look at it!" And she pointed dramatically to the wrecked mantelpiece.

Father cast a quick despairing glance at his handiwork, then bolted outside.

"There's a man for you!" Mother shouted, addressing Dora. "There's a beautiful father! His children ought to be proud of him—proud of him!"

Limpy, who all the while had looked very uneasy, shuffled quietly towards the door.

"You're off, too, are you!" Mother cried, rushing at him.

Limpy reached the door and pulled it open just in time for Mother to shove him right through on to the dog lying outside.

"A pair of lovely men!" she foamed, turning to her room. "Oh, a lovely pair of men! Brave men to run away from a woman! Brave! brave men!"

5. Burning Off

The wind was howling in the tops of the big ironbark trees, and chopping round ridges and through fallen timber the day we started burning off the twelve acres. And what a delight it was starting! The prospects of seeing a wheat-field waving where all was wilderness and waste, and the hope of rising to fortune on it filled us with joy.

"We mustn't waste any matches," Mother said, producing the box from her dress pocket, and handing Father one with no head to light the first fire with. "When you get that one going we can all take firesticks to light the rest."

Father bent down beside a pile of dry bushes and logs, and using his hat as a break-wind rubbed the match on his boot. He rubbed it several times; then looked at it, and declared they were "rotten matches".

"Come out of th' road! You'll waste all that's in th' box!" And squatting down beside Father, Mother struck a match on the box and set the bushes ablaze.

"It's been the same ever since you've been married," she said, reviling him. "You've never lit a fire yet that didn't cost us half a dozen boxes of matches!" Then she proceeded to arrange the lucifers so that none would fall out of the box, or the heads get jammed in the lid.

"I've made fires without a match at all," Father boasted, "just be rubbin' two sticks together same as th' blacks, an' sometimes be strikin' me knife on a bit o' flint." And lifting a scrap of ironstone that lay at his feet he began knocking it against the back of his knife. Martha and Tom attracted by the operation raced one another through the grass to reach him. Martha jostled Tom, and Tom, fouling Mother, bumped the matches out of her hand into the fire.

"Oh, my soul, look at that! Look what the wretch of a boy has done!" And Mother threw up her hands, and danced round the fire as though one of *us* were in it. Tom, though, made no attempt to rescue the matches. He pulled himself together, and raced to the nearest tree and hid behind the trunk of it.

Father put his knife away and gazed solemnly and uselessly into the fire.

"Where is he?" Mother cried, jumping round and lifting a stick.

Andy grinned, and pointed to the tree behind which Tom was concealed.

Mother, gripping the stick firmly, tip-toed to the tree. Andy threw up his hat, and rejoiced inwardly. Father and Aunt Sue and Dora, with amused looks on their faces, first watched Mother, then the tree. As Mother reached one side of the iron-bark Tom glided instinctively to the other. Then Mother darted round and struck at him. But Tom wasn't there! Mother looked surprised. Then she looked back at Andy, and cried: "I'll warm you, me shaver, for making a fool of me!"

Father and Aunt Sue and Dora joined together in mirth.

Andy started stealthily forward to capture Tom and hand him over to Mother. Andy possessed all the instincts of a mean policeman.

"*Run,* Tom, *run!*" Martha screamed. Tom left the tree and ran.

Then Mother turned to Father.

"Unless you do as a Father should," she said, "and see those children behave themselves and obey their mother, and do something for what they eat and wear, I'm not going to put up with it! I'll not suffer this place, nor them, nor YOU, not another day, not another hour. You can take me out of it—take me wherever you like, I'm sick of it!"

Father swung round, and facing the wilderness, roared: "Torm-m!" He roared "Torm-m!" twenty times. Tom, whining and hopping on one leg, at last emerged from a clump of green bushes. "Ooh! Ooh!" he groaned, holding up his foot, and showing a wound on the instep from which blood was trickling.

Father's heart softened.

"W-why, what's th' matter, eh? What's up?" he asked in a tender voice.

"Ooh! Ooh, s-s-s-s-!" And Tom's face filled with painful grimaces.

Father approached him and examined the wound; then called to Mother to know if she had a bit of rag about her.

Mother had no rag, and she had no sympathy for Tom, either. "I'll give him rag," she said, "if I lay my hands on him!"

Father tore the lining from the waistband of his trousers and clumsily bandaged Tom's foot with it.

"There y'are, me boy," he said, patting the patient on the head; "that'll be all right now! Never mind! Never mind! Where's Andy? *Andy!*"

"Oh, I'm ere!" Andy, standing by grumbled.

"Oh, yer there, are y'! I didn't see y'. Well, come on now, all o' y', everyone o' y', and get firesticks and make a start."

Andy took a firestick and went off swinging it about to keep it flaring; Martha secured another; Tom, with one eye on Mother, who stood near by, bent down and reached cautiously for a third.

"You tinker!" Mother cried, and aimed a kick at Tom's ribs. Tom flopped flat on the ground like a cattle pup, and, missing him, Mother's foot went up in the air and propelled her on to her back. Tom grabbed a fire-stick and forgetting his wounded foot, bounded off like a marsupial. Aunt Sue and Dora shrieked merrily at Mother. But Mother didn't rise and abuse them. She turned over on the grass, and burying her face between her arms, began to sob. Aunt Sue and Dora got a shock. They stopped laughing and stared at each other, and turned red in the face. They felt like criminals. Then they spoke apologetically and consolingly to Mother, and coaxed her to get up. "Leave me!" Mother said, in a sad, broken voice—"leave me!" and wept more. Aunt Sue and Dora started to blubber then! they shed tears all over Mother, and wailed as if someone were dead belonging to them. Mother couldn't stand much of Aunt Sue and Dora.

"Oh, I know I'm silly to take any notice," she said at last, and rising with an effort, smiled through her tears at them.

Then Aunt Sue and Dora wiped their tears away and smiled too. And they chatted and frisked round Mother, and fawned on her, and explained why it was they had laughed when she fell. They proceeded to illustrate the humour of the episode to her. First Dora made an imaginary kick at Tom and toppled over; then Aunt Sue, forgetting how prude and prim she always pretended to be, went one better than Dora. And as she fell and rolled amongst the grass a strange and unexpected voice called out:

"*Hi! yi! yi! yi!*"

Aunt Sue screamed and struggled to her feet. Mother and Dora looked round, and saw a robust, middle-aged man, in patched moleskin pants and brown whiskers, smiling at them.

Aunt Sue hung her head and hid behind Mother.

"You don't like dot, I see, yoong laty, hah?" the stranger said, grinning pleasantly at Aunt Sue. "Nefer mindt, I saay noding aboudt dot you make spordt mid yousselluf. Py heavens sake, n-no!"

Mother and Dora burst out laughing, and looked to see where Father was.

Removing his hat—a three-cornered old felt patched with pieces of moleskin, sewn with string—the stranger advanced and handed it to Aunt Sue. Aunt Sue shrank from it. "Take it," Mother said; "*take* it, and see what he wants."

Aunt Sue took the hat, and held it as though it were something that would bite her.

Stepping back a few paces the stranger hitched up his pants. "Now den," he said, "I shows you soomding. Oop mid him, yoong laty."

Aunt Sue didn't understand.

"Oop mid him, leedle creadure—oop so high as you head."

"Oh, he wants to kick it," Dora cried, the truth suddenly dawning upon her.

"Oh, indeed," said Aunt Sue, and she stood on tiptoes and held the hat up at arm's length.

"Yah!" exclaimed the Dane, "dot vas him. *He* nod like you"—he added, grimacing cheerfully at Aunt Sue. "*He* haf quick brain."

Great mirth from Dora.

Then fixing his eyes on the hat, the Dane took a short run, and bringing up both arms and legs, kicked it out of Aunt Sue's hand.

"Dere now," he said, smiling at Aunt Sue, "dot vas saamding for you. You make spordt mid him soom day." And securing his old felt, and pressing it tight on his head again, turned away and saluted Father with a series of friendly nods and grunts and smiles.

"You nod know Villiam Brandt, already yet. I dink so. Hah?" he said, introducing himself.

"Oh, you're Mr. Brandt," Father said, remembering we had a neighbour of that name living about two miles away.

Mr. Brandt shook hands with Father; then stared all round at the timber we were starting to burn off, and pulled ugly pessimistic faces at it. Then noticing Martha and Andy and Tom grinning at him, said:

"Py heaven't sake, vas all dem yours, my frien'?"

Father, with pride in his eyes, owned up to all of us.

Villiam Brandt patted him on the back.

"Vat for you vant to work?" he said. "You vill get rich too quick aldergedder. You go home, mein frien' und sleep."

Father stared.

"Yah, you off to sleeb," Villiam repeated, and wagging his head, strode off through the timber, and left us all laughing.

After that we settled down to work and commenced firing the timber in real earnest. Not a log, stump or standing tree escaped. And as the smoke and flames entered and roared up the hollow logs and hollow trees, and licked up tufts of long dry grass, kangaroo rats, 'possums, paddymelons, cats and the vermin of the bush, scorched and singed, left them, and careered stupidly around in search of fresh air and fresh cover. Talk about excitement! We *were* excited! Father, armed with a heavy stick, pursued a half-cremated rat; Andy chased one that staggered and hiccoughed like a drunken man; Martha and Tom took after a 'possum that was making off with some of the fire on its back; while Mother and Aunt Sue and Dora, shrieking at the top of their voices and holding their skirts wide with both hands, tried to make prisoners of everything that came their way. Joy! There was no end to it. Whenever we paused for breath, a fresh batch of scared vermin would present themselves, and the fun would begin all over again.

We tired of it at last, though, and together threw ourselves on the grass and laughed, and perspired. Mother and Aunt Sue said they "never, never had any idea that so many animals lived in the bush." And Father wished to heavens some of his relations in the Old Country were with us. "It'd open the eyes of some of them," he said, "that think there's nothing out here only hard work and blacks."

Next day we continued burning off. But somehow we didn't take so much interest in the vermin. And the day after that they had no interest for us at all. We weren't so enthusiastic about the burning-off, either—at least, we younger ones weren't. Father and Mother, though, were as warm on it as ever. They had a lot of faith in the burning-off, had Father and Mother. They rarely talked about anything else. According to them, the burning-off was the commencement, the middle and the end of everything. It was nearly the end of us.

"If we can only get the ground ready and the wheat in before the rain comes," Mother would say, "things will go on right enough—right enough." In those days the rain always came at the end of June—so the people and the papers, who were mostly liars, used to say.

For days, weeks and months we delved and slaved at the burning-off. At last we finished it—at least for the time being. We didn't finish it all till fifteen years later—till it had finished several ploughs and scores of swingle-trees, and broken the heart of every old horse that came on to the place. But we got the ground ready and the wheat in before the rain came. The rain came many months after the wheat was put in.

6. *Aunt Sue Meets Trouble*

Sunday morning.

Father on the verandah resting in an easy chair of his own manufacture, reading the newspaper; Mother and Aunt Sue and Dora, busy tiding up and preparing dinner; Andy in the front room telling Tom and Martha lies about Jerry Manning riding Edens' buckjumper, and disfiguring the pine table with a pocket knife; Limpy crossing the yard, blowing music from a split stick and a gum leaf. (Limpy spent most of his spare time blowing music from a split stick. And most of his time was spare time.) Father looked up and frowned as Limpy stepped under the verandah. Andy assailed him with shouts of, "Shut up, and clear out o' here with that bloomin' thing"—when he stepped inside.

"Dis id a good one," Limpy claimed, removing the contrivance from his mouth and admiring it.

"But yer can't play any toons on th' dash thing— on'y make a beggarin' noise!" Andy told him. "What's th' good o' that?"

Limpy reckoned he could "blay lods o' doons".

"Well, play us a step dance," Andy asked, grinning.

Limpy put the stick to his mouth again, and set up a series of screeches.

Andy, grinning more, mounted the table and commenced stepping to them.

Martha and Tom sat back and laughed.

Dora came to the back door; then ran back to the kitchen.

"Quicker," Andy shouted. Limpy blew himself red in the face.

Mother bounced in with the broom in her hands.

"Upon my soul!" she cried—and jabbing Limpy in the neck and in the stomach with the butt-end of it, propelled him through the door on to the broad of his back and stopped the music. Then she made a stroke at Andy's shins; but Andy jumped for the door, and trampled over Limpy in his haste to escape. Baffled by Andy. Mother raised the broom to take the full worth out of Limpy while he was down. The broom descended just as Father inserted his bald head through the door to see what was taking place. You'd have thought Father was a pithed bullock the way he dropped on his knees.

"And on Sunday morning, too." Mother foamed, throwing down the broom and violently bundling the furniture into position again. "Th' cheek o' them! No more respect for the Sabbath than a lot of barbarians! Now, look here!" She lifted the broom and went to the door again. But observing the arrival of a visitor she checked her temper, and withdrew to the kitchen, where, with Aunt Sue and Dora, she began laughing.

"Hello, Villiam!" Andy shouted joyfully and cheekily. "How you vas?"

"Good morning, Mr. Brandt," from Father. Father was always polite to the neighbours.

Villiam Brandt, wearing a spanking new shirt and tweed trousers wrinkled all over like a concertina, and carrying a square case by a leather handle, grinned and nodded his shaggy head in friendly greeting.

"You don't nod vork to-dah, mine friend. I dink so—huh?" he said, addressing Father.

"Not to-day; not on Sunday, Mr. Brandt," Father answered; and rising, offered him his patent easy chair.

"Oh, py goodness saake, nod at all," Villiam protested, putting the square case down beside the verandah post, and waving the chair away with both hands. "I vos not lazyie like dot. Sit on him youselluf, my poy," and playfully taking Father by the shoulders shoved him back into the patent.

The rest of us laughed. Villiam laughed with us, and patted Father on the head as he would a boy.

Limpy blew a blast from the split stick.

"Oh, I zee," Villiam said, jumping round and eyeing him curiously. "You makes museek mid youselluf—eh? Py shingo!"

Limpy, encouraged, blew some more.

Villiam shielded his ears with the palms of his hands, and made ugly faces.

The broom descended just as Father inserted his bald head through the door.

"You make people granky mid dot squealin' ding!" he said. "In Denmark, my poy, dey put you by youselluf in der mad place. You see, now? Yust you keep kviet mit dot rubbeedge und I show you soomdings."

"Take it away, can't yer! Go on!" and snatching the "music" from Limpy, Andy threw it almost as far as the sliprails.

"And how long is it since you left Denmark, Mr. Brandt?" Father inquired, settling himself for a yarn.

"Too long aldergedder, mine friend," Villiam answered. "I wish me all der vile somedimes dot I was baack dere already yet."

Mother, with a broad smile, appeared at the door, and said: "Good morning, Mr. Brandt."

Villiam snatched his hat off, and placing it under his left arm, curtsied extravagantly.

"Mine great greatness," he said, striking an astonished attitude, "you get most mighty fat efery day, Meesis Perrigrewd."

"Surely not?" and laughing, Mother placed her hands on her hips, and attempted to draw herself in.

"Oh, dot vos no good—no good ad all, mine goot voman!" Villiam cried, "you could squeeze youselluf oop der hollow log, und nod make soom deeference. Huh? You see now?"

"Oh, go along with you, Mr. Brandt," Mother said, stepping on to the verandah to make room for Aunt Sue and Dora, who came pushing behind her.

Both the latter smilingly bid Villiam good morning.

"Oh, py gracious saake!" Villiam gasped, placing his hat under his right arm and bowing and scraping all about the verandah. "Dem vas der laties!"

"It's a nice morning, Mr. Brandt," Aunt Sue said, blushing and smiling.

Dora thrust her head forward, and said:

"I saw you in the paddock yesterday, Mr. Brandt, but you wouldn't speak to me."

Villiam looked alarmed. He cocked his head to one side and thought hard. But his memory failed to assist him.

"You see me, you dink?" he said.

Dora nodded her head in the affirmative.

"Mighty saake!" and Villiam took himself by the ears. "I "I vos nod, you dink, behind some more dress? Eh? Noh? Huh? my laty?"

All of us, including Mother, burst out laughing.

"Oh, no! Oh, no!" Dora hastily assured him, "you were just walking alonk—just walking along, Mr. Brandt."

Villiam's eyes filled with joy and gratitude. He remembered that he had been in swimming that day.

"I am bleased," he said. "Oh, py great mighty greatness, I em bleased for dot."

Then turning to the square case, which Tom was turning upside down to see if anything was under it, placed it on his knee and brought forth an accordion.

Had he brought forth Noah's Ark with a brass band and a banquet on board we couldn't have been more surprised or delighted. Mother stared; Dora shoved Aunt Sue through the doorway, and came on to the verandah herself; Father sat up in his easy chair and smiled; Limpy put away the split stick, which he had secured again, and stood gaping, open-mouthed.

The rest of us crowded close to Villiam and endeavoured to touch the instrument with out finger-tips, while we watched him fixing his hands in the straps.

"I dole you, my boy, dot I shows you soomdings drekeley—you see now!" he said to Limpy.

Limpy was dumbfounded.

Seating himself comfortably on the ground Villiam wagged his head cheerfully and started playing.

Talk about joy! We were in Paradise. No man ever rose quicker or higher in a flying machine than Villiam rose in our estimation. We younger ones couldn't squeeze close enough to him. He had to motion and elbow us away to provide working room for his arms.

Villiam changed the tune.

"A waltz," Dora cried, excitedly. "A waltz!" and seizing Aunt Sue by the waist, forcibly twirled her along the verandah.

Villiam smiled and nodded in approval.

"Stop it, Dora! Stop it!" Aunt Sue cried "Don't you know it's Sunday?"

"Dot was rightd," Villiam shouted above the strain of the music to Dora. "Go id!"

Dora "went it," and dragged Aunt Sue with her.

Then Martha, becoming suddenly inspired, began careering over the grass on her own account. Tom up and followed her example. Andy gripped Limpy in catch-as-catch-can style, and joined in the fun as though it were a three-legged race.

"Stop it, children!" Mother called out. "Stop it. If it was any other day it wouldn't matter."

But the tone of Mother's voice was not convincing, and the smile on her face only encouraged the dancers. It also encouraged Father. Rising steadily in his chair, like a dish of dough, he finally came to his feet, with his cheeks bulged and his sides heaving with premeditation. Then suddenly thumping the earth with his big foot, opened his arms and shouted: "Come on!" to Mother. Mother came on; and into the thick of it they trundled furiously. Dora, releasing Aunt Sue, pointed to Father and Mother, and screamed till she dropped. But Father and Mother went on with the dance. They went on with it till the music suddenly stopped, and Villiam stood up and bowed

Into the thick of the dance Mother and Father trundled furiously

to them. Then Mother gasped out that she "never thought sho could be such an old fool," and ran inside and started setting the table for dinner.

After dinner.

Father and Villiam, with Martha and Tom slinking at their heels, strolled over the yard, talking about shelling corn and growing potatoes.

Mrs. Holstein and her daughter, Amelia Mary, a big, fat girl with a baby face and a thin, useless voice came walking along the cultivation paddock fence, holding their dresses above their knees to escape the grass seed.

Aunt Sue and Dora, calling out "You've come at last," ran to meet them.

"Dot vas a shplendeed voman, mine friend. Oh, py gracious! I can't dink me of her soomedimes!" Villiam said, bursting into raptures over Aunt Sue.

"What, my sister?" from Father, with a smile.

"Look you here at me," and Villiam waved his hands and grimaced tenderly at Father. "I gif mine blace: I gif everydings I hef no for myselluf to be der same like you, mine friend!"

"To be her brother?" And Father looked surprised.

"Nod egsagtly qvite dot, my friend—but vad you call id?" And Villiam shook his head in search of the right word.

"You mean her *husband?*" And Father smiled.

"My poy"—and Villiam patted him affectionately upon the back—"now you shpeakd id—her hoosban'."

"Go and ask her," Father said into his ear; "she might have you." There was a lot of humour in Father sometimes, though few people ever suspected it.

"You dink dot so, huh? eh? Oh-h, great greatness, mine friend." And Villiam heaved a succession of sighs at Father, and patted him on the back again.

Just here, Martha, who had been all eyes and ears, darted for the house, where Mother and Aunt Sue and Dora were endeavouring to entertain their visitors.

"Mother! Mother! Mother!" she shouted, bursting in upon them, "Villiam Brandt's going to be Aunt Sue's husband. He just told Father; and Father said he could!"

Mother of Mercy! Had a bull or a bomb-shell burst into the room more commotion could not have been made. Mrs. Holstein and Mary Amelia suddenly screamed and gesticulated at each other.

"You silly girl!" Aunt Sue gasped at Martha, "Go—go out of this! G-g-go outside." Dora rocked about on the sofa with merriment. Mother jumped to her feet and asked Mrs. Holstein "what was the matter?" "What was up?" Mrs. Holstein, striking an unfriendly attitude, turned the English language inside out in frantic efforts to inform Mother that Villiam Brandt "vas Amelia Mary's young shap," and that "Amelia Mary she lof him". And Amelia Mary, with tears trickling down her fat chubby cheeks, nodded endorsement.

"Well, I'm sure I don't want him," Aunt Sue said, forcing a smile.

"You a gruel ding!" Amelia Mary squeaked at her, "Vy nod you get one for youselluf?"

Martha dashed out again, and, breaking in upon Father and Villiam, yelled: "Mrs. Holstein's in a awful frightful scot about it, and sez Mr. Brandt is to be Amelia Mary's husband; and Amelia Mary sez it too; and they're all fightin' like anythink about him."

Villiam jumped right off his feet, and made use of several bad languages.

"I talk mid dem beople, py——! ——! ——!" he cried, and ran towards the house.

"Heigh! Heigh! Man!" Father called, running after him. *"Brandt!* VILLIAM!*"* But Villiam wasn't to be deterred in love matters. Into the presence of the enemy he bowled, and confronting Mrs. Holstein across the table, addressed her wildly in Danish. Mrs. Holstein gesticulated and shouted back at him. And Amelia Mary in a broken-hearted way approached him tenderly, and would have put her arms around his neck. But Villiam wanted none of her. He ducked from her embrace, and declaring himself in Danish, pointed meaningly to Aunt Sue. Aunt Sue went pale and gurgled: "Don't! don't! don't drag me into it!" Villiam placing a hand over his heart, indicated her again with his trembling finger. And Aunt Sue cried: "My heavens! what is the man saying?" Amelia Mary explained. She screamed, and spat at Aunt Sue, and tried to scratch her. Mrs. Holstein spat across the table at Villiam. Then Villiam spat back again at Mrs. Holstein, and throwing a kiss to Aunt Sue with his hand, turned on his heels and fled without the accordion.

Mrs. Holstein and Amelia Mary rushed out in pursuit of him. They pursued him noisily to the foot of the cultivation paddock, where they abandoned the chase, and slowly directed their steps homeward.

"Did you ever in all your born days!" gasped Aunt Sue, pale and terrified looking.

"No never! never! never!" Mother answered with anger and excitement.

But Dora wasn't at all perturbed.

"My word, you did keep it quiet, Aunt," she said with a titter.

"Shut up! Shut up! Shut up!" Aunt Sue squealed, and ran to her room.

7. *She Wouldn't Take Them*

"We've finished borin' all th' posts," Andy cheerfully announced as Father and Limpy and he, flushed with heat and perspiration, came in for dinner. "Want th' wire now, then th' two cultivation paddicks 'll be fenced all round, an' nothin' in th' world 'll ever get in."

"An' a tough job id was, doo, wid dem jolly rusty o'd augers," Limpy stammered, taking a dish of water and sluicing himself extravagantly near the back door.

"I don't know where the wire is to come from, then, I'm sure!" Mother said despondently. Mother, during the morning, had received the account from the store, and for hours did nothing but mope about thinking, thinking and thinking over it.

"Where does everything come from?" Andy answered carelessly.

"Yes, where does everything come from!" gloomily from Mother—"where!"

"From the store, I 'spect." And Andy scrutinised the dinner-table with hunger and disappointment in his eye.

"Then no more will come from the store," flashed from Mother—"not until we've paid for what has already been got, and every penny of it." And, worried-looking, she paced up and down the room, while the rest of us fixed our eyes on the floor and watched the wretched flies swarming over it, and felt miserable.

"Eighteen pounds, and not a fraction in the place to pay it with!" Mother murmured at intervals. "And the woman wants the money perhaps more than anyone!" Mother alluded to the storekeeper, a big, kind-hearted widow, struggling hard to support a large family with her modest little store.

"If der jolly whead had come ub," Limpy observed, combing his hair with the palm of his hand, "dat lot could hab been wibed oud quick an' libely."

"If *you* had come up!" Mother snapped, pausing and glaring angrily at him. Then to Dora, and in a sad, calm voice:

"Give them their dinner, girl—if there is any to give!" And, turning away, she went out to the commodious bark kitchen, and sitting on a hardwood stool, leaned her elbow on the corner of the table, and there thought more and more, and more.

"There isn't much for you to-day," Dora murmured apologetically, as we tumbled into our places around the scanty board.

Father gazed hard at the little there was, and said nothing. Limpy gazed at it, too, and said the same.

"No *meat?*" Andy asked, lifting his eyes to Dora.

Dora shook her head gloomily, and taking up the tea-pot, begun pouring out the tea.

"The Edens owe us some, don't they?" Father inquired thoughtfully.

"They owe us a roast," Dora answered, "but I s'pose they haven't it to spare yet. Mrs. Eden said last week that the boys were looking everywhere for a steer they were going to kill, but couldn't find it."

"That one-eyed one with the white flank?" Andy inquired. "He's runnin' at th' back o' our paddick—has been fer munce."

"Has he?" eagerly from Father. "Well, you go over an' tell them about him Andy—go as soon as you finish your dinner."

"Well, that won't be long, I don't think," and a grim, sickly grin passed over the face of Andy.

"Not unless you're very fond of spinage," Dora said, chuckling in spite of herself.

"Ah, well!" Father remarked, with an attempt at cheerfulness, as he spread himself over an enormous dish of spinage, as green as grass, and proceeded to divide it up, "it won't hurt any of us for once, at all events".

"Well, no, not if it's *only* for once." And Dora spoke as though she had doubts about the matter; then chuckled again, and passed round the tea.

"Things will soon be different—soon be different." And Father commenced on the spinage with an air of confidence and appreciation. Father was fortunate in that he could adjust his appetite to any kind of diet.

Andy wasn't eager to commence on the green stuff, though. And took some on his fork and smelled it. Then he asked Dora what the deuce it was, and where it was grown.

"Why, the spinage that grows about the yard, of course," Dora moving to the fireplace more to hide a smile than to replenish the teapot with hot water, informed him.

'*Spinage!* round about the yard?" Andy echoed. "Do y' mean those *weeds* out there?"

"Weeds, no; not at all. *Spinage* is the right name for it," and Father filled his mouth with a supply of the vegetable, and made a great noise eating it.

"It's nod der worst tack in der world, eider," Limpy said, following Father's example.

Andy tasted the green stuff cautiously.

"Yous can have it!" he said, pulling an ugly face. Then shoving his plate from him, he commenced on bread and salt, without further complaint. When there was no butter or cream, or dripping, or sugar to eat with our bread, Mother always insisted on us taking salt.

Aunt Sue sat down and comforted Mother

Tom, though, was hardest to appease. Tom started murmuring like an Israelite. He seemed to think the slump in provisions was due to mismanagement on the part of the home. But Tom, grown older, knows better now. Tom has a homestead of his own now—snug, prosperous little homestead—and a family growing up around him. And often by the fireside on a winter's evening, he sits and talks of the bitter hard times the old people went through, and his eyes fill with tears as recollection after recollection rises up and floods his memory, and the hearts of his offspring beat with pride and pity for the poor, brave old grandfather and grandmother, whose honest, care-worn, withered faces, treasured in frames of oak upon the wall, they have long since learned to love and reverence.

And, somehow, Aunt Sue didn't sit to dinner that day. She hung about outside. And when we all rose and left the table she went to the kitchen, and sitting beside Mother, talked to her in a kindly womanly way. Though Aunt Sue was often stiff, and touchy, and sensitive, and suspicious, yet never breathed a soul more unselfish or sympathetic when anguish and misfortune entered the home.

"What's the use of worrying any more, Alice?" she said softly. "You know I have some cows and calves left yet—there are six altogether—doing nothing but eating grass. Why not let Mrs. Brayton have them, and settle the account?"

"No! no!" Mother cried. "*No! no! no!* It wouldn't be fair to you, Sue; it wouldn't be fair at all."

But Aunt Sue persisted. She claimed some of the debt as hers, too; and said that when things improved, and there was a good crop, Father could give her other cows in place of them.

"If one could only be sure that they will improve!" Mother sighed, "it wouldn't matter. But think of what will happen if they don't! Think of you being without a beast or stick to your name!" And large, hot tears dropped from her eyes and formed into a miniature pool on the rough table.

"Well, if things get worse, Alice, *let* them get worse!" Aunt Sue said, with defiance in her eye. "And a pinch won't hurt me any more than it will hurt you—perhaps not as much."

Eventually Mother gave in, and accepted Aunt Sue's offer. Then she pulled herself together, and, after explaining matters to Dora, told her to catch old Cobby and run the cattle down to Mrs. Brayton.

And what a hard half-hour Dora put in on old Cobby before she induced those cows and calves—strong, rowdy bull calves they were—to leave the homestead! Cobby was a sterling horse, too, a stock-horse in a thousand. Where or how Father came by him I don't know; and Dora could ride him like an angel. "Dear me! dear me! that girl will kill herself!" Mother kept exclaiming, as Dora, in a wretched make-shift of a saddle, the girth tied with scraps of kangaroo hide, dashed and wheeled amongst the ironbarks, and followed the black cow across Father's two-rail fence more than once. But when she got the animals bunched together on the track leading to the main road they steadied down and trotted off without further trouble.

The sun had gone down, and night was closing in over the great, solemn, silent bushland when Dora was seen returning. And, what seemed strange, she was bringing the cattle home again.

Mother and Aunt Sue, surprised looking, went to the slip-rails to meet her. Neither of them spoke. Both stood waiting for Dora to explain.

"She wouldn't take them," Dora cried, sliding off Cobby, with a parcel under one arm. "Do you know what Mrs. Brayton said, Mother?"

Mother didn't. Mother looked into Dora's laughing face, and trembled.

"She told me to tell my mother that she would sooner tramp the roads and beg for bread than take her few head of cattle. And I was also to tell you," Dora rattled on, "that you weren't to worry about anything, but to send down and get just whatever you wanted and pay for them when there was a crop."

Then, holding up the parcel containing a tin of jam and two tins of fish: "And Mrs. Brayton gave me this to give you for yourself."

Mother's breathing could have been heard chains away. She took the parcel from Dora, and after holding it in her hands for several moments in silence, burst into a choking sob.

But Dora and Aunt Sue understood.

Thinking of Mrs. Brayton, the latter said: "A woman in a hundred!"

"A woman in a hundred?" repeated Dora, leading Cobby away to unsaddle him—"a woman in a million!"

At supper Mother was bright and cheerful again. She talked hopefully of the future to Father and Aunt Sue, and assured the rest of us that if we made up our minds and worked willingly and well, and had a little patience for a while longer, there would sure to be a crop, and we would all get new boots and new clothes after the harvest.

And when Dora, beaming with smiles, placed the jam, and the fish upon the table we thought the harvest had already begun.

8. We Start Dairying

Aunt Sue, returning from a visit to the Dorsetts one afternoon, hurried inside, and said excitedly to Mother:

"Do you know—they are making £8 a month over there out of butter that they send to town, Alice?"

Mother didn't know.

"All I know," she said, "is that *we* are not, anyway; and that we don't even make £8 out of the corn or out of the potatoes."

"Well, it surprised me, Alice, when they told me," Aunt Sue continued, "I wouldn't have believed a word of it only Mrs. Dorsett told me herself, and *showed* me. And out of THEIR few cows they're making it, too! Why, we've twice as many, and better ones. I've more than they have myself."

"Yes, maybe you have," thoughtfully and indifferently from Mother.

"Well, why shouldn't we make butter, and send it to town, too?" inquired Aunt Sue, earnestly.

"I'm sure I don't know," answered Mother.

"And I don't know, either, unless it is because we are a lot of fools," and Aunt Sue removed her hat and placed it on the table.

"Where would you send it if you made it?" Mother asked, brightening a little.

"To the place they send theirs—to Push and Push. And they want a lot more than Mrs. Dorsett is sending them, so they said in a letter she showed me. And they're giving half a crown a pound for it. But she makes lovely butter, Alice. Oh, it's simply beautiful!" Aunt Sue sat down, and clasping her hands and opening her eyes wide, rolled them about in admiration of Mrs. Dorsett.

"I can make butter, too, for that matter"—Mother said, the spirit of rivalry starting to assert itself—"make just as good butter as she can, and perhaps better if I tried."

"But you never saw richer butter in all your life, Alice," the other insisted. And the color of it—dear me, the *color* of it—it's as yaller—as yaller—as—as"——

"Oh, the color's nothing! Why, I made the *best* of butter before I was ten years old," Mother interrupted; and "more than ever she made, I'm sure of that."

"Then why can't we get all the cows in and make it now?" cried Aunt Sue, "and do the milking, and everything ourselves, and let the men go on with the farming?"

"Yes, and I'll do the stockriding"—Dora, entering the room with the frying pan in her hand, chimed in.

"Dora will do all the stockriding," repeated Aunt Sue with increased enthusiasm. "And I'll be the milkmaid."

"Mein sweet leettle meelk-maidens, I lof you," and Dora started singing in the voice of William Brandt; then burst out laughing.

The blood suddenly rushed to Aunt Sue's cheeks.

"Just when a person is trying to do the best for everyone you insult them," she sobbed; and snatching up her hat, rushed off in a temper to her room.

"What on earth do you mean?" And Mother flew into a passion with Dora. "Why do you come in here just to say things to annoy your aunt?"

"I don't say things just to annoy her," answered Dora.

"Heaven and mercy! Haven't I got ears?" in a loud voice from Mother.

"I suppose you have," quietly from Dora.

"You *suppose* I have! Don't you *know* I have?" And Mother approached Dora menacingly.

"Yes, I know you have," Dora admitted, coloring and edging away; "but what harm is there in singing William Brandt's silly old song to her; and why should it hurt her?"

"Don't you know it does hurt her?" demanded Mother. "Don't you?" and she ground her teeth and drew closer to Dora.

"I suppose it does!" sullenly from Dora.

"You SUPPOSE it does? Don't you *see* it does?" yelled Mother.

"Oh, she pretends it does!" And Dora turned to the fireplace.

"Then you stop it! I'm not going to have it; do you hear that?"

Dora made faces at the frying-pan, and Mother, receiving no answer swung on her heels and went off to make peace with Aunt Sue.

Martha, carrying things in Tom's hat, entered the room. Tom, with his hair in his eyes and a grin on his face, slunk at her heels.

"What are y' larfin' to yerself fer?" Martha asked of Dora.

Dora turned quickly from the fireplace and surveyed her sister.

"Mother'll give you laughing, my lady," she said, "when she she sees how you've torn all your dress getting up trees after bears."

"Well, it *wasn't*, then; so you're out of it," Martha replied. "It was after young parrots, and we got them, too—see!"

"Three o' them," Tom put in, his eyes beaming with joy. "Show them t' 'er!"

"There y' are, if y' don't like t' believe it"—and opening Tom's hat Martha exposed three wretched, miserable naked birds to view. Their heads were larger than their bodies, and scraps of shell were clinging to them.

Dora peeped into the hat, and gasped: "Oh, you'll get it! You'll get it when Mother comes; taking those poor, harmless little birds away from their mother before they have even a feather on, just to let them die of cold and hunger, for you'll never feed them. How would both of you like it if you had been taken away from your mother without a stitch of anything on when you were just babies, I'd like to know?"

Martha shrugged her shoulders, and gazed triumphantly into the hat.

"Well, then, I *was*," Tom answered proudly. "Didn't old Dolly Banks find me in a hollow log without anythin' on, and fetch me ten mile when it was a cold night?"

"And it's a pity she didn't leave you in the log," Dora snapped at him.

Then to Martha:

"Go and put those poor little birds back with their mothers at once, or look out when Mother comes."

"If they won't live then, why can't we eat them?" Tom suggested.

"Ugh! you young savage!" and Dora scowled.

"Well, I bet Father'd eat them," and Tom shook his head stubbornly.

Just then Mother was heard coming from Aunt Sue's quarters.

Martha hurried out the back door, and in her haste spilt two of the birds on the floor. Tom picked them up by the legs and ran after her.

When we sat to supper that night, Mother was in a high state of amiability. She spoke cheerfully of milking the cows and sending butter to Push and Push.

"The girls and myself," she said, "are going to start dairying. Other people are making money that way, and why shouldn't we?"

Aunt Sue nodded approval, then gazed round the table to see how the announcement was taken.

Andy laughed and said:

"Yous milk cows? Milk kangaroos, you mean!"

Martha and Tom enjoyed Andy, and kicked each other under the table.

"Yes, kangaroos, more like," Andy repeated, a smile spreading all over his round, fat face, which, from the rubbing he had given it with the towel, was shining like the moon.

"No, *not* kangaroos," Mother stated firmly, "but our own cows."

"It's easy enub milkin' der jolly cows," Limpy, straining with a mouthful of pumpkin, observed; "it's gettin' rid ob der beggarin' butter dat'll be d' trouble."

"There'll be no trouble while you're here," Mother said, without lifting her eyes from her plate.

We laughed; and when the mirth subsided Aunt Sue asked Father for his opinion on the dairying idea.

"Well," Father answered thoughtfully, "I've been thinkin' about it. And I dare say that money can be made that way as well as any other."

Father was a wise man.

"What other way can it be made?" Mother, looking Father straight in the eyes, asked.

"Oh, plenty other ways—plenty other ways," Father answered. "But, certainly, certainly, by all means," he added, "try th' cows an' see what y' can do".

"Whether it's the right way or the wrong way," said Mother —"whether there's money in it or whether there isn't, it's decided. And to-morrow," rising and thumping the table like a man—"to-morrow we commence dairying."

Next morning. Dora mounted on old Cobby went off to rake the bush for cows in profit. She returned late in the evening with seven of them tearing along in front of her, and only a fragment of her riding skirt hanging to her. The rest of it she left clinging to the up-turned roots of a fallen tree way back on the edge of the big scrub.

All of us rushed out, when we heard the stockwhip crack, and frightened the cows. At sight of us they turned and stampeded. And as Dora laid the whip on Cobby and raced abreast of the black cow, as wild as a wallaby, we heard her swear several times.

"As much sense as a lot o' blessed mad people!" she shouted through the dusk.

Andy guffawed. And Father cried, "Stand in behind the trees—in behind the trees, and the cattle won't see you."

Father was a good hand at yarding cattle.

All of us ran to trees and hid ourselves. And when Dora, slashing the stockwhip, and wheeling and propping and crying with temper, worked the cattle back to the yard, every iron-bark and gum in the vicinity of the rails concealed a human being.

The animals didn't rush the yard. They became suspicious and stared nervously on every side.

"Don't move! Don't move!" Father called out to the rest of us, and the cattle gave a jump and stared harder at the sound of his voice. Dora, with tears and venom in her voice, urged them hard in the rear, at intervals yelling: "Fools! Senseless goats!" to us and asking why we "didn't stay inside, where we should always be!"

An old red cow, with one teat as large as a black pudding, detected Aunt Sue's skirt fluttering round the foot of an iron-bark, and approached it cautiously. Aunt Sue glanced round, and finding the old red cow had discovered her, rushed out, screaming, into the open. Talk about cattle seeing ghosts! Those cattle saw eight ghosts in quick succession! All of us suddenly left cover and waved our arms. And no matter in what direction they rushed they were confronted with an apparition. The yard was the only avenue of escape open to them, and into it they bounded with their tails in the air. Father ran to secure the rails, and the rest of us, armed with sticks, posted ourselves at the various panels.

"It's a wonder to me y' didn't have the rails up all the time!" Dora snarled, tossing her hair back and sliding off Cobby.

All of us left cover and waved our arms

"They'd have gone in just the same," Father assured her with enthusiasm. "They'd have broken 'em down to get in, they would."

Then we started to pen up the calves—at least Dora did. She went into the yard and flogged them right and left with the whip. We remained on guard, outside of the yard, and hit at every head that showed itself between the rails or under them. Excited! We were excited. So were the cows.

"Only one more to go in, Dora," Mother in a pleased voice called through the rails.

"Merry Mag it is," Dora answered, dropping the whip on to a white bull calf. The calf careered frantically round the arena, then charged at the panel that Tom was protecting. "Look out, Tom! Look out!" All of us shouted. Tom swung his stick and kicked with both feet. But the calf forged its way under the rails and bolted off with Tom hanging to its tail. Rover, a useless, senseless canine, joined in the fun. He grabbed the calf in the rear, and made it bellow and go faster, and Tom lost his hold, and his feet. The calf butted into Father's new wire fence, and rebounded several lengths. It struggled to its feet, and butted the fence again, and got caught in it by every leg. Father deserted the rails of the yard, and ran to save his fence from the calf. Merry Mag attacked the rails in Father's absence, and carried most of them away on her back. She charged wildly in pursuit of her offspring, and arrived just when Father and Tom succeeded in freeing some of its legs. They hadn't time to free all of them. They fled in two directions. Merry Mag selected Father. Father yelled, and waved his hands and zig-zagged. It was wonderful, the ground Father covered before she caught him! And it was wonderful, too, the ground he covered when she did catch him! And if he had been a second later rolling under the fence, Andy reckoned, Merry Mag would have eaten him.

After a lot more excitement we secured the calf and dragged him by the neck and the tail to the pen.

"Now, over with the wretch!" Andy said.

Over we threw him, and when he landed amongst the others they burst the side of the pen down and escaped—every one of them.

"Oh, let them go to-night." Mother said in disgust. We let them go.

The calf bolted with Tom hanging to its tail

9. The First Consignment

Talk about butter! We *had* butter! Never before had we seen so much in one lot. And never before did we get less of it to eat. You would think it was gold or diamonds we were devouring, Mother was so sparing and jealous of it!

"We are not making it for you to gorge yourselves on, remember that," she would say. "If it's to be sold it's to *be* sold, and that's all about it."

And how she and Aunt Sue persevered in the preparation of it! What pains and trouble they took washing, tittivating and tattooing it! The night before the first consignment was to go to Push and Push we thought they would never go to bed. They sat up working at it and admiring it, and building castles in the air on the hopes of it till long after everyone else had retired and fallen asleep. In the middle of the night Martha and Tom woke up, and hearing voices in the kitchen stole silently out to reconnoitre. Mother and Aunt Sue, satisfied with the result of their labors, were enjoying a cup of tea and sampling the butter with hot bread they had just lifted from the oven.

"Y'ah!" Tom growled, rubbing his sleepy eyes against the sapling doorpost. "We found yous out!"

And Martha nodded:

"Thought yous wasn't goin' to eat any of it?"

"Just look at those two!" exclaimed Aunt Sue, "coming out here at this hour!"

Mother, in her haste to rebuke the intruders, nearly choked herself with butter and bread, and while she coughed and coughed, and Aunt Sue patted her on the back and laughed at her sudden distress, Martha and Tom went right in and began on the supper.

"Here!" Mother shouted, recovering her breath, "off with you! How dare you leave your warm beds and come out here without asking? Away with you!" And she waved her hands at them and coughed some more.

"Oh, let them be, Alice," Aunt Sue pleaded good-naturedly; "let them have some."

Mother relented.

"Well, go on then," in a softer tone; "take some and go back to your beds. But don't let the whole house know about it."

Martha and Tom took all they could lay hands on and cheerfully withdrew.

"Eh? What?" Andy said, sitting up in the dark and rubbing his eyes when Tom shook him, and breathed the breath of fresh butter and crumbs upon him. "Who? Where?"

"We's has been havin' a great feed," Tom chuckled into his ear. "Yous is all out of it."

Andy comprehended instantly.

"By cripes!" he cried, and knocked the fat lamp off the gin-case that stood beside the bed, as he jumped on to the floor.

Father heard the noise and called out: "What's th' matter?"

"Everythin'! By cripes!" Andy said, groping for the door. "Come on; get up, Father."

Then, grinning and sniffing like Rover, he glided into the kitchen.

"I thought I smelled somethin'," he said, grimacing pleasantly at the provender.

Mother stared in surprise at Aunt Sue; Aunt Sue stared at Mother; both stared together at Andy, then at the great dish of butter ready for the market.

"Oh, yous are pretty cunnin'," Andy said, drawing a seat into the table and making himself comfortable, "but y' can't beat a cove with a good scent."

"What—what's up? What's happened?" And Father, in his night gear, arrived at the door.

Aunt Sue burst out laughing.

"Did yer smell it, too, Father?" Andy asked, digging into the butter.

Father rolled his eyes about and grunted: "Oh-h, I thought there was a fire or somethin'!" and turned to go back to bed.

"So there is, Father," Andy chuckled, digging into the butter again.

"But it can't do any harm, th' kettle's sittin' on it.

"Come on, Abe," Aunt Sue called out. "Don't go away; have a cup o' tea now that you're out of bed."

Father didn't go away.

"Must be near mornin'?" he mumbled, taking a seat near Andy.

"Mornin'?" And Andy cut himself more bread; "it's breakfust time."

Aunt Sue poured out a cup of tea and handed it to Father.

"Well, you might have put your trousers on, man!" Mother said angrily.

"Oh, he's all right!" Aunt Sue said, forgivingly.

"All right!" Mother echoed with a sneer.

"It's a wonder you wouldn't have more sense!" And she scowled and curved her lip at Father.

" 'Tis a wonder yer wouldn't," Andy repeated, " 'cause a 'possum might get up under there and cling to yer back." And with his bare foot he took liberties with Father's nightshirt.

Father doubled himself up into a ball, and said:

"Never mind! Never mind! Never mind me," and began eating.

Mother rose and removed the consignment of butter.

"There, they can have that bit, Sue, if they want any more," she said, placing a spare slice on a saucer and shoving it into the centre of the table. "But no more of the other is going to be touched—not a scrap!"

Dora, with a blanket thrown round her, rushed in.

"Well, upon my soul!" Mother gasped.

"Yes, it is upon my soul!" Dora repeated, making straight for the eatables. "This is what you've been doin', is it?"

Limpy, without socks and his greenhide belt dangling behind him, came hopping along.

"Well, I declare!" And Mother started wrapping cloths hurriedly around the butter.

"Oh, he can't eat anythin'," Andy said, with his mouth full. "He ain't awake. He's one o' them whot-d'-y'-call-'ems, thet walks in their sleep."

"Goats!" Mother suggested.

The others laughed.

"Well, der goat was nearly walkin' too jolly lade for dis lot." And Limpy moved round the table as though it were a banquet.

Aunt Sue looked hard at Mother.

"Oh, let them make breakfast of it," Mother said, in a reckless sort of way, and removed the cloths from the butter.

Then, while Aunt Sue filled the teapot again and cut more bread, Andy took fresh liberties with Father's nightshirt.

"Have some manners, fellow! Have some manners!" Father growled, tugging at the bottom of the rag to make it cover his feet.

"Manners!" Andy guffawed. "Oh, I like that, Father! Tellin' a bloke t' have manners when yer ain't got any trousers on!"

Then Martha and Tom, looking as though they never had anything to eat in their lives, stole back again. And when the hot steaming tea was poured out we all squeezed round the table and began another meal. And though we often had better meals, and often had many worse ones, a merrier meal we never had at the Old Homestead.

10. Mrs. Dorihey Jumps to a Conclusion

"That blessed old yeast isn't a bit o' good!" Dora, sweeping out the front room, complained. "Th' flour has been set since yesterday morning, and hasn't shown any signs of rising yet."

"Keep th' dish well covered, and near the fire," Mother advised.

"Oh, it's been covered and at the fire all night long." And without any apparent reason Dora suddenly attacked Rover with the broom, and called him a mongrel, and abused the owners of him for keeping his likes about the place. We were all owners of him.

Rover, yelping, rushed out the front door, and was sauntering calmly in by the back once again, when Dora anticipating his cunning, met him there and assaulted him further. Rover snarled and retreated sullenly. Dora closed the back door and hastened to the front one. She met Rover again.

"*Damn* y'!" she exclaimed, throwing the broom at him.

"*Dora!*" Mother cried. "What on earth is that I hear you saying?"

"Well, th' wretch will come in th' house in spite of me!" answered Dora. "He's enough to make a saint swear."

"Don't let me hear you again, that's all," firmly from Mother.

"Very well, I won't let you next time, Mother," and Dora blushed and sniggered.

"What's that you say?" and Mother, with a determined step, came from her room.

"Oh, it was only a slip." And, putting down the broom, Dora inspected the dish of flour again. Then she tucked the flannel covering—a discarded old petticoat of Mother's—closely about it to keep it warm.

"We've just got enough bread to do the dinner," she said. "A damper would do for supper, I suppose? But if anyone comes this afternoon I don't know what on earth we'll do."

"Oh, there'll be nobody come," Mother said, confidently. "People don't come very often—unless," she added, after a silence, "you know of someone who is coming?"

Dora knew it was possible for Jerry Manning to come. Jerry frequently made brief visits when passing with cattle or horses. But Dora didn't say he might come on this occasion. Dora rarely said anything about Jerry in Mother's presence. And it was only when speaking of young George Dunn that Mother ever mentioned the name of Jerry to Dora. She mentioned his name to her now.

"That George Dunn," she said, thoughtfully, "is a decent young fellow, Dora! A young fellow, too, I should think that any girl would be proud to get for a husband. The only one in the family, isn't he? And he'll be well off some day, too."

Dora shrugged her shoulders and gave a light laugh.

"Oh, you can laugh," Mother snapped, getting into a temper. "You're just like all the rest of the girls of your age! The silly, empty lot of creatures that they are! But, believe me, my lady, if ever that scoury Jerry Manning, the cattle stealer that he be, comes here again, with his sly ways and his strapped trousers, I'll scald him with a kettleful of hot water!"

Dora hurriedly invented an excuse to run away to the kitchen.

About three o'clock that afternoon Mrs. Dorsett and her three grown-up daughters locked up their slab house by driving a peg in the door and crawling out through the window, and started off together to pay a visit to the Doriheys. At the same hour Mrs. Dorihey and old Mrs. Dorihey, her mother-in-law, locked up their home and went off to visit the Dorsetts.

The parties met half-way, at the back of our grass paddock. Talk about a surprise! and a disappointment! You could hear them expressing their feelings a mile away. Neither party could believe its eyes.

"Why, goodness, gracious me, if Mother and me wasn't just going across to your place!" young Mrs. Dorihey cried.

Old Mrs. Dorihey, energetically working her toothless gums and blinking her dim little eyes, said: "I declare to God that's the very truth!"

"Well, I never!" laugher Mrs. Dorsett; "and we were just going over to see yous."

And with that they all flopped down on the stony ground and laughed together. But there was nothing real or hearty in their mirth. It was strained and forced, and was followed by an awkward silence on both sides. The Doriheys, like ourselves that day, were right out of bread, and in their hearts were hoping and wishing that the Dorsetts would turn back and lead the way to their place. But the Dorsetts were also out of bread; they were also out of sugar, and had been out of it for three days. And rather than permit their friends to discover the fact were prepared to remain seated on those stones till next morning. Though the Dorsetts were poor, they possessed a wealth of pride.

"A Quaker's meeting," Jessie Dorsett remarked, with a sad effort to work up some more mirth.

Her mother said something about "the lovely view", while young Mrs. Dorihey became intensely interested in the blouse that Nora Dorsett was wearing. Finally, old Mrs. Dorihey came down with a brilliant idea. Like most mothers-in-law, she was as full of brilliant ideas as an oyster.

"Well, seein' we're all here, and don't know what to do," she said, "what if we all of us go and see Mrs. Pettigrew? We" (meaning the daughter-in-law and herself) "haven't seen any of them for munce."

The others all answered at the same time, and in loud, eager voices. There wasn't a dissenting one in the number; and next moment they were on their feet, hurrying and jostling each other as they stepped it out through the long, rank kangaroo grass in the direction of our homestead.

Dora and Aunt Sue, gazing meditatively through the window of the old kitchen, saw the crowd of laughing visitors approaching. Consternation! Had it been a tribe of war-like blacks, or an army of soldiers, or the Devil himself, they couldn't have been more surprised or excited or alarmed. Both of them rushed wildly into the house and danced a war-dance round Mother.

"Oh, great heavens!" And Mother, in her annoyance at the intelligence, almost shed tears.

"And every one of them dressed up to the very nines!" Aunt Sue cried, wringing her hands despairingly.

"And not a mouthful in th' place to offer them; not a blessed mouthful!" Dora moaned, flying uselessly from one corner of the room to another.

"Dear, oh dear, oh dear! Oh-h-h DAMN it!" distractedly from Mother. "And just look at the state I'm in! Just look at me!" And she clutched at her greasy, ragged workaday skirt as though the miserable raiment were to blame.

"It's awful! It's—it's—rotten to come at such a time!" And Dora ran and slammed the back door.

"Oh, for the mercy o' me!" Mother groaned, making a fresh discovery. "I haven't even a boot or a stocking on! Whatever are we going to do?"

Aunt Sue, with a long hopeless face, remained silent and motionless.

"You get into bed, Mother—into bed, Mother; into bed—into bed." And Dora threw herself excitedly upon Mother, and began hustling and forcing her towards the bedroom.

"Quick! quick! quick! Get in! Get in! and we'll cover you up, and tell them you're ill."

Mother resisted, and hissed: "Are y' mad; Are y' mad?"

Aunt Sue, suddenly seeing the sense of Dora's suggestion, cried:

"Yes, Alice; you get into bed, and they won't stay—they'll go." And she helped Dora to shove Mother into the room.

"For heaven's sake what does this mean? Are y' both cranky?" Mother kept hissing. She also kept working nearer to the bed.

At last she gave in, and was speedily covered over with the bedclothes.

"Try and look sick, Mother!" Dora enjoined, "and keep your head covered up as much as possible."

"And don't let your feet stick out—they're not very clean!" Aunt Sue advised.

Mother snatched her feet in quickly, and drew them up to the middle of the bed.

Then, with her head resting uneasily on the pillow and a

frown on her forehead, she looked a sour, bad tempered invalid.

"Now you go out and meet them, and tell them whatever you're going to tell them, and I'll sit here," Aunt Sue, taking her place beside the bed, whispered hoarsely to Dora.

Dora, hastily arming herself with a basin and the oil bottle, which contained only a few dead flies, and a spoon, and striving to look concerned about Mother's illness, sauntered out to the kitchen.

Mother's heart started thumping the bedclothes about. Mother felt she was committing a crime, and gave signs of rising and bursting up the conspiracy. Aunt Sue held up a finger warningly, and whispered: *"Sh-h-h. Still, Alice! They're here!"*

A clattering chorus of cheerful greetings was heard outside, to which Dora responded in a hushed and lying voice. A running fire of the tenderest expressions of sympathy then reached

Mother gave signs of bursting up the conspiracy

The Visitors gathered round the back door

Mother's ears through the cracks in the walls, and she groaned, and grimaced, and showed her teeth to Aunt Sue.

The latter became dreadfully anxious and uneasy. Motioning Mother to remain still, she rose, and tip-toeing her way to the back door so as not to disturb the quiet of the patient with unnecessary noise, said in a soft, tender voice:

"Dora, don't speak so loud, dear; she has just dozed off again."

Next instant, like a crowd of theatre-goers waiting for tickets, the visitors gathered round the back door, which Aunt Sue was careful only to partially open, and in subdued tones bombarded her with questions concerning Mother's illness.

Aunt Sue was an awkward, clumsy liar for a woman.

"And are you nursing her yourself, Miss Pettigrew?" old Mrs. Dorihey asked, blinking out of the hollows of her head at Aunt Sue.

Aunt Sue fidgeted, and nodded in the affirmative.

"And is it your first case?" the old dame further inquired.

And Aunt Sue nodded again, and clutched the door with both hands.

"Give her plenty of castor oil," old Mrs. Dorihey advised. "Two tablespoonful."

Aunt Sue started to cough.

Dora, in the kitchen, coughed, too.

"And how old is her youngest?" next inquired the old lady.

Aunt Sue looked dazed.

"Oh, dear me," Mrs. Dorsett whispered, "the youngest is quite a big boy now. He must be twelve or thirteen, I'm sure."

"Then she should think herself very fortunate," murmured old Mrs. Dorihey. And added: "Look at me"—gathering the simple thread-worn cape tightly about her aged shoulders—"look at me; I had sixteen of them—yes, sixteen—and there wasn't more than fifteen months between any of them, and only twelve and a half months between the last two, that's Jacob and William Henry."

Dora was seized with a violent fit of coughing over the kitchen fire.

I th-th-think I hear her . . . . good bye," and Aunt Sue, closing the door quietly, rushed back to Mother, and throwing herself across the bed hid her face in the blanket.

"Have they gone?" Mother inquired.

Aunt Sue shook and wriggled, but made no reply.

Mother, kicking her, repeated the question.

Dora stampeded into the room.

"They're gone!" she cried, flopping on the floor and scream-ing with merriment.

Aunt Sue lifted her head, and screamed louder than Dora.

Mother, with a black, angry look in her eye, sprang from the bed.

"Fool that I was; whatever will the people think!" she cried. "Never—*never* will I ever do such a thing again! Not if I have to say I'm starving, and offer them grass to eat!"

"Think?" yelled Aunt Sue, the tears running down her cheeks. "Only what they think now."

"What do they think now?" demanded Mother hotly.

"Old Mrs. Dorihey told me to give you—*oil*," screamed Aunt Sue—"and asked how old your—your YOUNGEST was?"

Mother stepped back and stared for quite a while.

"THE OLD WRETCH!" she said.

11. Going Into Figures

Mother herself took the butter to the railway siding; she took it in the old spring cart. And when a cheque for £3 15s, and a letter from Push and Push asking for more came to hand a few days later, she and Aunt Sue and Dora nearly went crazy with joy. The trio eagerly scanned the letter together, and before reading scarcely any of it threw up their hands and started jumping round the table. They shook hands with each other, too, and waved the cheque triumphantly at Father and Andy.

"Well, it shows y'—" Father said, eyeing the piece of paper with great gravity—"that there's plenty o' money to be made on th' place—plenty of it."

Father had a peculiar confidence in the Old Homestead.

"It's a wonder to me," Limpy said, "dat y' neber starded miltin' der jolly gows long enough ago."

"*What?*" and Mother scowled at him.

Aunt Sue with a smile advised Limpy to "shut up".

"My old peoble," Limpy rambled on, "milt gows der Sebenteen Mile long beford eber I could remember, an' done jolly well outer dem, too."

"*W-hat!*" and Mother scowled hard at him.

We laughed because we knew what a curious liar Limpy was.

"That was when th' nurst let y' go wallop off th' eighty-guinea pianer on to th' marble floor, an' lamed y', I s'pose?" drawled Andy, referring to an ancient lie of Limpy's.

Limpy wrinkled his brow, and thought hard.

"After dat a good whide," he answered.

We all laughed more—all except Mother. She stared at Limpy as though suspecting him of insanity.

"Four yeards after, if I can renember right," he added for Andy's information.

We laughed again, and this time Mother joined in the mirth. Then, taking his "music" from his pocket, Limpy started to entertain himself on the floor, and was forgotten.

Mother and Dora and Aunt Sue went into fresh raptures over the butter cheque. They rushed about, and searched the house high and low for a lead-pencil. And when Dora unearthed one barely an inch long, Aunt Sue, with a piece of paper before her, sat down and began working out the amount the cows would earn in a year.

She worked hard with the pencil for a long while.

"Surely not a *hundred* pounds?" Mother, all atremble with feelings of joy and fear, said when the result was announced.

Andy guffawed, and advised Aunt Sue to "do it again".

Aunt Sue wet the lead with her lips and started to check her arithmetic. And while she pondered her figures Mother and Dora stood restlessly by, clutching their fingers nervously and cracking every joint in them. They seemed to feel that the fate of the Empire depended on the accuracy of Aunt Sue's calculations.

At last Aunt reached the end. Mother and Dora almost reached their end. The suspense was telling on them.

"It's a few shillings *more,* if anything," cried Aunt Sue, with a tremour in her voice.

Mother gasped, and rattled her teeth. Dora clapped her hands and made a great fuss.

"A 'undred quid! Cripes!" Andy muttered solemnly.

"N-No! Sh-urely!" gasped Mother.

"A hundred pounds, three shillings, four pence, and five farthings," said Aunt Sue, positively.

Mother clutched at her heart to stop it from fluttering.

"Work it out for yourself, Alice," Aunt Sue said, "and you'll see that's what it is."

"Oh-h. I'm too excited!" Mother stammered. "Let me be—for—for—just a minute."

We let her be for several minutes.

"Now," she said, and began calculating on her fingers.

All of us watched her.

Presently she took her eyes off her fingers, and asked, thoughtfully:

"How much is 154 pence?"

"A hun-dred and fifty-four pence," Dora mumbled slowly, looking at Aunt Sue.

"A hundred and fifty-four pence." And Aunt Sue resorted to pencil and paper again.

"Ain't there no table-book in the house?" Father inquired of no one in particular.

Mother frowned and shook her head in signal to him to keep quiet.

Father played with his whiskers and kept quiet.

"A 'undred an' fifty pence was what old Stingy Diggler offered Tommy Moore for his piebald," Andy said, thinking hard, "and he paid him a half-sovereign. I see him get paid. And a half-sovereign bein' ten shillins, a 'undred an' fifty-*four* pence must be four more, mustn't it?——Four on to ten is fourteen. Fourteen bob."

"He's did it," Father said excitedly. "Andy's got it for y'. Fourteen shillings it be."

Andy's eyes started to glow with pride, and he asked Aunt Sue if "she was goin' to take all th' day to do *that* bit of a sum?"

"Well, it's not quite fourteen shillings," Aunt Sue said, looking up. "Thirteen shillings and eleven pence ha'-penny it is, Alice."

"Well, I wasn't far out o' it, anyway," Andy claimed. "A ha'-penny ain't much to blow about."

"How did y' do it?" Aunt Sue inquired of him.

"How did I do it? How d' y' think I do'd it?" And grinning, Andy tapped himself proudly on the forehead.

Mother continued her calculations. She manipulated her fingers as though talking to a deaf and dumb institution; then suddenly pausing, fixed her eyes intently on the cross beam where Dora's old one-horned saddle occupied a prominent position.

"Yer won't find it up there, Mother," Andy said. "If yer ain't got it 'ere," tapping himself on the forehead again, "ye're flummicksed."

The rest of us laughed, and made a great noise.

"There! bless it! You've made me lose it just when I had it!" Mother cried. Then snapping at Dora—"Keep quiet, can't you, for a minute. I've got to go right over it again, through your talking!"

She started over it again.

Dora began to titter.

"Quiet! quiet! Let her be!" Aunt Sue said, in Mother's interest.

"O' course, give 'er a charnce an' she'll do it orright," Andy said, grinning hopefully at Mother.

"Fifty and forty-one?" Mother asked, closing here left eye and nervously moving her fingers—"Fifty and forty-one—quick!"

"Fifty and *forty-one!*" Andy drawled in distressed tones. "Yer want a bloomin' schoolmaster for that!"

"Well, fifty and fifty," Dora said slowly, and doubtfully, "would be a hundred, wouldn't it?"

"A *what?*" Andy asked in surprise.

"A hundred," Dora repeated.

"Gerr out!" from Andy.

"Yes"—and Aunt Sue agreed with Dora.

"Well then," Dora continued, "subtract nine"—

"S'tract yer granny!" Andy broke in. "What's to s'tract? There's no s'traction about it—its addin' up."

"Well, ain't that what I want to do?" And Dora thought harder.

"An' what are y' talkin' about s'traction' for then?" Andy asked aggressively.

"Oh, shut up! You've put me out altogether now." And Dora abandoned the effort, and sat down on the sofa.

Mother, with one eye still on the rafters, kept moving her fingers as she waited for an answer.

"I've got it!" Aunt Sue cried, putting down the pencil; "a hundred and nineteen."

Father shook his head dismally and said he thought it "would be more'n than that".

"I'll swear it's a lot more, if y' mean it in 'orses or cattle," and Andy shook his head confidently.

Aunt Sue looked confused.

"But it doesn't matter what it's in, does it?" she murmured hesitatingly; "that can't make any difference, I don't think."

"Oh, can't it, but!" from Andy. "You're workin' it out in butter, ain't yer?"

Aunt Sue said she was; and her confusion increased.

"Well then"—Andy cleared his throat—"ain't there a different table to go by fer butter?"

Father nodded in agreement with Andy, and said: "Certainly!"

"Certainly!" Andy repeated with proud emphasis.

"Yes—but—but"—stammered Aunt Sue, frowning and puzzling and eating some of the pencil—"but we only want to know what fifty and forty-one *make*, ain't that all?"

"O' course! What else?" Andy concurred loudly. "Not what they *don't* make! We knows that a'ready."

"Well, how can it matter, then," Aunt Sue argued further, "whether it's in horses, or anything else? I can't see that it can."

"Oh, can't it, though! I can see how it can," Andy maintained. "It all derpends where Mother is got to in th' sum, don't it? An' whether she's fetchin' it into cows, or into pounds o' butter or what."

Addressing Mother:

"What are y' bringin' it into, Mother—into butter, or—er—"

"Into th' *devil!*" Mother shouted, and ran out of the room.

12. Breaking Up

Breaking up the twelve acres was the devil. It would have been as easy to break up a drought. We had only three draught horses to break up with and they were all broken up themselves. They were honest and willing enough though; and once they warmed up to their work and felt the collars, they never thought of "coming back". It took them a long time to warm up though. They had always to be warmed up. Andy mostly warmed them up. He held the reins and a stick, and drove the brutes. But Limpy helped him. Limpy carried a supply of stones, and dodged from one side to the other, and pelted them. Father's place was between the handles of the plough. That was the most important place. Father filled it well, too. He did good work between those handles. He shoved and grunted, and perspired, and called out "*Woh*" whenever he wanted a spell. He wanted a spell every twenty yards or so. "It's very heavy on them," he would gasp, dropping down on his haunches, "very heavy". Father was an unselfish, generous ploughman. He deserved a place in the book of martyrs. In an instant, though, he would rise and tackle the handles again.

They understood their work thoroughly, did those old horses. And in those days it was difficult to get horses to understand anything. There was nothing for them to understand. With our horses, though, it was a gift. I remember they had never seen corn until we grew some. And yet when Father merely rattled some of it in a nose-bag they knew all about it. They pursued him for it as greedily as though it had been a favourite dish with them all their lives. But more surprising still was their consideration for the plough. Their thoughts were on it the whole time it was behind them. Whenever it touched a root, no matter how small, or whenever it was likely to touch one, they would all three stop instantly, and stand at ease. And they *could* stand easy, those old horses! You'd think they had been trained in the army. Although there were numerous occasions when they didn't all pull together, there never was one when they didn't all stop together.

Once when the nose of the plough was right against a stiff root Andy called upon them to "get up". The quadrupeds got up several inches, then strained and groaned and grunted, and leaned heavily through their collars and blew holes in the dust with the breath of their nostrils. Andy, dancing and jumping up and down, jerked and tugged the reins, and yelled encouragingly to them to get up some more. Limpy threw stones and mud at them from the off-side, then hopped round and continued the attack from the rear. Father shoved and groaned, and broke up the earth with his toes; but the plough made no headway. Andy discarded the reins in disgust, and put all his energy into a bramble. He smashed a lot of it across the near-sider; some more of it across the middle brute; then he jumped over the plough, and got to work on the furrow horse.

"Up to it!" he shouted, "Stick to it. Now then!—*Now!"* and rushing back he rattled all that was left of the bramble on the fleshy part of Father. Father let go on the handles and wildly remonstrated with Andy.

"Dang it!" he cried, "d' y' think I'm one o' them?"

"I think you're better 'n any two o' them." And Andy, exhausted, dropped on the ploughed ground and laughed.

Limpy disapproved of Andy's methods.

"It's nod a jolly bit o' good," he said, "blayin' d' fool."

"No, it's not," Andy agreed, rising to his feet; "but it strikes me that's just what the lot of us is up t'!"

"No wonder! Not a bit o' wonder! No wonder at all they couldn't pull it," Father exclaimed, making a discovery, "why th' nose of her is against a root."

"I made sure dere musdt have been somethin' in d' way when d' little grey mare couldn't shift id," Limpy observed. Limpy had a peculiar affection for the little grey scarecrow.

"It's somethin' that'll *shift her,* y' mean!" Andy growled, "th' *cow!"* And he threw a lump of hard mud at the little grey, which struck Father on the back of the ear.

"Dang it!" Father roared, jumping round, and shaping up to Limpy, "what are y' doin'?"

Limpy jumped back, surprised, and becoming tangled in his own feet, fell down.

"Think because I don't take no notis that I'm to stand any dern nornsense?" Father shouted, standing over him with the plough scraper. "Do yer?"

Limpy shook and trembled, but made no answer.

"Don't think it no longer, then!" And Father lowered the scraper, and rubbing his neck turned the plough again.

Limpy sat up and glared at Andy.

"You're a jolly nice sord o' gentleman," he said, accusingly.

Andy grinned, and started whistling dance music through his teeth.

Father manipulated the plough so as to clear it of the root, then started the team again.

Jason Jerricks, one of our neighbours, came along nibbling the end of some kangaroo grass.

"Woh!" and Father stopped the team out of respect for Jason.

Jason looked the team over.

"They goes nice an' stiddy," he said. Father rubbed the sweat off himself with his hat, and looked proudly at the brutes.

"Oh, yes," he answered, "they're settlin' down well to it now, very well."

Andy sniggered, and squatting down on his heels, looked up from under his slouch hat at old Jerricks.

Limpy perched himself in front of Andy, and began playing his "music".

Jason looked at the plough then cast his eyes over the grass patch.

"You're gettin' over it," he said.

"Oh, yes; it don't take long when yer keeps to it constant," Father answered.

"Gettin' over more'n we're gettin' under," Andy observed, catching a fly and firing it, marble fashion, at Limpy.

"Yer don't wants to be under it yet a bit, do ye?" Jason said, failing to appreciate Andy's sarcasm. "All on us'll be there a good while soom day." Then the old fossil laughed, and Father laughed with him. Father had a rare regard for Jason Jerricks, and always enjoyed his society.

Andy caught a large horse fly, and aimed it at Limpy.

Limpy stood up, out of the line of fire, and finished the "piece" on his feet.

"Won't 'n take fright at that?" Jason, thinking of the horses and the music, asked gravely of Father.

"Oh, they're very quiet—very quiet," Father assured him. "The three o' them are."

"Nothin' only work frightens 'em." And lowering his head, Andy chuckled at the earth.

Father frowned at the crown of Andy's hat.

Jason, as though measuring the area of it with his eye, gazed over the grass patch again, and said, turning to Father:

"Could y' do that bit o' mine for me, when y' finish?"

"Oh yes," Father replied without thinking. "I dare say, certainly."

Father never had the heart to say "no" to anything. And if old Jerricks had asked him for his trousers, Father, without thinking, would have taken them off and given them to him.

"I wants to make a little this year soomhow or t'other," Jason explained, "and without I gets in a few taters I don't see how as where it's comin' from . . . . . . Not havin' no team of a man's own, it's awkid on a time like what is now."

"Quite so; quite so; I see," Father said, sympathetically.

"And when, think y', will yer finish this?" Jason asked.

"Well—see—," Father stared all round. "About a week, I've no doubt." And he appealed to Andy for confirmation.

Andy sprang to his feet, and shook the dirt off himself.

"What, with *these* mokes?" he said, pointing scornfully at the team.

"With *them*, o' course. What's wrong with them?" from Father.

"Well, we'll be lucky, I reckon, to finish it this side o' twenty years!" And Andy sat down again.

Father's mouth and eyes flew open like windows.

"Go away with y'," he mumbled, "talks some sense!"

Jason, ignoring Andy, suggested coming himself and giving a hand for a day or two to accelerate the work.

"Have yer a collar and chains to fit yer?" Andy asked of him with a grin.

"Dang it! Think y' I means to pull in th' plough, m'self?" Jason shouted wildly.

"It'd be no good comin' unlest y' did!" Andy shouted back at him. Andy wasn't afraid of old Jerricks. Andy wasn't afraid of anyone.

"Pshaw!" Jason growled. "Pshaw!"

"Anyway," Father said decisively, "we'll *do* it!"

Jason, who was a very religious man at times, grabbed Father by the hand and thanked him fervently.

"If I can't pay y', friend," he said, "then Some Body else will." And with his big, hard finger he pointed confidently and impressively to the great, glorious, blue sky above.

A fortnight later.

"Whatever on earth is up!" Dora, hearing Mother's voice raised heaven's high, in the yard, cried, and rushed out of the kitchen.

"*Alice! Alice!*" Aunt Sue called excitedly; and hurrying from the house arrived in the yard just in time to see Mother pull the harness off the team and assault Father with it.

"I declare to God!" she foamed, addressing the rest of us when Father had taken refuge behind the pig-sty, "if the man wasn't actually taking the horses away to do ploughing for other people. Actually taking them away and leaving his own ground standing there waiting to be done! Heavens above us! If he wasn't going off to help others before doing a hand's turn for himself—before earning a single shilling to keep the place and his family with!"

Dora and Aunt Sue, with their eyes fixed thoughtfully on their toes, silently retraced their steps to the house.

Father didn't go and break up for Jason Jerricks, though. And now old Jason tells everyone that Mother wears Father's pants.

Father had taken refuge behind the pig-sty

13. *Aunt Maria*

Tom one evening brought a letter from the post office for Aunt Sue; and when she opened it she rushed excitedly through the house, and round it, and down to the milking yard in search of Mother and Father and Dora. Martha and Tom joining in her excitement, ran beside her shouting: "What's it?" Tell us, Aunt. Tell us, quick!" But the contents of that letter were much too valuable to be wasted.

"Wherever have they gone?" And Aunt Sue stared in every direction.

"Tell us and we'll find them," Martha stipulated, eagerly.

But just then Mother and Father and Dora issued from the sorghum patch with bundles of it in their arms. Aunt Sue, waving the letter, shouted: *"Maria!* From Maria! She's coming Saturd'y!" And ran to them as fast as her legs could carry her.

"Maria!" Mother echoed, throwing down her bundle of sorghum.

"Aunt Maria?" and Dora let fall her burden.

"Be she?" And Father unloaded.

Aunt Sue proceeded to make a great fuss.

"She wonders if she'll know any of us?" she said; "but there's some words I can't make out. Such a long, nice letter it is—six pages. Read it out, Alice." And she handed the precious epistle to Mother.

Mother, smiling and flushing and trembling with excitement, wiped her hands on her old rag dress, and, taking the smudged screed proceeded to read laboriously. And as she spelt it out, Father, all eyes and attention, nodded and mumbled approval. Dora giggled and laughed, and at proper intervals Aunt Sue made complimentary references to her sister's startling composition. Martha and Tom, having grasped the introductory remarks, bounded off to enlighten Andy and Limpy, who were coming in from the paddock with the grubbing tools on their shoulders.

"Aunt Maria's comin'," they cried, "we's got a letter."

"Id she!" Limpy answered, brightening up and quickening his hop to top speed. Limpy had known Aunt Maria when she "wad ony a bid of a kid no higher dan hid little finger". But to Andy, as to the rest of us, she was a blank, except in name.

"Limpy's glad," Martha shouted, racing back again. "Look at 'im tryin' ter run!"

They all looked; also laughed.

Then, as they came nearer, Dora shouted the glad news to Andy.

"Go on!" Andy grunted. "Another Ant! There'll be a nest o' them here dreckly! Yer better put on plenty hot water."

Aunt Sue frowned and hung her bottom lip.

"Never mind him!" Mother advised, treating Andy with contempt. "Let's go inside and see about everything at once. And Dora, you'll have to bake some cakes to-night—there's enough dripping, I think; and to-morrow the house and everything will all have to be done out . . . . She don't say, I don't think, how long she's going to stay; but there's some of it I can't quite make out."

"I expect a couple o' weeks, surely?" Aunt Sue said.

"We won't let her back before a month." And Dora appealed to Father.

"Well, yes, quite so, no doubt," Father reckoned. "A month will soon pass here."

"I s'pose she'll stay till there's a bust-up!" Andy broke in, cold-bloodedly.

Mother turned on him like lightening. "A bust up? Why will there be a bust up?" she yelled. "Th' cheek o' you to say it! *You,* you thing of a fellow! How dare y'!"

"I'd like to bet a bit on it, all th' same," came stubbornly from Andy.

"*You'd* like to bet! *You* would! *You*"—and lifting a sorghum stalk Mother showed him the butt-end of it. "Very flash you're getting, my shaver! Very flash with your betting—your betting, indeed!"

Andy, grinning, wisely walked off to the old shed to put away the tools he was carrying.

Mother, foaming and puffing, and talking all the while to no one in particular, led the way to the house. We followed in a string.

At the door of the old shed Andy swung round and shouted: "What d' *you* reckon, Father?"

But Father didn't reckon anything. Father had had too much experience in domestic affairs to reckon things in Mother's presence.

"He's getting far too big for his boots lately, that's what he is!" Mother raged, sitting on the sofa and spreading the sheets of Aunt Maria's letter on her lap.

"Oh, Andy doesn't mean half what he says, Mother," Dora put in in the interests of her brother.

"Well, then, *I* mean *all* what *I* say!" And Mother wagged her head aggressively at Dora. "And I say if he doesn't take care how he talks to me he'll have to leave here and go and do for himself somewhere else."

"*Alice! Alice!*" pleadingly from Aunt Sue.

"Asking his Father what he thinks, indeed!" Mother stormed on. "As if it mattered a straw what he thinks!"

Father blinked, and rolled his big eyes about uneasily.

"I've no doubt his Father agrees with him, though—no doubt of it whatever; for it's just what"——

"Oh, never mind, Mother! Read the letter to us!" Dora interrupted trying to smile.

"Read th' letter? Read it yourselves!" and throwing the sheets from her, Mother bounced off the sofa and flew into her room.

Saturday arrived. Mother and Aunt Sue, with their best hats and boots on, drove off in the old spring cart to meet Aunt Maria at the railway siding. Dora, with a pot of paste and an assortment of newspapers on the table, applied herself to putting the finishing touches to the front room. Martha and Tom, charged with the responsibilities of cleaning up the front door and putting everything tidy, argued and fought for possession of the rake, and in lucid moments, excited and upset Dora by bellowing, "Here they comes".

At last, though, and just when Dora had finished dressing and was squinting frontways and sideways at herself in the looking-glass, they came. Talk about excitement!The coming of the coach or arrival of a new Governor was a dull circumstance beside it.

"Auntie! Hello, Auntie Maria!" Martha and Tom, rushing off to meet the cart, yelled repeatedly.

"Don't frighten the mare now; don't frighten th' mare!" Mother cried to them, as though it were possible to scare poor, sad, old Rosina.

Dora, leaving the house as if it were on fire, and making as much noise with her skirts as a rushing train, sped across the yard shouting: "You got her! She come?"

Simutaneously Father and Limpy crept from the old bark shed, which, for an hour or more had served them as a waiting-room. Father, his hair and whiskers combed out and rounded, resembled a grass-tree moving along on legs. Limpy, wearing a white drill suit that had been washed and done up for him when

the school was opened a year before, looked like an important member of a minstrel troupe.

Aunt Maria, smiling all over her face, descended from the cart and exchanged kisses with Dora and Father, and shook hands with Limpy. She would have kissed Martha and Tom, too, but they were not of her mind. They hung their heads and shuffled shyly away.

"Martha!" Mother said sharply, *"Martha!"*

"Never mind," Aunt Maria said, large heartedly, "I've something better for them." And, taking out a large leather purse bulging with letters and buttons, raked two threepenny pieces from the depths of it and gave one each to Martha and Tom. *"There!"* she added, *"there!"* And her voice was the voice of one conscious of penetrating a great philanthropic feat.

"Maria! oh, why did you do that?" Mother gasped; "giving your money away like that! They don't want it."

But the looks of unmistakable joy that spread over the faces of Martha and Tom gave a denial to her statement.

"That's her all over; that's Maria," Aunt Sue remarked proudly. "She never was happy if she wasn't giving something away."

"Well, and what do you say for it?" Mother said, prompting the lucky recipients.

Martha, grinning, waited for Tom to make a speech. Tom, turning the silver over and over in his hand, waited for Martha.

"What do you say?" And Mother raised her voice and scowled.

"God bless Auntie," Martha tittered.

"And make her good," Tom added, and bolted.

They all looked in surprise at each other, then burst out laughing.

"Here's Andy," Aunt Sue announced for the benefit of her sister, as the former, with clean shirt and pants on, his hat off, his hair brushed up in front like a cockatoo's "top-nut", and ten or twelve inches of his waist belt dangling in front of him, came round the corner of the house working his way with his shoulders, and sliding along on the ground on the heels of his boots.

"You don't know *me*, Andy?" Aunt Maria called pleasantly to him.

We all smiled, and waited for Andy to answer. He didn't answer till he came right close to her.

"I'd know yer 'ide on a fence," he said; "How're y' cookin', Ant?" And he shook her by the hand till she screamed to him to let go. He let go, and, looking hard into her face, suddenly cried: "Why, which o' yer is it? Or are yer both one in two or the same as th' sayin' is, or what, eh?"

Then we remembered that our two Aunts were twins, and that often we had been told that no one could ever distinguish one from the other, and all of us gathered round them and laughed at their similarity, and made them stand beside each other, front ways and back to back.

"Their mother couldn't never tell the difference," Father said solemnly.

"I can tell them by their clothes," Dora remarked.

"Yes, but if they hadn't any bloomin' clothes on?" Andy argued, wagging his head at Dora.

"*Andy!*" And Mother stamped her foot. "*Andy!*"

Father, smiling to himself, hobbled round to the back of the cart and began dragging out Maria's luggage—a pillow-slip bursting with clothes. The others, with Limpy at their heels, all hurried inside—all but Andy. Andy remained behind to sympathise with the old mare and take her out of the cart.

"Poor old Rosina!" he murmured, fondling her. "Did it knock it out o' yer draggin' them fat old fowls up the hill?"

Then he lowered the shafts to the ground, and invited her kindly to "get out, old girl". And when she didn't get out with a rush like a two-year-old he gave her a kick and called her a "silly old cow."

With Aunt Maria in the home the days and moments flew quickly by. All of us got on well with her, especially Martha and Tom and Dora. Martha and Tom pursued and pestered her every minute in the day. They dragged her here, there and everywhere, showed her everything about the place, and told her all they knew—told her things that Mother had warned them over and over again not to breathe a word of to any living soul. Dora confided her love for Jerry Manning to her, and complained of the way Mother always treated him. "Mother would like me to have George Dunn," Dora told her one day, "but I don't think I could like him; not well enough to marry him, y' know." Aunt Maria knew—at least, she said she did, and in return confided an old lovesore of her own to Dora. And when Dora heard the whole of the sad story she cried and kissed Aunt Maria and said she was "so, so sorry for her".

"But perhaps I'm just as well off," Aunt Maria sighed, "just as well." And she quietly hustled a tear away from her eye.

"But you might get a better catch yet," Dora, sniffing, said encouragingly. "How do you know who might take it into his head to come along?"

Aunt Maria sighed several more times, then added: "Some men do take silly things into their heads, but I don't think any of them will take that one." And she laughed a faint, miserable laugh.

"Well, look at Aunt Sue, she's had an offer," Dora went on; "and more than once, too."

'Sue?' And Aunt Maria jumped several feet and clutched Dora excitedly. "When? Who? Tell me, oh Dora, tell me!"

"Well, you won't let on if I do, will you?" Dora stipulated with a giggle.

Aunt Maria struck herself on the chest, and said she wouldn't let on for the world.

Then Dora leaned on her and whispered the name of Villiam Brandt into her ear. "And the poor fellow comes nearly every Sunday to see her," she said, "and she won't even come out of her room the whole time he's here."

Then they laughed and squealed together, and hugged each other for quite a while.

Presently a brilliant idea occurred to Aunt Maria, and throwing her arms around Dora again she laughed the inspiration into her ear.

Dora received it with a loud shriek, and said, "It would be great fun if you're game to do it."

Just then the voice of Aunt Sue calling them to dinner was heard. And when they appeared at the table their eyes were still wet with tears of joy, and neither could "eat anything for laughing".

Sunday afternoon. Aunt Maria and Dora, after conspiring together all the morning, said they were going for a walk down the paddock, They took Andy into their confidence, and he prepared to accompany them. He seemed proud of the privilege, too, and patted himself nobly on the chest.

"If yous two come follern'," he said, turning aggressively on Martha and Tom, "I'll interdooce me boot-maker to yer bloomin' tailor, if yous knows what that means."

Martha and Tom seemed to know what it meant, and promptly slunk out of the way. Then, together, the three conspirators started off cheerfully, and soon were lost sight of amongst the timber.

"This is 'im," Andy said with a chuckle, as Villiam Brandt, in his best clothes, was seen hurrying along the track in the direction of our Homestead.

Dora became excited and began giggling, and pinching Aunt Maria.

"Whatever will you say to him, Aunt?" she said, nervously: "what if—if"—

"I won't say anything," the other laughed. "He'll have to do all the saying. But you two mustn't go far away, now, will you? Mind that."

"We'll keep y' in sight," Andy assured her.

Then, raising his voice as Villiam came near: "Hello, General!"

"Vy you nod shalute me den, mein poy?" And coming to "attention", Villiam saluted in real, royal, military fashion.

Dora laughed and shook hands with him.

"You know me Ant Maria, Villiam?" Andy said.

Dora pinched Andy.

"Me Aunt Sue, I mean," and Andy corrected his mistake.

"Undrews mein poy!" Villiam said, placing his two hands affectionately on the former's shoulders. "Yust for von, dwo, three meenit I spheak mid Shoosan. I dake sharge mid her for you, eh? You go orf mid yourselluf und lose der vay. Mein gerracious, I dink so, Undrew?"

Meanwhile, Aunt Maria, like a bashful young maiden, hung her head and probed at the earth with the toe of her boot.

Andy poked Villiam in the ribs, and winked knowingly at him.

Then Dora put in a word.

"We're going over to see if there's much water at the rocks, Aunt," she said; "we'll only be a few minutes."

"You haf gerreat sense, mein gerracious." And Villiam patted Dora on the head.

Aunt Maria, with her eyes still fixed on the toe of her boot, remained silent.

"Come on then." And Andy hustled Dora off the field.

When they had gone about seventy yards they looked back and saw Villiam kneeling on the ground before Aunt Maria, gesticulating and holding out his two hands imploringly to her.

"Well, ain't 'e a goat!" Andy grunted.

"Look at him! look at him now, though! look! look! oh, *look!*" Dora cried. "He's kissing her hand— and she's letting him!"

"Lickin' it like a bloomin' dorg," Andy drawled.

"Whatever will he do next?" and Dora threatened to hurt herself with mirth.

"Kiss her on th' mug, I 'spect," Andy said.

"Oh, if he does—if he does!" And Dora started dancing about.

But Villiam took his time, and rising to his feet, stood for several moments facing Aunt Maria with his head thrown back and his arms out wide.

Aunt Maria stood playing with the corner of her handkerchief.

Suddenly Villiam sprang forward and clasped her in his arms. Aunt Maria struggled and wriggled, and succeeded in turning the back of her hat to his whiskers. Villiam poked his nose first at one side of her face then at the other.

"I reckon it's about time to blow th' whistle," Andy said, "or he'll be breakin' th' rules."

Dora thought so too, and they hurried back.

Andy coughed loud when they came up, and Villiam, smiling hard, released Aunt Maria and confronted him.

"I thought yous was havin' a fight!" Andy said.

Villiam laughed a deep, happy sort of laugh, and, placing his hands on Andy's shoulders, again whispered hoarsely:

"Undrews, I come nex Sund'y-daay and tol' you soomdings. I vent me home now, bleased mid mein-selluf. You see—eh-h?"

"Oh, is that it—a wedding, I s'pose?" And Andy poked Villiam in the ribs again.

"Eh-h, mein poy!" And Villiam returned the poke.

"Well, we're going home now, too," Andy further said; "so-long."

Villiam, smiling, bowed very low, and the parties went their separate ways rejoicing.

14.   A Set Back

Sunday again. Dinner over; and what a feast it was! Cabbage, beans, peas, potatoes, pudding! And all in honor of Aunt Maria!

"Well, I think I'll go and have a lie down for a few minutes." And Mother went off to her room.

"And I'm going to read one of the books Maria brought," Aunt Sue said, taking possession of the sofa.

Andy yawned and declared Sunday to be "th' rottenest day in th' week."

"Mond'y's der jolly day I don't like." And Limpy, elevating his chin, thoughtfully scratched his scraggy wiskers.

"And Toosd'y an' We'n'sd'y, I 'spect?" Andy added with a grin.

Limpy, without replying, rose and strolled on to the verandah. Presently he was joined by Father.

Dora, from the kitchen, called to Aunt Maria.

"Y-e-s-s-s," Maria answered, wonderingly, and ran out.

Dora, all smiles and giggles, pointed to the form of William Brandt coming along the cultivation paddock fence, and said: "For goodness sake run and hide yourself."

Aunt Maria flew into the skillion-room, and, throwing herself on Dora's bed, lay there pricking her ears and cocking her head from side to side, and trying to stop her heart from thumping.

Dora called to Andy.

Andy, feeling suspicious, sauntered to the kitchen.

Dora indicated Villiam Brandt.

Andy pulled a significant face, and, whistling steadily through his teeth, strolled across the yard and waited for Villiam to arrive.

Villiam arrived, and, smiling blandly, greeted Andy cheerfully.

Andy saluted him in extravagant military fashion.

"Undrews," Villiam inquired, "coom me der broper time, you dink so?"

"You're in splendid time," Andy answered, "she's waitin' for you inside on the sofa."

Villiam, pulling a large coloured handkerchief from his pocket and smelling it, made haste for the house. Andy hurried round the back way, where he grinned and rejoiced in the presence of Dora. Dora, red and flurried, placed her ear to the door.

"Hello, Mr. Brandt," Father said, as Villiam stepped on to the verandah.

"I spheaks mid you direkelys," Villiam answered; and straight inside he went.

Aunt Sue suddenly let her book fall and rose to a sitting position.

"You vas vait for me, eh-h, sweet greature?" And dropping down beside her, Villiam put his arms round her waist.

A scream that fairly rattled the roof came from Aunt Sue, and she attacked Villiam with both hands and feet, and, escaping from his embrace, rushed off screaming, "WRETCH! WRETCH!"

All of us hurried in to investigate—all of us except Aunt Maria. She crawled under the bed.

"What th' devil!" Father shouted in astonishment at Villiam.

"Dis sord o' ding won't do, y' know!" Limpy, hopping all round the culprit, declared bravely.

Villiam stared and gasped, and made several futile efforts to explain matters.

Mother, with her hair down, made her way through the rest of us like a policeman. She pulled Father backwards, sent Martha and Tom spinning in front of her, tossed Limpy off his legs, and furiously faced Villiam.

"What's this?" she cried. "What are you up to? Eh, what?" Then she reached for him and pulled his nose.

Villiam, astonished and stupefied, staggered back and placed the table between them.

"No! no! no! *No-h-h!*" he broke out, holding up both hands. "I do noding! I dinks"—staring wildly at all of us—"I dinks me I vas in der mad house!"

"You'll be there very soon, or in the lock-up, you bad man!" Mother shouted to him. "Away with you out of my house!" And she pointed to the door.

At this stage Andy squeezed into the room, and Villiam's eyes immediately rested upon him in a hopeful sort of way.

"Undrews," he gasped, "Shpeak for me vat I dink! Shpeak mid your Moder! You told her! Mighty gerracious!" And beads of perspiration broke out all over him.

"Yes, *I* know all about it, Villiam," Andy said. "I know, I know" (to Mother): "It's all right, Mother. I'll tell y' all about it, drekeley. Let him alone! Let him alone. (Then taking Villiam by the arm and leading him to the door): "You're all right, Villiam; come on with me! Come on! I'll tell them all about it when I come in."

Andy took Villiam out and escorted him part of the way home. When he returned, Mother, still furious, came from Aunt Sue's quarters and said:

"Now then what's this you know? Who's it about? And what have you to say for that man?"

"Well," Andy drawled, "Just this much; that if I 'adn't got him away quiet he might have done for someone! He's off 'is dot! An' none o' yer had the sense to see it!"

"You bad man! Away with you out of my house!"

15. *An Unexpected Development*

A bright beautiful day. All of us, including Aunt Maria, in the field pulling corn. We were anxious to take the crop off and get it out of the way—at least Father was. Not that it was a very valuable crop, or a particularly bounteous one; but Father wanted to start the plough going. Whether there was to be a crop or whether there wasn't was never the question with Father. Father's idea of good farming consisted entirely of keeping the plough moving. So long as the bit of ground was perpetually being turned upside down, Father reckoned things were just buzzing along, and that all our fortunes were being made.

For hours, long, heavy hours, too, we raced each other up and down the cranky, crooked rows, rattling and cracking the wretched stunted stalks in search of cobs, that for the most part were never there.

Andy and Dora worked in with Aunt Maria and helped to lighten her load by doing her share as well as their own. And the trio kept aloof from the rest of us, too, and always contrived to be at one end of the field when we were at the other. And those rounds of wretched drudgery seemed to give them pleasure. While we slogged on without exchanging a word one way or the other, except with the flies, they laughed and talked together about Villiam Brandt and Aunt Sue. And at intervals one or the other would look over the top of the miserable corn to make certain none of us was within hearing.

"He doesn't seem to be such a bad fellow, though?" Aunt Maria said as a mild reproach against her sister.

"*Bad?*" Andy echoed indignantly; "by cripes, Villiam's an orl right bloke, you take it from me. An' 'e ain't th' fool they think 'e is, neither. An' for work! He'd work half th' coots about here inter their grave in a day!"

Then Dora said a good word for Villiam.

"Indeed, *I* like him," she said, positively; "and he's a nice man if he's treated properly. And believe me, Aunt Sue, although she knows such a lot, could have done a lot worse."

Aunt Maria started chewing corn and thinking hard.

"I'm going down to give him a hand with *his* pulling when we finishes this," Andy announced after a silence.

Dora became excited.

"What do you say if we go down, too, some evening, Aunt?" she said.

Aunt Maria thought it a splendid idea, and asked Andy for his opinion.

Andy, pulling burr prickles from his fingers, shook his head gravely.

"Oh—no," he drawled, "I don't think so. He'd reckon you was Aunt Sue."

"But we'll tell him," Dora urged enthusiastically. "We'll introduce her properly as our other Aunt— Aunt Sue's sister upon a holiday, and tell him we've brought her down to see his place."

"Oh, that's right enough," Andy agreed. "That'd be orlright. Come down towards evenin' then, an' I'll tell him yer was comin'."

Aunt Maria became excited, and said she would wear clothes quite different to Sue's that day, and do her hair up differently too; in fact, make herself look as unlike her sister as it was possible for art to do. And Dora became even more excited. She wrung Aunt Maria by the hand and danced round about her, and left Andy to hunt for all the cobs.

Another bright, beautiful day. They were all bright, beautiful days now. Nothing else around was bright and beautiful though.

Dora and Aunt Maria cleaned their teeth with ashes, and fastened their hair with snoods, and started off merrily for Villiam Brandt's farmstead.

When they were gone, Aunt Sue turned to Mother and said she thought "they would have had more sense than to go near the place of a man like that!

"Well, they say they're not a bit afraid," Mother answered. "Besides, Andy is there, and surely the three of them can manage him!"

"In any case," growled Aunt Sue, "what do they want going near him at all for? Maria, anyway, ought to know better. If I'd been in her place I know I'd treat him differently to that!"

Mother went out to the kitchen and left Aunt Sue grumbling to herself.

"My word, Mr. Brandt," Dora cried, greeting Villiam in his maize paddock, *"You've* got a good crop!"

Villiam made faces at the corn-stalks and heaped pious imprecations on the dry weather and the gravelly soil and the country generally.

"This is my other Aunt, General," Andy said, introducing Aunt Maria.

Aunt Maria smiled and bowed, and extending her hand to Villiam asked him "how he was getting along, and if he was fond of farming?"

"Mighty Zake!" Villiam gasped. "Yeou vas so gereatly like Sushan!"

"Like my sister?" repeated Aunt Maria in a winning sort of way. "I believe I am in *some* things. But not in all—not in all, Mr. Brandt."

"Heavens Zake, n-no; I hope nod! Eh-h?" And Villiam shook his head and groaned.

"I'm afraid she's a great flirt," ventured Aunt Maria.

"Mighty, I dink so—yess!" sighed Villiam.

"They're *twins,* Aunt Sue and this one, did you know that?" Andy put in with a grin at Aunt Maria.

"Tvins?" echoed Villiam, with wide open eyes.

"Greatness, yeou told me dat, eh-h?"

"Oh, yes," Dora confirmed; "they were both born on the same day."

"Shiminey!" Villiam laughed. "Dink o' dot, now, eh-h . . . . Und mein heifer cow, Yellerboy, she too haf some tvins. Yah; dree day ol' soon now."

Dora and Aunt Maria started giggling.

"Bute dey vas nod d'same like yeou," Villiam added, smiling at the latter. "Von, der bull, vas plack; der odder shap, she vas shtrawperry."

Dora and Aunt Maria laughed aloud.

"Nefer mindt, laties," Villiam went on apologetically, "coom now, und make yousellufs soom tea, und I show yeou my blace."

Then to Andy:

"You make yourselluf a holiday for a vile, my poy."

"I'm goin' down to have some tea, too; my colonial," Andy answered, throwing some cobs he held in his hands on to a heap. "You're not going to lose me."

Then, leading the way along a track that wound in and out the rank grass and through a dog-legged fence, Villiam conducted the party to his hut.

And when Dora and Aunt Maria crossed the threshold they stood and gazed in astonishment at the interior. To their surprise, everything was spotlessly clean and tidy, and the room adorned with strong, comfortable furniture of Villiam's own making. They looked at each other, and complimented him upon the state of his home.

"I vants me yust von dring more to make happeeness," said he smiling and blushing and wagging his head.

"Oh, she'll come along directly, Mr. Brandt," Aunt Maria assured him, meaningly.

"I daught me dot, too, soom leetle vile beck!" And Villiam shook his head sadly. "But I makes me a meestake."

Dora laughed and said:

"There's just as good a fish in the sea as was ever caught, Mr. Brandt."

"Yah, dot is righd; bute I vish me I could ketch him." And Villiam grinned insinuatingly in the direction of Aunt Maria.

Pretending to take no notice, the latter interested herself in a quaint-looking arm chair that had once been a beer barrel.

Andy poked Villiam slyly in the ribs.

Villiam, indulging in a side view of Aunt Maria, suddenly discovered a further resemblance in her to Aunt Sue, and began enlarging on the matter.

"The only difference in us," Aunt Maria informed him, "is that I've got a mole just there, see?" bending down her head and showing him the nape of her neck, "and she hasn't."

Villiam touched the "difference" tenderly with his fingers, and laughed like an angel.

Andy nudged Dora, and drew her attention to a pair of military pictures ornamenting the wall. The daubs held no earthly interest for Dora, still she expressed a loud admiration for them, and hung round them, and killed a lot of time.

Meanwhile Villiam proceeded to make hay while the sun was shining on the backs of Andy and Dora. He produced an album and showed Aunt Maria a photo. of himself taken in military uniform; and photos of his father and mother and other curious looking folk "in Denmark". And he plunged into a long rigmarole about himself and his native land. And finally, venturing to touch her tenderly under the chin with one of his big, restless fingers, he hurried to the fireplace and made a billy of tea, and fried a panful of eggs.

When it was time to go, Aunt Maria gave Villiam's hand an extra squeeze, and said she and Dora would come down again another afternoon.

They went down another afternoon—they went down

several afternoons; then went down until Aunt Maria was head over ears in love with Villiam, and became engaged to be married to him. And when Villiam, in turn, started calling at our homestead to take Aunt Maria out for walks, Mother was quite puzzled. And she remained puzzled until Dora whispered a number of things into her ear. Then she threw back her head, kicked one of her blucher boots into the air, and laughed like a man.

"Well, I used to think it strange," she said, controlling her mirth, "if he would do anything wrong, for he was always such a very respectable man."

"And don't you think Aunt Sue was a fool, Mother?" Dora inquired.

"A fool?" Mother answered. "Would she be single so long if she was anything else?"

Then, one day, Mother in confidence asked Aunt Sue if she knew there was going to be a match between Maria and Villiam Brandt.

Aunt Sue, who for weeks had preserved a peculiar silence,

and didn't seem the same person at all, suddenly burst into sobs.

Mother couldn't understand her. "Why, don't you believe in it, Sue?" she asked anxiously.

"You n-n-know well enough I don't," blubbered Aunt Sue. "It's b-b-bad 'nough . . . . b-b-bad 'nough for others . . . . but wh-wh-when y'r own sister . . . . y'r own flesh and blood . . . . kuh-kuh-comes in y'r way . . . . *Oo! Oo!* Buh-*boo! hoo!*"

Mother understood her.

"Well, you *are* a curious woman," he said, "why bless me, it's your own fault, isn't it?"

"*No;* it *isn't* my own fault!" screamed Aunt Sue.

"Then why didn't you have him when he asked you to?" Mother snapped unsympathetically.

"*Why* should I—why should I have him the very first time he asked me to?" yelled Aunt Sue. "Do you think everyone is like yourself?"

"Like—like who?" . . . . . . And Mother, enraged, sprang to her feet.

But Aunt Sue was looking for fight.

"Like *you!*" she shouted through her falling hair.

"You lying wretch of a woman!" And Mother stamped her blucher boots one after the other, on the floor. "I was not like *you!* I was not like *you!* I could have had a dozen husbands if I had wanted them!"

"Then why didn't you have them?" And Aunt Sue threw a fistful of her hair from her eyes, and glared defiantly at Mother. "Why didn't y'—why didn't y'?"

"You—you screaming mad huzzie!" stammered Mother. "I didn't because"—poking her face into Aunt Sue's, and raising her voice to a yell—"*because* one fool was enough for me to slave for!"

"Well, anyway," squealed Aunt Sue, "she hasn't got him yet. And what's more, she *won't* get him— she *won't* get him! She won't! She won't! She WON'T!" And throwing the rest of hair out of her eyes she left Mother, and rushed off to her own end of the dwelling.

16. *A Birthday Honour*

"A hot day! Too hot to eat!" Father said, sitting back from the dinner-table.

A portly, well dressed, well-fed looking man, wearing a heavy gold chain and carrying a large gold-headed walking-stick, stepped on to the verandah and called out "Good-day" in a loud, cheerful voice.

"Mr. McFlosh," Father gasped, and went to the door.

"Th' Member o' Parliament," Andy said. And Mother whispered to him "Shut up!"

Father brought the M.L.A. inside, and he shook hands with all of us, from Mother down to Tom, and inquired after our health. He looked about the room and seemed disappointed when there was no baby to cuddle and kiss. Then he sat down and talked of the country's prosperity and progress, and mentioned a lot of things he had done for our district and more that he was going to do. Finally he supposed that Father knew there was going to be another election, and that he could depend on his support again?

"Oh, yes," Father stammered.

But Mother wasn't so sure.

"You only want our votes," she said. "As soon as you get in we won't see any more of you till next election." Then she asked him what the Government meant by making a J.P. of the publican, and the bank clerk, and the commission agent at the township, and leaving the men on the land out of it?

Mr. McFlosh pulled a note-book from his pocket and said: "What's your husband's full name, madam?"

"He's well enough able to tell you that himself," Mother answered.

The M.L.A. turned to Father. But, taken by surprise, Father seemed to forget what his name was, and sat staring stupidly.

"Abe," Andy answered coming to his parent's assistance.

"Abel," Martha said, correcting Andy.

"Its *Abraham,* isn't it, Father?" Dora inquired softly.

"Well, it doesn't matter about being exact to the letter—any of them is near enough." And Mr. McFlosh wet the pencil on his tongue and made a careful note in his book. Then he looked up at Father and said: "I'll see you are made a Justice of the Peace, Mr. Pettigrew. And no mistake about it, it should have been done years ago."

"No, not me!" Father, finding his tongue, and wagging his head, protested. "I don't want to be nothing!"

"You don't want to be nothing?" Mother roared at him. "Have you ever been anything else? And do you think no one in the family wants to be anything? If I was a man I would want to be everything—I'd want to be Premier!"

"And damme, Madam, if I don't think you would be, too." And the M.L.A. broke into a loud laugh in which all of us joined except Mother.

"Don't want to be nothing!" she repeated, scowling at Father.

"If Mr. Pettigrew won't take it, what about this young man?" And the M.L.A. looked at Andy.

Martha and Tom began to snigger.

"I'd make as good a one as them blokes at the township," Andy claimed. "Cripes, wouldn't I. But it would be no good to me. I don't want to be giving blokes six months for nothing!"

"Well, if no one else ith game to take id on!" Limpy put in. "I'll hab a go ad it."

Mr. McFosh stared hard at Limpy, and asked his name and what his politics were.

Mother explained Limpy's relationship, and said she "supposed his politics were all right". Limpy always voted Labour and Mr. McFlosh was a Liberal.

"Yes, of course," the latter said to Limpy; "I knew all your family as well as I know my own. Very well, my friend, I'll see that your name is put on the list of magistrates."

"Dey mightn't put it on," Limpy suggested.

"By jingo, if the Home Secretary refuses to do it," the M.L.A. answered, "there'll be a change in the Cabinet pretty soon."

Limpy thanked him, and Mother handed him a cup of tea.

Months after the election. A large letter with a red seal on it came addressed to Limpy. Had it been a summons, or an invitation to Government House we couldn't have been more excited.

Limpy opened it, and holding the communication upside down, gazed hard at it. Limpy's education was limited to drawing. He always drew his signature.

"Here y' are," he said, handing the communication to Mother. "What's der jolly ding all about?"

"I have the honour to inform you," Mother read, "that His Excellency the Governor, with the advice of the Executive Council, has been pleased to appoint you a Justice of the Peace for the State of Queensland."

Limpy's mouth opened wide. So did ours.

"The Governor himself has done it," Dora exclaimed.

"And he was pleased to do it," Martha added.

"He must know about everyone in the country," Father observed.

"They say he's a awfully nice man, the Governor," from Aunt Sue. "I saw him when he opened the show at Too-woomba. If Andy was a little older and not so straight and sunburnt, you wouldn't be able to tell one from the other."

"Look at that now!" And Mother's eyes, beaming with admiration, rested on Andy. Mother was proud to have a son who resembled the Governor.

"Cripes!" Andy said; "he must be a handsome bloke! Don't y' think so, Father?"

Father grinned.

"Read dat again," Limpy requested.

Mother read the official note again.

"Well it's somedun to be proud of," and Limpy rose and hobbled thoughtfully round the room. "And on me birthday, too!"

A week later. The local newspaper announced that "Thomas Sampson Muggles, of Ironbark, farmer, was appointed a Justice of the Peace."

Joy. One by one we lifted our heads from the columns of *The Sage* and regarded Limpy as Australia's Noblest Son.

"Everyone will soon know about it now," Mother chuckled; "and I wonder what they'll say?"

Days and weeks passed and no one said anything. They didn't say anything until one day Mother mentioned it to the Dorsetts. Then we discovered that none of our neighbours knew who Thomas Sampson Muggles was. But when they were enlightened they scoffed and sneered, and said anyone could be a J.P.

"Never mind what they say," Mother counselled Limpy; "but just do what I tell you!"

And Limpy did everything that Mother told him. And everyone said she was the J.P.

One day Limpy rebelled and reminded Mother that he was the magistrate.

'What!" Mother shouted. "Put on airs to me, will you?" And she poked the head of the broom under his chin and pinned him to the wall.

Limpy yelled for help, and Dora rushed to his rescue.

"For goodness sake, Mother," she cried. "What are you doing?"

"Doing!" And swinging the broom with both hands, Mother battered Limpy's head with it.

Ducking and dodging, and fouling the furniture, he blundered through the house and fell out on to the verandah. Mother pitched the broom after him and yelled:

"Tell me you're a J.P. will you?"

17. The Justice Receives a Call

Limpy preparing to visit the township; Paley calling excitedly, drove in to the yard in his milkcart.

"Stay inside," Mother counselled; "and I'll see what he wants."

"I want the Justice," Paley howled in reply to her.

"You can't see him, he's getting ready to attend a case."

"There's no case so important as mine," Paley urged. "Them Gilgrooms attack me every day when I'm goin' to th' facthry. They waits on the road for me with stones and waddies—th' cowards that they are!"

Mother doubted if Limpy would have any influence with such people as the Gilgrooms.

"He don't want influence!" Paley shouted angrily, "He have th' law on his side, and I want him to drive along with me in th' cart and ketch them in the act!"

Mother returned to the house and shook her finger at Limpy and warned him to be sure and side with the Gilgrooms. Mother had a warm place in her heart for the Gilgrooms. Mrs. Gilgroom used to swap settings of eggs with her, and once she gave her two pullets for a rooster that tried to snatch a piece of meat off a steel trap that Gilgroom had set for dingoes. And when Mother heard that it took the bird's head off, she had nothing but sympathy in her heart for Mrs. Gilgroom ever after.

"I know none of them would do anything to him," she went on, "unless he did something to them first—and even if he didn't, he deserves everything they do to him."

"I don't know about dat; I only got to hold d' scales of Justice." And Limpy hung his lip, and looked as important as a Chief Justice.

"The scales of your gradmother! If you don't take the Gilgroom's part I'll scale you when you come back with the poker." And Mother shook her fist at him.

Limpy put on his hat and slumped stubbornly out without making further reply.

"Remember what I have told you," Mother shouted after him," or you'll get it!"

"They never gives me a moment's peace," Paley spluttered in reply to Limpy. "And not satisfied with blackgardin' and scandalizin' me to everyone, they wants to stop me now from taking me milk to th' facthry."

"If dat's dere jolly game," the Justice said, crawling into the cart, "I'll make it hot for them."

"Ye're own eyes will tell you it is, there!" And whipping up the horse, Paley drove rapidly down the lane.

Nearing Gilgroom's place, which stood close to the road, Paley advised the J.P. to hide himself in the bottom of the conveyance. "If they sees th' least bit o' ye," he added, "they'll shmell a rat."

Limpy curled himself up among the empty cans in the bottom of the cart, and rolled and bumped about on the milk-stained floor like a corpse.

The Gilgrooms, moving peacefully about the farm, saw Paley approaching, but made no unfriendly demonstration towards him. Paley was disappointed. It wasn't the sort of reception he expected. He slowed down to a walk and stared insolently in their direction. Still the Gilgrooms disregarded his presence. Paley shook his first at them. The Gilgrooms took notice. They stared hard. Paley touched his nose with his fingers. Old Gilgroom and his eldest boy rushed and seized the horse by the head.

"I'll give ye both in charge," Paley shouted in grieved tones.

"I'll give you a broken head," old Gilgroom shouted back.

Then the horse started to rear, and Paley to roar "Woa!" and "Weh-h!"

Mrs. Gilgroom and one of the girls laden with bad eggs and over-ripe tomatoes arrived. They pelted Paley with the rapidity of machine-guns, and Paley dodged and ducked and spat and swore loudly in the presence of the hidden J.P.

"Give it to the dog!" old Gilgroom shouted at intervals to his wife. "Give it to him; he can't get away!"

Then Paley roared for the law to rise and do his duty.

The J.P. cautiously raised his head, and nervously peeped over the edge of the cart.

"There's a fellow in with him!" Annie Gilgroom cried, letting fly a shell that burst in the Justice's eye. Limpy dropped down on the floor of the cart and flattened himself like a turtle. Then Paley, with egg-flip and tomato dropping from him, seized an empty milkcan and heaved it at the Gilgrooms. Mrs. Gilgroom and Annie dodged it and responded with more eggs. William Gilgroom lifted the milk-can and threw it into the paddock. Paley called upon the J.P. to witness the theft. The J.P. ignored him.

"Damn you!" Paley roared, and grabbing him by the coat collar stood him on his legs. Fresh shells burst and bespattered his white coat. Limpy stuttered and struggled, but Paley, holding him firmly, used him as a shield.

"Run for more eggs, Annie!" Mrs. Gilgroom commanded. But just then old Gilgroom pulled the winkers off the horse and "hooshed" it. The brute swung round and bolted along the lane. Paley jumped out and rolled in a gully, but Limpy remained in the cart. He remained in it till it fouled a stump and turned over.

Then he got out and rolled on his head. And when he was carried home and questioned by the township policeman, he declined to make a statement. But next day Mrs. Gilgroom came over to our place and between intervals of mirth told Mother all about "the great fun they had".

18. Andy's Watch and a Kangaroo

Andy reared three calves on the bucket; three calves that old Bill Bush, who decided to go in for dairying on scientific principles, was going to knock on the head with his axe—and exchanged them with Jim Blaises for a silver watch. And a splendid watch it was, too. Father said he never saw a nicer, or felt a heavier one in his life.

"Don't y' think 'e was a fool to give it for th' poddies, Father?" Andy chuckled, pressing the turnip to his ear listening to its ticking.

Father did; and reckoned "a watch like that must have cost a good lot of money".

"Well, th' calves didn't cost much, anyway." And chuckling more, Andy opened all the lids of the timepiece and gazed learnedly at the mechanism.

Martha and Tom crowded round. "Now yous keep away," Andy commanded, "an' don't be shovin' near it!"

"Who's shovin' near it? Yer very fritent of th' old thing, ain't y'?" from Martha.

"No, I ain't fritent of th' old thing!" Andy repeated loudly; "but I'm fritent of a clumsy goat like you."

Martha poked her tongue out.

"Let's see what makes it go?" Tom pleaded humbly.

"Yer can see what makes it go, can't y', without wantin' to put your breath on it an' stop it from keepin' proper time?"

"What's the proper time on it now?" and Tom strained his neck to see.

"Yer can't tell th' proper time on that side!" Andy informed him. "Here's where yer've got to look for that." And closing the back of the watch with a loud snap, displayed the face of it to Tom.

"Half a hour past," Tom announced solemnly.

"Half an hour past! Yer galoot, that's not what th' time is!

"Can't yer see what makes it go without wantin' to put yer breath on it?"

Lovely bloke you'd be to tell how th' evenin' was goin' on a job!" And Andy laughed.

"Well, tell us yerself what time it is then, if yer so smart?" Martha demanded.

"Eh—tell yer—the er—what time?" Andy studied the turnip hard for several seconds. "It's twenty to; that's what it is if y' want to know."

"Well it *isn't,* then," snapped Martha. "An' yer can't tell th' time yerself, though you do own th' blessed old thing!"

Andy turned to Limpy.

"Ain't I right?"—showing the cripple the face of the watch —"Isn't that twenty to?"

"I tan alweds manage to tell der time od a clock," Limpy confessed; "but I neber could understand dem jolly things.

Andy appealed to Father.

Father stared at the Waterbury, and it seemed to perplex him.

"I can't quite make them hands out," he said. "On th' watch I used to have, one wer' a bit bigger'n other. Them's both th' one size.

Andy's blood went cold.

"Oh, I dunno," he growled; "they're th' same sort o' hands as is on all watches, ain't they?"

"Well, if that's the big hand," Father indicated one with his thumb, "it'd be now just erzactly ten minutes to ten. But if th' other's the biggest hand, it's—well—see (calculating) it's just th' other way about—ten minutes after ten."

"Oh, well, in any case, that ain't a big lot o' difference." And Andy cheerfully returned the jewellery to his pocket, and fondly pressed his hand over it.

"*You,* and your rubbishing watch!" Mother broke in like an explosion. "Much better indeed if you had kept the calves! They might have been some use on the place, and something made out of them! Taking a useless, trashy thing like that for them! It shows what a fool you are!"

"Well, they was me own proputty, wasn't they?" Andy protested sulkily.

"I don't know that they were your own proputty. I don't know that they were!" Mother swung her arms like a pugilist.

"Other people looked after them, and reared them just as much as you did, and a good deal more than you did. And whose milk was it they were reared on, I would like to ask; was it *your* milk, *was* it?"

"Oh, I dunno whose *milk* it was," Andy drawled. "It wasn't mine, I don't expect."

"No, it *wasn't* yours! Of course it wasn't yours!" yelled Mother. "And well you know it!"

"But this watch is mine, though." And grinning hard, Andy went off to the barn, where he took the Waterbury from his pocket again and studied the time some more.

Andy drove a large nail into the wall of his room, and having warned everyone in the home to "keep out an' let things alone that didn't belong to them," hung his watch carefully on it.

Several times a day he would race in from the paddock to see if the Waterbury was all right, and to wind it up. It was wonderful the amount of winding up it required, and how hard it was to wind. A windlass was no harder to wind. Being so strong and well made was the reason of it, Andy reckoned.

One day when he came in to see it, the face was open, and one of the hands was missing.

"By cripes, who's been at my watch an' broke it?" he bellowed, careering wildly into the front room with the damaged turnip in his hand.

"*Who* d' y' think would be at it!" Mother snorted. "No one but yourself. Ain't y' always at it? Are you ever doing anything else? When are you not wasting your time running to it and fooling an' humbugging with the rubbishing thing! And a blessed good job that it *is* broke, for perhaps you'll settle down and do something now!"

"Is it a good job!" howled Andy, with tears in his voice.

"Yes it *is!*" yelled Mother.

"Well, anyway," bellowed Andy, "whoever broke it I'll break their bloomin' necks for them!"

Martha and Tom outside, with their ears to the cracks in the slabs, suddenly scampered like rabbits for the barn.

"Will you! Oh, *will* you! You'll do a lot my fine fellow!" And Mother, tugging at her sleeves, moved menacingly towards Andy.

Andy backed cautiously in the directions of the front door, and was about to bolt when Limpy, in a strangely excited state, hopped in by the back way. He pointed at the wall, and gasped, and grimaced and gesticulated, but failed to make himself intelligible. Mother stared at him. So did Andy. Limpy hopped towards the door and wildly motioned them to follow. Mother remembered that Father was engaged sinking a well in the gully and jumped to a conclusion.

"It's your Father," she cried to Andy, "He's met with an accident—*run!*"

Andy ran. Mother ran, too, and Limpy dodged along behind.

A pack of strange dogs of all breeds and descriptions clamoring round the well, or hole—there was no windlass on it, and it was only down about twelve feet—caught Andy's eye.

"Somethin's up!" he yelled back to Mother, and ran harder. Arriving on the scene he kicked the yelping mongrels right and left and looked in to the hole. The anxious look on his face instantly changed to a curious, joyful grin. Then he burst out laughing, and shouted as Mother came puffing down the slope: "It's a kuh-kuh-*kangaroo!* Down th' bloomin' well along with Father!"

"What-what d' y' say!" Mother gasped, peering down the hole. And there, sure enough, was a good-sized kangaroo, standing erect on one side, and facing Father with fire and fight in his eyes.

"Merciful heavens!" she said, "what's to be done?"

"Get th' gun," Andy suggested, excitedly. *"I'll* shoot 'im."

"And shoot your Father, you fool!" Mother yelled in deprecation.

Then Father's voice, loud and terrible, rose from the hole.

"Lower th' ladder!" it said. "And keep them d—d dogs from shovin' stones in!"

"But can't yer brain him with the pick, Father? An' how did 'e get in there with y'?" Andy shouted back.

"D—n it, he's standin' on th' pick!" Father roared. "If I stoop won't he get me down! (To the 'roo) *Hoo! Hoo!* Would yer!" Bif! bif! thump! And for quite a while an interchange of scratches and clinches took place below.

Andy laughed and cheered, and counselled Father to "get him by the throat", and in his excitement shoved a quantity of blue metal down.

"Keep them d—n dorgs from shovin' stones in! An' get th' ladder!" howled Father.

Limpy knew where the ladder was.

Andy turned and attacked the mongrels with both feet, and two of them, a large black and white kangaroo dog and a small brute with no tail, in evading the kicks, fell down the well together. Mother threw up her hands when she saw them disappearing, and groaned.

Father cursed and swore worse than any bullockdriver we ever heard; but his words were soon drowned in the trouble those dogs made.

"Wad d' debil hab y' done now?" Limpy, struggling with the ladder, asked.

"Done!" yelled Andy, "two bloomin' dorgs gone down!"

Dora and Aunt Maria and Martha and Tom arrived and wanted to know what was the matter. But no one had time to tell them.

"Down with the ladder quick!" Mother cried.

All of them steadied the ladder, and as soon as it reached the bottom the kangaroo started to ascend it with the dog in his arms. He ascended in a spasmodic sort of way till he was nearly at the top.

"Loot oud for 'im! Loot oud for 'im!" Limpy shouted, hopping away from the well.

Andy reached down and struck at the 'roo with his hat. Then the big black and white kangaroo dog which had been worrying Father in a corner discovered his mistake and seized the marsupial by the tail. The marsupial dropped back to the bottom of the hole and kicked the big dog against the wall, and pranced all over Father.

Andy, leaning down, shouted to Father to get on the ladder. Father, his shirt scratched off his back and his chest all clawed and bitten and bleeding, feebly clutched the ladder with his two hands, and was struck on the top of the head with Andy's watch. Consternation! Andy danced round and round that well shouting: *"It's down!"*

"What's down now?" Mother yelled.

"Th' *watch!* Th' *watch!"* Andy groaned, clutching at his empty pocket like a drowning man at a straw.

"Then thank God!" Mother said, "and a pity you didn't go with it!" Then grabbing hold of Father as he struggled up the ladder, she laid him out on the grass, and sent Tom for some water.

Dora and Aunt Maria, looking down the hole, excitedly shouted:

"He's killing the poor dogs! He's killing them both!" And all of us gathered round the hole again—all of us—except Father.

"Th' *wretch!"* Andy hissed between his teeth; "An' he's standin' on my watch! I can see it. Where's that rope what was here? I'll fix him! I'll fix th' sod!"

Limpy, anticipating Andy, produced a hemp rope to which an old bucket was fastened.

Discarding the bucket Andy quickly adjusted a running noose on the end of the rope, and threw it down to the 'roo. The brute seized the hemp with both paws, and for several exciting seconds engaged the lot of us in a tug-of-war. When he found we were too many for him, though, he let go, and Mother fell heavily on Aunt Maria and hurt her leg.

Andy adjusted the noose again, and threw it a second time. "Got 'im roun' th' waist!" he shouted wildly. *"Pull!* PULL!*"* We fell in behind Andy and pulled for our lives.

The 'roo snorted and made a high standing jump, and when he jumped we hauled in the slack, and suspended him half way up the hole with his big feet kicking the ladder about.

"Hold him there! Hold him!" Andy cried. "Hold him while I throw the end over here," And taking the end of the rope he heaved it over the grim arm of a big dead tree that hung over the well like a gallows. Then all of us shifted our grips and pulled with Andy. Even Father, becoming excited at the prospects of publicly executing that marsupial, scrambled to his feet and got on the rope. Never before had we taken a prominent part in an execution, and the joy and novelty of it filled us with mirth.

The head of the condemned appeared over the hole.

"Look! he's comin'," Andy cried; "stick to 'im! Stick to 'im!"

We stuck to him, and gradually the great 'roo, his eyes bulging from their sockets, rose till his toes touched the top of the hole. Then, in a flash he made a mighty spring at the space above our heads and took all the strain off the hemp. We fell down and took all the slack with us, and the brute became suspended in mid-air.

"Blime!" Andy gasped. "If I could only get a look at me watch we'd know th' time it was when he was hanged."

Then the dogs became active again, and started biting the 'roo's tail. We all laughed at the dogs, and while we laughed the 'roo doubled himself into a ball, and sticking his long toe-nails under the rope around his waist, stiffened and strained and struggled till the muscles of his thighs stood out like

Gradually the 'roo rose

Samson's, and the sinews in his legs threatened to snap. And just when Andy called: "Now then! A little higher!" that rope flew into several fragments, and the marsupial fell on the dogs, and all of us fell on top of one another.

When we jumped up and looked round, the brute was jumping as hard as he could up the other side of the gully, and throwing dust and distance at the pack of mongrels limping in pursuit.

"Well, well, well!" Father murmured.

19. Tat-ta-a-a

When a month expired, Aunt Maria didn't say anything about returning to her situation. She didn't say anything about returning when two months expired. She settled calmly down to work, and became a permanent member of our household. As time went on she purchased a supply of drapery, and assisted by Mother and Dora, sat all the afternoon, and late into the nights, cutting out and making up pillow-slips, and sheets, and dresses, and night-gowns, and all sorts of unmentionable underclothing for herself to wear later on. And beautiful underclothing it was, too. The sight of it nearly turned Dora's head. She used to stop sewing to turn it over and over on the table and admire it. And several times she wondered if she would ever be lucky enough to own so many nice things. And the finishing touches that graced the bottoms of some of the articles were almost divine— they were ornamented with three and four rows of the most lovely lace Dora had ever seen. Mother, though, was not so delighted with Aunt Maria's finery. Mother didn't approved of such an elaborate display of lace. Mother always took an economical view of everything; and extravagance in dress was a crime in her eyes.

"Surely one row of lace should be enough to put on those things!" she said to Aunt Maria, one day. "In fact, I don't know what an old thing like you wants with any on them at all for! It's simply waste and flashness, and nothing else. I never had any on mine in all my life—and neither had anyone that ever I knew."

Aunt Maria turned red in the face and would have taken offence at Mother's remarks only for Dora.

"Indeed, Mother," Dora put in, "it's the right thing to have lace on them. Perhaps when you were getting married they mightn't have been so particular. But it's the fashion now with everyone; they all have lace put on."

"When I got married, me lady," Mother snorted, "they were

a lot more particular than they are now, and girls had a lot more sense. No one ever heard of anyone in my days wasting their bit of money on such trumpery! Sticking yards of good lace that costs money, where no one in the wide world will ever see it! Pshaw! It's dirty pride, that's what it is!"

Dora and Aunt Maria looked at each other, then burst into mirth.

"You may laugh and snigger," Mother grumbled on, "but I'm sure the money would be much better spent in boots, or a milk-bucket or something."

"Lots will see the lace on the clothes-line," Dora giggled.

"Yes, and laugh and sneer and poke fun at it, too," Mother answered.

"Villiam won't, will he, Aunt?" And Dora giggled more.

"No, Villiam won't," growled Mother. "No man ever sees the senselessness of anything when he gets married, and if his wife's as ugly as an ape he thinks she's a beauty. But wait awhile—wait for a month or two!" And shaking her hand she plunged the needle into the underclothing and started sewing furiously.

And while Aunt Maria was carrying out her share of the marriage preparations, Villiam Brandt knocked the end out of his humpy and totally changed its sad, lonely-looking appearance by adding two rooms and a verandah. Several times a week, too, he would put down the hammer and come along to our Homestead, and report progress to Aunt Maria. One day he came along when Aunt Maria, Mother and Dora were over at Bush's seeing Mrs. Bill Bush's little baby, and only Aunt Sue and Martha at home. When Aunt Sue saw him coming, she ran in and put on Aunt Maria's best hat and smiled at herself in the glass. Then leaving Martha staring and wondering, strutted out and met Villiam a short distance from the house. Villiam met her with a broad smile, and greeted her as "Mari"; and clasping her in his arms, playfully, lifted her several times off her feet. Then he stooped and kissed her on both cheeks, and on the mouth, and led her to a wild fig tree that spread itself all over the gully. There they sat close beside each other on the bare ground, their backs to the base of the tree, and murmured about the future into each other's ears. After a lapse, Aunt

They murmured about the future in each other's ears

Sue burst into tears, and in distressed tones told Villiam that all of us, especially her sister (she didn't mention her name) had turned against her, and were treating her shamefully, and wanted her to break off the engagement.

Villiam's eyes flashed, and his lips quivered; and he swore an oath that he would break all our heads.

"Sushan, dot wretch!" he cried excitedly. "She vos jealous of yeuo, mein sveet kerreature."

"So she is, Villiam," Aunt Sue stammered, letting her head fall on his shoulder; "and on that account we shouldn't wait any longer, don't y' think so?"

"I nod vait von more (unprintable) meenit!" Villiam exclaimed.

"I can't tell you *all* they've done and said just now," sobbed Aunt Sue; "but I think it's best not to wait."

"Mighty, I goes me home now and puts me der mare inter der spreeng cart and drive sweeftly to der train."

"Well, make haste and hurry, Villiam," Aunt Sue urged, drying her eyes, "and we'll be away before any of them comes back."

Villiam rushed home as fast as he could run. Aunt Sue hurried back to the house, and, to the astonishment of Martha, put on Aunt Maria's wedding dress, and packed all the new clothes that she and Mother and Dora had made, into a box.

"Oh, I know wot y're up to," Martha said, intruding, "think I deon't!"

Martha was on the side of Aunt Maria.

"You go out of this, you prying little cat, and mind your own business!" Aune Sue said, fumbling excitedly with a rope she was fastening the box with.

"You want t' make him believe yer Aunt Maria, doen't yer?" sneered Martha; "but she'll be here drekly, they're comin' now over th' hill."

"Don't you come here telling any of your lies, you little wretch," and Aunt Sue, greatly alarmed, began to perspire.

Martha darted out into the yard and shouted: "Aunt Maria-a-a! Aunt Maria-a-a! Hurry er-r-p!" to no one in particular.

Aunt Sue grabbed up the box and struggled to the verandah with it just as Villiam rattled up with the cart.

"Kvick, my sveet kerrature!" urged Villiam, jumping out and taking possession of the box.

"Don't you b'lieve 'er, Mr. Brandt, don't you b'lieve 'er! She's not Aunt Maria, she's Aunt Sue!" Martha squealed.

Villiam, seating himself beside Aunt Sue in the cart, and gathering up the reins, made ugly faces at Martha, and in broken language committed to her care a number of violent messages for "der oders ven dey cooms beck", and one special one for "her Aundt Sushan".

"Yer must be a galoot," Martha answered contemptuously, returning his ugly faces.

Just then the others, returning suddenly, appeared round the corner of the house. Mother excitedly screamed things to them. Mother and Aunt Maria grasped the situation in an instant. So

Aunt Sue waved her hand

did Dora. She collapsed in a fit of merriment. Mother, in her loudest voice called to Villiam to "Wait man! wait man!" Aunt Maria screamed and rushed towards the moving cart with her arms out. But Villiam wasn't to be deterred. Urging the mare to a fast trot, he looked round triumphantly and pulled faces at Aunt Maria. Then Aunt Sue, with one arm round Villiam, waved her other hand and cried: "Tat-ta-a! Tat-ta-a-a-a!"

20. The Wedding

When the cart containing Aunt Sue and Villiam Brandt had rolled away, Aunt Maria turned and ran inside and threw herself face downwards on the sofa and wept.

All of us, except Mother and Andy, stood gloomily round staring silently and sorrowfully at her. We were sorry, because we had been looking forward to her wedding with great joy, and to think that no marriage would now take place in the house was a great blow to us.

"It's a wonder they would do a thing like that, Father murmured.

"But I'm sure he doesn't know it's her 'es gone off with," Martha explained. "The first time 'e come, when all of you was away, and before he went to fetch the cart, she was wearin' Aunt Maria's dress, an' it seemed to strike me, somehow, then, that somethin' was wrong."

"Couldn't yer tell him?" Father asked thoughtfully.

Father was a deep thinker sometimes.

"Tell him," echoed Martha—"I might just as well have tried to tell things to a traction engine. She had him stuffed with her lies."

"If it had been anyone else," Aunt Maria moaned. "Oh-h-h! Anyone else—anyone else! Anyone but my own sister!—my own sis——"

"Baa!" Mother interrupted, suddenly entering the door. "Your own sister, indeed! What have you to cry about, let me ask? Didn't you treat her in the very same way yourself? And who has the most right to him—you, Maria, or her?"

Aunt Maria tried hard to take a fit, and when she stiffened out she kicked Limpy, who was seated sorrowfully on the end of the sofa watching her, on to the floor.

Martha and Tom laughed hard, and Mother ordered them outside. They went out cheerfully.

Aunt Maria's teeth began to chatter and she drew her knees almost up to her chin.

"Well, you needn't lie showing your legs to everyone," Mother shouted at her.

Aunt Maria screamed and sprang from the sofa, and said she wasn't showing her legs to anyone.

Turning to Father, Mother ordered him to put the horse in the cart at once.

"If Sue's to be married," she said determinedly, "I'm going to see it's done proper. She stuck to me all her life, and I'm not going to desert her just when she'll want someone near her."

Father went out and caught Marvellous, and we helped harness him and put him in the old spring cart. Then Mother flew round and dressed herself in her best clothes; and when she was stepping into the cart she thought Father had better accompany her.

"But I've got nothin' on!" Father mumbled, looking mournfully at his tattered shirt sleeves and mud-bespattered milking pants and unlaced "clodhoppers."

"You've got a shirt and trousers and boots on, haven't you? Do you want any more than that?" Mother snapped.

"Oh, I don't care," and Father mounted the cart. Father would do anything for the sake of peace. Father was always an obedient husband.

"Does that feather look all right in my hat, Martha?" Mother asked.

Martha said it did.

"Give me the reins!" And snatching them out of Father's hands, Mother drove off down the lane.

Nightfall. Aunt Maria sulking in her room. Dora came in from the yard and wondered aloud "if they were married yet?"

Aunt Maria, wiping her eyes came out from her room and said resolutely: "I'll break my heart over no man! If she marries him—let her. I don't care!" And she snapped her fingers and wagged her head.

"That's the right way to take it, Aunt!" Dora agreed. "And there's just as good fish in the sea as has ever been caught."

"There might be in the *sea*," Andy put in; "but accordin' to Father, them in the crick is nothin' to what they was twenty-five years ago."

"Pshaw! Neither is he!" And Dora shrugged her shoulders.

"Still, if I liked," Aunt Maria added thoughtfully, "I could have my noble William Brandt up for breach of promise."

"Could you, Aunt?" enthusiastically from Andy.

"Because both of you heard him ask me to have him." And Aunt Maria looked from one to the other for confirmation.

"I don't think *I* ever did, Aunt," Dora answered. Dora scented trouble. So did Andy.

"Nor me, by crimes, no!" he gasped; "I know nothin' about your courtin' business."

Andy had once been summoned to court as a witness in an assault case.

"But you *do!*" Aunt Maria insisted.

"But I DON'T!" stubbornly from Andy.

"Oh, let them get married, Aunt! What does it matter?" And Dora assumed a conciliatory attitude.

"You might do twenty times better yet, and I believe you will."

Aunt Maria swallowed a lump that was in her throat, and said: "He isn't worth worrying about, anyway, the old crawler that he is, but he's only like all the others."

Then she went off to her room again.

Next evening. The sun slowly sinking behind the range. Dora and Martha, and Andy and Tom in the milking-yard; Aunt Maria moping about the fowlhouse; the Paleys passing along the road behind their milking cows.

Andy, about to bail up his fourth cow, glanced through the rails and saw two carts approaching.

"There they are, back again," he called out; and letting the milking rip, bolted off with the empty bucket in his hand. The others followed excitedly. Aunt Maria ran into the house and hid herself.

Villiam and Aunt Sue, occupying the first cart, waved their hands; Mother and Father in the second one, waved pieces of white ribbon. Andy responded with the bucket, while the others threw their hats up.

The carts stopped at the rails and Mother and Martha said: "Hold on now—wait a while! Don't be in a hurry!" And when they had all alighted safely she gripped Father by the arm and proceeded to form a procession. Mother was a great believer in etiquette.

"I'll be der jolly band," Limpy said, producing his split stick and breaking into music.

Then Mother and Father led the way. Entering the home, the former lifted her voice and shouted "Welcome!" All of us echoed "Welcome!" and gave three cheers to boot. Then there was much kissing. And when Villiam kissed Dora and claimed her as a sister. Aunt Sue told him that she was "watching him".

"You vatch me, eh, little goosling?" And Villiam approached his bride and tickled her under the chin. She returned him a tender, loving smile.

Then Mother took the bride aside, and after whispering things to her, left the room with her. And while we talked to Villiam and asked him what it was like getting married, Aunt Maria, with paint on her cheeks and ribbons and roses in her hair, entered.

Villiam mistook her for the bride.

"You vas come back to me already, leetle goosling?" he said, throwing his arms round her.

We stared.

Aunt Maria broke angrily from his embrace and spat at him, and called him a deceiver.

We laughed.

Villiam was dumbfounded. But when Aunt Sue returned, he saw his mistake.

Then Aunt Maria spat at the two of them and hoping they would be "happy with each other", turned on her heel and went out.

21. An Unexpected Visitor

A glorious autumn day. There had been copious rains, and all the land was green and grand.

Father, standing in the doorway, looked out at the grass waving waist high, and wished he could afford to buy a hundred steers to fatten on it. Father was always crying for the moon.

A lady and gentleman, on stable-fed horses, rode briskly in through the gate, and gave Father a great surprise.

"Who's this?" he whispered.

Mother peeped over his shoulder. Dora squinted through the window, then fled into the bedroom, Martha and Tom slipped round the house and concealed themselves in the chimney corner.

"Helloa, Pettigrew!" the gentleman said, riding right up to the verandah—"and how are you getting along over here?"

"It's Harry Bellbridge—or Mr. Bellbridge, I should say!" And Father looked as proud and pleased as a schoolboy with a holiday.

"Harry is good enough," the other said, dismounting and shaking hands with Father.

Mother rapidly wiped the hand she was going to shake with in her apron, and flinging her hair back behind her ears, rushed out noisily.

Mr. Bellbridge shook hands with her, too, and Mother made a great fuss about him.

"And this is the young lady that was a baby when we left the station?" and Mother beamed proudly on Miss Bellbridge.

"That's the little Ida, then," the parent said.

"Well, well, well!" and Mother stared harder at her.

The young lady urged her restless horse forward, and leaning from the saddle, cheerfully put her gloved hand in Mother's.

"I can just remember when you and your husband were on the station, Mrs. Pettigrew," she said, and Mother quickly reckoned up her age and admitted "it were possible".

The heads of Martha and Tom appeared cautiously round the chimney corner.

Mother frowned at them.

"We just came from the wash-pool paddock," Mr. Bell-bridge explained, "where we were helping Sandersen to give delivery of a draft of bullocks to Will Springfield, the drover for the Meat Company now."

"Just so," Mother broke in, wagging and nodding her head.

"And my daughter was determined that we should give you a call before returning to the station."

Tears of joy and gratitude filled Mother's eyes, and Father tried hard to express the pride he felt at their favoured visit, but words failed him.

"That's all right, Abe!—that's all right!" Mr. Bellbridge interrupted sympathetically, "you were a good servant to me. And I hope you have never regretted leaving the station to go on your own."

"Oh, no!" Father mumbled, as if he wasn't quite sure. But Mother said she reckoned if he had it, over again he'd never go on a selection. Mother was always making Father out to be a liar some way or another.

"But we had a lot more ready money," she added, "when we was working on the station."

"Money is nothing!" the squatter said, and jokingly pre-dicted the time when Mother would be taking a trip round the world along with Father.

"That would be nice, wouldn't it, Mrs. Pettigrew?" the daughter laughed, and taking her foot out of the stirrup, jumped lightly from the saddle.

"A bit too nice for an old slave like me," and Mother laughed, too.

"Here, Tom, where away?" Father called—"Come and hold these horses."

Tom left the chimney corner like a startled rat leaving a hollow log, and fled for the hay-stacks.

"Don't bother, Abe," Bellbridge said. "I'll fasten them to this post for a few minutes, while I trouble you for a glass of water."

"Yes! Yes! Wait till I get you a glass," Father answered.

At mention of water, Martha, who knew they would have to pass her hiding-place to reach the tank, left the chimney-corner even more abruptly than Tom, and flew like an emu for the harness shed. And while Father went inside to procure the only glass we possessed, which he carefully wiped clean with the slack of his shirt, Mother inquired if Will Springfield would be passing our road with the cattle?

Bellbridge said he "thought he would be", and followed Father to the tank.

"A nice lad is Will Springfield," Mother remarked incidentally.

"I'm so glad you think so, Mrs. Pettigrew," and the young lady flushed the colour of a tomato and seemed inclined to embrace Mother.

Mother, who had a keen instinct for love affairs, displayed a quick interest, and gave Will Springfield, who often called at our place on his trips, a character that would have made a princess long to elope with him. And before the others returned from the tank the young lady opened her heart to Mother and confessed her love for Will, and told her how Pa didn't approve of her keeping company with him, and how he wanted her to have Sandersen, his manager, and the things he did to keep her from meeting Will. Then, hearing the others returning round the house, Mother squeezed the young lady's hand, and called her "dear", and told her not to be down-hearted, that it would all come right in the end, and promised to help her and Will all she could.

Just then who should turn off the road and ride straight in but Will Springfield himself.

There was mild confusion. Mother went forward hurriedly to meet him. Never before did she make half so much of Will. She greeted him as if he was the Governor come to open the new cheese factory, and told him it was in Parliament he ought to be and not droving cattle. Of course, Mother didn't know any better then; she thought Parliament was a place for intelligent and honest people. She knows better now. When she had finished welcoming Will, Mr. Bellbridge asked him how the cattle were shaping, and if he thought they would travel all right? And when Will told him they were moving along splendidly, the squatter grunted "H'm", and "Huh", and "Ah", then going to release the bridle reins from the post, said: "Come along, Ida."

It was here that Mother showed her ready resources.

"Wasn't you sayin' there was somethin' you wanted signed by a J.P.?" she said, with a sudden significant look at Father.

"Eh! No—I don't think so!" and a frown of perplexity came over Father's face. Father could rarely ever see through anything straight away—except it was a gate or a wide gap in the timber with a blue sky behind it.

"Of course there was." Mother tramped on his foot. "Something about tendering for the Board contract," and she tramped on his other foot.

Father began to follow the light.

"Oh, yes, of course!" he said. "I want you to sign something for me, Mr. Bellbridge."

Then Mother told Father to bring Mr. Bellbridge inside while she looked for the pen. Father brought him inside and Mother was a long time finding the pen. Having found it, she suggested that Father also tell Mr. Bellbridge all about a wretched feud he had had for years with old Maguire about a dividing fence, and ask his opinion about it. She made this suggestion so as to afford extended time for the young couple. Having waited till Mr. Bellbridge witnessed Father's signature, and was leaning back with a wise and attentive air listening to the dreary details of the endless squabble with old Maguire, she slipped outside and winked at the young lady. Then she ran inside again and contradicted Father in his statement of fact, and started at the beginning and gave the particulars all in her own way.

Father shook his head in disagreement with Mother.

"Nonsense, man," she persisted; "why you've got no memory at all." And to prove that her version was the right one, proceeded to mention everything that had happened in the district for ten years past and more. And while Mr. Bellbridge pressed his brow with the palm of his hand and stared bewilderingly at Mother, the angry voice of a stranger calling someone "a d——scoundrel", was heard outside.

"That's Sandersen!" And Mr. Bellbridge jumped off the chair and ran outside. Father and Mother ran out too. And there, ducking and side-stepping amongst the horses, were Sandersen and Springfield, with their coats off, dealing it out left and right to each other, while the young lady stood, pale and trembling.

"Here! What's this? What's this?" And Bellbridge forced himself between them. The fight stopped. Then scowling at Sandersen, he added: "Scandalous! Scandalous!"

The combatants, puffing and blowing and bleeding from the nose, started putting down their sleeves and walking aimlessly about. Three minutes later, Bellbridge and his daughter were cantering briskly away, and Sandersen and Springfield, hard at it again, were rolling about in the dirt and clutching each other by the throat and digging one another with long-necked spurs.

22. *Puttinga Puts Things in Order*

Everyone was saying the Bank had taken over Magoola Station and that Harry Bellbridge had "gone off his head". Father and Mother wouldn't believe it, but when Ida Bellbridge, who had no living relation other than her father, came one day and said it was true, and sobbed into her handkerchief, they *were* surprised.

"Dear, oh dear! oh dear!" Mother moaned; and Father said, "Good God!" Father in his young days had worked for many years on Magoola, and somehow always seemed to think that he owned an interest in the station.

To our delight, Ida consented to stay with us for a while, or, as Mother put it: "Until she got settled in her mind and saw how things were going to turn out". And if the way she used to sit sadly by the window, and other moments mope round the homestead shedding tears when Mother would condole with her, were circumstances to judge by, I fancy things were a long while turning out well with her.

At intervals the Bank manager would call and talk in confidence to Ida about her father's overdraft. We knew it was about his overdraft, because Martha and Tom used to listen outside with their ears to the cracks in the wall.

Once Sandersen called; but when Ida heard his voice telling the dogs to go to the hot place because they barked at him, she told Mother she didn't want to see him and hid herself in the bedroom.

Will Springfield, though, never called to see Ida, and all of us used to wonder why. At Tom's suggestion, Martha asked Ida the reason one day and made her blush to the ears.

"Martha!" Mother rebuked with a scowl, "run away and mind your own business."

Martha ran away and sneaked into Ida's room and looked into her box.

Three weeks passed. Christmas approaching. A scorching December sun baking and parching the earth; dogs, fowls, milking cows and all living things except Polly, the old spring-cart mare, vainly endeavouring to side-step the heat and the flies. (Polly never wasted her energies. She just stood in the open with her head down, her eyes closed, silently enduring everything, like the good, willing, uncomplaining, battered, dying old slave she was.) Ida, thinking of leaving us; all of us wishing she would change her mind and remain at the old homestead for ever.

Puttinga, a faithful, intelligent blackfellow, who was reared and employed on Magoola all his life, glided noiselessly to the back door and said he "wanted a speak alonga Miss Ida".

"Puttinga!" Ida exclaimed, when Tom delivered the message; and with tears of joy rushing to her eyes, ran out and greeted the black like a lost brother.

"Don't a you cry, Miss Ida!" the old servant said; "I come to tell a you secret"——

Ida pulled herself together.

"A secret, Puttinga?"

"I don't a want you to hear," and the black, glaring at Martha and Tom, waved them away.

Both slunk round the house.

"Yes, Puttinga?" And Ida clutched at his shirt sleeve.

Then, after glancing round the corner to assure himself that Martha and Tom were not lingering there.

"Someone who a you know been a steal big fella mob a bullock Magoola a moonlight a long a time now."

"Stealing Magoola bullocks for a long time, Puttinga? Who; tell me?" And the expression on Ida's face changed quickly.

Puttinga looked round the corner again, then whispered in her ear.

Ida started back and asked him "if he was sure it was true?"

"Been a true as hell, Miss Ida," and the eyes of the aboriginal rolled in their sockets like billiard balls.

Ida, clenching he white hands and biting at her lip, turned her head away.

When she relaxed and faced Puttinga again, he had vanished.

It had been a record frosty morning. Breakfast over; Mother, blue in the face and rubbing her hands together, came from the yard and told Ida "it was lovely out in the sun!"

Presently the latter went out and walked along the headlands of the wheat paddock. The warmth of the sun, though, seemed to find no place in her thoughts. Pausing at the farthest corner of the field, she leaned both elbows on the top of the round post and gazed thoughtfully down the bush track that led to old Magoola Homestead. Suddenly she heard a movement in the undergrowth outside the fence; then a man, pale, haggard and hunted-looking, appeared and hurriedly approached her.

"Will!" she gasped with a start.

Casting suspicious glances all around him, Springfield in a broken, agitated voice told her he was blamed for stealing Magoola cattle, and that the police had been hunting him for weeks to arrest him.

"But you haven't stolen any of the cattle, Will?" Ida asked calmly.

Before all in heaven and on earth Will declared he was innocent. Then added; "What you would think if I was arrested, makes me afraid to face them."

"I would think you were innocent," she answered; "because I know who has been stealing the cattle."

"You—know?" And Springfield stared.

But Ida was too excited to explain. She urged him to hurry with her and tell Father and Mother all about it.

Will hesitated and glanced back to where his horse was fastened in the dense undergrowth.

"Leave your horse and I will tell Andy to come and watch it." And Ida moved towards the house.

Will crept through the fence and joined her.

Noticing a man crossing the wheat paddock beside her, we stared and wondered what was up. We wondered more when Ida hustled Will, whom we recognised, straight into the

front room and called earnestly for Mother and Father. But
when she returned to the verandah and whispered things to
Andy, and warned the rest of us to keep our tongues in our
cheeks should anyone call to ask questions about Will Springfield, we knew then that something very serious was up.

Andy, who had been reconnoitering in the vicinity of
Will's horse, returned excitedly.

"Tom! Tom!" he called, "bring the gun, quick! There's a
big ole man wallaroo down in th' brigalow."

"What did y' say, Andy" from Tom.

Andy rushed into the kitchen and secured the gun himself.

"A what? A ole man wallaroo?" Tom repeated.

"An' he let me get right up to him 'fore he moved." And
Andy started ramming home a charge of shot.

"A big cove? A black one? And did he look at y'?"

"By cripes he did!" And to assure the gun going off, Andy
placed a pinch of powder in the nipple and put a cap on.

"Hurry up, quick! afore Father comes out," from Tom.

Andy hurried up and crept away with the loaded gun on
his shoulder just as Father came out of the house.

A few minutes later Sandersen rode into the yard and
dismounted.

"Well, Pettigrew, how are you getting along over here—
making a fortune?" he said jauntily to Father.

"Well enough; but no thanks to you," Father answered.
Father had got to hate Alf Sandersen, the manager of
Magoola.

Sandersen laughed ironically, and Father scowled at him.

Ida came to the verandah to ask if Andy had returned.
Sandersen raised his hat and said he had something very
important to say to her.

"Well, say it to yourself, if you have, Mr. Sandersen!"
And Ida turned her back on him and went inside.

Then Sandersen burst into profanity, and turning to
Father, asked if he knew a warrant was out for the arrest of
Will Springfield for stealing 5000 head of Magoola bullocks?
"*Do you?*" and he lifted his voice to a roar.

"No!" Father grunted, "an' I don't want to, either."

"Well, do you know he's hiding in that humpy from the police?" And the other pointed scornfully to our house and added: "Because if you don't, I DO!"

"You know a lot!" And Father tried to look unconcerned.

"And I know the police will be here in less than half an hour. But, listen to me!" and Sandersen shoved his angry-looking face near Father's, "If he'll take the last chance that will be given to him, there's time yet to get his horse and cross the border into New South Wales."

Father never said anything. But inside, Mother and Ida were fighting and struggling to restrain Will from rushing out to tear Sandersen to pieces.

Suddenly a gun-shot rang out, and a volume of smoke rose above the undergrowth.

Sandersen turned with a start. Father stared in the direction of the report, too, and wondered.

"The police! Didn't I tell you?" The former said, turning again to Father.

"Then I hope they'll make haste and arrest YOU!" And Ida's face appeared at the window.

"For God's sake don't be a fool! Do you know what this means?" Sandersen appealed to her.

"Perfectly!" she answered. "You think to get Will to prove himself guilty by running away, you villain! When it was yourself who stole the cattle!"

"A lie!" and Sandersen broke into fresh profanity.

Puttinga, who unnoticed had been lurking in the chimney corner, suddenly stepped forward and grinned at Sandersen.

"You been steal a bullock all a right, Alf a Sandersen," he said. "I been watch a you longa time in a moonlight."

Sandersen stepped back and glared fiercely at the aboriginal.

"Ebera time Will Springfield buy a mob," Puttinga went on, "you take a mob, too, and travel in a night alonga same tracks, and camp all a day in a scrub. I know. I been follow you."

Then there *was* excitement!

Like a madman Sandersen rushed Puttinga, and seizing him by the throat tried to tear his tongue out.

"Leave him alone! Leave him!" Father shouted, picking up a stick.

Sandersen swung round and knocked Father down.

Then Will Springfield, leaving fragments of his clothes in the clutches of Mother and Ida, jumped through the window and laid Sandersen out.

All of us hastily gathered round, and Mother and Ida knelt beside Sandersen to see if he was dead.

In the middle of it all, a dismounted sergeant of police, hopping and dancing on one leg and bellowing "I'm shot! I'm shot!" entered the yard.

Fresh consternation.

"My God!" And Father ran to the wounded officer.

Then Andy, trailing the gun after him, appeared and gave himself up.

"I didn't mean to do it!" he blubbered. "I thought he was th' wallaroo."

The trial of Sandersen, which lasted a fortnight, was the most sensational cattle-stealing case ever heard in Queensland. And the marriage of Will Springfield to Ida Bellbridge, six months later, which took place at our homestead, was the greatest and the liveliest wedding that Father or Mother or Limpy, or any of the Aunties, could ever remember.

THE END

The Emu Ran Through His Whiskers and over Him and Escaped with the Plow Reins Hanging to It

On Emu Creek

(with illustrations by Percy Lindsay)

Introduction to the University of Queensland Press Edition

This book was written in 1917, soon after my father returned to live in Brisbane for the second time, following nine years on the land at "The Firs", Nobby, on the Darling Downs.

My mother's health at the time, together with my parents' inability to run the farming property owing to my brothers' enlistment for the First World War, necessitated coming to the city.

The events in this book are basically factual, with literary embellishment here and there. In parts my father interspersed autobiographical sketches.

The chapter "The Death of Little Jens" is entirely true, even to the little fellow's name. This sad passing I can recall, and the numerous visitations to the Petersen home by another famous Australian, the late Sister Elizabeth Kenny, then a trained nursing sister whose family home was a short distance out from the township of Nobby.

This book was published as a paperback one shilling edition by New South Wales Bookstall Ltd., who paid £125 for the book rights.

ERIC DAVIS

BRISBANE

NOVEMBER 1971

1. Retrenched

The Duffs, except Mrs. Duff, all began life in the city. Mrs. Duff was a Rudd, the daughter of Joe Rudd, the son of Dad Rudd of Shingle Hut, and began life on a farm. Duff, himself, had been a public servant, and if he had had his own way, would still be one. But he hadn't his own way—the Government had it instead; and had all its own way as well. It was an ass of a Government—so Duff said. He said it because it ran the country into debt and tried to save it from disaster by dispensing with his services.

"There's what it's come to", he said, returning from the office one evening, and handing his wife an official letter in a blue envelope; "they've bulleted me, Kit! The 'native born Ministry'!"

Mrs. Duff turned pale.

"Malice!" Duff hissed viciously. "Malice and dirt!"

The wife read the official rigmarole dispensing with her husband's service, then dropping it on the floor, stared at him in dismay.

"Ain't it a knockout!" and Duff threw his leather hand-bag on the table and commenced cracking his fingers.

Mrs. Duff gazed on in silence.

"Let them keep their billet! Gad, if I can't make a living at something else!" and Duff started rolling himself a cigarette and pacing the floor. Duff always rolled himself a cigarette when he paced the floor—and often when he didn't pace the floor.

Still Mrs. Duff stared silently on.

"Fifteen years' service! A hundred and fifty quid a year! No rise for four years; 15 per cent deducted from me under 'Special retrenchment'; and now the dirty kick-out—and from a lot o' miserable political billet-hunters! Talk about reputation! It's the limit!"

Duff dropped into a chair and angrily blew smoke through his nose.

"Strike me!" and he jumped to his feet again—"if I were getting seven hundred a year, like a lot of blobs who go out lapping up whisky all day, I could understand it! But to sack a cove who's been doing his work honestly and trying to keep a family on a hundred and fifty quid a year, less 15 per cent— God love me! and they call themselves Australians and democrats!"

Mrs. Duff spoke.

"Never mind Titt!" she said putting a hand on his shoulder; "never mind! The service isn't the only place in the world, so don't worry!"

Then Duff sat down again; sprawled his long, thin, fork-like legs over the cheap carpet; dropped his sharp-pointed chin on his sunken chest, let the cigarette dangle from his lips, and reflected.

Mrs. Duff lifted the official letter from the floor; and listlessly folding and unfolding it, reflected with him.

Splinter, the eldest boy of the family, with school bag swung over his shoulder, marched into the hall, and, pausing at the sitting-room door, stood staring wonderingly at his parents.

"Home again?" Duff said, looking up slowly.

Splinter grinned and took the bag from his shoulder.

"No more cricket clubs or swimming baths for you after this, old chap!" regretfully, from the father.

"Oh, ain't there!" and Splinter stared rebelliously.

"Father's been retrenched by the Government, my son!" the mother explained, sadly.

"Retrenched!" Splinter repeated, staring hard.

"Retrenched—bulleted—speared!" Titt groaned.

"Dicken!" and turning away, Splinter went off to the kitchen to explore for provender.

"His troubles! Ah well!" and drawing in his long legs, Duff turned to his wife again.

"You're right, Kit," he said, "th' service isn't the only place in the world."

And it wasn't.

Six months later. Titt Duff left the city and came to Emu Creek, and brought his family with him. He also brought some furniture; a heart full of hope; a head empty of agricultural knowledge, and a pair of hands that had never done anything harder than roll a cigarette or wield a cricket bat.

"The Creek" was a subdivision of a famous station run—a run which the Government, after boring all over it with an augur to "test the quality of the soil" turned down at thirty-six shillings an acre, and was afterwards purchased by a "philanthropic" syndicate in the interests of closer settlement at £3 per acre. Said syndicate "close settled" it at prices ranging from £3/10/- to £9 per acre on "easy terms".

Wonderful looking country, though, was that famous run when Titt Duff, along with a persuasive commission agent, inspected it. Dairy farmers and sheep men from the South— men who knew a thing or two about farm lands—also inspected it. For months scarcely a day passed that didn't witness fresh contingents of prospective settlers, driving or riding or motoring over the run with lithographs protruding from their pockets, and land-hunger depicted on their faces. And when that run was cut up and thrown on the market, what a Godsend it was—to the philanthropic Syndicate and Commission Agents!

And the growth of grass that was on it was so high and so dense that neither man nor motor car could be seen amongst it; neither could the big stones, strewn over portion of it, nor the flourishing crop of young prickly pear sprouting from end to end of it. The genius who thought of "spelling" that famous run for a couple of seasons and letting the grass grow before inviting inspection will have something to think of on the Day of Judgment!

But when Sale day came—that was the day! People from all parts gathered at the auction room. Bankers from surrounding branches—farmers with mortgages round their necks— solicitors from the great metropolis to watch the interests of the benign Syndicate, and see they didn't give too much away for nothing! Commission Agents by the score were there shepherding their clients, advising them how to bid; how many portions to take; and urging them to keep on bidding till

all they required was knocked down to them, or the Banks
broke, or an earthquake or something happened! Great solace
at a land sale is a commission agent to a buyer! But Titt's
agent was one of the straight ones. And Titt secured the block
he was after, a bonser it was too! Two hundred and fifty acres
of the best scenery on the run, with grass as high as a house.
And the terms! They were enough to melt the nose on a Re-
patriation Committee. Five pounds ten per acre—one-sixth
cash; nothing the second year and the balance in five equal
instalments extending over five years, with interest at 7 per
cent! Seven per cent! Oh, Ikey, my Australian Uncle!

The Auctioneer opened the proceedings with a prophetic
speech, in which he painted that run dotted over with a
thousand rich prosperous homesteads flowing with milk and
honey, then read the provisional agreement and terms of sale
at the rate of 366 words to the minute so as no one would
understand.

"Those are the conditions of Sale, ladies and gentlemen,"
he concluded; "now I'll begin by offering portion 12—250
acres. Who'll make me an offer?"

Laws! Titt nearly dropped dead in his seat! Portion 12 was
the block he had set his heart on. For some seconds he was
struck speechless; and though his friend, the Commission
Agent, kept prodding him in the ribs, several bids were taken
before Titt could find his tongue. At last he started bidding at
the top of his voice, and when portion 12 was knocked down
to him he scrambled over the heads of six rows of astonished
people in his excitement to reach the table, and signed the
agreement without looking at it!

"Gee!" he said, wringing the hand of the Commission
Agent, "I was frightened I wouldn't get it!"

The Commission Agent, to be agreeable, said he "was feeling a bit funky about it himself". No one can lie so cordially
and naturally as a Commission Agent. It's a pleasure to listen
to him.

Then they slipped out and went up the street to the "Com-
mercial", where they celebrated the occasion in beer—celebrated it until Titt's double-jointed legs started bending beneath him in different directions—until he started talking of

returning to the auction room and bidding for the "homestead" block. There were five thousand acres in the homestead block, worth nearly £5 an acre, with fifteen hundred pounds of improvements on it, and Titt possessed something less than £500.

Months later. Duff's house was built—a modest weatherboard building of four rooms; and when the local contractor was paid, barely sufficient remained of Titt's money to purchase dairy cows and some machinery and a horse or two to go on with.

A stinging hot day. Titt and Mrs. Duff and Splinter and Araluen, the eldest of the family, were busy moving the furniture in, and cleaning up the mess left about the place by the carpenters. Titt, in shirt and pants, his sleeves rolled up, showing a pair of long lean arms, moved about on his calfless limbs as though he were on springs and couldn't get enough out of himself. At intervals he paused, and with hands resting on his wide bony hips—hips that held his pants up without the aid of a belt—enthused about the house, and the splendid view from the front door, and the clear air and the blue sky, and his future prospects.

"If we had only come here fifteen years ago, eh Kate?" he said making a seat of the corner of the table and swinging his legs about, "we'd be worth a bit now."

"Perhaps we wouldn't—you never know," his wife answered thoughtfully, wiping the dust from the crockery that had just been unpacked.

"If y' had come here fifteen years ago, you wouldn't have been worth me any way," Splinter chipped in, " 'cause I wasn't born then." Splinter possessed a wit inherited from his Uncle Joe.

"You!" Titt guffawed, springing from the table, and playfully swinging a feint at Splinter with his long, fleshless right; "if you could stand a punch I'd give y' one."

"Give me one then", and sparring up to his parent, Splinter rolled into him with both hands. The parent sparred and feinted and chuckled and ducked and side-stepped, and hopped all round the room; and the fixing of the furniture, and the splendid view from the front door and his future prospects and all the rest suddenly vanished.

"Oh, look at Splinter! Look at Splinter, Mother!" Araluen called, in delight, from the other end of the room.

"I don't want to look at him", the Mother answered. "I wish they'd both stop their nonsense and let us get on with the work."

But Mrs. Duff was forced to look at Splinter. Something went wrong with his legs—they twisted round each other like the cane of a cart-whip handle, and he flopped backwards into a dish of dough that stood in a corner of the room awaiting the oven, and became submerged to the hips in it.

"Holy!" Titt ejaculated, dropping his hands and pulling a serious face. Araluen flushed joyously. Splinter tried to rise, but sank deeper into the dough and squeezed a lot of it over the edge on to the floor, and cloyed his fingers in it.

Mrs. Duff stared at Splinter, then at Titt.

"Here!" the latter commanded of Splinter, "get out of it, can't y'. What did you want fallin' into it for?" then jerked him out of the dish by the two arms, Splinter taking enough dough with him on the seat of his pants to make a loaf with.

"It was your fault, father, as much as mine", the latter protested, plucking the dough from his clothes and returning it in fistfuls to the dish.

"My fault as much as yours?" from Titt.

"And there might have been a hole in his trousers, too!" Araluen suggested, with a giggle.

"Of course there might, and to say it was as much my fault as his!"

"And so it was!" doggedly from Splinter.

"Here! Don't you give me any more back-jaw!" and Titt struck an attitude.

"Well, it was!" and Splinter dashed for the open door. His parent dashed after him, and risking a flying kick, succeeded in scraping some of the dough off him with the toe of his boot.

"If he ain't a determined young hound", and Titt, with an injured expression, turned to Mrs. Duff; but instead of meeting with approval, found her crumpled up in a chair weeping copiously into her apron.

"What's th' matter, Kit?" he said, putting a hand on her head; "don't take it like that. Y' know it couldn't be helped."

The wife wept harder.

"Come on, be a sport. Look up, won't y'?

He was playfully forcing her face towards his when Splinter rushed back into the room again.

"Someone comin'," he shouted; "two swells right near th' house in a buggy."

Father and mother separated instantly. The latter sprang to her feet and began drying her eyes with her apron. The former moved to the door and looked cautiously out.

"How do I look—my eyes all right? Are they red?" Mrs. Duff hurriedly asked.

"Red? No!" Titt lied—"they're right as pie."

Then she wiped them some more, and rapidly smoothing her hair with her hands and removing her apron, looked ready to receive the King.

But it wasn't the Royal family that were coming—'twas two clerks from the office of the Syndicate; and coming with a completed agreement and a bag of promissory notes for Titt to sign in connection with the purchase of his block of land.

Two nice-looking young men they were, too, city bred, and one a J.P.—the Syndicate's own particular Justice of the Peace. Had they come with a bag full of yellow, golden sovereigns for free distribution amongst the family, Titt couldn't have been more pleased to see them.

"Go on!" he said, in surprise, to the J.P., "are you from Brisbane? What part?" And when the Magistrate answered "Woolloongabba", Titt shook him hard by the hand and called him "Townie", and asked him what school he went to.

Then they got down to business. Titt sat up to the table, squared his shoulders, flourished the pen and attached his signature to that completed agreement and those promissory notes with an air of importance that would make you think he was a Commonwealth Bank. And when the J.P. had witnessed everything, and initialled the alterations, he and his companion wished Titt "good luck", and, shaking hands with Mrs. Duff, went off to call upon their next victim, who was hiding somewhere on the adjoining block.

"That's the way to help people on to the land", Titt said, directing his wife's attention to the copy of the agreement lying on the table. "Now, why couldn't the Government have gone about it that way?" And taking up the agreement he opened its foolscap pages. "For £222/3/4 we are able to go on to this block worth £1525, with seven years, you might say, to pay it off, on terms as easy as falling off a log."

Mrs. Duff reached for the document, and began perusing it slowly and studiously.

"Just have a squint at it, old girl, to satisfy yourself", Titt said, encouragingly. Then sitting back, employed himself uselessly scribbling his name and address in fifty different ways on scraps of paper left by the Syndicate's clerks, at intervals glancing up to see how the wife was enjoying the terms.

But Mrs. Duff wasn't enjoying them at all.

"Seven per cent interest?" she questioned, wrinkling her brow. "Why, by the time the six years or whatever it is, are up, you'll have paid for the place twice over!"

"Get out!" Titt scoffed amusedly; "the interest'll get smaller and smaller every year, won't it?"

"And if at any time you're behind with the payment," the wife went on as though he had never spoken, "they can fine you and make you pay a higher rate."

"Well, of course," Titt acquiesced, cheerfully, "that's th' general thing in business, ain't it?"

"And all the improvements must be insured at your expense", and Mrs. Duff wrinkled her brows some more.

"But all the improvements will be mine, won't they? Bless me, Kit, you wouldn't expect a cove to get things for nothing, would you? You're a great business woman, YOU are!"

"All noxious weeds are to be kept down by you"—and the wife turned over a page of the agreement.

"Not necessarily by meself," Titt explained; "there's nothing to stop me from getting anyone else to keep them down, so long as I pay for it."

"You've to pay all rates and taxes, including the Local Government Tax and State and Federal Land Tax."

"Cer-certainly," Titt stammered, "all landholders have to do that, haven't they?"

"You've to pay the legal cost of this agreement and the stamp duty on it."

"Legal cost and stamp duty?" Titt echoed thoughtfully. "Are you sure?"

"And if you fail to pay any of the instalments," the wife went on, "the place will become the Syndicate's again, and all that you ever paid or did in the way of work, will be theirs, too!" And Mrs. Duff, her eyes swimming like two large lakes, looked up pitifully at Titt.

Just then the Syndicate's clerks unexpectedly returned. They returned because one of the P/N's had been overlooked.

"Oh, yes, I see", Titt said, sullenly, when the document was placed before him. Then taking up the pen he signed it with a trembling hand. And when the clerks, smiling and bowing, took their departure again, Titt, pale and funky looking, turned to his wife.

"What are you looking so worried for?" she laughed.

"Do y' think we'll come out of it all right, Kit?" he mumbled, hoarsely.

"Of course we will."

Then, taking up the broom, she started sweeping and singing, and whistling.

But deep down in her heart the woman knew that through the long years of hardship and toil and disappointment that lay ahead, hell itself must needs be faced before their souls could ever again be called their own. And if 'twas a lie she uttered, 'twas uttered in a good cause, and the tears that fell from her and mingled with the dust on the floor were surely noted by the good God above.

2. Weaning Mary Ellen

Early morning in December. The sun rising over Umbrella Mountain; locusts in thousands awakening the forest trees; flies—millions of wretched, sticky, savage flies—swarming from their sleeping haunts. Inside, breakfast ready. Titt, at the head of the table carving the remnant of yesterday's roast; Mrs. Duff at the end serving out the tea; Splinter and Araluen at either side, snarling, pulling faces, and backbiting each other; the baby perched in a high chair beside its father "goo-gooing" and sucking a strip of gristle that hung from its mouth like a worm in the beak of a young jackass.

The baby, Mary Ellen, was being weaned. For the third time it was being weaned, and for two long nights had squealed and squawked in protest and kept Mrs. Duff singing to it, and Titt grumbling, and everyone else awake.

"You nearly had to give in again last night, Kit", Titt grinned. Titt, when daylight came, was always inclined to side with the infant.

"But I didn't", the mother smiled. "Never again." Then addressing the infant as though it understood her:

"No more titty-bottle, Miss Bully—never, never any more."

"There's no bread on the table", Splinter discovered.

Araluen left her place and ran to the bread tin.

"Here, cut that out you!" Titt, rattling the knife on the steel, roared at Splinter, "What did y' snap that off your sister's plate for? Think I ain't got any eyes?"

" 'Cause I like it well done an' she don't", sulkily from Splinter.

"He's fibbin', Father", Araluen, returning with a loaf, protested. Then a scuffle commenced across the table.

"Araluen!" Mrs. Duff commanded. "Araluen!" Mrs. Duff, in quarrels with his sister, always sided with Splinter.

"Well, he's taken me meat, Mother, and won't put it back", stubbornly from Araluen.

"Never mind, Father will cut you some more."

But Araluen did mind. She cracked Splinter hard on the head with a spoon and told him to "take that, too!"

Splinter hurriedly stuffed the well-done slice into his mouth and started making headway. Splinter was a slick tactical thief.

"Look at him, Father!" and his sister burst into tears. Sisters always burst into tears when argument fails. "He's puttin' it in his mouth! Boo, hoo! hoo!"

"Now look here me noble young buck!" and dropping the carvers on the cloth and rising to his feet Titt eyed the erring one with great authority. "By Christmas! I'm gettin' tired of talkin' to you an' tellin' y' to mind yourself—do y' know that?"

Splinter, his eyes rolling, his cheeks bulging, his jaws working against time, regarded his parent complacently.

"Do y' hear what I'm sayin'?" loudly from the latter.

Splinter swallowed the meat at a gulp, and said, "Well can't I have me breakfast as well as her?"

"Have your breakfast as well as her!" the parent sneered Then lifting his voice: "Y' can't have her breakfast as well as your own, too, can y'? You ain't a carpet snake, are y'?"

Splinter quietly reached for some bread, and grinned.

Mrs. Duff pleaded for peace.

"That's right, my pet lamb, tell them to stop, and to behave themselves!" playfully to the "goo-gooing" youngster.

"It's a good job for him he's got his Mother to side with him! But by Christmas if there's to be any more of this squibbin'——"and Titt, whose bark was ever worse than his bite, sat down and renewed the carving.

Araluen, simpering into her apron, lifted her head and saw Splinter smiling.

"He's laughing now, Father," she said, "he's laughing!"

Titt never heard her.

"He's making faces, Father."

Still Titt didn't hear her.

"He's poking his tongue out at you, now, Father!"

"I ain't!" Splinter promptly lied.

But Titt could stand it no longer. Dropping the carvers again he jumped round the table at Splinter.

Splinter humped his shoulders, and, hanging over to one side, instinctively guarded his head with his elbow.

"You darned young dawg! What did I just tell y' awhile ago?" And, striking a fearsome attitude, Titt stood over the culprit like an eagle over a defenceless lamb. But just then fresh commotion broke out. A low gurgling sound came from the vicinity of the high chair.

"My God!" Mrs. Duff cried, "the baby's choking", and bounded from her seat.

"It's swallowed th' grizzle!" from Araluen.

Titt turned and grabbed the gasping infant in his arms and groaned, "Oh, oh." Then shook it and said, "My God! My God!"

Splinter and Araluen went pale and stared openmouthed. The brat stiffened out and went black in the face.

"Put your finger down its throat", Mrs. Duff shrieked, wringing her hands frantically. "Down its throat; its throat!"

Titt tried to put his finger down, but couldn't. It was a sore finger with rag and cotton wool rolled round it, and the lot saturated with "Farmer's Friend".

Mrs. Duff snatched the child from him, and holding it upside down, thumped it on the back, and every time she thumped it, Tit moaned, "My goodness! My goodness!"

Not a kick or whisper came from the youngster.

"Do something, some of you, or it'll be dead!" Mrs. Duff shrieked desperately. "Oh gracious heaven!"

Splinter and Araluen burst into blubbers, and bellowed like two calves. That was all they could do.

Titt rushed to the open window and looked to see if any first-aid was about. An old grey-bearded swagman, deaf as a beetle, with eyes half eaten out of his head by flies, and an empty black billycan in his hand, was approaching the place in search of hot water for breakfast.

"Quick, Mister! Quick!" Titt shouted and waved to him. "Our baby's chokin'!"

The deaf swagman, in doubt whether Titt's demonstrations were friendly or otherwise, stood stock still and stared. Titt jumped through the window and ran to fetch him.

*Mrs. Duff Snatched the Child from Him, and, Holding It Upside
Down, Thumped It on the Back*

The deaf one dropped his billycan, turned, and fled, and in his haste tumbled over a wheel track and hurt himself.

Mrs. Duff plunged her fingers down the youngster's throat and fished up the gristle. Then it got back its breath and screamed and kicked and nearly got out of her arms.

Titt rushed in again shouting, "Is it all right? Is it up?"

Splinter and Araluen ceased bellowing. The kid screamed harder.

"There, there, there, my poor wee lamb, it was Mother's fault! Mother's fault!" and opening her dress Mrs. Duff pressed the squalling offspring to her bosom. It grabbed the "bottle" with both hands and "teeth" and was soon silent.

"By Christmas!" Titt said, proudly, "that's all she was chokin' for, th' young devil!"

Then Splinter and Araluen, wiping their eyes, gathered round and laughed. Titt laughed some, too. But Mrs. Duff, bending over the precious brat and coddling it planted kisses on its brow and crooned: "Mother's little darling!"

That's eighteen years ago.

"Mother's little darling" is married now and will soon be weaning one of her own.

3. The Bereaved Bear

Titt took the grubbing tools and a drink of water and started burning off. Grubbing and burning off was an occupation new to Titt. He knew nothing about it then—he knows a wonderful lot about it now. He seemed to think then, that clearing land was an index to the glories of farming—glories he had often heard know-alls raving about in city streets and in offices and in Parliament, so rolling up his shirt sleeves and throwing off his hat, he went at it as though nothing but sport and pastime and pound notes were to be extracted from those huge box and iron bark trees—trees that had stood there stolidly defying the elements for ages and ages! 'Twas the trees that did the extracting—extracted sweat and groans and profanity from Titt till there wasn't any more left in him; and if he had had any fat about him, which, of course, he hadn't—there was nothing of the gohanna about Titt—every particle of that would have been extracted from him, too.

Waving the axe, Titt cheerfully indicated a heavily timbered portion of the holding—a fifty acre patch of dense heavy timber—and advanced determinedly on it to knock it all down and chop it all up into small pieces, and burn it all into ashes, and fence it all in with a new fence—a substantial cattle-proof fence—and break it all up with a plough, and plant it all with corn and pumpkin—the best of pumpkin, pumpkin that, when ripe, would take some getting into a dray. Ah, yes, Titt was going to tackle this land business with intelligence and a strong hand and tremendous self-determination. All the old hands on the land were only fooling and fiddling with the industry. They were afraid of it. Grit and pluck were all that was required to win through on. The old hands hadn't any such qualifications. Titt knew they hadn't. He had often heard politicians and produce merchants, and financial authorities, and shop-walkers, and gentlemen of the cloth and all the rest of the town men who loved good soft, easy jobs themselves, say

they hadn't. And no one in this world or any other world ever
knew so much about land settlement and soils and farming, as
politicians and produce merchants, and shop-walkers and
financial authorities did—or ever knew so little! Titt, theoret-
ically, was a goer, a scene shifter. In the space of one short
evening he could go right through life, right through the world
shifting every obstacle in it, material, spiritual or financial,
and end up with wads of wealth. 'Twas before the axe and
tongues of men like Titt that wildernesses succumbed and were
reclaimed. But settlers of his kind didn't grow on prickly pear
bushes! They weren't made either. They were born behind
counters and in Parliament and in pulpits and in offices—and
will be born there to the end of time! God bless them!

"And soon as I harvest the corn and pumpkin," Titt told
the Missus, "I'm going to plough it all over again, cross-
plough it, and keep on ploughing it till it has a mulch on it a
foot deep and fine as flour. Then I'm going to sow the lot
with wheat and lucerne—sow them all together——"

His wife stared at him in surprise. She couldn't conceive
where he had got his ideas from.

"That's th' surest way of getting crops", Titt went on, omit-
ting to explain that he'd been yarning with old O'Connor
round at Umbrella Mountain. "It gives y' two strings to your
bow, besides saving a lot of labour and time."

The Missus was deeply impressed.

"Y' see, the wheat grows the faster of the two," he explained
further, "and by the time it's ripe and harvested the lucerne
will be comin' on—it'll be about four or five inches high in
fact. Directly after that when the sun gets to it, it'll shoot up
like a mushroom, and before a month is out it'll be ready for
the mower."

Mrs. Duff, standing with a jug of hot tea and some home-
made scones in her hands, for Titt's "eleven o'clock", smiled
encouragingly; then set the provender down in a shady place
beneath the giant gum he was engaged in rooting, lock, stock
and barrel, out of the earth. Titt, flushed and perspiring,
stepped out of the huge excavation he had made round the
roots of the gum and threw himself down beside the tea and
scones, and proceeded to enjoy the new life.

"But I must"—pausing and noisily sipping the tea to test its temperature—"get all these trees down first, Kit", he added.

Mrs. Duff turned her head and ran her eyes over the "clearing" to see how many trees were down. She saw one solitary old iron bark lying prostrate, its great limbs smashed and shattered, its hacked and mutilated roots cocked in the air with junks of turf clinging to them, and its faded, withered leaves drooping in sullen, stricken contrast against the living green and blooming flowers of a glad and joyous world.

"How long were you grubbing that one?" she asked.

"About a week"—and opening his mouth wide, Titt put a scone into it.

"A week?" And the wife turned her eyes to the giant wall of timber yet standing, and a feeling of despair seemed to come over her.

There was an interval of silence. The chirping of the birds and the crowing of the roosters over at the house were the only audible sounds.

"A penny for your thoughts, Kit?" and Titt cheerfully attacked another scone.

His wife swallowed a lump that came into her throat, but kept her thoughts to herself.

Titt raised the jug of tea to his head and commenced to drink. Suddenly a sharp cry came from the tree top. Titt, whose eyes as he drank, chanced to be raised in the direction, nearly choked himself. Dropping the jug, he shouted, "A hawk! A bear! Look out!" And sprang excitedly to his feet as a baby bear, snatched from the back of its unsuspecting mother by a prowling eagle, fell to the ground with a thud and a squeak, within reach of the Missus. Talk about a fright! Mrs. Duff startled every living thing for a mile around with the shriek she gave.

"Holy!" Titt gasped, open-mouthed. "Holy!"

But while he was "holying", the winged Hun returned to the attack. It swooped brazenly down, this time striking its claws firmly into the furry coat of baby bear, tumbling blindly about in the grass, and rising with it in its clutch, shaped a

*Mrs. Bear Sprang on Titt's Shoulders, Dug Her Claws in, and Clung
to Him*

westerly course and soared triumphantly for the highest point on Mount Sibley.

Titt said he was "damned!"

His wife said nothing; but if her face was an index to her mind, she was solemnly thinking of all that was in the prayer book.

Up above mammy bear was springing frantically from limb to limb—running—literally running—up and down them, shedding tears and filling the air with cries and sobs.

Titt, with solemn countenance, gazed up at her.

"Poor thing! Listen to her!" And Mrs. Duff burst into tears.

"That'll do, Kit! Never mind!" and Titt struggled to restrain a sob himself.

Mammy bear paused for a moment to listen for some response from her missing offspring. She heard Mrs. Duff whimpering below. Down along these limbs she slithered head first. Reaching the lowest fork, a few feet higher than Titt's head, she hesitated. Then peering at her sympathisers with red glaring eye-balls, listened some more. A low sob came from Mrs. Duff, and a comforting murmur from Titt. Mrs. Bear didn't wait for any more. That her stolen young was concealed somewhere about their persons she hadn't any doubt. She sprang off that fork as though it were a spring-board and, flopping square on Titt's shoulders, dug her claws into his naked neck and clung to him. He bounded against the Missus and sent her spinning in the grass. "Oh! Oh-h! Oh-h-h!" he bellowed, running round and round with his back humped and mammy bear sitting on his neck. Then he threw himself down and roared, "Help!" and fought the air with his hands and feet. Mrs. Duff rose, and arming herself with a heavy stick, ran to his assistance. She aimed blows in rapid succession at Mrs. Bear, and every one that missed was stopped by some part or other of Titt's head. But the stick wore shorter and lighter, till one or two blows "got home", then the bear released her grip and skedaddled for the tree. Mrs. Duff threw the stick after her and shrieked, "You wretch!"

Titt, smeared with blood and dust, arised himself on hands and knees.

"That's what it was!" he groaned; "I —I—(another groan) thought it was the eagle!"

"Oh, you old Hun!" his wife shrieked again at Mrs. Bear, now gazing contentedly down from the highest limb. "A pity it wasn't yourself the hawk took!"

4. Charlie

Titt let the clearing slide and started hurriedly to erect a milking-yard. He started to erect a milking-yard because he suddenly decided to buy twelve good dairy cows from O'Connor, and make money quickly. He decided to buy them from O'Connor because O'Connor went in for Shorthorns, and Shorthorns were the best stamp, and most profitable class of dairy cattle to have about a farm, or about anything—so O'Connor reckoned. Growing grain was right enough in its way, there was nothing wrong about it, but Titt had learned that waiting till the ground was cleared, and the crop came up, and grew (especially grew) and was harvested, and carted to the railway station, and a cheque came in payment for it would take much time, but with twelve or so good Shorthorn cows on the go the farm would return money right from the word "off". A monthly cheque would come rolling in, and like the brook, keep on rolling and getting larger. Of course, meanwhile, between milking-time and banking hours, he would go on leisurely clearing the land, and ploughing and sowing, and hoping for rain, and in that way keep abundance of green fodder up to the herd, and cut and convert into hay all they wouldn't require. And all that the herd wouldn't require would be tremendous—enough to build dozens of mighty stacks and make the homestead look like a State Experimental Farm or an Art Gallery. And in addition to the ever-recurring monthly cheque he would make a big "scoop" out of these side-lines.

"That's the way to do it," he said brimming over with enthusiasm to Mrs. Duff, "wonder it never struck me before? And it ought to have, you know, because I 'spose I must have heard it dozens of times in the city—scores of times—hundreds of times. Bishops and parsons and University Senators and all th' bloomin' aristocracy were always preachin' and writin' about it down there. Wonderful when y' think of it what the educated blokes know about farming, and the best way to go about it to make it pay. They know twenty times more than the chaps here do, who've been at it all their lives!"

"They know so much about it," Mrs. Duff snapped, "that they never want to do any of it themselves, or make farmers of their sons."

Titt opened his eyes and stared. His enthusiasm got a rude shock.

"Still y' can't beat the educated coves, for all that", he mumbled feebly.

"No, not for talking and telling others how to do the hard part while they sit and ride about and have a good easy time themselves!" and Mrs. Duff walked away.

"There's a lot o' truth in that, too", and seating himself on the log he had been barking with the axe to prepare for a gate-post for the yard, Titt reflected silently.

Then after a minute or two.

"There is so!" and lifting a chip from the ground he care-lessly tossed it at a soldier ant lurking a few feet in the grass as though it were on scout duty. "A d——n lot of truth!"

Then resting his elbows on his knees, and his chin in the palms of his hands, he gave himself up to reflection.

Old Charlie, a bone collector, driving three horses and standing upright in a dray came blundering along—bumping over ruts and stones and timber hidden in the grass, and making as much noise as the retreat from Mons.

"Woh-h!" he roared, as the leader was about to walk over Titt, log and all, and trample him into the earth. "Woh-h!"

Titt's reflections were suddenly scattered. He bounced up from that log like an India-rubber man, and snatching the long-handled shovel, angrily glared at the grinning bone col-lector.

"Hoh! Hoh! Hoh!" the latter laughed from the depths of a tremendous stomach hanging in rolls over a tight-buckled waist strap. "Was y' sleepin' on th' job eh-h? Did y' think I was agoin' to run y' down? Did y'? Hoh! Hoh! Hoh!"

"Well, you might just as well," Titt gasped, "as to frighten the life out of a chap!"

"Oh, I wouldn't do thet", and calmly alighting from the dray, Charlie rolled the reins into a coil and hung them on the *harness* of the leader. "You wasn't afrightent I would, was y', eh?"

Titt made no answer.

Then casting a pair of small, black snakey-looking eyes at the yard Titt had started to build, Charlie, in a loud voice, inquired, "What are you been adoin' on, eh?"

"Building a milking-yard, I suppose!" and Titt eyed the boisterous intruder sullenly and curiously. Titt had never seen a person like him before—nor had anyone else, for that matter. He was a powerful looking man, a Samson of the bush, with hair and whiskers as black as the ninth plague of Egypt; he wore a flannel shirt and moleskin pants, wondrously dirty, and a pair of heavy boots, without laces. His bare arms were thick as Titt's thighs, his hands as small as a woman's, and his Gipsy-coloured skin as unwashed as his clothes.

"A milkin'-yard?" he echoed, amusedly; "Hoh! Hoh! Hoh!" and taking hold of the only panel Titt had erected, shook it mightily, with both hands, then pulled it to him and shoved it from him till the posts, rails and all, lay flat on the ground.

"What th' devil do y' mean?" and with fire in his eye, Titt took a short grip of the long-handle shovel and squared up to the offender.

"It tumbled down! Thet ain't no good? Hoh! Hoh! Hoh!" the other laughed.

"It did when you shoved it!" and Titt, swinging the shovel, jumped closer to Charlie.

"You wouldn't hit anyone, would y', eh?"

But just then a puff of wind gave Titt a sniff of Charlie, and suddenly dropping the shovel, he sprang back from him.

"Would y'?" the other repeated.

Titt stood spitting and coughing and grinning.

"Dorn't y' know who I be? Ain't y' seen I afore? Eh? Hoh! Hoh! Hoh!"

Titt hadn't.

"I'm Charlie. I be agatherin' oop the bones. There be a fine lot on 'em in the dray; look at 'em, eh?"

Titt turned and saw a smellsome pile of bullocks' horned

heads, bullocks' ribs, sheeps' heads and horses' heads, shoulder blades, shin bones, joints, knuckles, and whole carcases of defunct kangaroo and emu mingling with each other in the vehicle, and shuddered at the sight. They were more offensive than Charlie himself.

"Do y' know where old Jim Ruskin lay?" the bone monger, approaching Titt again, inquired covetously.

Titt, scowling and spitting and backing away, said he had never heard of Ruskin, and didn't want to.

"He lived round here onct, old Jim Ruskin did", Charlie informed him. "He quarrelled wi' I one day about a sheep, and took I to court. Hoh! Hoh! Hoh! he wer' a' old dog wer' Jim Ruskin."

"Yes?" Titt was getting interested.

"But I'm come back now, and they tells me old Jim's dead?"

"Perhaps he is?" Titt suggested.

"But I wants to find out where he lay." And Charlie looked concerned.

"Where he's buried?" from Titt.

"Yais", loudly from Charlie. "I wants to get his bones."

Titt fell backwards over a log, trying to get further away from his unwholesome visitor.

"Y' can't tell me where he lay, then, eh?" and with a sad far away look in his beady little eyes, Charlie viewed the horizon disappointedly.

Titt shook his head. (Later he learned that the missing one's last resting place was just inside the garden gate!)

"A chap in the township", Charlie went on, "said as you would be able to tell I where he lay"—then taking the reins from the harness, he climbed back into the dray, and, standing amongst his gruesome trophies, remained pondering the the position a moment or two.

Mrs. Duff, accompanied by Araluen, re-appeared. Standing beside Titt, they stared curiously at Charlie and his load of bones.

"Ask him what he does with them?" whispered Mrs. Duff. Titt asked him.

"I sends 'em away in a railway truck, and makes money out on 'em."

Bending down he lifted a human skull with neck and one shoulder and an arm attached, and held it up proudly.

"There's a good find I got this mornin', eh?" he enthused. "I be goin' to ask a big figure for that yun. I got 'em over there at King's Creek where th' shanty were. Were it a man or were it a laidy? I don't be sure about that, eh?" and he turned the face of the grinning skeleton towards them.

But Mrs. Duff and Araluen didn't wait to solve the question of sex. They both fled back to the house.

"Hoh! Hoh! Hoh!" Charlie chuckled looking after them; "they be frightened o' a dead yun."

Then carefully restoring the gruesome thing to the bed of the dray, he jerked the reins, told the horse to "get on", and drove off through the timber, roaring like a bull at every obstacle that impeded the way, all the while keeping a sharp look-out for any object bleaching whitely amongst the grass or that was newly dead or surely dying.

5. Real Life Commences

Though a small kitchen was attached to the house, the Duffs often used an outside fire-place. There was more room in the outside fire-place to hang pots, kettles and things, and to fix the camp-oven. And as Mrs. Duff made all her own bread, the camp-oven was constantly in use. And in the outside fire-place a good roasting fire could always be kept going without danger of burning the house down. The wood it consumed, too, didn't require much chopping—that, Titt and Splinter reckoned, was "the best thing about it".

And when first they went on the holding and everything was novel, new and strange, the Duffs delighted in taking their evening meals, picnic fashion, on the short grass before the outside fire-place. And what cheerful, merry meals they were! Seated round the steaming dish of boiled corned beef, with new potatoes in their jackets, the big black billy of boiling tea, the large "wheel-loaf" of home-made bread the size and shape of the camp-oven itself; eating, talking, jesting, while the glowing fire shedding its light around, and the stars coming out winking and blinking till the great dark dome that loomed over all was jewelled with a million silvery little lights, made it a Fairyland, and a world of wonder and enchantment.

"It's splendid having dinner out here", Araluen, glancing at the Southern Cross, enthused one evening.

"My word, ain't it?" And Splinter reached for another potato in its jacket.

"This is what I call life—real life!" from Titt, "not like being caged up down there in th' dirty city!"

"Imagine us hav'ng a meal like this in the city!" Mrs. Duff laughed, "the neighbours would all be staring over the fence at us!"

"They'd ring up for the police!" Titt reckoned cynically, "or write letters to the papers about us being a public nuisance."

"Or throw their dead cats over at us", Araluen thinking reminiscently, laughed.

"Cats!" And Splinter, removing the jacket from the potato preparatory to putting it to "bed" with others that had gone before, paused and grinned, "more like one of th' 'old pilgrims of th' night' would come bowlin' in on top of us and——"

"Splinter!" interrupted his Mother warningly.

"And walk on th' corned beef, and——"

"Splinter, did you hear me?" his Mother again interrupted.

"And put his big foot in th' jam."

A scream of mirth burst from Araluen, in which Splinter, himself, joined heartily.

"That's quite enough, now! You always carry a joke too far, Splinter!" Mrs. Duff, herself on the verge of bursting into merriment, concluded.

"Ah, well!" Titt, throwing some scraps to Bluey, the dog, standing watching with head in the light and the rest of him out in the dark, sighed independently, "we're done with the rubbishy, smelly city an' its dead cats and plague and thieves, and cadgers and bloomin' gentlemen swankin' round waitin' for the farmer to get a crop so as they can dig their claws into it, or waitin' to be made his representative in Parliament—done with it all, and forever more, thank God, amen!"

And when the dinner things were collected, and the washing-up finished and more wood thrown on the fire, they would remain lounging outside talking of the day's events, of their hopes and prospects and plans for the future, and listening to the native bears snoring, and the curlews shrieking and the mopokes calling and the dingoes howling as they descended the hill-sides in quest of something to steal or slay. Occasionally some of the neighbours—mostly old pioneers of the Creek —would happen along to while away an hour of two yarning and smoking. And no one loved more than those quiet, horny-handed, sunburnt patriarchs of the Bushland, to be counted amongst the circle seated before that old outside fire-place. With a flat stone, or a woodblock, or a chaff bag beneath them, they were happy and comfortable. A sitting-room, how-ever humble or luxurious, never appealed to those old pioneers. They were never themselves when surrounded with couches and chairs and cushions and antimacassars and such "fal-th'-ra-dols", as they termed them. Sitting-rooms, or any sort of rooms—except bedrooms perhaps—robbed them of their ease and naturalness. Sitting-rooms didn't suit those old pioneers, and they didn't suit sitting-rooms. They were only themselves where they could sprawl their limbs and turn their heads without looking into the faces of those about them or at the wall beside them—where they could smoke and spit and swear if they wanted to. And whenever a dazed snake, or an adder, wriggled from the hollow of a log that was thrown on the fire to keep it going, and excitement ensued, or the voice of a wild dog rang out within a few yards of the home, and gave the family the "creeps", and drove Bluey hurriedly into the light where he whimpered with fear, those smoke-dried Bush veterans would always be reminded of things that happened on the Creek when first they came to settle there. And no one, not even themselves, ever knew how long it was since first they settled there! The influence of the fire, and the clustering stars and the weird noises arising out of the darkness around, like lost souls crying from the depths of Eternity, thrilled those old denizens, stirred the very marrow in their brittle bones, revived the vital spark again and sent their thoughts flying back—back to fears and terrors and tragedies of days so far arrear! What weird happenings—what dream-haunting skeletons they would resurrect from the graves of their shattered memories! Once, when they had sat talking and whispering in weird hushed tones—their bearded visages well nigh inflexible—until nearly midnight, "the witching hour when churchyards yawn and graves give up their dead"—until the fire had nearly burnt itself out, and no one was inclined to venture into the darkness in search of a fresh supply of wood —about a shepherd names Jones having been murdered by the blacks at a spot not more than a stone's throw from Duff's gate, and his remains buried by the station-hands near Blain's water-hole, and a flat sand stone with his name and the date of his death chiselled on it, placed on the grave; and about the number of times they themselves had seen the ghost of Mrs. Mundle, a woman who got lost on Eton Vale, away back in the 60's, and was never heard of again—had seen it dressed in

white come to the door of their tent at the same hour each
night, and stand there till they braced themselves up and found
courage to speak to it and how, when they spoke, it answered
them quite distinctly, but low and soft, and pointing to the
Creek, and, beckoning them to follow, glided swiftly and
noiselessly away through the long grass and, disappearing
over the steep bank, would fade into the water without making
the least sign of a disturbance upon the surface—the Duffs
became unnerved with dread and superstitious fear, and were
afraid almost to rise and venture into the house. And when
they did go in and "light up", they were afraid to go to bed.
Araluen, who was most affected, insisted on sleeping with her
Mother. Splinter, who was very pale and thoughtful and kept
watching the door, said "he wasn't frightened to sleep by himself", but in the night or early morning, woke up yelling like a
dingo, and, bounding from the bed, rushed into Titt and
plunged in beside him, and made him swear and feel if his ribs
were broken.

Next evening Mrs. Duff set the table in the kitchen. "If
those old blowers come again with their silly ghost stories,"
she complained, "they'll have to sit inside—but I'll not listen
to them!"

The old hands, though, didn't go along the next evening.
Young Martin Drygrass went along instead. Martin didn't go
of his own free will—his father, who was going to town early
next morning to put a jibbing horse in the sale-yards—sent
him along to get the proper time so as he could set his clock
right. It hadn't been set right since Drygrass' last trip to town,
when he put it right by the sun. On reaching town, though, he
found it was all wrong, and he never trusted to the sun again.

Martin was a shy, nervous boy, and when he reached Duff's
yard-gate, which he slowly and silently opened, and saw the
light shining in the house and heard voices inside, his nerves
took possession of him. His feet went cold. He hesitated in
the gateway and stood thinking. To approach a strange house
and knock on the door and stand face to face with a group of
staring people and be your own spokesman, calls for a pro-
digious amount of courage and confidence in a bush-bred
youngster. And Martin possessed but little of either. For

several minutes he steadily watched the flashing, erratic movements of the light, occasioned by Araluen and Splinter bob-
bing their heads into it while leaning over the table, but
couldn't make up his mind to advance further. Presently Bluey
discovered his presence and started barking and growling menacingly. Martin took refuge behind one of the gate-posts—a
giant round ironbark post with a level-sawn surface top large
enough to dance on. Bluey, who had eyes that could see like
stars in the night, became suspicious. He cautiously
approached the gate and barked more. And Bluey could bark!
That was all he could do—except eat! And when it came to
eating, he could hold his own with Mayors and Aldermen, or
State banqueteers. The door of the house opened, and Titt,
poking his head out and scowling into the night, asked Bluey
"What th' devil he was barking at?" Bluey, whimpering and
whining and bounding about, did his best to inform him. But
no more than the gatepost, behind which Martin was trembling and shaking and perspiring, did Titt comprehend.

"You old fool! Go an' lie down!" he said, and closed the
door again.

But Bluey couldn't lie down—not in the night. He spent
himself at that throughout the day—and at it he went again,
bark! bark! bark! at intervals, moving near the gate and
bounding back again.

"I'm sure there must be something outside," Mrs. Duff
said nervously, "or the dog wouldn't keep going on like that!"

"Barkin' at his shadow", Titt grunted, taking up the newspaper and trying to read.

Mrs. Duff, not satisfied, sat listening.

"Mrs. Mundle's ghost, p'raps?" Splinter whispered, his
eyes and ears now wide open and alert.

"Oh!" and Araluen sprang from the table and crouched in
fear beside her Mother on the sofa.

"What are y' frightened of?" Titt rebuked, Splinter under
cover of "training th' cat to jump", left the chair he was kneeling on, and crouched under the table.

"I'll never stop in this place by myself if ever you are away!"
Mrs. Duff tremblingly warned Titt.

"Rot!" he grunted, and started reading the newspaper upside down. Though he didn't confess it, Titt had a notion himself that Bluey was "barking at something".

Meantime, Martin's trembling hand came in contact with a jam tin half full of tar, left by someone on the gate-post, and seizing it he heaved it through the darkness in the direction of Bluey. But before leaving his hand the tin emptied itself over him. Bluey, taken by surprise, retreated full speed for the house as though all the dingoes in the Ranges were on his heels, and noisily dug himself in on the verandah.

"Listen!" and Mrs. Duff fairly shook; "the dog wouldn't rush onto the verandah like that if there wasn't someone about."

"Nonsense!" Titt mumbled; but the short cough he gave to drown the tremor in his voice made his wife the more apprehensive.

"Where's Splinter?" she almost choked on missing him from the room; "where is he?"

Titt glared about the room, and failing to fix Splinter's whereabouts, began to look alarmed, too.

"Where is the boy!" And Mrs. Duff, throwing her arms round Araluen, held to her as though determined no one would steal her, too.

"Where (Titt paused to clear his throat) where are y'?" he called, looking towards the bedroom.

"N-Now then—j-j-jump, Pussy—jump", Splinter, beneath the table, where there wasn't any cat, lied by innuendo and inference.

"Well, you are a frightened woman!" Titt said, turning to the Mother, "what's gone wrong with y' all at once?" And he took up the newspaper again and tried to make it rattle loud enough to drown the row Bluey was making on the verandah.

Having disposed of the dog, Martin, with tar trickling from his face and chest, began weighing the consequences of returning home without the "proper time". He turned his head to see if the light at his own home was visible in the distance. Instantly all thought of the light fled from his mind. Quite near, and silently approaching him, he distinctly saw a tall white figure. Angels of mercy! His heart stood still. He was between the figure and the gate-post. Martin, too, had heard about Mrs.

Mundle's ghost. He tried to shriek for help, but couldn't. The tall white figure seemed to grow taller. It stood still. Then Martin remembered the gate was open. Through it he dived! Regardless of Bluey's barks, or Bluey's bites, or of anything else, he raced for Duff's house as fast as his legs and hard bare feet could take him. Bluey saw him coming and lost heart. He howled and yelped and scratched desperately on the door, and made those inside jump to their feet and stare. When the door didn't open to let him in, he bounded off the end of the verandah and got under the house.

"Oh, my heavens!" and Mrs. Duff clapped her hand over her heart. Mary Ellen, who had been asleep, awoke and screamed. Araluen turned pale, then pink. Splinter, still beneath the table, raised himself on hands and toes in readiness to dart at a moment's notice in any direction.

"Keep quiet, the lot of y'!" Titt growled irritably, "and I'll go again and see—if that'll satisfy y'!"

"Perhaps you better not!" And Mrs. Duff's teeth chatted audibly.

"Of course I will!" And with visible indecision, Titt moved to the door and turned the knob of it. At the same moment it suddenly burst in—there was a shriek and a bump, and he fell back heavily on the floor with a great noise, and his head under the table, and Martin sprawling over the top of him and smearing him with tar. Talk about a fright! And a screaming match! Nothing ever happened like it anywhere. Titt fought like an Anzac. He struggled and gurgled and spat out tar, and squeezed poor Martin's throat till his eyes nearly fell out. Meeting with no resistance, he jumped to his feet, grabbed a chair with both hands and, raising it above his head, was about to break it over Martin, when he saw who he was— when Araluen and Splinter saw who he was, too. "It's Martin Drygrass," they cried, "Martin", and leaving their hiding places, gathered joyously round him and held his head up, and helped him to stand on his feet, and wondered how he got the tar all over his face.

Titt put down the chair and for a moment or two walked the room puffing, gasping for breath, and struggling with himself. Then he turned to Martin again:

"What th' devil did y' rush in here like that for?" he foamed.

"Th' ghost!" Martin whispered, his bulging eyes roaming to the open door.

Just then a light footstep was heard on the verandah. Mrs. Duff and Araluen screamed again; Splinter, dragging Martin with him, took refuge once more under the table; Titt, himself, stood like a fixture, then Mrs. Weeviltopp, dressed all in white, glided in, and in a hoarse, despairing voice, said, "I lost me way".

6. A Lively Visitor

It happened one bright Monday morning. Titt wasn't in good humour that morning, and kept venting his feelings on the cranky plough and the two hairy unoffending quadrupeds that strained and tugged and did their best, which was a poor, feeble best, to till the land for him.

Dinner hour. Titt unyoked, and leaving the harness on Darby and Joan to save trouble and time, drove the hairy mokes to the door of the "shed".

"Keep your darn head steady, won't yer!" he roared, and was putting the nose-bag on the team over their winkers, when the voice of neighbour O'Connor, calling excitedly from the front of the house, attracted him.

The front of the house was distinguished from the back by a garden containing some cabbages and lettuce that went to seed, and a geranium bush that grew on the grave of old Ruskin, the man who first selected the holding, and died in the excitement of reclaiming it from the wilderness, and made room for Titt.

"Here's an Amu! An Amu!" O'Connor called.

"A what?" and Titt turned and stared.

"An Amu! Quick, till we catch ud!"

"You mean a plain turkey", from Titt.

"Do ye think I don't know a plain turkey! 'Tis an Amu!" sharply from O'Connor.

Titt left the horses and went to see; sure enough an emu, one as tall as himself, was stalking silently and inquisitively to and fro along the crude palings, poking its head in wherever there was a hole to admire the horticulture. O'Connor, his big brown hairy arms extended like wings, was shepherding it and trying to "hoosh" it through the open gate into the garden.

"Why, bless me, it must be a tame one!" Titt said, walking

up. "Where did it come from, O'Connor?" Titt looked upon
the leggy visitor as the Israelites had looked upon manna.

"It didn't come from anywhere; it was here admirin' ye're
garden when I came along. Look out! Block ud!"

Titt side-stepped in time to block the bird from slipping
round the corner. Then it stood, and facing them with its head
high in the air, looked sideways at them.

"Bedam, 'tis a beauty!" O'Connor enthused, keeping his
arms extended and his best leg forward in readiness to check
any sudden strategy on the bird's part.

"They're fine eatin', too, them coves", covetously from Titt.

"The man what wud ate an iligant beast like that,"
O'Connor reckoned, "would ate an angel. Block. Block ud!"

Titt blocked again.

Mrs. Duff and Araluen appeared on the verandah.

"Goodness!" they cried. "An emu!"

"Fetch a bucket of wather, Mam, and put ud near the gate,"
O'Connor advised, "an' when he goes in after ud, we'll bang
the gate and capture ud."

"Yes, bring a bucket of water, quick!" Titt approved.

"And come ye round here Araluen and help block ud!"
O'Connor added.

Araluen ran round the back way, and taking up a position
between her father and O'Connor, began waving her apron
at the bird and ordering it to "go in". The emu looked wonderingly at Araluen.

Mrs. Duff came from the house into the garden with a
bucket and placed it temptingly in the open gateway; then
returned to the verandah again and awaited results.

The emu turned and eyed the water suspiciously.

"Keep steady, keep steady, he'll go in directly", and Titt
speaking slowly and softly crept lightly toward the game.

Araluen, who had a sense of humour, giggled.

"Sh! Sh!" O'Connor whispered, shaking his head at her.
"Don't shpake; they're as cunning as the divil."

A large ladybird appeared overhead like a flying machine
and volplaned into the bucket. The emu reached through the
gate and promptly picked it off the water and interned it.

"Did ever ye see the like of that?" O'Connor asked in wonderment.

The bird's eye rested on a piece of scrap iron lying on the gate-post, which it leisurely swallowed; then turned its tail to the bucket.

"Hell, but look at that!" And O'Connor's eyes opened wide. But Titt showed no surprise.

"That ain't nothing", he said. "I've seen them pull the shoes off horses and swaller 'em."

O'Connor winked at Araluen.

Then, stooping, Titt quietly collected some fragments of blue metal and tossed one toward the emu. It rattled against the bucket. Suspecting treachery in the rear, the emu kicked out blindly and upset the bucket, and irrigated the garden.

Araluen burst into mirth.

" 'Tis no use", O'Connor said. "Run, fetch ye're plough reins and we'll lassoo ud."

"Lassoo it with my plough reins?" Titt objected, "and let it get away into the bush with them hangin' to it? Are y' mad, O'Connor?"

"Catch it with your hands, why don't y'?" Mrs. Duff advised from the verandah.

"That's what I'm goin' to do", and crouching like Cain when he slew Abel, Titt began creeping nearer the bird.

The emu strolled along the palings, and looking over the tops of them, plucked a geranium and dropped it on old Ruskin's grave.

"Now, Titt, now!" O'Connor whispered hoarsely.

"Quick, father!" And Araluen turned pale with excitement.

Then Titt dived low at the emu's legs. But the bird had had been attacked before. It jumped high in the air, and Titt knocked three palings out of the fence with his head. Mrs. Duff, when she saw Titt's head inside the garden, dropped down on the verandah in a fit of mirth; Araluen dropped down behind O'Connor, and O'Connor dropped on his hands and knees in the dirt, and tore up fistfuls of it; and glanced over his shoulder at Titt.

"Yes, that's right!" Titt growled, extracting his head from the splintery palings. "Laugh away! Laugh away!"

And O'Connor and Araluen laughed until they heard Mrs. Duff shouting:

"My! My! My! It's got its head in the back window and is eatin' all the hot pumpkin!"

Then, headed by O'Connor, they hurried to the back of the house.

"Hould on now, jist go steady!" And O'Connor directed operations. "Wait till he puts his head in the windy again, and is swallerin' a bit of pumpkin—then we'll all rush him!"

"If I get me hand on th' wretch," Titt with malice, murmured solemnly, "I'll screw its neck."

Then noticing that Darby and Joan had their heads in the air and were looking alarmed, he shouted, "Wa-a-y, yer fools!" to them, and grimly set his teeth again.

"Don't let it eat all the dinner—dont' let it!" Mrs. Duff cried. Then O'Connor and Titt charged, and both got a grip on the emu. But the bird plunged and struggled and twisted and bashed Titt with its stubby wings, and kicked O'Connor in the stomach with one of its long legs and put him out of action.

"Hold it tight, father, hold it!" Araluen cried, keeping out of the fight herself.

But Titt lost his footing and fell, and dragged the emu with him.

"Get the plough reins and tie its legs!" Mrs. Duff cried, coming to her husband's assistance.

Araluen ran for the plough reins. Darby and Joan must have taken her for the emu. They bolted and fell over the fence into the corn, and left most of the harness hanging on the wire posts. Araluen snatched the plough reins, and hurrying back with them, found her mother lying under the emu and Titt on top of it.

O'Connor, who had recovered himself, took the reins, and making a noose at one end, threw it over the bird's head and over Titt's head, too. Then he pulled hard.

"Stop! Stop! Dammit, it's me you got!" Titt shouted.

O'Connor stopped. Then Titt shook his head out, and O'Connor pulled again and cried:

"Lit the divil up! I have ud!"

The emu flapped its wings, struck at the rope with its feet like a horse, squawked, sprang in the air, then sat back and "scratch-pulled" till its head nearly came off.

"I've got ud!" And O'Connor, leaning back, pulled harder.

Suddenly the emu changed tactics. Taking long swift strides, it raced straight at O'Connor, giving him no time to haul in the slack. O'Connor lifted his foot to kick it, but kicked too soon, lost his balance and fell back. The emu ran through his whiskers and over him, and escaped with the plough reins hanging to it.

"Yer didn't let it go, did yer?" Titt roared, jumping to his feet, with a bunch of feathers in each hand.

"The divil go with ud!" O'Connor gasped, and sat down to regain his wind.

A week later. O'Connor with a hoe on his shoulder, called on Titt at the plough.

"We cot that amu, Titt," he said; "ud came to our dairy the morning after, and fed out ov the ould woman's hand like a dove. Sure, 'twas a tame one, all the time."

"Did it have my plough reins on it?" And Titt scowled at the broken make-shift things he was working the team with.

"A fut of them were round its neck; all the rest were in its crop."

"They were what?" And Titt regarded O'Connor with suspicion.

"Amu's ate greenhide like worms, ye know."

"You're a liar O'Connor!" And Titt shook his fist in his neighbour's face.

"Ye're another!" And tearing off his vest (O'Connor always wore an old vest), and throwing it on the ground, turned and walked away, calling out, "Come on to th' road! Come on to th' road!"

Titt's eyes rested on a fig of "twist" tobacco that had fallen from the pocket of O'Connor's vest. He picked it up, filled his pipe, and speaking to Darby and Joan, went on wobbling behind the old plough and blowing great clouds of smoke.

O'Connor, out on the road, danced about, shouting, "Come on!"

Splinter, driving the cows to the gully paddock, on Paddy

Grey, the new saddle horse, came along, and grinned at O'Connor.

"Hello, Mister O'Connor," he greeted, "did y' finish sinking th' well yet?"

"I'll finish ye, ye —— young shnipe!" and lifting a stick big enough to brain an elephant with, O'Connor went after Splinter.

"Yah!" Splinter yelled, labouring hard with his heels and his hat to make Paddy Grey shift himself, "I'd take you on one hand."

Then O'Connor went into Titt's again, and putting on his vest and taking out his empty pipe, waited calmly till he finished another round.

"By dam, Titt," he said, looking along the furrow and laughing, "but ye're ploughin' as straight as a dog's hind leg."

"Am I?" Titt grinned.

"Ye are: give us a bit of tobacco if y' have any on ye."

Titt gave him back his own; then they both sat down and smoked and talked and built castles in the air till dinner time.

7. Old Fred

Old Fred (a distant relation on Mrs. Duff's side), one day unexpectedly turned up on an old horse and filled the home with joy. None of them, except Mrs. Duff, had ever seen old Fred before, and Titt was delighted to meet him. He made Mrs. Duff give up their bed to him; saw that he was provided with water and a new towel. "And get a brush or something," he ordered, "and leave it in the room for him to do his hair with." Titt still retained all his city ideas of hospitality.

And when Old Fred objected to having so much consideration lavished upon him, and asked "what they are going to do themselves?" Titt laughed, and said, "they had plenty of room —enough to start a boardin' house with."

"Very well, just as you like", and Old Fred, a genial, kindly, silent bushman, rubbed his hands together and smiled agreeably.

Then Titt showed his guest the double bed he was to sleep in, and explained the working of the wash basin and the hair brush to him and showed him how to open the window and shut it without severing his fingers or getting his head jammed in it, or letting it fall on the floor, or right outside—and after saying "good-night" and hoping he would sleep sound and have pleasant dreams, slipped out and helped the missus to make a shake-down for themselves on the floor, in the front room; and then turned in as though he had been used to dossing on the floor all his life.

It was a hard, even floor, and Titt didn't sleep well on it. He didn't complain though; he was a martyr to the comfort of his new-found relation. He would have suffered death rather than Old Fred should be uncomfortable. But he was careful to rise before daylight next morning, so that the latter wouldn't know the sacrifices he had made for him. Titt was a modest man, even though he came from the city. He roused Mrs. Duff out, too, and promptly removed the bed. Titt always

believed in covering up his tracks. Like murder, though, it
all came out the next night. Old Fred had to get up the next
night to go outside for something. He groped his way in the
dark to the front door, and in his uncertainty trampled heavily
on the flat of Titt's stomach, Titt had a lean hollow stomach,
and got a great start when he felt the weight on it.

"Who's there?" he groaned, when he got his wind back.

Old Fred got a start, too.

"Eh, who is it?" Titt repeated nervously.

"Is that where y'are?" the other responded feebly.

"It's you, Old Fred? I thought it might be some one else
prowlin' about." And Titt turned over and rubbed his stomach.

"I—I'm trying to find me way to the door," Old Fred
explained in a voice full of anxiety, "but I don't know where
it is", and he fumbled the wall all over with his big palms, and
knocked down a framed photograph of Brisbane under flood.

"Why? What's the matter?" Titt inquired, brightening up.

Old Fred never replied, but continued fumbling the wall,
and knocked over a whatnot.

"What's up, man?" Titt asked again with increased nervous-
ness.

"Left me saddle on the fence; stray cattle about might chew
it." Old Fred said with a tremor.

Mrs. Duff gave Titt a silent dig in the ribs and whispered to
him. Then Titt changed his tone.

"Can't you find the door?" It's there, old chap", and sitting
up in bed he pointed through the darkness with his finger to
the place where the door should be.

"Wh—where?" And Old Fred groped some more.

"To your left a little." Titt was guided by the sound Old
Fred's horny hands were making. "It pulls in this way towards y'."

Old Fred turned to his left and mauled and fumbled and
moaned afresh, till his hands excitedly came in contact with
the new sideboard. He grabbed hold of it eagerly—clutched it
like a drowning man—and pulled. The side-board and everything on it fell with a great crash in comparison with which
the fall of Jerusalem was only a faint echo.

"Man alive!" Titt cried, "don't pull the bloomin' house down."

But Old Fred wasn't conscious of having pulled anything down.

"There's no door", he murmured.

"For heaven's sake, Titt," Mrs. Duff burst out, "get up and show him where it is."

"I suppose I'll have to!' and Titt got up slowly.

"Here it is, Old Fred", he said, throwing the door open without an effort and suddenly letting in streaks of moonlight.

Without a word, Old Fred, like a wild animal given its freedom, darted out.

Titt chuckled and returned to bed.

"It's not very nice to laugh at him", Mrs. Duff rebuked.

Then peals of pent-up merriment burst from Splinter's and Araluen's rooms.

"Children! you've a nice lot of manners, I must say", Mrs. Duff called to them.

Araluen promptly smothered her mirth with a pillow, but Splinter took all he could out of the situation.

"If I have to go into you, me noble, I'll soon shut y' up!" Titt threatened. Splinter shut up, and Araluen broke out again.

"Can't y' stop it?" Splinter giggled to her through the partition.

"I'll stop you, pretty quick, anyway", and feeling in the dark for one of his boots which he had left near his pillow, Titt heaved it over the partition at Splinter. But it didn't go over the partition. It hit the Bishop of Someplace hanging on the wall, and made a great crash.

"Now, what have you done?" and Mrs. Duff, in her alarm, clutched Titt and trembled.

Titt hardly knew.

But amidst the dead silence that prevailed, Old Fred crept in again; said it "was a beautiful night outside", and cheerfully found his way back to bed.

8. Fireworks

Fireworks, Old Fred's horse, wasn't welcomed in the warm way that Old Fred was, himself. Fireworks received a real hot reception. Duff's farm horses were not like the Duffs themselves—they were a selfish, jealous, inhospitable lot, and when Fireworks, on the first day of his arrival, greeted them in a friendly spirit and wanted to pal in with them and make himself at home, rushed at him, open-mouthed, and aimed heavy kicks at him, and squealing like demented brumbies, chased him round and round the farmyard till, scared of his life, he bailed up in a corner. Then they at him teeth and toes, kicked him below the belt or anywhere; made him cut his throat in three or four places with the barbwire, and would have eaten him alive if Splinter hadn't by chance come to the rescue in time. There were no manners or sense of hospitality about Duff's horses, whatever; ignorant as aboriginals, the lot of them.

An uncommon looking horse, too, Fireworks was. Superior and dignified. Stood up well on his legs—must have stood fully six feet high on his two hind ones. His back was the only part of him that was faulty. It had a dip in it—a hollow about a foot deep. But anyone could see in a glance that he had known better days. He must have known a lot of different owners, too, in his day, judging by the number of registered brands he carried. Most of the hair was burnt off him with brands, and from head to tail he was tattooed with numbers and letters in capitals and script, some straight on, some sideways, some upside down, and all mixed together. At a distance, you'd think he was a Chinaman's sign-board. Those brands were his references—his certificates of popularity.

On the second day, when Fireworks, after holding aloof till he couldn't hang out any longer, stealthily approached the trough, Duff's horses rushed at him again. In his hurry to escape them he slipped on the grass and fell down. At first he lay still, and didn't try to get up, thinking, maybe, they would regard him as dead and let him rest in peace. But when they all gathered round and began clawing and pawing and kneeling on him, and rejoicing over his death, he struggled for his feet. Every time he lifted his head, though, and raised himself on his forefeet, one or the other, or the lot of them at the same time, would kick him over again and walk on him.

"Heigh! Heigh!" Titt, returning from the township with a part of the plough that he had taken to the blacksmith for repair, shouted from the gate, "they're fightin' Old Fred's horse again; they've got him down!"

Old Fred ran and got the bridle, and while Titt drove the others off, caught Fireworks and led him to the trough.

"Put him in the yard over there", Titt, indicating a crude sapling enclosure with an old iron tub and some broken gin-cases that served for feed-boxes lying about, advised when Fireworks had blown himself out with water, and Old Fred was standing wondering what to do about him—"and give him a feed of corn—will he eat corn?"

Old Fred wasn't quite sure—he had never seen him eat any.

"Oh, well—at that rate," Titt suggested considerately, "we'll give him some in a nose-bag, and he can learn how to eat it!"

Then, while Old Fred placed Fireworks in the sapling enclosure and put up all the rails—altogether there were about twenty rails to put up, counting the broken ones and others that were several inches too short to "reach"—Titt half filled a nose-bag with corn and chaff, and brought it along.

"You put it on him," he said handing the bag to Old Fred, "you know him better than I do."

Titt was a cautious man where strange horses were concerned. And Fireworks wasn't looking at all friendly—he was surly and depressed.

Taking the bag, Old Fred said, "Come on, old chap", and held it invitingly in front of Fireworks. For several seconds he took no notice of it. It might as well have been a lump of wood. Old Fred gave the bag a shake and the corn rattled. Fireworks instantly pricked his ears and brightened up and stared all about in a most friendly way.

"Seems to know th' sound of it", Titt said.

Old Fred shoved it under his nose; and when Fireworks got a sniff of the contents he whinnied in surprise and plunged his snout into the bag and burrowed to the bottom in search of the corn—and he had to search, too!

"No! he don't know what it is!" Titt grinned, "not him!"

So ravenous and eager was Fireworks for it that Old Fred couldn't fasten the nose-bag to his head properly.

"Hold up!" he said, leaning over when the brute forced the bag to the ground and sneezed happily into it and slobbered,and made a great noise cracking the grain with his teeth, when he found some. "Hold up, fer a minute, can't y'?" And when he didn't respond as he should have done, Old Fred kicked the bag with the toe of his foot.

Gee! Fireworks must have thought it was the other horses making another assault on him. He threw up his head with such suddenness and hit Old Fred so hard under the chin that he knocked him right off his feet on to the broad of his back.

"Cripes!" Titt gasped, gathering him up, "did he hurt y'?"

But Old Fred was knocked out—right out—and never answered.

Titt, suddenly filled with fury, dropped Old Fred in the dust again, and grabbing up a broken rail hit Fireworks on the head with it and called him a "long ugly cow!" Fireworks swung round, switched his tail, and lowering his head, went on feeding, as if nothing had happened.

When Old Fred recovered and sat up, dazed looking, Titt explained how it happened, and told him where he was, and the time of day, then led him across to the house to "get a drink of something, and have a camp for awhile on the sofa".

No sooner had they gone than the draught horses gathered round the sapling enclosure and stared enviously through the rails at Fireworks. One would think they had never seen another horse having a feed before. Feeling himself secure, Fireworks bravely laid his ears back and stamped his feet as a sort of challenge to them, and ate faster.

Bounce, Titt's big ungainly shafter, thrust his head between the rails and craned his neck to reach the nose-bag. Fireworks laid his ears back some more, and moved further away.

Bounce withdrew his head, and to revenge himself on Fireworks, bit Diamond, who was dozing beside him, hard on the
rump. Diamond woke up with a start and jumped away and
tramped in the iron tub and pressed the bottom out of it. Then
Gypsy, a diplomatic old beast who always worked in the
furrow and was a great favourite with the women—so the
man said who sold her to Titt—shoved her nozzle between the
rails and tried to make love to Fireworks. But Fireworks
wasn't an emotional horse—flirting on the spur of the moment
wasn't in his line. He just shook his head and turned his rump
disdainfully to Gipsie. Binnie, the slick, brainy horse of the
farm, meanwhile, had been standing off doing some hard,
deep thinking. And in roguery or thieving, or anything where
direct action was required, Binnie was a prime mover. He was
also "Boss" of the farm; it was he who made Fireworks cut
his throat on the barb-wire, and was first to paw him and
trample on him while he was feigning death.

Separating from the others, Binnie strolled leisurely round
to the barricade of "slip-rails," and regarded them thoughtfully. Then he turned his rump to them and started scratching
himself against them as if he had the mange. From side to
side he rubbed and scrubbed, occasionally "sitting back in the
britchen" and putting all his weight into it. At last the top rail
became displaced and fell across his back. Without noticing it,
Binnie went on rubbing and shoving. But Fireworks took a lot
of notice of it. He heard the rail fall and looked round quickly.
When he saw Binnie and what he was up to, he designed his
motive instantly, and became alarmed. He suddenly lost his
appetite, too, and began trotting round the enclosure in search
of a place to get out. At intervals he would stand with head
high in the air and stare at Binnie to see what chances he had
of breaking in. Concluding he had the best of chances, he
took to galloping round and snorting into the nose-bag. When
at last all the rails fell down on top of Binnie with a crash,
Fireworks, as the last recourse, rushed at the highest panel,
which was about 7ft. high, to jump out, but changed his mind
in the last stride, and bumped his head. Then into the
enclosure Binnie bounded triumphantly, and roaring and

screaming like a stallion, took Fireworks by the back of the neck and shook him. Fireworks reared straight up on top of the yard; his fore feet became stuck in the top-rail, the nose-bag hung over the other side, and there he remained a curious helpless looking spectacle. Nothing could have pleased Binnie more. Dancing round, he shoved his rump up against that of Fireworks, and lowering his head, banged into him hard and fast with both heels. Bing! Bang! Biff! rang out all round the place. Fireworks could do nothing in the way of retaliation only roar into the bag. And while he roared, Bounce, outside, reached up and dragged the nose-bag off him, and spilling most of the feed on the ground, started cleaning it up and showing his teeth to the others when they approached to help him.

"Father! Father!" Araluen, flying into the house, shrieked, "they're killing Old Fred's horse!"

"Who's killing him?" and Titt came to the door.

"Binnie is—look at him!"

"Th' cow! he's broken into him! I thought he would!" And off Titt ran.

"Ahoh, you dog! Stop that!" he shouted, when he reached the rails. Then he let fly anything he could lay hands on at Binnie.

Binnie stopped it and rushing out of the enclosure, galloped away, bucking and kicking and showing off to "the gallery".

"Look at him now!" Titt said, when Old Fred, pale with excitement, came shuffling along. "Too much to eat an' not enough work! That's what's wrong with him."

But Old Fred just then could only look at Fireworks. There he hung (or stood), with patches of skin and half the brands kicked off him, grunting, groaning and moaning.

"Oh, dear! However did he get up there?" and Old Fred's eyes filled with tears.

"Binnie kicked him there, of course", Titt answered proudly. "He's a terrible powerful horse Binnie is. I paid £8 for him. And if I hadn't got here when I did he'd 'a' kicked him right over th' top on to his head an' perhaps broke his neck!"

"Oh, dear! what's to be done!" And Old Fred shivered and shook like a leaf.

"We'll have to chop him down, I 'spose," thoughtfully from Titt.

Splinter, with a magpie's nest hoisted proudly on the end of a long stick, appeared at the gate.

"Heigh, Splinter!" Titt shouted, "bring th' axe over here—quick! Look sharp!"

"Bring th' what?" and Splinter put his hand behind his ear.

"Th' axe! Dammit, th' axe!"

"Can't hear y' ", and Splinter shifted the magpie's nest from the end of the long stick to the top of his head.

"By Christmas you'll hear me if I go over to y'! Bring th' axe!" roared his parent.

Splinter started running towards the enclosure.

"Well! Well! Well!" Titt hissed hopelessly. "Damned if he ain't coming over here!"

Just as he arrived and was about to ask his parent what it was he wanted, Splinter's eyes rested on Fireworks. He never before saw such a strange sight.

"Holy!" he gasped, "wh—wh—what's up?"

Then, after a pause, and at the top of his voice: "An 'orse?"

Rushing to the rails and grimacing fiercely through them, Titt yelled: "Yes, a horse; but I want th' axe! Get th' axe! Blarst it, haven't y' got any ears?"

"What 'orse? an' how did he get up there like that?" in dreamy amazement from Splinter.

"Well, I'm damned!" and Titt, scratching his head desperately, turned to Old Fred.

"It's my horse", Old Fred murmured, sadly, for Splinter's information. "One of your father's kicked him up there, and we want the axe to chop the rails with."

"An' ain't y' got it here?" and Splinter started looking about.

"Would I have shouted so often to y' to bring it if we had? By cripes!" and Titt started unbuckling his belt.

"Oh! was that what y' said?" and away went Splinter full split, and returned in a few seconds with the axe.

*Old Fred Could only Look at Fireworks, Hung with Patches of Skin,
and Half the Brands Kicked off Him*

"Pretty near time, too!" Titt, reaching for the implement, snarled savagely. "Pshaw, y' chump!"

Then, mounting the enclosure, he severed the top saplings, and Fireworks' useless life was saved once more.

After a week or so Duff's horses changed their attitude towards Fireworks. They ceased to resent his presence, allowed him to graze peacefully in the paddock and permitted him to drink with them at the creek. A little later he had become one of them, and instead of standing aloof, a lonely, miserable, friendless outcast, took a leading part in everything they did—except farm work.

One Sunday Mickey Masuki, leading a lame horse, called and asked Titt if he could leave it to rest in the paddock until he returned from Felton the following day. Of course Titt said he could, and when Micky pulled the halter off his head the animal limped into a corner and stood there, gazing fretfully over the fence.

After a while Duff's draughts, with Fireworks bringing up the rear, came trailing along to spend a half-hour or so poking about the "farm-yard". All of them, at sight of the stranger, stopped and pricked their ears, then disregarding him, went on again—all of them, except Fireworks. He stared at the intruder for quite awhile, as if he was a foreign invasion, then arching his neck and raising his tail and putting a lot of frightfulness into himself, strode straight and aggressively towards him. On hearing his approach, the other turned his head slowly and looked dreamily round. But when he saw Fireworks he woke up and turned right round. One glance at him was enough. Off he went along the fence as fast as his three legs could take him, and off went Fireworks, his neck outstretched and mouth wide open, in pursuit. But finding he was losing instead of gaining, he quickly pulled up. Then shaking his head and kicking feebly up behind, to show he had plenty of go left in him, returned to the others.

Fireworks believed in doing to others when others had done to him. In that respect he resembled human beings.

9. Splinter Goes Out Working

One day, O'Connor called and after talking the matter over with Titt, engaged Splinter to work for him for ten shillings a week.

"We won't want him here for a while—not until we get th' cows going", Titt explained to Mrs. Duff. "And he'll learn a lot at O'Connor's, and be valuable to us when he comes home."

"He will then," O'Connor agreed, "and I'll make a man of him for yez."

Mrs. Duff consented reluctantly, and stipulated it "would only be for a little while". But Splinter was eager to go and earn some money—eager till his clothes were packed, and his father warned him to "keep out of mischief", and he saw tears in his Mother's and Araluen's eyes, then his enthusiasm left him; his heart sank; and he would have changed his mind if O'Connor, who was waiting, hadn't bustled him into the cart and driven hurriedly away.

"This is th' new mahn", O'Connor announced, referring to Splinter when the family ran to the front barb-wire gate to meet the cart.

Splinter regarded them sullenly. He wasn't used to being grinned and stared at and made a lot of.

"He's been cryin'", Barney O'Connor, who was about Splinter's own age, discovered.

Splinter scowled at Barney, and turned his eyes to the garden where pumpkins and melons were growing luxuriantly.

"Poor bhoi," Mrs. O'Connor sympathised, "sure an' he'll be after wantin' his dinner."

Splinter sniffed his nostrils noisily, and looked approvingly at Mrs. O'Connor.

A week passed. Splinter began to feel at home with O'Connor's: made himself familiar with everything about the place; noted the number of melons on the vines and calculated the time it would take them to ripen; and looked happy.

"Phwat's ye'er name again?" O'Connor inquired of him at breakfast one morning. Splinter grinned and told him for the twentieth time.

"Ov course," and O'Connor repeated it several times, "I do alez be forgettin' ud."

Then, after a pause, "I'll want y' with me at the well to-day; Barney he have to take pigs to the sale."

O'Connor had only the day before started to sink a well in the back yard.

"And if we shtrikes water, ould woman," he added for his wife's benefit, "we'll run it all over the house for ye'."

"Lord love ye, Tim", and Mrs. O'Connor helped herself to more breakfast.

O'Connor rose from the table, and went off. Splinter followed him.

Scrambling down the side of the well, the former dropped into the hole, and commenced working with the pick. Splinter sat on the top and caught flies, and in unguarded intervals, knocked loose earth down on top of O'Connor, and caused him to use bad language. No windlass was yet constructed, and whenever he picked enough mullock to fill the bucket, O'Connor would shout to Splinter: "Call Mrs. O'Connor to give ye a hand to haul it up."

And Mrs. O'Connor, protesting noisily, would come blundering along and knock more earth into the well.

"Shut up, what have ye to growl about?" O'Connor would shout up at her. "and don't be droppin' stones on me."

"If I drops the bucket on ye," Mrs. O'Connor would grunt. "ye'll have something to swear about."

Then O'Connor would crouch silently against the wall of the well, and closely watch the bucket till it was safely landed at the top.

After dinner Mrs. Pat Donovan, the nearest neighbour, came along, carrying her baby. Mrs. O'Connor greeted her loudly and warmly, and taking the infant out of her arms, hugged and cuddled it; then called to Susan, her eldest daughter, to make a cup of tea, "an set it out here on the table under the grape vine. An' cut some of th' rainbow cake if it's cooked."

Mrs. Donovan leaned over the well and looked down into it.

"What are y' doin' down there, Tim O'Connor?" she laughed, "digging a grave for yerself?"

O'Connor dropped the pick and looked up.

"Phwat th' divvle do ye be doin' up there wid yaller stockin's on, Mrs. Pat Donovan", he shouted back.

Mrs. Pat Donovan clutching her skirts, jumped away from the well and blushed at Mrs. O'Connor.

Mrs. O'Connor smiled.

"Yaller stockin's," Splinter chuckled, looking at Mrs. Donovan, "you haven't got any on, have y'?"

"Shut up, y' young divvle," Mrs. Donovan cried, "how do y' know whether I have or whether I haven't."

Then casting her eyes hurriedly about the yard. "If I could see somethin' to drop on Tim O'Connor, I would, for his imperdence."

"Drop the baby on him", Splinter grinned.

"Ye insolent brat, I'll—I'll", and Mrs. Donovan chased him round the well, but Splinter had often been chased before.

Susan came from the house and set the tea and the rainbow cake on the table beneath the grape vine.

Mrs. O'Connor called down the well to O'Connor to "come up and have some tay"; then turning to Susan, told her to bring out her new ball dress and show it to Mrs. Donovan.

Susan brought the dress, and Mrs. Donovan, placing the baby beneath the table, went into raptures about the "beautiful garmint".

While they were admiring the dress, Splinter approached the table and reached for the rainbow cake.

"Get the rope, Splinter, and trow me down an end of ud", came from O'Connor.

Splinter, stuffing his mouth with cake, procured the rope and lowered one end of it.

"Tie it to somethin' up there, and tie it tight," O'Connor further ordered, "and I'll pull myself up be ud."

Splinter said he could see nothin' much to tie the rope to.

"There's lots of things. Use your eyes!" O'Connor called back.

Splinter tied the rope to the leg of the table, and shouted, "Orright!"

Before trusting his weight to it, O'Connor pulled hard and suddenly with both hands. The table instantly reared up and plunged towards the well, threw a forward somersault and tossed the tea and what was left of the rainbow cake, and the crockery into the well on top of himself, and emptied the milk jug over the crooning infant.

"My God, the child!" Mrs. Donovan screamed.

Then there was pandemonium.

Suddenly the table somersaulted some more, and landed across the mouth of the well.

Mrs. O'Connor and Mrs. Donovan and Susan fled with the screaming infant into the house, and left the ball dress behind.

O'Connor, threatening in a loud, angry voice, to take Splinter's life, started scrambling out of the well.

Splinter waited till the other's head and body were above the ground, then threw the ball dress over him and ran.

But when O'Connor found his feet, he didn't run after Splinter. He tore the ball dress from his head, and for an instant stood viewing the wreckage. Then he rushed inside and, using violent language on Mrs. O'Connor and Mrs. Donovan, asked them "pwhat th' devil do ud all mean?"

10. The Cheese Factory

There had been a couple of good seasons, and dairying in South Queensland started ahead. People talked hopefully about the industry; some got excited over it, and one day a few of the leaders got together and decided to build a co-operative cheese factory. Then trouble commenced; some believed only in a butter factory; some in a creamery; some in no factory of any kind; others gave the venture a month to prepare its will and make peace with everyone. One-half of those who held shares wanted to become directors, the other half aspired to the position of manager and secretary. Dan O'Hearne and old Grogan, who decided to "wait and see if it was going to be a success before putting money into it", quarrelled over the contract for supplying wood for the engine, and went to law about it, and three weeks after the case was heard both lawyers in the township were wearing new tailor-made suits.

After numerous ordinary meetings, and special meetings, and secret meetings, were held, it was finally announced that the factory would open to receive milk on a certain morning.

Talk about excitement. Scarcely a supplier slept the night before for thinking and dreaming of it. All were anxious to secure the honour of being first to deliver the goods.

At 3 a.m. O'Connor pushed in the door of Splinter's room, and found the bed empty; an hour later the cows were in the yard, and milking started.

"Milk them dry now," O'Connor said, "an' don't leave a dhrop."

"Barney ain't strippin' his", Splinter grunted.

O'Connor rose from his block and threatened Barney with annihilation.

"How can he tell if I'm strippin' them or not?" Barney argued. "Can he see in the dark?"

"Can tell be the sound in yer bucket", Splinter answered.

"If ye got hit on the nose ye could tell be the sound of it, too, perhaps", and Barney chuckled aggressively.

"You couldn't hit it, though", Splinter said.

"Couldn't I?" from Barney.

"Now thin," O'Connor yelled, "if there's to be any foightin', I'll do ud, an' throw ye both out ob th' yard."

Then for quite a while nothing but the "swishing" of the milk was heard.

"Only three more", Splinter said, bailing up his last cow.

"Leave Mulberry for me, and ye two shove the milk-cans into the cart and put the horse in", O'Connor yelled.

Splinter and Barney handled the cans, and put the horse in the cart. A few minutes later O'Connor rushed from the bails, climbed into the cart, yelled "throw down th' gate", and flogged the horse into a canter.

The others stood watching him through the dawn till he passed Grogan's and was out of sight.

"Now, then," Splinter said, turning to Barney, "wot about hittin' me on th' nose?"

Barney was taken by surprise.

"You mind yerself", he said, and tactfully backed into the yard.

"Come on, if yer think yer fit", and Splinter sparred after him.

Barney jumped back and collided with the hind end of a cow. Plum kicked him hard and he dropped in the dust and bellowed.

Splinter declined to believe Barney.

"She ain't hurt y' ", he said. "Come on, get up, before I counts ten, or I'll hit y' down."

He started counting.

"One . . . . two . . . ."

Barney bellowed harder.

"Three . . . . four . . . . five."

Mrs. O'Connor, armed with the gridiron, ran from the kitchen.

"Six . . . . seven . . . . eight . . . . nine . . . ."

"Ten, ye young blackguard", and Mrs. O'Connor hit Splinter on the head and bent the gridiron.

Just then the rattle of the spring-cart and the angry voice of O'Connor were suddenly heard again.

Mrs. O'Connor turned quickly and stared.

"Whatever have brought ye back?" she shouted.

O'Connor sprang wildly to the ground.

It was Splinter's and Barney's turn to stare.

"Thim young divils", O'Connor yelled, "put the can of wather into th' carrt and left the milk shtandin' where it is, and made a d—— fool of me at th' fachtry."

Then he unbuckled his belt, but before he could enter the yard Splinter and Barney were through the rails and streaking like emus for the tall corn.

For twelve months the co-operative factory struggled bravely on, every day manufacturing some cheese, every month paying cheques to suppliers. Then one Saturday the first Annual Meeting happened. It happened in the factory building and an enthusiastic gathering it was! Shareholders crowded in till the room was packed and restlessly waited for proceedings to start. They didn't start until Duncan McClay, who was manager, secretary, cheese-maker, and the largest shareholder, sauntered in and took the chair.

When he was seated, he rose and spoke about the progress and prosperity of the industry, then began to read the balance-sheet and annual report.

"Can I ask y' a question?" Old O'Hearne said.

"Ye can, if it isna aboot my past heestory", Duncan answered.

"History! It's about the money that's been wasted makin' them cheese cases", O'Hearne shouted, angrily.

"Well, ye'll hear aboot that presently", and McClay went into finance. He read out sums for advertising and discount, and cartage, and insurance, and repairs, and directors' fees, and railway fares, and petty cash, and——

"Mercy, mon! You surely ain't paid away any more?" Mrs. Brown interrupted excitedly.

Old Streeton, who was a great believer in McClay's ability, and public integrity, turned in his seat and stared at Mrs. Brown. And when old Streeton stared at anyone they felt it.

"That isna a' ", Duncan answered. "There're plenty more, but I didna like tae pu' them a' doon."

Streeton laughed. Streeton always laughed at McClay's jokes. Besides being a man of business, Duncan was a humorist. But the meeting was not in a mood for merriment.

"An' who is ud that's payin' all this money ye hab shpent, Mr. Chairman?" O'Connor, with suspicion in his eye, inquired.

"It isna Mister O'Connor, anyway", McClay answered. "He has a'nely been a reg'lar supplier for a month and doesna always bring milk in his cans either."

Streeton laughed hard again, but no one else joined in his mirth.

"Thaives! Thaives!" O'Connor shouted.

"Shame!" Streeton said to O'Connor. "Shame!"

Hurried whispers passed from one to another, and the feeling of antagonism to the directors increased.

"Will ye read th' sums paid away again, Mr. Chairman?" O'Connor shouted. "Read thim!"

All eyes were turned on O'Connor. He became the hope of the opposition.

McClay read the item again, and said that every particle of the expenditure was justified.

"Don't take any notice of them", Streeton advised. "Get on with the business, Mr. Chairman."

"You shut up", Mrs. Brown, shaking her fist, said to Streeton. "And don't be looking at me with your old cow eyes!"

O'Connor, yelling out things at the top of his voice, sprang to his feet.

"Order! Order!" from the Chairman.

"Dam yer Order," O'Connor roared, "I'm not under any order, it's sthraight dealin' we want—an' it's nothin' but sthraight dealin' we'll hab."

"I object", and Streeton sprang to his feet, too.

"Who th' divvle are ye?" O'Connor asked of him.

"I'm a shareholder, an' have a right to me opinion", and Streeton punched his left palm with his right fist.

"I've twice as many shares as ye—three times as many, so

I have, and have a right to more opinions than ye", and O'Connor, turning his back on the Chair, shook his fist at Streeton.

"Then you got more shares than you got sense, or opinions either", and Streeton sat down and stroked his whiskers.

"Order!" the Chairman called again, and Tommy Ryan in a thin voice cried, "Chair! Chair!"

"I have the flure", O'Connor protested. "An' Oi'll sit down for no mahn."

"Sit doon", McClay ordered.

"I ask for your rulin' ", O'Connor demanded.

"Hear, hear", Mrs. Sawpitt said, applauding O'Connor. "Hear, hear."

"Rubbish!" Streeton said.

"Hauld yer tangs", and McClay waved the balance-sheet at the meeting.

"I'll give way to no wahn", and O'Connor stood upon his seat. "I'm here to hab my say, an' I'll hab ud!"

"Sit ye doon", and McClay pointed his big thick finger at O'Connor as though it were a rifle. "If ye dinna I'll go an' throw y' doon."

"Hear, hear! Hear, hear!" Streeton shouted approvingly.

"Shut up! You hairy old bear", Mrs. Brown called to Streeton.

"I'll shut you up", Streeton retorted, and Mrs. Brown poked her tongue out.

"There's manners for yer", and Streeton scowled at her.

"I'll shtay here till I know where all this money hab gone to", and O'Connor folded his arms and wagged his whiskers defiantly at the meeting.

"That's right; we want to know into whose pocket it went", Miss McOwen, an old maid who milked her own cows, squeaked.

"That's corperashin for y', if y' like!" Mrs. Daley interjected, and Mrs. Holmes declared it "wasn't corperashin at all, but robberation of poor, 'ard-workin' people."

"Hauld yer gab," McClay called to Mrs. Holmes, "an' talk sense, woman—ye an' your robberation!"

Then old Holmes jumped to his feet and said he "rose on a point of order."

"I thocht ye rose on the point o' a pitchfork", McClay answered, and filled Streeton with more mirth.

"You can laff," Holmes shouted, "but I'm goin' to stand here and dee-mand of the Chairman—yes, dee-mand———"

"But I hab the flure", yelled O'Connor.

"Chair!" Streeton shouted again. "Chair!"

"Oh, you shut up, and get yourself sheared", Mrs. Brown shrieked at Streeton again, and Streeton told her "it was a good job she wasn't a man".

Then Tommy Williams, and Billy Donkin, and Strawberry Smith all rose at the same time to say something.

"Order!" McClay cried to them, "Order!" but they didn't hear him.

"On whose ertority, Mr. Chairman?" Tom Williams began —but was interrupted by Bill Donkin.

"Mr. Chairman!" Bill roared, "was all that money———"

Then Sam Smith, in a louder voice than Bill Donkin's, said he "called it nothin' but rookin' the suppliers".

Here the meeting took an unexpected turn.

A mad-eyed, blood-stained, spear-horned bullock burst suddenly in through the open door, and made panic. Shouts, screams, flying cheese cases, and the minute book all greeted the intruder. A wild rush for the "escape door", a narrow opening in the wall leading to the rear of the building, set in. The Chairman and co-directors abandoned their places and joined in the retreat. The bewildered animal covered with foam and whip-marks stood dazed, till Brown's terrier noisily attacked it. Then it bellowed and turned on the terrier and upset the directors' table and tramped on the annual report and balance-sheet. The terrier skedaddled for the "escape door" and disappeared between the legs of McClay and O'Connor, who were last getting out. With a roar, the bullock pursued the terrier.

"Look out! Look out!" McClay cried, but O'Connor couldn't look out because McClay himself was before him, and McClay was big and broad. O'Connor abandoned the escape door, and took refuge behind the milk vat. The bullock bounded over the vat in pursuit of him. O'Connor jumped it back and faced the brute across it. "Help!" he shouted, "Help!" but no one but McClay rendered any aid. McClay put his head in at the door and shouted, "Tell him ye have the flure, O'Connor."

Then the local butcher and three dogs arrived, and the bullock bounded out the way it bounded in.

After that the meeting was adjourned *sine die*.

11. Why Splinter Came Home

O'Connor didn't put a windlass on the well; he hadn't time. Just when he was about to erect it, masses of black clouds rolled up, and the wind started to blow hard, and everyone said a change was on, and there was going to be rain, and O'Connor got excited.

He threw some harness on a pair of old horses, and hurrying them into the field, commenced planting corn; and when he had planted it all, the clouds rolled by without wetting anyone, and the sun came out again and shone brightly. Then Pat Donovan strolled across and spoke to O'Connor about branding colts.

"Come over in the morning, Pat and help me throw thim," the latter said, "an' I'll have the tackling all ready."

Donovan came, and they threw the colts and broke the tail of one, and the neck of another, or thought they did. Then O'Connor tore his hair and foamed, and blamed Splinter for the accidents and chased him out of the yard.

Donovan dragged at the fallen colt's tail to make the brute rise, but it remained motionless. It was apparently dead as Caesar.

O'Connor swore more and groaned and lamented his loss.

Donovan sat astride the prostrate animal and reasoned with O'Connor—told him there were plenty more horses in the world.

"Wouldn't it make y' woild, too," the latter said, "to see y' besht-bred colt disfigured for loife, and his half brither lyin' there under y'?"

"But the boy had no more to do with it than yerself", Donovan said, defending Splinter.

" 'Twas him did ud", roared O'Connor obstinately. "Didn't Oi yell and yell to him to shlack the rope, and he pulled it harder an' pulled him over!"

Donovan, who, absent-mindedly, had been scraping hair

off the fallen animal with his pocket-knife, suddenly pricked its rump with the blade point.

Talk about a surprise; Donovan did get a surprise!

That colt came to life again, bounded to his feet, and, carrying Donovan astride its back, face to tail, careered round the yard as though possessed of forty devils.

O'Connor, alarmed and delighted, mounted the rails and yelled to Donovan to "shtick to him".

Splinter climbed up beside O'Connor and waved his hat.

The sleeping dogs about the farm woke up and yelped and barked through the rails.

Mrs. O'Connor, with some of the washing in her hand, followed by the children, ran from the house and gathered round.

No circus ever gave such a performance. It was a thrilling entertainment. Donovan, in desperation, curled his long legs and arms round the maddened animal, and clung to it like a staghorn.

"For the love of heaven, childer, keep back", Mrs. O'Connor cried, when clouds of dust came flying through the rails.

The children crept closer.

"Shtick to him, Pat, shtick to him", O'Connor shouted.

Donovan's hat flew off. The colt met it with both heels, and kicked it past Splinter's head. Splinter tried to field it amid air, but missed, and, losing his balance, toppled over backwards and fell on Mrs. O'Connor, who was kneeling at the bottom rail. Mrs. O'Connor thought he was the colt, and shrieked. Then she slashed at Splinter with the washing, and chased him from the yard.

Splinter grinned, and, returning, mounted the rails again and proceeded to encourage Donovan some more with shouts of approbation.

But the colt began to tire, so did Donovan. His long legs and arms relinquished their grip and dangled limply down. The colt staggered and stood. Donovan swayed from side to side. The colt trembled and shook, and Donovan rolled off in a helpless heap. Then O'Connor and Splinter jumped into the yard to rescue him. Splinter seized the cowed and beaten animal by the mane and said:

"Give us a leg up; I'll ride 'im for y'."

O'Connor kicked Splinter hard in the rear, and shouted:

"Help me to lift th' mahn up."

Splinter rubbed the injured part, and scowled at O'Connor, then reluctantly gave a hand to drag Donovan through the dust and out the gate.

Mrs. O'Connor ran for a jug of water, and threw it over Donovan.

When Donovan recovered, O'Connor laughed and praised his horsemanship.

Donovan looked round and smiled feebly. Mrs. O'Connor inquired "if he felt all right?"

Donovan said he would "in a minute".

"If y' was t' train that colt t' alwez gammin' he was dead, Mister 'Connor," Splinter advised, "and sit on 'im yerself, and stick a knife inter 'im, you'd make——"

"Oi'll stick a knife into ye", and O'Connor rushed at Splinter before he could finish.

Splinter fled. O'Connor pursued him across the barn-yard, through the house, round the house, and round the house again. Then he gave up and held his sides with his hands and used bad language.

"Yah!" Splinter called to him, "I'm goin' home." And home he went.

12. *The Death Of Little Jens*

A sweltering hot day; not a breeze blowing; not a cloud in the sky; the sun beating fiercely, relentlessly down, withering the leaves of the great forest trees, scorching, burning every blade of grass, every particle of vegetation, parching, cracking, baking the very earth. In the creek-bed at the "crossing", where the oak tree stood, and where those whose tanks and water-casks had given out procured their house supplies, dairy herds and miscellaneous stock moaning with thirst hurriedly assembled. In dozens they walked knee-deep into the water, drank and gorged to their fill, then remained to puddle, and slobber and churn it all into "soup". They would loiter and puddle in that creek the whole day, or until someone with a real, live dog came and dogged them away. And it was the only creek there was for miles around!

Titt, with the help of an experienced "bush carpenter", whom he engaged at something a week, and Old Fred, had given the finishing touches to the new milking-yard, and with both hands in his pockets, was standing in the centre contemplating it all with silent satisfaction. Neils Jensen, a Danish neighbour, living on the plain where the grass-trees stood, dragging a lean, slab-sided dispirited-looking animal in the shape of a horse attached to a forked log sled, with an empty water-cask rolling about on it, drew up near the gateway and called "voe", an injunction hardly necessary to bring the leg-weary, heart-broken creature to a standstill!

"Hello, Jensen!" Titt greeted, cheerfully, "come to see my new yard?" And the rough, splintery three-rail enclosure, with its sapling gates and bails, took a firmer grip of his affections. But Jensen hadn't. Jensen had slaved too often and too long in his lifetime erecting similar yards and getting very little in return to go out of his way to admire Titt's, or even to take the slightest notice of it. His sunken eyes showed no gleam of appreciation or enthusiasm; no more than those of the jaded quadruped standing so dejectedly beside him, did. He just leaned his two bare, boney, freckled, scarred and hairy arms on one of the middle rails, poked his whiskered chin through, and speaking with a thick tongue in slow, broken English, proceeded to explain the object of his visit.

"What?" Titt said, crawling through the rails to him. "What did you say?"

Using his hands to assist his articulation, the Dane repeated that he had come for a cask of water. "Too many cows," he explained, "stand by der creek an' make der vorter no goot!"

"Oh, you want some tank water?" Titt responded cheerfully. "Certainly—come along—bring your moke an' trolly over to th' house and get what y' want." And marching off, swinging his arms, jauntily led the way.

With the aid of a couple of buckets the cask was soon filled and the lid hammered on with a stone over a wet bag to make it water-tight.

"Mooch eiblished, my frien'," Jensen said, shaking his benefactor by the hand, "yo' do my fambly a good turn."

"That's all right," Titt said, lightly, "a cask o' water is nothing: come back for more whenever you want it." Titt Duff was nothing if he wasn't generous and open-handed.

"It ees not for ourkellef ve vant it," and big tears started rolling from Jensen's eyes and mingling with the hair and dust on his big sinewy arms, "it ees for der little Jens."

"Why so?" wonderingly from Titt.

"He vos ver sick for so long time now!"

"Sick? One of your boys? I didn't know that."

"My tent poy, little Jens."

"Your tenth boy? Good God! How many have y' got?" and half-amazed, half-amused, Titt stared at the worried-looking Dane.

"Fifteen, countin' der lash fellow—twelf poy an' tree girl."

"Good God!" Titt said again. "Fifteen!" and stepping back a pace or two regarded Jensen with wonder and astonishment. "Why, I've only got three—yet", he added. And the emphasis he placed on the "yet," seemed prophetic.

"Der poor little Jens!" Jensen went on disregarding the other's astonishment, "for six week he lay on der bed an' scream wid pain, an' der vife she can make him not some better!"

"Send him to the General Hospital", Titt suggested. "Your wife can't look after him properly if he is very bad, neither can you, and there are doctors and nurses at the hospital to attend to him."

In his social isolation and ignorance, Jensen's only idea of a hospital was that it meant a big bill—a bill that his little homestead would, in the end, have to be sacrificed to pay! And how, in any case, to procure admittance to such an institution he had no more idea than an old man kangaroo. He and his family had always kept to themselves; made no friendship; attended no church; read no newspapers; voted for no politicians; took no part in the many minor public movements that tend to draw the scattered bush-folk to closer circles of intercourse where enlightenment and the hand of fellowship so often lessen their load of disappointment and misfortune. And the more Titt explained about the hospital, the more mysterious and impossible it all seemed to poor Jensen.

"Vould yo' come an' see der little chap?" he asked, "den yo' could tal my vife all vot yo' tol me vat dat place?"

Titt would—cheerfully.

"You go on with the water," he said, "while I go inside and get my coat, then I'll catch you up."

Jensen nodded, and started off dragging the horse and water-trolly after him.

Mrs. Duff, at work in the kitchen, got a surprise when she saw Titt brushing his hair and putting a coat on.

"Where are you going?" she asked, coming to the door with a dish of peeled potatoes in her hands.

Titt explained.

"They seem very quiet people," she mused, "I hardly ever see them going anywhere."

"Nor I," and Titt buttoned his coat and put on his hat; "and the old chap just told me", he continued, "that they have fifteen youngsters—twelve boys and three girls."

"Fifteen? Goodness!" from Mrs. Duff. "They've more children than we've got hens and chickens."

"But ye'll have more than that directly." And Titt glanced at himself in a hand mirror.

"What! More!" and Mrs. Duff let the dish of potatoes fall on the floor.

"More hens and chickens—yes, I won't be long away." And rushing off, Titt followed after Jensen.

Mrs. Duff sighed a sigh of relief, and collecting the scattered potatoes, went on with her work.

Having tarried along the way to exchange a few words with McNelson, the oldest inhabitant of the Creek, about the weather and the prospects of getting a school built, Titt didn't overtake Jensen until he had almost reached the door of his home. Dragging the horse and trolley into the shade of a peach tree amongst the foliage of which reared a formidable-looking scarecrow purporting to frighten the flying-foxes from the fruit, Jensen called "Voe!" to the tired brute, and turned to Titt.

"Him stan' dere," he said, "vile I take yo' in to see der little Jens."

But Titt didn't hear him. His mind was on the crowd of youngsters that came scampering from every corner of the farm—youngsters of all sizes and ages; fair-haired and freckle-faced; two of them with a hat and coat on several sizes too large for them; the rest quaint phenomenons of raggedness. Around the water cask they collected, jostling and scrimmaging for the honour of removing the lid and taking first peep at the water. Following the youngsters came swarms of fowl—fowl of every hue and variety—of every breed and mixture, with here and there amongst their ranks a waddling, quacking, dusty-looking duck; and behind the lot, but holding proudly aloof, a boisterous procession of high-stepping turkey gobblers. Disregarding the presence of the youngsters and the dejected horse, this conglomeration of poultry gathered about the cask with open beaks and widespread wings.

"Struth!" Titt said, "you've a lot of fowls and things!"

"But dey trink a lort o' vater, an' eat a lort o' tucker!" and Jensen led the way to the house across a bare, hoof-trodden yard, strewn with loose stones, shelled corn-cobs and horse manure. It wasn't a very imposing looking dwelling—'twas a long concern made of slabs and covered with a low-pitched, slanting roof of galvanized iron. At one end was a large square fire-place minus a chimney—the smoke, when a fire was burning, escaped between the slabs that lay across the top of it. At the other end was a gaping window with an "old man" grape vine twining round it; and right in the centre was the door. And at the threshold stood Mrs. Jensen, with the "last fellow", a six months old child, in her arms. A short, stout, weighty woman she was, wearing a sack-apron and heavy shoes. She had an abundance of faded hair, a portion of which was carelessly gathered together in a knot on top of her head, while the remainder fell anyhow about her neck and shoulders. A silent woman, too, the willing drudge and unselfish slave of the farm, who every year, as regularly as the world went round, presented her husband with a fresh contribution to the family.

Titt raised his hat; and by way of introduction, Jensen said:

"Meester Doff, he come to see der little Jens."

With a movement of the lips Mrs. Jensen turned inside and walked across the floor of the front-room, and standing at the foot of a sofa on which lay the invalid, waited for them to enter it.

"Min' yo don't knock yor head," Jensen stooping low himself, warned, "eet's not ver' high."

Titt "minded," and crept in after him.

One glance at the interior and the hard struggle the Jensens were having to exist upon the land was quickly revealed to Titt. Anyone else, probably, would have realised it as speedily as he—anyone else except Governments, legislators, and the like! The little there was in that home was clean and tidy enough, God knows; but its littleness was the tragedy of it! Corn sacks ripped up and stitched together covered the ground floor. The slab walls were lined with newspapers. No pictures, no clock, no chairs. Some boxes and bush-made stools took the place of the latter. A long pine table with pieces added to the ends of it to cope with the ever-increasing demand for accommodation stood in the centre of the floor. No cloth was on it; nothing was on it except an official letter lying open

—an official letter from the Land Tax Commissioner demanding the Government's pound of flesh!

"Here is der little shap", Jensen said, tenderly, taking a position at the head of the sofa. "Vos yo any better now, little Jens?"

The mother, by a despondent shake of the head, answered in the negative for the sufferer. Then Titt's eyes rested on the little Jens. All save the boy's face and hand were covered with a calico sheet showing much wear and tear and many specimens of neat patch-work of various shapes and dimensions. And such a pale little face! Such shrivelled little hands! Little Jens was the colour of a ghost, and so emaciated, so wasted! At sight of Titt the drooping eyes of the little fellow suddenly lit up with a ray of hope. They got bigger and brighter. Then he stretched out his little hands and pleaded:

"Make me better: I want to get better!"

For anything so pathetic Titt had not come prepared. Speech for the moment left him, and ghostlike, he stood gazing into those pallid features twitching and writhing in pain, and whereon death so unmistakably was written.

"We didn't think he would be so bad at first", the mother explained. "He was quite well six weeks ago, and playing with the other children about the haystack when all at once, he sat down and said he had a pain in the stomach."

"Did he?" Titt murmured, "poor little chap!"

"It never left him since", she continued, "and you can see how his stomach has got bigger and bigger and bigger!"

By the rising and falling of the sheet with the short sharp breathing of the boy, Titt could see it only too well, and the conviction that it was cancer made him shudder.

"You'll make me better", little Jens appealed.

Titt took one of the withered little hands in his, but a lump that was in his throat choked back any comforting words he might have uttered. He looked away, and his eyes rested sadly on the floor, and only a hopeless, desolate feeling filled his mind. For the power to heal the sick boy he would have given the whole world were it his. But the helplessness and impotence of mortals in the presence of Death were all he could realise or was conscious of. Remain there another minute he couldn't.

"I'll go and send for the ambulance to take him to the hospital", he said, suddenly, and taking his hat, rushed out.

Mrs. Duff was tidying herself for the afternoon when he entered his own home again.

"Well?" she said.

Titt told what he had seen, and added that he was going to the township to communicate with the ambulance.

"I'll run over and see if I can do anything." And pinning her hat on, Mrs. Duff left by the front door, while Titt, to save time, hurried out by the back one.

Nearing Jensen's place, a cry of pain met her ears, and Mrs. Duff quickened her steps. Without announcing herself she swiftly entered.

"Poor little fellow!" she said, fervently, and kneeling beside the sofa smoothed the long fair hair of little Jens back over his forehead with a hand that had not yet lost its city softness. "Poor dear little fellow!"

He slowly turned his eyes to hers, and murmured:

"Make me better; I want to get better."

"And you will get better", she answered. "Jesus is watching over you, little Jens—you know that, don't you?" And bending over him she kissed the pale forehead.

He made no answer. His eyes remained fixed upon the kindly face, that seemed to fill that gloomy room with a heavenly light. His sick little brain seemed puzzled.

"Jesus loves all little boys, Jens," she added; "and wants them to go to him."

Then his lips moved.

"Who is Jesus?" he asked.

The simple question struck Mrs. Duff like a bombshell. She turned and cast a look of surprise and pity at the mother, still seated at the foot of the sofa—a look that was plainly understood—and answered by a shake of the head.

"We not had time to tol him abort dosse dings", the father interposed, apologetically.

"I don't know Jesus", the little Jens added.

"But he knows you, Jens", from Mrs. Duff. "And you will know him, too."

Then as he lay perplexed and listening with his last feeble strength, she told him in tender earnest words of the birth and love of the Saviour. The rest of the children, crowding noiselessly into the room, she paused a moment to glance at them. That moment seemed an eternity to the soul that was swiftly passing away.

"Tell me about Jesus", he murmured. "I—I—never saw him."

Holding his hands between her own, she lifted her voice and repeated the children's prayer:

"Gentle Jesus meek and mild,
Look upon a little child;
Pity my simplicity;
Suffer me to come to Thee."

"And will Jesus make me better?" the boy inquired with a struggle.

"Yes, little Jens, He will—He will."

"S—soon?" he whispered feebly.

"Soon—very soon now!" And tears flowed from Mrs. Duff's eyes as she leaned over and smoothed the fair hair back over the pale little brow again.

Scarcely was her last word spoken when in the darkening gloom the eyes of little Jens closed themselves for ever and his soul passed out to the Silence of Eternity—to the world beyond the setting sun.

"He's gone!" Mrs. Duff whispered softly.

"Gone!" echoed the father. While large tears starting into the eyes of the mother, overflowed and fell upon the face of her suckling child. The rest of the children drew nervously to the death-bed. For a minute or more there was a solemn stillness within the house. Then in twos and threes they gave way to grief and wept aloud.

Outside, the sun went down behind the distant hill-tops, casting great black shadows over the rolling plains—the great grey plains filled with mists and land-marks and memories of coaching days and shepherds' huts and deserted homesteads. One by one the stars came out and twinkled like the eyes of a million angels watching from the windows of another world. The moon rose over the Great Dividing Range, spreading his light around, streaming through timber and trees, creeping up and up till, entering the window like a searchlight from Heaven, revealed a parting smile of peace and serenity on the face of the dead, and pains of affliction upon those of the living. Then the moaning, summer night winds sprang up, rustling the drooping corn-blades and tops of the weird grass trees, and crooning into every corner and angle of the home and farm sheds, seemed to be haunted with ghosts, and charged with messages of grief, and many, many unavailing sorrows and regrets.

13. Starting Dairying

It was Spring. The westerly winds had ceased; the frosts departed. Valleys and hills now were bright and green and gay. Gum-trees were in blossom; wattles in bloom; the birds of the bush whistling merrily, and the busy bees humming all around again.

Titt's block boasted of a patch of cultivation now—a patch of twelve acres, and twelve young Shorthorn cows—the Shorthorns Titt bought from Donovan. Eleven of them were in "profit"; the twelfth, an unbroken one, had yet to "come in". Titt didn't milk all the herd himself. Mrs. Duff, who had forgotten more about milking than he was ever likely to learn, accounted for six of them; Splinter and Araluen for four, and the remaining one, "Tulip", fell to the mercy of Titt himself. And little mercy did she receive at his hands. Milking didn't come natural to Titt, and whenever he pinched a teat or accidentally pulled the hair on her udder, Tulip would resent it and do her utmost to put her foot in the bucket or kick him off the block. Then Titt would rise and argue the point— sometimes with his mouth; more often with a short stick.

"Goodness me!" Mrs. Duff would say after letting go her last cow, "you are a milker! Why don't you take both hands to it like this." And bending over, would seize a teat with each hand and start playing a tune in the bucket. But Titt would never wait to be instructed; he couldn't bear anyone coming near Tulip when he was sitting under her. He would hurriedly leave the block, and in his haste spill what was in the bottom of the bucket over his boots.

"Do y' want a bloke to get his brains kicked out?" he would remonstrate; "she ain't used to a crowd draggin' at her, y' know!"

"Bah! no wonder! See how far you've got her leg tied back!"

Then his wife would slacken the rope till Tulip rested firmly on all fours, and seating herself on the block, and placing the bucket between her knees, and humming a tune, would milk away till Tulip was drained of her last drop.

"There you are," she would say, rising again, "now let her out."

"My Christmas, yes!" Titt would chuckle, "all very fine, to say 'let her out'. Easier to milk her, I reckon."

Then cautiously undoing huge ridiculous knots he had tied in the leg-rope, and unwinding it from the post, he'd talk coaxingly to Tulip for a moment or two, and when satisfied her mind was off him snatch stealthily for the loop encircling her leg to pull it off—the loop, not her leg. If he missed it, which he mostly did, the cow would let fly a kick which Titt would elude by springing back and bumping into Mrs. Duff or into the bucket of milk, and letting go the end of the rope. When Tulip felt four or five feet of hemp or greenhide dangling to her she'd mistake it for a snake or a cattle pup or something, and let fly a lot more kicks—savage, reckless kicks, every one harder and swifter than the last. And when the whirling, whizzing rope-end, instead of leaving her leg, would smack her hard on the back, or along the ribs, she'd get hysterical and flop down on her knees, and elevate her hindpart, and put out her tongue and bellow, and the cows that had been milked and let out would rush excitedly back and bellow too, and tear up the dust with their hoofs and throw it over their backs and fill the air with frightfulness.

"Oh dear me!" Mrs. Duff would sigh, coming to the rescue again, "what a way to take a leg-rope off!"

"Well, see what you can do," Titt would chuckle and cheerfully abandon the job, "a man wants a gun to take a leg-rope off a brute like her, I reckon."

"Nonsense!" and his wife would pat Tulip on the back and speak soothingly to her for a moment or two; then reach confidently for the loop and take it off her leg.

"There you are," she would say, tossing the greenhide to Titt, "but I'm sure I don't know how you'll ever manage a dairy herd yourself!"

"It's all very well for you to talk, Kit," he'd remind her, "you saw some farm life before you went to the city. But wait a while." Titt didn't mind how his wife criticised his efforts at farming.

Once, though, when Old Fred, who hated the sight of cows, but loved milk and cream, and spent a lot of time running in and out of the dairy, poked into the yard at milking time and smiled at Titt and reckoned he should never have left the city, there was nearly a separation.

"Here!" Titt barked at him, "get out of this and go and do something for your living! Go and get a hoe and cut th' prickly pear you were talkin' so much about at breakfast-time, go on!" And shooting out his right arm like a railway signal, pointed to the gate.

"It's no good anyone cuttin' pear," Old Fred argued, "it only makes it grow more; it's like cuttin' hair; anyone ought to know that. Pear must be pizened if y' want to 'radicate it!"

"Well pizen it, then!" Titt shouted, "and there's a bunch there outside the yard lookin' at y'; pizen that, too, and pizen yourself when you're about it!"

"Don't know about pizenin' meself," Old Fred murmured, "but I don't mind doin' th' pear. Where's th' pizen?"

Just then Titt's eye caught Mrs. Duff frowning and scowling at him, and he temporised.

"Oh, how do I know?" he mumbled, "and don't care a fig either whether you do it, or whether you don't it; or what you do about th' place or what you don't do about it!" and grabbing a bucket of milk in each hand, slipped away to the dairy.

"Seems I put me foot in it", Old Fred, taking his hat from his head and spinning it nervously on the first finger on his left hand, said.

Mrs. Duff laughed and was "sure Titt didn't mean a word he said".

"Sounded to me as if he did!" and the kindly Old Fred thoughtfully followed Titt to the dairy.

"Come for your mornin' allowance, Fred?" and Titt cheerfully held up a can of new milk level with his head.

Old Fred took down a pint from the shelf, and holding it out while the other filled it from the can, said:

"What did y' mean over at th' yard, Titt? Are you getting full up o' Old Fred?"

"What did I mean?" Titt echoed, sparring for time.

"Because if yous are," Fred went on, humbly, "they'll be startin' shearin' at Cecil Plains in a couple of months and th' boys 'll never have anyone there for cook but me. And I ain't a pauper, y' know."

"A couple of months?" Titt echoed. "But who said they were getting full up o' y'?" he chuckled. "Drink that milk and you'll fill yourself up." And he punched Old Fred playfully in the ribs.

Old Fred drained the pint without drawing breath and smacking his lips, said he never drank better milk anywhere in his life.

"They're good little cows all right", Titt grinned proudly.

"A good little gold mine to y' in a year or two", from Old Fred.

"Now for the factory", and Titt turned down his shirt sleeves.

"Is everything ready for you?" And Old Fred ran out and walked all round the horse and cart and viewed the harness to see if it was buckled properly. And when Titt took the reins and climbed up amongst the cans, Old Fred ran to the gate and swung it wide to let him out, then wished him luck and waved to him as he trotted away.

14. Billy Cattfish

Driving the milk to the factory was a work of love to Titt. He was in his element at the factory; there was always some company there and its atmosphere was congenial to him. A free and easy sort of place it was, no stiff collars or polished boots or fashionable hats. Nothing was worn there but "milking clothes", and then never more than was required by the local standard of bare respectability. Besides, it was a co-operative factory, and Titt had become a shareholder. And every morning when their milk was weighed, and taken charge of by the Manager, and they received their "empties", the suppliers would retire to the whey tank, and congregate about it as though it were a pub and discuss cows and milk and cheese and land and the Government and the district's "useless representative". And in these debates Titt became a central figure. He shone out like the morning star. He was not an orator—just a talker. And no matter how many tackled him in argument, he was never perturbed. He would talk and talk and talk until they were all silenced, and then he'd continue talking so as to keep them silent.

But one morning, Billy Cattfish, a sharp-faced slick-tongued, black-whiskered supplier with an inexhaustible flow of profanity suddenly jumped off the elevated box drain that led from the factory to the whey tank (the whey tank was lower than the factory) on which he had been seated, swinging his legs about and scratching and puncturing the drain with the rowel of an old spur that never left the heel of his boot, not even when he went to bed at night, and confronting Titt, aggressively rapped out:

"Just one —— word!"

Titt paused and stared at him. The others who knew Cattfish from childhood, rejoiced.

"You being such a wise ——coot," he proceeded spitting

to the right and then to the left, "now tell us if y' can—and I know you —— well can't—why cheese is so cheap?"

The crowd, grinning broadly, waited for Titt's reply.

"The reason is this"—and Titt crossed his two first fingers— "the farmers have always been mugs who worked for the middleman, and voted for him as well."

"I'm one of those —— farmers!" Cattfish interrupted, "and the man who calls me a mug gets one on th' —— jaw."

Great excitement!

"Do you mean that?" Titt said.

"Ask these —— blokes who know me, whether I'm a man that means what he says or not?" And swinging his clenched fists about Cattfish walked round Titt.

"My oath he do!" fully a dozen voices confirmed at once.

"All right—so do I." And Titt started rolling up his sleeves.

"Mine's —— well coming off!" giving his milk-stained shirt a savage tug, Cattfish stood stripped to the waist.

Greater excitement!

Though lean, lanky and bandy, Titt was no "slouch" with his hands. He had been an active member of the Brisbane Gymnasium for ten years, where his hobby was boxing and everything appertaining to it. There was nothing about the "art" that Titt didn't know. On the other hand, Cattfish had won some fights at a shearing shed; walloped a number of harmless old "sundowners" for having camped in his paddock without permission, and with the aid of his profanity had worked up a local "reputation".

"There's goin' to be a fight! There's goin' to be a fight!" several voices, like the sounding of Gabriel's dinner-horn, shouted. Next moment the Manager, and cheese-maker and all late arrivals came running from the factory and joined the "ring".

Bendy Sawpitt, who had often expressed a desire to see Cattfish "get a hiding from someone", appointed himself Titt's second. And Podgy Smith, "just to see fair play", stood behind Cattfish.

"I've got scales on me —— back," Cattfish bragged, "as hard as a bull's horn for the want of a good hiding, and I've never met the —— man who was able to give it to me."

Loud laughter from everyone, except Titt.

Titt silently toed the line and faced the foe.

"Go fer his short ribs. Billy", Podgy Smith advised.

"I'll go for the whole lot of th' long —— !" Cattfish hissed, with set teeth. "Now come on! Watch your —— skin!"

With that he rushed in like a dog at an emu. Titt side-stepped, and Cattfish went on an air-raid.

Loud mirth and looks of surprise all round the ring.

"You ——! ——! ——!" and Cattfish spat and prepared another offensive.

"I'd sunner be here thun home on th' farm", old Doughboy said to old Drygrass.

Cutting loose with both fists, Cattfish flew at Titt again; but the latter seemed to be part of the atmosphere. He was in every place except where his opponent's blows were landing.

"The cow!" Cattfish foamed, "he isn't game to stand up to me. He keeps running away!"

Titt, smiling, sparred for level ground.

"Now, you've got him agin th' tank, Billy," Podgy Smith shouted "he can't back away from there!"

Cattfish judged so, too.

With lowered head and glaring eye-balls, he sprung another wild rush. But instead of finding Titt's head or short ribs, he landed a heavy right on the whey tank, which rumbled like an approaching storm.

Loud guffaws and shouts of appreciation from everyone.

"Th' —— coward!" Cattfish foamed, rubbing his thumb; "someone hold th' ——! and make him stand!"

"I'll wait for you this time!" Titt chuckled, handing him a couple of love-pats on the nose, "but don't hit too hard."

Like a panther, Cattfish sprang at him. Titt stopped him with one—two in the ribs.

"Time!" Podgy Smith cried. "Time!" while his principal doubled up and walked round holding his side.

"Ready?" Titt said, after an interval; and both toed the line again, Titt looking resolute; Cattfish cocksure and uncompromising.

"Keep it up, an' you'll get him directly, Billy," Podgy Smith whispered, encouragingly.

"I'll keep it up, my —— oath!" the other responded. Then like a windmill in gear when the pump ain't working, he went after Titt. Titt's long right shot out and met him between the two eyes; then his left got him under the chin, and Cattfish's face suddenly looked skyward, and his head, for a moment, hung down his back.

"Oh! Oh-h!" from the spectators.

Cattfish straightened his head, staggered, swore feebly. Then Titt jumped in and using his hands like a quick-firing machine, punished his man all round that ring and nearly knocking a hole in the whey-tank with him. It was nothing but biff! biff! biff! followed by a mighty jaw-punch and down Cattfish dropped like a pithed bullock.

Consternation and alarm took possession of the onlookers. None of them had ever seen a man knocked out before except by a swingle-tree or a slip-rail, and as Cattfish lay motionless, visions of hand-cuffs and the gallows came to them. Then, suddenly they turned and fled, some into the factory, the rest into their carts; and leaving Titt himself to console Cattfish as best he could, careered out the gate and along the lanes, like Roman chariot races, for their homes.

15. The Unbroken Heifer

"Th' heifer—the unbroken heifer's calved!" Splinter, rushing breathlessly into the house one afternoon, shouted, "I saw her first."

"Has she? Where?" and Titt who, with Mrs. Duff and Araluen, was taking a cup of tea in the kitchen, jumped up from the table and tramped on the cat's tail and made Tom squeal and spit.

"Down in th' gully," from Splinter, "an' it's a bull—a little red and white bull."

"I must go and see it", and Titt started looking round for his hat.

"We'll all go and see it," Mrs. Duff enthused, "come along, Araluen." And they finished their tea hurriedly.

"Will we keep him for a bull, Father?" Splinter asked excitedly. "Will we?"

"I must see what he's like first", and Titt continued to look round for his hat.

Mrs. Duff and Araluen started tying their bonnets on.

"Now where th' diggings has that hat o' mine got to?" And Titt looked round the room.

"O'Connor is keepin' one of theirs for a bull", from Splinter.

"Oh, shut up! It's me hat I want just now!" from Titt.

"Look!" and Mrs. Duff, with a broad smile, pointed to Bluey, the dog, comfortably coiled up on the floor in the missing felt.

Araluen and Splinter laughed.

"My Christmas! if that ain't cool!" And taking a place kick at Bluey, Titt lifted him through the door into Splinter's room.

"Ah!" Mrs. Duff protested, "that's cruel!"

"Come outer that room, you mongrel!" Splinter yelled, "do y' hear?"

Bluey, cringing and calculating the direction in which every boot in the kitchen was facing, crept cautiously out till within measurable distance of the back door, then he made such a desperate dart that his toe-nails almost tore up the flooring.

"Cripes!" Splinter laughed, "I was just goin' to hand him another, but he was too quick!"

Then the whole family, led by Titt, ran out, and in single file, hastened to the gully.

Before they had gone fifty yards, they were joined by Bluey, who raced round Titt and bounded up at his shoulder and barked for sheer joy. There was no bitterness about Bluey. He was a real dog, and felt nothing but love and gratitude for those who put the boot into him.

"Don't go too near her!" Mrs. Duff cried when they came in sight of the heifer standing guard over her offspring, "it will only disturb her." Then she and Araluen halted. Titt and Splinter, however, prowled along a little nearer.

"My word," the former murmured, when he could get a full view of the calf, "it's a bonser!"

"Will y' keep him for a bull?" Splinter whispered back.

"Can't say quite yet", thoughtfully from his parent.

The heifer raised her head and regarded their presence jealously. She began to moan apprehensively, and, shaking her head, stood right over the calf.

"She was lickin' its head when I first saw her", Splinter proudly informed his parent.

"Well, you needn't be talkin' about it!" the other snapped.

"I wasn't talkin' about it! I only mentioned it, didn't I?" in an injured undertone from Splinter.

"Well, don't be mentionin' it again!"

"Who said I was goin' to mention it again?" obstinately from Splinter.

"Shut up!" the parent hissed, peremptorily.

"A bloke won't be able to open his mouth at all directly." And Splinter hung his bottom lip and contemplated his parent out of the corner of his eye.

Just then Bluey, who wasn't in the know, suddenly and joyously emerged, wringing wet, from a deep part of the gully within a few yards of the heifer, and started rolling himself gladly in the dust.

Unhappy stars! 'Twas like a Hun suddenly dropping into the Allied trenches in the Great War! That heifer let out a round of infamous bellows, prolonged and curly as chain lightning, and was on top of Bluey before he could get his legs down! And the howl that came from Bluey was a hair-raiser. And when he found his feet, his hair rose too, and whipping his tail between his legs, he raced straight for Titt and Splinter, the heifer bounding and snorting behind him.

"Look out!" Splinter yelled; "she's after us!" and in his blind haste to skedaddle, bumped into his parent and knocked him off his feet. Titt protested profanely; but at that moment nothing short of a wireless could have communicated anything to Splinter. Recovering himself Titt saw the form of Bluey flash past, and realising that nothing in the world lay between himself and the snorting heifer, but a pair of short, gleaming horns, he stretched his legs and his arms and his neck and ran. Oh, how he did run! Mrs. Duff and Araluen, a hundred yards ahead, their bonnets in their hands, their stockings coming down, were running, too, and squealing like two loco-motives. None of them had time to look behind until they reached the milking-yard, the nearest haven of safety; when they did look behind they found the heifer was nowhere in sight. She was still in the gully with her calf.

Three days later. Titt and Splinter and Old Fred in the yard, breaking in the heifer. Armed with heavy sticks they were endeavouring to induce her to put her head in the bail. But instead of putting it in and submitting quietly, she became excited and reckless, and poked her head into every place but the right place; then went down on her knees and tried to crawl under the bottom rail, and the bottom rail of Titt's yard nearly touched the ground; and finding she could only get her snout under, began to bellow as if she was being slaughtered, and started Bluey barking, and the roosters crowing, and all the hens cackling, and the plough horses neighing, and the clock inside striking, and some stray cattle on the road bucking about with their tails in the air and looking across the fence in wonderment.

'You'll have to rope her and pull her into it", Mrs. Duff, hurrying from the house amidst the turmoil, advised.

"We'll get her in if we have to cut her bloomin' head off!" Titt, pausing to wipe the perspiration from his face with the palm of his dusty, clammy hand, declared determinedly.

Old Fred shook his head and seriously agreed with Mrs. Duff.

"All right, then, we'll pull her in!" and Titt went off to the harness room and returned with brand new hemp rope almost as stiff as steel.

"Who's goin' to rope her—you, Father?" Splinter inquired, with a happy grin.

"Well, you don't think I'm goin' to ask you to do it, do y'?" his parent snapped.

"No, but I thought p'raps y' might ask Mother."

Old Fred hid himself behind one of the bails, and shook with silent mirth.

"Well, y' see I ain't", and Titt started adjusting a noose on one end of the rope, and tangling his legs and feet in the rest of it.

"Here," Splinter said, "I'll show you how to do it."

"Just you get out o' here before I throw you out!" and Titt glared indignantly at his son.

"Don't get so scotty", Mrs. Duff interceded through the rails.

"Ain't it enough to make a bloke scotty," Titt returned, "when a kid like him wants to tell his old man how to do things?"

"I didn't want to tell y' ", Splinter grumbled.

"Well, what did y' want, then?" and his parent glared at him harder.

"I was only goin' to show y'."

"Pshaw! goin' to show me!" and Titt, swinging the loop round and round his head, as he had seen experts do, approached the heifer, now anchored in a corner of the yard.

"I don't think you got that loop quite right, Boss", Old Fred muttered mildly.

"No, of course not," the other snarled, "I can't get anythin' right, accordin' to you blokes."

"Don't be scotty", Mrs. Duff said again, and Old Fred, deeming it wise to become neutral, sat down in the dust beside a bail post, and with a contented expression on his face, took out his pipe and started smoking placidly.

The heifer faced Titt with a wild, bewildered stare.

"Bet y' sixpence you don't throw it on her first shot?" Splinter, climbing on to a top rail to be out of danger, called bravely.

"Nor in the sixth", Mrs. Duff added, amusedly.

Titt made no response. He kept swinging the noose steadily, and cautiously approaching the animal.

"Don't throw it till she runs", Mrs. Duff advised.

Then the heifer ran. She came out of the corner at a gallop, and amidst a cloud of dust flew between Titt and Old Fred.

"Now!" Mrs. Duff screeched, merrily, and Splinter simultaneously yelled, "Now!"

Titt let fly the rope at the brute's head. It grazed her tail as she flew past, and the full force of the heavily knotted loop hit Old Fred hard and straight, and knocked his hat off, and sent his pipe flying from his mouth, and put hot tobacco ash in both his eyes, and lassooed him by the neck.

"Oh! Oh!" Mrs. Duff gasped.

Splinter clung to the top of the yard, and squealed with joy.

Titt looked dumbfounded.

Old Fred bounded to his feet with a dexterity that was next to marvellous, and clapping both hands over his eyes, and with yells that could only have come from the pangs of torture, rushed blindly through the yard with the rope hanging from his neck.

"Stop him!" Mrs. Duff shrieked, "he'll run against the heifer!"

But before Titt could pull in the slack, and jerk Old Fred back out of danger, he bumped right into the animals's hind quarters as she strained to shove the yard down with her head. Next instant, she kicked him in the stomach with both hind legs, and knocked him on his back; then she bounced round and kneeled on him, and bellowed into his ear, and slobbered

She Charged Titt, and Put Him out of the Yard

on him and mixed her horns up in his shirt, and shoved him over when she tried to get up; then she jumped over him and tangled her legs up in the rope and dragged him for several yards by the neck. After that she went fairly off her head. She charged at Titt and put him out of the yard, and snorted aggressively through the rails at Mrs. Duff. Then Splinter, squatting on the cap, attracted her notice. At him she went and made the jump of her life. Splinter made a great jump, too, but landed in the bunch of prickly pear aforementioned. The heifer reached the cap, and for several tragic moments hung on it with her head outside the yard and her tail inside. Then she toppled right over, and without her calf, and in full possession of her freedom, careered for the gully again.

That evening when the sun and the fowls and the birds and everything living had gone to rest, and Titt was sitting smoking peacefully on the verandah, building castles in the air and dreaming of a prosperous future, and Mrs. Duff was rattling the sewing machine inside, and Splinter and Araluen and Mary Ellen were showing a magic lantern to themselves in the darkened kitchen, and Old Fred was groaning in his bed, the voice of the unbroken heifer could be heard in the gully calling and calling for her calf.

16. *Another Go At Breaking The Heifer*

Day dawned, revealing the slumbering homesteads scattered over the black soil plains and the mountains looking down upon them. The golden streaks that flushed the eastern sky paled and diminished. The wheat fields, the grass paddocks, trees, shrubs, and bushes, all were wet and glistening with dew. The sun came softly over the mountain. The air grew clear and crisp; and life on Emu Creek seemed real and earnest, good and grand.

Titt, returning from the factory, standing upright in the milk cart, flicking the whip at the horse and throwing tobacco clouds behind him, drove into the yard and, alighting as if he were on springs, commenced unharnessing hurriedly.

"Hullo! Old Fred", he called cheerfully, as the former emerged from the dairy with milk froth clinging to his shaven lip like icicles. "Soon as I get some breakfast, I'm going to have another go at breaking in that heifer."

"Right-o," Old Fred agreed; "I'm with you." Then removing the "empties" from the cart, and grunting as though he were transporting the whole world on his back, conveyed them to the dairy.

"Bendy Sawpitt gave me a wrinkle this mornin' how to get her in without any trouble", Titt added as he passed into the house.

"Right-o", Old Fred responded again, and helped himself to another pint of milk.

After breakfast. The unbroken heifer and her calf in the milking-yard; the calf bunting and dragging at an empty black teat; the heifer, staring as though some impending misfortune was about to burst upon her, watched every movement of those outside.

"Now, what we've got to do is this", Titt, working his hands as though he were playing a piano, proceeded to explain to Splinter and Old Fred, "not to rope her at all", and he paused and grinned as if expecting them to be tremendously surprised.

"Not to rope her." And Old Fred nodded agreeably, and as though he never expected anything else.

"Not to rope her at all?" Splinter squeaked disappointedly. "Oh, go!" Splinter could conceive no satisfaction or joy in breaking a heifer without roping her.

"No, not to rope her," Titt repeated, with an air of great superiority, "but to catch the calf, and one of us drag it through the bail and hold it there. See?"

Neither Old Fred nor Splinter could quite "see". And when they shook their heads in the negative, Titt's feeling of superiority increased.

"Well, listen—when the calf is lugged right through the bail", he went on, "the heifer'll follow."

"An' what about th' bloke who's luggin' it through?" Splinter, with the first law of Nature uppermost in his mind, interrupted with a faint grin. At the same moment, Old Fred's hand went swiftly inside his shirt to feel if the bandage protecting the wounds the heifer had, the previous day, made on his ribs with her horns, was still in position, and the agreeable look that had been in his eyes started to die out.

"That's what I'm coming to," Titt snapped at Splinter, "if you'll only keep from puttin' your spoke in when it ain't wanted for a minute or two."

Splinter cocked his head to one side, folded his arms and "kept his spoke" to himself.

"An' when she goes to go through the bail," Titt poked his long, first finger into the atmosphere as if it were the open bail, "one of us will be standing close handy, see?"

Old Fred and Splinter both saw.

"And soon as her head goes through, whoever it is, he's got to shove the bail shut on her neck—hard—and then we'll have her." And Titt grinned as if it were all over.

Neither Old Fred nor Splinter even smiled. They were thinking hard, the former unconsciously feeling the bandage round his ribs again.

"Blow it; can't y' see how it's done?" and Titt growled and became restless and impatient.

"I see it all right!" Old Fred answered slowly, "but as he sez"—pointing with his thumb which had a rag on it, to Splinter—"who's goin' to drag th' calf?"

"Oh, anyone, for that matter", and Titt tossed his head about and walked round in a little circle. Then in a prolonged persuasive tone: "But I suppose I'd be th' best myself to stand close handy to the bail and shove it on her, because it's the most important."

"An' I'll keep behind her and see she follers th' calf", Splinter, allotting himself a portfolio, got in quickly.

Old Fred scratched his head:

"At that rate," he concluded, "you want me to drag the calf?"

"Don't want y' to do it!" and Titt shook his head indifferently, "but someone's got to. . . I'm goin' to stand by th' bail, an' he's goin' to keep behind th' heifer. . . . so—I dunno", and he scratched the dust with the toe of his boot contemplatively, and waited for old Fred to reply.

Old Fred kept on thinking.

"It won't be th' worst job, anyway," Titt went on, "you'll have the leg-rope round its neck to pull it by. It's me who'll be in th' dangerous position, no doubt about that."

"And what about me, if she turns round?" And Splinter started jumping about like a dog let off the chain.

"Oh, all right!" Old Fred assented at last, "but hurry up an' let us get it over."

Then the three of them crept into the yard.

"Go steady now", Titt said, mooching stealthily after the calf with the leg-rope in his hand, but keeping a sharp discerning eye on the movements of its mother.

Several efforts to lassoo the calf failed. At last an opportunity presented itself to Splinter. He jumped in and seized it with both hands by the tail, and hanging on like grim death, shouted "I got him!" The calf bellowed and pig-rooted, and went up and down in waves like a short switch-back railway. Splinter, at the end of him, went up and down, too. The heifer turned and let a roar out of her. Splinter broke up the "railway" and flew up the rails like a wild cat. Titt and Old Fred took shelter behind the bail posts.

"She's got her monkey up, now," Titt grumbled, "why didn't y' let th' calf alone when y' couldn't hold it?"

"I could 'a' held him,' Splinter boasted, "but his tail started crackin up near th' roots, an' I thought it was goin' to come off."

"Your own was, y' mean!" Titt snarled, and put Old Fred in a good humour. And when Titt heard Old Fred chuckling, he started chuckling too.

Their joint mirth touched Splinter in a sensitive place. He never could stand being made the cause of others' merriment.

"Yous blokes are very funny, ain't y'?" he said, sulkily, descending the rails.

"Who are you callin' 'blokes'?" And his parent frowned across the yard at him.

"Well, who are yous laughin' at?" stubbornly from Splinter.

"That don't matter. Don't you call me a bloke again, young man. I'm your father, and don't you forget it", and the parent clenched his fists and wagged his head and humped his back determinedly.

"Who said I was forgettin' it?" grumbled Splinter.

"I won't stand you or no one else callin' me a 'bloke' ", and gathering up the rope, Titt turned his attention to the calf again.

"I alez had to say 'Sir' to my old man, or else get a clout on th' head!" came reminiscently from Old Fred.

"But you never had a proper old man, had y'?" Splinter grinned. Splinter had heard that Old Fred's was a step-father.

Just then, by the merest fluke, Titt roped the calf.

"Quick!" he shouted; "keep her away! I got him!"

Old Fred and Splinter ran to his assistance.

"Here, take it! Take it!" And Titt shoved the end of the rope into Old Fred's hand—"and pull—pull him right through th' bail, an' I'll be ready to shove it shut on her when she goes to go through after him."

Old Fred pulled hard and went backwards to the bail. The calf "burr-ur-ed!" and reared and plunged after him. Old Fred fell over a milking block and burst the bandage round his ribs. When he found his feet again, he saw the heifer coming like a whole herd of devils. He let the rope go and ran through the bail on his own account. The calf with the rope hanging to it, raced blindly after him; the heifer anxiously pursued the calf; Splinter, shouting and waving his hat, pursued the heifer.

Titt, who was ready waiting, slammed the bail when he judged the heifer's head was in it. But her shoulders and two front legs were in it, too, and the bail couldn't close! But Titt put all his strength into the job, and shoved and held her by the body. She plunged and bellowed and looked like tearing the bail out of the ground and demolishing the whole yard.

"Quick! Give me a hand!" Titt shouted.

Splinter and Old Fred gave him a hand.

Finding she couldn't get through, the heifer started to pull back, to retreat. That was what Titt wanted.

"Let her back a bit," he cried, "till she gets her neck in it, then shove—but look out! Watch her! Watch her!"

They then cautiously eased the pressure little by little till at last the heifer came back with a bound. They shoved. The bail closed with a mighty three-man power push, and as many grunts, and missed her neck by a few inches! also her head!

"Lost her! I'm damned!" Titt said, hanging round the empty bail like a drunken man.

17. How They Came To Baptise Her "Stumpy"

The unbroken heifer and her calf were standing in the yard again.

"If that beast isn't milked very soon," Mrs. Duff said, "her udder will go bad, and she'll be spoilt."

"We're going to milk her to-day," Titt replied resolutely, "if we have to shoot her dead to do it!"

"It wouldn't be right to shoot one like her, Boss", Old Fred, always humane, said.

"Well, of course, I only mean we'd do for her," Titt explained, "in case we had to resort to direct action—see, Old Fred?"

Then he procured the new hemp-rope and started fixing a loop to the end of it again.

"What, yer goin' to rope her again?" Splinter, with a broad smile, questioned.

"Goin' to rope her again, me boy," the father confirmed as confidently as if he had really roped her before, "an' more than that", he added.

"More? How? What y' mean?" wonderingly from Splinter.

"Well, I'm goin' to hook old Derby to her as well, and pull her into th' bail—pull her bloomin' head off if she won't go in. That's what I harnessed him up for."

"Oh, crime!" And Splinter danced about in joyous expectation of more excitement. Old Fred philosophically spun his hat round like a wheel on the first finger of his left hand and chuckled like a frog. Mrs. Duff smiled and said "she had often seen Grandfather Rudd pulling a cow into the bail with a horse".

"And he knew somethin' about breakin'-in, didn't he, Kit?" proudly from Titt.

"He'd break them with a rail or anythin' if they wouldn't go in", Old Fred remembered.

"An' he got into Parliament, on th' strength of it, didn't he, Mother?" Splinter laughed, "and broke it up, too?"

"Good enough for it!" Titt, working away at the loop with hands and teeth, cynically approved; "wants a few brainy old bucks like him in Parliament now."

"A kind old man, anyway," Mrs. Duff gratefully reflected, "even if he was a bit wild. And he made money."

"Which was th' main thing", Titt decided. "Make money in this world Old Fred, and then you can talk. My oath, can't y'! Money's the recommendation, the qualification, the dinkum passport to anythin' and everythin' on this bloomin' earth."

There were times when Titt became eloquent.

"I suppose so, Boss", Old Fred agreed, cheerfully.

"My Christmas, yes," Titt went on, "if y' ain't got money— you're no bloomin' good in this world—but if y' have (tugging hard at a knot with his teeth), if y' have, you're a little Almighty standin' out on your own with everyone. Money'll get y' into anywhere!"

"It won't get y' into Heaven, Titt?" Old Fred ventured.

"No, it won't," Titt admitted, "and thank God for that. It will keep y' out of Heaven, though; and that's where you and me, at th' resurrection, Old Fred, are goin' to get th' laugh on these toff blokes in their flash motor cars."

"But I'm goin' to have a motor car, some day," Splinter reckoned, "and chance the ducks."

"That's right, Splinter," Mrs. Duff smiled, "and you can drive Mother about."

"You think they'll be able to drive their cars to hell, Titt," Old Fred grinned, "but——"

"But not to Heaven", Titt, taking the words out of his mouth, laughed; "not to Heaven, Old Fred. Ha! Ha! Ha!"

"Goodness me," Mrs. Duff interrupted, "shut up preaching and get the heifer milked."

"A little worldly discussion now and then does coves good", and throwing the rope over his shoulder, Titt led the way into the yard.

Soon as the heifer saw their approach, her tranquillity became perturbed and she prepared for action.

"She doesn't look any too affectionate, does she?" Titt soliloquised, as he started to swing the noose.

"What about lettin' Mother have a go at ropin' her this time?" Splinter suggested earnestly.

"All right, if she likes", and Titt paused and dropped the rope in the dust. "It's all one to me who ropes her, so long as she gets roped."

"I don't know if I could now," and Mrs. Duff blushed to the tips of her ears, "though I could when I was a girl."

"Yes, y' can, Mother," Splinter urged, eagerly, "you can do it better than him, anyway."

"Here! Who are you callin' 'him' to?" And facing round quickly Titt scowled. "Can't y' think of anything else to call me by, eh?"

"I s'pose so", and Splinter looked down at his toes.

"Why didn't y' call me be it, then?"

"S'pose I never thought."

"Yer s'pose y' never thought! My Christmas, then, you better think about it next time!"

Splinter looked up slyly from behind the drooping leaf of his hat at Old Fred.

"You needn't be squintin' at Old Fred!" the parent stormed. "He ain't laughin' at y; an' y' ain't said anythin' funny to laugh at, anyway."

"Never said I did", sullenly from Splinter.

"Never said y' did!" and Titt, wrinkling his face and showing his teeth like a dog, was looking right under the leaf of Splinter's hat when Old Fred, who had moved away to pick up a stone which he tossed over the rails, called: "Look out!" in warning to Mrs. Duff. Titt and Splinter both thought the warning was meant for them, and connecting the heifer with it, suddenly separated and rushed for safety to the nearest panel of the yard and climbed up on it. When Titt looked down and saw the heifer still standing in the corner, and Old Fred hugging a post to restrain his mirth, and heard Mrs. Duff laughing outright, he felt aggrieved and humiliated.

"Blooming old ass!" he mumbled, scowling across at Old

Fred, "might be another case of th' boy and the wolf some day!"

But Splinter, with more presence of mind and a keener appreciation of humour, shrieked:

"Look out, Old Fred! Look out! She's got y'!"

Old Fred was taken quite off his guard. He left the post he was hugging in the centre of the yard—a post for the stock to scratch themselves against, and plunging headlong to escape one of the bails, struck his head against it, and knocked himself out.

Titt's mood instantly changed. Old Fred's fright and fall delighted him. He lay across the rails and laughed till he reckoned he had pains and stitches all over his body.

"You're all wasting time!" Mrs. Duff said. "Give me the rope! I'll catch her."

In an instant Splinter left the rails, and gathered the rope together for his Mother to try her hand.

"Now we'll see somethin' ", Titt, descending from his perch, grinned.

Old Fred, rubbing his head, sat up and stared.

Mrs. Duff, swinging the noose round her head, turned to the heifer.

Old Fred rose to his feet and gazed in admiration.

Splinter waited breathlessly.

The heifer, deciding to change her quarters, came out of the corner at a run.

Mrs. Duff let her pass, then flung the rope.

"Caught her! Caught her!" Splinter shouted, as the animal went plunging and snorting with the loop fairly round her horns.

"You ain't forgotten th' way, Kitty", Old Fred grinned.

Titt was too surprised to say anything.

"In th' first shot, too! By go!" from Splinter.

"Only a fluke", Mrs. Duff laughed, and ran out of the yard.

"My Christmas, eh!" Titt said at last, "that's th' sort of wife to have", and grabbing the end of the rope, hung on to the startled animal.

Then the fun commenced.

"I can hold her!" he cried, jerking and playing with the

brute as an angler would a fish on a line. "One of you bring another rope to tie to this one, and the other get the horse and back him close to the rails. Be quick!"

"Right-o, Boss, I'll fetch another rope", and Old Fred crept through the rails and hurried to the harness shed, while Splinter raced off to bring Derby along.

"That's right! That's right!" Titt said, talking to the struggling heifer, "go on, fight and bellow away. But I got y'! Y' can't get out this time!"

Then Old Fred returned with another rope, and Splinter with Derby, whom he dragged along by the winkers.

Titt fastened the two ropes together, passed the end through the open bail, then through the rails to Splinter, who tied it securely to the swingle-tree behind Derby, and grinned expectantly.

"Now then," Titt commanded when all was ready, "you lead old Derby straight out of the yard, Splinter, as if you were goin' down the paddock somewhere; and Old Fred an' me'll get behind the heifer and keep her straight for the bail when the rope tightens, and Derby starts to pull. But when I sing out, 'Stop!' mind y' stop him sudden, or he might pull her head right off."

"Orright," Splinter returned, "I'll stop him." And away he went, leading Derby after him.

Titt and Old Fred "shooed" the heifer out of the corner. She bucked across the yard, then tried to force her head between the rails. The rope began to tighten. Old Derby felt the strain and began to pull. He pulled the heifer's head from between the rails and round to where her tail was. She now faced the bail. Splinter shouted, "Get up!" and Derby pulled harder. The heifer shook her head and roared, then planted her two front feet firmly in the dust and hung back. Derby grunted and tore up the ground with his toes. Splinter urged him louder to "Get up!" and kicked him in the hairy ribs with his bare toe. Derby hung in the collar and swayed from side to side. Titt and Old Fred, one on each side, waved their hats, and kicked dust at the jibbing heifer, and shouted, and made a great noise. But she wouldn't budge, and it looked as if Derby was really going to pull her head off and get away with it.

"Get up, Derby; get up!" Splinter kept shouting and between him outside, and the other two inside, you'd think a couple of bullock teams were stuck in a creek, and the drivers had "double banked" and were urging the bullocks to shift the creek!

"Why don't you screw her tail?" Mrs. Duff, returning to the scene, called out advisedly.

"Screw her tail?" and Titt, scratching his head looked puzzled. He'd never before heard of such a device for making a cow go.

"Yes, catch hold of it and give it a little twist near the butt", Mrs. Duff repeated.

"Yes," Titt grinned, "and get me bloomin' head butted off with her foot?"

The same probability seemed to present itself to Old Fred, and he shook his head and smiled dubiously.

"Well, you are a pair of cattle men!" and entering the yard again, Mrs. Duff took hold of the heifer's tail and gave it a twist. With a roar the brute instantly bounded forward, and Derby fell flop on his head, and in a desperate struggle to recover himself, tramped on the reins which Splinter had abandoned, and tore the whinkers right off his head. Gosh! Things that weren't on the programme then happened rapidly! When Derby saw himself in harness, a privilege he had never enjoyed before, he took fright and tried to bolt. But he couldn't get any forrader, because the heifer had her two fore feet stuck in front of her, and was hanging in the "breechen" again. So he snorted like a brumby and kicked up behind and came down with his legs outside the chains and swung to the right, and back to the left; then turned right round, and kept going round and round till all his legs were wound up in the rope; then utterly discouraged, he threw himself down in a heap and put out his tongue, showing his long brown teeth, and blew a crater in the dust with hot blasts from his red nostrils, and turned up the whites of his eyes, and groaned as though he were dying. Meantime, the heifer had wound herself around the "scratching post", and Titt, to save her neck, was throwing his hand about and bawling. "Stop! Stop! Dammit stop!"

Then howls of alarm and despair came from Splinter.

"Oh, look at th' horse! Look at th' horse!" Mrs. Duff shrieked.

Titt and Old Fred turned from the bellowing heifer and, bending down, looked between the rails at the horse.

"Oh, my hell!" Titt choked. But what to do to afford quick relief, neither he nor Old Fred had a baby's idea.

"Cut the rope! Cut the rope!" Mrs. Duff shrieked.

"Yes—cut th' rope," Titt, hardly knowing what he said, repeated in a thick, hoarse voice; "where's a —— a —— knife?" And he felt himself over twice. And Old Fred felt himself all over three or four times.

"Oh, what men you are!" And Mrs. Duff disappeared and, returning with the axe, chopped the rope in two against the rail of the yard.

"There!" And she heaved a sigh of relief.

Then old Derby struggled to his feet, and after surveying himself and his surroundings with a most indignant stare, snorted again and careered down the paddock with the swingle-tree flying in the air and at intervals hitting him on the head. The heifer, freeing herself from the post, rushed here, there, and everywhere, finally and passively coming to a standstill in the place where they had all been trying to force her.

"Struth, she's in the bail! She's in it!" Titt, with wide open eyes and mouth, cried.

"Where?" and Splinter, taking his eyes off Derby, rushed to the rails, and hung through them and gaped.

"She is, Boss", Old Fred confirmed, cheerfully.

"But if you go near her to close it," Mrs. Duff put in, "she'll run out again."

"Wonder if one of us could sneak up and shove it shut on her?" in a low, anxious voice from Titt.

Splinter giggled. His father turned and scowled at him.

"Might get something to shove it shut with", Old Fred thoughtfully suggested.

"A clothes prop!" And away Splinter scampered, returning with the longest prop available.

"My Christmas, the very thing!" Titt said, reaching for it

eagerly. Then stealthily advancing a pace or two nearer, poked it against the bail, and while Splinter held his breath and stood on one leg, and Old Fred contemplatively stroked his hairless lip with finger and thumb, and Mrs. Duff struggled to restrain her mirth, he suddenly shoved it.

"Got her! Got her!" Splinter shouted.

"Christmas, but I have!" and discarding the prop, Titt ran to the struggling captive and proudly and bravely placed both hands on her back and said she was his now, and inquired how she felt about it.

Old Fred leaned against the "scratching post" and shook with noiseless mirth.

Mrs. Duff said, "Well! Well! Well!" and went back to the house, smiling to herself.

"But you wouldn't have got her bailed if I hadn't fetched the clothes prop?" Splinter claimed.

"If you hadn't fetched th' clothes prop!" Titt jeered. "You did a lot, didn't y'?"

Then, taking the leg-rope he succeeded, after a lot of tumbling and nervous starts, in putting it on the heifer and tying her leg back.

Old Fred brought a bucket, and when the heifer heard it rattle, she bellowed and kicked all the hair off her leg against the rail.

Titt laughed, and punched her triumphantly in the girth, and she roared harder, and kicked more.

"I'll milk her", Splinter suggested.

"And make a mess of her," Titt chuckled, taking the bucket himself, "same as y' did old Derby. Don't y' think so, Old Fred?"

Old Fred smiled benevolently on the two of them. Old Fred never liked taking sides.

Titt discarded the milking block, and, standing with humped back, ready to jump away any moment, started milking. To Titt, milking a cow was a game of hazard; but he never regarded the animal as a partner.

"Is she tough or easy?" Splinter enquired.

"Easy as a beer pump", Titt answered, and for a while all went merry as a marriage bell.

Then the heifer started flogging him in the face with her tail, which was heavily loaded with mud and burr-seed.

"Darn y'!" Titt shouted and jumped away to take some dirt out of his eye.

Old Fred looked away and grinned.

"Here," Splinter said, taking possession of the tail, "do what O'Connor used to do", and he tied the offending append-age to the side-rail of the bail, and laughed when the beast made futile efforts to release it.

"That's the idea", Titt said, and returning, completed the milking in comfort.

"She'll be a great little milker when she's in for awhile", he enthused, showing Old Fred what was in the bucket, but ignoring all that was spilled on the ground.

Old Fred supposed she would be.

Then Titt patted her on the back, and talked in a friendly way to her.

"Let me take th' leg-rope off her!" Splinter said, eagerly.

Titt let him, and stood by her head while it was being taken off.

"Now, stand away yous two, and I'll let her out."

Old Fred and Splinter stood away. Titt cautiously opened the bail and jumped away himself. Out the heifer flew, and swung round with a snort. Then she started bucking and bellowing, but couldn't get away any further. She was tied to the rail by her tail.

"Oh, my hell!" Titt groaned and turned savagely upon Splinter.

"I forgot it was tied", Splinter squeaked and fled.

"Get her into the bail again, Titt, get her into the bail", Old Fred suggested.

They ran to her head and tried to "hoosh" her back into the bail. But all the maddened animal would do was roar and plunge, and scratch-pull, and kick up behind. Suddenly she got free, and careered round the yard wagging her tail and spattering blood on the rails, and looking quite a different animal altogether.

"Struth!" Titt gasped, "she's left half it behind!"

And that was how they came to baptise her "Stumpy."

18. School Commences

The oldest inhabitants of the Creek were few and far between. From time to time, as old years rolled out, and new ones drifted in, they would foregather and talk of their isolation, bewail the circumstances that compelled the up-bringing of the children in the wilderness, and resolve for the fiftieth time and more to ask the Government for a school, any sort of an old school, to send them to. And to their petition, the Department, for the fiftieth time and more, would answer in the same well-known weatherworn way: "When it is shown that there are sufficient children in the district of school age, as required by the Act, steps will be taken to comply with your request", or words to that effect. But the inhabitants of the Creek, like the inhabitants of any other place, or of the whole universe, for that matter, shifted and changed, and came and went, and at no time could they guarantee the essential number of kiddies. And, as far as Bendy Sawpitt could see, "they never would be able to without they manerfacted a foo of 'em of out of th' black mud".

"And then th' —— department," Billy Cattfish was of opinion, "would turn them down because they weren't white."

When, however, another old station run, which took in the best lands on the Creek, was cut up and sold in small areas, and the new settlers began to arrive, the position altered. The number of scholars was soon over-subscribed, and a brand-new school, spacious enough to accommodate over half a hundred, made of weather boards and boasting of a front verandah, and a wire fence all round, was erected. It stood off the main stock-route where the road to the Range branched away, and faced Dundonald's cultivation paddock.

Memories of the opening day of Emu Creek School have survived the emus themselves, and the brown kangaroos, so numerous that they seemed to set the whole wild bush in motion whenever they were on the move. It was a real St.

Crispian's Day—a wonderful gathering of the inhabitants, old and young, big and little, took place.

They greeted and congratulated each other noisily and merrily; ate and drank and danced, and talked about "learnin' ". The oldest inhabitants were overjoyed. "The youngsters that are still on our hands will now have a chance to get on," they said, "an' rise to somethin' better'n sloggin' all their lives on selections like their old fathers an' mothers, or workin' on wages for th' squatters, to make rich men of them."

Even those who had missed their chance and had entered manhood and womanhood weren't to be left out of the programme altogether. "They can go, too, sometimes," the old folk reckoned, "when there won't be much doin' at home, and make up for some of th' time they lost." And Dundonald, a vigorous sturdy Scot, who knew how to take his courage in both hands, told them to "look at Abraham Lincoln. When only a gossoon like a lot o' these young farllows here, he educated himself in the weeldernaiss of America and rose to be the graitest President the world ever knew; and why in th' naime o' conshuns, let me tail you, can na' a lot o' thee yokels do the same?"

"Anyway they can pick up somethin'," Bendy Sawpitt was convinced, "an' it will be a lot better to them than nothin'. I wish I only had the same chance at their age!" and he shook his old grey head sadly.

"I bet ye do, Bendy!" Dundonald said, shaking his head, too, "but ye've seen too mainy winters. Puttin' you into a school would be as rideeculous as shutting an old parrot in a cage and trying to teach it to wheestle 'Th' Red Flag.' "

"Well, I'm quite sure that that Susannah of ours," Mrs. Drygrass, with motherly pride, enthused, "would learn as quick as anyone, an' quicker, I believe, if she could only just be given th' chancet, as th' sayin' is."

"Dat's quite right, too", Mrs. Shuttlewood, nodding her head, as if it was on a hinge, and jumping her last baby—her very last baby—up and down in her arms, endorsed, smilingly. "Susannah only wants to get a chancet."

"Is that the one ye call Susie?" Dundonald inquired.

Mrs. Drygrass nodded, and said, "That's her ladyship, Mr. Dundonald."

"Oh, God blaiss me," he roared, "I've known her saince she was in napkins (shrieks and screams from a score of female voices), and, by gosh! I've naiver seen a man who could use a butcher's knife better than her."

"Nor anyone who could pick up things she hears like her, either", Mrs. Drygrass rattled on, proudly. "Did you, Mrs. Shuttlewood?"

But Mrs. Shuttlewood had a lot of daughters of her own, and deemed it wise to be cautious.

"N-n-no, dat's true," she stammered, "but we've got one in our family, too—Clara—who is awful quick at things."

"Oh, yes," Mrs. Drygrass conceded, grudgingly, "Clara isn't too bad when she likes—but that Susannah of ours!" turning to Dundonald, "can git hold of anything she hears jist like a tame magpie."

"But bless my soul!" Dundonald broke again, "what in the naime of gudeness do ye want tae worry about thaim for? Get thaim gude husbands, that's a' they want. Th' country wants populating. An' who's goin' tae do it? You an' th' like o' mysailf and Bendy Sawpitt can na' keep on multiplying and replainishing for ever!"

Another chorus of feminine shrieks and squeals; and laughing hoarsely and roughishly himself, Dundonald left them, and went off and started swinging the youngsters.

Later, when Splinter was told he would have to attend school, too, for a year or so, to be "topped off", he rebelled, and blubbered, and reckoned "he knew enough and wasn't goin' back any more".

"But I say you've got to, me noble!" the father put in, "and, my Christmas, if there's any nonsense about it, an' you ain't ready to go with your sister on Monday morning—look out for your skin, that's all!"

But when Splinter heard that Tom Dyer and Joe Shuttlewood, and Andy Drygrass and some more, all of whom were approaching the twenties, and starting to grow whiskers, were enrolled as scholars, he changed his mind and became cheerful and agreeable.

"What, them big blokes?" he questioned, with a grin.

"Well, unlike you, Splinter," his Mother explained, "the poor chaps never had a chance to go to school before."

"And will they have to start in the A B C?"

"I suppose so", Mrs. Duff smiled.

Splinter sat back and laughed hugely.

Just then Tom Dyer, who came to borrow a rope for his father, looked in.

"Hello, Tom," Mrs. Duff greeted, "we hear you are going to start school on Monday?"

"Yairs, I b'lieve so", Tom, dragging proudly at a little tuft of hair starting out of his chin, drawled. "Might as well go for a while an' see what sort of a game it is."

"You'll get on all right, Tom", encouragingly from Mrs. Duff. "Better late than never; and the master they have sent is a good teacher and a very nice man, I believe."

"Don't mind how nice he is, so long as he don't go for me with his waddy, like th' schoolmaster who father went to in the ol 'country, used to do", and Tom started filling his pipe.

"No fear of that", Mrs. Duff assured him.

"There'll be skin an' hair flyin' if he do", and Tom blew a great cloud, and aimed a kick at his dog for showing its teeth to Duff's Bluey.

Splinter was immediately transported to regions of endless delight. He saw in Tom a hero who would wipe his feet on the teacher and turn the school upside down. A revolutionary step that should have been taken years before, he thought. Nothing now, only gaol or small-pox, or the Federal police could keep him at home. His heart was all in the school. Visions of those big fellows defying the master and punching him, opened up a vista of undreamt-of excitement to Splinter, and made him restless as a cat on hot bricks. He worked himself into a pitch of high ecstatic fervour and thought Monday would never come.

But when Saturday and Sunday dragged slowly by, it came, and away went Splinter, leaving Araluen to make her own way to the seat of learning. And what a sight it was when those scholars, ranging from infants up to men and women, some in shirt sleeves, some in long dresses, entered the playground. First they peered all round the building, then commenced playing "Drop the Handkerchief", the only game the girls knew.

For a while the teacher, a kindly, prematurely bald pedagogue, stood on the verandah pulling at his moustache, and regarding them as though their presence involved him in a tremendous responsibility. Once or twice he paced the verandah, and pausing, stood gazing at them again. But when he saw big Susannah Drygrass drop the handkerchief on Joe Shuttlewood, who stood six feet in his stockings, and run away from him like a greyhound, and Joe run full split after her, and catch her, and struggle with her, and kiss her loud and square on the neck, he frowned and snapped his fingers, then, hurrying inside, put on his helmet (he always wore a murky-looking helmet), and rushed out and called them all to the front of the school. In twos and threes they assembled there, the big ones laughing and talking, the infants trembling and staring with fear, and nervous anticipation.

"Good morning", he said, forcing a smile of welcome, and nodding familiarly to those whom he remembered having seen on "opening day".

"Mornin', Master", several thin little voices squeaked timidly in response, while from several gruff thoats came, "Good day".

Joe Shuttlewood, standing between Andy Drygrass and Splinter, wondered in an undertone, "what time he got up; it's a pretty late sort o' mornin' ".

"Tell him it, Joe," Splinter urged, "sing it out loud, go on." Splinter was a thoughtful, unselfish sort of adviser.

Joe pulled his bottom eye-lid down with his thick middle finger, and asked Splinter if "he saw any green in it?"

Splinter looked into it and said he didn't—and Joe Shuttlewood and Andy Drygrass exchanged winks.

"I want you all to form two lines, according to your respective sizes, and face this way", the teacher said, taking up a position a few paces from the verandah. "Do you understand?"

Some understood; others didn't.

"Come on, you blokes with th' new coats on," Tom Dyer supplemented, "an' form into two bloomin' clothes-lines."

Splinter, bursting with joy, planted himself next to Tom, and squaring his shoulders and craning his neck, tried to look as tall as he.

Then there was much shifting and changing and talking and shoving.

"Here, you Joe Shuttlewood," Susannah Drygrass protested digging him in the ribs with her elbow, "don't you put yourself alongside o' me—I don't want y'!"

"Please, sir, she punched me ribs", Joe bawled, pulling an ugly face and pretending to shed tears.

His complaint was greeted with great laughter, Splinter laughing louder and longer than any of the rest.

"Serves y' glad, Joe," Andy Drygrass, taking his sister's part, drawled, "you shouldn't have kissed her on the neck, when she was expectin' it in th' mouth."

Another burst of merriment; and when it was over, Susannah, addressing the teacher, said: "Don't you believe that long-legged brother of mine, mister—he's a bigger liar than Tom Pepper."

The teacher, preserving a stern, inflexible countenance, returned Susannah a malevolent stare. Then lifting his voice, asked for silence, and said he had a few words to say to them before they went into school to commence work.

Here Splinter slyly pinched Tom Dyer on the back of the leg.

"Oh!" Tom yelled, in devilment, and jumped as high as the verandah, "somethin' bit me!"

The tears of mirth that came from the lines made Splinter's bosom heave with pride—made him feel a hero.

Then the teacher proceeded, and addressing the boys with hair on their faces, and the girls in long dresses, told them he could, if he wished, refuse to admit them to the school. But as a favour to their parents, for whom he had the greatest respect and admiration as brave pioneers of the country, and out of sympathy for themselves, he would admit them the same as the rest of the children, and do all he could to help them and bring them along. All he would ask in return was strict attention to their lessons, good behaviour and obedience.

"Oh, rather!" Tom Dyer interjected, in agreement, and Joe Shuttlewood added:

"All the time, governor! My oath!"

"One other matter he wished to impress upon them, and not the least in importance, was a rule that was strictly enforced at all schools he had ever been connected with: the boys and girls must not mix up or play together in play hours—the girls must use the eastern half of the ground; and the boys confine themselves to the western side."

This was received with an exchange of doubtful grins and smiles.

"Now—attention!"

Splinter, and those who had been to other schools, straightened up, put out their chests, and looked as if they had been in the army. The others remained standing easy and wondered what was coming next.

"Mark time!" and the teacher, holding up his chin and dropping his hands by his side, suited the action to the word.

Splinter bending his knees nearly to his chin, pounded the earth hard with the flat of his feet, and seemed to have it all his own way.

"Look at this bloke!" Tom Dyer, directing attention to Splinter, laughed; "he knows it."

"Altogether! Everyone! Everyone!" the teacher, vigorously marking-time himself, urged.

"Oh, I'm with you", and Tom Dyer, striking a higher knee-action than Splinter, began battering the ground like a draught horse. Then Andy Drygrass and Joe Shuttleworth entered into competition, then Susannah Drygrass and Judith Hammanegg, squealing as their skirts tangled above their knees, got going; then all of them became infected and entered into the exercise with great vigor and enjoyment.

"Right turn!" The teacher himself turned, but no one in the lines, except the few experienced ones, budged.

"Right turn!" and he motioned them with his hands and head, still spiritedly marking time himself.

In twos and threes they turned.

"This is somethin' new, Joe", Tom Dyer called to Shuttle wood.

"Like horses treadin' in th' thrasher", Joe called back.

"Quick march!" and the teacher marched.

Splinter kicked Tom Dyer hard on the heels and shoved him forward. Tom kicked Joe Shuttlewood and shoved him. Joe, who was one of the leading file, kicked violently at the atmosphere, and his boot flew off and caused delay to the column.

"Left turn!—and into school!" and the teacher led the way up the steps which were unprotected by side-rails. Nearing the top, Tom Dyer, at Splinter's whispered suggestion, seized Andy Drygrass's hat and heaved it over the heads of those crowding behind. Andy shoved Tom right off the steps on to the ground, and said: "Stay down there, you long cow, and get a thousand cuts for comin' in last."

Splinter and the others rejoiced.

"Hang all hats and lunch-bags on the pegs—girls on the right, boys on the left. Then all into school."

Much scuffling, scrimmaging and disorder at each end of the verandah followed this command. One would think there was only one peg at the boys' end, and all of them were claiming it! But when Tom Dyer mounted the steps again, the commotion had subsided; all had entered the school-room, and every peg in the rack was occupied by a hat and a bag—some held two hats. Tom removed the first two head-pieces his eyes rested on, tossed them over the verandah, and hung his old felt and his bag in their places. Then one by one he examined a number of lunch-bags till he came to what he took for Andy Drygrass's. Emptying it, he gulped down as much of Andy's lunch as was possible in the time, stuffed the rest into his pocket, returned the bag to the peg, and blundered into school with a cheerful grin on his face.

Splinter, who had been watching for Tom's entrance, caught his eye and slyly indicated a vacant place between himself and Andy Drygrass. Tom winked and strode straight into it.

"Wot kep' y'?" Splinter whispered.

"Havin' a snack", Tom said, and producing the remains of

the commandeered lunch, shoved it under Drygrass's nose, and invited him to have some.

Andy grinned and had some.

Tom offered the rest to Splinter; but Splinter was too overjoyed to eat, and wouldn't take the risk, anyway.

"It's a floggin', y' know," he warned Tom, "if you're caught eatin' in school."

"Is it?" Tom grunted, "if he tries it on me I'll break him agen th' wall."

"Would you go for him?" in a joyful whisper from Splinter.

"Would I not?" and Tom stuffed his mouth with sandwich.

Splinter rubbed his hands and gazed towards the teacher. Splinter longed to see him flog Tom. If he could, without Tom knowing it, he would even turn informer, so enthusiastic did he feel in the matter.

Tom diverted him with a dig in the ribs.

"Do y' know whose tucker that was I give Andy a bit of?"

Splinter's eyes nearly dropped out of his head.

"His own! I went through his bag before comin' in."

Splinter hung his head and tittered and giggled beneath the desk.

"He'll have to go hungry at dinner time!" he said, looking up.

"So he can! He won't get mine. . . Look at him", Tom grinned.

Splinter turned and saw Andy with mouth open trying to catch what the teacher was explaining to a class of infants—and let out an involuntary yell that made the teacher turn quickly and stare.

"He's got his eye on you blokes!" Andy Drygrass, turning to them, grunted.

Splinter's heart missed a couple of beats. He pulled an innocent face, sat up straight, and gazing along his nose, looked the embodiment of good behaviour.

A little later the teacher commanded "Silence!" and explaining that he was now going to call the roll, told them how to answer.

Everyone shouted "Present." or "Here, Sir", except "Squirrel" Sawpitt, and "Skebo" Woods, and "Snapper"

Smith, and "Dwodley" Dyer and "Blue-tongue" Black, and "Blowfly" Brown. When he questioned them and asked why didn't they answer, and if their names were not Archibald and Matthew and Arnold Jacob, and Josephus and Edward Samuel, and John Thomas, they hung their head and sniggered.

"Them's their Sunday names you got hold of, Boss," Joe Shuttlewood explained, "they had nothin' but week days on th' Creek afore you come, and they've forgotten 'em."

"Silence Shuttlewood!" the teacher rebuked; "you're in school, remember!"

"Oh, all right," Joe drawled, "if you won't let a bloke speak!"

"Silence!" and the teacher faced him firmly.

"Crimes!" Splinter whispered, "now there'll be a fight!"

Then Joe glanced side-ways at Andy Drygrass, and grinned, and the storm passed.

The rest of the morning the teacher devoted to organising the classes, serving out material and giving instructions for general guidance.

When one o'clock came, all were let out for lunch. Then Blowfly Brown and Squirrel Sawpitt found their hats were missing and began to weep. Everyone except Tom Dyer suspected some passing swagman of having stolen them.

"And they've stolen my dinner!" Splinter gasped, turning pale and holding open his empty bag.

"Yours?" and Tom Dyer stared in surprise.

"It's gone!" and the tears started swimming into Splinter's eyes.

"And what about yours, Andy?" Tom, puzzled looking, asked of Drygrass.

"Mine?" Andy said, unpacking a setting of boiled eggs, and starting to shell one; "if there ain't no chickens about, it's orlright."

"Isn't yours gone?" Splinter asked, in surprise, of Andy.

"It will be directly," and Andy put the shelled egg into his mouth, and chanced a chicken.

Splinter, with an injured look on his face, turned to Tom Dyer.

"It's all right, old chap," Tom said, patting him on the back, "I've enough here for the two of us." And opening his bag, he shared a cargo of buttered scones and corned round, and a bottle of homemade jam with Splinter.

That evening when four o'clock came, and the first day was over, and the yougsters tramped merrily home along the bush-tracks, the cheery faces of mothers watching at the door, the lowing of the cattle, the whistling and calling of the birds, the gentle noise of the wind in the trees, and the sunshine on the plains seemed to be all in unison with each other.

19. Some Nature Study

The school had been opened six months. It was making headway. Shyness and dread of the master were wearing off the infants, and giving place to confidence and fidelity. The hair on the faces of the bigger boys was spreading and taking distinctive colour; the dresses of the bigger girls getting longer, and between the lot of them they succeeded in making the school a real live institution that kept the teach busy. He was never out of employment. But Roger Garfield Wimblepip was a teacher! a learned indefatigable, dignified pedagogue. He was no round post in a square hole. No newspaper reporters or society wife or parliamentary, or lodge, or church influence made his reputation. His own hard-worked brains made it. He was a student of Nature, and studied the characters of his pupils, and got to know them as he did the A B C before beginning to teach them anything. "A teacher", he used to tell Titt, "might pass all the examinations in the world, and get loaded up with honours, yet not be able to teach worth tuppence. Unless he has been taught to teach or happens to be a born teacher, he's a professional counterfeit, a fly in the departmental ointment, a hired destroyer of the nation's greatest asset."

That was why he wavered on the matter of including "Nature Study" in the bill of fare for the Emu Creek School, and couldn't arrive at a definite conclusion. One day he chose fifteen of the most stalwart and intelligent boys to accompany him along the creek and through the intervening forest country to the top of Mt. Sibley, on a nature study stunt. Great crawling jew lizards! No stunt could have suited or delighted them more. A day out of school together was "into their hands". They grabbed their hats, poked faces at those who had not been selected, and away they went down the road, the teacher stepping it out in the centre of them like Bonaparte amidst his bodyguard.

Instead of spreading out to collect wild flowers and yams and blackfellows' fruit, and lizards and spiders and snakes, and all kinds of creeping things, and bring them to the teacher for scientific investigation and explanation, the boys promptly disappeared into water-holes and among grass trees and up the limbs of gums and coolibahs, and left the master waiting.

He waited and studied his watch till his patience gave out.

"God bless my heart and soul!" he mused anxiously; "what's become of them all?"

Then making a funnel of his two hands, he coo-eed, a high-pitched, mournful coo-ee, with a long melancholy tail to it, and placing his ear to the wind, listened.

No response came—not a sound could he hear save the creak-creaking of chafing limbs and the flapping of moving bark, dangling in strips from the forest trees.

Again and yet again he coo-eed; but no more than if those louts had all been swallowed up by the earth, was any indication of their whereabouts borne back to him on the breeze. Yet, while his throat was getting sore and hoarse and the perspiration breaking out in beads upon his brow, Tom Dyer and Joe Shuttlewood and Splinter, in the hidden bend of a steep gully, were splashing and wallowing in a murky water-hole not more than a hundred yards away. A little lower down, Andy, Drygrass and Bill Billygum and Ned Rudd were secreted in the foliage of a spreading coolibah, chewing grass-tree gum; the rest of the "nature students" were a mile and more away, giving mad chase to anything and everything that had the temerity to start from its hiding place and run, or fly, or creep, or crawl! They were death on Nature Study, were those bush scholars, with no more care or thought for the teacher than they had for the man in the moon.

"Listen to old Roger coo-eein' for us", Tom Dyer, shaping a mud-ball to paste Joe Shuttlewood with, grinned.

"If he comes this way," Joe answered perching himself on a miniature island adorning the centre of the water-hole, "he'll see some Nature Study."

All three laughed joyously.

Then Splinter scrambled up the bank and peeped cautiously over the edge to see what the teacher was "up to".

"There ain't a single jolly bloke left with him," he announced, clinging tight to the long grass on the parapet, "everyone of 'em's cleared."

Joe Shuttlewood grinned and pointed meaningly to the back view of Splinter.

"Has they?" and Tom Dyer stood up and flung the mud-ball he had prepared for Shuttlewood, at Splinter. It went straight and swift, and with a loud smack, fastened itself on to his bare skin like a parasite in clay.

"Oh!" he yelled, and losing grip of the grass, rolled down the bank into the water.

The others dropped down in helpless heaps and gave themselves up to mirth.

Splinter gathered himself together, and crawling out of the hole, began dressing silently and sulkily.

"Glod bless my heart and soul!" the teacher burst out again. "Well! Well! Well!" then went off to search for the absent students. He walked briskly for a couple of hundred yards, and entered a clump of grass-trees where he came upon foot prints and moist spots of expectorated chew-gum. Then he coo-eed hopefully and listened some more. Andy Drygrass and Bill Billygum and Ned Rudd, perched in the coolibah trees, were only fifty yards distant.

"Look out!" Andy warned his companions; "get up higher! Old Roger's comin' through th' grass-trees. I can see his helmet."

The others climbed higher, and squatting among the branches like scrub turkeys, listened and watched every movement below.

Emerging from the grass-trees, the teacher paused beneath the coolibah, and peered all round, but never once dreamed of looking up.

A word, a giggle, or the sound of a breaking twig among the branches, and those absconders would have been undone. But Fate befriended them. With their hats shoved half-way down their throats, they sat tight and motionless.

Once again the teacher woke the silence and solitude with a forlorn coo-ee. Those yahoos in the tree never, in their lives, before, experienced such a strange and trying sensation. None dare lift his head to look into the face of the other.

"God bless my heart and soul!" they heard him moan; "whatever has become of them! What ever shall I do?"

Starting off again, he crossed an old sheep-yard that had long been in disuse, and headed for a belt of thick forest timber.

"Oh, my side!" Andy Drygrass broke out, "if he hadn't gone the instant he did I'd have had to let go and fall right on him." His companions choked and gurgled, and said they "would have had to, too".

Then they laughed together like jackasses, and "reckoned it was th' best fun ever they had in their lives".

In vain the teacher kept up the search, and amidst red and crimson streaks along the sky, the sun started to go down. Then giving up hope, he began retracing his steps, and instead of returning to the school, got lost! became hopelessly, irre-trievably bushed!

Meanwhile, Mrs. Wimblepip, who was left in charge, when four o'clock came, let the scholars out. All of them, closely followed in dribs and drabs by the fifteen absconders, soon reached their respective homes.

Night, dark and cheerless, came on, but no Mr. Wimblepip.

At 8 o'clock, Mrs. Wimblepip, hatless, breathless, pale and almost overcome with alarm, hastened to Duff's place and asked if Splinter was home.

"Oh, long ago, Mrs. Wimblepip", and Titt and Mrs. Duff stared in surprise.

"Long ago?" Mrs. Wimblepip echoed. "Oh, dear! dear!" and dropping into a chair, fainted, and looked as if her end had come.

The Duffs grew frantic. They shook her, pleaded with her to speak, and broke into lamentations. Not until they gave her water to drink and poured some down her back did Mrs. Wimblepip revive again, and state her trouble.

Splinter, listening through the kitchen door, took time by the forelock, and in fear and trembling, prepared his defence. For the first time in his life he seriously exploited the regions of thought.

His father called him, and in he slunk, his hands twitching, his lip quivering, a tragic stare in his eye.

"Here," Titt questioned, "was you one 'o them who went out with Mr. Wimblepip to-day?"

Splinter was.

"Where did yous go?"

Splinter told him (in part).

"How was it Mr. Wimblepip didn't come home with you?"

Splinter didn't know.

"Where did he go? Did he stop behind or go somewhere be himself, or what? You ought to know, and mind you tell th' truth, or by cripes, I'll kill y'!"

"Me and Tom Dyer and Joe Shuttlewood", Splinter stammered, "left him with all th' others, an'— an'——"

"Well? Yes? An' what?"

Splinter lost the thread of his defence, and was ransacking his paralysed brain to find it.

"Can't y' remember?"

"Oh, you must know, Splinter?" anxiously and kindly from his mother.

"Yairs!" Splinter spluttered.

"Well, tell Mrs. Wimblepip!" Titt yelled, "an' don't be standin' there lookin' like a jolly goat!"

"An' we went to get a yaller flower", Splinter remembered. "A yaller flower"—and he faltered again.

"You told us that before! By Christmas, young man, look out for yourself if you're tellin' any lie! Do you know what all this means, do y', eh?" Looking into Splinter's face; "it might mean—murder!"

Mrs. Wimblepip screamed; Splinter bellowed.

"Don't frighten th' boy, Titt!" Mrs. Duff protested. "Let him tell what he knows about it in his own way!"

"How can he tell anythin' in any way, when he's bellerin' the way he is!"

"Yes, of course," Mrs. Duff agreed; "but he's nervous about it, when I'm sure he has no reason to be!"

Then softly and encouragingly to Splinter:

"You were going to tell us about the yellow flower, son? Yes? Don't be afraid; no one will hurt you."

"One growin' out of a rock that Tom knew about," Splinter blubbered, "an'—an' we was to bring it back to—(sob)—to—him——"

"To who?" Titt interrupted.

"To (sob) old Roger."

"What? Who? By cripes, me noble, I——"

"To the teacher", and Splinter blubbered harder by way of apology.

"And did you bring it to him?" from Mrs. Duff; "now don't cry about it."

"N—No; he was gone when we came back, an'—an' we couldn't find him."

"They have done something terrible to my husband—I know they have!" Mrs. Wimblepip wept, "my intuition tells me there has been foul play! Oh, why did he ever come to such a school! —such an ill-bred, barbarous school!"

"Don't go on like that, Mrs. Wimblepip," Mrs. Duff said, "Mr. Wimblepip will turn up all right, never you fear. It won't surprise me if he is at home when you go back—not in the least", and she sat down and put her arms around her.

"And did y' look for him?" Titt asked further of Splinter.

"We waited for them all to come back, and when they didn't come, Tom Dyer said they must have have gone home, and then we come home."

"I see", Titt reflected wisely.

"Oh, Splinter is not to blame," Mrs. Duff asserted, positively, "he and Tom Dyer and Joe Shuttlewood merely did what Mr. Wimblepip told them to do, isn't that so, son?"

"Y—yes, that's it", Splinter lied.

"I didn't see it that way at first," Titt said, apologetically; "but I understand now."

"I never saw it any other way," from Mrs. Duff, "and I knew my boy wouldn't tell a lie."

"At that rate," Titt summed up, "Mr. Wimblepip must have went home with some o' them others. Perhaps one of 'em took sick or got sunstruck, and he carried him home——?"

It was a brilliant and timely suggestion. It came just when Mrs. Wimblepip was working up for another fantod.

"That's just what really happened!" Mrs. Duff exclaimed,

"just what Mr. Wimblepip would do; he's so thoughtful and kind. He has taken one of them home—young Hamlet, perhaps—he often takes fits, you know."

"My Christmas, you've struck it, Kit!" Titt laughed, and clapped himself on the thigh, "Hamlet took a fit. He took one here one morning, y' remember, and nearly fell in the fire."

Then they both laughed; and their mirth inspired Mrs. Wimblepip with confidence, and dispelled all her anxiety.

"I don't know what you must think of me?" she smiled. "It was awful foolish and weak-minded to become so anxious."

"Not a bit of it; anyone else would have felt the same," Mrs. Duff assured her, "and lots of women wouldn't have had the courage to cross the paddocks alone on a dark night, as you did."

"But, to make sure," Titt said, procuring his hat, "me and Old Fred will drive round to Hamlet's and if Mr. Wimblepip is still there, we'll drive him home."

Mrs. Wimblepip didn't know how she would ever repay Titt for all his kindness.

"And when I see Mary Ellen to bed," Mrs. Duff added, "I'll walk back to the school with Mrs. Wimblepip and come home with you and Old Fred, in the sulky."

Then everything seemed to be unravelling and terminating beautifully.

Splinter and Araluen alone in the home; the former restless and silent.

"I don't think you were telling father the truth, Splinter?" his sister said, looking up from her home lessons.

"Not all of it, I didn't", he confessed, twisting and screwing his body, and pulling painful faces. "We didn't look for any flowers—we went bogeying—an'—an'—— I'm all sunburnt," he blubbered; "it's painin' me; an' they'll find it out!"

"Where? Show me—let me see?" And Araluen, always sympathetic, rose from the table and went to him.

"Don't touch it, don't! Oh! it's stingin' me all over!"

"Get into bed," his sister advised; "then I'll some and put oil and ointment on you and father and mother won't know anything about it."

Splinter got into bed; and at intervals, Araluen, bending lightly over him, applied oil and ointment to his red roasted-looking back and shoulders with a feather. When at last he fell asleep, dreams of the day's misdeeds kept appearing before him like spectres of the dead, and he moaned and talked and tossed about.

Meanwhile, Titt arrived at the home of Hamlet and found that youth in the highest spirits.

"What did you blokes do with the teacher, when you were out in the bush with him to-day?" Titt asked abruptly. "He ain't come home yet, and Mrs. Wimblepip is over at my place lookin' for him and cryin' like winky."

Hamlet got a shock. His eyes started rolling in their sockets; his muscles began twitching, and his whole frame working.

"Don't excite him! Don't excite him!" his uncle (Hamlet was an orphan) cried, jumping up from the table. But the damage was done. Hamlet gave a lurch, and next minute was upon his back on the floor in a fit, fighting the atmosphere with hands and feet, and kicking over the furniture, and everything within reach of his limbs.

Having helped as best they could to soothe the sufferer, Titt and Old Fred hurried to the rest of the homes and inquired for the missing master. In turn, every boy who had been in the "study stunt" was questioned and cross-questioned. And the bad, unreliable memories most of them had were a feature of the investigation.

Tom Dyer was the last to be interrogated. Tom said that "he and Joe Shuttlewood and young Splinter went off up the big gully and got divin' in th' round water-hole to see if they could get the bunyip that everyone reckoned was there, to show old Roger".

"Splinter said you went to get a flower of some kind that was growin' out of a rock somewhere", Titt, displeased and suspicious-looking, interrupted.

"Eh!" Tom said, pausing and thinking rapidly.

Titt repeated the correction.

"That's right, quite right", and Tom quickly amended his statement. Then, monopolising all the talk, waved his hands

about and added a rambling, disconnected string of immortal
and transcendent lies on Splinter's account. Tom wasn't the
chap to desert a confederate once he knew how the land lay.

Then everyone came to the conclusion that the teacher had
either got lost in the forest or had met with an accident, and
in very short time the whole countryside, per horse and per
boot, were out searching for traces of him. Supplied with
hurricane lamps and matches, some with a bit of food, others
with a drop of spirits, they went off through the darkness in
every possible direction. Time was the essence of the search.
They took short cuts across paddocks, and where there were
no gates or slip-rails, a panel of the fence was pulled down or
the wires cut with a file. It was a night of memorable excitement, and rare privileges.

The women, too, after putting the children to bed, and
ordering them to sleep, left their homes and congregated at
the teacher's residence. They joined Mrs. Duff, and sympathised with Mrs. Wimblepip, and increased her distress. Then,
in a spirit of helpfulness, they over-ran her home, took possession of the kitchen, raided the wood-heap, set the table, made
tea for all hands, and insisted on Mrs. Wimblepip "eating
something to keep up her strength".

At intervals they would crowd on the verandah, and, gazing
into the night, would turn their eyes to the star strewn sky and
listen intently. Now and again some would hear a distant coo-
ee; others would discover fires showing simultaneously on top
of Mt. Sibley, and Keefer's Mountain, and Ryan's Mountain,
and the one in Eton Vale. And they knew they were signals
sent up to catch the eye of the lost teacher and guide him to
safety and home.

After midnight, as the lingering moon came over the range,
the sound of galloping hoofs were heard approaching. The
women became excited. It was Tom Dyer and Joe Shuttlewood. They reined in; dismounted quickly, fastened their
horses to the palings, and hurried through the garden.

"Have you found him?" a dozen eager voices inquired.

"No," they answered, bounding breathlessly on to the
verandah and pausing in the light of the door, "but we got his
helmet", and Tom, who was wearing it over his old felt, took it

off and displayed it proudly in the light, "and there's blood on it of some kind", he added.

A high-pitched, prolonged shriek came from Mrs. Wimblepip, and before any of them could reach her, she flopped on the floor and struck her head against the leg of the sofa. There was a confused rush to her assistance. Mrs. Drygrass, a large, clumsy woman, bumped the table with her hip and knocked the kerosene lamp on to the floor. It crashed and flared in a most alarming manner, threatening to set fire to the house and burn it down. Those who expected an explosion, screamed and, grabbing their skirts in their hands, flew to the verandah. Mrs. Shuttlewood was the only one who showed any presence of mind.

"Throw something on it—something on it!" she cried, crawfishing herself into a corner and holding her hands over her face.

"A blanket!" Mrs. O'Connor suggested, trying to squeeze behind Mrs. Shuttlewood.

Tom Dyer sprang forward and clapped the helmet over the flames; then jumped on it with both feet and pounded it, lamp and all, until the room was dark and smoky, and smelt of kerosene.

Then all thought again of Mrs. Wimblepip. They lifted her from the floor, placed her full length on the sofa; dragged her shoes off, opened the neck of her dress, rubbed her hands, and said everything and did everything they could to bring her to life again. When she revived, and looked as if making up her mind to stay in this world for ever, whether her husband was found or not, Tom and Joe started explaining how it was they came across the helmet.

"We saw a fire in Botkin's Gully," they exulted, "and when we come up to it, here was two swagmen camped at it and lying alongside one of them was th' bloomin' helmet!"

"They've murdered him! I knew it!" Mrs. Wimblepip shrieked again, and a second time rolled off the sofa on to the floor. Her large dark eyes went white; her red lips went blue, her small feet quivered, she gave several spasmodic kicks, such as a beheaded rooster gives for a finish, then one hand fell beside the sofa, the other showing several lovely rings, rested lightly on her breast.

Great commotion.

"My hokey!" Tom said, looking gloomy as the inside of an old man kangaroo, "she's done for this time!"

"Undo her dress—and her stays! Quick! Quick!" Mrs. Drygrass cried, "and leave the room, you boys—leave the room!"

Tom and Joe left the room slowly and clumsily, both gaping back over their shoulders as they went.

The rest of the women, feeling they were in the way, left the master's wife to the care of Mrs. Drygrass and Mrs. Duff, and withdrew on tip-toes to the kitchen. There they stirred up the smouldering fire, put some more wood on it, and sat round conversing in whispers and pricking their ears for any hopeful sounds outside.

From time to time, Mrs. Drygrass or Mrs. Duff would trip in in quest of hot water or something, and in hushed tones all would inquire from her how Mrs. Wimblepip was. Once she screwed her face significantly, and said "she didn't believe she was really half as bad as she made herself out to be!"

The others all nodded in silent agreement.

"And do y' think she's so fond of him as all that?" Mrs. Sawpitt asked.

Mrs. Drygrass pulled a more significant face than before, and returned to the front room.

The others then talked about the absent master and discussed his good qualities and his domestic affairs and wondered if "he was really lost" and "if there wasn't something else at the bottom of it all".

After that they fell into reflection, and a heavy drowsiness came over them as they sat looking into the dying fire. Mrs. Crosscut, who had been going hard since five o'clock the morning before, fell right off to sleep and started dreaming aloud. The others smiled and some spoke to her; but she slept and dreamed on. Suddenly she said:

"Mr. Wimbletop!" and leaning forward, put out her hand touched the fire with it. Then she jumped right out of her sleep in to the lap of Mrs. Sawpitt, and both fell heavily on the floor and shook the house, and all the others squealed.

"Good heavens!" her companions cried, jumping up, "did you burn yourself?"

"My God!" Mrs. Crosscut gasped, "I must have been dreaming? I thought I found the schoolmaster, and he was dead, and I was going to pull him out of some place!"

"It must have been out of the Hot Place," Mrs. Shuttle-wood said, "or you woudn't have put your hand among them coals."

The others all laughed. They were laughing when Tom Dyer and Joe Shuttlewood returned again, shouting: "They got him! They're comin' with him!"

Then there was more commotion! and all stampeded through the house on to the verandah.

Mrs. Wimblepip raised herself on the sofa and said she wouldn't believe it until she saw her husband walk in at the door!

A few seconds later when he walked in, she scarcely knew him. He was bare-headed, was mud all over; his clothes torn to tatters; boots wet, and his face conveyed no feelings of joy or pleasure or thankfulness or gratitude. He looked as if he were rehearsing the part of "The Remorseful Drunk". He was in a bad humour, too—the worst humour he was ever in his life.

"Roger!" his wife cried, throwing her arms around his neck. "My husband! My ——"

"Stop! Stop! Stop!" he snapped, trying to shove her off, "what's all this fuss about?"

"I thought you were murdered—oh, I did! I did!"

"Stuff and nonsense!" and freeing himself from her embraces, the master dropped into a chair and with elbows on his knees and his face in his hands, seemed to be undergoing great mortification.

His wife dropped on her knees beside him and rested her chin affectionately and gratefully on his bald crown, and murmured love things to him.

"Rubbish!" he barked, and rising from her paced the room.

That his bump of locality should have failed him as it did injured the master's professional pride and dignity. He had been lost and found within a few miles of his home, and was humiliated.

Tom Dyer, having heard all he wished to hear from the rescue party, collected about the verandah steps, sauntered inside to see the master.

"Hello, Mister Wimblepip", he grinned, sympathetically.

The sound of his voice seemed to awaken angry memories in the master and bring him out of his remorse. Turning quickly and facing Tom, he pointed dramatically to the door and said: "Go!"

"I was only goin' to say——", Tom mumbled.

"Go!" shouted the master.

"Oh, alright," Tom said, "if that's all th' thanks you got I will"—and he went.

Then Mrs. Drygrass and Mrs. Shuttlewood and all the rest stole softly from the verandah, and joining their husbands, whispered:

"Leave them to theirselves; we better all go home now."

And though the breaking dawn could not be seen through the gathering fog that was enveloping the Bushland, by the lowing of the cows, the laughing of the jackasses and the twittering of the ground larks, they knew another day had come.

20. School Goes On Merrily

Though the master decided to lead no more boys into the forests on Nature-study stunts, there came moments when he found it difficult to restrain them from breaking out on their own account. Such moments came when a mob of kangaroos would gather round and hop over the fence into the playground to sample the grass growing there. Then only by placing his back firmly against the door, and brandishing his black ruler and angrily shouting a fusilade of threats and warnings to the leaders, was he able to stem the rush and prevent a stampede in pursuit of those marsupials.

"Oh, blow it, Boss!" Tom Dyer, when calm was restored and most of the scholars returned to their places, would grumble, "if you'd let us out, we'd have caught one of them and brought y' th' tail to make soup o' ".

"Go back to your studies, Dyer!" with a final flourish of the black ruler, Mr. Wimblepip would order, "or you'll compel me to expel you from the school!"

"Oh, beggar the expellin'!" and with a surly grin at those in the desks, Tom would reluctantly obey. Then giving Joe Shuttlewood, or whoever happened to be nearest him, a malicious dig in the ribs, he would proceed to clean his slate with his big bony elbow. That done he would look up when Mr. Wimblepip's back was turned, and in mimicking tones, sneer. "Go back to your studies!" Those within hearing would giggle, and lower their heads to escape detection.

"Shut up!" Joe Shuttlewood would whisper, "he can hear y'." Tom would shut up.

Then pencils would start scratching again, the hum and din of voices would pervade the room, and once more discipline would be restored.

Out on the floor, at one end, the infant class, which included girls in long dresses and broad leather belts drawn tightly around their waists to preserve their figures, half sang, half shouted, "two and one are three", and "two and two are four". At the other end another class, the "low second", boisterously related to anyone within hearing, the sad story of two unhappy frogs that went off "one hot day to look for water". And up and down the room the voice of the master, correcting and directing this pandemonium, rang out clearly above the lot.

In the middle of it all the restless gaze of Tom Dyer or Splinter or Joe Shuttlewood or someone would suddenly discover the presence of the "big black gohanna" on the verandah. The "big black gohanna" had developed a habit of visiting the school at convenient moments in search of crumbs and fragments of food left lying about and soon as his ugly form appeared, word was speedily passed around. Then would come a lull. The "two and one are three" sing-song would terminate abruptly. The two frogs who went to look for water would expire instantly. Every eye would be strained and every neck stretched to secure a glimpse of the long-tailed visitor. All worries, too, would disappear. Cheerful grins would brighten and broaden faces, that only a moment before were filled with misery and despair.

Without a word, the master, with eyes wide open, would promptly put down his chalk, and reach for the black ruler. Then stealing softly and cautiously towards the open door, would pause for a moment, take in a deep breath, secure a firmer grip of the ruler, motion the grinning school to perfect silence, then jumping out, to the accompaniment of a tumult of guffaws, would let fly the ruler with all his might at the lurking reptile, and make a dent in the verandah boards, and another in the water tank. Then he'd pursue the startled vermin down the steps, with all the school shouting encouragingly at his heels, and race it to the nearest tree. The nearest tree was about twenty yards away, and the gohanna always arrived there first, and wriggling hurriedly up the trunk, would be half an inch beyond reach, when his pursuer made a spring for the tail-grip.

"Well! well! well! Missed the brute again!" he would murmur when a shower of sticks and stones would fly at the gohanna, and if Garfield Roger Wimblepip didn't duck a dozen different ways at once, or suddenly drop flat on the ground, he stood a better chance of being brained or maimed than ever the "big black gohanna" did!

As much as the boys of the school hunted and molested the animals and birds of the bush, making their lives a misery to them, the injured creatures seemed to cherish a fondness for their society, notwithstanding. Scarcely had the institution been in full swing when numbers of birds and possums found their way into it. They built nests in the crude ceiling, the boards in which, for mean departmental reasons, were an inch apart, and made their homes there. And talk about a surprise! Talk about mirth! The first time their presence was discovered, there was a surprise! And there was mirth! The discovery happened one sultry afternoon at three o'clock. The fifth class was in the front desk writing a composition "out of their own heads" on "Australian Wild Animals"; some were deep in thought, some writing rapidly. Suddenly Maggie Murphy, sitting about the middle of the desk, next to Splinter, jumped to her feet with a squeal; then stood looking at the ceiling. Splinter gazed at the part of the desk that Maggie had abandoned, then up at the ceiling also, and seeing the tail of a possum dangling through one of the cracks, laughed and shoved further away from Maggie. Then all the class rose up and fixed their eyes on the ceiling, and burst into great merriment.

Next moment the master was brandishing the cane in their faces, and loudly demanding "Silence!" Splinter, for the master's information, cheerfully pointed to the desk, others directed his attention to the dangling tail with a curl showing on the end of it. He looked at both.

"Possums in the ceiling!" he said.

"My word!" Andy Drygrass, who had left his class to be in the fun said, with a grin, "and they ain't got any sanitary system up there, either."

Then Mr. Wimblepip's sense of humour revealed itself. For the first time in school, he burst into laughter like a man whose very soul was in the mirth, and the whole school, excepting Maggie Murphy, followed his example. Maggie Murphy thought they were all laughing at her, and like a good, illogical little girl, started crying.

Luncheon hour; the boys, in their half of the ground, playing "dogs and kangaroos"; the girls, in theirs, forming sides for a game of "rounders".

Joe Shuttlewood, one of the "dogs", having been mauled badly by the 'roos, retired to the shade of a tree and lay down. The rest of the "dogs" continued in their efforts to exterminate the 'roos.

Joe looked across and saw the girls playing rounders and enjoying themselves.

"Blow 'roos and dogs!" he mumbled, and rising again, leisurely slouched into the forbidden ground, and joining the girls, took the ball and started bowling to them.

"Here hold on a bit!" Tom Dyer, who was master of the hounds, yelled in protest to the 'roos, "we've lost a dawg!"

They all paused and gazed about in quest of the missing canine, and when they located him, shouted lusty commands to Joe "to come outer that".

Joe grinned, and waving his hand to them, went on bowling to the girls.

Then in a spirit of devilry, the dogs and 'roos made trumpets of their hands, and in one loud voice, shouted in the direction of the master's residence that "Shuttlewood is over playing amongst th' gir-rls".

Joe waved cheerfully to them again. But Susannah Drygrass, who approved of Joe's presence there, called to them in sneering tones to "shut their big mouths!"

Ignoring Susannah, the "dogs" and " 'roos" shouted again, "Shuttlewood is over playing amongst th' gir-rls".

The echo had scarcely died away when Mr. Wimblepip, adjusting his helmet, issued from the house, and came striding towards the playground.

"By crimes! Here he comes! Look out!" and the "dogs" and the "'roos" made off, laughing joyously.

"Run, y' tittle-tattles—y' mean lot o' tell-tales!" Susannah Drygrass shrieked after them on Joe's behalf.

But the valiant "dogs" and " 'roos" on reaching a patch of long grass from whence they could see and hear anything that might take place, dropped down amongst it and concealed themselves. And all the girls, excepting Susannah, anticipating trouble, deserted Joe and fled to the farthest corner of the ground and started swinging on the wire fence. Susannah struck a defiant attitude, and standing before Joe, resolutely awaited the worst.

Next moment Mr. Wimblepip approached the pair.

"Listen!" the "dogs" hissed though the grass at the " 'roos"; "keep quiet!"

"If he hits Joe," Tom Dyer mumbled prophetically, "there'll be a bloomin' fight!"

"An' will you be in it, Tom?" Splinter whispered earnestly.

"Up to me neck!" Tom answered back.

"Cripes! I hope he hits Joe!" and Splinter raised his head to get a better view.

But the master displayed no aggressive signs whatever. He spoke kindly and advisedly to Joe, and when he had said all he wished to say, the latter nodded in agreement, and smiling down at his toes as he mooched along, re-crossed the "border-line" and returned to his own part of the ground. Susannah turned, too, and ran off in pursuit of her companions; while Mr. Wimblepip himself strolled back to finish his lunch.

A little later, school went in again. For awhile all went smoothly. As the hand of the clock pointed to three, Joe and Susannah, after being warned several times for talking, suddenly put down their books, and walking on to the verandah, returned to the room with their hats on their heads and broad smiles on their faces. No roomful of youngsters ever looked more astonished! Nor any schoolmaster, either.

"What does this mean?" Mr. Wimblepip, when he got over the first of the shock, demanded.

"Oh, nothin' much—only—", and Joe paused to grin and chuckle shyly at Susannah. Susannah turned partially away, and hanging her head and patting the floor with her foot, smiled from beneath her home-made bonnet at the rows of gaping faces in the desks.

"Only what?" indignantly from the master.

"Well—only—y' see——", and catching the eyes of Tom Dyer and Andy Drygrass, Joe broke into a chuckle again.

"I insist on an explanation Shuttlewood!" roared Mr. Wimblepip.

Great alarm! All the school rose to their feet, and some of the girls commenced blubbering.

"Well, th' short an' long of it is———", Joe cast another cheerful side-glance at Susannah; "we finish up here to-day— we're cut out———"

"Cut out?" and Mr. Wimblepip tugged at the collar of his coat with one hand and scratched his head with the other.

"Yes, we've gradeated," Joe grinned, "an' are goin' to a uneversity."

Loud laughter from Tom Dyer and Andy Drygrass.

"Silence!" and the master turned sharply upon them.

Then facing Joe and Susannah again.

"A university! I don't understand you!"

"One of our own", Joe responded.

Susannah hung her head again and giggled.

"Well me an' Susannah is goin' to get MARRIED!" and Joe made the grand announcement with a boisterous guffaw.

Mr. Wimblepip's eyes and mouth flew wide open, and his head went right back. For a few moments he was speechless— all his breath seemed to leave him.

"It seems to give y' a surprise, Mr. Wimblepip?" Susannah, looking up at him with a beaming face, put in; "but it's quite true—we are!"

Then suddenly his demeanour changed. The blood mounted quickly to his face. Instead of scholars of his school he saw them now as man and woman. Taking both their hands in his, he shook them warmly and kindly, and said:

"Good luck, and may you both do well."

Turning to the rows of staring faces, Joe and Susannah gave them all a parting smile, and a wave of the hand, and went out. Following them to the door the big human-hearted master stood and watched them descend the steps—watched them pass out of the gate—watched them enter the wide, grassy lane where, hand in hand, step by step, they started slowly, happily, aimlessly along. Above them the sky was bright and blue and clear; beneath their feet carpets of wild daisies and immortelles doffed their gay little heads; among the trees the birds sang merrily, and the soft winds sighed through the leaves like a breath of many ages past and gone.

"Simple, innocent souls!" he reflected, "knowing nothing of the dark, troubled road that's before you—nothing!"

He started, and turned quickly round.

The scholars had formed themselves into a circle on the floor, and led by Araluen, suddenly lifted their voices and sang:

> "Should auld acquaintance be forgot,
> And never brought to mind?
> Should auld acquaintance be forgot,
> And auld lang syne?"

Sound travels fast. The ring of those voices fell on the ears of Joe and Susannah. They paused and turning their faces to the school again, listened. When the words "We twa hae run about the braes, and pou'd the gowan fine", were reached, they both stopped and each plucking a wild flower, waved in response. And when the last note of the old refrain was sung, and the voices died away, they waved and waved again; then went on—on—but to what end in Life's mystery, whether weal or woe, sunshine or shadow, richer or poorer, better or worse, only the God above could reveal.

21. Drought and The Devil

Taking a leaf from the book of an old hand who had succeeded on the Creek, Titt Duff resolved to do the same or die.
He started out, and slaved and "bullocked" from daylight till
dark; sacrificed every pleasure, every moment of leisure to
free the homestead from its financial encumbrance, and make
it his own. He developed a restless, untiring energy; work
became his life, and life held nothing for him but work. No
one in the district toiled so hard as he—no one ever did—
unless it was those who had worked themselves to death, and
died in their tracks. If Titt was lean and bendy when first he
went on the land, he was much leaner and more bent now.
There was little left of him but courage and sinew, his hands
were hard and knotted, his face weather-beaten and burnt
almost black with the fierce winds and heat of summer.

"Slogging the way he does is only madness", Bill Sawpitt,
who for eighteen months worked for Titt on wages, used to
say. "I never knew him to finish his breakfast the whole time
I was with him. Havin' breakfast or dinner or anything like
that was waste of time to him! He'd gulp down a cup of tea and
a mouthful of bread and meat and rush off to work before the
rest of us had hardly stirred our tea! And at night, after he'd
had supper, he wouldn't sit down and have a smoke or a yarn
like anyone else, not him! He'd grab a hurricane lamp, and
rush out to the barn or some place, to patch wheat sacks or
mend harness, or make new swingletrees, or kill a sheep and
hang it ready for th' mornin'. And to be pullin' corn with him,
and cartin' it in——" Bill would sigh—"was deadly! He'd
kill y' in a couple o' days if y' tried to keep up with him! You'd
think it was all a matter of life an' death to him, and when he
saw you gettin' behind a bit, blowed if he would want to do
your share as well as his own. No good to me!" Bill would
conclude; "life's too short an' uncertain for that sort o' thing!

And Titt Duff one of these fine days'll drop dead, an' that'll
be the end of him!"

And so several years passed—years that had started full of
hope and promise of plenty—years that had seen the few
heifers increase to a dairy herd of five and thirty good and
profitable cows, and the eight or ten acres of cultivation
expand to a hundred—years through which Titt, in the mistaken impulses that were always bubbling within him, made
prophecies that never came to pass—years that changed, that
led to bad seasons, and worse seasons, ending in drought,
disappointment, and disaster, leaving the Duffs to face a
promissory note for £200, a land tax assessment, the local
government tax, a marsupial tax, and a large bill at the local
store!

"My God!" Titt groaned, when the impending disaster
fairly revealed itself; "what is to be done?"

Yes! What was to be done? That was the question. How
many poor broken hearts upon the land, before and since,
have asked themselves the same hopeless, unanswerable
question? And echo ever answered mockingly back: "What is
to be done?"

Titt's total liabilities amounted to nearly £300. Another
year of drought and the debt would easily double itself. Should
sufficient rain come by that time, however, another six months
at least must elapse before there would be any return from the
farm. Even if it rained ever so hard, the crop might be a
failure, and the cows all be dry for a period, and the dairy
deserted. Or the storekeeper might press for payment of his
account, and refuse further credit! This chain of gloomy
probabilities careered in procession through Titt's bewildered
brain till they appeared realities, and drove him to the verge
of despair. His nights became long and sleepless. He went off
his meals. Depressed by a sense of remorse and distraction, he
walked aimlessly about the farm to compose his spirits. Day
after day he turned his eyes from the cloudless, waterless sky
to the moaning, starving animals around. The straw-stacks
that he had long held as a "stand-by" had disappeared. The
cheapest fodder in the market was £14 a ton, and he hadn't a
shilling left to his name! Even if he had hundreds of pounds,

there were now forty head of stock to feed, and forty head would eat a ton a day, and a ton a day would absorb £98 a week! "My God!" Titt moaned again. "My God!"

"Don't let it worry you!" Mrs. Duff, woman-like, pleaded. "Lots of people have been in the same position—in a worse position, perhaps, than we are, and came through all right in the end."

"No one could be in a much worse position than we are in, Kit", Titt groaned. "If they were, I'm sure they never got out of it—never! Never——"

"Faith is everything", she assured him. "Put your trust in Providence, and you'll yet lift up your eyes and look on the fields, and see them white all ready for the harvest."

"I hope so," Titt groaned. "I hope so!"

But when discussing the prospects with Old Fred and the others, Mrs. Duff herself was inclined to lose heart and become despondent. She came, however, from a pioneer stock, whose spirit was never broken, and with an effort she always pulled herself together and smiled in the face of adversity.

Another month passed, and the drought still raged. Some of the stock now were lying about the farmyard unable to rise; others raised in "slings" were hanging between earth and heaven, while those that were still able to stagger about were almost demented.

Realising that his bit of capital, his hard toil, and everything were now lost, Titt was filled with fresh remorse and useless regrets for having left the city and dragged his family on to the wretched land. Remorse and dread became his constant companions.

Prickly pear was the only available food to feed the starving stock with. The whole family took a hand in cutting the wretched plant, and roasting it at open fires to destroy the prickles. The animals ate it eagerly, contracted disorders of the bowels, grew thinner and thinner every day, and then started dying, one by one, till the farmyard was a hospital, a morgue, and cemetery all in one. It had to be a cemetery because there was no horse power left to haul the corpses away. And when Titt and Old Fred and Splinter, the eldest son, had dug a dozen graves or so, and rolled the bodies in and covered them with earth, and in some cases, having misjudged the depth, left the four hoofs protruding and pointing skyward, a grim, humorous-looking cemetery it was! Poor old Diamond, Titt's favourite draught mare, a huge Clydesdale, died right across the gateway, and there she had to be interred. And so high was the mound when she was covered in that for years after when anyone was driving through the gate, their trap, or car, or whatever it was, would go up and down like a switchback railway. And children who had learned the stories of that drought would call in reverent warning to whomever chanced to be driving, to "go slowly over poor old Diamond!"

No wonder Titt couldn't sleep at night. Often he would lie down without undressing, and rising again at midnight would go to the door and through the pale, ghostly moonlight, gaze on the ghastly scene in all its desolate calm. Returning to his bed of wretchedness, he would lie awake in burning restlessness, while the groans of the starving animals rang in his ears till daybreak.

Fall of evening. Everything calm, peaceful. The broad, shadowy plain-lands, black and bare, lay lifeless, and all the world seemed wrapped in the mysteries of life and death.

Titt Duff, sitting on the verandah, his head in his hands, brooding, heard the sound of a horse's hoofs, and looked up slowly.

Ned Scantleton rode into the yard, dismounted, and fastened his horse to the palings.

"That you, Duff?" he called.

Titt descended the steps without answering, and went to the garden gate.

Scantleton, with a stockwhip hanging loosely over his shoulder, approached from the other side. Both leaned on the top bar and eyed each other in the growing darkness.

"You remember me, I suppose?" the former said.

Titt did.

"You called one day when passing with cattle," he said, "but you didn't have a cabbage-tree hat then."

"You've been having a bad time here?" And the visitor,

through the gloom, glanced over his shoulder at the "hospital and cemetery".

"Ah, well! It can't be helped", and Titt struggled with a lump that came into his throat.

"You're not the only one—if that's any satisfaction." And Scantleton knocked the ashes from his pipe on the gate.

Titt struggled again with the feeling in his throat, then said: "We'll be having some tea in a minute or two; you better come in."

But Scantleton was in a hurry. He was always in a hurry at that hour of the evening.

"I'm making over for over the Range," he added ("over the Range", to people of the plains and tablelands was a world away), "and just dropped in on my way to put a little proposition to you."

"Yes?" Titt said, wonderingly.

"Would you like to make a couple of hundred quid—perhaps a thousand?"

Titt clutched the gate till it rattled, and strained his eyes in the gloom to see if the other's face was serious.

"Anyway, a couple of hundred for a dead certainty", and Scantleton started filling his pipe from a pouch.

Titt's heart beat violently. Two hundred pounds just then would save him from financial disaster, would lift the load of worry from his mind, and brighten his heart and home again.

"H-how?" he stammered.

"Simply by holding some bullocks here for me for a day or two till the Western Butchering Company's buyer calls, and selling them to him in your name!"

"In my name?" Titt echoed, trembling with excitement, and the hope that had suddenly sprung to his breast.

"It's just this way." And Scantleton proceeded calmly to explain that running on one of the creeks over the Range amongst scrub and prickly pear he had 150 head of fat bullocks—bullocks he had bought when calves four years ago for half-a-crown a head.

"By cripes!" Titt interrupted, "you're a lucky dog!"

"And fats being so scarce now, as you know," Scantleton went on, "they're worth anything from £15 to £20 a nob."

"Ghost!" Titt gushed. "I'd have sold them long ago if they had been mine!"

"No doubt," the other agreed, "but here's the difficulty I'm in; I'm not a land-holder, and having got into a bit of trouble about three years ago, through a misunderstanding over a cow and calf that I really had nothing at all to do with, I don't like to sell these bullocks in my own name now. Some of these chaps who are always trying to be very smart, might try to make out that I didn't own them, and put me to all sorts of trouble; and I'm a chap who would sooner do anything or give all I got, rather than be put to the bother of going to law or seeing Government officials and all that sort of thing."

"I see", Titt said eagerly.

"So if you care to take the bullocks and sell them in your name, and you being a land-holder, there'd be no questions asked, you can keep half of what they fetch, and give me the rest!"

"I'll do that quick enough," Titt gasped, "and if anyone asks any questions—well, I bought them, that's all."

"Quite so, but not from me!"

"Oh, no," Titt readily agreed, "anyone but you."

"Then, if you wake up one morning next week," Scantleton concluded, "and find fifty head of bullocks in your paddock, for a start, you'll know what to do."

"Leave that to me", and feeling in the dark for the other's hand, Titt shook it warmly.

But in his excitement, Titt never suspected that those bullocks in which he saw his salvation, and more than salvation, were stolen by Scantleton and a gang of confederates from a border station hundreds of miles away, and skilfully travelled by night to Smuggling Gorge, over the Range. And if he had suspected, we wonder if, under the circumstances, he would have had the moral strength to resist and turn the matter down. Ah, well! who hasn't at some time or other realised that needs must when the devil drives!

So Scantleton mounted his horse again, and rode silently away into the night and over the Range—over the Range, a world of its own—a world of solitude, of great gloomy scrubs, of deep dark mountain gorges, of wild dogs, wild cattle, and saddle-marked horses—a world of mystery, of robbery and romance.

That evening at tea the family wondered what had come over Titt. His worried look, his restless, depressed spirits had left him. He came to the table with a brisk, confident step, and a broad smile, and was consumed in cheerfulness.

"What's up?" Splinter grinned, "was it goin' to rain when y' came in, father?"

"It's goin' to rain sovereigns this time, lad," he smiled, "and I don't care now what happens—if every bloomin' cow and hen an' dawg on the place croaks before mornin'—or if all th' fences get burnt as well. That's how I feel."

"My word," Mrs. Duff smiled, "something good must have happened all at once."

"Something good just did happen, Kit", and Titt started rubbing his hands together, and grinning with increased cheerfulness.

"Has someone left y' a fortune?" Old Fred inquired.

"Remembered you in their will, father?" from Araluen.

"Not exactly," Titt smiled, "but Scantleton has just put me on to a great wicket—on to a little goldmine, an' saved th' situation."

Old Fred, in the act of conveying a spoonful of kangaroo-tail soup to his mouth, suddenly paused, spilled the soup, and stared first at Titt, then at Mrs. Duff.

"Scantleton?" the latter repeated thoughtfully.

"Ned Scantleton?" Old Fred echoed, dropping the spoon in his plate with a rattle.

"Do y' know him?" Titt replied. "I've just been having a long yarn to him at the gate."

"Everyone knows him! An' I'd steer clear of him if I was you, Boss!" And lowering his head, Old Fred went on with his meal in grave silence.

"If it's the Scantleton they used to talk about at Ruddville years ago," Mrs. Duff reflected, "he was a notorious charac-ter!"

"Notorious or not notorious," Titt laughed, "he's doin' me

a good turn, for him and me are going into a cattle deal together that'll see me out of me trouble in no time."

"That'll see y 'in trouble in no time!" and rising abruptly, Old Fred left the table and went off to his room on the verandah.

Next morning while Ttit was roasting pear for the few surviving head of cows and whistling merrily as a butcher bird in summer, Mrs. Duff, her heart full of worry and eyes wet with tears, sought Old Fred in the garden and asked him "to tell her truly what he really thought about this Scantleton affair".

"Just this, Kittie," and Old Fred looked her solemnly in the face, "Ned Scantleton was always the ringleader of cattle-stealers, and if the Boss has any dealin's with that gentlemun he'll land him where he's landed many another, an' where he ought to have been himself twinty year ago—in gaol!"

"You must come and tell that to Titt himself, Old Fred", Mrs. Duff implored. "He won't listen to me; he thinks I'm too particular. and expect people to be angels."

"Don't worry about it, Kittie," he responded, "I'll tell him all I know about Scantleton directly—I'll tell him."

And a few mornings later, while Titt was standing admiring fifty bullocks that he found locked carefully in the yard, Old Fred approached and, disregarding the sight of the surging animals, told him all he knew of the career of Scantleton.

"That might be," Titt mumbled sullenly, "he might have done worse things, perhaps, than the Marsdens or Starlight in 'Robbery Under Arms', but it don't prove there's anything wrong about these bullocks does it?"

"Them bullocks", and Old Fred, with his long bony finger, pointed dramatically through the rails at them—"are stolen! Ned Scantleton wouldn't have anything to do with them if they weren't! And you won't if you don't want to get five years in gaol!"

"And then—what?" Titt groaned. "I'll be without a bean! Without an animal left on the farm! Smashed! Broke! Insolvent! A beggar!"

"No, you needn't be anything of th' sort, Boss", Old Fred

*The Fifty Head of Bullocks Bounded Through and Stampeded down
the Main Road*

answered kindly. "I'm not a pauper, altogether. I've always managed to save a little one way an' another (taking a bank book from inside his shirt), and if £300 will put you on your feet, it's here for you."

Titt started, and stared. Then his head hung down; his chin rested on his bosom; big tears swam into his eyes, his tongue cleaved to the roof of his mouth, and he could say nothing.

Taking his arm, Old Fred led him back to the house, which they both entered in silence.

A little later Splinter and Araluen ran out and threw open the gate of the stock-yard. Then the fifty head of bullocks bounded through, and, with Bluey hard at their heels, stampeded down the main road, and were never heard of again.

22. A Tight Place

The drought was over. Fields and pastures looked green and grand again. The creek was flowing fast and full. People who had struggled and lost and suffered were "bucking up" and cheerfully facing the odds once more—hope became the comfort of their adversity, and, with all her treacherous moods and changes, the world seemed a good old world, after all.

Titt, having squared most of his accounts, and replaced some of the dead stock with live ones from the loan Old Fred advanced him, started out to make up lost ground. A crop in and well above ground, he dceided to subdivide the "big paddock", and go in heavily for lucerne. The soil was low and silty, and rich in the big paddock, with water beneath at shallow depth for the lucerne to dip its roots into. To plant it in any other quality of land, Titt had learned, was only throwing labour and money away. So, along with Old Fred, he began by felling an aged ironbark tree that had been left standing near the cowyard, to convert it into fencing posts. It wasn't an ideal splitting tree—it was windy and a bit hollow. With the cross-cut they sawed the butt into two 6ft. lengths. Stripping the bark from one of them, they took the maul and wedges, and commenced to burst it in halves. It was tough work. Titt swung the maul while Old Fred, looking on sympathetically, did the grunting. At last the log yielded slightly to the touch of the entering wedge, and began crack-crack-cracking.

"Now, she's going!" Old Fred announced jubilantly. "Give her another!"

Titt gave it another thump, and Old Fred grunted his loudest. Then Titt took a larger wedge, and, inserting the point of it in the crack that had begun to traverse the face of the log, spat on his hands, opened his shoulders, swung the maul again. and gave the wedge a mighty bump. It sank half-way in; the log opened with a rip and a tear, leaving the crack gaping an inch or so wide and extending halfway along the log.

"It takes you, Boss!" Old Fred complimented.

"My oath!" Titt grinned.

Just then Charlie, the bone collector, with his three horses and dray, and shouting and roaring just for the love of making a noise, came rattling in through the gate.

Titt looked up and stared. Old Fred turned and stared, too.

"What's he after?" the latter proposed.

"What's he always after?" Titt reckoned, "a drink of water —or beer, if there was any about!"

"Whoa!" Charlie roared, steadying the horses beside the head of the fallen tree, and jumping from the dray. "What are y' doin' on neow, cootin' dahn a tree, eh? Hoh! Hoh! Hoh!" And he beamed a quaint smile first on Titt, then on Old Fred.

"Trying to knock up some fencing posts", Titt answered. "What do y' think you're after?"

"I'm lookin' for boanes—what did y' do wi' all your dead cows, eh? Hoh! Hoh! Hoh!" And Charlie sat down leisurely on the log inside the wedge.

"Burned them!" Titt said sulkily.

"There's one of them, under there, alongside of y' ", Old Fred added, pointing to the grave of Tulip, and taking up the empty billy-can, he strode across to the house to replenish it.

"So-h? Hoh! Hoh! Hoh!" from Charlie.

"It was no laughing matter", Titt grunted.

"Hoh! Hoh! Hoh! Charlie rumbled on. "We heard at th' township how y' had a cemeteery out here. But what abaht lettin' I dig 'em all oop, an' take on of 'em all away—eh?"

"Let them rip where they are!" Titt said restlessly. He always fidgetted when reminded about the drought—and sitting down on the log faced the opposite way to Charlie, and frowned.

Splinter, crying out, "The gully's runnin'!" came along and grinned familiarly to the bone collector, then, idly lifting the maul which his parent had thrown down, started thumping the earth with it.

"It wouldn't take I long to dig 'em all oop", Charlie persisted. "An' I'd fill the hoales all in agen for y'?"

"No!" Titt snapped. "Let th' poor beggars rest. They're doing no one any harm, and I've seen enough of them."

"Will y' then if I pays y' somethin' for 'em?" and leaning back over the log, and stretching out his right leg, Charlie dipped a hand into his pocket, and produced a match to light his pipe with.

"How much would y' pay?" quickly from Titt.

"Oh—well——", and the other lit his pipe and started spitting and pondering.

Tired of thumping the earth, Splinter brought the maul down heavily on the end of the log. Mother of Miracles! That wedge shot out like a cork from a bottle, and the split closed with a snap on the fleshy parts of Charlie and Titt, and like the jaws of a mighty steel trap, held them captives! Oh, the howls and roars of them! Their yells of pain and profanity were appalling! Their faces writhed in agony. The pipe fell from Charlie's mouth; tears gushed from both their eyes and rushed down their cheeks; both clenched their fists and shook them at Splinter, but neither made any attempt to break loose. They couldn't. And for the life of him, Splinter, for the moment, couldn't conceive the cause of their sudden distress. He stood dumb, dazed, alarmed, staring wild-eyed, and trembling like some newly-captured animal of the bush.

Louder and louder the victims bellowed and swore, until Charlie's horses, taking fright, bolted with the dray. Glad of any excuse to make off, Splinter turned and pursued the runaway animals with a speed and determination next to marvellous.

Attracted by the roaring and bellowing of Charlie and Titt, Old Fred, closely followed by Mrs. Duff and Araluen, hurried from the house.

"What's up?" Old Fred cried breathlessly. But a glance at their faces and at the closed split in the log conveyed everything to him in a flash.

"They're caught in the log!" Araluen squealed, "caught in it!"

"Oh, goodness!" Mrs. Duff gasped.

"I see they are!" and lifting the maul, Old Fred drove the wedge into the log again. The split opened instantly and

Charlie and Titt rose cautiously to their feet, pulled more ugly faces, and bending backwards and forwards, hobbled about, moaning and groaning.

"That d——d young scoun'rel of a boy did it!" Charlie yelled. "He wants killin', he do!"

Then Old Fred and Mrs. Duff and Araluen broke into mirth.

"If it'd got a grip of any of you, you wouldn't be so funny!" And Titt, walking wide and cautiously, directed his steps towards the house.

Splinter, in charge of Charlie's horses and dray, returned grinning triumphantly. He seemed to anticipate a reward.

"I caught them!" he called; "but what was th' matter with yous two?"

When he came a little nearer, though, and saw the scalding tears and the look of murder in Charlie's eye, and heard his teeth grinding, he threw the reins to him and fled.

It was a week before Titt could move about with confidence again; and a year passed before Charlie paid another visit to Duff's—then it was in the night—the night they heard a great commotion in the fowl-house, and next morning missed two of the fattest roosters.

23. *Araluen Attracts Admirers*

Whatever obstacles and adversities the Duffs had encountered during the year just passed, the growth of the family had in no way been retarded. There were six of them now—"six little Australians"—and both Araluen and Splinter were as tall as their parents.

Never on Emu Creek was a girl so fair and favoured as Araluen. She grew up a vision of the bush-land. Hers was not a paint and powder and fine feathers over Nature, for in home-made gowns and the sun's complexion, Araluen was good to look upon. Kindly, sensible, human-hearted, she was, too, and beloved by everyone around.

Ever rounding up cows and horses—galloping here, there, and everywhere, she easily became a good horsewoman. The "egg money" she earned by caring for fowls enabled her to take music-lessons once a week, from Mrs. Brophy, at the township. Thursday was her day for lessons, and it was remarkable how soon Thursday became the day when every single man on the creek and every beardless youth over the age of 16 had business at the township! And somehow just when Araluen's lessons would be over, and she was ready to return to "Coondalloo", the name Titt gave to the holding, and the aboriginal word for "emu", they would all be prepared to leave the township, too! And no matter in what direction their respective homes lay or how far off, the road that led to "Coondalloo" led to theirs as well! And bachelors residing in the township fell into the habit of going for a ride on Thursdays about 5 p.m., and would always take the road that led past "Coondalloo". The bachelors of the township, though, never left when Araluen was leaving—they always waited till she was well on the road, then "set sail", and caught up to her. And when she would bow to them, they would feign surprise at seeing her, and tell her they "thought she had gone home

long ago". Of course, Araluen always knew they were lying—
any intelligent girl would—but bachelors, out of their vanity,
always build a fool's paradise around themselves where attractive girls are concerned.

One evening Johnny Crosscut and Jimmie Shuttlewood
(Joe's brother), and Danny Jones were ready to leave the
township for their homesteads when Araluen came out of
Brophy's to mount her horse. Johnny and Jimmie and Danny,
aged 18, 19, and 20 respectively, were all long, lean, shy,
silent, beardless young men.

With bridle reins on their arms, they stood around "Beeswing", a mare Old Fred had given Araluen on her birthday,
with a nervous desire to lift her into the saddle, an act of
gallantry that every country youth feels he must achieve to
earn the favour of a nice girl. Greeting them by their Christian
names, Araluen threw the reins over the mare's neck and
proceeded to tighten the girths. Johnnie's and Jimmie's and
Danny's hearts beat fast; their faces turned crimson; their big,
brown hands closed and opened, yet they never shifted an
inch; they stood there as if spiked to the earth.

"My word"—Mrs. Brophy called cheerfully from her
verandah—"it's well to be you, Araluen, with three fine looking young men dancing attendance on you."

Mrs. Brophy, besides a musical talent, possessed a keen
sense of humour. Araluen, blushing like a rose, dallied with
the girths to hide her blushing face.

Johnnie Crosscutt, remembering he had purchased his first
pipe at the store, took it from his pocket and bravely put it
in his mouth. Jimmy and Danny, who had made similar
purchases, followed his example and in turn all three grinned
and began feeling their pockets for tobacco and matches.

From the opposite side of the street—a two-chain wide
thoroughfare, gravelled with big stones and good intentions,
and with a network of narrow hideous gutters running through
the centre of it—the loud masculine voice of big Mrs. Frawley,
the "popular" proprietress of the Horse and Collar Hotel,
rang out from the bar verandah.

"Araluen!" she cried, "'tis a pity ye're not a quadruped, for
then ye could give each of them bhois a fut to lift ye on be."

Araluen looked across the mare's neck in the direction of the Horse and Collar, and smiled and blushed more.

Mrs. Brophy hung over her verandah rails and laughed joyously.

Filled with an embarrassment that even the thick smoke-screens they were now raising from their pipes couldn't conceal the three lanky timid loons grinned awkwardly at each other.

Just then the burly dusky form of the bone collector appeared. He was blundering along the "footpath", where herbage and noxious weeds grew luxuriantly, on his way to the store.

"Here's Charlie coming, Araluen," Mrs. Brophy laughed again, "don't be in a hurry; he'll lift you on."

Glancing over her shoulder as she gathered the reins together and placed a hand on the saddle. Araluen caught a glimpse of the familiar figure, unwashed, uncombed, unbarbered and pausing, leaned against the mare and laughed to herself.

"Charlie!" called Mrs. Frawley. The bone collector stopped and stared across at her.

"Hello, old woman!" he yelled back. "What be wrong wi' you? Gotten a long beer for I over theree, eh? Have you? You owe me one, don't you, eh, for cuttin' y' wood o' Sunday?"

"Charlie!" she repeated, as though he had never spoken, "give Araluen a leg up on to her horse!"

"Eh?" and looking ahead, Charlie saw Araluen standing beside the mare and the three shy loons looking uselessly at her. "What! can't y' get on, girl?" And he strode straight to her. "Don't some o' these young coves know how to lift a lady on?"

"That's right, Charlie", Mrs. Brophy encouraged. "Show them how to do it."

"My word, 'n I will. Hoh! Hoh! Hoh!" he laughed. "Giv us your leg?"

With a merry giggle Araluen placed her foot in the palm of his hand, and into the saddle he hoisted her without an effort.

"Thank you, Charlie", she laughed. Then shaking her riding

whip, first at Mrs. Brophy, then at Mrs. Frawley, touched the mare and cantered away.

Charlie winked proudly at Johnny and Jimmy and Danny, and went his way to the store.

"Well, you are three beautiful ladies' *'men'*!" Mrs. Brophy jibed. "Fancy letting old Charlie beat you! I thought you had more go in you than that!"

"I was goin' to lift her on," Johnny mumbled, in defence, "but these two seemed anxious—an'—so—I——"

"Gerrout!" Jimmy interrupted, "only for yous two pokin' your nose in, I would 'a done it!"

"Gerrout yourself!" Danny protested, sulkily. "Didn't I bring her mare round for her when yous two goats came messin' about, like y' alez do!"

"Haven't any of them got th' courage to see her home?" Mrs. Frawley's voice rang out again.

Mrs. Brophy didn't think they had.

"By cripes, I have, anyway!" and springing on to his clumsy looking half-draught Johnny Crosscutt blundered over the stones and ruts in determined pursuit of Araluen.

"Blowed if I'm goin' to be left behind!" and Jimmy vaulted on to his "three-legged" piebald and pursued Johnny.

"Well, I ain't goin' to be out of it!" and, getting astride his ancient "bob-tail" creamy Danny rattled over the stones at great pace after Jimmy.

"Did ever y' seen such chumps!" and, shaking her head across at Mrs. Brophy, Mrs. Frawley turned to answer a bar call.

"Never!" and Mrs. Brophy went inside, chuckling.

One after the other, those loons overtook Araluen. Johnny, who was first, lay right back in the saddle, and, hanging to the reins, made an imposing display of pulling in his hairy, wooden-headed half-draught beside her.

"Hard to hold, is he, Johnny?" Araluen asked, steadying her mare to a brisk walk.

"It's the corn he's got in him", Johnny explained.

"I'm feedin' him twice a day now", and leaning forward on the saddle he proudly patted the brute on what little neck it possessed.

"Y' can't beat corn for puttin' life into them", he added, after a pause.

Then Jimmy, standing in the stirrups, came up. He jerked and "propped" his piebald into position on Araluen's left, and grinned blandly when she greeted him with a smile.

"You wasn't long before y' followed me!" Johnny on the right of Araluen, grunted over her mare's neck accusingly at Jimmy.

"Wasn't follerin' you!" Jimmy snivelled. "What would I want to foller you for?"

Before he could answer Johnny's "corn-fed" mount stumbled badly, and went down on its knees and nose.

Araluen thought the brute was right over and got a start.

"The third time to-day he's said his prayers with me!" Johnny grunted, squaring himself in the saddle, as the animal recovered. "Th' third time, y' keow!" Then he jerked the offender's mouth hard with the reins, dug his heels into its ribs: again called it a "keow", and, suddenly hauling it to the "left about turn", nearly shoved Araluen out of her saddle with the half-draught's heavy slobbery snout.

In the mix-up that followed, Danny came up full tilt, and commandeered Johnny's place beside Araluen.

"Caught up to y' ", he said, grinning at her, happily.

"Everyone catches up to me, Danny; I must be a slow-coach' , Araluen said.

Johnny, having finished chastising the half-draught, drew up on the outside of Danny, and gave him a sly dig in the ribs.

Danny turned and frowned indignantly upon him for daring to interrupt his love-making.

"That was my place you teook", Johnny, springing lightly to the jogging of the half-draught, hissed into the other's ear.

Danny turned from him with contempt, and grinning lusciously at Araluen, inquired, "was it as hard to learn th' pianer as th' concertina?"

The query suddenly sharpened Araluen's memory.

"Oh!" she cried bringing the mare to a stand-still. "I left my music-roll at Mrs. Brophy's!"

"Eh!" Jimmy gasped.

"What?" from Johnny.

"Did y'? I'll get it", and wheeling round, Danny put heels to the bob-tail cream again, and off back he went for the roll.

"So'll I", and putting the piebald under the whip once more, away went Jimmy hot on the heels of Danny.

"Yer music, was it?" Johnny, taking a short hold of his steed's head, paused to interrogate.

"I forgot it!" Araluen added. "How silly of me!"

"I'll soon have it for y' ", and belabouring the half-draught, Johnny set off midst a cloud of dust and gravel and dead leaves.

In quick succession they met Sam Jackson cantering along, and shouted haughtily to him, "Clear th' road, or get run over!"

Sam smiled, and clearing the road, kept cantering till he overtook Araluen.

"Mrs. Brophy asked me to give this to you", he said, handing her the music-roll.

With a look of surprise, Araluen thanked him.

The Jacksons were the latest arrivals on Emu Creek, and it was the first time Araluen and Sam had met.

"Goodness!" she added, with concern, "and those poor boys have gone all the way back for it!"

Sam said he met them: was sorry he didn't know it was her music they were going for, or he would have stopped them, and turned them back.

Then he and Araluen rode steadily along together, and made friends with each other.

Meanwhile, Johnny and Jimmy and Danny reined in excitedly at Brophy's, and throwing themselves from their saddles as though competing in a polo gymkkana, rushed to open the garden gate, just as the lady herself, attracted by the rattling of hoofs, appeared again.

"Araluen forgot her music, Mrs. Brophy", the three of them shouted in one voice.

"And I got to get it for her", Johnny added quickly.

"No, I have!" from Jimmy.

"It's me that has!" from Danny.

Mrs. Bophy laughed and said she gave it to Sam Jackson

to give to Araluen, and asked if they hadn't met him along the road?

All three looked surprised and disappointed.

"That bloke!" Johnny sneered.

"Him!" Jimmy said.

"I nearly run over him. Wish I had!" Danny lamented, sulkily.

A loud peal of mirth came from Mrs. Brophy.

Then, like movie actors, the three turned, and remounting their horses, galloped back again.

When they overtook Araluen Sam was riding close beside her, talking and laughing, and carrying the music roll. Araluen sympathised with them; told them Mr. Jackson had brought the music along, and thought it was a pity they hadn't noticed it with him.

None of them said anything. But all three eyed Sam sullenly, and cast envious glances at the music roll in his hand.

Then Araluen introduced them to Sam, and Sam to them. Sam nodded and said he was pleased to meet them but neither Johnny, Jimmy, or Danny took any notice of Sam. Somehow, their steeds seemed to demand all their attention at that particular moment.

"You clumsy keow! Mind where you are walkin'!" and Johnny spitefully rattled both his heels against the half-draught's ribs.

"Hold yer bloomin' head up, can't y'!" Jimmy said to the piebald; while Danny unexpectedly jerked the creamy's mouth, and grunted, "I'll make yer walk, yer mule!"

Approaching the school where the road leading to his homestead branched off, Sam returned the music-roll to Araluen, said "Good-bye", nodded to the others, and raising his hat went his way alone.

"He's a perlite bloke!" Johnny grinned.

"My oath!" Jimmy sneered.

"Good-bye", Danny, mimicking Sam, echoed, and raising his slouch hat to the horse under him.

All three guffawed.

Araluen smiled amusedly, and suggested a canter.

Away they all scrambled and kept cantering till Duff's gate

was reached. There Araluen said "Good-night, boys".

"So-long, Araluen," Johnny and Jimmy and Danny answered cheerfully, "so-long, till another time."

Then, quickly separating, each took a different track through the bush. Night fell on the Budgee hills. The mellow, milky moon came up; the stars peeped out and winked. Stirred by a sense of triumph the softening influence of song swelled their bosoms and Johnny and Jimmy and Danny, though a mile apart, lifted their voices and shouted:—

"Hoh! fare-thee-wel me only love!
Hoh! fare-thee-wel awhile!
For I will come again me love
Tho' 'twere ten million mile!"

And the startled 'possums and owls and mopokes in the weird moonlit trees heard the noise and knowing nought of the strange forms in which the love of striplings manifests itself or the floodgates of sentiment through which it lets itself loose, stared wonderingly down and blinked and blinked.

24. *Tragedy, Comedy And Love*

It was while Titt Duff lay 'between life and death in the hospital. Splinter and Old Fred, to fill in time, were putting in a supply of firewood. They had gone for the last load, and Araluen was the sole occupant of the home. As afternoon wore on, she finished the ironing, and having put everything away, went out into the garden to work among the flowers. The garden was Araluen's special pride and care. All her spare time was devoted to it, and wherever she went she collected seeds and plants, and cuttings of fresh varieties to set in it. And when long dry spells came she always "got round" Old Fred to cart water to it. And no one, so well as Araluen, could "get round" Old Fred. No other member of the family cared for gardening. Titt, when at home and well, reckoned he wanted all his time, and more, if he had it, for the farm work, without "bothering about a blessed old garden". Splinter, on the other hand, was always going to "put in a couple of days at it", as soon as the ploughing or the harrowing, or the mowing, or something or other was finished, but the ploughing and the harrowing, and the mowing, so far as the garden was concerned, was never finished. All of them, though, when a drought was over the land, and fields and the country around were brown and bare, would turn in wonder and admiration to the garden.

"Come out here", Titt would enthuse to despondent neighbours, dropping in to ease their minds of their worries, and leading them through the house into the garden, would point to the beds of blooming roses and carnation and sunflowers and things, wagging their dainty heads in defiance of the weather. "Look at that! In the middle of all your drought! Ain't that beautiful? Ain't it!— eh? Shows what can be done with water, and a bit o' brains, no matter how dry it is; don't it, eh?"

And when the neighbours would shake their heads in admiration, and ask Titt if he had done it all himself, he many times wished he could truthfully answer in the affirmative.

"My gad, no!" he'd chuckle; "like yourselves, I've hardly time to finish my breakfast as a rule; Araluen's our gardener. But when she works at it, I'm blowed if I could tell you! I think she must get up in the middle of the night and get at it."

Splinter, too, when dressed up on Sundays, to go out riding (when there was a horse fit to ride), with a meaning grin, would ask Araluen, "how th' garden was getting on?" Then he'd saunter leisurely into it, have a good look around, and taking French leave, would cut a bunch of the best blooms to take to his "girl". But Splinter in his indifferent, flippant way, didn't grant Araluen so much credit for the garden as her father did. Araluen discovered that sin of omission in her brother the first time Splinter brought his "girl" to the home. After kissing Mrs. Duff and Araluen, and taking off her hat, the young lady went into raptures about Splinter's manly qualities, and his good looks, and the "funny way he had of saying everything", and said "there was one thing before everything else that she particularly wanted to see, before she returned home—and that was his garden!"

"Oh, my!" and the look of incredulity Mrs. Duff gave Araluen was enough to convict Splinter of perjury and breach of promise. But Araluen was ever a loyal sister.

"And you shall see it, Julia," she said, "as soon as you have had a cup of tea, but it's not looking so well now as it was a few weeks ago."

"Oh-h!" Julia gushed, "the great bunches of beautiful roses! And the carnations! And the sweet peas he brings me! However does he manage to grow them through such dry weather? That's what none of us can ever understand. Father thinks Splinter must be wonderful—a real genius on the land."

Mrs. Duff assured her that Splinter was going to be a splendid farmer, then deserting Araluen, she hurried to the kitchen, promptly closed the door, and let her mirth go till Bluey started barking through the window at her.

But on this afternoon Araluen's mind was not running on
the garden or what was growing there. She moved moodily
around the beds, stooped to pull a casual weed, took up the
fork, dug for a moment or two, then stood the implement in
the ground, plucked a pink rose, fastened it in the bosom of
her dress, and, hardly knowing why, stood scanning a clump
of box trees afar off to the eastward in the wide lane that led
to the township. It was while gazing at these box trees the
previous afternoon at about the same hour that her eyes
chanced to rest on a horseman emerging from them—a horseman that turned out, as he came nearer, to be Sam Jackson.
Sam, having heard of Titt's illness, came along to see Splinter
and to ask about the invalid. He saw Araluen as well as
Splinter, and remained for tea. And now, as Araluen turned
her eyes to the road winding out of those box trees, the smile
that dimpled her cheeks revealed a secret. No moving object
taking shape, she turned away, and taking up the fork again,
commenced digging in earnest, picturing in her mind the bed
of pansies that would bloom and flourish there in days to be.
So absorbed did she become in her work and her flower-
dreams, that she failed to hear the garden gate being shoved
open, and heavy footsteps coming along the crude gravel path,
and dug on, unconscious that Moneygrub Garr, with a grass
stem hanging loosely in his teeth and an ugly accusing leer on
his scowling face, was standing beside her.

"You seem very busy", he sneered.

Araluen let fall the fork with fright.

"Oh!" she cried, staggering on to the dug ground, and facing
him, "it's you—Mr. Garr!"

"Yes, it's me! "and he glared at her in savage silence.

"Do you want to see—Splinter—or anyone, Mr. Garr?" in
a halting, trembling voice from Araluen.

"No! I don't want to see Splinter or anyone!" he barked. "I
want to see you. . . You played a rotten game on me last week!
Had me sitting in the house waiting for you to come back from
Weeviltopps', like a d—— fool, while you were in your room
laughing at me!"

"Oh, please forgive me—I really didn't—er—mean anything to——"

"No, you didn't mean anything," he hissed; "d——young flirts like you never do mean anything!"

"Please go now, Mr. Garr", and Araluen found her courage. "You've said enough—go before I scream for my brother!"

"Your brother! . . . I'll go when I've settled with you!" and he grabbed hold of her.

Araluen screamed, struck, scratched, and struggled to free herself from his grip. But her puny efforts were in vain; she was as a dove held in the coils of a serpent.

Just then, as though he had dropped from a flying machine, Sam Jackson came over the garden fence like a kangaroo, and throwing himself on Moneygrub, seized him with both hands by the throat. Instantly the other released his hold of Araluen and closed with Sam. Sam's heart was in the right place, but Moneygrub had all the weight and age and savagery. Both fell and rolled amongst the roses—Moneygrub on top, roaring like an enraged bull. Araluen, in the hope that Splinter and Old Fred, returning with their last load, might be within hearing, screamed her hardest. Splinter and Old Fred, as it happened, were not within hearing; but Johnny Crosscutt and Jimmy Shuttlewood and Danny Jones, riding by in hopes of catching a glimpse of herself, were. Johnny and Jimmy wheeled their horses to the wire fence, dismounted hurriedly, and ran full split for the garden. Danny thought to outdo his companions, rushed his mount at the fence to jump it. But the old bob-tail creamy had only been accustomed to facing logs and gullies. He stopped "dead", and Danny went over his head on to the fence. His two big feet got twisted in the top wires, and there he hung—his head touching the ground, like an old-man kangaroo.

But Johnny and Jimmy were, in themselves, sufficient reinforcements. Taking the garden fence in their stride, they were beside Araluen in a twinkle. Araluen shrieked, "He's killing Sam!" and indicated the struggle going on under the rose bushes.

"Moneygrub!" they both yelled. Then on to his back, regardless of rose-thorns, they sprang like a pair of tigers. It was a bad moment for Garr. To those bush striplings the chance of a lifetime had come. They tore him from Sam;

belted, butted into him, played havoc with his clothes, threw
him heavily every time he tried to rise, and put the boot into
him; and only that Araluen, taking fresh alarm, appealed to
them to desist and let him go about his business, awkward consequences might have ensued.

"Just th' cove we've always been wantin' to give a good
lambacin' too," they foamed, when Moneygrub, bleeding and
battered, dragged himself out of the gate and laboured for the
road, where his horse and sulky were standing. "But what did
the old dawg tackle you for, Sam?" they added eagerly, "what
was the matter?"

But before Sam or Araluen could explain, yells for deliver-
ance from Danny reached their ears.

"Cripes!" they cried, "what's up with Danny?" and back
over the palings they bounded again. When they saw the
ridiculous plight Danny was in, they burst into mirth—a
mirth that was resented by a round of profanity from Danny.

"Why th' devil couldn't y' come and let a bloke out before?"
he complained when they lifted him up and released him from
the entanglement.

"Because we were stoushing old Moneygrub", they answered, excitedly. "He had Sam Jackson down in Duff's
garden, and was strangling him! By gee, we gave him hell!
. . . . Look at th' blood from him!" and with pride they displayed their blood-stained shirt sleeves.

"Where is he? I must have a cut at the cow!" and glaring
round, Danny saw Moneygrubb Garr, like a wounded beast,
crawling into his sulky. Along the fence he rushed and reached
the sulky just as Moneygrub started the horse going.

"You ugly old dawg!" Danny, running beside the step,
called to him, "come down outer that and I'll settle y' myself!"

Moneygrub, who still had some life in him, leaned over and
slashed the whip fiercely across Danny's face: then applied it
to the horse.

"Hell!" Danny shrieked, and instantly buckling himself up,
sprinted his best; and Danny at his best was like a shot out of a
gun for fifty yards. Past the horse's flank he flashed, then up
to its neck. Shouts of laughter from Johnny and Jimmy rang
after him; and Araluen and Sam, watching from the garden,

There 'Midst the Fragrance of Blooms and Blossoms, He Spoke of Love

wondered what was going to happen. Placing his right hand on the animal's mane, with his left, Danny slipped the winkers off its head! Then dropping out of the race, he sank down as the affrighted animal propelled Moneygrub along that lane at a mad break-neck gallop.

Riding off together again, Johnny, Jimmy and Danny agreed that while they "didn't mind being beaten for Araluen by a decent bloke like Sam Jackson, they'd sooner be all hung together at the end of a bit of greenhide, than let a rich dawg like Moneygrub get her".

And that evening, when tea was over—when Splinter and Old Fred had expressed their scorn for Moneygrub Garr, and solemnly decreed never more to leave Araluen alone on the farm, she and Sam went out into the garden again. There, 'midst the fragrance of blooms and blossoms, surrounded by the soft murmuring of the night breeze in the trees under an archway of running roses, in the presence of the silvery moon, they held each other's hand and spoke of love, of truth, of life; and as the moon shone down upon them in all the brightness of its orb, they kissed their first kiss, a long, warm kiss, an old, old kiss.

25. *The Great Harvest*

Like snakes emerging from their winter sleep in new skins, the man on the land, after slaving all down the years through cycles of bad seasons for nothing in return, and slaving again through good ones for the benefit of the middleman, began to wake up and shed his ancient suicidal ways in favour of reforms and united methods, promulgated by a few revolutionary spirits that had suddenly risen from the ashes of their fathers, and the "temple of their gods". Too long had the easy-going, dependent, short-sighted, mortgage-bound old "cockie" been the silent victim of the city exploiter; too long had he been the blind man in the game of industrial "bluff", too long had he been the dupe of braying politicians and paid scribes. And so now the worm was turning.

The farmer, grey and bent, and broken, as most of him was, tired of fighting in the camp of his foes—weary of trying to gather grapes of thorns and figs of thistles, was at last awakening. He was realising the fool, the flat, the dumb-driven mule, he had been all the years—years when it only wanted a feed of thistles to make him a real donkey, with long ridiculous ears, and a stripe down the back! That he never before woke up to the arrant folly of claiming no real voice in the law-making of his country, in the shaping of market prices for what he produced by the sweat of his brow, and made his own; that he had never realised it was the simple difference between the prices he had been paid for his produce and the prices in all reason and justice he should have been paid but wasn't that had kept his nose to the grind-stone, his neck in a mortgage, and his family in slavery all down those hopeless, hapless years, was now a matter of stupendous wonder to him. And the slow awakening of the man on the land was the quickening of a young nation.

The bread question had assumed serious aspects— there was a world's shortage of wheat, and Government for the first time in the history of the State, as an inducement to the farmer to step out and save the situation, guaranteed the price of wheat at 9/- a bushel.

Talk about a stir! You'd think the millennium had come. The public announcement of that guarantee started the farmers of Emu Creek going like alarm clocks. Never before was so much activity seen there. All the ploughs in the district, heavy and light, up-to-date and obsolete, were set going, and all the horses, draught and saddle, old and young, were yoked to them. Old lucerne paddocks, sheep paddocks, neglected gardens, and waste patches, and every available inch of land were marked out for the plough.

Concentrating all their efforts on the land, Titt and Splinter went at it like tigers. There was no delaying—no stopping every moment to tie a rein, or tighten a bolt, or to oil something that didn't want oiling; no watching the roads to see who was passing; no leaving the team and strolling lazily to the house to fill the water bag or to get some matches, or something. They kept their eyes on the neighbours nearby, and setting the pace, made a race of it. Everyone made a race of it. Like shearers cutting for the biggest tally those farmers raced each other to see who would put the largest area under crop and finish first. And they raced against time and against weather and equipments. Those fortunate enough to possess steam-power or abundance of horse-power, worked by moonlight and starlight, as well as by daylight; but the want of "horse-flesh" was a brake on the will and energy of most.

"By strike," Splinter used to say to Old Fred, when a family of emus would go striding along the fences, "pity we couldn't yoke forty or fifty of those beggars to the ploughs, or put 'em in th' harrows to make a team for you."

Then encouraged by a approving nod from Old Fred, he'd shout, "Heigh!" across the field to his parent.

Thinking something had gone wrong Titt would suddenly stop his team, and putting his ear to the wind would yell back: "What?"

"There's some good plough horses for y' ", Splinter, indicating the birds, would laugh.

"Good grandmothers", and grunting to himself, Titt would start his team again.

Taffey Corrigan, a bachelor, who kept more horses on his place than he had work for, told Titt over the fence one morning when he (Taffey) wasn't quite sober, that he could have the use of two of the best, if he went for them. Titt, before Taffey had time to get sober, went for them. Then with the help of an old stager of his own, he made up a team for Old Fred, and started him off tramping behind the harrows.

Then there was activity! Such a sight as three teams operating in the field at once had never been seen on "Coondalloo" before. Up and down and round about they went—Titt going one way, Splinter another and Old Fred a course of his own. And from 8 a.m. till 4 p.m., they kept going almost without cessation. Titt believed in only "one yoke". Unyoking at midday for dinner and a spell, and continuing again till night, Titt reckoned meant loss of time and extra work.

And when the whole of "Coondalloo" was turned over and harrowed up, the chance of leasing an abandoned farm of 160 acres, from the bank, came Titt's way, and he promptly seized it. Then into that farm he and Splinter and Old Fred went with their teams, and ploughed and harrowed it all, too.

Three hundred acres were ready when seeding-time came, and the horses and men had still a "kick" left in them. Then came fresh problems. What varieties of wheat to sow? When and how to sow? Would he start and sow some of it "dry", or would he wait till there was rain? These were questions that now confronted Titt! They were questions, too, upon which every farmer in the district had doubts and differences. All of them at some time or other, and under some conditions or other, had obtained good, bad, and indifferent results from all the best known varieties of wheat. They had known every variety to fail, and every variety to succeed. Their early wheat one year was a success, and their late wheat a failure. Their late wheat some other year was a success, and their early wheat a despicable failure. From deep-ploughed land they had harvested heavy crops, and from land that was prepared with only a springtooth cultivator, they harvested nothing. Another year they reaped heavy yields from land that had only been "scratched with a cultivator", and the grain that was sown in the deep-ploughed fields didn't come up. All of them had, at some time or other, sown "dry" and got splendid "strikes", and on other occasions had sown "dry" and didn't get any strike. All of them had sown without "pickling", and never got any rust; and again had sown without "pickling", and "got full of rust". All of them had known every variety to "stool out" beautifully, and had known every variety not to stool out worth tuppence. They had known every variety to escape frost and every variety to get "hit up" with it; had known every variety to take rust and smut, and to have "white lead"; and every variety to pan out well-filled and free of rust and everything else. And to make matters worse, there was no Solomon anywhere in the district for Titt, or anyone else, to appeal to. True a "State Department" existed with a number of "experimental farms" and agricultural colleges under its control, where students, whose parents could afford it, were taught to dress smartly and polish their boots before putting them on, and brand pigs, and white-wash cow bails, and where good and popular spreads were prepared for "distinguished visitors", and wonderful results obtained from the farms by manuring them with bank notes and overdrafts, and the whole lot cheerfully presided over by a Minister for Agriculture. But that was all. So nothing startling was to be gained by seeking advice in that quarter.

"I don't think I would sow before rain came", Mrs. Duff suggested, "and I'd sow several kinds of wheat when I did sow."

Splinter reckoned he'd sow before rain came because it could then be planted deeper and cleaner, and quicker, and would come up evenly when the rain came—if ever it did come—and "you could be in bed listenin' to it fallin' on the roof, an' be warm an' happy, instead of jumpin' up in the dark to find th' horses and go muckin' round the fields with th' drill, n' comin' in again all wet and with enough mud hangin' to your boots to sprain your ankles with."

"But what if the rain doesn't come?" his mother suggested;

"or if only just enough to germinate the seed, and then it dies off?"

"Then it will be all up with it", Splinter admitted.

"Ah, well", Titt drawled, coming at last to a decision. "I'll leave it to the last penny I have in the world to decide: 'heads we sow dry, tails we sow wet'." And he tossed the brownie into the air.

"Tails! A wet sowing!" Splinter cried, picking up the coin. And a wet sowing it was.

"Now for the sort of wheat to put in", and Titt wrote the name of nine varieties on three separate slips of paper, three names on each slip, and placing them in Old Fred's hat, invited Mrs. Duff to draw one of them. She drew one, on which was written, "Allera Spring", "Gluya", and "Bungee", then got excited about her chances.

"Fancy that!" she exclaimed "the very three I have always been saying you should plant. Isn't that curious?"

"Just a coincidence", Titt remarked.

"There must have been something more than coincidence in it", Mrs. Duff claimed. "I'm sure there must."

"I often heer'd y' tellin' him to sow 'Gluya' and 'Allera Spring' ", Old Fred remembered.

"And 'Bungee' too," Mrs. Duff insisted—"Didn't I?" and she appealed to Titt.

"You did, Kit", he confirmed. "But perhaps you watched me writing down the names?"

"There!" and she struck her breast ."As sure as I'm living, I didn't."

Splinter, who had silently been examining the "voting papers", suddenly discovered that they all had "Allera Spring", "Gluya" and "Bungee" written on them. Then, with a loud laugh, Titt fled from Mrs. Duff, who pursued him through the house with the yard broom.

To the joy and excitement of all, rain came at the right time; and it kept on raining till the land was soaked—kept on till it was flooded—kept on till people grew weary, and sick, and tired of rain, and began to get alarmed lest it would never stop. But one day, thank goodness, it eased off; and the weather cleared and remained fair till all the grain was sown, and the drills returned to the shelter sheds. Then it rained again, and cleared up again; rained some more, cleared some more, and kept on raining and clearing, raining and clearing, till agricultural areas, far and white, were awave with wheat and barley and oats, the like of which had never been seen before on Emu Creek, or any other creek.

Titt's three hundred acres were perfection—they were pictures for a painter. And how he guarded those wheat paddocks! How he strolled along the headlands from day to day, from week to week, watching to see if the crop was "stooling out"—watching it emerging into shot-blade, from shot-blade into flower and from flower to grain, and then anxiously watching for signs of rust, and hoping to God there would be no late frosts!

Ah! those are the exciting moments in the life of the wheat grower!—moments when he realises how recklessly he is gambling with frost and caterpillar, rust, smut, storm, flood, Heaven, Hell, and Earth!

And when the crop began to "turn" and harden, how Titt and Old Fred and Splinter, and all the family, would poke amongst it, sampling it—plucking ears, measuring the length of them, and shelling them in the palm of their hands to estimate the probable yield! Ten, eleven, and as high as twelve bags to the acre, they repeatedly concluded. Titt always smiled and shook his head, and said, "He'd be satisfied with eight—twenty-four hundred bags at nine bob a bushel would do him."

And when the first field had nearly ripened, how eagerly the reaper and binder was taken from the shed and transported to the paddock! And how all the family gathered round to wait and watch if the machine would start working without giving any trouble! There had been occasions in the past when all sorts of mishaps took place and all manner of things went wrong before a start could be effected. The "knotter" wouldn't "knot" — or the knife wouldn't cut or would break—or a cog would slip—or the driving chain come off—or something wouldn't be "put on right"—and much time and "language" would be wasted trying to locate the trouble and fix it up, or waiting for an "expert" to arrive to do it. As a last resource,

Titt, like everybody else in the same fix, used to wire for an expert. And when that "genius amongst machinery" would arrive per train or sulky or "footback", he'd stand scratching his head and gazing at the binder with a heavy frown on his perspiring brow. Suddenly inspired, he'd look in the twine box to see if they had been trying to make her bind without twine. If the twine was in its place, which, of course, it mostly was, he'd unthread the needle and thread it again the same way that it was threaded before, and mumble. "Too much tension! —too much tension!" After that he'd nose round the "knotter" and scrape the dust off it and put some oil on it, and condemn the oil, and recommend some other brand to Titt. Then he'd take off his coat and, if he wasn't too fat—which he mostly was—would crawl right under the machine, and lie there on his back gazing up at the works like a poet looking to the stars for inspiration.

"A wrench!" he would call suddenly; and the rush that Titt and Old Fred and Splinter would make to procure the wrench for him, would make you think he had called for a stick to kill a snake with. Then he'd groan and swear at the flies, and unscrew several nuts, and screw them on again. "I see-e!" he would mutter, meditatively, after a long, anxious silence; "I see-e—", then emit a low, tragic whistle that would fall on Titt's ears like a death-knell. "You'll have to get a new part here; this is worn," he would shout, decisively; "she'll never work the way she is. I wonder you haven't bust her up to blazes!"

After that he'd crawl out again, sigh triumphantly, and wipe the oil and grease from his hands with good ripe ears of wheat, and put on his coat, and look hurriedly at his watch; "I'll wire to them to send you a duplicate as soon as I get back to the township." And away he would drive again, leaving Titt and Old Fred and Splinter scowling at the useless jibbing old binder.

And when that expert reached the township he would perhaps meet some farmer there who wanted to buy a new binder from his firm; and he would promptly invite that farmer to have a drink; and the farmer, who wanted to buy a new binder would invite the expert to drink with him; then they would both drink to each other; then to the success of the new binder, coupled with the names of the great season everyone was having, and the Empire, and the girl behind the bar— and between all the "happy days" and "good lucks" and "prosperous seasons", the wire would be forgotten, until days later, until a telegram from Titt would reach the firm, saying: "No duplicate yet arrived, crop getting destroyed". When at last it would arrive, carefully sewn up in a piece of bagging like a ham, and accompanied by an account, and Titt and Old Fred and Splinter had spent a whole day trying to adjust it to the machine, they would suddenly discover it was a part belonging to a lucerne mower! Then Titt would swear, and heave that duplicate as far as he could heave it, and regret he hadn't punched the expert, fat and old as he was, till nothing of him had been left!

But things were different now. When Splinter climbed into the seat and put the machine in gear, and called to the others to stand clear, and cracked the whip at the horses, the old binder rattled off like a German band, cutting the crop clean, delivering it beautifully, leisurely feeding the rollers, tieing accurately, and throwing the sheaves out like a live thing.

Titt and Old Fred kicked their heels up with joy.

"She's going great!" Titt said—"making a lovely sheaf."

Splinter looked round in his seat and waved the whip by way of congratulations. Mrs. Duff and Araluen waved back and smiled. Then Titt and Old Fred bent their backs and started stooking. For days and weeks—from morning till night under a flaming noonday sun, in the cool of the evening breeze they followed after that old binder, stooking, stooking, and "keeping the way clear for her".

Providence this time was surely watching over the man on the land. Not a drop of rain fell while the crops were down. And weeks later when all the stuff had been carted off the fields, and stacked, what a sight Coondalloo presented! Rows of bright new stacks looming in the distance like the Pyramids could be seen for miles. There they stood in grand manifestation of the wealth to be wrung from the soil when all things are favourable and the seasons pregnant with rains. All that was required now was the thrasher. And the thrasher, with the host of men who followed it from farm to farm, and all the worry and excitement of preparing and cooking for them wasn't far off. All day long a cloud of dust and chaff flying from the machine could be seen at Drygrass's; while the droning and buzzing of it all came floating in waves upon the wind.

Every now and again Mrs. Duff or Araluen would go to the verandah to see if they had "commenced on Drygrass's last stack", then anxiously hope they wouldn't "finish before Sunday". To have the "thrashers" on your hands over Sunday was tragedy. Everyone—especially mothers and daughters—longed for them to come on Monday, put the stacks through, clean up, pull out and take themselves off before Sunday. Men on thrashers are always hungry men, often crabby men, and mostly fault-finders; and how much to cook, how many to cook for, and what to cook for them are fitful nightmares to the women of the farms. And the men themselves, even though they may never have been on the thrasher before, always seemed to know beforehand the places that "tuckered well", from those that didn't. And when they "pulled in" to a farm that "tuckered well" they were never in a hurry to pull out again; and if it came on to rain they were always pleased to throw the tarpaulins over the stacks and camp in the huts and barns, turning up regularly for meals, until the weather broke again. But whether it broke the day after or a week after never concerned them.

And one morning, at 9 o'clock, when the engine's whistle was heard, announcing the thrashing at Drygrass's had finished, and Mrs. Duff and Araluen flew excitedly to the kitchen and started rattling pots and pans, you'd have thought it was the Royal Family they were expecting.

Splinter was rushed off in the sulky to the township for supplies of bread and meat; Old Fred told off to put on an outside fire, and to see to wood and water, while Titt on pins and needles lest the gateway might prove too narrow to admit the machine, and a panel of the fence had to be taken down, was called upon to ascertain the number of men who would be sitting to dinner. At intervals, Natt and Jimmie, perched on either post, watching the plant approaching, would scramble to the ground and rush inside to inform their mother that it was "comin' across th' gully" or was "just down at th' corner", and increase her excitement.

At last the "puff—puff—puff" of the grimy old engine could be heard outside on the road. Next minute, with the lumbering plant trailing behind it, and boisterous, dusty-looking men and their swags perched all over it, it rumbled through the gate and headed for the rows of wheat stacks. Hardly had it drawn up amongst them when, manned by all hands, it was set in position. Then the engine whistled again, and every man fell into his allotted place; "outside" shirts were discarded, pitchforks gleamed, the engine started, the belt flew round, the thrasher rattled and hummed, sheaves started flying from the stack, a whirl of dust went up, chaff flew with the wind, the straw went climbing up the elevator and toppling over, and into the bags poured the plump golden grain, like streams of water.

"And how is it going?" Mrs. Duff inquired, when the men knocked off and came in for dinner.

"Splendid, Missus," they said; "the best we've struck yet, if it's all as good as what we've put through this morning."

It was all as good—some of it better. And when the last stack was put through, and the final whistle sounded, Old Fred and Splinter counted 3000 bags.

A parting lunch, and the men collected their belongings, tossed them on to the machine again, climbed up themselves, found seats wherever they could, and the lumbering thrasher went on its way whistling a warning to the next farm.

Then Titt and Mrs. Duff, while the children in proud delight clambered all over it, stood in silent admiration beside that imposing stack of grain piled high, sack upon sack. The sound of the departing thrasher rumbling along the black soil lane was no longer distinguishable. In deep reflection they gazed on the great harvest. A vista of the past—of those years of loss and failure, disappointment and gloom, came vividly to their minds, then quickly faded away. Bright sunshine lit up their faces, and in the light of their eyes, animated with the joy of triumph, was reflected the dawning of prosperity.

And in the years that followed, the days of the Duffs were days of joy and plenty; were as the butterflies that drifted by and the flowers that garlanded the hills and headlands.

The Romance of Runnibede

Author's Note to First Edition

I am indebted to my parents, who resided on the Balonne River, Queensland, during the early 50's, for the various incidents and impressions gleaned from them during my boyhood days, which now appear in these pages. And also for the kindly help given by my friend W.H. when writing "The Romance of Runnibede".

Steele Rudd

Introduction to the University of Queensland Press Edition

This, his second last book, my father commenced in 1925. He was running *Steele Rudd's Magazine* at the time from an office fronting the footpath in John Mills Himself building at the upper end of Charlotte Street, Brisbane; it still stands. It was there that his sub-editor, Winifred Hamilton, encouraged him to press on with this novel, particularly during those not infrequent times of depressed state of mind when he was inclined to forgo any further effort towards completion of it. He subsequently recorded his appreciation to "W.H." for her assistance in the foreword.

In 1931 she wrote:

I was fortunate in being privileged to read *The Romance of Runnibede* chapter by chapter as it came from his pen, and today, six years later, I feel justified in thinking it will stand as great a book and as true a story of Australian life as was *On Our Selection* [Steele Rudd's first book in 1899 — in all he wrote twenty-four books].

In *Runnibede* the writer chose a totally different side of Australian life, though it is a life he knows if possible even better than that of the *Selection*. "Runnibede" is a cattle station of wide extent occupied by an English family — a strikingly different type of family to the "Rudds", and the writer's absorption of this life in his work bears fine fruit here.

What he knows of horses does justice to the horses in a manner vastly more interesting to the true horse lover than D. H. Lawrence ever did in *The Boy in the Bush*.

And what Steele Rudd knows of cattle is an eye opener. And what he knows of the Aboriginal is amazing and is intensely vivid. In *Runnibede* he still gives rein to his ironic humour, but breaks out in a new way, pictorially and philosophically.

On Our Selection was the work of a comparatively immature man, whereas *Runnibede* shows all the breadth, and the thought and memories of youth portrayed by maturity, and to that extent is a bigger, better thing than the work which played, to a great extent, a part in putting Australia on the literary map. I think *Runnibede* truly reflects the colour of Australian life as it was lived on a cattle station some fifty years ago. Upon *On Our Selection* and *The Romance of Runnibede* he will probably be judged . . .

This book of father's was a complete departure from his earlier *Selection* characterizations of incidents around the Queensland farming communities. In *Runnibede,* as he referred to it, he found a new theme in the domain of the larger property holdings on which he had worked as a stockman in his early teens.

The incidents relating to the Aborigines, as they appear, allowing for literary embellishment, stem largely from stories told him by his father and mother (my grandparents). And in this regard he drew upon his remarkable, retentive memory to pen picture some happenings.

Both my grandparents, Thomas and Mary Davis, had had very early associations with and recollections of the pioneering days on the Balonne, Maranoa, and the Dawson Rivers districts of southern Queensland; and as a result of their close associations with the Aborigines both of them could speak and understand the tribal dialects of the natives of those vast areas, then only very sparsely inhabited by white settlers.

Grandmother is credited with being the first white woman in Surat, arriving there as a seventeen-year-old bride in 1852 with grandfather by bullock dray after their marriage in Drayton by that celebrated pioneer clergyman the Reverend B. Glennie. In the Balonne district the Aborigines affectionately called grandmother "White Mary".

In those days the areas mentioned were included in the northwestern section of New South Wales and known as the "Never-Never". Queensland became a crown colony in 1859.

Several foolscap pages of Aboriginal words and their meanings of tribal dialects written by grandfather Thomas Davis are now in the care of the Royal Queensland Historical Society at Newstead House, Brisbane. A more voluminous manuscript of his on Aboriginal folklore and word meanings was unfortunately destroyed when "Shingle Hut", the original family home on the "old Selection" at Emu Creek, East Greenmount on the Darling Downs, Queensland, was burnt down in the middle nineties.

Most of the material of *Runnibede* went through the columns of *Steele Rudd's Magazine* in Brisbane up to the end of 1925. During 1926 in Sydney it appeared in *Steele Rudd's and The Shop Assistants' Magazine,* a periodical my father edited on a joint ownership basis.

In 1927 Mr. Fred Phillips, a bustling American businessman, arrived in Sydney with his mind set on putting Australia on the map in the film industry. Phillips Film Productions Ltd. was formed with the paramount objective of making and producing films in Australia featuring the works of Australian writers. Steele Rudd became a shareholder, being largely influenced by an agreement made with the promoters to feature *The Romance of Runnibede* as its first production.

As the film featured scenes which included numbers of Aborigines, permission was obtained from the Queensland government to shoot scenes at the Barambah Mission Station (now Cherbourg Aboriginal Settlement) outside the town of Murgon in the south Burnett district of Queensland.

Miss Eva Novak, then a leading American film actress, was brought to Australia (at considerable expense it was subsequently known) to take the leading female role of Dorothy in the production.

The formation of this company and the decision to film *Runnibede* evidently appeared enterprising enough to my father at the time, but alas! it was the rock on which he perished — financially. He was induced to put into it his very limited resources. Of course he was always a keen protagonist for Australia's making and exhibiting its own films, and always forthright in his views against the tremendous hold that American interests had on the industry.

Despite filled theatres, in a somewhat limited exhibiting circuit, the venture failed for reasons too many to expound upon here.

Reviewing the book in February 1928, the Sydney *Bulletin* said (in part): "Without excluding the vein of humour that is peculiarly his own the popular creator (Steele Rudd) of 'Dad' and his family (of the 'Selection' series) has treated the characters in the present novel in more serious mood. The days he pictures, and the types that filled them are undergoing the process film folk describe as 'the fade away'. 'Runnibede' will do something to preserve the fine pioneering tradition. Quite as good as any piece of work the author has submitted for the past 20 years; vibrant with life and rich in local colour . . . "

In his agreement with the New South Wales Bookstall Company dated 12 December 1927 father sold the book publishing rights for £150, but retained the picture and dramatic rights.

ERIC DAVIS
BRISBANE
JUNE 1974

Chapter 1

I remember well when father selected Runnibede for a cattle run. A great run it was, too, a hundred thousand acres — stretches of sheltered valleys and scrubs, lofty ranges and wide grass plains. To the north loomed the Great Dividing Range; on the south the winding, bending Condamine, and most of it watered by creeks, lagoons, and great waterholes that never went dry — so father and others reckoned. The homestead, then, was different to what it is today — rougher and wilder, and more romantic. The "big house", as it was called, with father's office at the end of a wide, high verandah, was walled and floored with dressed slabs — wonderful slabs they were, too; and the roof was covered with stringy bark. The "store" and butcher's shop and men's huts were of similar architecture, and standing in a row amongst the wild limes and brigalow, looked like a lost township of primitive days. And the cattle yards that Sam Mann and Bill Hawkes erected on the bank of the station creek — all made of round saplings — I remember well. They have crumbled and rotted away since then, and only a few shaky panels are standing now.

But the wide-spreading wild fig tree that stood between the wings of the old yard thrives the same as ever. And how the tired, sun-baked stockmen used to gather in the shade of it when the breaking, rushing, crushing mobs were safely yarded, to lunch on damper and steaming billy tea. Splendid horsemen and cattlemen were those old stockmen — reckless, cheerful prodigals for the most part! And tossing junks of damper to each other, as they knelt round the "hamper", what accounts they had to tell of the gallops and spills and escapes they had in the muster! And carved with pocket knives and skinning knives on the trunk of the fig tree are still to be seen the crude initials of most of them — or what is left of the initials, for the bark has long since grown over, leaving but the scars, Ned Kearney and Jack Holloway are the only two I know of living now; the others all are gone — buried in different parts of Runnibede — and passing drovers will tell you that, when on their lonely night watches round the resting, silent mobs, they often see them—

> "Seeing their faces stealing, stealing,
> Hearing their laughter pealing, pealing,
> Watching their grey forms wheeling, wheeling,
> Round where the cattle lie."

Drovers used to say that in the weird wailings of the curlew and the plover they could discern the voices of the lonely dead souls of the bushland. I remember them telling this to father, one morning at the store, while getting a supply of rations from him.

"What!" he laughed. "Curlews and plovers the reincarnation of dead stockmen? My gosh, imagine Bill Bent, who broke his neck on Hodgson's Creek, with the thick legs and raucous voice he had, turning into a curlew! If poor old Bill ever turns into anything other than a fat, red worm, it'll be into a scrub bull."

Father — or as the station hands called him — "The Governor" — was an Englishman, with all his hopes of treasure in Australia, and his heart in England. A good style of man the Governor was — in build neither thick nor thin; a shaved chin and "muttonchop" whiskers; ruddy complexion, cheerful, generous, and, in a quiet way, daring as the devil. He was schooled at Eton, and like most well-educated men, his intellectual gifts were mediocre. Sometimes he talked about books and literature, sometimes of politics, but more often it was about prices of cattle or sport. An incurable optimist the Governor was, full of theory and ideas. But his ideas were mostly English — so was his seat in the saddle. The English in a saddle are "players to the gallery", and little better than gymnasium riders. Maybe one in a thousand could be called a horseman in the Australian bush. Like most of the pioneer squatters, the Governor plunged into Australian station life without any knowledge of the Australian bush, or of its moods and changes, and so he had a lot to learn — and he learnt it.

Whenever the mails reached Runnibede — the mailman only happened along at irregular intervals — the Governor would hurry away to his office and shut himself up with the newspapers — most of them English periodicals, back numbers half a year old. And often on reading of the happenings to people or friends known to him far over the sea, he would put the paper down and lose himself in meditation, until mother, perhaps, would seek him out with a sheaf of closely written and cross-written letters in her hand to communicate their contents to him. She, too, was English and educated; and in her heart, even more than any other, she showed a tendency to fret for old associations and friends, and to weary of the isolation and loneliness that the new life on Runnibede brought to her.

"And are we always going to remain here in this Australian bush, Edward?" she would sigh as she folded the letters again and gazed out at the belts of brigalow on the distant landscape.

"Not on your life, my dear", the Governor would assure her. "Cattle will become gold mines here directly — most of them are animated nuggets now. And in a year or two, we'll be able to spare a thousand or so on a trip back to London to see them all again."

"I hope so, Edward."

"There's no need to 'hope', Dorrie, my dear — it's as sure as night follows day and day follows night — which seems something of a paradox."

"In any case, Edward," she would remind him in her soft, appealing way, "the boys and Dorothy will be sent home to be properly educated when they are old enough, won't they?" (The "boys" were Ted, ten years; myself, twelve; and Dorothy was eight.)

"My good woman," and the Governor would pat her on the head, "what else do you think I'll do with them — send them to the blacks' camp down the river to have 'King Sandy' and his tribe of linguists put the finishing touches on them? They shall go to Eton, where their father put in a number of joyful, unproductive years, my dear; and we shall both go with them to witness their enrolment."

Whatever anxiety mother might have felt at such moments would soon be dispelled, and next minute she would be heard humming airs in her room or talking happily with the governess, or Mrs. Channing in the kitchen. But what a woman mother was! If beauty, combined with gentleness of manner, sympathy and kindness, were qualities that went to make a lady, then she was truly one. More practical-minded than the Governor, yet while having confidence enough in his plans for the future, she knew that high spirits and optimism alone would not turn mobs of cattle into profit or secure a bank overdraft.

And now I remember the first draft — two thousand head of young steers the Governor bought. (Till then the run was carrying eight hundred breeding cows and their progeny only). What station the steers came off I don't remember, but the Governor paid two pounds a head for them through the bank, and John Strean was the drover in charge. When word came in that the mob was coming up the Condamine and had crossed Myall creek, Joe Eustace, the head stockman, was sent to meet them, and I went with him, as proud as a prince, on a little grey mare called Whitewings. Next morning the Governor, with mother beside him in the trap, drove out to inspect the mob on the run.

"What are they like, Eustace?" he asked, as the latter, in a few short, sharp props, reined up beside the trap.

"Not bad stuff, Governor — some good growers — a few brindles among them."

"What should they be worth in a couple of years, Eustace?"

"A couple of years?" And the head stockman pulled thoughtfully at his horse's mane, and toyed the stirrup irons with the toes of his boots. "That's pretty hard to say . . . they might be worth a fiver . . . and they might be all dead by that time! Depends on the seasons."

"The seasons will be all right", the Governor chuckled confidently, and starting the trap again, drove rapidly around the mob and interviewed the drover.

And while they talked mother sat silently reflecting on Eustace's words: "They all might be dead by that time."

Returning to the homestead the Governor was elated.

"Five pounds a head in two years means a profit of six thousand my dear ... the natural increase on the run by that time will leave another four thousand, about ten thousand in five years ... in twenty years, an Australian cattle king and millionaire — a blooming multi-millionaire, Dorrie."

"Then, Edward, you don't think what Eustace said—"

"To Hong Kong with Eustace. He ought to have his head cut off and given to the blacks ... why, look it's coming on to rain now, you goose. This bushland is full of rain — it teems with it."

Then giving whip to the horse and echoing at the top of his voice: "Cattle king and millionaire, my dear", the Governor drove over the tufty grasses and round through the undergrowth and clumps of myall like a rising cyclone — at least, he thought he was going like a cyclone. But that's fifty years ago now!

Chapter 2

A year passed and midsummer came. And such a summer! There had been worse ones, I know, numbers of them, but for some reason that summer left a more lasting impression upon my memory than any other. The heat, I remember, was terrific. And the flies and other insect hosts swarmed everywhere. They seemed to come in a night; and you'd think they came to remain for ever. They were insufferable, and savage as bull ants. Everyone so inclined cursed them, and in that way, at least, got some imaginary revenge and relief — but to dumb brutes they were Sheol. No rain had fallen for ten months, and all the fresh running creeks which the Governor and other cheerful optimists predicted would run on and babble musically for ever, were fast giving out and turning into bogs and traps for weak stock. And the big waterholes were getting very low and "sick" on it — so were some of the cattle, for the land was in the initial grip of a drought, and Runnibede already threatened with desolation.

Still, no one was idle, and work went on apace, for the Governor was a goer. If he didn't do a great deal himself, he knew how to get the best out of others, and to get it from them willingly and cheerfully. And so the axe and the maul rang out at different parts of the run to some purpose. A home paddock of three hundred acres, with swing gates painted white, had been fenced off, and only animals that were in work were grazed there. A stable with a loft and outside stalls and a small yard adjoining were added to the improvements. What was to be a "great garden" — the garden of Runnibede — according to the Governor, who never grew tired of rhapsodising over everything that was done, or was going to be done — was laid out in gravel walks — fine gravel it was, too, hauled from the creek's bed with the bullock team — and avenues of trees and rows of hedges. In the centre of it all stood the "big house", which one day, when big cheques began to roll in for fat mobs off Runnibede, was to be rebuilt into a castle of stone, with fittings and furniture all of native timber. Such was the home of the Governor's dreams, and the future home of some of us who had not then been dreamt of. Temporary yards, too, to save time in the musters were erected out on Wallaby Creek, and the fencing of the eastern boundary was in progress. I remember the Governor taking Ted and me out with him one day to see how the men were getting along with it. He wasn't a hard rider on such occasions, just took things easily — it was only when there was something "worth while" that the Governor would shake his mount up and make the pace, and how Ted and I shortened our reins and fidgeted in our saddle whenever an emu or a kangaroo, perhaps a mob of them, started up. If we had had our own way that day we would have given the lot of them the run of their lives, but whenever we shot out in pursuit of something we'd hear the Governor's voice thundering after us to "come back here, you young scoundrels; do you want to break your necks?" But we kids, when across a horse, hadn't time to think of a broken neck. Unless we could keep the animal going like the wind we were never contented. Advice from our elders to "go steady and let the ponies alone" was uncalled for interference by "silly old coves" afraid to put a horse out of a canter, and who didn't want to see anybody else enjoying themselves. That's what we reckoned, but we were truly very young those days, Ted and I.

"And when the eastern boundary is finished," I recollect the Governor telling mother one day, "that'll be the last I'll do in the way of improvements for a while ... the range makes a good enough fence on the northern side, and the stock rarely cross the Condamine on the south — not even now when it's little more than a chain of waterholes. And it doesn't matter about the western end — they may go in that direction as far as they please."

Though wages in those days were about as low as possible

the Governor must have paid out a lot of money for labour before he got the old run into anything like working order. But that didn't worry him — nothing, I fancy, ever worried him much at that time. The Australian bush was all new and strange to him then. It was his Eldorado. Besides, the spirit of romance and adventure was strong in the Governor. But what often makes me wonder now is that he ever got men to do the work at all for him, considering the rough and isolated conditions that prevailed. Still they did it — for him, and what great work they did, too. Some of it has lasted to this day.

A quiet, drowsy afternoon — scarcely any life about the homestead. Only the flies and the wild bees had any life in them. The Governor, with Joe Eustace and Ned Kearney and Warabah, an aboriginal recommended to the Governor by Haly of Taabinga, were out mustering cows towards the Condamine, to wean the calves and give the mothers a chance in the drought. They had been away three or four days, and were expected to return some time that afternoon with the mob. What wouldn't Ted and I, kids and all that we were, have given to be in the muster! But mustering wasn't for us — not then. Instead, we had to go to school, along with Dorothy and Zulu and Tarpot, two ebony-skinned, frizzle-haired aboriginal kids that had become separated from a tribe on the river during a "dispersal" by the police patrol, and to whom mother had taken a fancy. A slab and bark edifice stood about a hundred yards away from the "big house". It was known as the station school, and was furnished with a couple of short desks, blackboards, maps, a globe, just like any other school, and big Miss Mary Rumble, the teacher — Lord, how I remember the old girl, with her red nose, and her white stockings falling over her elastic-side boots! She was also "governess". But why we were kept shut up in that dull school with Mary Rumble trying to hammer things into our heads that didn't matter tuppence to us or to anyone else, while so much excitement was going on outside was something Ted and I couldn't understand . . . It seemed to us that the Governor, mother and the governess hadn't an ounce of sense between them, so far as our interests were concerned! And on this day Ted and I were on pins and needles.

"Ted Winchester!" said big Mary, "you've not done a thing for th' last hour but stare and glare out the window. If you don't pay attention and listen to what I'm saying, I'll tell your father on you when he returns — it's no use telling your mother, she won't believe anything about you."

"I can't look at you, teacher," Ted said to her, hanging his lip, "without seein' the back of Zulu's head!" And Ted's big honest eyes rolled round in their sockets as if they had broken loose.

"You can see over his head very well, if you want to, for he's smaller than you, and he's sitting on a lower seat."

"Yes," Ted admitted, "but there's a great big flea on him, teacher."

That was something Mary Rumble wasn't prepared for.

"A what?" she said, crossing the floor to investigate Zulu.

"There isn't, Miss Rumble, don't you believe him", from Dorothy, who took a delight in helping mother every morning to bath the nigger kids and keep them clean. "It's grasshopper eggs they've been putting in his hair."

As that incriminated me, I invented a charge against Tarpot, who was sitting front, and accused him of "smelling like a dead snake", and holding my nose, turned my head way to emphasise the falsehood.

"That's a fib, teacher", indignantly from Dorothy. "Tarpot smells cleaner than he does", and in proof she put her nose close to Tarpot and sniffed noisily.

"Attention, the lot of you," commanded big Mary, "and don't let me hear any more of your nonsense, me noble Ted and Jim [Jim was my name], or I'll box the ears of the two of you myself, without waiting for your father to do it."

"They want it, too", and Dorothy, sister-like, screwed a mouth at Ted and me. Poor Dorothy! It was only a couple of weeks later when she had to run for her life from the myall trees to the big house to escape from the old black gin — mother of the two abo. kids. Our lessons continued for another hour or so, when the faint echo of a stock whip crack rumbled into the room. Ted caught the sound and looked at me, open-mouthed. I looked quickly at Ted . . .

Two more echoes in quick succession, and sounding nearer.

"That's them!" And Ted and I, disregarding Miss Mary Rumble, cocked our ears and listened.

A volley of stockwhip cracks then rang out, stirring us more than the guns of Waterloo stirred the Brussels ball party. I can see Ted even now, jumping over the desk, and myself jumping after him, and both of us scrambling for our hats.

"Have you young wretches been eating indigo and gone mad, too, like the cattle?" was all I can remember Mary saying as we bounded out the door like brumbies leaving a yard when the rails are thrown down.

"Father said we were to go and meet them", I shouted at her, then off we went to the stable as fast as our legs could take us.

At the stable, their heads hanging dreamily over the stall-rail, were our two ponies, Whitewings and Wallaroo, bridled and saddled and girthed to the last hole. They had been saddled since breakfast, and at invervals during the day when we had asked the governess if we could "please go out", it was to stuff bush hay and more bush hay into those ponies, till sickening of it they turned from it and went to sleep. But, when we rushed under the rail, panting, and started scrambling into the saddles without giving any warning, those ponies woke up with a fright. What they thought for the moment was attacking them goodness only knows; anyway, Wallaroo, with a loud snort, flew round, and with her hindquarters knocked Ted under the rail, while Whitewings stood up on her hind legs and fell back wallop against the wall of the stable. Neither of us was prepared for a reception of that kind from ponies we had been feeding and fondling and galloping about for a year and more. "Hang y'! Don't y' know who I am?" Ted gasped — and, "you little brute, I'll pay y' out when I get on y'!" But the ponies soon took in the situation, and became apologetic and tried to rub their bridles off against our shoulders. Then into the saddles we climbed with fresh haste — but in the excitement, forgot to throw down the stall-rail before mounting, and there we sat for a moment or two, riding as the crowd "ride" on the grandstands at a race meeting. I managed to reach far enough out of the saddle to drop my rail, and out bounded White-wings; and off round the stable and down the home paddock we went, like Dick Turpin and Black Bess. Ted, though, essaying to follow my example, wasn't so successful. Wallaroo jumped back when he reached out for the rail, and he fell over her shoulder on to his head. "Wait, wait for me, Jim", I heard him shout. But I couldn't lose any more time. Besides, I wanted to be the first to meet the mob and do some "stock-riding". All the same, I was scarcely abreast of the cattle yards when I heard him coming in the wake of me, crashing through the broom-bush and stunted wattles, lashing into Wallaroo with the double of a saddle strap, and shouting, "I can see them crossin' the creek!" Up to that I had a pretty good hold of Whitewings, and was keeping a sharp eye on the saplings and overhanging limbs. But when Wallaroo came romping up alongside of me, I let her go. Then neck to neck we raced — and a mad, harum-scarum go it was, but only what you'd expect from a pair of excited kids who were beginning to fancy themselves in the saddle. And knowing really nothing, we didn't fear anything. So we hustled and jostled, and bumped into each other, taking everything before us, and shooting between saplings and solid old gums and coolibahs that might have smashed us to pieces had the ponies misjudged the spaces by a foot between any of them.

Across the point of the sand ridge and past the old sawpit we fairly flew, then rounding the wild lime trees, swooped right in amongst the leaders of the coming mob ... Surprise! Gad! What the old Governor and the stockmen thought when they caught sight of us, I don't know! But I do know that we fouled a number of startled calves that jumped in our way, and only the cleverness of the ponies saved us from coming to grief over the top of them. Then, in our flight we cut off a two-year-old bull, a brindle brute they were bringing in to unsex, that had been breaking from the mob on every opportunity and giving a lot of trouble. He was better conditioned, of course, than the cows, and was pretty flash, and fretting to get back to his own mob — a mixed lot than ran on Dingo Creek, a short branch of the Myall. Anyway, as soon as we dashed between him and the mob he up with his tail and away. Then, to hear the shouts of the Governor and the stockmen! But what they were shouting for we had no idea, and didn't wait to ascertain. We had come to meet them and to do some stock-riding. And here was our chance to show what we were made of. So, lurching the ponies almost off their feet, and in a cloud of dust, we turned at right angles and took after that bull. Then more yells — yells of great profanity went up on the wind, and Eustace and Warabah spurred their horses in pursuit of the bull, and of us. But we wanted no help — we were out to head the brute and return him to the mob alone and unassisted.

Riding wide and all over the ponies, we drew on to him on either side — Ted on the near, and I on the off. Of course, we didn't try to "shoulder" him or go for his tail and try to throw him. Our object was to head him and wheel him back into the mob. As we both drew ahead, we were watching and thinking only of the bull — so were the ponies. And we were indulging in some loud, triumphant shouting; so round in front of him we circled full speed. Then, right under his foaming snout, almost, our mounts collided — bang! bash! like two loco engines . . . I remember being propelled out of the saddle into the air; but after that, nothing, until I found myself lying in bed with mother standing over me, and Ted sitting in a chair with his arm in a sling and a bandage round his head, his bottom lip hanging and his eyes drooping . . . But that was three days later.

Chapter 3

And there were the Channings — old Harry and his wife, the first married couple engaged on Runnibede, and what a lot of years they must have spent there. Old Harry was killed at last, which was just as well, perhaps, by a kick from a horse while nearly blind with sandy blight — Harry, I mean, not the horse. And the missus, as he called her, died shortly after, but not, I fancy, from anything corresponding with grief at the loss of Harry; and though they were on Runnibede for quite half a century, I don't suppose either of them were ever further than the bark of a dog from the smoke of the head station, or ever got on the back of a horse! And Harry, I remember, always counted himself among "bushmen". Yet, I suppose, it would have been hard to class him as anything else, for truly he lived — in a way — and died there — in a rather unusual way. A queer couple if ever there was one. Hired to work for the Governor by Billy Handcock of Drayton, publican, storekeeper, commission agent, and Parliamentarian before separation, the Channings turned up at Runnibede late one evening on a bullock dray. And how excited and brimful they were of adventures with the blacks on the way out! So frightened of their lives had they been that I recollect them telling the Governor they would stay and work on the station for ever, without pay, rather than face a return trip until the bush became civilised. Yet, as time went on and the bush not only became civilised but baptised and colonised as well, old Harry and "the missus" never displayed any inclination to go back, although the Governor gave them their "walking ticket" often enough! Still, Mrs. Channing was a help to mother in the housework, and, in a way, company for her at times. In addition she cooked for the station hands, while Harry chopped wood and brought water, and pottered about the homestead growling and grumbling habitually of the hard work he had to do. But how they did quarrel with each other, that happy married couple. They would engage in real stand-up fights at times, always over paltry, trifling things that mattered little to anyone and often enough they had no idea what they were rowing about themselves . . . Comfortably quartered they were, too, in the kitchen, a detachment of three rooms, connected with the big house by a wide "gangway", shaded with flowering scrub vines.

"Now, Harry," I recollect mother almost pleading one night, while visiting the kitchen to procure some necessity or other before retiring to bed, "I hope you will let Mrs. Channing have a good rest to-night, and don't fight with her any more, like a good man! She worked very hard to-day, and I'm sure she must be tired." Mother, kind soul, ever had a sympathetic thought in her heart for others, and always made allowance for the weaknesses and deficiencies of humans.

"I don't fight with her, ma'am", and Harry, leaning his elbows on the kitchen table, and sucking at a clay pipe as black as the nose of a nigger, stared vacantly at the moths flying about the lamp. "It's herself what does all that."

"Me! Do you say it's me what does it all — and to my mistress's face?" and Mrs. Channing, who had been dropping some salt junk into the pot to soak overnight, flew round and faced her husband . . . Gad! I can see her now glaring at him with fight all over her, and only a thin, bony wizard of a woman she was, too. But mother — she fled, shuffling along the gangway to our living room as fast as her slippers would allow her. There was none who understood the married couple as well as mother.

"I'm sure they'll have another row out there", she confided to the Governor, as she closed the door firmly behind her, to keep the noise out should a row commence.

"Don't mind them, my dear, don't mind them", and the Governor quietly raised his eyes from the paper he was reading.

"Harry and the missus could never get along together if they were not fighting like cat and dog."

"It does seem like it, but it's a dreadful pity", mother sighed, seating herself near the open window that looked out on to the home paddock flat. "And Mrs. Channing has worked so hard to-day."

"It's only medicine and recreation to them, my dear", the Governor smiled. "Keeps them from contracting this weird melancholy of the Australian bush, and from forgetting the beautiful side of it; and prevents them from becoming like the flowers that haven't any perfume, and the birds that don't sing."

As concerned as mother was for Mrs. Channing, her face brightened with a smile.

"You see," the Governor went on, "it's these little differences that break the monotony of their existence and make them glad to be alive when so many are dead. It's just their exclusive way of making love to each other, my dear."

"Oh, nonsense, Edward. I've seen them when they have been quite nice and thoughtful to each other."

"They must have been in bed, asleep, my dear, where I shall be in a very few minutes", and the Governor yawned noisily as a tiger. But before his jaws closed again screams and yells came from the kitchen that rang all through the big house.

"There! My goodness, what did I tell you!" Mother shuddered and shook, and held her hand over her heart.

The Governor tossed the newspaper about and chuckled indifferently. Ted, with the wits frightened out of him, sprang from the couch where he had been "camping", and huddled alongside of me. Fancy him getting alongside of me for safety, when my hair was standing on end and I was thinking about crawling under the table! ... But the Governor calmly indulged in another yawn; then sat back with his eyes closed as though calls of the mopokes outside in the myall trees were the only sounds to be heard. But another volley of screams, with hoarse roars in between, came from the kitchen.

"Dear, oh dear, listen to them!" Poor mother covered her ears with her hands. "He'll kill the woman, Edward. For mercy's sake go and stop them! Oh do — do!"

"If he kills her, my dear," drawled the Governor, "we'll arrest him without a warrant, and try him in the school, and hang him here on the station ourselves, and save the Government all the trouble and expense."

"Will y', father? And how will y' hang him — an' when will y' — to-morrer?" And gad, didn't Ted's face light up at the prospect of seeing old Harry's execution.

"We'll swing him up on the gallows of the killing yard", replied the Governor. "Same as we do the bullocks, my boy."

"An' can we come and help to pull him up?" and Ted's eyes glistened more, and his jaws rattled with enthusiasm. And, of course, I had a word to say in approbation.

"Whatever are you putting such things into the boy's heads for, Edward?"

But ere the Governor could answer mother, there was a shriek, followed by screams of "murder!"

Mother half fainted. My heart stood still, if anyone's ever did. Ted got under the table. It was even more than the Governor could stand. He gave a start and bumped the table.

"Dern the fellow!" he broke out, jumping to his feet. "What does he mean?"

Then off to the kitchen he hurried, Ted and I, despite mother's entreaties to "stop here, boys", crept excitedly after him.

"What th' hang's all this row about in here?" and flinging wide the kitchen door the Governor bounced in.

"He's going to kill me, master, he is! He is!" And Mrs. Channing, her hair all down (though I can't remember that it was ever all up), threw herself at his feet, sobbing, and embraced him round the knees. And old Harry certainly looked as if he was guilty, for there he stood in the centre of the floor with a huge American axe gripped firmly in both hands.

"Don't believe her, boss; I weren't goin' to at all", he declared.

"Then what are you doing with that axe?" Never had we heard the Governor in such voice or seen him tremble as he did with rage.

"I was puttin' a edge on it, boss, so as to have it ready for th' mornin' " — old Harry lifted a file from the table and tapped the face of the axe with it — "and she wanted me to stop it 'cause it give her a headache, and when I wouldn't and she wouldn't shut up talkin' I said I would chop her head off with it — that wer' all."

"Woman! Let go my legs and get up out of that", and the Governor had almost to kick himself free of Mrs. Channing. And though she relaxed her grip she remained kneeling and sobbing out fresh accusations against her husband. A heavy, slow-moving man was Harry, of giant's figure, with a scraggy, faded whisker and a big stomach that filled his coloured shirt and hung over his waist strap like a large pudding in a bag.

"Now look here, Channing," and the Governor, his gray-granite eyes flashing, his arms stiffened and fists clenched, stood up to the dull-eyed, weak-hearted, hulking giant, "we've had enough of your mad squabbling, and for two pins I'd rouse the men out of their huts to drag you to the bank of the creek and rope you to a tree for the dingoes to feed on you, or the blacks to get you."

Then to hear Harry begging mercy and promising on oath and word of honour never to offend again. Oh, my! Never was there anything so contemptuous, yet it was comedy, for I know that Ted and I could always look back upon it with outbreaks of mirth.

"No! I don't see why they shouldn't — and strip every stitch of clothes off you", the Governor was thundering, when the "missus" jumped to her feet, and, only that he ducked in time, would have thrown her lean arms about his neck. Strong and weighty the Governor was, and he just shoved the "missus" from him with one hand like brushing away a fly.

"Don't let them touch him, master — don't", and she made another grab at his neck. "Eustace would do anything to hurt Harry. He's got a grouch against him. Don't let them take him, master! He didn't want to kill me . . . he didn't at all . . . and he's English, too, like you, master."

Never did anyone look more disgusted than the old Governor. He eyed her in silence for a moment or two, then: "Pshaw! The pair of you ought to be dealt with."

"But won't y' hang Harry, father?" Ted piped out disappointedly. And gee, how old Harry jumped round to see where the voice came from.

"Come away, boys", and hustling the two of us out the door, the Governor banged it angrily, and went back to the dining-room.

Meantime, the governess in night attire had joined mother, and from the look in the face of big Mary, you'd think the homestead was being attacked by the blacks — which, by the way, did happen a few months later. But that is another story.

"Nothing the matter with them at all", the Governor assured mother, with a smile. And sat at the table again.

Mother was thankful, and sighed in relief.

"They'd be sent off to live with the blacks, or do what they liked, if I was their master . . . disturbing people's rest, and bringing them out of bed the way they do!" And big Mary gathered herself together and waddled back to bed again. Ted returned to the couch.

Then there was a long silence.

"It's as bright and clear as day outside, Edward", mother said, gazing dreamily through the open window into the moonlight, that soft, eerie, mystic moonlight of the bushland. And her voice seemed filled with sadness.

"We get some beautiful moonlights here, my dear", the Governor said.

"The trees beside the creek, and the shadows out there beneath the mountain, do remind me of Warwickshire."

"Yes — ah, yes! But I think it's bedtime, my dear", and the Governor rose from the table.

Chapter 4

Nearly a year had passed, and still no rain other than a few shattered showers, which mostly fell about the homestead. Reports were plentiful, though, of "heavy downfalls" and "terrible big storms" way out, on Wild Bee Creek, or somewhere down along the Condamine. But they were only rumours, or the misinterpretations by stockmen of what members of aboriginal tribes roaming round on hunting expeditions had to say about the weather, or state of the country. And nothing that one knows of was more unreliable than "information" derived from the blacks concerning rain, grass, or the country.

So the drought continued to increase its grip upon the land. The days were hot and fierce — every new day seeming worse than the one before it. The creeks on most parts of Runnibede were rapidly giving out, necessitating mustering and removing of mobs to more favoured spots. Still they were hanging out pretty well, though what another couple of months would mean, no man just then could tell. But an inch or two of rain might fall any day, and settle all doubt and anxiety.

"I don't know what to think of it, I'm sure", I remember the Governor would say, when remarking on the outlook to Eustace and the other stockmen. "No one seeing this country a couple of years ago would have thought it possible for it to look as it does now."

Eustace and Kearney, men somewhere in their thirties I suppose, then, and both natives of the colony, having first seen the light somewhere round Moreton Bay, would shake their heads and reckon the Runnibede country must have always been subject to droughts, and mighty big ones, except, they supposed, in odd seasons, when it must have rained mighty hard to make up for it. "And it must have been just at the end of one of those blanky good years," they would tell the Governor, "that you first came and saw this place." And often enough they would recite the fate of Burke and Wills, to prove "what sort of bloody country it must always have been as far west as a man could go". Little they knew of it, to be sure. Though kings amongst horsemen and cattlemen, theirs wasn't the spirit that the Governor could expect to find solace in.

But there was one other, Tom Merton, only a young chap then, of eighteen or nineteen, who always backed the Governor up. And what a favourite Tom was right from the first day he started work on Runnibede. I was at the store the morning he rode up leading a pack-horse, to ask the Governor if there was any chance of a job of stock-riding.

"You're a young looking chap," the Governor said to him, "to be out this far looking for a job by yourself."

"I can't help that, Mr. Winchester", he laughed — that pleasant laugh he always had, no matter what was happening — and he tilted back a big cabbage tree hat and showed those big grey eyes and freckled face of his. "I was quite young when I was born, y' know."

"Can you sit on a buck-jumper?" the Governor asked. "Oh, yes, sometimes", and Tom laughed again. "But I'd much sooner sit on a quiet horse, or in the shade of a tree." And I couldn't explain how pleased I felt when the Governor told him to let his horses go and put his swag in the hut.

And when Eustace and Kearney were as wet blankets to the Governor, it was good to hear Tom Merton chaffing them, to give him a bit of hope and encouragement.

"Don't you take any notice of them, Governor," he would cheerfully advise, "they've only dreamed about it being a dry country out here. They've been used to inside, along the coast where the big waves are, and where there's always plenty of wet. Can't you tell that by their hard salt faces, and their flat, swampy feet, like the hooves on horses that are bred in the big swamps." And Tom, himself, would laugh with the Governor.

"But let me tell you", he'd go on, "that my old man, old Jim Merton, who was no sea-gull, was two hundred miles west of this place thirty years ago, and there was always boggins of rains and grass that he used to lose his horses in."

"Well, where th' blaze has it all gone to, Tom?" Eustace, a pug-nosed, thick set, bow-legged, surly fellow would inquire through his nose.

"Sweet man", a great expression of Tom Merton's. "It's taking a spell for a while, that's all, and any day at all now, it won't surprise me to see you fellows out on the run stripping off your shirts and pants and sticking them up a hollow log to keep them dry."

But how Tom could use his head in the bush; his resourcefulness was almost uncanny, and there was no hole once into that he couldn't find a way out of. There were few who could ride like him in the pine scrub, and how he could hurtle a horse down the sides of mountain ranges! The part he played, and the way he rode those blacks down in rescuing Dorothy when the Cooby tribe kidnapped her, was the greatest thing ever done by man on Runnibede. And how she loved him! But that, too, is another story.

Though the homestead tanks had all gone dry and the creeks seemed as if they didn't want to run any more, there still was Curlew Lagoon. And what a wonderful lagoon that was! I really wonder if in the best of seasons the Garden of Eden was ever anything like it. It was the most charming spot I have ever known. About two miles outside the home paddock boundary it spread itself, a broad, calm, silvery shimmering sheet of deep, clean water. Curlews out of number haunted it, screaming their dirges like the cries of a whole kingdom of lost souls. The Station Creek rising in the pine-clad ranges rippled into the northern end of it, and out again at the southern, to wind along on its way to join the Condamine. Here and there on its smooth surface you could see the splashes of fish, and many a huge cod, and swags of jew were hauled out of it. And around it the blacks often camped, swimming and fishing and holding their weird, wild corrobborees. Over the great rock-slides the thin smoke of their fires curled by day, and by night the sparks from them leaped high into the air. The trees growing along the water's edge twisted about each other, and swayed in gentle motion as the soft, summer breezes crooned through their branches. All the wild animals and feathered tribes of the bushland made their way there, till Curlew Lagoon seemed the Mecca and centre of their universe. Wild ducks would rise from the seclusion of its reeds and lilies in such numbers that they looked like black storm clouds. And what a gorgeous sight it was when all the bright plumaged birds that gathered there were astir in the sun. And the armfuls and baskets of wild flowers and orchids and ferns that mother and Dorothy used to gather around its banks, in what profusion they must have been! They knew the names of all the varieties, too! Derned if ever I could remember one. The fragrance that came from those wild flowers and blossoms of the trees made one linger to inhale deep breaths of it. It was the very essence of poetry and perfume. Dingo scrub came right to the edge of the rock cliff that walled the western side, and what a place for pigeons! 'Twas a spot that made the bush endear itself to you — a spot right in the heart of the silences and solitudes of the bushland.

From Curlew Lagoon all the water required now for use at the homestead was drawn. That was work given to old Harry. Several times a week he went off with a small iron tank on a dray, and a nuggetty grey horse between the shafts; and all the way there and back Harry yapped and tugged at the mouth of that horse. A hollow-eyed rogue of a horse he was, too, that always kept himself in good condition on the fodder he rifled from the others. Had he been bred a man instead of a common grey horse he would more than likely have been a great success in business. He was a horse with moods. In some of his moods he would pull enough for three horses. In other moods he wouldn't pull the hat off your head. When leaving the homestead with only old Harry and the empty tank on the dray he would crawl sulkily along, stopping at intervals to wait till Harry got down and humoured him, and led him along affectionately. But on the way back he would be in such a hurry to get home and be freed of the load and his worries that Harry would have to run as best he could, under anatomical disadvantages, to keep with him. But the day "Tommy", as Harry called him, jibbed with a load of wood on the other side of the Station Creek — oh! that was a comedy! How he managed it I don't know, but Harry induced, or seduced, a couple of stalwart aboriginals belonging to the tribe that paid visits to Curlew lagoon — chaps about twenty-five or thirty, who, through the Governor's friendly attitude to them, were gaining confidence in the whites and getting pretty tame — to accompany him for the load of wood. They were tall, lithe niggers, as black as the ace of spades, and naked as the day they were born. The wonder was, as Eustace and others afterwards said, they didn't knock old Harry on the head. Perhaps they didn't think him worth while, or they were not hungry. Anyway, they didn't. Instead, they enjoyed the dray-ride over the creek, and said things to Harry when he said things to them, no word of which he or they understood. All the same, they followed old Harry's example when he started to load the dray with fire-wood. Like big black school-boys they entered into the fun of it with the spirit of rivalry. In no time there was a load of iron-bark and box-wood stacked on the dray that would have made a couple of horses much more willing than Tommy scratch pretty hard to shift it far. Then Harry ordered a stop-work, and throwing a rope this way and that way over the load, twitched it tight in several places. By making signs and gesticulating at the grinning abos., he managed to make them understand that they could ride on top of the load if they wished. Nothing could have pleased them more. They climbed over the wheel and on to the top like twin' Mephistopheles, and sat there showing their splendid teeth, and making their own jokes as they grinned down at old Harry and Tommy.

"Now then, stick tight up there, you black skins", said old Harry, taking the reins and starting to turn Tommy and the loaded dray in the direction of home. But he might as well have told those blacks to tumble off and break their necks for all the difference it would have made to their understanding. Anyway, when Tommy wheeled to the right about and scratched and strained and grunted for a yard or so, he stopped trying and gave in with a definite purpose. His purpose was to pull not another stroke until that load of wood was reduced and lightened to his liking. But horses in harness, like humans, don't always attain their objective. Though old Harry did his best to urge Tommy into further effort by belting him with the double of the reins, and kicking him on his full belly with an ugly crinkled boot, and using insulting language, the grey horse remained obdurate, and stubbornly stood his ground. But, when old Harry anathematised Tommy's pedigree and relations, and profanely mentioned things that really had nothing to do with the case, the nuggetty grey shook his head violently and cow-kicked under the shaft at his tormentor. Seeing his mistake, old Harry resorted to coaxing. But, being a horse with principle and pride, Tommy wasn't to be degraded with smooge. Then old Harry seemed to think he had lowered his own prestige by smooging, especially when it wasn't effective, and taking up a long waddy he broke it into small pieces against Tommy's back and his rump and against the harness. Combo and Curricomb, as the two niggers afterwards became known, had all this time risen to the occasion. They were showing their appreciation of the position by standing upright on the load like bronze gladiators, holding each other with one arm, while with the other they did to the atmosphere what Harry was doing to the horse. In addition, they let out yells that rent the heavens, and were echoed back from the silent gorges of the home mountain. With perspiration rolling off his angered features, old Harry looked up for a moment or two at his joyous helpmates. "Oh! none of that b——y row up there," he objected, forgetting that, unlike himself, they hadn't been educated, "but get down and go round to the other side and give th' cow a kick." But all that Combo and Curricomb did in response was point two long black fingers of scorn at the grey then laugh the rich mirth of their tribe, and out of excessive joy with themselves and their new job, embraced each other till they nearly overbalanced.

"Well, if y' can't be any other dam use —" snorted old Harry in disgust, "keep your eyes on him till I go and cut one of them saplin's over there. I'll make the——go!" Whereon he took the axe from its place on the dray and strode off. The niggers, seeing him depart, suddenly exchanged serious words and looks. Disregarding his injunctions, they descended from the load and pursued him. Harry only became aware of their action when, as he was cutting the sapling, Combo peered curiously over his shoulder like Dick Whittington's cat.

"Why, dammit," old Harry said, "didn't I tell y' to stay an' keep a eye on him?" They said nothing in reply that afforded him any help or information.

Taking up the sapling just as it had fallen, Harry started back to the dray. Anticipating him, the blacks raced ahead, and up on to the load again they climbed like two gorillas. They seemed to think they had risked the chances of losing their box seats. They marked their joy at recovering them by once more awakening the echoes of the home mountain with their unearthly yells. For a moment or two old Harry, holding the sapling with both hands, stood contemplating the jib in an undecided sort of way. Finally, he thrust the bushy top beneath his flanks. Whether from the unexpectedness of it, or the rustle of the leaves, or what it was, I don't know, but Tommy plunged in violent action like a horse gone mad, rose on his hind legs, plunged again, swung round and capsized everything, including himself and the wildly joyous niggers, into a gully that was lying in wait nearby. Who it was, the grey or the blacks or Harry himself, that got the biggest surprise would be hard to say, but true it is Tommy came out of the gully free of the shafts and stripped of all his harness except the winkers, and a fragment of the reins, and away he bolted. Combo and Curricomb, after reaching the bottom of the gully into which they had been forced, disentangled their ebony limbs, then sprang to their feet and regarded the bewildered Harry for a moment, as though they suspected him of playing them a dirty trick. But all that Harry had in mind was the flying steed, after whom he waved his two hands, and cursed shameslessly. Whether from a sense of understanding, or the inherent love of pursuit and capture, or the sudden determination not to be done out of their joy-ride, it is hard to say, but one quick glance at the absconding grey, then swift as eagles and noisy as hounds those blacks pursued him — pursued him in all their glossy nudity to the very verandah of the station store, where the Governor and big Mary Rumble and mother were holding converse . . . but my stars! It calls for the old Governor himself to tell the rest of the happening for it to be fully appreciated.

Chapter 5

Mid-day. A fierce, sweltering mid-day it was, too, in November. Joe, Eustace, Kearney, Tom Merton and Warabah had gone off down Station Creek early that morning to keep the cattle from boxing with a mob of bullocks — a thousand head — that had come over from New South Wales and were crossing Runnibede on their way to Bowen Downs. The drover in charge had sent one of his hands on ahead the evening before to ask the Governor's permission to water the mob at Curlew Lagoon. To do this they had to travel seven miles off their route and to divide into two mobs.

"That travelling mob can't be far off the lagoon now," the Governor remarked to mother, as he finished an early lunch, "so I'll jog off down and see what they look like."

"I'd like to go with you and see them, too, Edward," mother said, "but it's so hot to-day, and I've a lot to do this afternoon, and the sight of the country just now only makes one sad."

At other times she rode out with the Governor when there was something special to see, or a part of the run to visit that was new to her.

A good seat on a horse, and good hands had mother, with a lot more nerve than one would expect to find in one so sweet and so gentle. And the brown blood mare, Kenilworth, that she always rode was a beauty. Yet, I've often wondered since then how she, or any woman, could ride at all in the old abominable side-saddle! But she could, and never gave much thought to the risks she often ran from the saddle rolling under the horse's belly; or her riding habit catching on tree stumps and brambles; or herself getting stuck in the horns if anything went wrong. On the other hand, I suppose mother would have been horrified at the very suggestion of riding astride. And I know the first time that one of the black gins were seen straddling a horse it became the joke of the station for long enough. But human prejudices and human ideas of what is modest or immodest, proper or improper, seem to change with the period.

So putting on his hat and buckling a pair of spurs to his heels, the Governor strode across to the stable to get old Hyperion, a solid grey cob that no one but himself ever rode. But if the truth would out, I must confess that Ted and I — before Ted was sent away to the Grammar School in Brisbane — took quite a lot of turns out of him on the quiet. Few big logs were lying about the homestead, I fancy, that we didn't put Hyperion over more than once; and what a jumper he was! Mighty big pine and ironbark logs, most of them were, too, that no "clouting" could shift. And at them he would go, his ears pricked, looking straight ahead, then a couple of short strides and — over! And by gad, he'd go up so high sometimes, that when he landed we'd be astride his neck. We double-banked him for a change, one day; and putting him at two big logs not more than twenty yards from each other, he took the second before we had regained our balance after negotiating the first, and jumped both of us from the saddle on to our heads. Mother and the old Governor, I remember, sat up all night treating Ted for a "touch of the sun". How far astray they were in their diagnosis, they, of course, never knew — but just as far as the sun was from the ground.

But about the Governor; he had his arm in the reins, leading Hyperion from the stable, and was pencilling some memoranda in a notebook, when school came out for lunch.

"Well, Miss Rumble?" he smiled, "how are these young savages getting along?" Zulu and Tarpot he referred to. "Are they making much progress in mathematics or at speaking English?"

"At speaking English they are, Mr. Winchester," the governess laughed, "but I don't know who's teaching it all to them — I'm sure I'm not."

"This little rascal here, I suppose?" And the Governor squeezed Dorothy's sharp little nose with his finger and thumb, as she pressed her rosy cheek against Hyperion's shoulder.

"No, indeed it's not, for what they know is far too advanced for Dorothy."

The Governor eyed the two little darkies.

"What can you fellows say in English?" Not understanding, Zulu and Tarpot merely looked pleasant and scratched holes in the sand with their bare toes.

Then big Miss Rumble took them in hand.

"You, Zulu — you, Tarpot," said she, "talk English", and she moved her lips in dumb fashion to give them the cue.

"Gov'nor big ass", responded Zulu, in a tenor voice.

"Gov'nor him fool", came gruffly from Tarpot.

The Governor dropped his notebook, he got such a surprise, while the shrieks of the governess echoing round the homestead scared all the crows.

"Ooh, you young monkeys, that's naughty to say that!" and Dorothy held up her finger to them.

"Gov'nor, ass", repeated Zulu, a note higher, and "Gov'nor fool", croaked Tarpot, a tone lower.

"Just so", the old Governor nodded amusedly at Tarpot, and throwing the reins over Hyperion's head, mounted and started to ride away. But he had only gone a few paces when Ted, standing aloof, taking no interest in Zulu and Tarpot "talking English", burst into blubbers, and bellowed like a calf being branded with a hot iron. The Governor stopped the horse and turned half-round.

"Can't we go, too, father, and see the mob?" blubbered Ted, while I remained downcast and miserable looking. In fact, we had pestered the Governor up to bed-time the evening before for leave to go and see the travelling mob being watered at Curlew Lagoon, and so renewed the appeal again that morning; had, in fact, gone off breakfast, fretting over it. So between Ted's tears and bellows, and my look of utter misery, the Governor weakened at the last moment. We had an idea he would.

"Very well, then," he said, "if Miss Rumble will let you out of school half-an-hour earlier, you can go. The mob will be camped about the lagoon all night, so you needn't be in any great hurry."

That was all we wanted. And whether big Mary was willing to let us out of the infernal school half-an-hour earlier, or whether she wasn't, we didn't wait to inquire. We bolted for the big house, and rushing inside, hustled Mrs. Channing to get our lunch.

"You'll get it when 'tis ready for y', and not a minute before! Great men you're getting", was all the notice Mrs. Channing took of us. But when it was ready, never did youths, or men for that matter, dispose of a meal in less time or require less waiting upon in the process than we. In face of mother's kindly injunctions to take our time, we veritably poked it down with our fists; and in grave silence eyeing the other across the table.

When we had taken enough to go on with, we suddenly remembered that our ponies "hadn't had a drink yet". We remembered them, because it was a rule that we were never to leave the table till everyone else had finished. But mother stretched a point in the interests of the ponies, and off we rushed, nearly upsetting Mrs. Channing as she came from the kitchen; then bounding off the verandah we scrambled over the top of the big white gate to save time, then down to the stable. And there, faithfully waiting with their heads over the stall rails, those ponies greeted us with short affectionate whinnies. Wonderful what friendly, forgiving natures have horses! And when I think back, how much superior in spirit those ponies were to ourselves, dumb and subordinated and all as they were! 'Twas with their heels, not with their hearts, that they should often enough have greeted us young beggars. And if we had been allowed to have everything our own way, I fancy those ponies would never have been out of the stalls, except when they had us on their backs. What cricket, "footy", hoops, pictures, shop windows, cigarettes, chew gum and the rest are to city youths, so is the horse to the bush youngster. So we talked patronisingly to them; patted and stroked them from nose to heels, as we thrilled with the pride of ownership and fancied heroism. Then we took down our spurs from the rafters, where they were kept in hiding, and buckled them with care and pride to the heels of our boots. Our spurs were old, rusty pairs that had been discarded by the stockmen; but the rowels that were still in them were sharp enough to make those ponies fairly jump out of their skins. And on occasions they'd draw blood, too.

Having adjusted my spurs so that they wouldn't turn back to front, or drop off, I thought I'd give Whitewings a drink before saddling her. And what a model saddle I had for a kid, too! English made it was, of course. A steel tree, pigskin seat, small knee pads and thigh pads; strong and light, and with a double girth and surcingle. And Ted's was of similar pattern. Gad, when I think of it, how indulgent the old Governor was with us boys. Lots of youths in the bush to-day are glad enough to ride about bareback, and with a greenhide bridle that they make themselves to guide the moke with. But that kind of gear wouldn't have suited us.

"You can give yours a drink if you like," Ted said in a worldly-wise sort of way, as he shoved the saddle on Wallaroo, "but I won't give mine. It makes them too full, and gives them gripes after a gallop."

So instead of carrying water to them from the tank, we tightened the girths, then got into the saddles to build castles in the air and rest ourselves. It was much more comfortable lolloping in our saddles than sitting on the floor of the stall; besides, there was something romantic about it. Indeed, we were so contented with ourselves that we dozed into slumber and lay there with our cheeks on the animals' withers and our arms around their necks.

"Jim and Ted!"

It was the voice of Dorothy; and it woke us up.

"School's gone in. The teachers's waiting for you. She sent me to tell you. You'll get it!"

"Been in how long, Dorothy?" we asked, scrambling to adjust the bridles, and in dread lest we had slumbered for hours, and missed the mob at Curlew Lagoon.

"Ever so long." And Dorothy ran back to school. Then down dropped the rails, and away flew Ted and I, rattling down the dusty track, hands, heels and heads working as we raced for Curlew Lagoon. Pulled up in a few short strides at the home paddock gate; threw it open; closed it, and off again. Half a mile down we overtook old Harry in the water-cart, going to the lagoon for water, his second trip that day. We yelled like Red Indians for his benefit, and startled Tommy, the dray-horse. Then we reined up in a few short props on either side the watercart, and cheeked old Harry; asked him why he didn't grease the cart-wheels, and advised him to get down and walk to take the fat off himself.

"Now both y' get on away from here, wherever you be goin'," Harry roared angrily, "or I'll get down and lift both of you off they ponies."

Then out of the fulness of our joy we jeered him, and Ted, riding close to Tommy and reaching for his head, said, "I'm goin' to pull the winkers off him and let him go."

Old Harry roared "whoa!" and stopped the dray. Then he called Ted and me "a pair of young imps", and started to get off the dray.

"When you catch us, Harry", we yelled. And putting spurs to the ponies, we raced on again, standing in the stirrups to give Harry a full view of our backs and increase his wrath by our impudence.

So at full speed we arrived at Curlew lagoon; and not a sign was there of the travelling mob, nor was the Governor anywhere about. Riding round to the edge of the granite wall overlooking the lagoon and affording a view of the vast valley through which the dry creek bed lay in curves and bends, we sat up in the saddles and cooeed. No one answered. But a flight of wild duck rose from the water and what a swarm there was! And great pelicans with their long bills floated gracefully out from the reeds and rushes. "By gad!" we sighed, "if we only had guns!"

We cooeed again, and the heads of black divers and turtle bobbed up inquisitively from beneath the blue water. Shy waterhens called to their mates and fluttered close in to the high bank for safety. And up in the trees overhanging the water, gay plumaged parrots, jabbering among the blossoms, lifted their heads and screamed.

Concluding that the Governor must have gone on down the creek to meet the mob there, we fastened the ponies to the branch of a tree and started out to hunt round the lagoon and kill time till the travelling bullocks would come along. Hardly had we fastened the reins when two curlews rose suddenly from the ground, and with spread wings flew at us aggressively. We knew at once that their nest was somewhere thereabouts, else our presence wouldn't concern them so. Then we became bent on finding it, no matter if there were a hundred curlews weeping and flapping their wings at us. So, while the two old birds stood a short distance away on their long thin legs, watching us anxiously, we hunted round and jumped about like two bloodhounds.

"Here it is! I found it! It's mine! Three eggs!" And Ted dropped to his knees amongst some short brown grass tufts that afforded but little shelter for a nest of any kind.

I leaned over the back of him and viewed the find.

"Look out! Keep them old beggars away!" he shouted, as the parent birds, half-running, half flying, advanced to the attack again.

I threw my hat at the enemy, and leaned over Ted again.

"There's a chicken in one! Look at 'im moving, Jim! It's kickin' – it's comin' out! Look at it!"

Curiously enough, and as much as I have been in the bush since then, I never had the opportunity of seeing it happen again – the eggs suddenly divided, and to our astonishment, that young curlew took to its long legs and ran in search of cover, stopping every few yards, looking about suspiciously, and exhibiting all the fear and scent of danger of an experienced bird. We refrained from pursuing or aiming missiles at the lanky, moist-looking fugitive, and to our honour, let it be recorded for once, anyway, we did no harm to the other two eggs.

Going further afield, we gave chase to a family of young ducks; tricky, cute little beggars they were, too! They dodged in and out of the water and under the banks, and played hide and seek with us amongst the clumps of reeds, until, tiring of them, we left them to themselves. Then we got down on our knees and groped under the water's edge for mussels, and when we had collected a supply, stood and pelted them at the nose of every turtle that showed above water. Fed up with this diversion, we turned our attention to an inoffensive jew lizard that lay sleeping on a log. We woke him up by taking hold of his tail and swinging him round and round. Then we heaved him into the lagoon to ascertain if he could swim. He swam back to the bank as fast as if he had an oil engine inside him. And Ted and I made a note of the fact that when he came out of the water he wasn't wet.

Abandoning the jew lizard, we looked over the bank and saw the mob of bullocks coming into view — a dark mass moving slowly over the brow of Pinnacle Ridge.

"Here they come!" and back to the ponies we cut like redshanks. On to their backs again, and off round the bend of the creek. In and out of the deep gullies, around another bend, and pulling up short in front of Tom Merton and Warabah. They were riding in advance of the mob to clear away any station cattle that might be about.

"Any cattle on the lagoon when you passed, you young blackguards?" Tom inquired mirthfully.

"None," we told him, "only a jew lizard."

"All right, then — the pair of you keep along with us, and don't get too close to any of the mob, or they'll make jew lizards of you. What do you think, Warabah?"

"My word," Warabah grinned, showing his white regular teeth, "stickit a horn in little fella horses all a same time, and pitch dem alonga moon", and the gentlemanly aboriginal, for such was Warabah, looked up at the sky and chuckled.

A low, rumbling muttering — a weird sort of gladness came from the foremost of the mob, and almost instantly was echoed by the others. Then out of a walk they all broke into a trot.

"They smell the water, Warabah. They're making for it", Tom Merton called out. And in a few seconds the first division had quickened pace, the strong outpacing the weak. And what a herd they were! Great bodied beasts with dusty skins; wild staring eyes; red, white and black; roan spotted and starred; spear-horned, hoop-horned, cock-horned and curly; some with one horn; others with broken shattered horns; all of them hollow as could be. Over the black soil bank that looked down on the clean deep water of Curlew Lagoon, the leaders surged. Suddenly they halted, surprised, and stood staring with their heads held square. Something had arrested them.

"What the deuce is there?" asked Tom Merton, who, knowing they were looking at some object strange to them, raised himself in the stirrups to get a better view.

"Ol' a Harry been there with it water tank. Big fool!" Warabah discovered.

"Mighty! They'll smother him, dray and all, if he don't get out quick!" and putting spurs to his horse, Tom, followed by Warabah, Ted and me, galloped to the head.

"Put out of that for your life, there's a thousand bullocks on top of you!" Tom shouted, as old Harry, hanging over the tail of the dray, was hauling up a bucket of water to pour into the tank. And what a fright he got! He had no knowledge that a mob of travellers were going to be watered there, to say nothing of their being right upon him!

Tom and Warabah swung round in the face of the staring leaders, and got to work with the stockwhips; but nothing short of quick-firing guns could now keep those bullocks, several days without water, back. And though Tom shouted to him, and Warabah shouted to him, and Ted and I chipped in, old Harry had scarcely time to drop the empty bucket and look round, before bullocks, moaning, muttering bullocks, four deep, eight deep and twenty deep, were plunging and ploughing into the water, churning, slobbering it, and hustling and squeezing and poking one another on both sides and all round the dray. Tommy, the grey horse, took alarm, and swinging blindly round into the water, hooked the reins on the hoop-horns of a red bullock. The brute bellowed and plunged to free itself of them. But the others paid no attention to his troubles.

More and more of them poured down the embankment, running up and down and all round that great lagoon seeking a place to stick their snouts. It soon was difficult to distinguish the horse and dray amongst the seething mass. Gad, it was a sight! And it took the breath out of Ted and me. Then along came the Governor and the drover in charge, at a hand-gallop, calling out, "What's up? What's the matter?"

They soon saw what was up, and what they didn't see Ted and I took delight in pointing out to them. But beyond sitting on their horses and shouting words of advice to Harry, they

were unable to afford him any help. Harry, fearing the dray
would be shoved over, struck all round at the nearest bullocks
with the empty buckets.

He struck the spear horn of one with it, and the bucket
became impaled on it, and Harry, overreaching, nearly fell out
of the dray trying to rescue it. Ted and I yelled joyously to the
Governor "to look at the bucket on the red fellow's horns".
But I remember that the Governor looked very sour at Ted.
Handicapped with the shafts and his harness, and with bullocks
raking him hip and thigh and ribs and shoulder with their horns
as they shoved their heads under him and over him and around
him in their thirst, the wretched horse, Tommy, plunged and
reared, and fought desperately for life. Poor Harry perched
himself on the tank, which wasn't much higher than the
guard-iron, and occupied three-fourths of the dray, and gazed
distractedly at the mass of horned heads on every side of him.
Reaching out above his head and drooping over the water was
the stout limb of an aged gum tree.

"Have you a rope?" the Governor shouted to him. "If you
have, fasten it to the limb above your head and hold fast to it.
They might upset the dray!" Poor old Harry heard every word,
and looking up and seeing the limb, clumsily stood on the tank
and clutched it with both hands as though it were a human
being or a gold mine. "Put your belt around it, Harry", Tom
Merton called. "You've got one on." Harry unbuckled his belt,
and putting it round the limb, hung on like a passenger to a
strap in a tram-car. Tommy meantime, finding the pressure
easing a little, made further desperate plunges; and as the dray
came after him, the wheels went down into several feet of
water. But laws, what a predicament it put poor old Harry in!
The tank went too far forward, and left him hanging by the
strap from the limb with his feet eight inches or so off the bed
of the dray.

"We can't do anything for him", the Governor, almost in
tears, said to the drover. But another plunge and the brave
Tommy got free of the shafts. Then out rang yells and shouts
of joy as the grey horse went swimming round amongst the
cattle. But with that first plunge of Tommy's the dray went
right away from old Harry into deep water, and there in the air

he hung above the backs of the bullocks! And as he hung he kicked — why, in the name of everyone, he kicked, I never could understand — and as he kicked, his boots and grimy moleskin pants, in the absence of the belt, kept slip-slip-slipping till they slipped right down and fell off on to the back of a beast.

"Goodness, look at that!" the Governor said solemnly. Warabah yelled the wild mirth of his lost tribe, and Ted and I, pointing to the unhappy Harry, joined in with him. "Confound it, boys!" the Governor shouted to us, "what do you mean by jeering?"

"There's nothing else for him, now, Governor", Tom Merton called out. "He'll have to let go and fall amongst them, and take a chance." Everyone else seemed breathless.

"Let go, Harry, and drop on them", Tom shouted, as he and Warabah made a further effort to flog a way through the bullocks.

Then old Harry let go, and fell flop and heavily on the backs of heaven only knows how many bullocks. Holy wars! Didn't we get excited. Where those bullocks thought Harry had come from, no one could tell. And when at the thud and feel of him, they struggled and heaved and bumped together, and made a water upheaval, you'd think old Harry was riding on a tidal wave. But for once anyway, his luck was in, for his two bare legs slipped between two hairy bodies, one each side the same body, and to his grim astonishment, and the astonishment of all of us, he was sitting astride a black bullock with tremendous horns. But when the black bullock stopped drinking, and began fighting his way back through the crush, Harry's legs kept getting in the way of horns that were not on the head of his mount. And as soon as the black brute found room enough he came out from the ruck at a run, then buck, unloaded old Harry beside a log, then turned round and bellowed vindictively at him. Laws! How Tom Merton rushed his horse on to that bullock and sent him spinning, big framed and all that he was! But old Harry, with just enough life left in him, had rolled under the log in time, and so saved himself.

That night, after tea, Ted and I had a lot to tell mother and big Mary Rumble about the watering of the travelling mob at Curlew Lagoon — a lot more than I can remember now.

Chapter 6

Following upon Combo and Curricomb's adventure with Old Harry and the load of wood, other aboriginals grew bolder and began to come round the homestead. Shy as a lot of kids they were, and for some time suspicious of everyone and of everything that was done. The Governor wasn't long, though, in making friends with those children of Cain and wanderers of the bush. He gave them supplies of food and all the discarded clothes on the station, and now and again a blanket or two. But I remember he often regretted ever having introduced clothing amongst them at all. They were a hardier and healthier people, he reckoned, without them. The clothes were not sufficient to cover their skins comfortably, and made them sensitive and susceptible to cold and heat, and vain as white people. They brought colds and coughs amongst some of them, changed their natures, and in time impaired their constitutions by taking the toughness out of them and weakening their powers of resistance.

It was wonderful how quickly the Governor acquired a knowledge of their language, and in a short while used to "yabber" for hours with Combo and Curricomb and "Captain", interrogating them on all sorts of things, sawing the air with his hands, and slapping himself on the thighs, and grunting and braking, in suiting the action to the word, and the word to the action. It wasn't long before those blackfellows fairly worshipped the Governor, and if ever man was a guide, mentor and friend to anyone in this world, "Missus Guv-nor", as they called him, was to those blacks of Runnibede. But to Ted and

me, for long enough, "King Henry of Curlew Lagoon", the
Governor afterwards crowned him, and "Combo" and
"Curricomb" and "The Captain" and all the rest of the tribe,
with their nakedness, and their "war wounds" and scars, and
high cheek bones and black eyes, and flat noses and thick
matted hair, were just plain savages, who would knock us on
the head as soon as look at us, and roast and eat us as they
would a 'possum. They appeared to us in our dreams, yabbering
and brandishing spears and boomerangs and nulla nullas, and
gave us nightmares, in the throes of which we would wake the
whole house up, yelling blue murder, and shouting for father.
Gad! it took Ted and me a long time to become reconciled to
those bare-footed, sleeky skinned barbarians of the Australian
bush, and to take them to our tents as long lost uncles and
cousins. But when we did, we too became fond of them.

Mother, too, took a human interest in the black gins. She
even become more perfect, I fancy, than the Governor in
speaking their dialect. And one day, I remember, she
discovered, when one from the Dawson tribe wandered into the
station, that different dialects were spoken, and that they might
as well have tried to converse with each other in German.

But the day she and big Mary Rumble lured the three lubras,
wives of Combo, Curricomb, and the "Captain", into the big
house to show them what it was like, and to advance their
ideas of civilised life, one could never forget. The gins had paid
a call to the homestead, in company with their gallant
husbands, who were loaded up with offerings of wild honey,
and 'possum skins, and spears and boomerangs. The Governor
sat on the store verandah, after accepting the gifts, discoursing
with them on the moon and the stars, the kangaroos, and dry
water holes, while mother and the governess took charge of the
lubras. It was, of course, the first home those simple-minded
black gins had ever put foot in – unless their own wretched
gunyahs of a couple of sheets of bark propped slantways
against each other could be called a home. And all the covering
they had to their bodies were strips of 'possum tied round their
waists, suggesting a girdle. They were very light on clothes,
those gins, and couldn't have been very costly wives. When they
mounted the verandah of the big house, they stood rubbing

their flat bare feet over the boards, as if astonished at the smoothness of them. Then in quick, timid, glances, they looked curiously about in at the open door, as if suspecting it was a mysterious sort of cave, or place of captivity. After much coaxing and caution on the part of mother and Mary Rumble the nude, straight-limbed visitors entered slowly on the heels of each other, pausing at every step — and what light, silent, angelic steps to stretch their necks and peer this way and that like emus. Visions of sinewy symmetry they were, yet with eyes and nostrils of wild horses. And then to hear the hosts endeavouring to assure those shy, wild women of the bush, in pidgin English, and by making signs with their hands and their heads, that everything was quite all right, that they needn't be afraid, was more enjoyable than any comedy. But laws! what a surprise Ted and I got when, from the sofa where we were doing penance by having to learn pages of history, we saw those ladies stealing in with only 'possum skin girdles on them. Gee!

"Will you boys please go on with your books, and behave yourselves?" Mother frowned at us. Mother would always have us keep silent and proper in the home when she had visitors. No sooner were the gins right inside, gazing at every bit of furniture with the bewildered glances of yarded brumbies, than grandfather's clock began to strike the hour. Heavens! Mrs. Combo and Mrs. Curricomb and Mrs. Captain must have thought it was the voice of Old Nick. They let out a wild whoop and tried to get out of the house, but in their bewilderment couldn't find a hole anywhere to go out by, for the door had closed. If they had suspicions before, they were positive now, that they were trapped. For a moment their eyes rolled wildly about in their sockets, their tight held lips projected, then in an outburst of violent yabbering they exchanged views with each other on the situation, and while they yabbered they shook and trembled all over. And it's different watching women who've only got a 'possum skin girdle on, trembling all over, to what it is watching those who are covered in petticoats and things — so Ted and I found out. And how we ourselves shook with mirth behind those history books. Often have I wondered since if our merriment really helped to allay or increase the fears of those simple women. But when mother hurriedly opened the grandfather's clock and no devil or anything in human or animal form jumped out of it, and when she crossed the room and threw up the window, and made all sorts of childish displays of good feeling, the gins calmed down and took fresh confidence. So much so, that after a while the knick-knacks and attractive ornaments that Big Mary took from the shelves and placed in their hands to admire and enjoy, were regarded as gifts; and they stacked them in their arms, so as they wouldn't forget them when leaving. Gad, didn't mother and Big Mary look concerned when they realised the simple intentions of their dark guests! And how happy Ted and I felt about it all!

"Oh, you not been take them home with you", Big Mary informed them, shaking her head gravely, while mother, forgetting that her speech, like Big Mary's pidgin English, was double Dutch to them, added, "No, my dears, you must put them all back on the shelves again." Laws, didn't Ted and I shriek! Instead of putting them back on the shelves again, one of the gins stuck a silver pepper pot in her girdle, as if it were a tomahawk she was taking care of.

"You can't take-it that home with you", repeated Big Mary. "You only to look at them — they stop here — they belonga Missus." Oh, dear! What a pantomime it was, watching those gins yielding up the "present" reluctantly and sulkily. The look of disappointment on their faces was beautiful. It was like giving a baby your watch to amuse itself with, then telling it you wanted the jewellery returned, and having to force it out of its hands at the same time. And in their simplicity, those wild women were little more than babies. For only after much smiling and coaxing and sisterly persuasion on the part of the governess was Mrs. Curricomb, who had sandy hair and red eyes, induced to disgorge the Governor's silver-mounted tobacco box; then the lady gave a most weird exhibition of wailing over the loss of it that ever Ted and I heard. We had listened to dogs lamenting, and native bears weeping, but the moans and lamentations of Mrs. Curricomb gave us more joy than the efforts of all such things put together.

As the moment went by, though, the guests seemed to

forget their disappointments and to gain more confidence in their hosts and in themselves. They moved freely about the room, sitting, or rather squatting — first in one chair, then in another; peeping under the table and behind the window curtains — our windows were then draped with the richest Venetian brocade — and even closely scrutinising Ted and me, and grinning broadly upon us. And at one stage, while mother was decorating the three of them with necklaces of glass beads, Mrs. Captain and Mrs. Combo, both brunettes with bobbed hair, barbered with a lighted fire stick as was the fashion, stood so close to the sofa that the back muscles of their sinewy limbs were nearly touching Ted and me. Whether it was telepathy or what the inspiration I really don't know, but each of us at the same moment conceived the same happy piece of villainy, and put it to the test at the same instant. Each of us took a pin from the breast of our coat and jabbed it into the fleshy part of the unsuspecting lady nearest us — Mrs. Combo getting the benefit of my pin, and Mrs. Captain the full measure of Ted's. Great kangaroos! how they jumped, at the same time! They bumped against mother and Big Mary, and sent them kicking on the floor. Then how they yelled (Mrs. Combo and Mrs. Captain I mean, not mother and Mary Rumble). And they glared about the room in search of the hidden dog, or whatever it was they suspected had bitten them, while mother and the governess looked as if they weren't sure that the bump wasn't part of a planned attack on their lives. Their sudden alarm, however, was as suddenly dispersed, when, strange as it might seem, Mrs. Curricomb (she with the sandy hair and red eyes), displaying a gallant and sisterly spirit, helped mother to her feet again; then, by gesture and wild demonstrative language, upbraided the other two for their clumsiness and lack of good breeding — at least, that's how Ted and I interpreted her. All the same, we deemed it discreet to appear composed and innocent looking through it all, a fraudulent frame of mind that was difficult to sustain.

Either Mrs. Curricomb possessed a sense of humour that was lacking in her black sisters, or else she had a deeper curiosity and a greater desire to find things out for herself. Whichever it was, she kept running her red, restless eyes over the white women's skirts which in those days trailed the floor and kept their ankles and legs a secret. And while Big Mary, with her back turned to the company, was restoring an ornament of some kind to its place on the mantelpiece, Mrs. Curricomb crossed over to her and, bending down, calmly lifted her dress, revealing a back view of the governess's thick, stockinged legs and two gaping holes in the stockings! Then poor old Mary, feeling something, nearly knocked the whole mantelpiece down, she jumped so high.

Just then, the old Governor, mounting the front verandah at the moment, and poking his head in at the window, spoilt everything.

"Here are three jealous husbands waiting out here for their better halves," he said, "to take them home."

Simultaneously from the steps rang out a chorus of wild sounding mandates to which the lubras inside answered in humble rigmaroles of gutteral noises. Then, in haste to obey their dear lords, the ladies would have departed through the window, but for the Governor blocking the way. So mother opened the door for them. They didn't offer any thanks for the pleasant afternoon, or say good-bye to anyone; just "bucked", rather than walked out, and joining their stalwart, black visaged hubbies, who carried long spears balanced on their naked shoulders, went off noisily to their camp on Curlew Lagoon.

In after years the three lubras became known to everyone as Annie, Sally and Maria; and never, as we shall find later, had woman a more faithful, devoted trinity of friends than had our mother in those wild and simple-minded women of the bush, who for years loyally served and loved her as their own "White Mary".

Chapter 7

It was sunset — a brilliant sunset that mocked the parched, drought-gripped earth; strips and streaks and streams of it were slashed across a violet sky. Also beautiful, yet so heartless, so hopeless! God! the earth was crying for rain! Rain! No one wanted glorious sunsets — no one then wanted sun of any kind — the sun was hell!

And it was then that the Governor, with Warabah jogging along behind him, came into view at the wild lime trees inside the home paddock gate, and neither of them, I fancy, turned in the saddle to admire the sunset. They rode along slowly, heeling their tired, weary horses at every stride, for the animals were pretty well done in — so were they themselves. Nothing in the bush world takes more out of you than the last stage of a long, hard ride. And the Governor and Warabah were at the end of a very hard ride. They had been away a week and more at Brisbane, where the Governor had gone to interview his banker and the stock agents. They returned in two days, covering 220 miles as the crow flies. But at Westbrook Station they were given fresh horses by McLean, a friend of the Governor's; so, leaving their own there to rest and to be looked after, got them again when returning. How those early squatters assisted each other! They were as brothers, and always ready to help one another over the stile. Gad! how excited Ted and Dorothy and I were when we saw the Governor coming! Didn't we rush to greet him at the stable! You'd think he had been absent from home for a year or two. Of course, we knew he'd never think of returning from Brisbane, even if he had to walk and lead the horse, without bringing something or other for us. And this time his valise was heavily packed. We attached a lot of importance to that valise too. All of us wanted to carry it into the big house for him lest it might be forgotten, or some unseen person suddenly appear and run off with it. And we all wanted to carry it at the same time — neither of us could trust the other with it. So the Governor himself, to some extent, settled our apprehensions by saying "Let me!" and hoisted it up on to his shoulder. And, laws! when we had time to look at Warabah, what a swell he was! Tweed trousers and flaring red shirt, a flash belt, a new cabbage-tree hat covering his black head, and elastic side boots on his feet, with new spurs jangling on the heels of them.

"Lit' a Dor'ty," he called, grinning over his shoulder, as his long fingers tipped with nails ivory white got busy unbuckling the straps of his saddle pouch, before taking the saddle off his horse, "I bringa you some'ing this time." Oil of angels! What a bound Dorothy gave! And what a picture she made — dancing all round the stately black, her flowing brown hair and pink ribbons flying about her, commending him in all the terms of endearment she could command, as he pressed a packet of lollies into her open hands. Poor Warabah! The look of pride her girlish fuss and gratitude brought to his dark, open, happy features has remained a vivid memory! And when Ted, bored a bit, I fancy, by Dorothy's good luck and excessive gratitude, grunted "Why don't you kiss him for it?" how quickly Warabah took him up. Pointing with his long piebald finger — white inside and black outside — he said: "You go alonga cowyard and kiss a red fellow bull calf."

"Warabah," Ted retorted, half in jest, and half in earnest, "you go alonga Curlew Lagoon and kiss old black gin."

"TED! You young rascal!" And the Governor nearly threw the valise at him. "Apologise for that to Warabah — tell him you're sorry, or —"

"Norn, no, Ted been all a right; he be a good lit' a boy, Gov'nor." And Warabah, while Ted blubbered like an ox, patted him consolingly on the head. A big, unselfish mind and a soft heart had Warabah, and many's the time did he rescue Ted and me from the rounds of the Governor's waist strap.

That evening, when tea was over, and the things cleared from the table, and as the light of the blazing glorious moon, silvering everything around, came streaming into the room through the open windows, the Governor sat talking earnestly to mother of the result of his mission to the capital. The seriousness of their conversation was not, of course, understood by us light-hearted youngsters. That the Governor was standing on the brink of disaster never entered our minds. At intervals they would become silent and thoughtful, and now and again he, looking tired, would lean forward in his chair and, eyeing the floor, would say, "There's no need to be so alarmed, Dorrie; a few inches of rain any moment, and everything will be alright."

"But Edward, what a mistake it was to put all our money into mobs of cattle before you knew more about the place and the country itself. You should at least have waited until you knew how your father's estate was to be settled!" And I can see mother now, pacing the room, nervous and anxious, and quite oblivious of the efforts of us youngsters to rouse the old Governor into telling us all about his trip to the city.

"As things are just now, it was perhaps a mistake, Dorrie," he admitted, "and I'm sorry my father took it into his head to marry again, but that cannot be helped."

"I suppose it is his own affair, Edward", mother sighed. What the words meant then, I did not know — but all of us know now!

"Everything might come out all right, and I think they will."

"Twelve thousand head was a lot to have bought," mother went on, "before getting some return. And the men said yesterday that some of them have been dying while you were away."

" Only a few out on Wallaby Creek, Eustace tells me. And the poorest of the herds are running there."

"Th' blacks are helpin' them to pull out some what got bogged in Curlew Lagoon, yesterd'y, father", Ted, thinking to afford the Governor some cheerful news for which he might draw all the credit, chipped in.

The Governor lifted his head quickly and stared in surprise at him. Mother, pausing near the table, said earnestly, "I did not hear of that, my son."

" Yes, they did", I, like an idiot, confirmed, so that I wouldn't be quite outdone by Ted in appearing important. "They helped Joe, Eustace and Tom Merton to pull a lot out."

"How many, Jim?" the Governor spoke quietly but gravely.

"Fifty!" from Ted, who rushed the question to get in before me.

"No, not fifty," I reckoned; "there might have been forty-eight." And now, when I reflect upon it, I daresay there were twenty or so bogged that day in a mild sort of way, most of which struggled safely out unaided at sight of the well-meaning black men.

"And Joe Eustace told Tom Merton," Ted, with wide-open eyes and stammering in his enthusiasm gushed innocently — "told him — that you'll lose every hoof on th' station before long, an' they'll all lose their jobs."

A smothered cry came from mother, and before anyone knew what was happening, she fell across the table and lay as if she were dead.

"Heavens!" and springing to his feet, the Governor seized her in his arms.

"Dorrie! Dorrie!" He shook her excitedly.

"You shouldn't have said that", I said, looking at Ted. Poor Ted, more innocent and more concerned perhaps than anyone, broke into tears. So did Dorothy.

" Quick, Jim!" the Governor said. "Tell Miss Rumble or Mrs. Channing to come here; get me the brandy."

I bounded out, calling for Miss Rumble.

But, to the relief of all, though I'll never forget those few moments, mother recovered; and, after a deep breath or two, looked up at the Governor, and at Big Mary standing there with the brandy bottle in her hand, and said quietly, "It was very foolish of me, I know."

Then, with his arms around her waist, the Governor took her out on to the verandah into the cool air. All the same, we youngsters were still greatly concerned. And as we watched in anxious silence through the window, while they paced up and down, up and down, how different, how gloomy and lonely seemed the striking of the clock! And over the garden trees, beyond the creek, beneath the everlasting stars, the Home mountain, so full of gloom and grandeur, was wrapped in a glow of sombre fires.

"How do you feel now, Mrs. Winchester?" Miss Rumble, having put away the brandy, called over our heads.

"She's quite all right," the Governor answered, "a long way better than a hundred dead ones yet ", and his cheerfulness made us a lot happier, and more like ourselves again.

Coming inside, mother smiled and said, " It was just a passing faintness, Mary. It' s gone now."

Then, as the Governor sat in his chair and talked to the rest of us: " You must be very tired, Edward, I'll get you a cup of coffee before you to to bed."

And though Big Mary begged her to sit down, too, and rest herself, and offered to go to the kitchen and make the coffee, mother insisted and went off briskly to attend to it.

Meantime, the Governor and Big Mary talked of trifling things, as they thought. Trifling things! If I live a hundred lives, I shall never forget their conversation of that evening. Oh, the grim humour, the unconscious foolishness and tragedy of it! There sat Big Mary at the table, fingering the cloth, looking wondrously wise and endeavouring to talk politely. It was always difficult to converse with her, because, whether by impediment or affectation, she drowned her speech in mouthfuls of breath, which made her articulation sound like the noises of a person inhaling soup through his whiskers. And the Governor, straining his ears to listen, would answer: "Yes — quite so — I didn't quite catch you — 'tis indeed."

And then:

"You remember those thick leaved plants that you set along the garden fence the last time you returned from Drayton, Mr. Winchester?" Big Mary questioned proudly.

"I do," from the Governor.

"Yes — them prickly pear that you and us set, father," Ted and Dorothy, anticipating Big Mary, broke in with enthusiasm, "they're all growin' — growin' like winky."

"Growing, are they, in all this dry weather?" and the old Governor sat up and looked quite wide awake again.

"There are a lot of young leaves coming on them," Big Mary added, which was about all that was left for her to add, "and they looked quite fresh and green. And we only discovered them yesterday."

"Curious," the Governor mused, "that they should grow through a drought like this. And they've never been watered."

"Me and Jim watered them, though, this evenin' ", Ted said, while Dorothy also claimed to have tended them.

"McLean, when he was giving me the cuttings from the bunch he has growing in his garden at Westbrook", the Governor told us, "said he thought they would do well out here. I must have a look at them in the morning. But don't you youngsters put too much water on them or you might kill them." My stars! Kill prickly pear! How young the Governor was!

"What is that, Edward?" mother asked, as she arrived with the coffee.

"Those prickly pear cuttings McLean gave me, I believe are doing well."

"Oh, they're shooting splendidly, and in all this dry weather, too", and mother handed the Governor his coffee and some biscuits.

Mighty! When you think that that was how the accursed thing first got its hold! To think that we were nursing an invader, a prolific viper! And now, after all those years of silent, stealthy growth, creeping ruthlessly on in advance of the march of settlement, this green-eyed monster reaches out and by day and by night, from year end to year end, its tentacles close upon acre after acre, until within its resistless grasp is enfolded what once was a veritable land of Canaan. God's own country — where hills and valleys and plains once teemed with the wealth of grasses and timbers. After all those years, to look now on Runnibede — poor Runnibede!

But when Ted and Dorothy said good-night and went away to bed, and when Big Mary Rumble, sighing and yawning as she mostly had a habit of doing, retired too. I remember that mother and the Governor sat again by the window, silently looking out into the moonlight, where everything was so still, save eerie echoes that seemed to come from out the dried-up bed of the distant creek.

"This silence of the bush, I wonder what it all means,

Edward?" mother questioned dreamly. "It is not the silence of the starry sky, nor the silence of sleep, or of death, but a strange silence full of weird noises."

"A silence that is golden for us, I hope, Dorrie", was all the Governor said, and went to bed.

Chapter 8

Another month passed and yet no signs were there of the breaking of the drought. On parts of the run less favoured than others and along some of the slimy creek beds, more cattle were down and dying, and not a day was there that the men didn't find a beast or two to skin. Between scratching for food and long drags to water it was becoming a case of the survival of the fittest. As with humans there is no equality among cattle, and as though nature were putting her own ingenuity to the test to be adopted or scrapped, the drought demon had fairly commenced to cull the herds at Runnibede. But the old Governor didn't get panicky; he kept his block and a bright face when out with the men. He was no Israelite; he didn't murmur and brood over things, neither did he assume any forced gaiety. He just shook his head in sympathy when a beast was down, and gave a hand to stand it on its legs again, or if it were dead, helped to skin it. All the same there must have been moments when his heart weighed heavily within him, for he was surely realising that the paths in life of the cattle raiser in Australia were not strewn with blossoms and primroses.

And one evening when Tom Merton came in after being out all day on Dingo Gully and said there were about a score out there that would be the better for being knocked on the head and skinned, the Governor smiled resignedly and said: "It's getting a bit of a terror, isn't it, Tom?" And Tom, rarely addicted to the use of bad language, shoved his hat back to the middle of his head and answered feelingly, "It's getting just hell and all, Governor."

The Governor merely shook his head. Then Tom denounced

the clerk of the weather of whoever it was he reckoned had charge of it for an "ass". "I'd like to make a slit in his ear and shove his foot through it, Governor", he added. Poor Tom! a quaint serio-comic soul was he, and to the old Governor a sort of spring tide upon which his gloom and anxiety would float off. Pulling the saddle off his horse — Daybreak — an iron grey, fully sixteen hands, and one of the first of the Beeza blood that afterwards became famous as the Runnibede greys, he patted him before getting him a feed and talked to him as though the animal understood. "Just have patience a bit longer, Daybreak, old boy, until the dry weather breaks, and then you're going out to Wallaby Creek to spell for six months. You can take that from Thomas, old chap, and there's no mistake about it!"

Wallaby Creek was the favoured part of the run for horses. They fattened quickly there, and came off it with clean glossy coats, and the limestone flint-strewn ridges which it watered hardened their hoofs and shaped them like a saucer.

"I hope you'll be able to turn him out very soon, Tom", the Governor said.

"Oh, I think so, Governor," and grinning broadly, Tom turned away from Daybreak, "for there was a moulty whiskered old miracle at the blacks' camp when I passed Curlew Lagoon this morning, and he's going to make a devil of a lot of rain to come, I believe."

"He's the tribe's rain-god", from the Governor. "I tried to converse with him on the subject one day, but I'm afraid, Tom, he's not a true prophet."

Then Eustace and Kearney, who had been up to the head of Station Creek, in the ranges, appeared round the corner of the garden, heeling their jaded mounts along and flicking their shoulders with the slack of the reins.

"Don't know what to make of things up the creek, Governor", Eustace said, tossing the reins over the horse's head, as he had a habit of doing before dismounting. "Th' feed is not so bad up some of the gullies — dry of course, but a fair amount of it."

"And how were the stock looking?" the Governor asked.

"There wasn't any — or devilish few." Kearney, with his

head under the saddle-flap unbuckling his girth, grunted.

"There were seven hundred head put out there, or was it eight hundred, Eustace?" the Governor queried.

"All the C.O.B. cattle were put there", Eustace answered.

"Strange you didn't see any," the Governor mused, "and on a hot day like this you'd think they'd all be on the water."

"What we saw were weak enough looking, but not too bad", Eustace went on. "But we didn't see more than a hundred head altogether, and there were very few tracks."

"A fortnight ago," Tom Merton, having attended to Daybreak in his stall, put in, "the creek was full of tracks, and I have seen five hundred head at the least." Then after a pause: "Did you see the mob that those roan poley cows run with, in that wattle gorge at the junction of Spinnach Creek?"

Kearney answering, said there "wasn't a hoof there".

"That's strange", Tom said, thoughtfully.

"Lots of them would be on the water at daybreak this sort of weather," Eustace reckoned, "and then work back into the ranges again."

"But they'd leave their tracks", from the Governor. "Did you go right to the head of the creek?"

"Not up on the range; our horses were too weak to do any climbing."

"What do you think has become of them?" and the Governor looked troubled.

"They might have all poked back into that spare country on the other side and got cornered in some dry hole or other", Eustace suggested.

"Or the blacks might have come over and rounded them up", from Kearney.

But the Governor, I remember, only pooh-poohed the latter idea. He was one of those who didn't regard the blacks as the terrible menace that others made them out to be, and which they certainly never were when treated decently.

"There are some white men on a skelp of country somewhere on the other side," Tom Merton chuckled, "and from all accounts they're a darn sight worse than the myalls."

I can see the old Governor now, after he had said "good-night" to them all, and gone into the big house, sitting reflecting in his chair, taking no notice of anyone until mother asked him not to worry about things, and enthused for his benefit over the splendid meal that was prepared, and told him to hurry up and get ready to do the carving. But later, when he took his place at the head of the table, rattling the carver on the steel, and chaffing Big Mary Rumble about looking lovesick, and suggesting that one of the station hands must have proposed to her, he was quite himself again. And on the table of the big house at Runnibede there was always full and plenty to carve, and few were there as expert with a set of carvers as the Governor, for it was wonderful how far he could make even a small joint go amongst a circle of hungry people and leave them all satisfied.

*   *   *

It was the Queen's birthday, and the Governor decided to spend it looking over the southern side of the run. And Tom Merton, rather than "camp in", saddled up Daybreak to go with him. As there was no school that day Ted and I were allowed to accompany them. Gad! Talk about joy! You'd think when we got across our ponies that we were off to a war, or to a circus. We were not calamity seekers, Ted and I. There was nothing but adventure and magic in the bush for us. And so we all rode away, taking the old track that turned off at the lime tree ridge just before you came to Curlew Lagoon. Ted and I, I remember, made the watering of our ponies the excuse for cantering over to the lagoon to see if there was anything of interest there. And as we loitered on its banks I remember how upon its surface there was reflected the relentless blue sky, till its depth seemed to palpitate with the shadows of the trees around its edges. And then, to overtake the others, we had to have a "flutter". As we came up suddenly behind them, Hyperion gave a bound that nearly unseated the old Governor, and raised his anger. Tom turned his head and grinned at something imaginary far out across the dull, leaden horizon.

"Couldn't you come up gently?" the Governor scowled when he had recovered his equilibrium.

"What are you always racing the ponies about for? There'll be no feed left for them directly, and you won't be able to ride them at all, then."

But in our hearts we knew that if he hadn't nearly fallen off, he wouldn't have cared two straws how we hustled Whitewings and Zulu. All the same, it must have been costing him a great deal for horse feed brought out on the bullock dray for the working stock. We all know now what it meant. And we hadn't ridden many miles over the country side, slow, miserable miles they were, too, when the desolate sights and scenes of grassless, dusty stretches, dancing mirages, slimy waterholes, gaunt, hollowsided, staggering stock and dead stock, leafless trees, famine stricken turkeys and emus, too weak to take wing, saddened even our youthful, careless hearts. Here a red bullock lying on its stomach, its legs tucked under it, its snout resting on the earth, looking as though death had come to it in its dreams of grass and herbage and running water in plenty again. There, a spotted beast, 15 cwt. if he had been a lb., before the drought, moaning on its side, the earth where he lay swept bare and scooped hollow with days of helpless struggling. Further along, tilted into a narrow shallow gully, as if it were a coffin, a roan cow, her legs stiffened in death, pointing to the heavens, her withered udder ravaged by wild dogs; and so on.

"Ah, well!" the Governor would sigh, "it's no use leaving them like this, Tom. Better to put them out of their misery." And getting down from his horse, he would take out his revolver, and level it at the head of a hopeless, pitiful beast. And with a groan that was more a sigh of happy release, the wretched animal would succumb peacefully. Though they differed much in life, lying outstretched they were very much alike in death. How many times we heard the crack of his revolver that day would be hard to say, now, but I know that every time it rang out it performed a kindly, humane act.

Returning home, as the sun dipped behind the Western Range, leaving the miseries to become buried in the mists and gloom of night, Tom Merton suddenly pulled rein, and pointed to the strangest sight we had seen that day, or any other day. "Well, if that ain't my old pack-horse hanging by the neck, I'll eat my hat!"

"Well, well, well!" the Governor said, staring at the object. Then crossing a gully that lay between, all of us sat in our saddles, gazing in wonder at Tom's pack-horse, hanging by the neck from the fork of a tree, as dead as any of the cattle the Governor had fired a bullet into.

"Well, now, if that ain't a caution", Tom mused, slighting from Daybreak to inspect the tragedy.

"He suicided, Tom", the Governor grinned. "You must have treated him badly."

Ted and I, shifting round the tree, discovered that his eyes were nearly bulging right out.

"He's been scratching his neck in the fork," Tom concluded, "and got his head stuck, then pulled back till he strangled himself."

"H'm!" the Governor said, and rode on again.

Nearing the home paddock, Tom, in a confiding tone, said: "If you don't mind, Governor, I'd like you to send me up Station Creek next time, instead of Eustace and Kearney."

"All right, Tom," and the Governor looked hard at him, but no more was said.

That evening, after tea, when mother inquired how he had found the stock faring, the Governor tapped her on the shoulder and said: "Dorrie, I'm not the only one who is losing by the drought. One man has already lost just half of what he owned."

Mother's face saddened as she inquired who it was.

"Tom Merton", he answered solemnly, and when he recounted the fate of the pack-horse mother's heart went out to Tom.

"The poor fellow!" she said, "you must give him another in its place, Edward."

"A dead one or a live one, Dorrie?"

Then Ted and I broke into mirth.

Chapter 9

"Bless my soul, it is a dull morning!" I remember the Governor saying when he left his bed and stepped on to the verandah.

"Dull?" mother echoed in surprise from below the blankets. "The sky was a wilderness of stars when we came to bed last night, Edward."

And old Harry, rubbing his eyes as he approached the wood heap, called out: "Why, damme — I thought there wer' someit up."

"What have y' thought?" his wife, poking her head through the kitchen window, asked. "We're all late", she added. "Whatever is the reason of it this mornin'. I don't know."

"Damme if it ain't goin' to rain!" and Harry, before lifting the axe, scanned the dark rolling clouds curiously. "I could feel there was somethin' in the air makin' everyone sleep late."

Then Mrs. Channing left the kitchen and hurried along the verandah, calling out, "there's big black clouds, Mrs. Winchester, and Channing sez it's goin' to rain. I hope it are. An' we're all behind on account of it."

"I hope he's right, Rachel! We want the rain more than we want breakfast", mother called back.

"He'll be right about it, I think — though that's all he ever could be right in!" responded Mrs. Channing.

Then all of us left our beds and hurried out to attend to our respective duties, for everyone at Runnibede down to Dorothy had some kind of work or other to attend to before breakfast. The Governor saw rightly to that.

"What do you think of it, Harry?" the Governor, strolling

round to the wood heap, asked with a light of joy in his eyes
and a hopeful ring in his voice.

"We're goin' to get it. Governor", and Harry brought down
the axe with a grunt. Harry was no newspaper weather prophet.
He gave his forecasts without an "if" or a "perhaps" or a
"providing".

"It looks like it, Harry", and the Governor rubbed his hands
gleefully, and regarded him proudly. Had the burly wife-bully
asked for a rise in wages just then the Governor would hardly
have refused him.

"Th' wind's in the right quarter for it, Governor", and Harry
with a smile rather than a grunt, swung the axe harder.

Pleased with everything, the Governor walked off down to
the men's quarters. Seeing him go out the gate, Ted and I
abandoned our work of "digging" and scampered on his heels.
Just then Tom Merton was running up the horses – his
stockwhip echoing across the creek. Eustace and Warabah were
round at the killing-yard, and only Kearney was visible.
"Grizzly Ned", we youngsters called him, and he was outside
the hut, with only his trousers and boots on, bending over a
dish of water sluicing his bearded face. A dense beard he had,
too, in which he concealed a long, suspicious smile, like a snake
hidden in the grass – at least we used to think so. And while
he sluiced himself, he made a noise with his mouth that
sounded like a dog swimming with a stick between its teeth. It
seems unkind to think of him that way, but he was never a
"good egg", was Kearney.

"Good morning, Kearney, and what do you think of the look
of things now?" the Governor enthused.

Kearney tossed the dish of water into the air, watched it
come down in a shower on the bare ground, then taking up a
cloudy-looking towel and starting to rub his hairy breast with
it, said:

"Nothing much in it, I fancy; might get a drizzle or two, but
th' wind's th' wrong way, I reckon, Governor."

"Nonsense!" the Governor frowned angrily. "What way
would you want it to come?"

"Not from there, Governor – from over this direction we
get all the rain." And the other swept the horizon with the
moist towel.

"All th' rain!" the Governor echoed with irony. "There's been hardly any at all, since I've been here."

"You're pretty right there!" and portion of the smile that lurked in Kearney's beard became visible, "but I mean all over th' colony."

"Why, it's raining now", and the old Governor held out his hand to secure some of the drops. Gad! I can see the expression on his face, as he stood with open palm out-stretched.

Then Ted and I held out our hands for the fun of it, and in the hope of helping to undo Kearney, for whom we had no affection. But scowling like a bow-legged bear he joined in and held out his own hand in derisive silence.

"There's one," the Governor jerked out, "on my arm — see it?" And his eyes glistened as though a sovereign had dropped upon him from heaven.

"A drop o'spit", Kearney drawled, and, my stars, I'll never forget the look the Governor gave him. Had it been upon one of us, I would have expected his boot to follow, and out of reach we would have danced quickly enough.

But when Ted and I were also visited with a drop — then two, three and four drops — and Kearney himself felt a few, the latter slightly changed his views.

"It might come on", he said. "You never can tell."

"Confound it, anyone with a nose can smell rain!" declared the Governor. "I've had enough darn drought, Kearney, if you haven't." And in a temper he swung round and started back to the big house. He had been suppressing his true state of mind so long, I suppose, that for anyone now to cast doubt upon the likelihood of it raining and saving the Runnibede from disaster was the last straw. Gad! We had scarcely entered the house grounds and closed the gate, when down it came, and in heavy blinding drops, driven before a rushing gale.

"Here it is!" shouted the Governor, and ran his hardest to the back verandah, while Ted and I, kicking up our heels in jubilation like bull calves after having sucked their mothers dry, ran much harder than he.

"It's here, Dorrie!" he gasped, holding on to his hat. "We're getting it at last!"

Mother, standing with her hands clasped, and looking out, could scarcely speak; she seemed to be muttering a prayer of thanksgiving.

Then Big Mary Rumble and Mrs. Channing and Dorothy and the two nigger boys gathered round, and all filled with excitement.

"Look how thick it's falling — you can't see th' mountains. Listen to it!"

Laws, it was something to listen to, too! The rattle of it on the roof, and swishing and sweeping of it into every corner was real music, and to Halifax with your Schumann and your Mozart and Beethoven. Old Harry in the middle of it all, without hat or coat, his shirt and long unkempt hair nearly getting washed off him, came to the verandah rails and yelled: "What y' think of it now, Governor?"

"Look at him out'n it all!" his wife rasped, while Big Mary above the din greeted him as an "old fool", and advised him to "get in out the wet if he didn't want his wife to be a widow".

"At that rate just let him stop where he are", and Mrs. Channing withdrew to resume her work. But the old Governor said nothing — just sat back and listened in a dreamy silence.

Inspired with the joy of everything, Dorothy opened the piano, and with the grinning abo. kids, one on each side of her, began banging the keyboard, but only an intermittent note or two could be heard above the God-sent music on that wind-driven rain.

And so it rained on, and on, while we breakfasted, and while we had lunch, and while we had tea. All night it rained unabated; poured and pelted until it found or made weak spots in the roof, and came down on Mary Rumble's bed, causing a stir amongst the women. Women don't like rain to come in the house, no matter how badly they are in need of it! They would almost as soon have a visitation of serpents.

But it didn't excite the Governor. The bush environment was stamping its influence firmly upon him now, and he was falling into the way of taking most things as a matter of course.

"It doesn't matter if it is", he said, as if speaking on the wave of a beautiful dream. "A little rain water will do Mary good, after all the dry weather we've had."

And it rained away until we got tired of being "weather bound", and began wondering when it would stop, until the Station Creek rose to a banker — rose till it spread itself a quarter of a mile on either side, carrying down logs and uprooted trees and the carcases of dead bullocks and dead brumbies, and dead-an'-alive marsupials, and goodness knows what — until we were faced with a milk and butter famine, for the milch cows, being wiser for once than we humans, saw what was coming, and inducing their calves to follow them, crossed the creek while there was yet time, and made for the safety and shelter of the home mountains.

And so from the first flood that we saw at Runnibede we learnt a few lasting lessons, and never again that I can remmeber did ever the cows get across the creek when it was rising. They went into the "ten acres" instead, and there were left to slop round and "moo" over the fence, same as Strawberry and Cherry did in the Ark.

There were many floods after that, though, and so will there be again. Yet, if ever they cease to be, it will not mean that the millenium has arrived, but Eternity.

Chapter 10

Though only a few months since it had ended, the drought now was nearly forgotten. But what recuperation! What a transformation! from dust, desolation and death the great bushland changed to scenes of splendour and plenty; to a wilderness of joy and life — a bush banquet of God's own catering, and all in a few months of rain and sunshine. Gad! how the creeks ran again. How the grasses and herbage grew. And the stock that came through it all, how they heartened and fattened, and went trotting and bellowing down the mountain tracks to roam the creeks and swamps and billabongs. And at the crack of a whip or sound of human voice, throwing high their heads and tails and — off! breaking and crashing through grass trees, and limes and wattles. Their sleek, glossy skins red, roan, spotted, magpied and starred, glistening in the sun like the bright plumage of birds in their flight. And so it was that summer again with all her green banners was marching over the land. But what had been the actual losses suffered no one yet could tell — not until a muster of every hoof on the run was made could that be known. So with such end in view, the Governor gave instructions for "all hands and the cook" to prepare to start on a certain Monday morning for the cattle yards at Wallaby Creek. The yards would be made the centre of operations for the southern and western portions of the run. But how long it would take to complete the muster none at that stage could say. So many things undreamt of, as in Horatio's philosophy, were so liable to happen per misadventure, lost horses, broken yards, missing herds, and all the rest, in a muster.

Mother, when the house was quiet of an evening, would question the Governor as to what he thought — "just what he thought — the losses would probably be?" And what anxious looks would come into her face!

"The two boys and little Dorothy are to finish their education, you know", she would remind him. "It would kill me if that couldn't be done, Edward."

Poor mother! It was always "the two boys and little Dorothy". Her own pleasures and comforts were never part of her plans for the future, at all.

"Don't worry yourself about that, Dorrie", the Governor would answer lightly. "That's a trifle."

All the worry of life seemed to have left his mind now, and he met everything and everyone with a smile. Indeed, he had more faith now in Runnibede than ever before.

"You've got to know a country like this," he'd say, "and the knowledge is worth paying for. It's something like finding out the qualities of a horse. And a horse that never stumbles or blunders with you, you never get the full strength of and never know properly. But the one, like Hyperion, for instance, or Daybreak, that Merton rides, that blunders at times and makes a recovery with the strength of a lion, that's the animal to stake your life on — not the one, no matter how good and confident he seems, that makes a slip is gone with you, and all the beggaring hands and reins in the world won't hold him up. He's down and out, and you can't stop him. It's something the same with a country."

Mother though, wasn't one to allow her cause to be lost in the Governor's rush of enthusiasm, and in her persistency would give as a last word: "I don't mind, Edward, what happens so long as the boys and Dorothy complete their schooling."

But when, a few evenings before the musterers were to leave for Wallaby Creek, the Governor spoke disappointedly of Willie Williams having asked "for his cheque", and thought he'd take me with the men to give what assistance I could, for the first week at all events, until someone else came along seeking a job, mother, poor soul, almost wept. The idea of taking "Jim", who was only a boy, out mustering with a lot of rough men! And fill him with a desire to follow the life and hate his books, "was too much for her". "What would the boy be, Edward?" she almost sobbed. "Just a plain uncouth bushman. They never read; scarcely know what their religion is, and have hardly an idea in their heads, no matter how good they might be in other ways as men. As to expressing themselves on anything, except the weather or the time of day, and cattle and horses, they simply can't, and I pity them for it. And would you see Jim become the same, Edward?"

"But Tom Merton can express things, mother", I put in, feeling that she was unacquainted with the efficiency of Tom, for in the eyes of us boys he was a prototype. We looked up to Tom. Though he might not have had any delicate breeding, there was a lot of gentility about him — at least we thought so. And how the Governor looked at me and smiled. But mother regarded me almost with pity.

"Tom knows music", I went on rapturously. "You haven't heard him playing his concertina, have you, mother?" (A chuckle came from the regions of the Governor's stomach.) "Gee! I wish I could play it like him!"

In truth, my youthful notion was that Tom was wasting his time stock-riding on a cattle station, and should be making a fortune playing the concertina to the multitudes. No finer or more praiseworthy profession could exist, I thought, than that of a concertina player.

"I'm glad you can't play one, Jim", the Governor chuckled.

"And you should hear Tom telling the other men down in the hut a lot of things they don't know, mother", I went ahead. "My word, he told them one day a lot they didn't know about young kangaroos being born — and about the blacks — he can talk all their language now. You ask young Ted, if you don't believe me, mother — ask him —"

"Oh, will you be quiet", she suddenly snapped, and the Governor, I fancy, feeling glad I had come into the discussion, echoed: "The black's language? I don't think so, Jim."

"Yes, he can", I maintained. "I heard him talking away like fury to that young black gin. Mother knows her, old fat Maria's daughter, that comes with her to the kitchen sometimes."

Mother opened her eyes and fixed them on the Governor.

But that wasn't all, for I felt myself getting important.

"And my word, she understood every word that Tom said, too. You should have heard her giggle, mother, and seen her look sideways at Tom when he —"

"Jim!" mother interrupted in anger. But as the Governor didn't seem to mind I thought I'd keep going — "when he poked her in the ribs —"

Just then mother rose and whacked me on the ear, and cried: "How dare you talk of what you see the men do, you bad fellow. Be off to bed this minute!"

I went off sullenly.

A furious storm rose one night, and among the things it damaged was the single men's hut. While trying to get out before it fell on him, Warabah nearly broke his ankle, and was put right out of action as far as the mustering was concerned.

"There's nothing else for it now, as far as I can see," the Governor said regretfully, "but for Jim to give us a hand."

"Well, if he does, it must be the first and last time, Edward", mother answered, as she bowed to the inevitable.

So when the Governor told me next morning to see to my riding gear, and take Wallaroo for a second mount, I thought myself a full grown man shaking hands with whole world. Laws, though, when Ted found I was to go stock-riding on his pony he protested in howls and bellows, and went near threatening to suicide. Man, after all, I do believe, merely proposes. And while the men, after seeing to final preparations for the morning, were lounging in their huts that Sunday afternoon, something happened to upset all our calculations, and throw the station suddenly into excitement. Having "heard" them their Sunday school lessons on the verandah, Dorothy pulled a red bonnet over her head, and ran inside to tell mother she was taking Tarpot and Zulu for a walk to the edge of the myall scrub to gather wild flowers. Mother warned her not to go where there were any bullocks for fear they would come after her again, as they had done once ·before. Dorothy wouldn't be long — "not very long" — she said, for the wild flowers were in such abundance that gathering of armfuls was a matter of minutes. So off the trio went. As they crossed the ridge to the back of the garden where bronzewing pigeons used to rise by the dozen, Ted and I noted how Tarpot and Zulu vied with each other for the honour of securing the first flower that peeped out of the grass.

In a moment they had disappeared from view over the brow of the ridge beyond which was a narrow grassy valley, and beyond that again, the myall scrub, with its foliage glistening in the sun, its wall-like edges proclaiming it the home of Nature in her wildest mood. A home by day full of divine tranquillity, and by night seeming to be haunted by all the dead souls and evil spirits of generations and generations.

A couple of hours passed and mother began to feel anxious. A little later she and big Mary Rumble passed out of the gate and sauntered quietly over the ridge, "cooeeing" as women do, for Dorothy. No one else gave thought until screams and cries came from the vicinity of the ridge. Then everyone who heard knew that something was amiss. The Governor was up from his verandah chair and out like a shot. Ted and I followed. Taking a short cut through the garden and over the back fence, we saw that something was wrong. There was Mary Rumble not twenty paces away holding mother in her arms, while the two abo. kids with scarcely a stitch of their Sunday suits left on them were bellowing and pointing frantically back across the valley to the myall scrub, around which the shades of coming night were falling.

"What has happened? Where's Dorothy?" the Governor questioned, running towards them. Between the cries of Mary on mother's account, and the bellowing of the two darkies on account of Dorothy, it was hard to make anything of them for a moment or two.

"Tarpot says black women took Dorothy into the scrub — and Mrs. Winchester has fainted", Big Mary at last explained. Then Tarpot in his own way made it fairly clear that they had all three been seized by black women and dragged into the scrub. That he and Zulu had got away and had eluded recapture. Zulu, poor kid, all he could do was to weep and howl weirdly and make frantic signs.

The Governor wanted to hear no more.

"Get Mrs. Channing to help Mrs. Winchester to the house, Mary."

Then to Ted and me: "Run for your life, boys, and tell the men to follow me as fast as they can", and off he hurried to the myall scrub; and off we dashed to the men's huts ... Lord! What a stir there was then! Eustace, Tom Merton and Kearney seated round the table to an early tea, dropped their knives and forks, and jumping to their feet before we had half explained, in a few seconds were striding over the ridge as fast as their legs could take them. They crossed the valley and arrived at the scrub puffing like winded horses. A cooee from Tom was answered by the Governor, who emerged from the gloomy shades of the myall with a grave face. In his hand were fragments of clothing that had been torn from the abo. kids. Not a trace had he found of Dorothy. The men stood still and silent, their faces filled with deep concern. Of themselves only they seemed to ask and answer questions. Whether one black woman, or a number of black women, or a whole tribe were concerned· in the abduction of Dorothy they could only contemplate, and realised that something had to be done quickly.

The light of day was going — and inside the scrub it was already dark. Of the area of that myall scrub belt no one at that time had an idea. That it covered a vast stretch of country extending to the north and west, alternating in brigalow, sandalwood and intricate vine scrubs far beyond the boundaries of Runnibede into the ranges, was as much as anyone, except the aboriginals themselves, knew about it. So dividing into two parties, the Governor with Kearney and Ted forming one, and Eustace, Tom Merton and I the other, we commenced to search the rim of that scrub, they going to the left and we to the right, all of us listening for sounds and straining our eyes in the fading light for tracks that might lead to the camping place of the blacks.

"Look here", and stooping down Tom Merton began collecting an assortment of wild flowers that were strewn for yards around near a huge old bottle tree.

Eustace stared.

"They've taken her, all right," he said. "and she had a struggle ... see here. The heels of her boots scraped the ground as she was dragged along. And look at these bare foot-marks —

they're MEN'S."

"God, Eustace, what will they do with her?" and Ted Merton stared at the footprints.

Eustace hesitated, and I remember the clumsy attempt he made at signalling Tom to say no more in my presence. Tom for the moment had forgotten I was one of the party. And how he tried to turn it off and make light of those bruised and scattered bush flowers and the footprints of aboriginal men and their women!

"My opinion it's some of those quiet blacks having a joke", Eustace said. "Some of them from Curlew Lagoon. Perhaps Combo and Curricomb and their better halves", and he forced a laugh for my benefit. Then, as he slapped me on the shoulder: "Jim, lad, when you get back home you'll find your little sister having supper."

Oh! we humans! To what vain ruses we resort to postpone for others their inevitable grief! That Dorothy was in the hands of the blacks rushed as rapidly through my boyish brain as it had rushed through theirs. But of course Eustace and Tom meant well; and time and again have I, myself, since then, attempted to stem the flow of grief in others by the same false assurance . . .

"Take charge of those for her, Jim", and Tom pressed into my arms a bundle of daisies and immortelles and orchids. As they covered my chest and poked their nodding heads under my chin, the perfume from them remained a sensitive memory with me ever after. It was not a collection of wild flowers, but Dorothy herself I seemed to be holding.

"They went in here, Tom", Eustace said, indicating a passage winding through the myall wide enough to admit a team. "We'll poke in as far as we can and see if there's any signs of a camp. You stop here, Jim, till we come out again."

They proceeded cautiously into the scrub. I remained leaning against a bottle tree, my mind flooded with confused imaginings, my eyes running with tears that fell in warm trickles upon those wild flowers. For half an hour I must have leaned there, while the night shades closed and deepened, making the narrow valley where ghostly curlews were screaming seem miles and miles in width, and the vast bushland itself to appear a world gone out, without end.

Suddenly I jumped like a startled marsupial. Rustling through the bushes came old Harry and Warabah — the latter hopping with the aid of two sticks and swinging his bandaged foot. For the moment I thought the blacks had prowled from the scrub and were upon me. And not until Harry asked: "Where're the others . . . ain't they found Dorothy yet?" could I grip myself and tell them what we had discovered. Old Harry, though, so far as my feelings went, only made matters worse. For he was a Job's comforter.

"I don't give much hope o' seein' of her alive again," said the old heathen, "for th' blacks that got her'll be some o' them bloodthirsty dogs that come over the ranges to spear the cattle — don't y' think I'm right, Warabah?" And he appealed to the manly aboriginal now kneeling on the ground examining the footprints with the aid of a lighted match.

"Don't you be big fool, old Harry", and striking another match, Warabah crawled further along.

"Well, that's what everyone'll tell y' about them, anyway", the other persisted sulkily.

"Two — three blackfellow been here along gins!" Warabah, rising on his improvised crutches, declared solemnly.

"That was what Eustace said, Warabah", I told him. And as though he didn't hear me, he added:

"They drag Dor'ty into scrub alonga that way", pointing through the gloom to the passage beneath the trees where Eustace and Tom Merton had gone. What a helpless, sinking feeling came over me at his words! And how I listened for sounds of Eustace and Tom returning, bringing Dorothy with them!

"Now what's your real opinion, Warabah?" Harry asked. "Do y' think they'll let her go again — or kill her with their tommyhawks? You ought to know more'n th' rest of us about it."

Warabah deigned to reply. His gleaming dark eyes were raised to the sky, and he seemed to be studying the moon and the conditions of the night. At no time was he a talkative person, but there was a silent bush dignity, a racial resignation about Warabah. "Fool!" he said, reproaching himself, "for breakin' it leg! . . . Dammit storm!" Then lifting his voice and addressing those who had kidnapped Dorothy: "By gum tree, Cooby tribe; touch it that lil' girl an' you die!"

Just then Eustace and Tom Merton came silently out of the shadows of the scrub. But no Dorothy was with them. How sick I felt. Disregarding old Harry, they talked in low tones to Warabah.

Presently came a low cooee, which Tom Merton answered.

"That's them coming back", Eustace said. Then we could hear them trailing beneath the hanging boughs and over crackling twigs and branches. Again, how I listened and strained for sight or sound of Dorothy! But at the sound of the Governor's voice my blood ran cold again.

"That you, boys?" he called softly, almost reverently, yet in it a deep note of terror was sounded.

"It's us, Governor", and Tom lowered his voice as though we were in the presence of the dead. Then in hushed voices they conversed beneath the soft rustling foliage. And when the Governor had listened to Eustace and Tom, he stepped close to me, and putting out his hand touched those wild flowers as though they were the hair of Dorothy's head. Without a word, and breathing as though his heart would burst, poor Ted did the same. And in those wild blooms with the moon shining down upon them were reflected the very eyes and soul of our lost sister.

In answer to the Governor, Warabah, who had been silent, spoke out:

"No," he said, "blackfellow not kill Dor'ty. They keep her for something. P'raps, might be gins, mothers belong Tarpot and Zulu come to steal them away. Something I don't know go wrong and boys get away; blackfellows keep Dor'ty and go back tonight over range all through scrub . . . You go to Curley Lagoon, get Combo and Curricomb; they track 'em tribe along daylight and find Dor'ty . . . Fool me, break 'it leg, else Warabah track 'em all night."

"I know you would", and the Governor patted him kindly on the back. Then turning to the others:

"Now, back to the house, quick boys", and striding off he led the way across the valley.

"And, Tom," he called back as he hurried along, "saddle the night horse and run all the others into the yard. Some of us will go at once to Curlew Lagoon."

It took little time to cross the valley; and when the Governor and Ted and I mounted the verandah and entered the home there was mother and Mary Rumble and Mrs. Channing beside her, pale as death, and watching the door with looks in her eyes that no one could ever forget.

"Where is she?" she cried. "Where is Dorothy — have you brought my girl?"

"She's all right, Dorrie — she's coming directly. She isn't harmed", and the poor old Governor put his big arm around mother. But she refused to listen or to be consoled.

"My God, Edward! Tell me, is she dead? Have they killed her?"

"No, no", he assured her. "We are going to bring her now; but you must calm yourself, Dorrie."

Ted, who had not spoken, now threw himself upon the sofa and burst into sobs. And in the midst of it all there stood I in a sort of stupor, still clasping the wild flowers to my breast. Mother's eyes rested upon them. I shall never forget that moment.

"Hers!" she screamed, "her wild flowers!" and dropped her head on the Governor's shoulder.

Chapter 11

How clearly that night all comes back! The clouds drifting across the moon; the coolibah trees standing beside the gate swaying and rustling in mournful tune; the station hands grouped in silence together beside their horses at the stable; the Governor hurrying from the big house, and out at the gate fumbling a pair of revolvers, unconscious that I was at his side.

"We're all ready, Governor", Tom Merton called quietly, leading Hyperion forward along with his own horse, their sharp ears pricked, and in the light of the moon their fiery eyes flashing expectantly.

"Tom, we must hurry; and put this in your pocket." And as he took the reins the Governor passed one of the revolvers to him.

"Do you want us all with you?" Eustace asked.

"Kearney had better stay with Warabah and Harry," the Governor answered "in case something might happen while we're away." Then to Kearney: "Tell Miss Rumble you will be about all the time, so that they won't be nervous."

"I will, Governor, and I'll keep a horse in the stall."

Then into their saddles the Governor and Eustace and Tom swung, and I, following suit, scrambled on to Whitewings. The Governor, without a word, took the lead, but instructions were not necessary just then. We knew where we were heading for. Even those horses seemed to know that something serious was in the air, for they required no urging. Off they plunged, tossing their heads, pulling on the reins and reefing. Through shadowy lime and brigalow, crashing into brambles and bush, in

and out, and around the head of rugged, shapeless gullies we
rattled at a half gallop, heading for the blacks' camp at Curlew
Lagoon. Not until we had covered more than half the distance,
and on Whitewings cannoning into Hyperion as we swerved to
avoid the spiked roots on a fallen tree, did the Governor realise
that I was in the party.

"That you, Jim?" he called, glancing back over his shoulder.
Then, fixing his eyes on the dim objects ahead, quickened the
pace. And how those horses, striding out abreast, swept over
the ground! As the mountain peak beyond began to take shape,
the Governor, taking a pull on Hyperion, called a warning to
"go steady".

We pulled in, and when the noise of galloping hoofs beneath
us was silenced, how the sound of clinking stirrup-irons, the
beating of hoofs on the ground, the horses' nostrils blowing and
steaming, broke upon the stillness of the eerie sleeping bush
around! Coming to the edge of the lagoon, the Governor
stopped, and resting his hand upon Hyperion's withers, engaged
Eustace and Tom in low conversation. While they spoke across
the horses to each other, the animals clamped the bridle-bits
and pawed the ground restlessly, and flung foam into our faces.
And looking down from the saddle upon that calm, silvery
water of Curlew Lagoon, what impressions of divine serenity it
made on one! The moon reflected in its depth, the rock walls
beyond looming grim and massive, and the waterfalls above
roaring as the waters tumbled over the rocks like breakers. And
well I remember my feelings as I sat there watching through the
moonlight on Whitewings, ears open, listening to the croaking
frogs, the calling of wild ducks to each other among the reeds,
and the swishing flights of night birds overhead. How eerie,
how sad, how terrible it all seemed!

"The camp is on the edge of the scrub over the rock walls",
Tom Merton said. "We'll have to cross at the waterfalls,
Governor. The creek is shallow there."

The Governor agreed. Then, turning our horses' heads, we
rode up the creek for a quarter of a mile, and entered its bed
in single file. How our mounts slid and ploughed on all fours
down the steep bank of loose soil! I was the last of the file.
Gad! when for a moment I lost sight of the others as they took

the track zig-zagging up the opposite bank, a sudden fear that I'd be speared or cut off seized me. Poor little Whitewings. She blundered to her knees, nearly tossing me over her head, then plunging and bounding, struggled up on a course of her own when I touched her with the spur.

Up the steepest part of that bank she scrambled, and colliding at the top with Tom Merton, gave Daybreak a broadsider than nearly toppled them back into the bed below.

"Great Scott!" Tom gasped, "where did you come from?" But all I was concerned about just then was getting safely out of that creek into company again.

Following the creek to where dingo scrub hung over the rock walls, we saw before us a half circle of smouldering fires.

"Here it is", Eustace said, breaking the heavy silence. And here and there, with the glooming scrub sheltering a camp of miserable gunyahs made of sheets of stringy bark, leaning slantwise against each other, took shape in the moonlight.

"Careful awhile", the Governor counselled beneath his breath. And again we halted. "It won't do to alarm them. We don't know how they might regard our coming at this hour of night."

Though friendly relationships had been established with these wild people, and in a sense the Governor had become the guardian of their happiness, the referee and arbiter of their disputes, in truth a wonderful being in their eyes, yet they had moods and fancies of their own, and were liable to misunderstandings. Mother, too, on her side had been moving peacefully amongst them in their sicknesses, providing them with clothing and food till her visits to the camp became a feature in their wild lives, and she had become known as "White Mary". Still, a surprise visit to the camp by night, when the fires were dying low, and all asleep in the gunyas, was an innovation not unattended with risks. So instinct told the Governor that wisdom lay in prudence.

For me, at least, those moments held a thousand terrors. While the others spoke in hushed voices, and the horses tossing their heads, jerked at the reins and snatched for mouthfuls of grass, I stared around, mentally measuring, as a nervous boy will do, the chances of a clear gallop in the event of trouble, for there before us, not more than fifty yards off, slumbered a couple of hundred people, men, women and children, wanderers of the Australian bushland.

And, as we paused, sparks started out the smouldering embers, and flickering heavenward, raced each other into oblivion.

"Listen to them snoring", Tom Merton whispered. And what a medley of strange, weird noises came from those sleepers! Some of the notes were deep and long-drawn; some high-pitched and shrill. Some seemed the groans and moans of tortured souls. And all so unearthly, so awesome, that you fancied you were standing in a hostile world filled with all the menaces and terrors of the night. Even the mangy, miserable dogs — and there was a pack of them — slept and snored. And from the lonely trees squirrels chattered as though keeping tryst. Curlews screamed all around. Dingoes howled from the scrub. Mopokes called their dismal note from the shelves of the great rock walls. While over all the everlasting stars twinkled and blinked down at the camp of those primitive, precarious people, just as they had twinkled a million years before.

Presently the Governor lifted his voice and called: "King Henry and Combo and Curricomb and Captain!" How the echoes of his voice answered back from the silent rocks and scrub! Gad! And how I shook in the saddle!

In an instant the camp was awake and on the alert. From every gunyah voices called the alarm. Even the miserable dogs set up a chorus of snappy barks. Nude men were on their feet, their hands reaching for war weapons, and the camp became a bedlam of excited jargon.

Again the Governor called those names. We, sitting in the saddle, listened intently. In the dead silence that followed he added: "Gov'nor Runnibede here, want yabba alonga you."

Then rang out yells of recognition. A rush of men, their black silky skins shining in the moonlight, came hurrying forward, giving our horses a start. What feelings of surprise and curiosity and joy our visit seemed to give them as they crowded round us. They knocked and rapped their war weapons together in their wonder and delight. Though their attitude was full of friendship, I could feel my hair rising on end. The Governor dismounted from Hyperion, and standing calmly in the centre of them, spoke with the "King", "Curricomb", "Combo" and the "Captain", telling them in their own dialect and broken English the object of our visit. Then he questioned them to ascertain if they knew anything of Dorothy. Eustace and Tom Merton put questions to others of the tribe whom they knew. How the horses distrusted them — snorting in their faces, and turning this way and that. Whitewings, when a tall, long whiskered warrior attempted to put his hand on her mane, reared on her hind legs. Gad! What a scatter she made!

"Whoa, you little beggar", and reaching from his saddle, Tom patted her on the neck to calm her, while I, shaking all over, wasn't sure if I was still in the saddle or not. "She don't like the smell of them, Jim."

The interview was soon over. Then, saluting the king and wishing all the tribe a good-night, the Governor turned to Hyperion and Whitewings, and, as silent as the stars, he led the way back to Runnibede. When he mounted the verandah we found the lights still burning brightly, with Mary Rumble and Mrs. Channing sitting up, waiting and watching, their eyes red and tear-stained.

"Don't make a noise", they whispered to the Governor, as we entered the room. "Mrs. Winchester has just fallen asleep." Poor mother.

Chapter 12

An hour before dawn and dark as pitch. The sound of snorting, rushing horses; the jangle of stirrup-irons and bridle-bits. The dropping of rails, and subdued voices at the stable yard. Lights moving about and disappearing again down at the huts.

The latch of the big white gate clicked, and the Governor's footsteps patted the beaten pathway leading to the stable.

"We're all here, sir", Eustace spoke, to indicate their whereabouts, for the waiting men were standing in a cluster at the heads of their horses, saddled and ready. "I could see the star in the black horse's forehead from the gate", the Governor answered, peering through the darkness. Just then Tom Merton struck a match to light his pipe, and back jumped every horse as though some evil spirit had appeared to them, wrenching the arms of the stockmen. Strange how horses are startled by a sudden burst of light while possessing eyesight to see as well by night with as by day.

"What are you scared of, you!" was mumbled by more than one, as the affrighted animals, recovering, stood snorting nervously, while Tom, groping for the pipe that was jerked from his hand, chuckled: "You'd think they wer' a lot o' dam brumbies and had never seen a match struck before."

The Governor spoke to Hyperion, and taking the reins from Eustace, fumbled for the saddle-bag to put some provender into it. Then to the men: "Have you all thought of bringing a snack with you?"

All of them had — a precaution they would hardly have forgotten.

THE ROMANCE OF RUNNIBEDE

"They ought to be here soon?" Kearney spoke now, and referred to the three blacks, Combo, Curricomb and Captain.

"Not before it's clear daylight", Tom Merton reckoned. "Nothing will coax them away from the camp in the dark, if they're anything like the coastal tribes."

"They're a bit different out here", from Kearney. "They don't mind how dark it is if they're out to tomahawk you! Those dogs that murdered the family at Hornet Bank surrounded the hut long before daylight and travelled a long way through scrub to get there."

"The whole mob were there, though", Tom reminded him. "When there's only a couple of them they're afraid of their own shadows in the dark."

The horses gave another sudden start, and with heads turned sideways; then with pricked ears silhouetted against the grey skyline, they remained stationary. The men knew the signal, and watched silently in the direction indicated. An unnerving stillness followed, lasting for minutes. The brigalows on the flat near the home paddock boundary, where the morning star was sinking, lay in the direction the horses were watching. An owl fluttered from the stable roof and perched noiselessly on a yard post within arm's length of Tom. Its big, ghostly eyes blinked. Tom peered at it, and felt a shivery feeling run through him.

"Ho! Ho!" said the owl.

"Go to blazes!" Tom hissed.

Eustace and Kearney chuckled.

The foolish bird fluttered off as silently as it had come. Still the horses kept their heads turned and their ears pricked.

"What th' h —l do they see?" Eustace mumbled sotto voce.

"They see something", wondering from the Governor.

"There it is", from Tom. "A light among the trees — see it?"

All eyes saw it now. Not one light, but a fantastic display of approaching fireworks. It was Combo and Curricomb and Captain swinging lighted firesticks about in the dark to keep off the evil spirits. And as they came nearer what excitement those horses were thrown into! They pulled back, bumped the yard and the stables, and got mixed up with each other. And in their efforts to hold them the men were nearly carried off their feet, and they choked back a lot of violent language. When Tom Merton at last called out, "Put out those firesticks, Combo, you blighter; you're frightening the devil out of my horse", his voice came from somewhere down the paddock.

Then from the Governor came a grateful welcome, and his voice was magic to those blackfellows. They responded with a round of wild whoops, their way of expressing joy at having come through safely, rather than as a greeting. And while they drew round him and the restless form of the nervous, distrusting Hyperion, and jabbered and grunted in complex vocabulary, the rest of us, leading our reluctant horses, assembled again.

Presently the day broke, and soon the bushland was arrayed in all its earliest light.

All were ready now, and the Governor rode off, the blackfellows swinging along on either side of the lofty grey. At the myall scrub the tracks discovered the evening before were shown to them. With bent heads they eyed them with the caution and curiosity that one might regard the bruised length of a snake coiled there with a blood-stained waddy lying beside it. Together they consulted earnestly, pointing at intervals to the scrub. And as they put their heads together, I remember how moist their matted hair and black beards were with the morning dew. Signalling their decision to the Governor in gesticulations they started off to run the tracks. It was apparent they had agreed to do it in relays, for Curricomb stepped off in the lead, his eyes riveted to the ground. The others strolled leisurely along at his heels. The Governor and the rest of us remaining mounted formed a rearguard, silent, watchful and expectant. Combo and Captain, though, seemed to find a deal of humour in the proceedings, for they made fun of Curricomb, imitating his gait, and pulling faces behind his back. But after penetrating the scrub some five or six miles to where the tracks led into an area of kangaroo grass, in the hollow of which was a soakage (Curricomb Spring we called it afterwards), Curricomb stopped to consult with his black brothers. Then Combo, dropping his levity and assuming solemn countenance, took up the tracking. Curricomb joining with the Captain, now made Combo the butt of ridicule. He even snapped off short

ends of dead sticks that impeded his way to toss at the back of
the other's woolly head. But nothing would induce Combo to
take his eyes off his work, and I remember how the Governor,
watching their antics, would pass meaning glances to the rest of
us.

"Just like us fellows when we were kids, Governor", Tom
Merton said, as he bent low in the saddle to clear the loop of a
vine and save his neck.

Emerging from the kangaroo grass on to a patch of loamy
soil covered with dead leaves and crumbling bark. Combo
pointed to the left and to the right. Curricomb and Captain
glanced sharply round about, then became grave. Leaning from
the saddle the Governor questioned them, only to learn that
the tracks at the spot had been reinforced and that the whole
tribe had passed over there. From there on there was no more
skylarking. The prospect of coming upon the mob of their
hostile countrymen set those three blacks thinking very hard.
Indeed the bare footprints were so plain and plentiful on either
side of our line of march that all of us could distinguish them
at a glance. God, how affected the Governor became!

"Hurry on!" he urged, and with difficulty restrained from
galloping forward. But instantly he was calm and thoughtful
again.

Now it was Combo's turn to step back and Captain's to take
up the trail. Scarcely had the latter run the tracks for a quarter
of a mile over country where wattles and wild limes grew thick,
when suddenly he halted, and, walking in a circle, kept pointing
to the ground.

"Her boot marks", came from the Governor, as he leaned
down over Hyperion's shoulder. "Thank God she's alive, men."

Since the tracking commenced these were the first footprints
of Dorothy's that had been discovered, and Curricomb
demonstrated the cause of it by carrying Combo round on his
back and letting him down again, denoting how the kidnappers
had been carrying Dorothy, and put her on the ground while
they rested or transferred her to other shoulders.

"Hurry on! Hurry!" came from the Governor, his eyes set
like steel on the pine scrub in the distance at the head of Wild
Bee Creek. Circus scrub they call it these days. And at that

time, before the inception of forest fires, the pines spread over
the great range and its pointed peaks and rock channelled sides
like a flowing leafy blanket of many tints and shades.

The blackfellows kept close together, and were no longer
studying or watching the trail. All three walked firmly, their
dark faces grim and solemn, their shifty white eyes fixed
intently on the nearest point of the scrub. It was plain they
knew the abductors of Dorothy were encamped there. The
Governor and the others felt for their revolvers. A set, resolute
stare was in all their eyes. What a rush of thought flooded my
mind as I gazed from one to the other. I was the only one who
carried no firearms. Perhaps it was well, too, that I didn't. But
Whitewings I knew was under me. What courage and confidence
a horse that you know will inspire even in a youth. A bush boy
on the back of a good horse has the pluck and spirit of a man
of years. A hundred yards from the scrub, and the trackers
paused. They yabbered excitedly, casting furtive glances behind
and before them. The Governor asked what the matter was.
Combo, speaking for the others, made it clear they were afraid
to go further. That the tribe camped in the scrub were
numerous and powerful enough to make short work of the lot
of us. The Governor and Tom displayed their firearms to
convince them of our advantage over the tribe with their spears
and boomerangs. The trackers grinned and remained obstinate.
Suddenly one of the animals pricked its ears, and stared toward
the scrub. That was enough for Combo and Co. Like
pedestrians starting off the the crack of a pistol in a foot-race,
they fled for home. We gazed after them in silence and
disappointment. Halting in their stride for a moment to glance
back to see what was happening — off they went again, and we
saw no more of them that day.

Closely scanning the edge of the scrub, the Governor told
the rest to look carefully to their guns. "We might have to use
them," he said, "but not until it's really necessary. Better get
across to the trees over there," he counselled, taking note of a
clump of coolibahs, "and one of you hold my horse while I go
in and see if I can locate their camp."

But Tom Merton, revolver in one hand, and hitching his
pants with the other, was on the ground before him.

"That's my job, Governor", he smiled. "I'm not such a good target for a spear as you, and I can run a bit faster." Tom was lean and muscular, and could run like an emu. "But keep hold of old Daybreak for me," he added, glancing at Kearney, "in a way that I can jump right on to him if I've got to make a run for it."

Then boldly he stalked through the long grass, while we sat in our saddles, our eyes roaming the edge of the pine jungle for signs of danger. Presently he entered it and disappeared from view. What moments followed! For how long we watched the spot where the thick foliage closed behind Tom I don't know. No sounds other than those of a shaken bridle, or the stamping of restless hoofs, were heard. Was Dorothy there, in that silent bush? Would Tom see anything of her, or would he come rushing back with the blacks in hot pursuit, were thoughts that well-nigh strangled one. But just as the Governor, finding the strain of waiting too much for him, had dismounted to go after Tom, the latter reappeared, making signs to the others to join him.

"He's spotted them, Governor", Eustace said, as we rode forward abreast.

Tom motioned us to be silent, as we came near, while his eyes glistened and the blood rose to his cheeks.

"What is it, Tom?" in a low voice from the Governor.

"I have seen Dorothy — she is alive", he stammered.

"Thank God!"

How my heart jumped. I felt like bursting into shouts of joy. But quick gestures from the others suddenly strangled the impulse.

"The mob's camped in an open space at a waterfall in through there", Tom pointed. "Dorothy's sitting up on a rock, and they're all holding a corroboree."

The horses were made fast, and, following Tom, we crept lightly through the scrub, our boots sinking deep in the mulch-soil, manured by fallen leaves and bark and vegetable matter over generations and generations. On the inner edge of the jungle he stopped and pointed to an area of bountiful grass-lands hemmed in on every side by the jungle. There, beside a waterfall that roared like the billows, we could see

Dorothy in her red frock, elevated on the rock, while around her in a wide circle squatted the tribe, men, women and children, chanting a dirge, and keeping time to it by beating their thighs with the palms of their hands.

The Governor alone remained calm. His was the silent, determined, calculating temperament.

"Don't be in a hurry — take your time!" he whispered hoarsely, and his hand felt for his revolver. What my own boyish feelings were would be hard to describe. "Just let us think what is best to do."

And, while they exchanged whispers, how my eyes stayed fixed on poor Dorothy. There she was, the red frock so familiar, conspicuous against the circle of black skins and heads, her long brown hair, that mother had taken such a pride in from the time she was a mere baby, hanging all about her. Without a hat, she was crouched on the rock, her head bowed in an attitude of dejection. As the doleful chant continued, several tall, sinewy warriors, fearsome in their nudity, and feathers adorning their heads, marched round and round the rock, rapping their nullah-nullahs and boomerangs together, and an intervals crouching down and hopping as marsupials. Eustace and Kearney reminded the Governor that this was the Cooby tribe. That they were full of bitterness and revenge because of poisoned flour having been distributed amongst them by a cowardly station-owner. So any attempt at friendly parley, they reckoned, would be fatal. On his side the Governor discounted the idea of attacking them, or making any display of violence unless there was no escape from it. Such attitude could only increase the danger to Dorothy. Then Tom Merton made a suggestion.

"All right, Tom", the Governor agreed. "Eustace and Kearney will come with me. And you, my boy [to me], go back with Tom, get on Whitewings, stay on her, and be ready to go for your life if you see any blacks coming. Never mind about any of us."

With my heart choking me, I went back to the horses with Tom. On the way he didn't speak a word. Pale and resolute, he mounted old Daybreak, and patted him affectionately on the neck. Rare companions had Tom and Daybreak become.

"It's do or die, Daybreak", he said, and rode back into the scrub. When he had disappeared, and the sound of the horse forcing a way through had died out of my ears, the feeling of isolation and dread was more than I could bear. Casabianca had thrilled me in the schoolroom, but my sense of obedience wasn't up to the level of the boy who "stood on the burning deck". I must see all that was going on, even if I were to be tomahawked for it. I followed on Daybreak's tracks, and came up with Tom just as he pulled rein and took up a position on the inner edge of the pines, where he could observe the movements of the blacks, and study the lay of the surroundings without being observed. He signalled me to keep behind him, and to remain silent. And so I remained, a length or two from him, holding my breath, and wondering what was to happen next. To the right of the circle of chanting blacks I could see the smoke from roasting flesh. I noticed two women with something in their hands resembling feather dusters rise from their places in the circle and approach my unfortunate little sister. They crossed the feathered things over her bowed head, like swords, keeping them poised for a moment while they turned their ugly black faces to those continuing the corroboree. How the hot blood surged through my veins! Had I been entrusted with firearms nothing could have stopped me from firing point-blank at those women! Not a word or movement came from Tom. He sat gazing across the heads of the tribe to a point in the scrub on the other side, about a quarter a mile off. Once he reached down and gave his girths a pull to test their security. Suddenly a puff of white smoke spurted into the air, followed by the report of a gun, that rang and echoed all around with a loud, prolonged boo-m-m! A second one rang out, and then:

The Governor, with Eustace and Kearney, could be seen, a few paces out from the scrub, all three looking up into the branches of a great gum, making pretensions of aiming at some object in it. Thieves and invaders! What a stir was made amongst those chanting blacks! Every man of them sprang to his feet, and to his weapons of war. For a moment they stood staring at the white man who dared to encroach on the sancity of their camping-ground! Up rose a savage war-cry, blood

curdling, and lifted my hair on end. Then, brandishing their
spears, they started off full split, a hundred strong, to settle
matters with the intruders. It was what the whites were playing
for, and back into the scrub went the Governor and his
companions. For a moment Dorothy was forgotten. Oblivious
to all that was happening, she remained motionless on the rock.
The warriors had advanced about a hundred yards when out
dashed Tom Merton full gallop on to the camp ground.
Swinging clear of low hanging limbs, and shouting a war cry to
confuse the black women and their offspring, he let Daybreak
out. Lord, how I held my breath as I watched! And how the
women and piccaninnies went flying for shelter when Daybreak
went pounding amongst them!

"Stay where you are, Dorothy," I heard him shout, "stay
where you are." And round the rock he swept. Daybreak
circled it in his stride; dust and ashes rising under his heels.
Tom carried Dorothy on to his knees, and before one could
realise it, was racing back with her, and urging Daybreak with
both heels and the slack of the bridle-reins. I nearly tumbled
off Whitewings with excitement. Attracted by the commotion
in the camp, the warriors paused, looked round, then with a
fresh burst of war-whoops changed their minds, and came
running back.

"I've got her", Tom puffed, pulling up short to enter the
scrub where I was hidden. Then:

"Get through as slick as you can, lad; they'll be after us."

So overjoyed was I that I couldn't speak a word, but went
ahead, guiding Whitewings through the jungle as speedily as I
could. How Tom steered Daybreak, and kept the limp, fainting
form of Dorothy clear of trees and vines, I know not. Every
other second I glanced nervously back, making sure we'd be
overtaken.

Out into the open we came again — just as the Governor and
Eustace and Kearney, their guns and ammunition rattling as
they hurriedly reached their horses. At the same moment the
fierce yells of the blacks as they entered the scrub behind us
fell on our ears like the cries of bloodhounds.

"I have her here", Tom called triumphantly to the Governor,
as he tightened his grip on Dorothy.

"On men, and away", the Governor ordered as he sprang to Hyperion; and on they scrambled, and off the lot of us galloped abreast.

We kept the pace up till we came to the hollow where the old wooden wind-mill now stands. Then, jumping from his saddle, the Governor rushed to Dorothy, took her from Tom, and never shall I forget how he held and hugged her, nor the sobs that broke from her as her arms went around his neck.

But later, when we reached the homestead, as the sun was setting in all its grandeur and glory, and Mary Rumble and Mrs. Channing, holding mother between them, and Reg and the two nigger kids, and old Warabah, the big tears loitering on his boney cheeks, were outside the big gate, waiting — when the Governor reached down from Hyperion, and put Dorothy into their arms, and said, "Here she is, Dorrie, a little frightened and upset, but quite safe and unharmed" — there was a burst of feeling that memory can never efface, and which one must always hold sacred.

Chapter 13

The Governor was a lover of good horses, with a faith in the demand that was in store for them as settlement advanced, and towns and cities increased. Looking to the time when there would be a big oversea market for the Australian horse of the right type for military purposes in India, he purchased "Exile", an imported blood stallion, and brought him to Runnibede. He was a rich chestnut horse, standing fifteen and a half hands, with big bone, a perfect barrel, massive sloping shoulders, and flashing eyes, set wide in a game, noble-looking head that glowed like the back of a beetle.

In the summer months Exile ran loose with the mares among the ranges and valleys of Wild Bee Creek; and many a time had horsemen who crossed his path when mounted on a gelding to ride for their lives to escape his jealous attacks.

In winter he was stabled, and groomed, and fed to perfection. Grooming and tending him was Warabah's work, and what a proud, jealous groom he was! No mother ever nursed her child with more affection than Warabah bestowed on Exile. No matter when one approached the stable, the faithful abo. could be heard "purring" as he applied the brushes and cloths to the silky coat of the beautiful stallion. And Warabah never spared the "elbow grease". He gloried in it.

When he wasn't purring and working at him, he was standing at the head of the stall talking to Exile like a brother, sometimes in pidgin English, often in his own Aboriginal dialect. And Exile seemed to understand everything he said, for when he spoke in coaxing flattering terms, the brilliant chestnut would listen with lowered head and dreamy eyes; but when he lifted his voice to rebuke him, Exile would stand to every inch of his height and strike a lordly, defiant attitude. Even then, if Warabah, pointing to a front or hind foot, called, "Lift 'im", Exile would promptly raise his foot. And when the order was "Stand it over", the stallion would sidle to the other side of his stall. And how visitors to Runnibede, chiefly neighbouring squatters, or stock-buyers, or land-seekers, loved to look Exile over, for through his stock turning out so well he became known to station owners and people far and wide.

And how Warabah loved the light of the horse's reflected glory as the visitors gazed at him in admiration. He got more of it than the Governor did himself. Gad, I can see Warabah now, standing there, his eyes glistening, holding the halter and stroking the friendly velvety nose of Exile. A familiar sight, too, was that of the black groom taking the horse across the yard to the water-trough every morning with only the halter on him. My! how Exile would career round and play up! He would leave the stable in a flying jump and a squeal, then round Warabah he'd spin with head down, ears back, and snorting as though he meant to devour him clothes and all. But, unperturbed, and stolid as a statue, the black would walk ahead to the trough.

As if giving variety to his exuberance, the stallion would playfully lash out with his heels, easing only when Warabah, thinking the sport had gone far enough, would lift his voice, and, jerking the halter, yell, "damn it you!" Then up he'd go on his hind legs, raising his majestic figure to the perpendicular, and in that attitude would approach the trough. If any of us chanced to be loitering there, as sometimes we would, what a scatter there'd be!

Among the mares that the Governor gathered together, some purchased from Mt. Abundance, others from Mt. Brisbane and Port Stephens, he struck a lot that "nicked" happily with Exile. The stock they threw him nearly all turned out perfect hacks, and clever, enduring stockhorses. Most of them were chestnuts, with tough constitutions, none that ever we knew was "washy", or was a cocktail. Upstanding, good-tempered animals they were, full of muscle and intelligence, and with a rare turn of speed. Nothing on the whole of Runnibede in those days thrilled one like the sight of an unbroken mob of Exiles in the ranges, or on the meadow lands of the forest along Wild Bee Creek. Standing in line, staring at you, their heads held high, tails well out, trotting around, high-spirited and proud, they were pictures that no oil painting could mock. An ideal horse-country, too, was Wild Bee Creek — plenty of shelter in the winter time, clean open country where it junctioned with the river, rich with blue grass knee deep high. And at the head of it were limestone ridges that formed and developed hoofs and fetlocks unknown to horses of the plains and the coastal swamp lands.

The first lot of Exile stock were growing and coming on about the time that Ted and Dorothy and I were in Brisbane at the Grammar. But my term lasting barely two years, I was back again at the station in time to see the handling of them. The Governor, I remember, met the train at the terminus to the railway line. Headed for home, we drove all through the afternoon and night and the whole of the next day in a buggy, behind a pair of big walloping greys that looked more like chestnuts with the dust clinging to their heated, hairy coats. For most of the journey the Governor talked of those young horses, echoing and re-echoing all that he meant to do with them, and what he would make out of them. Ted and Dorothy, much against Ted's grain at first, remained four or five years in Brisbane, and their course and schemes in life were shaped different to mine. Both Neil and Geof, too, were born while I was at the Grammar. Neil came to light under the buggy, ten miles out of Oakey. Gad! when one thinks of it, how the mater and women like her had to rough it in those days! And what other women, worse off than they, who went West for a home, for mateship and motherhood, silently endured in those wild pioneering days of the outback bush, no one now will ever know! Though the Governor as we drove had lots to tell about Neil and the baby (Geof), yet I fancy he enthused more as his thoughts turned to the young Exiles. In all, there were eighty head to be handled and broken that year, all beautiful four and five year olds.

"We'll send sixty of them to the saleyards," he said, "and

the rest will be kept in work on the station. There's one of them," he added, "just about up to your weight, Jim, a black colt out of one of the Mt. Abundance mares. A bit small, but looks like a derby winner."

I was over sixteen then, and weighed about eight and a half stone.

"I've my eye on a big chestnut for myself", he concluded as I hopped out of the buggy to open the horse-paddock gate. And how different were my feelings as I flung it wide, to the heavy heart I had when opening it going away a few years before! If there's a sadness at heart in doing things we have been in the habit of doing for the last time, I can vouch for the joy and lightness of heart there is in returning to do the old familiar things once again!

What a scene there was at the yards when we started to draft those young Exiles, and to tackle the first of them! A noble, magnificent mob they were. And what snorting and reckless rushing and crushing! Bunches of shapely chestnuts, with here and there a bay and a grey and a brown mingled with them to relieve the sameness. Willie Williams, who had returned again to Runnibede, and Eustace and Warabah and Kearney were all there in their element "woh-ing" and "werping" and "shoo-ing" amidst clouds of dust, and scrambling and trampling of hoofs. Astride the yard-caps at every viewpoint, sat a contingent of the Curlew Lagoon blacks, dusky, grinning, mirth-making spectators. Combo, Curricomb, the Captain, and even old "King Henry", with his long, grey crop of curly whiskers, had all gathered there. The tribe was part of the homestead now, with a "suburban" camp pitched on the ridge at the back of the stables; but the lagoon, of course, remained their headquarters. And though many of them, men and women, did odd jobs about the station, in return for rations and blankets, they never missed any fun or excitement that was going on. They would "down tools" and off, helter-skelter to the scene the moment they heard the ring of voices, the cracking of stockwhips, or saw a mob coming in.

"He's the one I meant for you, Jim" — the Governor laughed as a beautifully modelled black colt, in plunging to evade Eustace, nearly knocked the two of us over. Gad! he was a "one", too! Shorter in the body and limbs than any of the others, and with the head of an aristocrat. Though a lot smaller, his lofty, proud carriage made him look bigger than he really was. "He's the Napoleon of them", the Governor remarked, studying him. And Napoleon he was ever after — the same grand, game, swift little Napoleon that everyone for a hundred miles around got to know as if he was their own; the same Napoleon that was stolen from the station no less than three times, and who at the end brought more sorrow and regrets and tears to a lot of us, the day the cur of a scrub bull gored the life out him under me, than ever did human grief! And what days, ah! weeks of excitement, we had handling and breaking those youngsters! It was my first real apprenticeship to horsebreaking. But it was not all excitement — there was a lot of hard work and hard knocks, and sun-baking attached to it, too.

They were not hard horses to catch or handle. A few of them bucked, due to a hereditary streak on the side of their dams, but most of them made no more than a mad rush or two, or reared a bit. A couple of nondescripts, though, the progeny of two mares that were in foal to a brumby stallion when the Governor bought them from a passing drover, did enough bucking to do the lot. Undersized, vicious brutes they were, with eyes as treacherous as their heels. A more nervous or wilder pair of animals never entered a yard. Their hearts thumped like hammers, and their eyes glared at you in terror and distrust. Whenever the balls of mud that clung to the ends of their long tails touched their heels they let fly at them, first one foot, then the other, sometimes both together, till the joints of their legs fairly cracked again! To the dusky spectators they were the joy and delight of the earth. But the morning one of them was saddled and ridden by Tom Merton, the niggers went wilder than the bush had ever made them. It was a yellow bay, a well-set thing, with hairy legs, and eyes like an eagle-hawk's. Mother and Dorothy were at the yard, too, to see it ridden. Eustace, a good hand at holding a young horse, held the brute by the ear in the centre of the yard while Tom mounted. And holding a raw, terror-stricken animal while another mounts it is neither a pleasant nor a safe undertaking.

It calls for strength, and knack, and courage and coolness. Numbers of good horsemen would rather take their chance of the brute's back than at its head. But the wisdom of that, one only learns from experience.

"Now then," Tom called to the merry blacks on the yard-top, as he hitched his pants and approached the outstretched quivering outlaw, "if he bucks me off some of you fellows will have to get on him."

And when the Governor passed along a clear interpretation of what he had said, fully a dozen of them, men and boys — "yarman" they called the latter — started hurriedly to ascend the rails in readiness for a seat in the saddle. Eustace hung on to the ear and the bridle ring, and pulled the horse's head well round. Tom took the reins in his left, gripped the off-side of the pommel with the right, made a couple of feints from off the ball of his left boot, pulled the saddle to test the yellow bay's sensibility and intentions; then, as he made no movement beyond quivering more intensely, rose lightly, deftly, into the saddle and sneaked his foot into the off iron. With the reins in both hands, his eyes on the yellow bay's head, his lips tight-pressed, Tom sat there as light as the sun on the grass for just an instant. Only those who have ever crossed a young horse, knowing that no one had ever sat astride him before, and that if they fail to anticipate his first movement they'll hit the ground, can understand all that rushed through Tom's brain in those few seconds.

"Right?" Eustace queried, looking back over his shoulder. "Let her go!" Tom said. And Eustace let go gladly, and danced out of the way.

Brumbies! and broken necks! How that yellow bay went to market! With his head between his legs he bounced in a ball off all-fours at lightning speed across that yard, giving an exhibition of straight, hard, speedy bucking, no pig-rooting, and looking as if he meant to suicide, and make a wet spot of himself and Tom on the blood-wood rails. but he didn't. He went close enough to hit them, though, as he swerved cat-like in a whirl of dust, then back across the full length of the enclosure straight for the crowd of yelling niggers. But if they didn't scatter and climb that yard faster than ever they climbed any tree on an empty stomach, say nothing! Again he scraped the rails, this time swinging the other way round, as if by instinct to test the eye and hands and head of the rider. But Tom anticipated him to the blink of an eye; went with him as if he had grown on his back like a staghorn. Into the centre of the yard again, bucking a hurricane, the niggers, yelling, the Governor and the rest of us shouting to Tom to "hang to him". Now the tussle commenced in grim earnest. It was man or horse for it, and any tactics was fair. The horse had never bucked or rehearsed the art or any of its manouevres before, so what brain-thought he had showed instantly when he changed his attack, or whatever one pleases to call it. Round to the off he spun, completing the circle in four or five high bucks that lifted Tom towards the sky every time. Ninety and nine riders out of every hundred would have taken it for granted that the horse would repeat the circle. Tom was one of the ninety and nine. The yellowbay rose his highest, screwed his body mid-air, and, hitting the ground at the reverse, spun to the near side instead of the off. His head wasn't where Tom was looking for it at the moment, so he slipped in the saddle, and lurched to the off. He clutched, and his rein flopped. "Tom's a gonner! He's got him!" Eustace and Kearney reckoned. Gad! how I held my breath as Tom, lithe as an eel, struggled to regain his lost balance. But the yellow bay saw his chance, and put the bucks in faster; he knew he now had an advantage. He squealed maliciously. The niggers yelled joyously. The reverse circle was completed. Tom was still unbalanced, but clung with desperate grip of the pommel. Then one, two, three rapid corkscrew bucks, neither straight ahead nor in a circle, but backwards! The ugliest bucks of all — and right over the head of the yellow bay on to his hands and knees went Tom, beaten for the first time for years! Gad, how the blacks rushed in to pick him up! Some of them almost turned pale for fear of his being hurt. But Tom wasn't even scratched. When he got his wind and finished spitting and thinking, he told Eustace to "get hold of him again". Eustace held the horse again. And such an exhibition of horsemanship, and of horse-bucking, was never after seen in the Runnibede yard. Tom won, but when he dropped off, how exhausted he was! And in front of everybody, the Governor and mother included, Dorothy, carried away by the excitement of Tom's achievement, squeezed through the rails and threw her arms around him. Poor Tom! How bashful it made him look! But for him what a fatal kiss that was!

Chapter 14

Figuring everything, the blacks gave us little trouble in those early days at Runnibede — not nearly as much, I vow, as the whites would have given them could the positions, by any form of miracle, be reversed. The wonder, indeed, was that they suffered their hunting-grounds and living places to be commandeered and overrun by cattle, sheep, and horses with scarcely a protest! Generally speaking, those wild black people were an innocent, harmless race. Still, from neighbouring stations reports of crimes committed by them would reach Runnibede from time to time, and warnings "telegraphed" to the Governor to be on the watch for a visit from this tribe or that tribe. Rarely did the Governor take any serious notice. He'd merely shake his head, and blame the white settlers themselves as the cause of any trouble. "If they'll only have the sense to make friends with the tribes, and treat them fairly," he would say, "they need never be afraid."

And so it was with us at Runnibede, for as the years went on the blacks became a help and not a hindrance to us, and were our friends, and not our enemies. Of course our relations with them didn't bring a millenium, or turn Runnibede into a Utopia. There came occasions when a beast, or a couple of them, would be found slain, speared to make an abo's holiday, far out somewhere on the boundary line. But whenever the Governor heard of it he didn't tear his hair out, and play the devil about it, or in his mind see the valleys and gorges soaked with the blood of his best bullocks, and himself ruined and carrying his swag, and the rest of us starving. He wasn't like that. He was something of a humanist and a philosopher; knew the blacks had to live, and that necessity knows no law. And on those grounds he shut his eyes to the butchering of a bullock or two. Indeed, he saw the value and virtue of giving the chiefs of tribes an open order to take a beast every few moons to slay in their own way and make a tribal feast of it. It became a boon to them; gave them the time of their lives, and so far as ever I knew the privilege was never abused. Rather, it gave them a slight proprietary interest in the herds, which often in their rambles they would guard by turning any they found straying over the boundary lines back on to the run again.

But squatters there were in the Never-Never Land who nursed bitter grudges against the black people. It was difficult for them to keep their guns silent whenever they came in contact with any of them; and in retaliation the tribes attacked the lonely shepherds, and at times a homestead, fired the grasses, and speared the stock. These depredations were reported to the police, and at long intervals after their occurrences a body of mounted "trackers" would scour the country in search of the accused ones, and the accusations were mostly made wholesale. When they came across a tribe, or the remnant of one, that "dropped their bundles and ran", they judged them guilty, and would gallop rings round them, give any that looked dangerous a taste of shot, and head them all like cattle from that locality to some other corner in the Back of Beyond. Such official displays were called "Dispersals by the Police", and thereby many a pretty bush daisy bloomed on the innocent blood of the wild blacks.

It was a day in December, and as hot as an oven, and I remember it as well as I remember yesterday. The Governor and Eustace took me with them out on to Yalcalbah Plains – a name, by the way, that has long since disappeared from the map of Queensland, but is preserved on a humble selection nearer in. Some of the Exile stock had been seen out there running with a mob of brumbies, and we rode out to locate them. We had ridden far over the run, and were rounding a belt of brigalow bordering Yalcalbah Plains, keeping a sharp look-out for the brumbies, or horses of any description, when all at once we got a start, and so did our horses. The report of a gun, two barrels in quick succession, rang out ahead of us. Our horses had hardly recovered from the bounds they gave, when bang! and up rose a blanket of smoke from the bushes not fifty yards away!

"Who the deuce is shooting?" the Governor queried, staring and straining, a wild, frantic scene suddenly opened before us. A whole tribe of black people — men, women and children — crossed a sort of inlet in the belt of brigalow, running for their lives. Then in pursuit of them galloped a body of police, shouting, yelling and waving their guns as stockmen might do when on the heels of a mob of scrub-cattle.

The Governor went black with rage and shook all over with indignation.

"Surely to God they are not riding them down and shooting them?" and he was about to put spurs to his horse to get up with the police when Eustace halted him by exclaiming: "Hell, look here!" As he spoke an immense blackfellow, hopping and staggering, came from where the blanket of smoke had risen, toppled over almost beside us, and sank into the grass. His thigh bone was shattered by the gunshot. Gad! what a pathetic sight lying there, the bone protruding through the flesh and muscles, and the long grass about him smeared with his warm red blood! Our horses nearly knocked each other over in the bounds they gave to avoid him. But down and disabled as he was, he still clutched a deadly-looking spear, and was on the verge of throwing it even in that position. And perhaps if it had not been for Eustace we wouldn't have noticed. The first law of nature was inherent in Eustace, and in a voice of frenzy he shouted: "Don't you throw that bloody thing!" There was grim humour in the mandate, because he might just as well have urged the man to throw with all his might, for all he could understand. Still, something in the way of an intervention of Providence seemed to stay his hand, all the credit for which, I remember, was later claimed by Eustace. Though the Governor threw himself from the saddle to go to his aid, and made friendly signs to him, that black crouched there, his wild white eyes rolling like billiard balls, his sides heaving, his ebony skin glistening with perspiration, regarded him as an enemy. He obviously expected no quarter, and no one could say that courage had deserted him. And how he glared from one to the other of us as we came round him, our horses straining on the reins and snorting. He looked to me more as a wild animal than a man. And Eustace, I remember, kept his eyes on the spear until he had rescued it from him and tossed it aside. But when the Governor, instead of showing murderous intentions, took the puggaree from his hat and proceeded to bandage the broken limb with it, and to handle him carefully, the look of defiance and terror began to leave the black, and he lay there passive and still while the thigh was put in splints, made of switch sticks that we cut from the brigalows, and bound with straddle-straps. The blackfellow never flinched during the "operation", though merely looking on, I know, made me shudder through and through. It was the first broken bone I had seen set, and having witnessed quite a number since then, I have learnt that the old Governor was not by any means the worst surgeon in this world. And as I stood by, curiously observing the black-fellow stretched out in the long blood-stained grass, how the white skin on the soles of his feet, and on the palms of his hands interested me. And the ridgy scars across his heaving chest, not unlike old brand marks that had been burnt heavily into animals, started me wondering. What was working in his mind as he turned those rolling white eyes on me, and met mine, I would have given anything to know; and about those eyes too, I remember, lurked a couple of tears such as one sometimes sees in the optics of a beast just released from the pangs of pain. No sooner was the bandaging completed than the tragedy of it all turned into comedy.

"I think that will keep it together", the Governor said to Eustace, and rose from his knees to review his handiwork.

"He's lucky to get that much done for him out here", from Eustace. And as though he understood them, or had been turned out of a hospital, the black started to get up to run off.

"No, no", the Governor objected, placing his hands on the wild man's woolly head to restrain him.

"Tchat! You damn fool; what are you trying to get up for?" And Eustace forced him on to his back again. But for a while it was like trying to keep an old man kangaroo down, and he struggled and strained as though he held broken thighs in the highest contempt. But soon he became passive again, and the Governor was wondering what was best to do with him, when the police body, riding back in our direction, showed in sight.

The Governor coo-eed, and waved his hat to them. They came on at a hand-gallop, and, pulling up short all about us, asked what was the matter?

"Are you the officer in charge?" And the Governor closely eyed a young-looking fellow with an open, happy cast of features, and a smart seat on a horse.

"Yes," he said, "but what's up with this chap?" and he glanced at the injured black.

"He's got a broken thigh — shattered by a gunshot", and an unfriendly look of protest was on the Governor's face.

The Governor nodded coldly. Then: "Do you think it justice or a fair deal to shoot these people without giving them a trial or the chance of a word being said in their defence?"

For a moment or two there was a silence that hung heavy, even way out there in the stillness and solitude of that Never-Never Land.

"No, Mr. Winchester, I do not", was the answer, and he looked steadily into the Governor's face. "Nor do I think it justice or a fair deal that whites should take this country from the blacks without giving them some compensation or a voice in the matter."

It was an answer the Governor hadn't expected from an officer of police, and it was one that in his heart he could not disagree with.

"Perhaps so", and the sub-inspector met his gaze calmly enough.

The Governor was puzzled. So were Eustace and I.

"But we heard the shot, and saw the fellow fall", Eustace confirmed, pointing to the spot.

The officer reflected.

"There were two shots fired," he said. "I fired them myself, over the heads of a lot that turned to throw their spears, but it was a quarter of a mile from here."

"There was a third shot," the Governor insisted, "in the Brigalow there."

"Not fifty yards away", Eustace confirmed again, while I

couldn't resist hearing testimony, too.

The sub-inspector scented something. He stepped back and faced his men.

"Who fired that third shot?" he demanded. None, either white or black, answered. But so many of them glanced at Charlie Wallaby, a sly-looking member of the black brigade, as if expecting him to say something, and Charlie himself looked so unutterably guilty, that the sub-inspector instantly accused him. "What for did you shoot at this man?" he asked, "when I said no one was to shoot at all?"

The answer came from "Sam Johnson".

"Charlie Wallaby been waitin' a long time for this fellow Murrummi," he said, "two—six—four fella moons."

"What for?" and ignoring Sam Johnson, the sub-inspector addressed himself to Charlie Wallaby. But again Sam Johnson acted as counsel for his black brother-in-trouble.

"He been walk about along his lubra", he said.

"A matter of jealousy," the sub-inspector said, turning to the Governor, "but I assure you I never heard the shot, and my instructions to the men were to frighten them off, but not to shoot unless ordered to do so. It's my first visit to these parts, and while I remain in charge of the patrol I assure you these people will be treated differently to what they have been. You are Mr. Winchester of Runnibede? I'm Sub-inspector Dale." Then they shook hands, and there began between them a great friendship way out there on Yalcalbah Plains that lasted a lifetime.

Turning to the injured black, Dale wondered "what could be done with him?"

"Take him into Runnibede," the Governor suggested. "I'll go back along with you, and see what can be done for him. It's a bad smash."

Then Sub-inspector Dale ordered the injured one to be lifted on to Charlie Wallaby's horse. "And take Chalie Wallaby into camp," he added, "and keep him there till I return to deal with him."

And when they bent over the casualty to lift him up he surely must have thought they meant to put an end to him, for he clawed at them and spat in their faces like a huge tiger cat.

But in a bedlam of dialects every tracker there made effort to assure him of the white man's goodly intentions. And what a figure he cut in his nakedness when hoisted into the saddle — his bandaged leg dangling, his face filled with doubt and distrust, his black beard spread all over his chest, and his hands clutching the horse's mane. The Lord only could tell what his thoughts were! But what torture must have been his when they started off, and that horse jogged and jolted along after the sub-inspector for fully a dozen miles.

Meantime, Charlie Wallaby, holding to the stirrup of one of the police, and crestfallen and sulky, was hustled along in any old way down the river to the police camp. Eustace and I, with a few words of instruction from the Governor, went on over Yalcalbah Plains to continue the search for the brumby mob. And a hot, silent ride it was way out there in that open, treeless land — a silence that was broken only by the creaking of our saddles and the rising of quail out of the grass. We crossed to the centre of that plain, then struck north to the timber land again. Nothing did we see but plain turkeys. And what numbers of them! Great grey fellows would raise their long necks out of the grass and stalk off to clear the way on either side of us, but keeping a watchful eye on us all the time, and nodding their heads to every step. Once our horses nearly jumped out of their skins as a huge pair of wings beat the air frantically between them and a turkey rose up.

"A hen!" Eustace said, turning his horse round on the spot. "She has a nest there somewhere." And leaning from our saddles we twisted about, curiously eyeing the grass tufts. I discovered some feathers.

"Feathers are no good", Eustace grunted. "Find her blanky eggs."

Almost in the same breath he cried: "Here they are! I got 'em — two!" And off he got to secure them. A pair of large ones they were. And when he held them up way out there on that silent, sunlit plain, they seemed as something mysterious and beautiful and strange — something that suddenly broke the sameness of everything around, and gave a fascinating spell to the monotony of that mystery land of the Never-Never.

It was late in the evening when Eustace and I returned to

the homestead, and with nothing to report in regard to the brumby mob beyond the seeing of numerous tracks. To my delight when we opened the stable door the sub-inspector's horse was there staring at us. So he himself was still at the homestead! I put my saddle away hurriedly, left Eustace to attend to the horses, and skidaddled inside lest the sub-inspector might leave before I could see him again. At that age, like most boys of the bushland, a police officer in uniform to me was something of a hero to gaze upon. He was more in my mind just then than the wretched black with the shattered thigh. But when I bounded on to the back verandah I was met and surrounded by Reg and the two nigger boys, Zulu and Tarpot. Reg and Dorothy were both home on holidays.

"Heigh, Jim!" Reg gasped, "come and see the wild black-fellow they got in the back room. He's got a broke leg all strapped up. They put a shirt on him."

Here Zulu and Tarpot broke into giggles. And Tarpot said: "He wild myall, and got no trouser on, Jim."

"Warabah is talkin' to him," Reg went on, "and keeping him from getting up. And old Harry is frightened, and has got his gun ready in the kitchen."

"Oh, he wild fellow, all naked", Zulu put in with a giggle.

"The mater gave him soup," Reg went on, shoving the little nigger aside, "and he spat it all over the bed. Warabah said he reckoned it was poison. Oh, Holy! come and see his whiskers, Jim."

"I know about him," I answered, speaking with a wise and important air. "Wasn't I at Yalcalbah Plains to-day when he was shot; and helped to set his thigh? But where's the sub-inspector, Reg? Is he here yet?"

"Can't you hear him?" Reg answered. "That's him, singin' in the drawing-room with Dorothy."

So, before seeking the water-bag and the bathroom, I stole quietly along the corridor and glanced in at the officer in uniform, little thinking that before a year had passed I'd be calling him "Dick", and he'd be greeting me as "Jim", and inviting me often enough to accompany him on his patrol work. When I glanced in the sub-inspector was paying Dorothy as much attention as he might have paid to a princess, and

Dorothy herself, tho' girl as she was, you'd think had known him for years. But how wildly improbable then would have been the thought that there in that old drawing-room at Runnibede was beginning in all innocence an attachment between two people that shaped its end through rivalry, sacrifice, unselfishness, and death, and a love that no man had greater.

Chapter 15

A feature of Runnibede now was the presence of so many
aboriginals at the homestead. From a "suburban" residence, the
Curlew Lagoon tribe had pretty well made it their headquarters.
And what a change had come over those simple black people!
For years the Governor and mater had patiently striven to
enlighten them and improve their condition. Tried to show
them how to create a happier state of things for themselves, till
at last their crude camp ground on Yapparappa ridge, behind
the homestead, changed to a civilised, well kept progressive
settlement where a spirit of labour and production and law' n'
order prevailed. While they still observed their tribal rites and
many ways of the wilderness, and roamed round hunting the
'roo and the emu, and climbing trees for 'possums, they learned
between times to till the soil sufficiently to produce vegetables
for themselves and for the station use. And in season, grew
maize to provide the camp with rare feasts of roast cob.

In front of their rude gunyahs — and there was quite a street
of these — garden plots that the Governor allotted them sprang
up, and all fenced round with saplings almost lofty enough to
keep the moon and the stars from looking over, to say nothing
of keeping the station stock from breaking in to steal, and
quickly some of them, though not experts, understood the
culture and nourishment of plants and trees. With forks and
spades they turned up the soil and in buckets and oil drums
carried water from the station pump, and in dry times, from
the creek a mile away. When shown the uses of manure, every
lump of cow dung ever after was "budgeree" to them. To

establish a "market" for their surplus products, the Governor, through King Henry, explained that the station would utilise it, and give them tobacco and rations in exchange. What a scene there was at the big house when the first consignments were brought along! Without waiting to estimate whether or not there would be a surplus after their "home consumption", they rushed their produce along by the arm-load as fast as their long spindle shanks could carry them. Laws you'd think a gold mine had been found the way they hurried over the ridge and in through the garden gate! Stacks of giant cabbages stood all round the kitchen door, with more and more arriving, while the proud looking producers grinned and waited for the "tea, tchugar and 'bacca". And what a time the mater and Mrs. Channing had! After distributing the house patronage as equally and liberally as they could, they then had to make the poor niggers understand that the market was glutted, and they would have to take the rest back to camp and eat the stuff themselves . . . And the artful Combo, I remember, in pleading his case, told them that his family had "plenty fella 'possum" to eat that day, and so didn't want the cabbage for themselves. And not until the Governor arrived on the scene and made the situation plain to them, did they take up their produce and go off.

An hour or two later, when the gins started cooking cabbage for the first time, the camp became a scene of clamour and kitchen fragrance. Their billy cans and stone vessels were to small to boil the vegetables in, and there were not oil drums enough to go round. So the Governor provided them with a huge copper boiler — one that the station butcher boiled down the shin bones of bullocks in. Into the copper the gins jammed all the heads of cabbage till the water flowed over and put the fire out . . . "Baal budgeree him!" they mused, staring at the catastrophe. But Uncle Jackie, more observant than the women, explained their mistake in a long, excited lecture, and started the fire going again. Though the gins were supposed to be doing all the cooking, the men gathered round the steaming cauldron two and three deep, poking the stewing cabbage with discarded spears, and rescuing fragments of it on the ends of them, and dropping them hilariously into the open mouths of each other

– like parent birds feeding their young.

One way and another, the blacks did a deal of work about the station, though they slouched through it in their own way, taking their own time over it. Only when the mood was upon them would they commence a job, and they would leave it the moment they felt tired, or it began to bore them. Hard work really didn't appeal to any of them. But in the garden when there was an abundance of ripe fruit on the trees, or lying about under them, they laboured well. The gins, though, could never do enough housework for the mater. They gloried in the washing and scrubbing, and each envied the other the joy of using the broom or belting the dust out of the carpets when hung across the clothes lines. How loyal and devoted, too, were those black women to "White Mary". If ever she was ill, and lay up for a day, how they missed her! They would loiter round the home peering through open doors and windows for a glimpse of her. And would chant a doleful sort of requiem until allowed into the room to satisfy themselves that she hadn't "gone bung". At other times, when any whisperings were going on in the camp, a projected attack on the homestead by a hostile tribe being "telegraphed" through the bush they would seek out the mater to warn her in confidence. The mater, of course, would pass the information over to the Governor. And more than once he was able to frustrate an attempt to set fire to the outbuildings by the Cooby blacks, and to bring them to reason.

When the Curlew Lagoon people had progressed further along the lines of civilisation, the Governor and the mater set out to develop a taste for music in them. They tested the capabilities of the tribe and sifted out those with ears for melody, which most of them had to a lesser or greater degree. And how quickly they responded and picked up airs that were sung over a few times to them. It is hard to imagine anything more strange, or that fills one with deeper reflection, than listening to voices hitherto only heard chanting wild, eerie corrobborees being lifted in song in your own tongue. Uncle Jackie, the father of Curricomb, and an old favourite of Dorothy's, had a rare gift of song in his wild make-up. No sooner was a verse sung to him, than he'd spark up and echo it back. They regarded him as a "discovery". Gad! I can see the Governor and Uncle Jackie now, just as I saw them together one Sunday evening, when I had run the night horse in. At that hour the camp was all peace and quietness, and the sun was dipping behind the clouds in the west. No other blacks were there at the time. They hadn't returned from the lagoon, where they were spending the afternoon fishing and swimming. Uncle Jackie, with his back to the garden patch, his head to one side, was listening soulfully, while the Governor sang "Abide with Me". I pulled up about fifty paces from them, and waited to listen to Uncle Jackie. I hadn't yet heard him in song. So when the Governor concluded and his voice died away, Uncle Jackie rose up to his full height — a majestic looking figure he was, in dark moles, open shirt front, bootless feet and bare head. With uplifted head, he faced the tree-clad slopes of the ranges of his native wilds that looked down from the back of the homestead, raised his voice, and sang the hymn in a way that pulled at one's heart-strings. What made it perhaps more impressive was the knowledge that only a year or so before, the sight of him made you feel you were in the presence of the evil spirit that led the swine of Gadarea down into the sea! But standing there singing that sacred song, he appeared a reincarnation of one of the Apostles who went down into the wilderness. So the practice of singing went on and developed until the tribe brought forth its own choir. And what a surprise old Parson Glennie got when he visited Runnibede to hold service there one Sunday and heard them sing! Glennie, in years after, became an archbishop. He was the thinnest, leanest, and toughest man I ever remember, and he could walk like a world-beater. He did all the rounds of his "parish" on foot, often enough taking his life in his hands. How many hundred miles it was round his "parish" the Lord only could tell. Anyway, when he turned up at Runnibede, the Governor led into the service more black people with rolling white eyes and huge grins than the big house and verandah could hold. And at the close of the service the mater at the piano took charge, and the black choir, led by Uncle Jackie, sang the last hymn.

*   *   *

How the whole tribe would gather from every hole and corner of the camp and homestead to greet Dorothy on days that she arrived back on her school vacations! Gad, how they idolised and worshipped her! And as the days went by and she paid visits to the camp, or met the gins on the verandah of the big house, they loaded her up with gifts of all kinds — necklets of shells and acorns, quaint dillibags made from the skins of birds, and bundles (not bouquets) of wild flowers and wattle blooms. What joy was theirs, too, when she appeared at their camp along with the Governor or some of us, and stayed to sit with them around the fires, joining in their songs and stories and jests. Dorothy was a lovable girl, and grew into a tall, handsome woman, and how old Jackie adored her! I can see the two of them now as I pen this, as they sauntered along one afternoon past the open doors of the huts — the old black in spotless white shirt and pants, and a wide-rimmed grass hat on his head. Dorothy with a sun bonnet and a smart print frock, and a leather belt encircling her waist. She held the black's arm and looked up into his happy, black visage as he talked to her of the mysteries of his race, and told what this, that, and the other was called in his tribe's dialect.

An impressive memory, too, was the big currajong tree at the foot of the garden, when Dorothy gave tea parties under the shade of it to all the black kiddies. Old Uncle Jackie would be seated in the centre of them, telling stories of the tribe's adventures, of hunting big game, and singing songs to them. One song that he always ended up with, was one that Dorothy herself wrote for him. The whole of it I never knew, but these were its last lines:

"I hear 'em callin', Jackie, I'm going home to-night!
No longer will I play and sing for you.
Oh, yes, I'm comin', brothers — I see th' kindly light
A-shinin' down along the old Barcoo."

Chapter 16

Time went on. "Fat mobs off Runnibede" and "the Runnibede horses" were by-words along the stock routes to the coastal towns. And what droving trips we had! From Runnibede down over the border to New South Wales, and on to Maitland! The gallops in the big musters — cutting out fats on the camp at Curlew Lagoon. Ah, what exciting days they were! See the mobs stringing through the timber from all directions, roaring, snorting, sniffing, tearing the earth up, raking skin and hair off each other with gleaming sapling-polished horns, boxing and mingling together. What a ring of stockwhips! What ripping and tearing and swearing! The sight of it! Ten thousand head at least! What a mob for the stockmen to hold together! The risks that were taken — and the thrills we got! What life for a lad in his teens!

"See the proud swell of 'em, mighty pell-mell of 'em."

The mater never worried herself now about what was to become of me in the future. My occupation so far was fixed. I was to follow the Governor's footsteps, and one day take over the management of Runnibede. But before that came to pass I was to throw off my coat and take my place beside the men for many a long, hard day. There was no false pride or snobbery about the Governor. But he was no "nigger driver", and he didn't mind if a bit of sport entered into most things. So that is how I came to be one of the hands who took the thousand head of bullocks to Maitland — a thousand mile droving trip. And it was while we were away that the big mob was stolen off Runnibede. Gad, what a sensation that was! I had been back from school then about eighteen months, and Napoleon, after being broken and ridden for a year, and spelled, was brought back into work again. A wonderful little horse he turned out to be. What an intelligent, lovable animal he was! In the saddle he seemed to apply all he knew of his own kind to outwit them and all I had to do was to sit steady on him and let his head alone. The number of horses that are spoiled by men who can't ride them without pulling and dragging at their mouths is legion. And so many of them, good riders, too, and yet they don't know the weight of their own hands. No matter how freely or fast a horse answers to them they lurch him round as if its mouth were of cast iron. But Napoleon was always on the alert. His dark fiery eyes, projecting ever so much, seemed always fixed on everything around. How he would answer to the pressure of your knees, and jump off into his stride in response to the swing of your body like a hare. No wonder we got to understand each other in after years, for I had the shaping and the making of him all in my own hands. He would have been a difficult horse for anyone to spoil.

How elated I was the morning we left Runnibede with those thousand head! The sights I was to see. The life I would have by day and at night around the camp fire! How it all went scampering through my brain. In the party were Tom Merton (in charge), Willie Williams, Warabah, old Harry as cook, Bill Tymes (off Mt. Abundance), and myself.

"Take care of yourself, Jim", said the old Governor, when he shook hands after seeing us off the run. "Drop a line whenever you get a chance along the road, and let me know how everything is going. Nearly all that we made last year had to go to reduce the bank overdraft; but all that this mob brings will be profit — and it's wanted, my boy."

That was the first time the Governor ever spoke to me of the financial affairs of Runnibede, though many and many a time in after years did we sit talking them over together in his little office at the rear of the old store.

Over the steep chocolate bank, across the shallow water-bed of the Condamine, and up the other side moved the great mass

of reds and roans, ballies and brindles, across the boundary of
Runnibede, and away eastward. And how soon they accepted
the situation and settled down to a silent, moving, tractable
mob. Like humans they showed a lot of class distinction by
seeking company congenial to each other, and before night
came on most of them were swinging along in pairs and
quartettes, groups and cliques that scarcely altered right
throughout that long droving trip. And soon the drovers
themselves settled down to lolloping lazily in the saddle. For
little, if any, real hard riding is done behind a mob on the road.
It is only one of the quaint ideas of the city man that a
drover's life is a galloping one. Gad! If it were, what a supply
of horseflesh would be required along the way! 'Tis only when
emergency rises, and the unexpected happens, that galloping
enters into the day's work — when something is sprung on the
mob when they are down and resting. Something that starts
some of them — then there's a rush, a ghostly affection sets in
till the whole mob, in a frenzy, becomes terrified, and makes
off in a mad, break-neck stampede. Some galloping has to be
done to "ring" them and steady them to their senses, and to be
done, perhaps, without a saddle, and in your shirt-tails, for time
and tact are the essence of the contract in steadying a
stampeding mob. A team of horses startled by something
invisible behind the winkers are just as liable to stampede as a
mob of bullocks, and with the same blind fury.

As to horsemanship, a very ordinary sort of horseman might
make quite a good enough drover. And after droving cattle year
in and year out, from north to south, from west to east, he
then mightn't be more than a fair horseman. But give him a
dozen vigorous bull calves, just separated from their mothers, to
drive ten or twelve miles across an open plain, single-handed,
and he would perhaps be a much better horseman at the end of
those few miles than he would on finishing a droving trip
behind a thousand head of fats. Horsemen will understand.

We had only left the Condamine a few miles behind, though,
when the spare horses started to give trouble. Three of them,
after showing signs of mutiny, suddenly wheeled from the
cattle and broke back at a devil of a pace. A chestnut mare, a
mount of Warabah's, led the rush. By some mischance she had

had a foal that year, and as it had only gone to the weaning paddock during the muster, she was still fretting for her offspring. Bushmen know how a mare will fret like a mother over her babe. And if ever animal cut out the pace that chestnut mare did in the rush she made for home. Warabah himself, on Two Bob, a big brown horse with white spots the size of a two shilling piece on his neck and rump, took the first spin out of her. But before reaching the river she raced clear of him. I was riding in the wake of Warabah, at the head of the others, with Napoleon pulling all his might, and jumping every obstacle that happened in his path magnificently. I could see Two Bob floundering and failing to answer to the flapping of Warabah's long limbs. But when the aboriginal glanced back to see where was I the "S.O.S." was in the glances he gave. Then it was my turn, and so I gave Napoleon his head. Gad! How he responded! I can feel him doubling under me now. It was the first time he showed his real mettle. Passing the floundering Two Bob in a few strides, he drew on to the flying chestnut at every stride, till we came level. My knee was brushing her shoulder as we descended pell-mell into the shallows of the river. Wars! How we splashed into the water and churned it into foam! Then up over the bank by a long, grassy grade. Across a box tree flat, where we raced locked together. Instead of swinging wide, and resorting to tactics, the mare seemed to welcome Napoleon's steaming nostrils to her side — to regard him more as a pacemaker than a pursuer. At first I made no attempt to draw the stockwhip. We were too close together, and the pace was so hot that my attention was all on the reins and where we were heading for. But another idea flashed into my mind. Tossing the double of the whip over her neck, I coupled it over her throat. Then tightening the grip, I hauled her in gradually with one hand and Napoleon with the other.

The rest was easy. And when we returned with the rebels, Warabah was so full of our achievement that Napoleon's reputation was ever after established.

The first and second night out were perhaps the worst to pull through with those bellowing, moaning, restless bullocks during the whole of that long, slow trip. We struck good camps, though, those first nights on the banks of the creeks, where there were splendid grass and good watering places, and piles of firewood, carried down by floods and left there heaped up around the butts of trees in the bends. But the mob took a power of nursing and steadying before they settled to camp for the night. When the sun had gone down over those great western plains, and the camp fire began to blaze, those bullocks still mooched up and down the creek, poking and mooing, and slobbering round first one waterhole, then another. When the watchful eyes of the stockmen left them for a moment, some would hurry round a bend in the hope of getting away. Cunning as foxes, they were! In fancy I can hear Tom Merton now, as he rode along the banks like a field-marshal surveying troops, calling across the creek to us:

"Fetch them out now, boys; they've had enough filling."

Then how the stockwhips would ring out, and our voices echo:

"Wherp! Wherp! Woh there. Werp! You cock-horned, sneaking crawler!" The "sneaking crawler" would imply one that was discovered in his attempt to prowl off, and back to his mates again he would come with one of us close on his heels. And, again, the voice of Tom:

"Steady! Steady there, lads! Don't rush them. They've a long way to go."

Though it was his first undertaking, a more efficient drover than Tom Merton never took charge of a mob of bullocks. When we rounded them on to the camp, a sheltered spot between the creek and the blazing fire, where the busy, stooping figure of the cook was reflected in the dusk, how in the shadows they surged and ringed, then stood like a wall studded with gleaming, animate horns, and rolling, flashing eyes! How quietly and vigilantly we rode round them! That is an hour on the first night that is filled with anxious moments for the drover, for what might be working in the minds of them he has disturbing doubts. So he moves round, keeping well out, so as not to irritate them, but watching closely through the thickening gloom. He knows that those glinting, ghostly eyes are upon him and his horse, and lowering his voice he talks to them in a friendly, crooning, wooing way as he moves about. Not until a beast here, and two or three there, drop to their knees, then flop their carcases on to the soft grass with a grunt, does he begin to slacken the strain and to breathe freely again. Once a few of them make up their minds to camp, how soon the rest, in twos and half dozens, and dozens follow, till soon the whole mob are down in one dark, breathing mass.

Long watches we had those first two nights. Little more than half the mob rested, then only at intervals. Often enough if a close eye wasn't kept on them numbers would have slipped away under cover of the darkness. It fell to my lot to take part in the last watch. My stars! When Warabah gave my blanket a tug, and shook me to rouse me up, I felt as though I had only turned in for a minute or two. And sitting up, booted and spurred, just as I had rolled into the blanket, and rubbing my half-open eyes, I would have given the world had it been mine to tumble back again and sleep for another couple of hours. Then, riding slowly round to the other side, how one watched the gleaming horns in strange confusion, and listened to the eerie breathing of those bullocks! What ghostly impressions the whole scene made on one as dawn started to break, and rising here and there, stretching themselves, and moaning, the mob began to take shape.

So we crept along through the wide bush mile after mile, day after day, through sunshine, wind and storm and rain, from camp to camp. Lolloping in the saddle, now sitting upright, now sitting "side-saddle", making crackers for our whips from the manes and tails of our horses, snatching a word, here and there, as we moved to the head or the tail of them, hailing some passer-by for the "right time" and information about the grass and water on ahead, sometimes sighting a mob of kangaroos or a string of scurrying emus, or a coach of Cobb and Co.'s rolling westward, or northward, but all the time watching, watching, and thinking of those bullocks! Like the beasts themselves, our clothes in a few weeks were as dusty as some of the plains; and, gad! how our hair grew! And my pants, how soon they got greasy, and fell into an uncomfortable state of disrepair! It was then I realised how far away I was from home.

Though many of the days were long and dull, and uneventful, some were exciting enough. When about a hundred miles or so from Maitland, we came to a comfortable-looking selection, the home of an Irishman with a turn for horse racing, not unusual in an Irishman. His name was Rafferty, and he came out to his slip-rails to watch the bullocks as they passed. It was about noon, and Tom and I, creeping along at the tail of them, stopped to yarn with him. Unlike most of the folk we had encountered along the route, Rafferty was more interested in our horses than the bullocks.

"Not a bad little hoss ye're riding, young fellow", he said, eyeing Napoleon, who was a bit fresh after a fortnight's spell along the way. "Can he gallop?"

"He's not too slow", Tom grinned, answering for me, while the Irishman walked round Napoleon, studying his points.

"I'll give ye a chance to win a fiver with him", he suggested after looking wisely at Napoleon's teeth. "There's a little mare over in the yard, there, I'll run ye with f'r a mile."

"Let's have a look at her", Tom suggested. "She might be a thoroughbred."

Rafferty opened his lungs and yelled to his son to "fetch Lady McCree out here".

In turn Tom shouted to Warabah to let the bullocks spread out and feed on a reserve that was a short distance ahead.

From the seclusion of a number of sheds came a freckled boy of thirteen or fourteen, mounted on a prancing, glossy-skinned mare — a herring-gutted, racey-looking thing that was hand fed.

"There she is", Rafferty affirmed proudly. "Will ye take me on, a mile along the road, f'r a fiver? Money down."

And pulling a bank-note from his pocket, he approached Lady McCree and twisted it round the ring of the bridle-bit.

"Ye drovers," he added, "have all th' besht hosses, but Rafferty 'll have a go at ye f'r the sport of it with this old screw of his that he bred himself."

And he chuckled merrily, yet somehow suspiciously.

Tom glanced over Lady McCree and looked meaningly at me.

"All right," I agreed, "I'll whack it with you, Tom, for the fun of it."

"It's a wager", said Rafferty. "Put th' stakes on the posht,

here", and taking the bank-note from the bridle-bit he placed it
on top of a corner-post. Tom produced a fiver and covered it.
Rafferty tightened the girths for his son, gave him a rigmarole
of directions as to how he was to ride the mare to victory.
Then to me, as I shortened my leathers and threw my hat to
Tom: " 'Tis just a mile and a bit fr'm th' first lot of trees ye
seen up th' road there to here. Flannigan will go 'long with th'
pair of ye and be starter. Ourselves will be th' judges."

Flannigan, a long-whiskered person in dusky moleskins and a
cabbage-tree hat, had just ridden on the scene, his eyes staring
and his mouth full of questions. Tom agreed to the arrangements, and unbuckling the jackshay from the saddle, said:

"Send him for his life all the way, Jim."

So, along with Flannigan, we went to the starting post. On
the way I learned that Lady McCree was in training for the
local race meeting to be held on the coming Saturday, and had
done some wonderful "trials".

"Line up", said Flannigan, and we drew together. Then,
standing well away from us, he dropped his hat and said "Go!"

We shot off together and for a distance were side by side.
Then Lady McCree's head came back to my knee. I could feel
the loins of Napoleon doubling under me, and his whipcord
muscles fairly lifting the saddle. At the quarter mile he had
drawn right away from her, and I could hear the whip going.
After that it was no race at all. I won holding Napoleon with
both hands. So astonished was Rafferty that he didn't notice
Tom collecting the stakes from the post.

"What happened to ye?" he asked when his son pulled in.

"Nothin' ", the boy answered, gasping for breath.

"H'm!" and from Lady McCree the Irishman turned to
Napoleon, capering round excitedly, and repeatedly dragging me
over his withers.

"And ye haven't fed him on corn or oats, do ye say?" he
asked.

"Grass fed", Tom laughed. And he could afford to laugh.

"Well, he's a champion. And is he f'r sale?"

"I don't think so", and Tom grinned at me.

I shook my head, and patted Napoleon jealously on his
warm, moist neck.

"I'll give ye fifteen pounds f'r him, young fellow."

"Money wouldn't buy him", Tom told him, speaking for me again. "His father owns those bullocks, as well as the station they come off in Queensland."

"Oh! oh! oh! And what might ye' name be? I'm plaised to meet ye."

Tom enlightened him, and Rafferty and I shook hands cordially. Then each of us, two pounds ten the richer, parted with him and cantered on to pick up the mob.

Five or six miles further along, where two creeks junctioned near a belt of gums, we pitched camp that evening. From the reserve the men had got a birds'-eye view of the race, and while we sat round the fire having supper, and went on and came off watch, the match with Lady McCree supplied us all with something fresh to talk about.

Next morning, to our astonishment, when Bill Tymes went out to round up the spare horses, he found Napoleon was missing. Af first we thought he had missed him somewhere in the low bushes that grew dense there. But when Warabah and Willie Williams, after scouring the surrounding country for a couple of hours, failed to find him, we concluded he was stolen, and my heart sank within me like lead. Napoleon stolen, and perhaps I'd never see him again. So proud had I become of the fiery little black horse that now I felt useless, lonely, and like something adrift in my little world.

"You fellows look after the mob", Tom ordered.

"Camp them for a couple of hours at dinner time, and Jim and I will ride back to that Irishman's place and have a yarn with him."

So back rode Tom and I on fresh horses, or as fresh as it was for spares to be on such a trip, scanning the country closely on either side, and thinking hard as we slipped along.

We found Rafferty in his yard rubbing down Lady McCree with brushes and cloth, and at intervals shouting to her to desist from biting at him. When we told him about Napoleon he seemed genuinely surprised and upset.

"Who do ye think would steal the hoss?" he asked.

We had no idea. But Tom asked him a question or two about his friend Flannigan.

A faraway look came into Rafferty's eyes.

"Well," he drawled, "a wise man keeps a still tongue in his head, and no one should speak ill of his neighbour. For all that, Flannigan, I will tell you, is not a great friend of mine."

He paused, and we remained silent. "But, if I were ye, I would come back to this part next Saturday for th' races and have a look at th'm. If ye understand me?"

Tom thought he understood, and, thanking him, we turned to go off again.

"Ye have nothing to thank em f'r," he called out, "f'r I have told ye nawthin'."

On the way back to the mob Tom formulated a plan of action. "The grass is good now, they say, all the way to Maitland, so we'll camp the bullocks all day Saturday, Jim, while you and I'll cut back to the races and keep our eyes out for Napoleon. Our friend Rafferty didn't tell us very much, but he meant a hell of a lot."

They were miserable hours for me on watch that night, and the next night, too! Banish Napoleon from my mind for a single moment I couldn't. Not until Saturday morning broke — and a fresh, beautiful morning it was — and we were well on our way to the races, did I brighten up and listen to some of the yarns that Tom had to tell.

They were the usual class of bush races, and the course, we found, was a couple of miles off the stock route. And what a crowd of horsemen had gathered there! And the buggies and carts packed with people standing in them to view the events were a sight to remember. A race had just started. We joined the hustling horsemen lined along either side of the straight, and, standing in our stirrups, watched the field racing down the slope, around the back of the course, and into the straight. They entered it in a bunch. The crowd began to wave their hats, and roar "Currajong! Currajong!" Suddenly a horse on the outside came right away, and the shouting ceased. The favourite was being donkey-licked; and as the winning colours flew past, with the rider looking behind him, Tom and I gasped: "Napoleon!" and gazed in astonishment at each other. "Almighty!" Tom cried, and through the thick of the crowd he spurred his horse. Then up alongside him he propped short, as the jockey pulled up and turned round. Tom snatched the reins, and held Napoleon while I wheeled to the other side of him.

"You rode him well," Tom chuckled, "but this horse is stolen, and belongs to this young man here."

Then there was commotion. The mob gathered round shouting out questions. The officials fought their way through them. The jockey protested nervously. Tom, sticking to the bridle reins, stated our case. Then Rafferty pushed his way in. He declared he "knew the horse belonged to these gentlemen", and told how he had matched his mare against Napoleon for a wager, and lost. Calls for the man who brought Napoleon on to the course and entered him for the race were not responded to. He wasn't to be found. The jockey said he had been engaged by Flannigan to ride him for a friend of his. Flannigan was not present either, and the "friend" had disappeared. That ended it — and we gladly left the course, leading Napoleon between us. Gad! How pleased I was when we got well away! And what joy there was in camp that evening!

With only a few head short, Tom delivered the mob in good condition to the agents in Maitland. They netted, I think, about four pounds a head. Then, after a few days' spell, we started back on a long, weary ride for Queensland and home. How long it took to do the journey I forget now. The last couple of days, though, when nearing the old station boundary, were the longest stretches of all. Yet what feelings of joy and gladness came to us when familiar landmarks began to reveal themselves. Creek crossings on the Queensland side. Table-top Mountain, on the Darling Downs. Bushmen coming east, starting their evening fires. Mountain gorges, and towering peaks where eagles built their nests. Stalking flocks of high-browed, hollow-eyed emus of aboriginal mould. Curlew Lagoon. And then — Runnibede, old Runnibede again.

Chapter 17

Contrary to what was expected, the Cooby tribe resorted to no treachery or acts of revenge, but as time went on showed a disposition to become friendly with us at the homestead. At certain seasons they would travel down from the ranges to pitch camp by the edge of Myall Scrub, where they corroboreed and feasted on the fruit of the bunya that grew there, but now, like many other timbers of those pioneer days, is pretty well denuded from those parts. It was only a temporary camp, however, little care being taken in erecting gunyas. The clouds served as blankets for many of the tribe, and the tufts of kangaroo grass were their pillows. It was pitched well in sight of the big house, where, looking from the back verandah at night, we could see their fires, and often by day watched the smoke from them curling above the gunyas up into the sky.

Gad! How nervous and restless the mater would get while the "Coobies" were camped in the old scrub! She could never forget that they had once kidnapped Dorothy, and though the Governor laughed at her fears, and assured her that our black neighbours merely wanted to corroboree now and roam in peace, and to be friendly, she took consolation only in the thought that Dorothy was away at school. But the day the Governor decided that he and I would ride over to the camp and take with us a supply of bread and beef as an offering of peace and goodwill to the tribe, Lawd! you'd have thought the mater had received word that we had been captured and roasted alive by the mob. Nothing could persuade her that we wouldn't be speared through and through if we went near them, and "then what will happen to us, Edward; and to the station?" she asked. "The place would be surrounded and set fire to."

"Not a bit of it, Dorrie", the Governor assured her. "They're nearly as harmless now as 'King Henry' and Curricomb, and Captain, and all these of the Curlew Lagoon tribe." But not until Mary Rumble broke into mirth, and expressed some confidence in the Cooby people, were the mater's fears allayed at all. And then she insisted on the Governor carrying fire-arms, and warned me to be sure and ride Napoleon, and not to go too near them.

"Put a pair of running shoes on Napoleon, Jim", the Governor jested as we rose from lunch to go to the stables.

Most of the tribe were away hunting in the scrub when we rode up to the camp. A number of old people — grey-haired grandfathers and grandmothers — were in possession, squatting before the doors of the gunyas — their sunken eyes fixed strangely upon us as we approached, for be it remembered the aged and infirm were not deserted by these wild people of the never-never land. Those melancholy, emaciated old folk crouched there like ghosts of the dead sitting by their old camp fires. The Governor greeted them cheerfully, and tried hard to start a conversation, but they only gazed on in strange silence at us. And not as much as a grunt came from any of them. And not until we dismounted and revealed the bag of provender, and the Governor patted one of the old women on the head, did they begin to realise that we hadn't come while they were alone to destroy them and fire the camp. But even then it was plain they had some bitter memories of white men's dealings, for, when the Governor proffered one of the "grannies" a scone, she shook her head, while her dim, sunken eyes clouded over with distrust. The Governor understood, and, turning to me, said:

"Eat one, Jim, and let them see there's no strychine in them", at the same time taking a bite from one himself and munching it up.

I ate a scone in quick time, but before I could gulp down the last of it, a half dozen pairs of long black bony hands were held out to the Governor. Next minute he was doing great business serving out the scones. Gad! What a picnic it was. The old men, after the first taste, in the greed plugged their mouths with whole ones, and went nigh choking themselves. They behaved like big hungry kids at a school treat when the cakes came round. And while the Governor was joyously feeding these poor old things a contingent of the tribe, returning from their hunting exploits, suddenly stalked with the silence of emus from the scrub and stood before us. My stars! If I got a start, they looked a bit surprised, too. For the moment I was for jumping on to Napoleon and clearing for my life. But on a sharp "stay where you are, Jim", from the old Governor, I stayed, with little credit to myself, though, and took my chance. There must have been twenty of them at least, and all men, tall, lithe looking fellows, some with spears in their hands, others holding dead 'possums and a couple of wallabies by the tails. And the more I stared at them the more I noticed what fierce, stubborn, black devils they mostly were, with their naked bodies streaked with the scars of adventure. For a moment or two they seemed to be trying to take in the position of affiars. The Governor, too, was silent, perhaps waiting for some of the old people to say something . . . Then suddenly a round of terrifying interrogations directed at them broke the spell, and cracked like thunder upon the solitude. Exactly what their words were, I don't know, but pretty sure it was they demanded to know of the old folk what the hell we whites were doing in the camp, and what was it they were eating. Anyway, the old people were not much perturbed by the questions, for, with self-satisfied expressions on their sunken faces, they rubbed their bingies with their hands and went on eating. Then the Governor made some friendly signs, and got off a few words in their dialect, which set them at ease and brought them all round us like long lost brothers who had gone bush, and formed themselves into a new tribe. All the same, I confess I was still ready at any moment to take a flying jump on to the back of Napoleon and head for the homestead. The old people, however, had nothing to explain to them. They couldn't have spoken, anyway, for they stuffed their mouths more and more with scones. Indeed, a couple of the old fellows resented their home-coming, for, when one of them essayed to sample the scones, they rose to crouching positions and waved their lean hands and stamped their bare feet in protest. The Governor, however, was able to treat them all to some meat, which they devoured greedily. They talked and laughed a lot among themselves, and when we mounted our horses to come home they gave us a boomerang apiece, and to assure us, I suppose, that they were the genuine article, two of the warriors took them and, stepping out into the open, threw them simultaneously in different directions. I have seen many boomerangs thrown since them, but never such an exhibition as that. No two birds could have been trained to leave the hand, and taking flight in opposite directions, rise gradually into the sky, circle round and return together at different angles with greater accuracy than those boomerangs were made to do.

It was six months or so later, while the Cooby tribe were again camped by Myall Scrub, that Moom, a beautiful girl of eighteen, the daughter of Hippee and Cobbotha, fell ill and died there. The wailings of sorrow and grief that the death caused in the camp, I can well remember. How distinctly their lamentations could be heard at the homestead on the night air! On that occasion, too, the Governor and I visited them, and Warabah went with us. It was the second day of their mourning, and we learned that the dead girl had been a great favourite with the tribe and was looked upon in the light of a princess. Also, that the death had been the work of some mysterious spirit. News of Moom's death was telegraphed throughout the bushland that lay far back in the ranges, and in wonderfully quick time, instead of fifty or sixty mourners, there must have been a couple of hundred gathered there. They turned up from every point of that realm of ranges in unaccountable fashion, coming at a long swinging trot, and announcing their approach in weird cooees that made the bush seem haunted with lost and tormented souls.

What preparations they made, too, for the burial of the dead girl! The choosing of a last resting place. The making of a bier, and the tribal requiem. The solemnity of their black visages, and the noisy howling consultations they shared! Sheets of stringy bark were stripped from two trees as similar in size, shape and foliage as could be found (one of them, with a new growth of bark, still flourishes by the old scrub; the other has long since disappeared), and between the sheets the corpse of Moom was bound fast by vines cut from the scrub. Upon the bier, formed of green boughs placed on the grass, she was laid in her coffin. Around it the mourners collected in a large circle. The women and children sat in the inside; the men knelt or stood round at the back. Though a form of religious ceremony, it was filled with childish antics. And as we stood there as witnesses, well can I remember the Governor giving me a dig with his elbow and saying, "Don't be laughing at them, boy." Gad! How difficult it was to watch their faces and refrain from chuckling. The day was a sweltering one, too. The sun blazed down from a white sky, while the leaves of the myalls and kurrajongs sparkled and shimmered in the glaring light. In the throes of their grief, those wild men twisted their bodies, rapped their war weapons together, and waved their long, fierce beards and marched round and round while they drooled and chanted a dirge. The women joined in and beat time by slapping their naked thighs with the palms of their hands, much the same as when they kidnapped Dorothy. This ceremony or corroboree ceased only when a scarred and heavily bearded patriarch, as fierce looking as any wild animal, rose to address them. What class orator he was, I can't say, but he was the tribe's prophet, rainmaker, priest and oracle, in whom they had the simple, unshaken faith of children. For, upon his premonitions as to the fate of the dead girl, they placed their dependence. Strange, I have often thought, that a wild, primitive people, who had so much fear of a devil-devil and no idea of a Providence, should hold, however crude, a belief in reincarnation! For such was the hope and consolation that this scarred and bare-limbed prophet — Goondi-Goondi — held out to them in their grief.

"Don't you mind about it, my children", he told them, according to the old Governor's interpretation. And Gad, I can see the latter listening, now, leaning forward with a hand behind his ear, as though on the prophet's words hung the fate of the bushland. "Our beautiful Moom, she go bung now, but in six moon she jump up white, and come back to Cooby people to be their white queen."

And when he had pronounced the benediction, which he interpolated with a high jump and a self-inflicted spank on the calf of his leg, in response to an attack by a wandering jumper ant, a confusion of willing pall-bearers surrounded the bier. As many as were able laid hold of the coffin, and, raising it to their shoulders, marched off with it along the rim of the scrub, followed by the others, all groaning and lamenting harder than before. Halting by the trunk of a crooked old gum tree with low-spreading branches, "grave yard tree", as it was called ever after, they hoisted the remains of Moom on to a frame that was fixed in the first fork, and there they left her in her last resting place, among the scented blossoms, above the nodding dandelions and daisies, near to the everlasting stars, and out of reaching of the prowling, slinking dingoes — left her to come down again on the sixth moon to a new life; and without further weeping or smacking of thighs, silently dispersed and went their different ways, into the wilds of their own land, the great Australian bushland.

Chapter 18

Though we had gone in the waggonette to meet Dorothy at the railway terminus numerous times before, it somehow seemed different now. Her school days were over, and how the years had passed! She was coming home for good, to be a help and comfort to mother at the homestead. There would be no more "few short weeks at home", no more partings and seeing her off midst tears and sobs and sad good-byes and remembrances! And so it was in the feeling that she was coming as a joy for ever that we waited for the train to come in, and in those days it only came in on two days of the week.

"There she is!" and, as the carriage rolled past the little platform siding with Dorothy smiling and waving from a window, the old Governor left me standing, and jostled his way through teamsters, station hands, blacks, half-castes, dogs, oil drums and wool packs, to be up in time to open the door for her. I was forced to limp carefully after him because of a stiff knee that I had from being run against a tree during a muster at Wild Bee Creek a few days before. But for the mishap I might not have been there at all ... And when I reached the carriage door, not only had the Governor lifted Dorothy to the ground, but he was tossing her up and down like a doll, to find out how much heavier she had got, with the motley crowd of spectators enjoying the performance. And gad! what a swag of luggage she had with her! Bags, baskets, cloaks, coats and hat-boxes without end! When the lot were stacked on the old waggonette, along with the usual station parcels, it was with hard squeezing that the three of us could find sitting room amongst the pile.

"So long as I can get my feet somewhere, and have room to handle the reins," the Governor chuckled, "I'll be all right", and Dorothy wedged between the two of us, was sure she "wouldn't fall out, 'less Jim did". So away we went, and at a slashing pace behind the pair of greys that the Governor wouldn't sell for love or money — and big money he was offered more than once for them, too. He was a great "whip", like many station owners; and driving was driving those days. And how the feet of those greys soon had the dust flying along that stock route! It was a splendid season, too, one of the best that ever we had on Runnibede, the sort that puts a lot of heart into you and makes you forget you ever had an overdraft or that there ever was a drought. And the day was a real stock-rider's day — the air so crisp and ripe with the scent of blossoms, of green, fresh herbage and brushwood. Spreading out to either side as we rolled along were miles of wattles in bloom, and red gum tips were splashed against the green of the grass. And far on ahead, as far as the eye could see, stretched the great wide plains that beckoned west, forever west ... Rattling over those old scenes again in all their glory, what a joy it was to Dorothy. There was nothing she missed — no rock slide, skyline, tree, shade or sun effect escaped her attention. Objects that passed under the eyes of the Governor and myself in dull procession, Dorothy enthused over as things of beauty, the joys and delights of the bushland ... At first her outbursts of admiration were full of amusement for me and inducive to fits of merriment, but before we were a quarter way along the road I found myself tuning my eye to searching out quaint old gums, unique coolibahs, battlemented rock slopes and land-scapes, lest Dorothy should miss them between the rolling of the waggonette and her snatches of conversation with the Governor. And how I remember when we came up the bank out of Bungeworgaori Creek, a name that is well-known now, the pair of great grey kangaroos that was there! Laws, they were a size! Down on their paws picking at the young grass that was shooting after a forest fire had been across that way, their huge tails resting along the ground, they seemed, for a moment or two, to be animals we had never seen or heard of before . . . As we swung round a bend in the road and came close to them, they rose up like a pair of giants, and stood as a couple of soldiers at the attention, gazing at us fearlessly, and as though we were an every day happening in their lives. We must have been near enough to those old 'roos to have roped them without much effort — I could feel Dorothy fairly tremble with the thrill they gave her, and the old Governor was so amused at the cool daring of the 'roos that he stopped the horses.

"Get out, Jim," he chuckled, "and catch them," I was nearest them, but instead of getting out, I let go fly more than half an apple that I had been munching, at Dorothy's invitation, and it struck one of the old 'roos fair in the paunch. Falling stars! That "old man" got the surprise of his life. He jumped so hard and so blindly that he knocked his mate over, and lost his own balance and his head. They both sprawled on the ground, each struggling to rise before the other. And when they found their legs and tails again, they made off, flying from our yells of mirth as if were dogs pursuing them.

The incident filled Dorothy with thoughts of a kangaroo hunt on a big scale, when her school friends, whom she had been telling us a lot about along the way, would come to spend their vacations with her at Runnibede.

"Jim and Tom Merton will be able to get up a hunt for you", the Governor suggested. He was never an ardent kangaroo hunter himself, always reckoning he could get more galloping than he wanted out of mustering the cattle.

Then, leaving the hunt to me, he talked of other things. Dorothy, I remember, asked a lot of questions about Tom, just as though the mere mention of his name had prompted them. But I know now that there was much more at the back of those questions than most people might dream of. I didn't know, either, that more than one letter had come in the station mail bag for Tom in her handwriting, and they had set the mater and the old Governor thinking and wondering very earnestly. And I could understand more clearly, a year or so later, why it was that the Governor, while not speaking much of Tom, had a lot to tell her of Sub-inspector Dale (Dick Dale, as he called him), and his visits to Runnibede. "A fine young fellow", the Governor would say. "He's taking my advice as to the way the blacks should be treated. He'll go a long way in the service, will Dick." And dropping Tom Merton for the moment, Dorothy was soon interested in all that the Governor had to say about Dick Dale. So much so that she began recalling the few memories she had kept of him. She remembered the mater and she "thought him a very nice man the first time he came to the station", and that he "had a fine seat on a horse".

"A splendid horseman", the Governor enthused.

"But not the horseman that Tom is", I put in, always feeling that Tom had no equal anywhere in the saddle.

"A different style of horseman, Jim," the old Governor reminded me, taking a shorter grip of the reins to steer the greys through a number of close-growing cherry woods — "quite a different style."

And then when Dorothy almost sighed: "Oh, the day Tom rode that outlaw!" and sat back, without saying any more for quite a long distance. I should, when I think of it now, been a lot wiser than I was to the understanding and sympathy between them.

But the lull in the conversation made no difference to the greys. They continued to step it out over those rolling plains — foam gathering at their flanks and hot steam coming from their nostrils — at intervals new-shorn sheep scampering out of their way, and quail and ground larks rising in confusion from the long grass. It was a long drive, travelling hour after hour throughout most of the day. But as the last miles were thrown behind, as the sun sank lower and lower, we drew nearer and nearer to the old homestead. The winding track threaded a clump of black wattles, taking us on to the turn-off at the northern side of the home paddock. The "new gate" had just been put there — it's a crumbling old tumbledown gate these days — and the road made a mile shorter. Some distance off we could see a gathering of blacks there, with a horseman in the centre of them. A mild form of excitement was going on, the cause of which, for a moment or two, wasn't clear to us.

"It's Tom Merton", I discovered at last. "He's riding one of those fillies we handled last week — couldn't get through the gate by herself, I suppose."

"And some of the Cooby blacks", the Governor said, as we came closer . . . What a start Dorothy gave! We couldn't fail to notice it, and laughed at her . . . but it was only a nervous flush, for next moment she was wondering aloud if any of them would remember the time they kidnapped her?

"They don't forget anything," the Governor said, "but they've been tamed a lot since then and you were very small, and they understand us whites better now."

Then as we came to the gate: "What's going on, Tom?"

"Helloa! . . . Oh, nothing, Governor", Tom shouted, as the filly sidled and capered about, after bounding through the gate which was held open by enough black hands to pull it down and toss it away. "She didn't want to come through while so many were looking at her."

"I thought, perhaps, they wanted to buy her from you", the Governor jested, as he drove the waggonette through into the home paddock and reined up the greys again.

Poor Tom! We were almost beside him now, and how he blushed, like a ripe tomato, when Dorothy smiled upon him and asked how he was. I felt sorry for him, he was so self-conscious, and how he did his best to answer questions the Governor was asking, and at the same time to raise his hat to Dorothy. And by touching his hat, however stealthily, he was taking risks on a nervous, flighty thing, the first time out. Horsemen will understand.

"Are you breaking in, Tom?" Dorothy observing the caution with which he sat the filly, asked. "What a pretty head it has!"

Tom, as he made answer, blushed more and more.

"Miss Winchester will want a kangaroo hunt arranged, Tom", the Governor began, when he was interrupted. Goondi, the oracle of the tribe, who was one of those in the gateway, suddenly approached the waggonette on the side on which I was sitting, and with mouth and eyes agape pointed right straight at Dorothy. What a start she got! and I could feel her clutching my arm, and with her other hand, I suppose, clutching the Governor as well. At first I thought Goondi merely wanted to shake hands with her, and perhaps apologise on behalf of the tribe for having stolen her away to Circus

Scrub on that memorable evening, and from the look on his face, for a moment, I got some grim amusement. But the light in his eyes imparted a different meaning to Dorothy. A strange stare came into them, and he stood there with finger poised; his scarred chest, as he leaned over, pressed against my knee. And the breathing of the old beggar suddenly speeded up to a pitch of excitement.

"What's the matter?" I said to him, with a grin, but instead of answering, he crooned something to Dorothy, and held out both hands to her in a beseeching way, as if he wanted to make love to her. Gad, I would have laughed into his big black ear, only that I felt Dorothy's clutch fasten like a vice. Then the Governor took a hand. "You know her? You want to speak with Dorothy?" he asked. But ignoring him, the prophet turned his head and said things to the other blacks that brought them hurriedly to the waggonette, and there they stood, all yabbering to each other and gazing up at Dorothy. I could see there was no joke in it now, and Dorothy became so alarmed that she appealed to the Governor not to let them touch her! The Governor had to think quickly. Tom Merton, calling to them to "get back out of that", tried to work the filly nearer the waggonette, but she reared and shied off. Still, their manner was not violently aggressive, and at last, among all the excited yabber, we several times caught the name "Moom", then "Moom" again and again. Quickly the cause of the clamour dawned on the Governor. Dorothy was Moom, the dead girl, returned in six moons as their white queen. And exactly six months it was since the black girl had been left in the fork of the gum tree by the rim of the scrub.

"Baal Moom — Baal Moom!" the Governor said, shaking his head at them as he placed his hand on Dorothy's shoulder ... But his words had no effect. Their Moom, she was, jumped up white woman to be their queen. And out went all their hands. Laws, it looked awkward! But the old Governor wasn't the one to put up with a lot of nonsense too long.

"Get out of the road", he called, and not caring a darn if they understood him or not, or got run over, whipped up the greys and away we went. When well away we looked back. Instead of them following, as we expected to see, they were all running for their lives towards their camp at the scrub.

"They are going to tell the rest of the tribe that Moom has returned", the Governor said. And in his voice there was a note of anxiety. Then steadying the horses to give Dorothy time to recover herself, he told her not to mind; that it was just a mistake on the part of the blacks, and that she had nothing to fear from them. "But say nothing to mother", he added. "I'll tell her all about it myself, to-morrow."

Chapter 19

Next morning. We were finished breakfast when Maria, the wife of "Captain", suddenly darkened the door. Rolling her eyes about to locate the mater, she said excitedly: "You tell him Governor, plenty fella wild black sit down to yabba along gum tree ... you tell him White Mary." And while we looked up at each other in surprise, she withdrew and was gone. The gestures of the old gin, her earnestness, gave us a start that brought silence to the table.

"Whatever does she mean?" and the mater stared hard at the Governor.

"Don't be alarmed, Dorrie", he said. "She meant the Cooby tribe, I suppose; they'll be looking for some rations — run short at their camp, I expect." And rising quietly from his chair, the Governor walked out on to the verandah from the northern end of which a clear view of the clump of blue gums that in those days grew on the flat in front of the homestead was to be obtained. But time has passed since them and seen those trees reduced to stumps and ashes. And as he went out, how the women's eyes followed him, then were questioningly turned to each other. That they dreaded some mischief behind the sudden appearance of these wild blacks was plain, and for my part, somehow, I didn't want to partake of any more breakfast. So, leaving the table, I stole out on to the verandah and stood beside the Governor. "Slip out through the garden, Jim," he said, in a low tone, "and tell the men to load their guns and come up quietly to the big gate ... but not make a fuss."

Laws! I never carried out an order with such feelings of awe and responsibility, never before or since. And through the gardens and down to the huts in full view of the loitering blacks I went full split . . . before I had scarcely opened my mouth the men anticipated the message . . .

"It's all right, Jim," they said, "we've been watching them for the last half-hour, whatever it is they've come about." Then they saw to the firearms that were always at hand though seldom used . . . and I remember how they joked about Curricomb and Captain and others of the Lagoon tribe running for dear life over Yabberrappa Ridge (named after the bronze-wing pigeon) to their camp when they saw the Cooby men gather at the blue gums. The Lagoon tribe were anything but warlike themselves, which, I suppose, made easy prey of them, and accounted for their diminished numbers. Anyway, if there was going to be trouble at the station, it was clear King Henry and his people were not going to become involved . . . and the warning that old Maria had given us was undertaken only because of her great attachment for "White Mary" (the mater).

"That black devil, Goondi-Goondi, the prophet, is egging them on to something", Tom Merton said, snapping the trigger of his gun. "And if the Governor was only away in Brisbane instead of here, I'd walk straight over and put a charge of rock salt into his hindquarters." Then, as in fancy we saw the big grizzly aboriginal careering off under the pangs of salt, we laughed outright at Tom.

Closing the door and fastening it on the outside when ready to leave, Eustace added: "Since he has come back to the tribe after being amongst the whites at Barambah, he's got as cunning as a mongrel dingo, and is putting a lot of villainy into the tribe."

"Look at him now," and Kearney drew attention to Goondi-Goondi addressing the others as we started off for the big gate — "look at him laying down the law to them!"

"I'd like to counterline my saddle with his grizzly hair," Tom chuckled, striding carelessly along with his gun on his shoulder, "and eat his fat in a damper."

"Don't take any notice of them, Jim", I heard Eustace say, as he came behind me. "Walk on as if you didn't know they were there." But what the others did, or how they looked or

walked over the distance that separated the huts from the big
gate, I can't now say. I know, though, that with the corner of
my eye I took in every movement of those tall, lithe blacks as
they moved about yabbering among themselves in the shelter of
those gums. And had any sudden demonstration on their part
necessitated our making a dash for the big gate, I reckon I
would have reached it first. There must have been at least one
hundred of them, and as we passed along they were within
three hundred yards or so of us. But they merely watched us,
though two of their number, I remember, the humorists of the
tribe, stumped about mimicking Kearney, who walked with a
limp and was very bandy.

"I don't know what's in the wind down there", the
Governor said, meeting us at the gate. "They mightn't mean
anything; but stand your guns in here and just go on catching
your horses, as though nothing mattered . . . Keep your eyes
about, though, till we see what's going to develop."

"It's Goondi-Goondi, Governor", Tom Merton repeated.
"He's got them stuffed with the idea that Miss Winchester is
the dead girl come back to life again."

"Lot o' black dawgs", old Harry, who came to join our
forces, bewailed. "They oughtn't to be allowed on the station."

"The tribe, themselves, have been very friendly for a long
while", the Governor mused.

"That fellow, Goondi-Goondi", Willie Williams put in
quietly, "has picked up some words in English and doesn't
know their meanin' . . . I said 'good-day' to him yes'day, when
passing their camp, and he called out: 'you fella liar . . . fella
fool'."

"Hold on", from the Governor, as they were about to go to
the yard. "Here he comes now, and two others with him . . ."

Sure enough Goondi-Goondi, with a tall warrior either side
of him, had left the others and was approaching us on some
errand or other.

"They're carrying no weapon, so sit down, men, and smoke
your pipes while we hear what they have to say." Then to me:
"Run into the house, Jim, and tell mother that everything is all
right, and not to be nervous." Gad, the way I sped along the
garden walk and flew into the house must have been enough to

alarm anyone. When I burst in, the women, including Mrs. Channing, snatched at things to defend themselves with. If they had had firearms in their hands they would surely have let them all off at me. I rattled off the Governor's message to them, and was away again before they had time to recover.

On came the three nude stalwarts, quite fearless, and talking audibly . . . when about fifty yards away they gestured and waved their hands to signify friendship. Stepping forward a pace or two the Governor called: "Hello, Cooby men", and saluted in a friendly manner. The three grunted in response and came to a standstill. Then Goondi-Goondi, as spokesman, addressed the Governor excitedly, while his two supports grinned at the rest of us. The station hands, lying on the couch grass, their heads propped up on their elbows, looked up from under their slouch hats as they nodded and smoked. So near were the abos that one was standing right over the form of Tom Merton, and Tom seemed to be studying his bare feet. Of what Goondi-Goondi was declaiming, the Governor seemed to have a fair understanding, but I certainly had but a vague idea.

"Look, you Goondi-Goondi," he responded warmly, "you ben tell your people lies that Moom come back a white woman — young woman that come back here is my daughter, not your Moom." Then he translated his words into their own dialect. Still, Goondi-Goondi was not silenced. He jabbered louder, made a series of fierce gestures, mentioned the name of Moom repeatedly, and stamped his bare feet. The Governor shook his head and said: "Bah, you might fool your tribe with your nonsense, but don't try it on em, else —" and again he resorted to the abo dialect. Once he conferred with Warabah, who addressed Goondi-Goondi, but with little apparent satisfaction, for they concluded with an exchange of angry grunts. Then the "prophet" turned and waved a black hand to those assembled at the gum trees, and faced the Governor again. The Governor waved him off with both hands, and said: "Be off with you, you're only a humbug."

"We'll soon send him, if you want us to, Governor", Tom Merton chuckled.

"No, no," he answered, "let him take his own time."

Goondi-Goondi then delivered a harangue to his supports, in

the course of which he pointed to the big house, and several times mentioned Moom again.

"He say", Warabah interpreted, "that Moom jump up white to be his wife, and you hold her inside, and they will go back and tell king you won't give her up."

Gad! I shall never forget the look that came over the Governor.

"What!" he said, clinching those solid fists of his and edging closer to Goondi-Goondi. "You black imposter, you want my daughter?" But just as he was about to crack the prophet hard on the chin, Tom Merton, having struck a match to light his pipe, mischievously laid the flaming wax calmly on the bare instep of one of the abos as he stood glaring at the Governor. Laws! That unsuspecting black let out such a yell, and jumped so high and sideways, that he took the punch the Governor aimed at Goondi-Goondi right on his bingie, and went down to it in a heap, but in a second he was on his feet again and running for his life, with Goondi-Goondi and the other warrior hard on his heels. The incident gave such a sudden and surprising turn to the interview that even the Governor looked confounded, then amused, as we gazed after the skedaddling delegates. Then Tom Merton and the rest scrambled to their feet, and as they went off to the stable the echoes of their mirth rang back mockingly from the side of Yabberappa Ridge.

"God bless me," the Governor broke in, with increased amusement, "they are all running." And so, indeed, they were, every man of them, without even waiting to hear what Goondi-Goondi and his friend had to report.

What with a run of splendid seasons, a big rise in cattle, the old house turned into a cedar mansion, Dorothy home for good, the Cooby tribe persistently claiming her as their white queen, Dick Dale paying his attention to her, and the mater and the Governor worried because of a secret attachment between her and Tom Merton, Runnibede was indeed in the throes of romance! Though I couldn't understand then — I can well understand now what the old Governor's feelings must have been when the knowledge of love between Dorothy and Tom first came to light. And how the mater used to press him to speak to Tom about it — to "tell him he mustn't think of

Dorothy any more, but go back to his own people and forget her". What a delicate duty it was for the Governor! For he himself was no snob or class distinctionist, but a big-hearted, broad-minded humanist. Find fault with Tom Merton as a man — straight, honest, courageous, capable and white — he couldn't, nor could any honest, manly person ... True, he wasn't educated as Dorothy was, and his people were not well off like hers, and for those reasons, perhaps, and it was only a perhaps, mateship for such a pair would be inadvisable. The Governor, he could advance no other sane or friendly objection ... The mater, on her side, had something different in view for her daughter ... If she married at all, she wished to see her marry someone with a position and some standing. In her heart she had nothing against Tom. She was fond of him, in fact, and openly admired his courage and manliness. But not until one day when out on Wild Bee, and while we were waiting there in the shade of a myall to meet Eustace and Kearney, was it that the Governor opened his mind and spoke to Tom of his love affair. Poor Tom! How the blood rushed to his sun-tanned cheeks when the Governor got out the first few words. His soft grey eyes seemed to loom larger, and he didn't know what to do with his hands. And half turning his head he gazed at his horse standing over him, while the Governor was speaking. And when the latter, softening his voice, said: "You know, Tom, while I don't think Dorothy is one bit better than you, she's hardly the sort of girl, all things considered, who would make a good helpmate for a man in your position."

"Yes — I know, Governor!" was all that Tom could say, and anyone could say, and anyone could see that it was with a struggle he found his voice even to say so little. In what way the mater broke the matter to Dorothy I never knew; but one afternoon when I came upon them together in the garden, beneath the English oak tree that stands sighing there in the cool breezes to this day, "Tom loves me, mother, and I love him", Dorothy sobbed. "He is a good fellow, and it's nothing if he hasn't got money or position ... those who have are not the best men."

I didn't hear any more. But I remember she always had a strong will of her own, and could be stubborn as a wall. Tom, I know, did his best to meet the Governor's wishes, and many times after avoided Dorothy's company in his daily rounds. But it was in the periodical visits of Dick Dale that both the mater and Governor, I fancy, began to see a hopeful solution of the trouble. Apart from his position of Sub-inspector of Police, which in those days was of some degree in a young colony, Dick had a rare personality that assured him unusual popularity. He was a handsome, free and capable fellow. And instead of Tom regarding him as a rival and harbouring feelings of jealousy towards him he met him openly as a friend ... They came together way out on the run on occasions and joined in dare-devil feats of horsemanship in the wake of a wild dog or a fugitive kangaroo. Yet, thinking back now one is pretty sure that had Dorothy at any time during those days been called on suddenly to choose between them she would have been thrown into a dilemma.

It was in the old home, though, when Dick Dale was on a visit, and Tom invited along by Dorothy for the evening, that the former seemed to put Tom in the shade. Dick could play and sing and dance well, while Tom only danced, and then clumsily and under much persuasion. And how noticeable it was on those evenings, though by no means neglected by Dorothy, that poor Tom felt himself at a social disadvantage.

The months went by and Dick's visits to Runnibede were continued. Tom seemed to take the former's attentions to Dorothy as a matter of course. And how pleased the mater became! But with his inner self Tom was having a harder fight than anyone knew ... for in the height and blindness of his love he acknowledged to himself that Dorothy would be happier with Dick ... But I never thought, and do not now believe, that ever Dorothy came to any such understanding with him. No one so much as I, perhaps, knew how really heart-broken poor old Tom used to become when on occasions he found himself alone. And I only became aware of it when stealing to the rear of his hut, one evening, to surprise a strange dog there. Then it was I saw Tom, through his window, bowed in grief over a photo of Dorothy, that she had given him! For a second or two I was in doubt whether to speak to him in sympathy, or creep silently away. I obeyed the latter impulse.

But that glimpse of the big soft-hearted fellow sorrowing in solitude has remained with me ever since!

It was a day in September. Old Runnibede, following a hard, drab, cold winter, had burst into a green gay world of warmth, and teeming with beauty and bird song again ... Spring had returned to the bushland; and the burnt-off grass of the plains and uplands had sprouted into blade as green and tender as young wheat ... The great grey kangaroos, in families and communities, spread themselves over it. The humped backs of those nibbling at the shoots, and trailing their grey forms in silence from patch to patch, contrasted in strange wild homeliness with the white flanks and flapping ears of those lounging in the early sun, and others sitting erect and alert.

The long-talked-of kangaroo hunt, organised for the dual purpose of a holiday for Dorothy's city girl friends, and a thinning out process in the interests of the stock, for the station was being over-run and eaten out by them, happened on this September day. And never did kangaroo hunt end so tragically, nor a season of plenty change so abruptly to a season of sorrow! The Governor spared neither money nor labour to make the hunt a success. On the boundary fence of the mustering paddock in a wide-spreading valley, thinly timbered with box tree, where galloping was good, he had a high paling enclosure erected, with a calico wing running out for a quarter of a mile from the southern corner. According to Eustace and Kearney, who had a hand in the erecting of it, there was standing room in that enclosure for fully a thousand 'roos. So numerous were the marsupials on Runnibede at that time that even a thousand or a couple of thousand, could they be yarded, would not have made much of a gap in them.

What a troupe of merry, joyous horse-people rode out from the homestead that memorable morning! All hands employed on the station, except old Harry and Mrs. Channing, who were left in charge, were of the party. Neighbouring squatters and their women folk, all good riders, came to Runnibede on the evening before, bringing with them changes of horses. And what ripping, rattling horses they were! A few carried revolvers, but not many, for hard riding, not shooting, was the order of the day. In the way of hounds there were a few cattle dogs that followed on their own initiative, and a couple of house things that were always coming along somewhere behind with their tongues out.

The Governor's plan of campaign was to work the 'roos on the lines of a big cattle muster, by separating into parties, spreading out and heading, or endeavouring to head them to the centre of the drive ... The success of it would depend on horseflesh, horsemanship and co-operation. All of us, I remember, excepting the mater, and she remained true to her old love, were mounted on Exile progeny. And it was the last occasion but one, I think, that the matchless little Napoleon carried me to the front in the maddest of mad gallops ... Dorothy was on Beeswing, a dark chestnut mare, a beautiful, faultless beast that Tom had schooled and ridden at all sorts of work for several years. Dick Dale, too, was astride an Exile horse, a tall roan that had just come in after a six months' spell, and was so fresh and touchy that for the first mile or two Dick could take no chances with him.

As we all moved out into the broken forest country that flanked the great myall scrub, the party began to spread out, and Tom Merton and I came together; and for a while we rode on the heels of Dorothy and Dick.

"If Beeswing puts her head down, Dorothy, and pulls on you when the others start," I remember Tom calling to her, "don't take much notice, she'll throw it up again before she goes far."

"And what about this fellow, Tom?" Dick, still closely watching the capers of the tall roan, threw back with a smile.

"You've only to sit tight on him, Dick, and remember your life's insured", Tom laughed ... "And when you reach down to get hold on an old 'roo by the tail, keep your spur out of his flank ..."

A few minutes later, as some of the party appeared over Black Wattle Hollow, the first mob of 'roos started up — a mixed mob of eighty or a hundred — "old men", stiff and slow and heavy; huge mammies, flyers, and others little larger than "joeys" ... Then the excitement commenced. The Governor's voice rang out and echoed as the mob made for the high, rough ground, as all wild animals will when hunted. And remembering his orders, Tom and I and a couple of boys from Mt. Abundance rode to head them towards the centre. What a rattle of hoofs and rapping of heels! As we went to the front Dick and Dorothy were galloping behind the thick of the mob, and that was the last that I saw of them for the rest of the hunt. The 'roos, unsuspecting at first, hopped along leisurely, and Tom and I, riding wide, soon were on a level with them before they realised they were being pursued on all sides . . . But when they saw us, and heard the yelling in the rear, hell's bells! how they woke up! A string of "flyers" in the lead suddenly bent and stretched and bounded to it as swift and light as the wind! The "mammies" kept close up, but the "old men", taking long, slow, measured jumps, soon were left behind. In quick time the mob had strung out and those flyers, superbly as Tom and I were mounted, outpaced Tom and me for the sheltered ridges. But we broke the line on them, and, confounded, the others changed their course and made for the lower open country. Then fresh mob after fresh mob, as the pursuers and pursued tore in amongst them, took to their heels and became part of the hunt. Soon the whole countryside was in motion, with kangaroos flying for their lives . . . The whole bush seemed to be alive and lifting, so numerous were they. And confused some became! Rushing in opposite directions, numbers coming through the ranks of the huntspeople like footballers, to be met with shouts and jeers. Some turned and careered the other way in fresh terror, while others stuck to their course and went the harder. Verily it was a day of wild reckless excitement. If we threw one of those 'roos on the top of his head at full gallop by swinging down, placing a hand under his tail and tossing him as he rose in his leap, we threw scores. Like humans the speed of the 'roo varies with age and condition. While the half-growns, or "flyers", were swifter than greyhounds, many of the "old men" were in difficulties after spurting a few hundred yards. And how the does, when hotly pressed, would fumble for the joeys and heave them from them into the long grass! And in most cases the soft skinned, long limbed young imp would lie motionless where it fell, as though its neck were broken. And if by any chance the mothers escaped, they would make back to the spot, from no matter what angle of the compass, and restore the joeys to their pouches. But what scenes, what excitement in the vicinity of that paling yard when mob after mob, fugitive after fugitive, struck the calico wing, an obstruction so new and strange that they were bewildered and thrown into fresh confusion. And when the hunters came up, in some instances followed by yapping, breathless dogs, closing in at every angle, the deluded marsupials, believing the wide open gate was an avenue of escape, rushed and poured through it into the yard ... Moses! No circus arena or stadium ever filled to overflowing at such a rate, or in such numbers! Gad, when they found it was a snare, what frenzy set in! And when we charged forward to close the gate, the mad stampede of those who couldn't gain admittance! Hundreds of them terror-stricken, bounced round, baulked and dodged, sprang over each other, bumped our horses, and off like the wind for their beloved hills again ... Little did any of them know how fortunate they had been!

When the gate was secured and we dropped out of our saddles to put our eyes to the palings, what a memorable sight was there! The yard was a packed mass of breathing, struggling, snorting, jumping 'roos. Innocent, beautiful things, and all for the slaughter!

But all the huntspeople hadn't yet arrived; some were still coming up, their horses blown and in a lather of foam; themselves excited, exhausted, bruised and torn. Various forms of adventure had happened to many — several had had harmless spills, others got bushed for a while, while another was pulled out of the saddle by an "old man" that bailed up and gave fight. The Governor and the mater, I remember, were far from being last in the hunt; and the first thought of the mater's, on seeing the yard crammed with 'roos, was to "let the poor things go again, Edward!"

But when all had dismounted, and some were securing the horses, others making a fire to boil the tea bucket, the roll was called and Dorothy and Dick were still missing. All manners of reasons were lightly advanced for their slow coming. One of the stockmen remembered having galloped past them way back beneath Bloodwood Ridge, where both were on the heels of an old man 'roo. Several others had noticed them, and were sure no mishap could have come their way ... But after waiting and watching for a half hour or so, and one and another began to show some anxiety, Dick's tall roan, to the amazement of us all, came tearing along the fence with the saddle empty, and the bridle reins over his neck! Consternation! That there had been an accident of some kind most of us now knew! Straightway a wet blanket fell over the hunt. We caught the roan, but there were no marks about him to show that he had fallen. But why hadn't Dorothy, a good horsewoman and well mounted, followed him, or overtaken and caught him was what flashed through most of our minds. And though none expressed it, each knew that the other was thinking it.

"A couple of you go back and find out what's the matter," the Governor said, "and take the horse with you."

The mater, who only a few minutes before was flushed and happy with the excitement of the chase, was now thoughtful, and as pale looking as death ... The other women, with their riding habits pinned up, stood round her and in their wisdom still strove to treat the matter lightly.

"Come on, Jim," Tom Merton said, taking hold of the tall roan and mounting his own, "hop on to Napoleon and we'll soon pick them up." So back into the forest we went and at no steady pace, either. And rattling behind us came the stockman who had passed them beneath Bloodwood Ridge. He was a young fellow from Warra Warra, who had brought some mares across to the station the day before on a visit to Exile ... And as he followed he shouted directions to guide us to the place he had seen them last. For a mile or two we made the pace, keeping a sharp lookout on all sides.

"Around this bend, I think it was," but the youth had hardly got the words out, when Dick himself shouted to us from a log he was standing on, scanning the bush around ... Gad! what relief the sound and sight of him gave to one! And to find he was safe and whole! In an instant, though, we realised the strangeness of his being alone, that neither Dorothy or Beeswing were visible. Before we could ask a question Dick had jumped from the log and came running towards us, calling anxiously: "Where's Dorothy? Have you seen Dorothy?" That was the strangest of all.

"Isn't she with you?" we asked, staring at him. Dick could scarcely speak, "My horse got away from me," he stammered, "when I got off just there," pointing to the foot of a big tree, "to tackle an old man kangaroo that we bailed up, and Dorothy galloped after him. But haven't you seen her?"

Tom explained how the tall roan came galloping to the yard.

"But he went off this way, round that ridge", and Dick pointed due north. The kangaroo yard lay to the south.

"She's got a spill, then!" we concluded, "while reaching out for your horse, and he worked round and followed the rest to the yard."

No more time was to be lost.

"Get on Dick, quick," Tom said, handing him the bridle of the tall roan, "and we'll follow her tracks. And you, young fellow," turning to the stockman from Warra Warra, "slither back to the yard and tell Mr. Winchester to come along after us as fast as he can and bring Warabah with him."

With a touch of his heels, and a rap of the reins, that youth was gone full rip through the timber, while Tom and I picked up the tracks of Beeswing nearby.

All of us knew that if Dorothy had got a fall and lost grip of Beeswing, that the mare would make for the country adjacent to Myall Scrub, where she had been foaled and reared, and which now lay to our right, on the north-east. So fixing on the tracks of both horses, Beeswing and the tall roan, and keeping wide apart, we ran them for awhile at the canter. For some distance they kept fully fifty yards apart, where the timber was thick and the ground fairly rough. Crossing an ironbark ridge, then down a long slope to an open valley, the tracks of Beeswing began to veer to those of the tall roan, coming closer and closer. We knew it was there Dorothy was matching her mare against the horse, and making a run to get up with him and seize the reins. It was a close tussle, for the tracks ran together for a couple of hundred yards. And as we anxiously studied the ground, all three suddenly made the same discovery! Beeswing had galloped into a burnt-out stump hole and fallen heavily!

"God! how she came down!" Tom murmured. And I picked up Dorothy's riding whip. A dozen paces or so away, Dick distinguished her footprints. They showed she had picked herself up all right, and had walked round about as if searching for something, perhaps the whip, or trying to get her bearings. Then they led off, not back to where she had left Dick, or for the kangaroo yard, but right in the direction of Myall Scrub!

"Thank heaven she can't be hurt much," both Dick and Tom burst out, "but she's turned round — she's lost for a certainty."

Then Tom looked at me.

"Go back over the ridge and keep a look-out for the Governor and Warabah, Jim," he said, "and we'll go on following Dorothy's tracks." Before we separated Dick set up a long cooee. He had a voice that carried like a trumpet, and after listening with our ears on the wind, back came an answer clear and prolonged, far off in the vicinity of Myall Scrub.

"Blacks!" Tom said in a voice hushed and pregnant with alarm. The three of us gazed into the faces of each other.

"Hurry, Jim and bring the Governor along after us as hard as you can."

I left them and was going for my life, while they took up Dorothy's footprints.

I had hardly reined in on the ironbark ridge when the Governor and Warabah came in sight, and along with them the mater and one of her lady friends. And how they came bowling along, and in such grim silence! But when they pulled up beside me, all gazing with questioning eyes, what a state of mind the mater was in! In few words I told them what we had found, then led the way off the ridge to overtake Tom and Dick. And whenever I threw back a glance at them, how all their horses were pulling and reefing behind me! We overtook Tom and Dick almost on the creek; then Warabah took up the tracking. And what a great tracker he was. Leaning over his horse's shoulder with his keen eyes fixed on the earth, he skirted the creek for a quarter of a mile or so, almost at a hand gallop. His sight seemed as something uncanny. But when he turned into the creek, crossed it, surmounted the opposite bank, and headed straight for the Myall Scrub, where we knew the Cooby blacks had several camping grounds, our anxiety grew to real alarm. Still we rode to keep up with Warabah, and none dared put their thoughts into words. And all the time our eyes were strained to catch a glimpse of Dorothy somewhere on ahead. Rounding a bower of wild brier Warabah came face to face with two stalwart blacks, both carrying spears and boomerangs. There was a halt, and we at once recognised them as members of the Cooby tribe. They showed little surprise at meeting us there, and certainly no signs of fear. Warabah and the Governor questioned them in their own dialect about Dorothy, if they had seen her, and where was she? Instantly they exhibited a strange excitement, and speaking rapidly and at the same time, pointed their spears to the dark scrub looming nearby. The name "Moom" frequently fell from them, and though one hadn't a good knowledge of their language, it was plain that it was Dorothy they spoke of. When the Governor and Warabah had finished questioning them, Dick Dale introduced himself officially, and was giving them a message to convey to their king, when suddenly, with a shout of defiance, they turned and fled back to the tribe.

"Come on, don't let us lose any time", Tom urged. But the Governor, before approaching nearer, turned to the mater and her companion.

"What did they say about Dorothy, Edward?" the mater questioned in tones of dread, while her horse turned restlessly about.

"That she walked into their camp, over in the scrub there", he answered. "She's all right; we'll go and get her. But better that you wait here with Mrs. Carter, till we return."

Mrs. Carter thought it would be better, also, and while they remained there, the rest of us, led by Warabah, rode forward to the blacks' headquarters, concealed almost from view in a pocket on the rim of the great myall scrub. Laws, no matter how long I might live, I shall never forget that camp. There must have been a couple of hundred of the tribe there, and as we drew near, the women sitting round in a huge circle began wailing and drooling and slapping their thighs with their hands, while the men in what seemed to me a defiant attitude, stood rapping their war weapons together. They had learned from the two men whom the Governor had questioned that we came to seek Dorothy, their Moom. But instead of being aggressive, the whole camp were rejoicing that their dead Moom had come back of her own free will to be the tribe's white queen, and to be taken in marriage by the prophet, Goondi. They had already welcomed her, and in reply to the Governor and Dick, who asked where the white girl was, an old gin who knew some English, pointed through an avenue of scattered myall trees skirting the main scrub, and answered: "Goondi take her to gunya, make her his lubra."

"Quick, boys!... that damn scoundrel has her", the Governor shouted, and turning and spurring our horses, we galloped down that bush avenue. God, we were just in time! There at the front of his gunya as we pulled our horses in, lurching and propping, was the black giant of the tribe with Dorothy struggling and screaming in his naked arms. In what haste we all dismounted, calling at the same time to the scoundrel to desist, and to Dorothy, to encourage her... Goondi had succeeded in imposing on the innocent faith of his tribe, and he was not unprepared for us. Goondi was ready for anything. With one arm around Dorothy, who was getting exhausted he straightened up and savagely threw a spear that went within hair's breadth of Tom Merton and pierced the body of Dick Dale. Flinging Dorothy from him, the murderer fled, but retribution was close at hand. A sharp report from Tom Merton's revolver was heard, and Goondi, his evil career ended, swayed, and fell lifeless at the edge of the scrub. Wild-eyed with terror, Dorothy, when she saw Dick lying there on the ground, realised that he had given his life for her, dropped on her knees beside him. He did not speak, but his gaze wandered steadily from Dorothy to Tom, who knelt with her. Dick wanted something, and a woman's intuition made Dorothy understand. She placed her hand in his. With a last effort he sought Tom's also, and a smile flickered across his face. As their two hands met, he gave them a gentle pressure. There kneeling hand in hand beside the stricken form of Dick Dale, Dorothy and Tom knew that a power greater than that of mortal man had at least drawn them together. Then as we gazed awestruck on the tragic scene, the Governor uttered one word.

"Dead", he whispered.

*   *   *

In the old station cemetery on the slope of Yabberrappah Ridge, where wild roses peep from among the tall rank grass, may, to this day, be seen a crude slab stone, on which is inscribed in simple words: "In memory of Richard Dale." And close beside it another stone intimating that "Eustace and Kearney sleep here." A little further away: "Warabah, a faithful servant." And beneath a gum tree left standing, "Jackie," and the lines:

> "I hear 'em callin', Jackie, I'm going home to-night!
> No longer will I play an' sing for you.
> Oh, yes, I'm comin', brothers, I see the kindly light
> A-shinin' down along the old Barcoo."

Green Grey Homestead

To O.B.S. . . . Recalling spent hours that were flooded with gladness . . . gladness that sparkled in quip and in quest; bringing back thoughts of bluest blue mountains, mem'ries of shade-trees when winds in their boughs crooned songs that were old, crooned songs that were new, crooned songs to the future . . . the songs that came true.

S.R.

Publisher's Note to First Edition

Most of this book appeared from time to time in the *Sydney Bulletin,* and chapter four, under the title of "The Letter Under the Mirror", was published in O'Brien's *Best Short Stories of the World.*

Introduction to the University of Queensland Press Edition

In this, his last book published, I feel father's thoughts carried him back down memory lane, a characteristic not uncommon in most, if not all of his twenty-four books.

Many of the people as he has characterized them here I cannot label, but some I can. The identities of the Philp brothers mentioned, Willie, Eddie and Artie, are not in any way concealed from the reader. The manner of their introduction and the relevant subject matter no doubt represent the way father wanted their association to suit his pen. They were lifelong friends of his, and like him they were all products of the bush, excellent horsemen, and outstanding polo players. In a letter I recently received from W.H. ("Phil") Philp (a son of Eddie Philp) of Cracow Station, Cracow, Queensland, writing of his father, his two uncles, and my father he said: "Our fathers and my uncles were brought up in a tough environment, but they were *men* with the milk of human kindness to the fore . . . "

In the chapter in which father describes the wild pig hunt on old Wallumbilla Station, the "city chap out of an office" was himself. During the late nineties he and my mother spent some of his holidays from the Queensland Justice Department with his brother Richard ("Dick") Davis and his wife Agnes (Agnes was a sister of my mother's) at Wallumbilla, where Dick was the stationmaster for the Queensland Railways.

Nettie Palmer, wife of Vance Palmer, was a friend of Steele Rudd's and a skilful literary critic. Here is a brief extract from a letter written to her by my father on 27 February 1930. She had evidently written a press review on one of his stories at that time.

... Your little note addressed to "The Courier" (Brisbane) [she had evidently mislaid his Sydney address] was a pleasure and a surprise. Women like yourself and two others I know, by your liberal unselfish notices [press] should make one feel more like a wild pig than a fellow human. Like lots more I read and read the many kind and lenient things you all write about the efforts of others, and always without ever thinking of giving a grunt of thanks or gratitude in return – quite like the pigs! Fortunately however, Scott paid a lot of our accounts in advance when he endorsed the bill with "Ministering Angels".

I can hardly tell you how many sketches I have now written of "Green Grey Homestead". They are piling up in the safe of New South Wales Bookstall Company. A week or so ago I had a talk over the table with the Managing Director about the terms but no finality was reached. But it appears so many manuscripts were purchased in the past, that the present management doesn't know what to do about them all – they are suffering from over production. And when I accused them of cornering my manuscripts, instead of wheat or onions, they wanted to know would I "buy a few cheap". I said I would take one of my own from them "cheap" but there was nothing doing.

As to the "supply" possibilities of "Green Grey Homestead", I fancy I might spin it out till I grow young again were I so inclined – it takes so little to recall some incident in life to me ...

The book is dedicated, as will be seen, to "O.B.S." – Olive Beatrice Sharp, then of Vaucluse, Sydney, to whom he had become engaged on 23 March 1934. But contrary to the belief of some, they never married.

Green Grey Homestead was published by Frank Johnson, Macquarie Head Press, Sydney, in September 1934. (A little over twelve months later my father died, on 11 October 1935, in the Brisbane General Hospital.) The book was well presented in cloth and paperback editions, of a limited output, so the sales could not have been very extensive. I cannot find any record of the terms of the agreement concerning the sale of the book rights.

In their review of 26 September 1934 the Sydney *Bulletin* wrote: "Much of Steele Rudd's *Green Grey Homestead* appeared originally in the *Bulletin.* The stories have now been linked . . . the linking has been well done; there is no halting of the story, nor is there any of the rough burlesque that characterised the author's earlier books. It leaves an impression of personal reminiscence and the design of placing the readers in the position of Dick Gall has the effect, when one has grown accustomed to it, of heightening reality . . ."

I prize an autographed copy of the first edition that father sent to me from Sydney in 1934.

To conclude. This will be the last foreword I have had the pride and pleasure of doing for the book works of Arthur Hoey Davis, "Steele Rudd " This was his last book, and also the last to be republished, of a total of nineteen, by the University of Queensland Press. As administrator of his estate I would be remiss if I did not warmly express my sincere thanks and gratitude to the University Senate, the manager and editors and printers of the Press for their ready co-operation and the excellent presentations of the various editions of Steele Rudd's works, enabling Australian and overseas readers of today to study the efforts of a young Queensland writer whom J. F. Archibald and A. G. Stephens of the Sydney *Bulletin* discovered and encouraged in the early nineties.

ERIC DAVIS
BRISBANE
JUNE 1974

Chapter 1

You'll be single when the idea of taking up a homestead first gets you; sober and steady-going, too. You'll be sick of knocking round, working for wages which you don't always collect. You'll be longing to settle down on a place of your own; to be your own boss and have a little wife, and nice kids.

So you'll decide one night, when in bed feeling lonely, to take the plunge, and chance the ducks. When you tell your friends — there won't be many of them — they'll be amused at first and will figure you're contemplating matrimony — getting the cage ready to put the bird in. They'll be old homesteaders themselves, and their wives, who'll be grandmothers, will stir your vanity by approving of your intentions and telling you you're wise for not doing what their husbands did; and they'll screw faces at the old men squatting there at the fire gazing into the flame as if waiting for a shower of money to come flying out of it. "Caught their birds before they had the cage to put them in", they'll upbraid. "And hawked us round the country with them looking for work, instead of having houses ready for us to live in."

"There'll be nothing like that about *me*", you'll grin. And those old women will be working all the time they're talking, slashing into basins of cream with spoons and licking their fingers as the butter comes.

So by-and-by, you'll begin to save your wages to pay the first instalments on the homestead, and make the start. Old Silas King, the big gun of the district, who'll have scraped areas of land together during his sixty-odd years and is a J.P., and a

church man, will have advised you when working for him to get
a homestead and take a wife to help you do something *big* in
the world.

"Pshaw!" he had scoffed. "A strong healthy young man like
you, Dick Gall, shouldn't be afraid to tackle a homestead. Tut!
Tut! Get hold of a block, no matter how small," he urged,
"whether you have the money or not – get it before the land
is all gone, and think about paying it off after. Look at me;
when I selected my first block I hadn't sixpence left to work it
with; the Lands Office took it all. But I stuck it, and by
attending church regularly I've come through; and look at me
now."

So in a year or two you'll hear of a block of good land open
for homestead selection, and you'll find out all about it from
the storekeeper, or someone who reads the newspaper. You'll
be told to "keep it quiet", and not let on to a soul that you're
going in for it. Then you'll withdraw your savings from the
bank and into the Lands Office you'll go with your application.
There'll be anxious moments for you after that, and for a lot
of others, too! Though you'll hope it will be someone worse
off than yourself who'll draw the block if *you* don't draw it,
you'll be praying hard all the same that all the applications will
be informal except your own!

But your luck'll be in. Your bread will be cast on the water,
for in time you'll get a Government letter telling you you've
drawn "homestead block No. 0000, situate in the Parish of
Maloney, County Joe, containing 160 acres, more or less."

Laws! how you'll shake when you read it, as if it was a
summons! But when you finish the last word you'll smile and
poke your chest out, and feel taller.

When the first Sunday comes round you'll mount your horse
and off out to inspect your property.

You'll ride all over it filled with the proud spirit of
ownership. Every inch of it and everything on it will be yours
– the growing timber; the logs and firewood lying about;
hundreds of fencing-posts that some poor cove's split and had
to abandon; the old sheepyard and shepherd's hut that were
erected by someone who went insolvent; even the wild flowers
and darn stones'll be yours! How you'll admire it all!

And while your horse'll be snatching at the grass as if he knew it was yours and wanted to sample it and give opinion on its quality, you'll remain in the saddle gazing and trying to calculate its total worth.

There'll be a couple of hills to take your fancy as sites for houses and yards, but you won't know which to decide on. It'll be a wonderful look-out, and that homestead'll seem just a big Christmas-tree to you, hanging with prizes. Then you'll start wondering what would be a good name for it? Being Australian, you'll think of "Wonggonggera" and "Turmurrumi" and "Yalcalbah" and other fancy abo names. Perhaps you'll be in a joking mood and think of calling it "Saint Elmo Square", or "The Boulevard", or "Imperial Paradise", then you'll laugh and ride on a bit further.

You'll strike up along Red Rock Gully, to see the water in the spring. It'll be because of the water that you and everyone applied for the block. And it will be the only waterhole for miles around that was never known to go dry in a drought. At least, that will be what you've heard from the old hands who used to camp near it when they were kangaroo-shooting for a living.

Following a beaten track you'll "switch-back" that gully till you come to a grassy flat in a hollow of the range. The flat will be bare as bark and sprinkled over with cowdung that's mostly out of season, and bleached bones and horns. The hollow will be a camping-ground for all beasts that come to water there. And how your eyes will sparkle and your heart beat fast when you see the water shining under a high clay wall, with wavelets no bigger than a gum-leaf rippling to the wind! It *will* be a spectacle! You'll just miss colliding with a couple of old cows in your hurry to get to that waterhole to look down into it. And the longer you look into it the deeper it will seem to be. The deepest part, though, won't be more than a couple of feet — according to the amount of mud and bones that will be in it. But it will be twelve feet wide and more. And the water will be very clear — that is if the cattle haven't been puddling in it.

Though old yellow bones will protrude round the edges, you won't see them; you'll only have eyes for the beauty and the gold in it. After a while, you'll see your horse and yourself reflected in it.

That homestead will grow on you as a wonderful discovery, and you'll look down the gully and up at the rock sides feeling like Captain Cook when he found Australia. There'll be green grass three feet long, hanging down draping the cliff; and the bones lying underneath on the rock bottom will give tragic evidence of what became of animals that were tempted to reach down for it! And the bees coming to the water and flying off at every angle will tell of the honey on your homestead, so you'll decide to stop coves from trespassing in search of bees' nests, by writing a public notice to them, soon as you get home.

There'll be gums and wattle and wild apple trees hanging over that spring, too — all rich in blossom. The smell of them'll be everywhere. And the gathering of birds hopping about the limbs and on the rocks, greeting you as if they had word of your coming, will make you feel you created the homestead yourself, and everything on it.

But while standing there in thought, your horse'll be fidgeting for a drink. He isn't concerned about birds and bees or with making a fortune; so you'll hop off his back, give him the reins, and let him help himself. While he's inching cautiously into the water, stretching his neck snorting at the bees to blow them out of reach of his nose, you'll remove your hat and get down to it on the flat of your stomach yourself. Lovely and cool it'll be; and in the middle of your thirst you'll lift your head to take breath, and smack your lips as if it was a brewery you'd come into. You'll glance up to see how the horse is enjoying it, and will notice he's taking it in like a pump. His tail and ears will work as if they were handles, and you'll see the water hurling up along his neck as if there was an elevator in him. You'll grin at the hurry he's in,too, then start into it again yourself. Keeping time with the horse.

While you'll be sucking it up there'll be a string of quiet cattle sauntering along a track skimming the edge of the clay cliff way above you, a hundred feet and more. Like cattle often do, they'll get shoving one another at the most dangerous angles, till one slips a cloven hoof over the edge and disturbs a hundredweight of loose cliff that's been on the balance for many a year. Then it will leap out and come whistling down, touching nothing but air till it squashes the water, right where you and your horse are drinking, and between your heads! Laws! You won't know what happened. But when you find your feet, and wipe the mud out of your eyes and the water from your hair and look around, there won't be a living thing near. Your horse will be turning round about eighty yards away, holding his head high, his tail up in line, the bridle-reins hanging. He'll be all splashed, too, and looking scared and indignant. And all the old cows that were lying about when you came up, as if they had finished with the world and were only waiting for a pass to the next, will be on their feet staring at you, taking you for an evil spirit, and ready to stampede. The silvery-throated birds, too, will scent something amiss, for there won't be a sound coming from them. And, way up above, the brutes that made all the trouble will be staring innocently down in line at you. Even a black goanna scooting round a tree-butt will keep his beady eye on you till he climbs high enough to feel safe. Every living thing round that waterhole, and above, and below it, will regard you as a disturbing element. When you look on the water again, which will have changed colour, there'll be a jagged corner of that hundred-weight of cliff poking over its surface, and a couple of dragon-flies will be holding a love meeting on it. A shudder will creep down your back and run up it again, and you'll ask yourself, "What *would* I have done if that dam' rock had landed on my head?"

Then you'll move off, thankful, and sneaking round your horse, and keeping wide so as not to startle him. The dull-brained, quizzing old cows will move curiously after you, making sure you're a spook. And not till you're on the horse again and looking yourself will they believe it is you. But when you roar at them, waking the gorge with echoes they'll just lower their heads, close their eyes again and look satisfied; and the birds will all start chirping as if it had just come daylight. Then you'll round up those cattle, waving your hat at them for a whip, to see what their brands and earmarks are. Gee! They'll all belong to old Silas King! Every hoof of them. And the brutes eating your grass, and drinking your good water! He has had the use of your homestead without paying rent for it for half a life-time! And his boundary-fence, in which is an opening four panels wide for the cattle to go in and out, will only be a few hundred yards off! "To take some of your advice is all right," you'll reason, "but that don't mean I'm going to let you have the use of my property for nothing, Mr. King." So you'll rush them away, shouting at them, hustling them through the opening back into his paddock. Then you'll dismount to hang your horse up while you mend the fence, so that they won't return to commit further trespass. And when you're riding off feeling you've done good work those cattle will be standing watching, indignant-looking; and you'll wish you had a good dog to put on their heels and send them stampeding to Halifax.

Crossing a ridge covered with broom-brush, pebbles and flint stones, from where you'll get a close view of the sunlit plains beyond, bronzewing pigeons and quail will fly up, and you'll recollect how Mrs. Fitzpatrick said that country where there are plenty of pigeons is best for raising turkeys. And all in a moment you'll see yourself growing great flaming gobblers by the hundred, at a time when no one has any, and getting top price for them in the market. And as you move on over the ridge, there'll be so many big goannas creeping about, dragging their long tails after them, that you'll figure another couple of quid a week revenue from the oil that's inside them.

Leaning here and there against trees will be snares set to catch 'possums, by someone. You'll stare hard at them. "The darn cheek. Setting snares on a bloke's land to catch his 'possums with!" You'll say, "None of that any longer!" And you'll kick those snares over, taking away the copperwire for your own use.

Before you've ridden all over it, the value of your homestead will go up and up till it's worth twenty quid an acre. You'll see the house and barn and yards built. The house will have a verandah all round, painted chocolate; the barn and stable roofed with iron; a windmill will be twirling beside them, and the yards full of cows walking in and out of the bails, and a big roan bull shaking his head, expostulating and looking angrily through the rails because he's not allowed in to have all his own way.

The world will move rapidly with you now; and after another look round you'll head for home again. Your home will be at "Caledonia", old Bob Sankey's farm, where you worked for five years. And of course it will be Sunday — you wouldn't be away from "Caledonia" if it wasn't. You'll catch up to old Silas King himself on the way. He'll be driving home from church in his new sulky. He always drives by himself on Sunday. His thoughts don't get crowded in it and it gives him room for pious reflection. But he'll have a hymn-book beside him on the seat for company. And as you come up, proud that you know him to speak to, and bursting to tell him the good news, you'll feel like a sinner breaking the Sabbath.

"Getting back from church, Mr. King?" you'll call out humbly across the wheel as you come up springing in the saddle.

"Yes — yes," he'll answer, surprised, and clutching the reins tight, "and it's where everyone should be getting back from."

Though you know old Silas would make a low pass in a test for keeping the Commandments, you'll be shy of starting an argument. So you'll be tactful and tell him you acted on his advice, and applied for a homestead block for yourself, and got it.

"A homestead — where?" he'll ask, looking hard at you. Not knowing that he wanted that block of land for years because of water on it, or that he had moved Members of Parliament, and Government officials and friends to have it thrown open for selection "on the quiet", and had put in a dozen dummy applications for it, you'll innocently tell him all, and ask his opinion of it.

"WHAT! Spring Gully!" he'll snarl. "That country is no good for you; 'twouldn't feed a bandicoot!"

You will think him a curious old man, and put it down to liver.

Then he'll look closer at you, and talk of the costly improvements you'll have to make, and that you'll be called upon to pay him half the cost of a boundary-fence he put up twenty years ago, "at the rate of fifty pounds a mile!"

You won't have anything to say after that. And when leaving him at the cross-roads you'll hardly hear him chuckling "you were a fool to go in for it — a damn young fool!"

But that night in bed when you put out the light, you'll see your homestead gleaming out there under the range, with all its grass and timber, and animals and birds. And you'll see it in the years ahead with a railway to it; a procession of farm-hands, of plough-teams and waggons at work; a dairy herd in full swing. Buyers of wheat coming and going; agents offering you forty pounds an acre, walk in walk out; the local banker calling and lifting his hat to you — and you'll laugh beneath the blankets and reckon old Silas King can go and hang himself.

Chapter 2

You'll be three years on the little grey homestead, working hard and becoming well-known and respected; you'll receive kindly handturns from one and another, and be known to them all as Dick Gall. At the township your neighbours when they call for their mail will ask if "there's anything for Dick Gall?" and take back goods for you from the store.

But you'll have a couple of years to go yet before getting your deeds and the little homestead is your own and you are properly settled. And you won't be properly settled till you get the right kind of woman for a wife to look after you.

You're battling along all right, though, one way and another, going your hardest from the rising of the sun unto the going down of the same; and most of the old homesteaders around, careful of overwork themselves, will appraise you favourably and reckon you're a goer, and admit you are knocking your place into shape pretty well. You'll get tired of it though, sometimes. Cooking and sweeping, and washing and chambermaiding weren't in the picture when you took up the holding. And after a year or two it begins to get pretty lonesome away back there by yourself, and no one but the dog and cat — who are not always on friendly terms — to pass the time with.

Still, there are hours when it's far from lonesome — nights when there's a dry storm on, and the lightning is superb, making flicker screens of the walls and darting down the chimney and out the door; and the thunder cracking, and bursting so close and continuous that your heart troubles you, and the cat gets panic and scoots about as if it was scalded, rushing into your bedroom, and planting under your bunk, and rushing out again when the next crack comes and the house rocks like a wooden horse, to surrender near the fire waiting its doom with its back up and fur ruffled ... Jerusalem! the electricity flashing round is like the fire that went out from the Lord and devoured Nadab and Alihu, the two meddling fool-sons of Aaron! And all the bombarding will make you feel the heaven over your head has turned to brass and sulphur, and the Lord in His wrath is making powder and dust of the little grey homestead. Gee! You'll think of flying out the door, then fleeing seven different ways to escape destruction. But remembering the long arm of the Lord, you'll prefer being struck dead in your own home to rolling over outside in the dark, and in some hole, perhaps, where you'd never be found and your carcase become as meat unto the native dogs and all the fowls of the air. But after a while — a terrible while it will seem to you and the cat — the storm starts to die instead, and to get out of range, and the flicker screen fades out, too. Your heart will stop kettle-drumming, and so opening the door which you closed when you found the lightning make a thoroughfare of the home, an inch or two, you'll squint out into the night. Seeing a window somewhere in the sky, with a star shining in it, you'll know the Lord isn't going to destroy the earth yet awhile, or smite you in the knees, or on the legs, or make you and your little homestead a proverb or a byword ... Opening it a little wider, you'll begin talking to the dog again. "It's all over, I reckon, Rover," you'll say, "but it was pretty rough while it lasted, eh, old chap?" And Rover, who was snorting all through the distrubance, you having thrown him a shoulder of mutton that went unhealthy on you during the day, will open his eyes and look up at you in sympathy, and without shifting his head. His head is between his paws, which are protruding on either side of his nose like two splints with nails in them. Looking out again, you'll see the storm had begun an offensive against the new settlement way over on Washpool Plain, where a community of migrants are settled for life. You'll get a new feeling then. you'll laugh and give it to Rover as your opinion that those chums over there will be under their beds saying their prayers, and wishing they had hold of the good Bishop of

London, or whoever it was lured them into a life of velvety days and pale peaceful nights of a new land!

But in the daytime your neighbours, the McClevertys, and the Ryans, and the Moriartys, and the rest, will remember you in your hours of melancholy, and will want to care for you, and make your life brighter — especially those of them who have marriageable daughters, and they'll all have a few over twenty-seven anyway. Most homestead mothers feel it's hard for a single man, when he comes in at the end of a long day, to have to prepare his own supper, and they reckon a place gets dull and uninhabitable without the touch of a woman's hand — and that a man does, too, if he's a bachelor. So, after talking it over among themselves, and wondering how you might take it, Mrs. Ryan, one day when you happen to be at their place having a cup of tea, will offer to go over with one of the girls one morning and scrub the place out for you; and if you have any shirts and collars and things you'd like washed and ironed, they'll be glad to laundry them along with their own; also if you have any currants or raisins, and a few fresh eggs over there they'll bake you enough cakes to do you the whole of the week . . . And it won't be any trouble to them. You're not prepared for anything like that, for it will mean their seeing the inside of you, and knowing how you live! And while they all wait for you to say what you think, you'll blush and grin, and shake your head and get self-conscious, and you will tell them you're used to doing it, and don't mind at all; that you prefer doing it. And while you are lying you'll reach for your hat, so as to get away before they can press you any further. But you want to show them you're grateful, so you'll pull your hat on at the door, and tell Mrs. Ryan that you reckon she and the girls have enough to do in their own place, without thinking about yours. Then old Tim Ryan himself will rise up, smiling placidly, and placing his big hand on your shoulder will look down into your face and tell you: "Not at all, Dick, not at all . . . Divil th' bit o' bother will it be to th'm. Sure it's nothing. Just look at th'm — as big an' sthrong as cattle — all exceptin' little Katie, perhaps!" And old Tim, who has more whiskers than wealth, and, taken lengthways, is the biggest man in the district, will shake you in a burst of friendship till you

are compelled to stiffen the joints of your neck to hold your
head on. A well-wishing neighbour old Tim is, and ever ready
to help with the services of the family, and the cheerful
dignified spirit he does it in is a pleasant feature.

"I won't want anything done — not for a while", you'll kind
of choke. Then off you'll go, blasting old Tim, and wishing you
hadn't gone near him to help load his pigs at all.

That evening though, when you finish supper, you'll start on
the verandah, and house, with a long-handle shovel, cleaning
away the mud. Then you'll get down on your knees inside, and
do some scrubbing. And before you go to bed, which will be
late, everything in the little homestead, in case of surprises, will
be clean and healthy, and in apple-pie order.

Chapter 3

There'll be nights in the little grey homestead when you'll sit smoking and meditating and planning for the future. The cat will be curled up contented at your feet before the fire, and thoughts that come to a man when married life begins to call to him will be passing through your brain.

You'll be disturbed by hearing footsteps on the verandah and voices making friends with Rover. And Rover will be rapping his toenails on the hardwood boards and frantically whimpering a welcome, instead of raising Cain, as he does when someone arrives without the password. You'll know at once it's young Bob McCleverty and his brother, little Artie, coming for a yarn, and you'll return to life again. You'll feel glad, too, for you've got to like those two quiet, drawling homestead lads, though at first you were slow to admit them to your circle. And they've got a liking for you that's uncommon. There's a novelty or something about the solitude of your little homestead — an air of romance of some kind — that's absent from their own abode. Perhaps it's because there's no restraint and no "old man" to consider. The furniture is more comfortable, and there's more light and company in their own home, yet they'll leave it all, no matter how cold or dark the night, to prowl and fossick across paddocks, helping each other through barb-wire fences, bounding high over grass patches likely to harbour snakes — so as not to disturb the vermin — and go to yours. If your light isn't visible when they come over the last ridge and you seem to be in darkness, they'll pause to consider; and if young Bob reckons you've turned in — little

Artie never reckons anything; he's a silent, faithful follower of
the other — they'll retrace their steps and make the most of
whatever's going on at home.

So you'll give young Bob and little Artie a royal welcome,
pointing to seats and telling them not to be bashful and to
make themselves at home. Perhaps you'll hop up and drag the
seat across to the fire for them — that's if you haven't twisted
your ankle, or chopped your toe half-off, or jambed your hand
in something that day. And soon as they've taken a look round
to see what changes have happened to the scenery since they
visited you last, and addressed a few words to the cat, you'll
ask if there's anything fresh over their way, or what's doing.
And young Bob will drawl: "On'y the same ol' thing." But you
know it isn't the harvest, or the weather, or the cows they've
come to yarn about. They're sick to death of such things and
hate the sight and sound and smell of them.

You retailed to them on their last visit some of your
adventures when droving 'way out back and doing horse-
breaking and stock-riding at Wonggongera and Pickenjinnie, and
the thrills you put into it all seduced the minds of young Bob
and little Artie, fired their imaginations and left them with a
desire for more. But a fight that you mentioned in particular
and didn't finish got a grip of them, and they've been burning
ever since to hear all about it and to hear you tell it again from
the beginning. And soon as young Bob reminds you of it, little
Artie will draw close to the table, rest his elbows on it, wedge
his chin between his hands, and fix his eyes on you as if you
were the Oracle. Young Bob himself will lean back and pull out
a pipe in anticipation of something unusual.

"Oh, yairs," you'll chuckle, "it was all over an argument
about a horse." And when you pause a moment to refresh your
memory, young Bob, thinking you mightn't be going to
proceed further, will echo encouragingly: "A argument about a
'orse?" And little Artie's twinkling eyes will be riveted on yours
like a snake contemplating murder, and not a hair of him will
move.

A city boob he looked like, you'll remember; one of them
cranks who spends his time working out cross-word puzzles — a
spare, wiry cove, medium tall, stooped in the shoulders; might

have been a shade past twenty. You forget whose horse it was, but because you just happened to mention that its brand was blotched this city coot pulled out a quid and wanted to make a bet about it. You knew you'd be betting on a certainty, and told him you didn't want to take his money. But, spare your days, if he didn't stick his nose into your face and tell you he had met swags of mugs like you who didn't want to take money; so you asked him quiet what it was he was trying to get at.

"Don't y' understand King's English? Didn't y' ever go to school?" And he pokes his nose in a bit closer to you. There was only one answer to that stuff; so you gave it to him, peeled off your coat and started rolling up your sleeves.

"You did?"

Young Bob will put down his pipe and leave his mouth open, and little Artie's bulging eyes will shine and twinkle. But you're not concerned about them; you're thinking now seven years back. And in your minds is a close-up of a cleared patch among some myall-trees; several horses with saddles on and four or five phantom forms in whiskers . . . So off went *his* coat, too, and it became a dramatic moment. Then off went his shirt. Cripes! When he stripped you saw he was a different cove; his muscles stood out, and he had a chest on him! A suspicion went through you that you had struck a pug — one of the crowd that travel round on the lookout for boobs. You verified your suspicions when his mate chipped in offering to back him for a fiver an' fight to a finish.

"Moses!" from young Bob, but not a sound from little Artie.

Of course you didn't want your mates to go taking bets on you; you weren't looking for fight — only defending yourself from insult. All you knew about fighting, anyway, was what you learned at old Condamine school, where you were king, and along the droving routes in years after. But mates are mates out back, and they out with their money, and brought it to a head. Then the backers all started kicking the dead sticks and leaves and things away to clear a ring. Well, darn him, you thought, if he is a blasted pug, he's only got two hands and two eyes; and so you squared up to him. No hand-shaking —

none o' that make-believe business — and he started putting on frill, crouching, working round you, moving his fists like pendulums, and glaring at you like a wild dog watching his chance to spring. You never had a cove face you like this before, and you began to feel a burden on your mind. All the same, you decided to give him all you had. Behind, you could hear your mates kicking away more dead leaves and stuff, otherwise they were silent as if it was all a burial service. So he kept on crouching and side-stepping, and you made up your mind to let him break the ice, and whatever move he made you'd swing the right at him and put every ounce of punch you had into it. All at once he made a feint at you and you let go the right at his head and got it! Cripes, it was a sensation! Like hitting a cricket ball fair and hard when you couldn't see it coming and expected to hear the wickets rattling. The sensation it gave him was different. His head went back so far that he must have seen his backer, who was behind him, throw up his hands in astonishment.

"Holy!" from young Bob, but little Artie is dumb and his eyes won't leave yours.

You didn't get over the surprise you got soon enough to give him the other, and another, and another; and, like a roped bull with its head down, he came at you, shooting both hands into your body, you catching them on your ribs and forearms and a final one shaving the down off the point of your chin. Ghost! And the cow all the time was hissing and calling you a bum, and scum, till he landed you one on your nose that made you feel it was decapitated. The blood trickled into the corners of your mouth and in your fury kept you busy blowing it out . . . Stars! how you remembered he could hit, and when he saw how the fluid was flowing from you, it maddened him more, and he came at you again. Gee! But somehow or other his head got under your arm, and you squeezed down hard on it, holding him like a cow in a bail. Out of it he couldn't get, and you jabbed and punched and bashed his face and mouth and eyes, while your mates yelled to you to stick to him and give him hell, and his mates danced round, distracted, shouting "Break! Break! Break!" But only when your arms got aching and you thought you'd broke him into mince did you break, and then he danced away sniffing and spitting and slandering you more. But you grinned at the mess you'd made of him and asked him how he was liking it.

And by the living Mike you went after the crawler with the fury of Jack Dempsey. But he was clever. He ducked and side-stepped, then swung a right and left at your jaw, as if they were fired from a cannon. If it wasn't instinct, you don't know what it was; but you saw them both coming, got your head out of the way, and uppercut him under the chin just when he slipped toward you, and, mother o' Mike! his head went up and his—

"Here, cripes, look at this cove!" young Bob interrupts, calling attention to little Artie, who has gradually risen to his feet and is leaning across the table still gazing at you, but trembling, showing his teeth, crunching them, as if he had got tetanus or had taken poison. In a second the fight will go out of your mind. But young Bob is disgusted at the behaviour of his young brother for spoiling the finish.

"Sit down, y' goat!" he'll protest, "and don't make an ass of yourself."

But you can see the little chap can't help himself, and you'll reach for a grip of him, talking kindly to him, asking him what's the matter, telling him not to be excited, and calling to young Bob to bring a pannikin of water and to be quick about it. And young Bob will see there's something the matter, too, and in his hurry to bring the water will tramp on the cat, who'll make a startling noise under his feet. And pale as a ghost he'll stand staring while you're administering the water; but instead of taking a drink little Artie's jaws will suddenly spring open and a yell will come from him that will out-do the cat and start Rover rushing round outside trying to get in to investigate. After a while his yells will tail off into weeping and sobbing, and you and young Bob will feel a lot easier in your minds. But in the end you'll be putting on the kettle to make hot tea for him, before letting him go home, and all the time you'll be helping young Bob to think of things that will make the kid laugh.

Chapter 4

Next morning, perhaps about ten o'clock, you're returning from the factory in the milk-cart, sitting up singing and swaying with the motion of it, and light-hearted and hopeful among the jangling empty cans, and one that's full of whey. You'll drive in through the gate into the little grey homestead as if it was the land of Canaan, and your eyes will fall on two startling figures coming across your pumpkin ground, carrying parcels and a basket, looking like two movie stars on location. They'll be big Nellie Ryan and little Katie Ryan, and Mrs. Ryan won't be with them at all.

"Ghost!" you'll mumble, turning a bit pale, "they meant to come all right!" And then you'll fold up. On the way to the piggery, where you'll deliver the can of whey to a family of expectant squeaking swine, you'll be blessing yourself again for going near old Tim Ryan, and getting into all this woman's business! But it can't be helped now, and as big Nellie and little Katie approach the house you'll be taking the horse out and fumbling the harness. Rover will be barking hard, too, making out they're enemies and that he's got a stiff job on, though he knows them as well as he knows you; and looking across to Ryan's homestead, "Tuam", they call it, you'll see Mrs. Ryan watching from the verandah to see how the girls get on.

Of course you'll have to go round to the front of your quarters to meet them, and when you are nearly there you'll order Rover to go and lie down, and ask him what he thinks he's barking at? You do this to keep cool and collected . . . A little nearer, and you'll grin and say: "Hello, did y' think he was going to eat y'?" And big Nellie will smile, and dragging the sides of her hat down over her cheeks will tell you they've come over to tidy up the place for you, if you'll just show them the run of it, and where the things are they've to take back? You'll stammer and blush and be sorry for all the jolly trouble they're going to for nothing. And Nellie will say, "Oh, no!" while Katie will screw up her nose and look about. "There it is — that's it", and you'll open the door to them — "but you won't want me any longer." And off you'll bolt before big Nellie can fix her smile on you again, or little Katie stretch her neck far enough to see all that's inside.

They'll throw the windows open, and put something against the door to keep it from closing; then stare hard at your housekeeping and your furniture for a minute or so as if they had come to learn something new. But soon big Nellie will have her cape off and an apron on and be hard at work in the kitchen. And while she's firing the stove and getting hot water ready, and clearing your shelves of dishes and things, little Katie, who is a girl of twelve or thirteen and just coming on, will tip-toe to the door of your bedroom and peep in as though she suspected someone was in hiding or in bed there. When no one jumps up or sings out to her she'll go right in and look around at the little that's there and handle whatever is on the table. Your brush and comb she'll drop and pull faces at as if they harboured plague; but your silver watch she'll open and fool with, and put to her ear, and wind up. There'll be a letter of five or six pages kept from flying away by your murky little mirror which serves as a paperweight. It's a letter from Sarah McCleverty to Bill Baker, which was dropped along the factory road by Bill for you to find . . . You hadn't read it all yet because you haven't had time, and you know it's Bill Baker's letter by the envelope, which you used soon as you got home to light the fire with. "Your sweetheart, Sarah", told you near enough who the author of it was, and you'll be going to restore it to Bill next time you meet him. Little Katie will see that letter and wonder what you have stood the mirror on it for? Girls, like grown-ups, always like to see things kept in their proper places. That's the difference between them and men. So while she's looking at herself in the glass and smiling different ways to see which of them suits her best, her hand will be fondling the letter as if it was a doll. Deciding on one of the smiles as the best for her complexion, she takes more interest in the letter. The first two words of it: "My lovest", will hold her and she'll open her eyes, and the smile will be forgotten. Then she'll rush to the last page, and when she reads "Your sweetheart, Sarah", you can tell she's found a great gold mine ... She'll turn back quick to the beginning, and when she's taken in the first few lines there'll be a broad grin on her face, but she's pretty careful of the step is little Katie. So she'll put the letter down and run to the front door to see where you are, and what kind of work you're setting yourself. She'll see you hooking the horses to the plough. Then taking the broom she'll tell big Nellie, who's turning the kitchen inside out and decorating the shelves with nicked paper, and looking as pleased as though you had just brought her into it as your bride, that she'll give the rooms a sweep over; and off back little Katie will skip to your bedroom and to Baker's love letter ... She'll sit on your bunk with it, and hold the broom between her knees so as to be ready for work at the sound of someone coming. She isn't a rapid reader of love-letters, not having had much practice as yet, and Sarah McCleverty doesn't write copperplate or spell according to the dictionary or the local schoolmaster. But she's worrying through it all right, smiling, and gaping, and getting red sometimes, and excited-looking at others; then putting it down sudden, but without losing the place, and slipping to the door again she'll see how you're getting on with your job. A word or two more with Nellie, then making a flourish on the floor with the broom, back she'll creep to Sarah and Bill again ... Though some of it will seem to be shocking to her, little Katie will want to read every word of that letter.

Meantime you'll be ploughing away up and down, singing out to the horses to make yourself more important because you think someone's listening, and stopping always at the headland nearest to the house to clean the plough ... And when you've cleaned it you'll be keeping an eye on the house; and you'll see homely-looking smoke coming out of the chimney, and big Nellie coming out of the house with papers and rags and all kinds of rubbish to burn; and sometimes she'll be getting water out of the tank, or throwing some out of a dish, and looking up at you as she throws it ... And seeing the smoke, and her moving about and looking across at you, will make the little homestead seem a different place; and you'll begin to feel what it must be like to fellows who have their own wives on theirs. You'll notice too, that big Nellie is a fine stamp of a woman, and that she's smart on her feet. You'll be taking longer and longer after each round to clean the plough, too; and when little Katie leaves the house and comes running across to the fence calling out: "Nellie says will you come and have a cup of tea now, Mr. Gall?" your heart'll give a jump! ... Hokey! "Tea!" you'll echo, as if you didn't quite understand. "It's all waiting on the table —" and back will fly the busy little Katie.

"Cripes!" you'll mutter; and leaving the horses standing there — they would stand there all day if you asked them to — you'll rub the soil off your hands on to your trousers, and rake your moist hair with your fingers, and creep cautiously through the fence. You'll drag a fistful of leaves from a gum bush as you saunter across the green patch to the house and be crunching them as you wonder what to say when you go in ... Big Nellie meeting you at the door with real mountain bloom on her cheeks will invite you to "Come along, Mr. Gall, before your tea gets cold." Angels of light! You were never met at your own door like this before! But somehow you feel it's *her* door, and you're a visitor being welcomed. Cripes, though! When you come in and look round you hardly recognise it! It's undergone a metamorphosis. You look down on the floor but don't like walking on it with your dusty, milk-stained bluchers. And the sight of the table! At one end of it is spread a white linen cloth, wherever it came from, ironed like a dress shirt, and on it, set in fashion, are the teapot, a cup and saucer, the sugar basin with a spoon in it, a big bowl of butter that's not yours, a plate of scones, a bottle of home-made melon jam, that isn't yours either, the milk jug all brightened up, and a serviette, wherever it also came from! At the other end will be a big bunch of flowers leaning over and ducking their heads about. Heavens! You feel it's your wedding breakfast you're sitting down to without the parson, or a best man, and you don't seem to know where the chair is when you are going to sit.

"Do you like milk an' sugar in your tea, Mister Gall?" And Nellie, while you'll be nodding you do, because you can't find your voice, will start pouring you out a cup, and calling to little Katie to see that "the cake in the oven doesn't burn, like a good girl".

Your cloudy, milk-splashed shirt and pants and dusty brown arms don't silhouette well against the white linen table cloth, and bright tea things, and the comparison will make you uncomfortable in your own home. You nearly spill the tea over it in consequence. Then when you lift your cup with precaution you get a nervous attack and the cup stops half-way up like a hotel lift, and wobbles in your hand. My! how you'll put it down, quick, and reach for the scones to kill time with — that'll be till big Nellie makes herself scarce. But when she suddenly runs out to the kitchen to take the cake out of the oven that little Katie, who has found a Jews' harp, doesn't know is burning like Rome was when Nero was fiddling, you'll hurl that cup of tea down like beer and send a scone or two and most of the butter after it.

In a minute or two more you'll be getting composed and feel a bit at home. You'll lean back in the chair and look out to see if the horses are standing all right. Of course you know they'll be half asleep, and that no one but yourself or someone shaking a feed of corn at their heads could awaken them. You have drunk all the tea but you sit there wondering if big Nellie will come in again before you go out. You feel you would like to have a wise conversation with her. She doesn't seem to be coming so you'll start to go. But when you make a noise getting up she'll come hurrying in apologizing, and asking would you have liked another cup of tea. Laws! How you'll wish you could reel off compliments like the goofy city swanks who charm the women on steamers and in tea-shops! But you only shake your head and smile, and twirl your old hat, and tell her you must be getting over to the plough again, now.

"My word, you're getting on with it; you'll soon have all that paddock finished, won't you?" she'll say. And the way she'll say it will burn your ears, and the skin on your face will shine like Moses' did when he came down off Mount Sinai after the big interview.

"If I only had someone always here to do the housekeeping for me" — you'll say, laughing amiably, and backing to the door, "I could do a lot more — and better, don't you think so?" "A good many of them don't, though —" And big Nellie, who will know what you are hinting at, will also know that some family men do a lot of ploughing inside, beside the kitchen fire. "I wouldn't be one of them sort —" And you'll step out and be off smiling, and reckoning you got in a good word for yourself, anyway.

When you start the plough again you'll talk like a brother to the horses and feel as if you are cultivating the Garden of Eden. More and more you will keep your eyes on the home, and when little Katie issues from it to empty a dish or something, you'll wave to her like a brother-in-law, and she'll shake the dish at you like a relation.

Meanwhile, big Nellie having done all she can see to do in the kitchen and living-room will turn her energies to your bedroom. And while she's hanging things up on nails, and making your bed, and wondering if you wear pyjamas and where they can be, little Katie will be hovering about watching to see if she will observe Baker's love-letter which she takes for granted was written to you. But big Nellie, who isn't there to pry into your correspondence, passes it over, as a matter of respect, and little Katie will get restless and point to it, and pull inviting little faces.

"A letter from some of his people, I suppose", big Nellie will observe at last, but giving attention to the arranging of some red roses on your table. But little Katie won't be satisfied. She must have big Nellie read that letter somehow or other without giving herself away.

"It starts with 'My lovest' ", and little Katie will start humming a tune—

"With what?" and suddenly evincing some interest big Nellie will glance at the love-letter.

"And it looks like Sarah McCleverty's writing too", little Katie will pause to add, and then go on humming more. Big Nellie's face will flush, and she'll look closer at the epistle, and little Katie, pleased with herself, will run out to the door to see if you're sticking well to your work, and to give her sister a good chance to enjoy the letter as she did herself. You'll be scraping mud from the mould board when she looks out, and you'll wave to her when you're putting the scraper back in its place, and she'll wave to you, and for big Nellie's benefit she'll remain a while, waving more. And big Nellie, who also will conclude without evidence to the contrary, that the letter was written to you, will be rushing her eyes over its pages like wireless, and with blood mounting to her cheeks and fire flying from her eyes. But she'll drop it like poison when she hears little Katie coming in again, and start cleaning the mirror, and striving to appear disinterested. But little Katie will know a lot, too.

"What's in it? Is it from Sarah McCleverty?" she'll want to know, looking innocent and anxious, and breathing short.

"Do you think I would read Mr. Gall's letters, or anyone's, you silly girl?" Nellie will choke, hardly knowing what to do about it; she'll be disappointed in you, and hateful of the McCleverty girl.

"*Oh, you have!* That's not how it was!" and lifting one of the displaced sheets, little Katie will start perusing it boldly.

"Don't you! ... What if Mr. Gall was to come in!" and Nellie will take it from her ... "Run out and see if the towel I hung on the line is dry — and bring me the broom."

And little Katie will fly off faster than ever, but only because she wants big Nellie to finish the letter so that she can talk to her about it on equal terms and without being accused of wrong-doing. And she knows from what's in it that big Nellie will be bursting to read it all. Women are curious like that. But this time little Katie will stay out much longer, and be waving the towel to you; and when she's going inside again she'll sneak on tip-toe and catch Nellie glaring in hate at the last lines and clenching her teeth. "Oh! you've read it," she'll shout, pouncing on her triumphantly. And then: "I know what's in it ... it's from S—— M——, who I said, isn't it?"

Big Nellie won't say anything. She'll be confounded — "And there's a lot of bad things in it, isn't there?"

Then big Nellie will put the letter under the mirror again, and say: "Get our basket, Katie! ... And we'll take back the jam and scones and everything we brought. He can bring his washing over to Mother, himself, if he likes . . . Come away out; and don't do any more for him. Booh, don't let his old dog touch you!"

And out they go.

Crossing the paddock they'll be holding their heads down and keeping a deaf ear. And when you wave and call out to them: "So long; are you going?" they won't see or hear you. Little Katie would like to look at you though, and give you a smile, too; but big Nellie will be telling her not to.

And so you'll stare after them, and think and puzzle, but you can't make it out.

Chapter 5

When first you took up the little grey homestead you counted on growing wheat and barley and maize, and leaving milk alone. Grain-growing was more dignified and manlier than strumming on Strawberry's teats while she chewed her cud and beat time with her tail. And being a bachelor — what all young home-steaders with any real respect for women ought to be — you'd have time to cook yourself good meals, and attend to your laundry occasionally. And you'd be able to go for a ride to some of the places on Sunday afternoons — perhaps on holidays as well, if you heard about them in time. Instead of slaving morning, noon, and night, you'd make a white man's job of farming and show a lot of them how to be their own bosses and masters of their own fate.

So contrary to local wisdom and tradition, you start off and plough and harrow and sow, and then pray and wait for the seed to come up and grow, and, when it grows, for it to escape blight and all other afflictions that old hands warn you crops are heir to if you don't look out. And after a couple of seasons of ploughing and sowing and the rest, you find you haven't "looked out" hard enough or something, and then you meditate a lot at night, instead of sleeping, till you lose flesh and look as if you had been put through a clothes-wringer; and you move and mope about like a shell with the life gone from it. When you're out of kerosene and candles at the same time, and you have to meditate and smoke in the dark, it will come home to you what a great part a little illumination plays in the comforts of a homestead, even one like yours; almost as great a part as a little hanging plays in the discomforts of gaol life. But it all helps to get you into the habit of going to bed early and beating the birds in the morning, and makes you well versed in the secrets of homesteading, and teaches you how hard it is to stand on your own feet, and that as far as society is concerned you are fairly in the wilds.

At last when the old hands, who paid dearer for their knowledge than you, keep on shaking their heads and warning you not to leave Strawberry out, and telling you that ten or twelve of her, which would be enough for one man to manage, would mean as many pounds a month regular in your pocket, and at the same time, if you couldn't shake off the habit, you could still keep on ploughing and sowing, you decide on a change of policy, and chance the ducks.

So out of meditating and smoking in the dark, one day comes a close conversation with the storekeeper. You've conversed closely with him before, and found him sympathetic and white all over. You've sold him the remnant of a crop you harvested and he's got a contra account against you. It's been against you for eight or ten months and growing faster than the corn did. But he's not reminding you of the account — he's listening to your conversation about Strawberry, to the fresh hopes you see in her success, but more especially to the difficulty you see in squaring his bill and buying a few of her from the proceeds of the crop at the same time. And when he says, "That's all right, Dick, don't worry; I'll pay you in full for the corn and you can buy the cows and repay me monthly from your milk money", your heart will weigh light again, and you'll canter all the way home with your hat hanging to the back of your neck, whistling and feeling like Napoleon hurrying from Elba to mobilise a new army.

All that night cows bulging with milk will trail through your brain, tramping all over you, poking you out of bed with their horns — herds of them there'll be. Next day in clean shirt and pants you'll get across your saddle-horse and ride into Terence Riley's farmyard at milking-time with a hand fumbling in your pocket, and running your eye over any of his herd that are lying about, like a butcher looking for fats.

"Hello, Dick, me bhoy", Terence himself from under the flank of young Rosie will greet you as your head shows over the yard-rails. "An' where is it ye're off to?"

"Looking for a few head o' cows," you'll tell him, dismounting — "if I can pick 'em up cheap enough."

"Well, you've come to the right place", Terence will say, winking at the boy in the next bail. "No one ever got anything else but cheap cows from Riley's."

And while he empties his bucket and calls to someone to fetch Polly and Kittie an' Gooseberry into the yard, you move amongst the soft-eyed creatures regarding them critically and covetously.

"Money wouldn't buy *her*", Terence, joining you, will declare as you stroke the back of a satin-skinned, companion-able little beast. "She's pure bred, be an imported Government bull, and has been givin' her five gallons for the last twelve months an' more. But there's Biddie standin' in th' corner there just as good, if not better, that I'll sell cheap to you. An' 'tis only because the farm's carrying more than it should that I would sell her, or any of th'm at all. 'Tis like parting with me heart's blood."

Then you'll examine Biddie, and a host of others that Terence will lead you to, studying them hard. And while you're studying them and he's fondling them, and reciting pedigrees, a conviction that you don't know so much about dairy-cows as you thought you did will grow on you. So far as you can judge they're all good milkers and super-animals. But as to how much milk any of them is capable of giving and the quality of it you've nothing but Riley's word to guide you. You know enough, however, not to delude yourself that he's going to dispose of six of the best if he can unload six of the worst on to you. So after chopping and changing you decide to take a half-dozen — "Beautiful animals, the like of 'em can't be got anywhere in th' distric' " — and because Riley "never likes to see anyone go away feelin' dissatisfaction", you're getting them "cheaper than anyone else would get them". Then off you go, the pride of ownership filling you with fresh hopes as you flick those milkers along the lane to your little homestead. You'll be a much prouder man in twelve months' time, though, when a dairy expert visits the homestead and teaches you something about testing and grading, and you learn, what Riley himself didn't know, that you bought for a fiver a head cows worth a tenner and more!

You're a man of the milking-yard now, and you talk cow and think cow. You're a shareholder in the local Co-operative Dairying Co., too, and every morning when you deliver your couple of cans and see them weighed you walk through with hands in your pockets inspecting the plant and appurtenances, and wondering if the hands are earning their screws and if the cheese-maker couldn't perform the duties of secretary as well and save the shareholders a hundred or two a year.

The spirit of the employer will get into your blood, too, and you'll think about engaging a man — one who knows how to handle and work horses, and can milk with both hands, and doesn't mind roughing it a bit until you get further on your feet.

"You'll have a 'ard job to get one", the old hands will tell you. "It's not work, it's waitin' on that men want now — until they get a few quid together, and then away they go." But someone tells you that Macpherson found one at the township for a quid a week — a pretty good man he was, only he got sick and had to go away to the hospital. So one day you go off in your new secondhand spring-cart to the township specially to hunt for a man.

"There was a chap here only a little while ago," the publican will tell you, "and he was askin' about a job, too. He might be just the cove to suit you. Hold on till I see if he's about."

And while you hold on, looking up at the bottles, and packets of cigarettes and dice on the shelves and sniffing the odour of stale beer rising out of a cask in a corner, he goes out and yells like a bullock-puncher (he *was* one in fact, before going into business) to all who can hear to tell that red-whiskered cove he's wanted in the bar, and to look lively. Then, returning, he'll take a murky cloth and start wiping some glasses. And he'll be forecasting the weather for you when the red-whiskered cove — who also has red eyes and a red nose and a red handkerchief — appears, hesitating and staring as if he suspected it might be April Fool's Day or some other catch.

"You were wanting a job, weren't you, Whiskers?" the publican will question, and so great will be the other's relief on finding it isn't April Fool's Day, or that you aren't a policeman, that for the moment he can't remember if he wants a job or not.

"Well, this chap wants a man for his farm. There's a chance for you." And the publican will pass him round the counter into your presence and take up the murky cloth again.

You'll ask Whiskers what sort of a hand he is amongst horses? If he can plough? And has he ever done any milking?

"Horses? Plough? Milk?" Whiskers seems surprised at you asking such questions.

"And what about your wages?"

Whiskers will leave that to you. But you would rather he stated a figure himself. You're afraid of slipping by mentioning something bigger than he expects. Whiskers has no idea, not having been long in the district.

"A quid?" you question, timorously.

Whiskers, undecided, turns his red face on the publican in search of guidance.

"That's the usual thing", Boniface will lie promptly, more in his own interests than yours, as he places three glasses on the counter. "And you're darn lucky to get it. Now, what's it going to be?"

Whiskers calls for a rum. Not being a drinking man you shake your head.

"Have a ginger-ale — that won't hurt you", the publican will advise, filling his own from a bottle of tea. You change your mind and agree to a ginger-beer. The publican lifts his and wishes you both the best of luck. Whiskers puts his down first; then, telling you he's going to get his swag and will meet you outside, he vanishes.

You'll reckon he ought to suit you and will be turning to the door to go off, when Bung will out with: "That'll be eighteen pence!"

As well as being surprised, you'll get a scare, because money is the last thing you carry about with you. You want all your pockets for carrying washers, and nuts, and nails, and twine and stuff that comes in handy. But you remember that by a piece of good luck there's a florin somewhere about you that you've been hawking round for months, and you start searching for it.

And when you discover it among some binder-twine you toss it on the counter as if you were darn pleased to get rid of it. In your hurry to be off before Bung in his generous way calls for another round of drinks, you forget your change.

Arrived at the homestead, you tell Whiskers he can make his quarters in the house along with yourself. Though you're his employer, you don't want to draw a social line or look down on him. And you apologize to him for the untidy state he's found the place in. But Whiskers does not mind — he's been accommodated in places a lot worse. So long as there are no fleas he doesn't care. Fleas keep him awake when he ought to be asleep. And Whiskers will be a man who requires a lot of sleep.

And while you're putting the kettle on and buzzing round preparing a bit of dinner before starting him on the plough, Whiskers will unfold his swag and be making a bed for himself in a corner, on the floor. He won't have any sheets or pillows, but he'll sort out his hairbrush and comb and clay-pipes and tobacco and matches; and there'll be a bottle which he'll keep covered, and handle gently as if it were a baby and he its mother putting it to bed.

When you both have dined — Whiskers better than you — you'll be scurrying round again returning the butter and bread and beef to their different places in the kitchen, and stacking up the dirty dishes, putting off the evil hour of washing-up till night, and at the same time communicating to Whiskers all that it will mean to you if you can, with his help, get thirty acres of wheat under in time for the rain, and some new land broken up before Christmas. And while you're scurrying and enthusing Whiskers will be standing in the doorway smoking and agreeing with you, and stepping aside whenever you want to go out or come in.

Putting on your hat and closing the door, you'll take him out and introduce him to the plough-team. You'll harness them up in his presence, showing him certain marks by which to identify their respective collars and winkers — the backbands won't matter so much. Whiskers won't be listening, but he'll be stroking the horses' foreheads and filling their eyes with smoke, and grinning.

"Now then", and you take hold of the reins eagerly and start off, driving the team to the paddock. Whiskers will follow, covering you and keeping in step like a soldier. When you "Waay!" the team at the barb-wire gate, he'll "Waay!" too, and stand while you drop the reins and open it. You'll hook them to the plough while he knocks the ashes from his pipe; and taking the handles you'll go a round or two, giving him hints and calling his attention to little things to keep in view; and all the time he'll be stalking behind you, studying the footprints you're leaving in the moist furrow, and looking back at intervals to see if you're doing straight work.

"There you are," you'll gasp at the finish; "now go ahead" — and you'll hand the plough over to him. He'll tighten his hat and dawdle a while, hoping you'll depart to your own job without waiting to watch how he starts his. He would sooner you returned in an hour's time, after he's had some practice. But you'll be anxious to see how he shapes. So you'll speak to the horses for him, and off they go. You'll stand watching, expecting to see an exhibition of ploughing — something unusual. And you see it. The plough will start wriggling and jumping, and Whiskers will wriggle and jump with it. And what the mould-board fails to turn over he'll be trying to kick over. He'll soon be trying to kick it all over. You'll feel as if you had lost heavily at the races; then, trying to cheer yourself by remembering that everything is new to Whiskers, and thinking he might do better after a while, you'll go off to the milking-yard to fix up another bail.

You're putting finishing touches to the bail now, trying to see how it works; humming tunes to yourself, and thinking about bringing the cows in, when loud profanity is wirelessed across the gully to you in waves. Looking through the yard-rails you see the plough-horses facing one another across the plough, and, rearing and shaking their heads and falling back on their rumps; and Whiskers will be running round, first to the tail of one, then to the tail of another. Love me, how you leave the yard and run to the rescue, ripping your pants and your flesh in falling through the barb-wire fence without being aware of it!

"Pshaw!" and Whiskers will spit when you've pacified the

team and collected the broken harness. "This is no good to me! Those — horses ought to be running with brumbies."

But you won't feel offended. You'll know that men sometimes make a smoke-screen of their tempers to hide incompetency; so you do your best to smile.

Later, in the milking-yard, when Whiskers struggles through with one cow while you're polishing off the other five, you'll try to smile again and tell him that you know it's always hard for a man to strike form at first. But Whiskers, on whom bad humour will seem to be settled for good, will tell you it's not his (unprintable) game. "Stockriding is what I've been at — dashing through the mulga on a good horse — throwin' scrubbers head over tip and tying them down — not messin' round with blanky plough-horses and cows."

After supper, though, when you've washed up and Whiskers is lounging on his bed stealing swigs from the bottle whenever you go out to the kitchen, he'll be in better humour, and you'll like his company. He'll relate weird accounts of his experiences out west 'midst thirst and privation and death. And while he's relating them to you the wind-haunted trees outside will be swaying and sobbing, and the dog, in fear of lurking dingoes, will be whimpering at the door.

"Did ever you read any of the po'try a cove called Boake used to write?" he'll ask.

You haven't, of course, but you've heard some of Henry Lawson.

"Not him — this cove, Boake, was a stockman on the Thompson when I was out there. He was a drover an' a 'orseman ... And you, livin' in a hole like this, never read 'Where the dead men lie?' Well I'll give it to y' ..."

And when, to the accompaniment of the moaning trees and the scratching of the dog at the door, Whiskers, his big eyes fixed on you like red mantles burning in the dim light, droles:

"Out where the grinning skulls bleach whitely,
Out where the wild dogs chorus nightly,
Under the salt-bush sparkling brightly—
That's where the dead men lie!"

You'll think ghosts and fancy the hand of one is feeling your hair. And just as he concludes, and the dog suddenly shoves the door open, and the wind rushes in, you'll let out *"Hell!"* and give a jump. So will Whiskers himself.

* * *

Next morning. Instead of rushing off, after you call and shake him a number of times, to round up the cows, Whiskers will mope round in a homesick sort of way. And when you tell him cheerfully that you can see all the horses on the ridge-side, he'll shake his head and say: "Oh, blime me, Boss — I think I'll chuck it in."

Of course you're not sorry; you'll be pleased, but you don't want to show your pleasure, so you'll tell him that it rests with himself.

"Full pay for yesterday, then, an' we'll be quits?"

You won't object to that even though he only put in half a day, and a dog darn bad half!

"And you'll run me up in the cart after breakfast?"

That'll make you bite your lip, but you'll say "orright!" And confounding him under your breath, you'll go off for the cows.

* * *

But next day when you discover that Whiskers had your fancy stockwhip, and your razor, and snake-skin belt, in his swag while you were driving him in, and hoping he'd come and see you again sometime, you'll curse him hard and far above your breath!

Chapter 6

It'll be a damp, drizzling day, a day when homesteaders turn their hands to plaiting green-hide into rope and reins, or to ring-barking. And you, with the help of Wattie Nutt, who, in passing, has taken refuge at the back of the old shed from a sharp shower, will be sharpening your axe on the grindstone; for you'll have a notion of "doing a bit of ringing in one of the gorges where the grass always seems to be sour". And as Wattie turns the grindstone and you hold the axe you'll both talk between jolts and grunts and stoppages about scrubs and timber.

"There isn't much of the good stuff left now, Dick", Wattie will lament. "Most of the rosewood and blackbutt and oak has pretty well disappeared from these parts altogether. There's a fair amount of silky oak left in the ranges, but it's so darn hard to get at that it takes more than it's worth to cut and haul."

"That's so, Wattie", you'll grunt in agreement, for he'll be tugging and jerking your rickety grindstone in such a way to speed it up that you'll require your two eyes and two hands to hold the axe in position, and save your fingers from being amputated.

"And as for the cedar, though my old man used to reckon that it once was as plentiful around here as ironbark and box, you never see a tree standing now."

"I've never seen a cedar sapling in my life that I can remember, unless on a precipice in some of those mountain hollows, where a beggaring goat could hardly keep its feet, to say nothing of a man with a team of bullocks."

"Strange thing that, Wattie." You'll snatch the implement from the creaking, jolting grindstone. Taken unawares Wattie will put in several rapid revolutions of waste energy.

"I've noticed it, too" — you'll pass your thumb over the edge of the axe to test it — "and never by any chance do you see any of the old stumps about either."

"What did they do with it all?" Wattie will wonder; "there was no market much for it then."

"Knocked it all down and burnt it up to clear their holdings and fulfil conditions, I suppose", you'll muse, taking up a billy of water and pouring some of the contents over the face of the axe and over the grindstone. "But lots of the old homes, even cow-sheds and lofts and gate-posts, still standing, have the best cedar in them."

As you cautiously apply the axe to the grindstone again, at the same time warning Wattie to "turn a bit slower this time", his thoughts will be carried back to boyhood, and, lifting his voice above the rocking and "clock-clocking" of the whirling, grating grindstone, will reveal a philosophic side to his nature.

"I can remember old man McGarry sawing down the last of the big cypress pines that grew near his place under the Macpherson Ranges", he'll tell you almost sadly. "I was only a kid then, but I felt that the old man and the fellow he had helping him were murderers!"

You'll risk taking your eyes from the wobbling grindstone to cast a glance of understanding at Wattie. His eyes, though, won't meet yours. They'll be fixed on the ground, and he'll be absorbed in reflection as he turns the handle. Changing his mind, he'll continue:

"And I'll never forget my feelings, Dick, when staring up at that lonely, lofty, silent tree, standing there before it fell. It had become a link in the lives of us boys when hunting the bush for bears and birds' nests. To us that old tree was a monarch — the king of trees in the ranges, and some mighty big box and ironbark grew about the Macpherson then, Dick."

"Wonder it didn't die of loneliness when it was the only one left standing," you'll jerk out, "for a tree will fret itself to death, you know!"

"It didn't, Dick, and though 'maggies' were always warbling

and yabbering amongst its green boughs in summer time, and parrots screaming, we never thought of pelting them there."

You'll flash another glance of understanding at Wattie as you make a non-stop change to turn the blade of the axe ... "And gad, Dick, as the darned old cross-cut see-sawed and see-sawed at its trunk, I felt it was myself it was going through! And so acutely that I was on the verge of running away so as not to be in sight when it fell, for I trembled at the thought of hearing it fall ... and of seeing it down and dying with its old green cloak around it! And then, though I didn't know why, just as it gave the first crack, I ran in shouting to them to stop! Not to cut that old tree down! and tugged at old McGarry's dangling shirt-tail!"

You'll suddenly lift the axe from the grindstone again to grin curiously at Wattie.

"I've had that feeling too, Wattie," you'll tell him, "but what a risky thing you did running in when the darn tree was starting to crack!"

"Wasn't it!" he'll admit. "But if you'd heard those old bent-backs yelling to me 'to run to hell from there — it's going to fall', and had seen how, when the tree gave several cracks, they abandoned the saw and ran for safety themselves, you'd have had your feelings changed as I had mine. Instead of protesting you'd have thrown yourself down in the long grass and laughed."

"I can see it all," you'll smile, passing your thumb over the edge of the axe-blade again, "but I suppose the old vandals made no use of the tree — just left it to the weather or the first bush fire."

"I suppose so, Dick," he'll agree, wistfully, "but I could have cried when I heard the crash and saw the old monarch down full length on the earth, never to rise again. For there it lay when I ran back, filled with a kid's idea of doing something to save it, its limbs broken and crushed and the sap oozing from its wounds like blood from one of us."

"I know, Wattie, I know" — and you'll take a seat on the ground with your back against the wall of the old shed and the axe across your knees — "I've seen it all, and felt the same as you."

"And what seemed strange to me" — he'll continue — "was how soon the sun started to ravish it in its helplessness, just like a wild animal devouring its crippled prey. For almost immediately the fresh green foliage began to droop and curl, and the song that it crooned to the winds, even when the cross-cut was severing its vitals, was silenced! And on my soul, Dick, you couldn't imagine how I hated those old fellows as I hung over the stump."

"I can, Wattie", you'll affirm.

"The same sort of pity came to me, Dick, that fellows often feel when they stand over a bullock they've just pethed or bulleted in a killing-yard, and put their hands on its still warm body. Even though the brute had done its best to put its horns through them they feel a bit sorry for having ended its life."

"I've felt it, Wattie", you'll admit reflectively.

Then as he rakes away the loose earth to shape a place to sit opposite you, you'll ask, "Did you ever look down upon a scrub of cypress pine from the top of a high mountain?"

"Lots of times, Dick — and never wanted to take my eyes off it."

"What a sight it is!" you'll remember; "no other timber that I know of makes such a picture. Though crowded together the tops of the trees seem set evenly, all pointing skyward like church spires, and tumbling away for miles in massed squares and triangles."

"And when you're down amongst them, Dick, the masses of ferny branches hang round the trunks like cloaks, but what clinging things they are to gallop through!"

"Gad, don't I know", thoughtfully from you.

"Of course you saw a lot of it one time, Dick", and a glow of admiration in his face will stir your memory.

"On Western Creek," you'll recall — "along with Jim Houston and Jack Fitz."

"Great horsemen, the pair of them, Dick."

"I hunted wild cattle with them in the pine scrubs out there" — you'll tell him — "and what scrubs they were. They had been at it for years, and how they knew the lay of the country, those two fellows, and every move of the wild mobs! But the game was new to me. Though you could ride like hell in the ranges and sit bucks with your pipe in your mouth, you soon found you had a lot to learn in the pines."

"It makes a new-chum of you, doesn't it?" from him.

"It did of me, Wattie, for I blundered behind Houston and Fitz for a whole week, often losing sight of them altogether, and hardly ever seeing a sign of the mob we were after!"

"And you one of the best horsemen on the ranges then, Dick!"

"Till one day, Wattie, we struck the biggest, wildest, and swiftest mob ever met out there, and yarded over a hundred of them."

"You did!" in astonishment from Wattie.

"I had a good mount that day — a black horse called Trooper, three-parts thoroughbred, by Leopold, fast and handy; a horse I gave an old stockman who was quitting the game ten pounds for, and he had had a couple of weeks' spell."

"I know the sort, Dick."

"It was about midday, and the mob was camping well out from the pine scrub when we came on them. A curious thing, too, Wattie, that Fitz, as we rode quietly along, had just said what a find it would be if we started a mob there! And no sooner were the words out of his mouth when, gad! there in front of us were five hundred if there was a hoof, covering three or four acres of ground, most of them lying down, the rest standing in the shade of scattered collibah trees, chewing the cud and flicking the flies off with their tails."

"Wars! What luck!" Wattie will gasp.

"Luck! We could hardly believe they were scrub cattle at all, just for the moment . . . 'Hell! Look out, chaps!' I remember Houston calling, then in an instant all that were lying on their feet, and the whole mob, with an affrighted snort that stirred the air, jumped into their stride, tails up over their backs, and thundered off. In open order, in massed formation, in line, but all following the lead of two bulls, a black and a red, they made for the pine scrub a quarter of a mile away.

"'Stick to them, chaps, one of you on each side', Fitz shouted — I can almost hear him now — as we rapped our heels into our horses, and grabbed a short grip of the reins — 'I'll follow them up.'

"What a race it was! But we never caught sight of each other again until it was all over."

"Ghost! I see them going, Dick, with you fellows after them", Wattie will chuckle excitedly.

"They cut the pace, too, Wattie," you'll continue, "reaching the pines almost abreast of each other. I flashed level with the ned ones, a young bull and a white cow were nearest me, I remember, just as we hit the thick of it. But Trooper, with eyes set, had chosen his path. I crouched on his neck, dropped him the reins, and into the cypress we dashed and 'swished'. There were no thorns and entanglements; but how dense and dark it all was! Had I time to think I must have thought that scrub was filled with spirits of darkness. But I clung with my heels as I crouched, my head tucked under, leaving the pace and the course to Trooper. And how he tore and swept me as part of himself through those clustering pines!"

"Holy, I can see the two of you, Dick."

"The going was soft though, and level as a table, Wattie; there wasn't a stone or a gully, but the swishing and tearing of the mob was like the roaring of the sea, and I kept in touch with the mob by ear. Suddenly there came brief flashes of light, and into the narrow open space we raced. Trooper crossed it like crossing a lane, and as I lifted my head I saw the white cow on my left, and let out a whoop of triumph for the others to hear. Then into more pines and dimness again! . . . But that narrow break was only the first of others much wider to follow. They came in rapid succession until right out in the open we burst, scrubbers and horsemen together. Gad, Wattie! if I live to be a hundred I shall never forget the riding and shouting and charging that followed!"

"You yarded a lot of them, though, Dick?" and Wattie'll rise excitedly.

"But they broke through the yard in the night, old chap, and got back to the cypress again!" you'll answer.

Chapter 7

You've pulled through two more years on your little home-stead, and the deeds are in sight. The Crown Lands ranger has been along taking stock of your improvements, and giving you advice on the making of farms and farmers. The knowledge he reveals will be wonderful — equalled only by the super-knowledge of the Intelligence Bureau man. He'll stay the night with you, too, and eat you out of bread, and sleep as sound as Bunyan's pilgrim in your bed while you toss about on a shakedown in your living-room.

But you battle on, following the plough and the sun from day to day, tailing the dairy herd, and trotting along to and from the factory. And though you've seen the main creek desolate of water, and your hay withered, and the grass eaten out, and very little green anywhere about, and heard the chums in the migrant colony over on the plain murmuring like a remnant of Philistines despairing, you're still smiling.

You're still a bachelor, too, doing your own laundry and chambermaiding, and cooking — putting junks of salt beef on to boil before going to bed, and making dampers whenever you have unexpected guests to your table, or the township baker runs out of dough, or forgets to leave your loaf on the gate-post.

Your methods of housekeeping, too, haven't improved like your dairy herd, or your ideas of gathering corn and reaping ears. Still, you are getting on; you are called a landholder now, which carries weight; and you're among those who have a stake in the country, and are its backbone . . . You're invited to join in movements afoot for the good of the district. Agents for separators, and harvesters and headers, and milking machines, and sewing machines, and insurances, all put you on their visiting list; and the local M.L.A., as well as his numerous rivals, call to see you, and blather inspiration about taxation, and a railway past the green-grey homestead, and a station at your gate. Even your old cowyard hat with all its air holes will be a lot too small for you, you're feeling so important.

You're asked to attend progress meetings, too, to get the telephone extended from the township to Smith, and a post office opened there ... Smith is the latest name given your area by someone in authority down in the city ... It is given to perpetuate to posterity a notable who crammed a lot into a short busy life before being called to account. You're asked to sign petitions, too, praying the Shire Council to put a culvert over Dog's Gully, and to deal with a diseased quadruped that is playing dog-in-the-manger at the creek-crossing. And when you've put your quavering signature to them, below old Silas King's and Tim Ryan's, and crossed the "h" instead of the "t", and placed a pool of ink over the "i" instead of a dot, you'll thrill with the brief authority of a ratepayer.

Because you think a lot and say little, and look as if the spirit of the dove has descended on you, you'll be reckoned a brainy chap — a man with a wealth of knowledge hidden in him. So one day when the Lukins, and Miskins, and Abrahams and others, who for years have been sending their kids per horse, and per milk-cart, and German waggon, to school at the township, decide to fight for their rights and apply for a school all to themselves at Smith, you'll bolt your supper and go along to a meeting of parents. It will be a historic meeting. At first you'll feel doubtful about going, thinking you might be out of order, being a bachelor. But Murphy, in whose house the meeting will be held, will rule you well in order.

"G'hon with you!" he'll pipe, "what difference do ud make, man, if you haven't e'er a chisseler? It dersent say you won't have be the time the school is builded. Our own have stopped goin' for long enough, plaise God, and it isn't lookin' as if there was goin' to be any more in their plaice —"

Mrs. Murphy, who is wearing long ear-rings, and has a shawl

about her shoulders, and is seated in a corner of the room sewing and listening, will interrupt him: "No, indeed, it isn't, thanks to goodness, and you needn't be sorry about it either." And after a big laugh he'll go on:

"Well, there's Abrahams and Lukin and Miskin there, though they can pool a fair lot between them, they kant make up what's required by the Department before the school can be builded, so Murphy here is goin' to put down his monigram for a couple more anyway, and Dick Gall can surely do the same?"

"Just listen to the talk of him —" Mrs. Murphy will break in again. "Why, 'tis conspiracy you're after, Pat."

"Who the divil's to know if it is?" Murphy will retort — "and a school at Smith — Wallaby Valley is the right name — will send up the value of Dick Gall's homestead, anyone can tell him that."

So you'll accept the situation by merely remarking, "I don't mind — if you're satisfied, I am." And add a couple of offspring to the list of eligibles.

"An' what's better still —" Murphy will determine with shining face — "just hand over that writing pin to him, Abrahams, and we'll app'int Dick Gall secretary to the movement, for no man is abler than him to do 'ud. And I'm not jokin' about it naither . . ."

"And why should anyone be jokin'?" Mrs. Murphy will pause to bite off another thread — "for doesn't us all know he can do it better than any wan widout such a cradle of talk, Pat."

And so, blushing and grinning, you'll adjust the pen to your hard, stiff fingers, and record the names of those present, and that Mr. Pat Murphy was voted to the chair. Then after a mixed argument about a chairman's casting vote, and a bet between Miskin and Murphy as to when the school at the township was first opened, you'll put down: "It was moved by Mr. Miskin, and seconded by Mr. Abrahams, that in the opinion of this meeting of parents the time has come for the Department to build a school at Smith, late Wallaby Valley, and that the secretary writes giving the number of children — carried unanimously."

"And put this to ud", the chairman will modestly direct:

"Mr. Pat Murphy, the oldest resident in the distric', who was in the chair, offered to give for nothing an acre of his land to build the school, providin' — and don't leave it out — providin' that he don't have to pay for the surveyin'..."

"In his usual generous-hearted style, why don't you put? —" from Mrs. Murphy.

Then the meeting will close with thanks to the chairman, and when you've gathered up the minutes and are looking round to see where you left your hat, Murphy, who is very proud of himself at the moment, will ask: "What's your hurry — sure there's lots of time, man. Ye've no old woman waitin' to see how'll you get to bed."

And Mrs. Murphy, gnawing at the cotton thread again, will chuckle: "Sure when you've given him a couple o' childer why kant y' be daicent and let him have a wife?"

While the room is ringing with mirth you'll feel the blood tingling through your spine and gathering in your cheeks, and a suspicion that you're being made a joke of will haunt you and start you wishing you had stayed at home and gone to bed. But Wally Lukin, who was dumb all through the meeting, will wake up and come to your rescue.

"You didn't put in it —" he'll remark — "how far the youngsters have to go to school from here, I don't think, did yer?"

"We didn't then, Wally —" Murphy will approve — "nor how many there are, either, an' 'tis important, 'tis very important. So let us take the number of them: — see — there's your own, how many is there of th'm?"

"Six of th' young Lukins —" from Mrs. Murphy, as she tosses her sewing about.

"Six Lukins — put it down, Misther Secretary."

"And nine of the Miskins —" confidently from Mrs. Murphy.

"Oh, good Lord!" and Murphy will stare incredulously at Miskin before bursting into laughter.

"And seven Abrahams", from Mrs. Murphy above the noise.

"Seven for you?" and shifting his amused gaze to Abrahams, Murphy will break into fresh mirth, and wiping the tears from his eyes with his knuckles will conclude: "It isn't a school you fellows want, it's a *reformat'ry.*"

"For themselves, Pat, or for the childer?" Mrs. Murphy will ask as she takes out some stitches.

And as the mirth sinks again, Murphy will continue: "Well, now, that's how many altogether, Dick?"

You'll tell him, "Twenty-two."

"And yours and my own, another four — but we better make it half a dozen between us, three each, what do you think, Dick?"

And while you're thinking and grinning Mrs. Murphy will suggest: "And as ye men have childer so easily put them down *triplets.*" There will come another outburst; and then the chairman will mention distances.

"Eight miles and a half, mine has to go," Abrahams will testify meekly.

"That's as good as nine. Put down *nine* miles for them," the chairman will direct — "and they goes over a mountain, too, doan't them, Abrahams? And through a scrub hangin' alive with snakes and death adders, and runnin' wild with dingoes?"

Abrahams will hesitate, and Mrs. Murphy, surveying a half-finished garment, will add: "And with lions an' tigers an' leopards."

"Put down about the snakes and adders and dingoes", the chairman, ignoring Mrs. Murphy, will instruct.

Then Miskin, who has been to factory meetings, will raise a point.

"Oughtn't it to be in a motion, Mr. Chairman?"

"It can be put in a motion if you like or in a 'mendment, it doesn't matter a gradle which —"

"If it's to go in a letter what in the name o' God do you want it in a motion or a 'mendment for?" Mrs. Murphy, tiring of stitching, will ask spiritedly.

"Order! will ye ower there — Mr. Miskin have the floor!"

"Well, I declare!" and Mrs. Murphy, smiling to herself, will renew the sewing.

But Miskin won't move any motion, so you'll complete the minutes, and the chairman will close the business again with the hope that if they get a male teacher it'll be one with wit and breeding.

"You old fool, Pat," Mrs. Murphy will intrude once more,

"a schoolmaster with wit an' breeding would be kept for the Zoo."

With a broad grin you'll find your hat, and when you've said "good night, everyone", Murphy will accompany you out to your horse ... He'll walk silently beside you as if there's something on his mind ... and when you throw the reins over the horse's head he'll take hold of the bridle bit.

"I spose that'll be all right, Dick?" he'll question looking up at you, "puttin' the names of childer down to ourselves?"

Cripes! you'll suddenly feel it's all wrong; your blood'll kind of freeze, and you'll stare between your horse's ears and drag hairs from his mane.

"And wan other thing, Dick —" Murphy'll whisper in a way that will make the night seem more haunted than the mopokes behind the sheds — "Dersent y' think for a small school like it will be that Julia, my daughter, would suit well to teach th' chisseler? ... I'm only askin' your opinion, you understan'."

You haven't any opinion that matters much about Julia; but under the light of the blazing stars and a sinking moon, you'll go home brooding over the youngsters you have parented, and wondering how you can get rid of that secretaryship.

Chapter 8

A bright velvety afternoon. You're working on your cowyard, bringing it up to date, and putting in round stuff, throwing out sheets of old iron and curls of ironbark and scraps of barb-wire. Old Tim Ryan and young Bob McCleverty are giving you a hand. Old Tim will be standing pawing his whiskers, recalling the massacre of station sheep in '68, on the very spot where your homestead stands, and Young Bob will be standing taking it all in, while you're grunting and straining to hold up the heavy end of a mighty sapling-rail that will bruise the feet off you if you fumble and let it drop, and when suddenly Rover will let the world know that a sulky with two ladies in it is making for the front door of the home. Their appearance will be a surprise. Old Tim, in the act of demonstrating a squatter dodging a flying spear, will break off suddenly to glance round. Young Bob will put his head through a panel of the yard and discover, "It's Mrs. Juba Lee and Josie King."

Ghost! You'll drop the mighty sapling with a crash and jump back bursting to call them a pair o' dam' fools. But you won't get your intentions recorded. Instead, you'll smile through the blood that's rushing to your face, and stare with them at the movements of the sulky. It will stop at your front verandah — you haven't got a back one yet — and Mrs. Juba Lee, who has charge of the reins, will be looking about for sight of you.

"They're lookin' for ye, Dick", Old Tim will suggest, concernedly, and Young Bob, with a rising temperature because they might drive across the yard, will urge you to "cut over quick, an' see them, an' me an' Mister Ryan will be putting up

th' next panel". Then he'll bend slowly over the sapling that
you dropped, and be looking back between his legs for Old Tim
to co-operate. Though he's Young Bob, he's fairly old, and has
a shyness about meeting women when they're dressed up,
equalled only by your own.

"Yes, *gahn,* man! *Gahn!*" and Old Tim will attach himself to
the sapling alongside Young Bob.

So you'll crawl out of the enclosure, casting perturbed
glances at the dirt on yourself and tightening your belt. And as
you slouch along the crooked little track that you and Rover
and the 'possums have worn, you're lost in an abyss of
discomfiture; your courage falls like the leaves of a tree; you're
in a sort of dream, and you look down at the red ants going
along ahead of you, and coming forward to meet you; and
while you walk on them as if they had no feelings, and no right
to live, you wish to heavens you could be turned into one of
them. Just when you've only ten or twelve more yards to
cover, and the wind sporting with the drooping leaf of your old
hat will show you the two women sitting under their flashing
red and blue parasols, watching you coming, and the horse
pricking his ears at you, you'll suddenly remember having burst
the seat of your pants straining to up-end a gatepost before Old
Tim and Young Bob arrived to give a hand. Mighty! You don't
know if your shirt is protruding through the rent or not, and
it's too late now to put your hand behind to feel. And,
conscious all at once of the gentle breezes finding their way to
your bare skin, the aperture will feel enormous, and it will prey
on your mind.

"Hello, Mister Dick Gall!" Mrs. Juba Lee, who has a pleasing
way and charming informality, will greet you. She's one in a
roomful is Mrs. Lee. What you'll answer won't be clearly heard
by them — nor by yourself either — and you'll lift your hand
as if you were going to stop your hat from flying off instead of
raising it. Then Mrs. Lee will be sorry they didn't notice you
were working at the yard or they would have driven over and
saved you the walk. And she'll ask, "Don't you know Miss King
— Josie King?" Of course you know her in a sort of a way —
you used to see her about the home when you worked for Old
Silas, her father; but you didn't look right at her because you

were propping yourself as close to the horses as you could squeeze on account of the sudden trouble on your mind.

Crossing your legs to steady yourself, and looking like a section in a dog-leg fence, your eyes will meet Josie's by accident. And, what will be surprising, she'll be smiling down at you. She who was always reckoned proud and stuck up, and was never allowed by her father to speak to working men! And she'll show such a set of teeth when she smiles that you'll want to see them again.

And the flush in your face, and the shaking of your hands, and the shortness of your speech will all be put down by them to your modesty. They've heard you talked of as being very modest.

Flashing her large, motherly eyes round the homestead, Mrs. Lee will mentally note your methods and habits. In a glance or two she'll measure you as correctly as a cobbler would measure you for a pair of boots. She's been through a lot of pioneering herself has Mrs. Lee — worked beside Juba in the fields; lived with him under canvas; shed gallons of tears over his shattered hopes; helped to make a man of him in the end. She'll take stock of your improvements, and the plan you've laid out the little homestead on.

And while you're uncomfortable because you can't think of anything to say to Josie, she'll rescue you by breaking into admiration of the splendid avenue of trees you have formed by leaving the gums that were growing in line with each other and grubbing out the others. Not having noticed your ingenuity and sense of the artistic before, she'll be full of enthusiasm. She'll infect Josie with it, too, and the combined compliments and the smiles they'll give you will make you blush more than ever; and you'll grin and shake your head till your forget all about your pants.

You'll be going to uncross your legs, too, to square yourself and put out your chest, when by chance you'll look down and catch a view of your shadow. Holy! You'll see a part of yourself projecting and moving when you move, like the ear of a calf. For a moment you can't make out what part of you it is, and you'll be wondering, till suddenly it will explode on you like a bomb that the tail of your shirt is hanging out. Laws, what a start you'll get! And how you'll change your position, dropping your hands by your thighs and spreading out your fingers! And you'll be wondering if they noticed it.

"But it's substance, not shadows, that interests women." So Mrs. Lee, enthusing more, will remark the simple handy way you've hung your gate; and the patent boot-scraper you have. Your little vegetable garden, too, and fowl roost, will take her attention, and you'll begin to feel proud and comfortable and be getting carried away again. But when Josie, who's been looking round, is suddenly taken with the patent armchair on your verandah, shaped out of a hollow log, the approbation they both bestow on it is nearly your undoing. Without thinking you'll turn round to look at the patent yourself; but all at once you'll front face again, and look up into their faces, with your eyes blinking, and your hands twitching.

Changing the subject, Mrs. Lee will start pulling at her glove, and telling you what it is they've really come to see you about. Miss King and she are collecting a little money to give the school kids over their way a Christmas treat. And she'll give you to understand that they haven't called to dun you, but they've come out of respect and as a courtesy.

Mrs. Lee knows to the sixpence, pretty well, what your farm revenue amounts to, and what you can afford in donations and what you can't. She also knows that to pass you by, out of pity and sympathy, would cut you deeper and leave more on your mind than waking up in the morning and finding one of your cows had turned up her heels. So, producing the list, which is flowing over with names and looks like a diagram of wireless waves, she'll tell you they only expect a small contribution, "as you're a single man, Dick". But when you're married and have a lot of children to send along to eat their share of the cakes and sandwiches, you'll be expected to donate a lot more. And though she'll beam first on Josie while she's saying all this, and then on you, a queer feeling will come over you — an intuition — which will keep you from looking at Josie, and Josie from looking at you. But it's the first time you've been asked for a subscription, and it comes on you as a first-born, and so your heart will open to it like a door. But it's Josie's job to record the donations, so while she taps her pink lips with the head of a silver-mounted pencil she'll be looking down with her brown eyes, waiting for you to name the amount. That will be a trying moment. You'll be overwhelmed with a spirit of bigheartedness; figures will fly to your brain as if you were a bank; your eyes will dance and glisten as though you're enjoying a new sensation; your shadow will be neglected again, and at last you'll blurt out: "Make it a quid."

"Oh, Dick Gall!" Mrs. Lee will laugh, blushing crimson for your dog-gone recklessness. And Josie, when she gets her breath, will gasp, "*Mister* Gall!"

"That's all right," you'll endorse with a grin — "it doesn't often happen."

But, like a mother to you, Mrs. Lee will tell Josie to put down two shillings, reckoning it's quite enough, and more than some who'll be sending along a cart-load of youngsters are giving.

"Quite enough, Mr. Gall", Josie will confirm, and her voice will sound as music to you.

"All right, if y' think so," you'll chuckle agreeably — "an' if you wait a while I'll go in an' get it for y'."

You'll be in the act of turning right round again to go off into your castle, when the shadow will once more catch your eye. Laws! What a predicament you'll be in then. They'll notice your hesitation, and the fresh colour that rushed to your cheeks. But they'll think it occurred to you that your treasury is empty, and so Mrs. Lee, to help you out, will tell you "not to mind — it doesn't matter; it'll do anytime". But you don't want to let them think you haven't got any money, so you'll get a sublime idea, and waving your hand to a big gum swaying on the other side of them, you'll observe that it isn't often four native bears can be seen up one tree. And while they're looking round, laughing, and trying to locate the fourth bear, you'll be taking three long fox-trot steps backwards, telling them at the same time where the fourth one is perched, till suddenly you turn round on to the verandah like a hunted wallaby.

Though you fancy you managed it all right, the ladies will turn their heads just in time to see your shirt-tail wagging as you disappear into your castle!

Next minute you'll be sitting on the corner of the table

holding your heart and your breath, and sighing, "Oh, hell!" But, of course, you won't see the pathetic smile they'll give each other, or hear Mrs. Lee whisper, "Th' poor fellow!" They'll be real understanding women, acting to others as they would have others act to them.

But having got your breath back, and feeling safe inside, you'll be breaking your neck screwing and twisting to find out the total damage to your pants. Hokey! You would never have believed it! They are nearly split in halves! And thanking the Lord, in your delusion, that the women didn't see them, you'll get out of those pants as though they were infested with bull-ants, and pull on others in great haste.

Putting your hand on a couple of bob, out you'll go again, smiling confidently and looking a different chap, as you slouch forward to the sulky, asking if they have seen the fourth bear yet? And out of the corner of her eye Mrs. Lee will notice your lightning change, and that you rubbed them on the floor before putting them on, thinking to make them look like a pair you discarded. But you won't be aware of what she's noticed; so you'll go on reckoning that women are as most people think.

When they're ready to go, and are shaking hands with you, and you're blushing up again, you'll promise faithfully to go to the picnic, and to go early, so as to help put up the swings, and collect the wood for boiling the tea-buckets. Then you'll open the gate for them, and stand by ready to wave when they look back. But you won't have to wave.

Still, when you turn away to go off to Old Tim and Young Bob again, you'll be uplifted, and you'll grin broadly, and feel like a martyred hero rising out of his own ashes.

Chapter 9

It will be a cold night at Green Grey Homestead, the coldest
you remember (you've forgotten all the others), and after
you've had supper and washed up and put the bread away and
scattered the crumbs from the table on to the floor with the
dish cloth and made the humpy look shipshape, you'll be
crouched in front of the fire, not reading the paper as some
would, but smoking hard and thinking. It'll run through your
head that now when fats are scarce is the time to get a good
price from the butcher for the two steers he offered you a low
figure for in the middle of summer. Finally deciding to sell
them for a fiver apiece, you'll turn your thoughts to the bees'
nest in the gully near your cultivation paddock. It's been there
in that silver-leaf ironbark for three years. Your neighbours
know of it, too, and some have wondered why you have never
robbed it. Just now you feel you would like a feed of honey;
you're tired of the same old jam — melon jam mostly, with
pumpkin-seeds in it, bought at the local store. You haven't
tackled a bees' nest since you were a kid; still, you were pretty
good at ribbing them then; never getting more than a dozen
stings or so; and you'll reckon that, this old silver-leaf being
hollow as a cave, there should be a couple of kerosene-tins of
honey in it at least — more than enough to do you for the rest
of the winter, and perhaps another half a tin or so that you
could pass to the Murphys. You can give liberally when it's
your own honey and is not costing you anything.

But just when you're wondering if you've got a piece of
mosquito-net anywhere in the humpy to wear as a veil so as the

bees won't have it all their own way, Curly Ginty, from down on the plain, will walk in on top of you, complaining of the "blasted cold", and telling you you're "all right in here, Dick, beside a burning fire".

Of course, your thoughts will be suddenly scattered, and for the moment you'll feel kind of shamed that he caught you sitting there thinking to yourself. For Curly, a big fellow with longish hair and a constant grin and a loud voice, isn't a close friend of yours and has rarely paid you a visit before. You'll know, though, that he's in with the Rileys, who do a bit of horse-dealing and horse-breaking, and you'll go to rise to welcome him. But Curly won't know any ceremony.

"Stop where you are", he'll tell you. "What do you think I am — a prince who can't look after himself?" Then reaching for a stool he'll adjust it near the fire, and he'll look curiously round your humpy before beginning to talk. Then he'll talk loud, and laugh loud, too, and often. He'll ask what you did with the little jumping horse you used to have? And while you're trying to tell him and feeling proud about it, he'll be standing up stirring the fire by kicking it together with his boot and talking about something else. Then he'll sit again, not having listened to a word you said, and start telling you the pranks the Rileys and he got up to one time over the Range with "Hungry" Hawran's cattle and horses. He'll tell you how they took a mob of Old Hungry's cows as "coachers" to the scrub one moonlight night and "lost the whole jolly lot"; and how they used to ride the tails of Hungry's horses that were spelling there, and swim them in a waterhole the next day to wash the sweat marks off 'em.

You'll get so interested in all Curly is telling you, and the *way* he's telling you, that you won't notice the sparks that fly out of the fire and lodge in your lap and burn small holes in your moleskins. And the number of times he'll rise and swing his arms about demonstrating and kicking the box over will make you laugh. And when you fancy — which you will — in the middle of it that you heard a tree fall, he'll remember a song Dan Riley used to sing in the camp at night, and break out loudly into the first verse of it. Then you'll laugh till you hear the report of a gun somewhere, when you'll suddenly stop and listen curiously. He'll listen with you.

"That sounded in the gully somewhere", you'll reckon wonderingly, with your ears still cocked.

"If there's going to be any shooting here I'll leave it to you, Dick", Curly will say. "You got a gun. I haven't. I'm off!" And snatching his hat, out the door and into the night he'll go without even saying so-long.

Beyond the report of that gun there'll be nothing, except fleas perhaps, to disturb your rest during the night. But in the morning, when you're rounding up the milkers that camp in the fully, you'll wonder for a moment if you're really awake or walking in your sleep. The tree with the bees' nest will be cut down and lying across your cultivation fence, and robbed of the honey!

"So that was your — game, Mr. Curly Ginty!" you'll explode, and almost choke. And in your mind you'll see the Rileys felling the tree and getting the honey while he was entertaining you. Then you'll hear the gun-report again, signalling him that the job was finished.

Turning away you'll vent your feelings on the loitering cows. "Get along, *blast* you, get along!" you'll hiss. And you'll keep on blasting them till they're in the yard, and you're sitting under one of them, squeezing the milk from her.

Chapter 10

It will be a crisp, velvety Queensland morning in May — one of
those mornings when, though fighting against irregular rainfall,
middlemen and officialdom, you'll feel it's grand to be alive
and amongst it all. You'll have returned to your little homestead after having delivered the morning's milk to the factory,
and will be preparing to carry on where you had left off late
the evening before, pulling your bit of corn, while round about
the yard the dairy cows will still be camped, contentedly
chewing at the cud. Dissimulating, willie-wagtails will be
hopping and dancing about the backs of them, waltzing from
their tails to their horns, and serenading them, even giving the
unsophisticated, unsuspecting, surly old Jersey bull a turn at
the same time, plucking and pinching beaksful of hair from
their coats, and flying off to upholster their nests with the
stolen goods. In the art of cheerful and barefaced purloining,
the "sweet-pretty-little-William" has no equal in the feathered
world. But you'll pay no attention as you pass him by.

Before you reach the corn-paddock, however, a string of
polo-players sporting white breeches and top-boots, with polo-
sticks strapped behind their shoulders, each mounted on a good
style of hack and leading a pair of clipped, corn-fed ponies, all
in the pink of condition, and looking hard and tough and fit to
play for an empire, will suddenly catch your eye. Then you'll
stand and stare while your heart'll go faster. Those polo men
will pull up short out of a canter — a long, long canter it will
have been, too — and passing through your open gate in treble
file will hail you loud and joyously by your Christian name,

inquiring in chorus: "Why the devil ain't you getting ready to
go in to see the match?"

Great stars! Before you can get over your surprise and make
answer, they'll be riding right up to you, asking:

"Don't you play at all now, Dick? Have you given the game
up altogether?"

"Darn me eyes! Why, it's th' Philp boys!" you'll jerk out,
grinning in happy recognition of them.

And, failing to ride you down, they'll draw in, gathering all
round you, chuckling and laughing like the real sportsmen they
are. Of course you'll know them — the three famous mountain
riders who, since the time their father used to strap them to
the saddle, have known no life other than that on the back of a
horse, and with whom in days past you played polo and rode
scores of miles and locomoted hundreds more to play it — you
could hardly forget *them!*

Ah, me, you'll be pleased to see those old mates again, even
though on appearances they have done better than you in the
world since you separated. And you'll notice they've scarcely
grown a day older in the saddle. And they'll be just as pleased
to see you.

"Willie, Eddie, and Artie," you'll repeat proudly, almost
inaudibly, as you look at their troop of ponies, greys, bays and
browns, all over. And when one by one, while adjusting their
reins, they'll reach down from the saddle to shake hands with
you, the ponies will be champing the bits, stamping, swinging
about in a half right and left kind of fashion, crowding you,
shoving you with shoulders and hindquarters as if ready and
eager to trample you in the dust of your own little homestead.

But you won't be thinking of the law of self-preservation:
your blood will start tingling and your eyes dancing at sound of
those voices and sight of the top-boots and spurs, bright
stirrups and polo-sticks again. And when you gush impulsively:
"Ghost! Wouldn't I like to be one of you going to have another
smack at it!" you'll have said all that your heart will allow you
at the moment.

Then when those mountain-reared brothers, filled with quiet
gladness, will hope to see you playing with them again one day,
and making those runs you used to make on Hippy down the

side and round the wings, putting in those near-side forward
hits on her that used to paralyze those who tried to ride you
off, your memory will fly back to matches at Toowoomba,
Spring Creek, Ipswich, Emu Creek, Brisbane and other places,
and your eyes will glimmer till the scene before you and the
green sward beneath is a phantom polo-ground with the dairy-
cows portion of the spectators, and you yourself standing there
booted and spurred, puffing and leaning on a polo-stick!

But on the boys asking, "Have you got a pair of
shoeing-pincers on the homestead, Dick?" you'll come quickly
out of that day-dream.

"Yes, course!" you'll say with feelings of fresh pride — the
pride of proprietorship.

As the ponies swing round you'll scurry across, leading the
way to your blacksmith shop, a flat-roofed bark shed, with two
sides and one end to it. The other end is its open door. Inside
there'll be a forge with a small bellows installed and other
fittings — an anvil, a heap of old iron, a pile of miscellaneous
horseshoes, tongs, hammers, hooks, broken swingle-trees, scraps
of wire, and greenhide, and a broken dray-shaft. You'll be
proud of your blacksmith shop, too — proud because you
designed and built it yourself, and collected everything that is
in it. And while the Philp boys are dismounting at the
shop-door sorting out the ponies and fastening the reins of
some of them, you'll be tossing tools about in search of the
pincers and a hammer.

"Which of them first?" you'll ask, brandishing a rasp as well
as the pincers; but when on looking round you'll see one of the
boys bent double with the gray pony's front foot held fast
between his knees, at the same time motioning you to hand
him the tools, you'll think of his snow-white riding-pants and
the chances of their getting ripped by the nails, and him having
to take the field, as you have had to do yourself times before,
with a handkerchief tied round his leg to hide his shame. Then
you'll ask him what he's up to, and bending beside him, you'll
reach for the pony's foot and place it between your own knees.
He'll stand by hitching at his belt and holding the halter-rein to
keep the animal still for your benefit. Like a skilled craftsman
you'll handle the rasp and pincers, and in a minute or so you'll

be lugging and twisting that shoe till you toss it aside. And when the others, looking on, will compliment you, you'll grin proudly, and go on attending to the rest, putting the rasp on them and trimming their hooves. You'll straighten up at the finish, perspiring; and with a pain in your back you'll move amongst those ponies, patting them, scrutinizing them and asking about their breeding and the rest.

And when the brothers, without discounting the merits of any, will assure you with enthusiasm that none of them ever was and never will be as good, or half as good, as the Hippy mare you used to play on in the days gone by, your memory will fly back to her achievements, and to the thrills and triumphs you shared with her.

"That little bay bloke there of Artie's beside you", one will suggest, indicating a pony on whose hindquarters you will be leaning, "is something like Hippy was when you first played her, Dick".

"Something," you'll agree — "a bit higher perhaps, but hasn't her rein or chest."

"He hasn't Hippy's face either," another brother will supplement as they all start collecting the ponies and gathering the reins together — "nor her brains and gameness." Then, as all three reach the saddles: "Her sort, Dick, are few and far between!"

You won't say anything at the moment, for you can't help picturing the little mare in your mind, and thinking what a wonder she really was. One you had bred and reared and trained yourself; one that had carried you so often into the limelight; and a faithful companion to you in the saddle and out of it. And the thoughts of her will stir feelings that will dim your eyes, till a further question or two will lift you out of your brief reverie.

"She was out of a Blackbutt mare," you'll answer, "by Young Olympic, a trotter on the Clifton side, if you remember?"

And as they gaze down on you, their eyes brimming with the light of fellowship of horse, while they adjust their halter reins and fumble with neatly-booted feet for the off stirrup-irons, you'll go on to explain feelingly, as though you were speaking of a lost relation, that you had her for two or three years after leaving their part of the world and giving up the game. And, stroking the pony nearest you on his arched and glowing neck, you'll add after a silence: "I took her with me on a big droving trip to the Cooper, and across the Barkly, and just as she used to follow a polo-ball she would keep on the heels of a beast. A marvellous mare at 'cutting out' on a camp, Gad she was!"

The others, shaking their heads approvingly as they sit erect in the saddles, will "guess she would be!"

"She would never take up with other horses at night," you'll continue, "and no matter where it was or what sort of country we were going through, no brumby mobs could entice her away with them."

"And the stallions at the head of some of those mobs running along the Culgoa and the Warrego were a daring darn bad lot, too!" the eldest brother reminded of past adventures of his own, will put in.

"No matter how dark the night was," you'll go on, "if I lifted my head from under the blanket and called out her name — or if I was mooching round quietly by myself, as you know a fellow does out there sometimes, or along with a mate — she'd whinny to me to let me know she was about. And if I didn't answer she'd come closer and whinny again.

"Great as she was at polo," you'll tell them, "I think she was even better after stock. The last time I rode her was after cattle over the Dividing Range, not many miles from here, on Ma-Ma Creek. After mustering most of the day on her, I was making back with young Gower, carrying a tomahawk that we'd found near an old sawpit."

"In a red-cedar gully off the creek?" one of them will suggest, and you'll nod in agreement.

"And coming along under Tipsy Point," you'll proceed, "one of those long herring-gutted, yellow-and-white goannas, not unlike three or four feet of centipede, about a hundred yards on ahead of us, was scurrying for its life across our track, making for a big old-man gum-tree. There'd been no rain for a good while, so the grass was pretty well eaten out and bare."

Anticipating you, the boys will start chuckling.

" 'Watch me head that cove before he reaches th' tree!' I said to Gower. And the darn goanna had only about twenty yards or so to go to reach it. But before Gower had time to grin I touched Hippy with my heels and off she went like a shotgun; and holding the tomahawk as a polo-stick I rode like a bushranger, making record reckonings of pace and distance. Gad! When the yellow crawler heard the rattle of her hooves he put the pace on, working his stumpy legs like machinery and wriggling from his head to his tail."

The brothers, leaning back in their saddles, will applaud the goanna in mirth, idly chorusing: "And who won, Dick?"

"Th' darn yellow wriggler beat us for the tree by a yard, and was starting up it as Hippy flashed past, darn near putting her off-front foot on his tail."

"Remember the match we played against Spring Creek, Dick?" one in no hurry to go will ask with fervour. And slowly shaking your head and seeming to smile away back to the past, you'll stroke the coat of the flea-bitten grey before you in silent thought.

"You won that match on Hippy for us, Dick, when you went right through the lot of them, and got that last goal with an under-th'-neck cut — a beauty it was!"

You'll remember it all.

"They had us walloped up to that. Marsden and Caswell were playing the game of their lives — Marsden reckless as Hell, riding across us and over us and on our heels."

You'll chuckle, thinking of Marsden swinging out, wheeling at racing pace, swerving and riding off without ever pulling a rein.

"We took you out of No. 3 and put you up in the front", they'll remind you with gleaming eyes. "And by the terrors, if Hippy didn't shake them up that day nothing ever did! From side to side and end to end she kept them riding after her like Hell, and I don't think you missed a stroke, Dick. Derned if you did!"

Seeing them still smiling down on you, and making no signs of going, you'll find your voice again.

Their mirth will broaden.

"But you know what a champion Hippy was at wheeling full

gallop?" you'll continue. "Well, soon as she passed the tree — scattering dust and dead leaves over th' goanna, too — I brought her round in her stride, right on her haunches, an' back she raced, taking the old gum on the opposite side; and as we flew past again the tail of the dog-scared goanna was wriggling level with my shoulder. Taking a potshot at it with the tommy, darned if I didn't amputate it at the butt — the cleanest job you ever saw!"

The roars that will come from the polo men will start the ponies jumping.

"And when I wheeled her again," you'll grin, "and looked up into the tree with Gower, there was our noble goanna perched on the highest branch, and when he turned his eyes down on us you never saw anyone look so darned indignant!"

As the mirth subsides the brothers will enquire: "What did you do with Hippy, Dick — sell her?"

"In a way I did", you'll tell them. "I let Tom Allen have her for twenty quid after she got in foal to a hairy-legged, wooden-headed draught-horse. Tom played her a while, and then sold her for a hundred to a cove who came along buying polo-ponies for the Hordens. But I can't imagine city fellows doing any good on a mare like Hippy."

Then in turn the Philp boys will reach down across their horses to bid you so-long and shake hands warmly. And as you watch their mounted forms stringing out through your gateway, you'll live again in fancy those days when you, too, rode through mountain passes, and over sunlit plains to line-up and mark your man on the polo fields of the south and east of Queensland.

Chapter 11

It'll be Christmas Week. The annual change in the solemn, plodding homesteaders will have set in strong. They'll be making special trips to the township to buy a "few little extra things"; and some will take their wives and families with them, though most times it will be the wives who will take the husbands.

You yourself, thóugh still a bachelor doing your own bit of washing and cooking and sweeping out, will trot along like the rest for a pound or two of raisins to try your hand on a pudding, and perhaps you'll plunge on a hat and a couple of flannels as well.

And what a bureau of information the store will be to the lot of you!

"D'you know who's come home for Christmas?" you'll hear from the bustling storekeeper as you step on the verandah and reach the door. But before he can get any further his wife, who's at the other end of the counter helping in the rush, will broadcast: "Willie Hagon and the two McNamaras."

"And is it true?" the oldest customer will ask as he squeezes one of his feet into a new blucher, "that Sam Telford is back after being in th' Never-Never for fifteen or seventeen years?"

"That's so", the storekeeper, scooping currants out of a bin for Mrs. Flinn, will proclaim. "He came back a day or two ago." Then there'll be a pause to place the currants on the scales. And in the pause Mrs. Storekeeper will take up Sam Telford and give full details of his arrival, adding that "he's going to stay at Rudd's place, so they told us."

Mention of Sam Telford will almost take your breath away. "What's that?" you'll ask, pushing your way in among the women and kids. "You mean Sam Telford whose father was killed by th' blacks?"

"Th' same", proudly from the storekeeper, as he squints closely at the scales for the third or fourth time.

"And a smart-looking man he's turned out, too," will come from Mrs. Storekeeper, for the benefit of the lady customers, "with his beard and strapped trousers, though he must be middle-aged now."

"Sam Telford back, eh?" you'll smile, letting the raisins and the hat and flannels slip out of your head. "Me an' him were pals for years out on the Warrego and the Cooper. Gad, I must see old Sam before he's off again, wherever he is."

"You'll see him, Dick", the storekeeper, taking back a few more of Mrs. Flinn's currants to make the load lighter for her to carry, will assure you — "He's sure to be in here again with some of the Rudds. We'll tell him about you, and where your place is."

"And tell him I've got whips of room for him", you'll say and out you'll stride as if you've finished your shopping. But before reaching your horse you'll stop abruptly and return with a foolish looking grin on your face.

It'll be Christmas Eve now. Having had your dinner you'll be standing in the doorway filling your pipe. The rubbish lying about will catch your eye and start you wondering if it wouldn't be as well to clean it up and make the place look a bit tidy in case you might have a visitor or two. The thought has scarcely entered your head when you'll realise that three horsemen have entered the gate and are almost at your door. How on earth you didn't see them sooner has got you beat! And while you're feeling puzzled, two of them, one a boy, will greet you mirthfully, the first addressing you as Dick, the other as R-R-Richard. The third will regard you with twinkling eyes and a broad smile. In an instant, of course, you'll recognise Dave and Joe Rudd, though you will have seen little of them for over a year.

"Don't you know who this bloke is, Dick?" Dave will ask, pointing proudly to Sam Telford as they all dismount.

"We've b-b-brought him over to s-s-see y' and to have after-n-n-noon tea, Dick", Joe'll stutter with even more pride that Dave, for they'll both be in charge of the lion.

"Sam!" you'll exclaim proudly, and, bounding from the verandah, you'll grab his hand and he'll grab yours. Then looking you up and down he'll reckon you haven't altered a darn bit.

Leading the way, you'll invite him into "the castle" (Dave and Joe will require no invitation). "And tell us what you've been doing since that Christmas — how many years ago? when we parted out on Maguire's old cattle station."

"About seventeen", Sam will remember.

"I s-s-say, Dick," Joe will break in, "them hens o' yours has been eatin' pumpkin s-s-seed."

"Why?" you'll ask indifferently, looking at the fowls that are dodging about. "What makes you think that, Joe?"

"Be th' w-w-way they l-l-lean back when they walk an' shove their hind p-p-part along like p-p-penguins."

"Like your gran'mother!" Dave will guffaw •at his young brother.

"They won't l-l-lay any m-m-more eggs for y', Dick," Joe, ignoring Dave, will persist as they step on to the verandah, "unless y' give them p-plenty o' s-s-salts."

"Was that what they used to give 'em to you for?" Dave will guffaw again; and Sam and you will break into mirth as you enter the castle.

"You're surprised, I suppose, Sam," you'll begin, dragging the chairs together, "to find I've turned out a cockie? But tell us something about the West. I suppose if a fellow like me was taken there now blindfold and let go, he wouldn't know where he was. And how did old Maguire get on — make his pile?"

"Oh, the old man passed out long ago, Dick", Sam, who's a good talker and no ordinary bushman, will answer as he rests the left boot on his right knee and toys with the rowel of his spur. "Fay — the daughter — you remember her — came in for everything when he died, and took over the station herself, and managed it splendidly, too."

You'll look surprised that a bit of a girl as she'll appear to your mind could run a large cattle station — a job that lots of men wouldn't tackle.

"A girl managin' a station?" Dave will grin doubtingly. "Cripes, there must be a lot of the man in her."

"No," Sam will answer quietly; "a fine-looking girl she is, very tall, a great horsewoman, very game, very determined, and quite at home, day or night, in any part of the Bush. Very few men better than her."

"And how big is th' s-s-station, S-S-Sam?" Joe will want to know; "and how many kuk-kuk-cattle has she got on it?"

"Well I suppose you could ride in a straight line for a hundred miles or so without crossing the boundary of it", he'll be told.

"W-w-what?" from Joe. "A 'undred m-m-mile?"

"Ghost!" Dave will add.

"And about twenty thousand head of cattle when I was there. But for a while she lost some big mobs. A couple of 'gentlemen' buyers used to call and take a hundred or so off her hands at her own price and hand them over to their men, staying over-night themselves playing and singing songs, while a second lot of men moved off with a thousand head or so, keeping in the tracks of the others, but travelling by night."

"Hokey!" Dave will gasp, leaning across the table, while Joe will echo: "A th-th-thousand!"

"The time came, though" — Sam will pause to put down his foot and stretch out his two long bowlegs in comfort — "when she got even with them."

"W-what did she d-d-do, Sam?" from Joe.

"Lay a trap for them?" from Dave.

"Well, this is one instance. I was up to my eyes in it with her, as it happened."

"Cripes! He never told us *this* one before", Dave will gush in anticipation.

Then Sam will lean forward, press his palms down hard on his thighs, and with eyes opening wide, and glistening like the leaves of the myall in a sun-shower, will proceed:

"We were mustering on the western side along Boomerong Creek — you'll remember it, Dick?"

You'll nod, of course, whether you remember it or not.

"There was Fitzmaurice, the head stockman; Gongoola, a

half-caste reared on the station; Fay Maguire, and yours truly. Fay was riding her grey mare, Britomarte, a splendid beast among stock; in fact, we were all mounted on the station's best."

"I reckon *you* would be, Sam," you'll break in reminiscently, your eyes starting to light up as in fancy you see and scent the mobs and the mulga; "but the old place never had a bad horse on it."

"As a rule we could muster a couple of thousand head of cattle at that end of the run, but this time we hadn't been a couple of hours on the Creek when Gongoola, with a shake of his head, decided, 'No cattle been runnin' here for long time!'

"I agreed with him, but Fitzmaurice kept a still tongue. So we worked Boomerong Creek the whole of that day, only coming across about a hundred head, and made the old hut out there our headquarters."

"And did the girl", Dave will put in with a curious grin, "camp with all you blokes?"

"Safety in numbers, Dave", Sam will answer. "Besides, Gongoola took care of her. Well, next day we came across some tracks 'way up the river. At first only an odd one or two, stragglers. But further along we got on the tracks of a mob. They came out of a belt of mulga, swam the river, crossed the boundary and headed due west. As it happened, we were all together, having made the spot where we picked up the first tracks our meeting-place. The time would be about noon. As each of us rode studying those tracks in silence, our thoughts all ran in the one direction. For there it was written on the ground, as plain as if it was printed on paper, that a mixed mob of at least a thousand head had been driven off the run — and driven by five horsemen, two of them on shod horses!"

"Holy! Eh!" And Dave will gape open-mouthed.

" 'Gone about three days', Gongoola said as we all came together again. For a few moments we just sat in our saddles looking at one another.

" 'What do you want us to do, Miss Maguire?' Fitzmaurice asked at last, speaking slowly while he dragged hairs from his horse's mane.

" 'To follow them up as fast as we can, of course', she

answered sharply. And when we caught the look that flashed
from her eyes we knew that she meant it, too, woman or no
woman.

" 'Not much use rushing after them now when they've got
three days' start', he demurred. 'There's no cattle country to
the west of here that I know of, and you'll find those tracks
will swing right south before going far and get lost in the
lagoon country.'

" 'That will be for us to find out', she answered. 'Now
hurry, men, get the spare horses and packs, and we'll follow
them.' "

"And sh-sh-she was a woo-woo-*woman*, was she?" Joe will
stutter in astonishment.

To which Dave will answer: "You don't think she was a
man, do y'?"

"N-n-no," from Joe again — "an' I d-d-don't think you are
either, D-D-Dave."

"In less than a couple of hours we were on those tracks
again, trailing them at a fair pace with our faces to the west,
Gongoola leading the way. I can see him now as plain as I
could see him then — leaning over his horse's shoulder, his eyes
scanning the ground, while his silence made him seem uncanny.
Towards nightfall those tracks increased, showing another mob
had joined in, the grass and herbage became scarcer and the
water we came to was only soakage.

"Gongoola at intervals would turn his head to tell us it was
right, but Fitzmaurice all the time was troubled with doubts."

"W-W-What was that y' s-s-said, Sam?" Joe not understanding will inquire.

Sam will explain and go on: "Before it got dark we came
upon a fair-sized water-hole untouched by cattle or stock of
any kind, and camped beside it for the night."

"Cripes, and wasn't she frightened?" Dave will wonder.

"Not the least; anyway, she didn't show it. Y'see the Bush
had been mother to Fay Maguire. Besides, Gongoola kept an
eye on her sleeping-place, lifting his head at intervals to see she
was not disturbed. I can see that camp now. A solitary owl, I
remember, looked down upon the lot of us from the branch of
a withered tree, blinking in the dim light of the stars."

"I seen them l-l-like that, round our culti-v-v-vation", Joe will say.

"Oh, shut up!" and Dave in reproval will press his foot on Joe's. Joe will rescue it and kick out at Dave.

"Next morning we got going early and followed on till about three or four o'clock in the afternoon, when Fitzmaurice seemed to lose hope. Though he said little he looked back at every turn. He seemed to be making calculations of the distance we had come — of the number of miles it was to the fringe of mulga that now lay behind far over the plain. To the rest of us who gazed ahead in search of new objects, the gleaming stretches seemed to be dipping over a horizon that led to God knows where."

"Cripes!" Dave, leaning back from the table, will whisper to you — "Sam can tell it all right!" But you'll nudge him to keep silent.

"As we trailed along the horses suddenly made a bound and snorted. To our surprise a calf staggered to its feet from the shade of a salt-bush. It had knocked up, and been abandoned by the raiders. The poor little brute was famishing, and hadn't long to live, and at sight of it we figured that that driven mob was not far off. As it staggered from horse to horse mistaking them in turn for its mother, Fitzmaurice took out his revolver and looked meaningly at Fay Maguire.

" 'It's the kindest thing to do, I suppose', she said."

"And d-d-did he sh-sh-shoot it, S-S-Sam?" Joe will ask.

"Of course he did, y' goat!" Dave will snigger disrespectfully.

"Another hour and a hot wind blew up — the hottest I was ever in. You'd think it was coming out of a furnace. It seemed to finally decide Fitzmaurice and suddenly he reined in. 'It's madness, Miss Maguire,' he said, 'to go any further. We've scarcely any rations left; and if there's no grass and water on ahead, what's going to happen to the lot of us?'

"She put it to Gongoola.

" 'Cattle-stealers know plenty of good country out here,' he grinned, 'or they wouldn't take big mob.' Gongoola was always logical.

" 'But this mob might only be wandering off to Halifax!'

Fitzmaurice argued. 'Cattle take those fits sometimes.'

" 'Are you becoming afraid?' she asked, her brown eyes flashing. 'If you are, I expect you can find your way home.'

" 'I'm not afraid,' he protested, 'but I'm not going to be a darn fool any longer either, not for all the cattle on earth.' With that he turned his horse and left us."

"Cripes! Went back on his own, eh!" from Dave.

"Yes, and Gongoola and I went on with her to see it out."

"She was pup-pup-plucky all right!" Joe decided.

" 'It's hard to believe a man could be such a cur', was all she said as we continued to run those tracks into the setting sun.

"The wide plain now appeared to be coming to an end. Two pinnacles came in sight; and we could see that the country sloped away on either side of them into lightly-timbered valleys. Gongoola, pointing his whip-handle, grinned. Fay Maguire could only stammer a word or two in her excitement.

"Passing between these pinnacles, standing there like a natural gateway, we got the surprise of our lives. Before us as fas as we could see were rich grass lands, with clumps of forest trees. 'What country is this, Gongoola?' Fay Maguire asked in wonder. But the half-caste was as much astonished as she. A little further on we reined in to gaze with amazement upon a lake, and all along it, and out from it, cattle, cattle, sleek fat contented cattle! We hadn't gone above a mile further before Gongoola cried out, pointing to a dozen head or so grazing quite near: 'Here — look! Them been Homestead bullocks — got 'm our brand — T.M. — look it!'

" 'So this is where they all are!' Fay Maguire muttered. 'The plant of cattle-thieves!'

"And all I could say was that I was damned.

"We'd hardly recovered from the surprise when a well-mounted chap came riding leisurely across to us. 'Hello, you Billy Fitzmaurice!' Gongoola called to him. Then I gasped 'Mighty!' For he was our head stockman's brother!"

"Cripes!" Dave will break out, "so that was why the cow went back! He knew."

Then there will be an interruption. The doorway of your home will be darkened by a burly, bewhiskered figure standing in it gazing on the group of you, and brandishing a green switch that he used as a riding-whip.

"D-D-*Dad*!" Joe, looking up, will stutter, and turn attentively to Sam again. But Sam will be looking up, too.

"Cripes!" Dave will whine in protest to Dad — "you spoilt it, comin' in!"

"So this is where you all are?" Dad will roar. "With your heads together like sheep in a storm hidin' from the thunder an' lightnin', an' a hundred of someone's pigs out there in your cultivation, Dick, spoilin' your corn an' pumpkins!"

"Pigs!" and you foul Sam and the table in your haste to get out to the rescue.

And Sam and the others will follow to give you a hand.

Chapter 12

You'll find the evenings getting long and hard to put in at the little homestead. They'll pall on you sometimes and fill you with memories of the old home you knew years now far arear. And it will all be because you've at last made up your mind to get married. You'll sit thinking and wondering if you are going to do the right thing or not. With no one to consult or confide in, it will be harder for you to decide. So you'll continue thinking on and dreaming back, turning over little mistakes, false steps and chances let slip, while your pipe will burn out and Rover, stretched as usual at your feet, will sigh and snore in his sleep.

Knocking the ash from the pipe into the fire and pondering more and more, you'll start counting up what you've got to marry on. You'll estimate the value of your stock and improvements, including the horse-collar you found on the way home from the factory, and a new bucket and a good two-inch rope that some absent-minded beggar left at your windmill; then you'll add the increased value of your holding as per the shire rate-notice, which, of course, will be fifty per cent, below real value, for the shire councillors, as you'll know, are shareholders themselves. Then, when you've appraised the cash value of your growing wheat-crop and included factory returns for six months ahead as a fair thing, you'll have made your assets look so satisfactory that you'll start smiling and liberally filling your pipe again. You'll confess to the snoring Rover that you feel you were a dashed fool ever to have been afriad of getting married, and that you're dog-darn sorry you didn't do it long ago.

Soon you'll be chuckling to yourself, "Now who the deuce would have thought I'd ever, be worth so much as that?" when a friendly kick on the door and sounds of welcome voices outside will bring you back to yourself again. Even Rover will prick his ears and look pleased for your sake, jealous as he is of you.

The visitors will be the two Ryan boys and young McCleverty; knowing that you are soon to be spliced, they've come over to spend the last of many good evenings with you. Single fellows in the bush all know that when one of themselves gets married it's the last of him as far as his old mates are concerned. On the Ryan boys and young McCleverty, who've always found your bachelor quarters more of a home to them than their own abode, your passing into married life will have a very melancholy influence; though, of course, they'd be the last to make you aware of it. Bush youths are like women in that respect.

"Here he is," they'll chuckle gladly as they file in out of the darkness, "filling his old cherry pipe as usual, and talkin' to th' bloomin' dawg, an' lettin' th' darn fire go out — and us blokes freezin'. Cripes!"

Grinning happily, you'll greet them with a "Hello!" and motion them to sit down. But Mickie Ryan, the leader of the trio, remarking censoriously that "he hasn't got a darn stick to put on it", will go out to visit the woodheap while the others, seating themselves in their accustomed places, will cheerfully advise the dog to keep his feet and tail out of the way if he doesn't want them squashed.

Then Mickie Ryan will enter again loaded up with wood, and when the fire is blazing brightly and Rover sitting up blinking his eyes in appreciation of it and everyone settled comfortably, you'll want to know what the latest is.

On past occasions they'd invariably drawl, "Nothin' much; only the same thing, Dick!" But on this evening their eyes will light up, and, turning beaming faces on each other, they will hesitate, each expecting one of the others to make answer. Then Mickie Ryan, remembering he's the eldest, will act as spokesman.

"By laws, Dick," he'll smile, "we've got something fresh this time — something that the four of us here could make money out of."

"Money!" you'll grin; and you'll feel your blood beginning to tingle.

"It's right, Dick," the other two, their eyes sparkling, will confirm, "but wait till *he* tells you."

"Ghost, yes, Dick," Mickie will proceed; "you'll think so, too, directly. Remember the time you and me saw those wild pigs at the head of King's Creek, near Stevenhausen's, close up three years ago?"

"There wasn't more than half a dozen of them, was there?" you'll say — you'll remember that, too.

"Well, us coves were up at the head of the creek a couple of days ago, these two chaps and me, and instead of half a dozen — Christopher! we came across *sixty* or *seventy* of them."

"I counted fifty myself from where I was", young McCleverty will put in excitedly.

"But you didn't see all those that I saw", Johnny Ryan in turn will claim proudly.

"Course there must have been a 'ell of a lot more that none of us seen," Mickie will go on, impressing you; "and there were all kinds of them, too, Dick, some fat as fools, and they all went like hunted devils for the undergrowth along the creek soon as they saw us."

You'll get interested and start visualising those wild pigs. You'll think of their increasing numbers — begin estimating the value of them, calculating the chances of securing them — till your blood in anticipatory pride of possession will circulate rapidly.

"The ones that I got close to were round and sleek as any you've got topped off in your sties now, Dick — would have brought a fiver a head easy, the way pigs were going a couple of weeks ago", young McCleverty will exaggerate; and Johnnie Ryan will vouchsafe that this old man "never sent better away, with all the feed he puts into them".

After moments of silence, during which you'll be thinking profoundly, and Rover will be settling his hairy form snugly round about your feet again, the others will wonder if it would be possible to get the beggars into a yard somehow or other, all the time looking to you for the solution.

"Well," you'll respond slowly, "they're a good distance from the railway to do much with them after you'd put them in the yard, but the four of us here could get a lot of sport yarding them."

That will rouse the hunting spirit in your visitors, and their eyes will flash suddenly as street-lamps just lighted.

"I never did any yarding of wild pigs", young McCleverty will stutter with enthusiasm, wriggling into a more uncomfortable position on his box seat, while the Ryan boys will reckon that "a cove would want to be on a pretty good horse — and a pretty handy one, too — to yard 'em in that sort of country, wouldn't he?"

Not only will the spirit of pursuit and of possession have gripped you, but you'll be stirred now to a consciousness of superiority by the way they're looking to you. And while they're regarding you with eyes brimming with expectation your mind will rush back to those reckless years you spent 'way back in the wilds of the West; and your visitors, remembering the thrilling tales you had recounted in evenings gone by, will ask:

"What sort of horses did you fellows have when you used to hunt the wild pigs on the Maranoa, Dick?"

"Gad, they were the best that ever any fellow put a leg across", you'll be pleased to answer, for it will be back to those very horses and pig-hunts your mind had taken you.

"Tell us about it, Dick!"

And again you'll recount to them how Wallumbilla Creek, below the old head station and across by Pickenjinnie flats, was alive with wild pigs when you were there. That was after the banks had taken over and the station was pretty well deserted and getting over-run with prickly-pear. The few head of cattle, some of them cleanskins, you'll remember, were worked by the hands on Blythedale, further up. Long Alec MacLennan was in charge of the two places, and you were one of the stockmen. You'll smile reflectively as you confess that all any of you did most of the year was to watch the prickly-pear spreading and the wild pigs breeding in it as fast as rabbits.

"How many were there, Dick?" will come eagerly from young McCleverty.

"God knows, youngster," you'll grin, shaking your head —
"as many as the stars."

"And all sorts of them, too, I suppose?" and with unceasing
enthusiasm the Ryan boys will jerk their seats closer to you
regardless of Rover exhibiting a nervous vigilance lest they
stood on his toes or his tail.

"All sorts and all sizes," you'll continue; "but on the day
I'm thinking of no one had any time to tell how many or see
what they were like!" The day you'll be thinking of was one
filled with scrub pigs — rushing, barking, savage hogs.

"It was a hunt got up by MacLennan to help the cockies
who had chanced taking up selections from the Government on
the northern end of Wallumbilla, among the wallabies," you'll
explain. "There was nothing else there that I remember except
sand and scrubs of sandalwood. The Government, though, was
supplying the cockies with wire-netting on time-payment to
keep the wallabies off their selections; so MacLennan offered
them pigs for nothing to stock their sties so long as they would
come along and take a hand in catching them."

"That wasn't too bad of him", the Ryan boys will enthuse.
And young McCleverty will add: "Cripes it wasn't!"

"And there was a city chap MacLennan was looking after,"
you'll proceed — "visiting the station, he was, on a holiday. He
was out of an office, and wrote books. He had never before
been among wild pigs, he said; so Mac, who was always out for
sport, even with the station-hands, reckoned we'd have a bit of
fun. Of course, our fellows kept taking it in turns to tell him of
the dangers that were in pig-hunting, and warning him to hold
his reins and the pommel tight when the galloping started, and
not to get up into the front nor fall too far into the rear, and
especially to keep wide of trees. I heard him ask one of the
station-hands if any of the pigs had greasy tails, and out of the
corner of my eye I noticed a look of simplicity on his face that
you'd think could only have been put there by Nature."

As the others burst into mirth and Rover yawns and
whimpers you'll take a moment or two off to join the
merriment.

"Anyway," you'll begin again, "everyone had to meet at the
yards of the old Wallumbilla homestead pretty early in the

morning of the pig-hunt to get a fresh horse. It was a glorious
morning, too; but the big homestead house, with its verandahs
and cedar fittings — built half a century before, and with Lawd
knows how many rooms — was fast decaying because of
neglect, and was empty of everything but an eating-table, an
old chair or two, and a couple of miserable bunks; while in the
fruit and flower gardens that once were all around it, now grew
only rank grass, amongst which an old cow poked and foraged.
But as the pig-hunters met and dismounted it was the horses in
the yards rather than the old homestead that held their interest.
There must have been at least twenty head of them — blacks,
greys, bays and piebalds, all clean-skinned, fresh and fit-looking,
staring and whinnying through the rails as the huntsmen
approached from different quarters."

"Hokey, eh!" and the eyes of your audience will gleam again
in the dull light.

"Those who had decided to change on to station mounts
were off their own before you could say 'knife', hoisting their
saddles on to the cap of the yard, and pulling their bridles off.
But the cockies, who had come only a couple of miles, most of
'em, remained seated in their saddles waiting for the party to
get ready. They had empty sacks strapped across the pommels
to bring back a sucker or two as part of their share of the
spoils."

"They reckoned they were going to be in the harvest all
right" — and Mickie Ryan will cause another round of cheerful
cackle.

"And all of them on their old draught nags," you'll admit
with a smile; "but those station horses, as they stood there in
the yard, flash and well-bred, staring, snorting and crushing
each other — I can see them now as plain as I could then —
their eyes flashing, their heads lifted, looking at you as if they
had never seen a white man before."

"Cripes! and *they* all broke-in horses?" in amazement from
young McCleverty.

"Yes, broken," you'll admit, "and most of 'em eight- and
ten- and twelve-year old; but there hadn't been much work for
them to do, and they'd had long spells. I can see us all hurrying
and scrambling through the rails of the yards now, with the

bridles in our hands, bustling one another for the pick of the mob — or what we reckoned was the pick."

"And what sort did you get, Dick?" young McCleverty will interrupt. "The best one?"

"What sort!" you'll repeat significantly. "The sort you don't see much of now — a strong, low-set, well-put-together little bay, with a quick eye, a broad chest and clean legs."

"One that would carry you all day, and be hard to hold at the end of it, I bet", Mickie Ryan will add in proud endorsement.

"Two chaps from Mount Hutton — both good judges of a horse, too — had fixed their eyes on him, and I just beat them for him by a couple of inches. Of course, when I saw he was their pick, too, I felt as if I had drawn first prize in Tattersall's big sweep."

"And wasn't he all right, Dick?" anxiously from young McCleverty.

"I'll tell you directly", and you'll start grinning meaningly again.

"Was he broken-winded?" from Mickie Ryan. Mickie knew a lot about broken-winded horses.

"No, he wasn't," you'll admit, broadening your grin, "but he darn nearly had mine broken."

Your audience will chuckle in chorus and kick about, and disturb Rover, who'll wisely draw in his feet and shift his tail.

"I led him out and was saddling him up in a bit of a hurry," you'll explain, "when MacLennan himself, girthing up a tall, brown stockhorse beside him, looked across and said: 'You're not a bad judge of horseflesh, Dick; but running wild pigs in the pear isn't cutting-out on a cattle-camp, you know, and you better girth that fellow tight and put a crupper on him'."

"Cripes!" — from the Ryan boys — "you struck a' outlaw?"

"Not exactly", and you'll adjust yourself in your chair, at the same time resting one of your feet on Rover's soft ribs. "He was always quiet enough after he'd settled down; but before he'd settle down with you he was the damnedest buckjumper the station ever knew."

"Oh, 'ell!" and all three will regard you with expressions of sympathy.

"And he'd get to it the moment anyone was on him. Before I'd hardly hit the saddle he was at it — round and round, and squealing, and nearly getting me in the first couple. Gad, the girths strained and creaked. His head went clean out of sight — must have gone somewhere between his hind legs. Between the fright I got and the squeals he gave and the yells of the other fellows to hang on, I didn't know what was happening, or where the diggings I was till he bumped like a blooming flywheel into the cockies' horses, scattering them like forty mad armed policemen, and straightening me right up in the saddle and giving me a fresh grip of the reins and placing my feet back in the stirrups again. Then I knew my luck was in and I was right and —"

You'll pause to smile at the others for gaping and looking so excited; and while you are pausing you'll put your other foot on Rover's ribs and he'll pretend not to notice any difference.

"And from out amongst them he came with his head in sight, but between his knees, and down the slope from the yard he went bucking as if he had a flank-rope on and a lot of ginger under his tail. I got to him then; but he was crumpling and bucking himself into such a ball that I was rapping my heels together behind his hindquarters. When he got on to the open flat he gave the bucking best, and started stretching himself to a gallop. It was a question then of pulling him or letting him go for his blasted life till he pumped himself out."

"I'd have let the cow go — I would!" Mickie will say vindictively.

"That's what I had to do, as it happened," you'll renew; "for just when I had given a couple of pulls at the reins and was snatching for breath, who should come rattling up beside me but the novice from the city, and on one of the swanky piebalds! Right up, brushin' the little bay's flanks, he came; then right beside me, his stirrup-irons clashing mine."

"What! The city cove who knew nothing?" young McCleverty will echo.

"I could only just flash a glance at him, for a cove has to watch a horse that's been bucking with him, not knowing when he might suddenly down with his head again and into it. But in that one glance I saw it was him. And he started talking to me as if we were both in here, or sitting on the cap of the yard, instead of reefing and swinging through trees that might knock your brains out. 'You stuck to him well, but he nearly had you', I remember him shouting; then, lifting his voice louder, 'Let him go! Take it out of him! A couple of furlongs — come on!' He let the piebald out, laughing at me over his shoulder. And I let go the little bay. Through the wild lime-trees and sandalwoods we went hammer and tongs and close together. And just behind us all the others were coming like blazes."

"*He* was no blooming novice, Dick!" from Johnny Ryan.

"*Novice*!" you'll repeat, grinning. "A couple of looks across at him, and I saw he had the best hands I'd ever seen on a pair of bridle-reins in thick timber."

"And he came out of an office, you said", with a puzzled expression from Mickie Ryan.

"There was nothing of the office about him now", you'll smile. "He wasn't only sitting the piebald as light as a blade of grass, but was riding with his head half-turned screwed in line with the horse's ears, both his hands pressed down on the shoulder blades; the crown of his head set down against the wind, to keep his hat on; his face towards me, and all the time looking out of the tail of one eye to watch where he was going. And we *were* going, too. Gad, how the sandalwood crashed!"

"Holy! He didn't learn to ride like that in a' office!" the others will exclaim in admiration.

"He was part of his horse if ever a rider was, wherever he learned it, that's all I can say", you'll answer. "And while the hanging boughs and limbs — you know what they mean — were smacking and belting me hard enough, he was gliding and swinging clear of the whole darn lot; and getting ahead of me, too! When he was a length or two in the lead he rose in the saddle and took hold of the piebald's head. Then I took a pull, too, and as we were steadying down chuckling breathlessly to each other, he began dropping me friendly hints on riding in thick timber."

"What!" the Ryan boys will break in. "Giving *you* hints, Dick — a city cove?"

"Yes", you'll smile. "But remember that I had only about an hour before been advising him what snags to look out for, and how to guide his horse when the galloping started — well, it made me feel a bit of a fool, though he didn't seem to remember anything about it."

A burst of merriment at your expense will come from the others.

"A lot of fellows have only themselves to blame", he said, when he had reined up, leaning over and patting the piebald on the neck, "for getting hurt in the timber. They never seem to learn that a horse has more brains than his rider, is a better judge of space and has quicker and surer eyesight. All you have to do when you have the pace up, and the timber is getting thicker and thicker, is to get your eye into sympathy with his, leave his mouth alone, swing with him and guide him if you want to with your knees and your body."

"And what did you reckon about it, Dick?" young McCleverty will ask curiously.

"I knew darned well he was right, for I had seen him demonstrate it", you'll answer. "But before I could say anything about it to him up came the whole army of pig-hunters again, MacLennan himself at the head of them, and the selectors with their heavy draught mounts and empty sacks bringing up the rear. Wallumbilla Creek was only a few hundred yards ahead of us then, and a bend in one of its long, narrow, deep waterholes, with ti-trees overhanging the banks, had just come into view. They were hailing us with shouts of laughter, when suddenly their voices changed to cries of 'Look out! Look at th' blanky pigs leaving the water!' And sure enough there were pigs all colours by the score scrambling over the opposite bank — and in the Devil's own hurry, too!"

" 'After them for your lives, chaps!' shouted MacLennan, heeling and whipping his tall, brown camp-horse. And by the Lord Harry we went for our lives, too, and for the lives of those pigs. Every cove there had his horse under the whip from the first bound. We were on to the creek, striking at an angle, MacLennan still in the lead, the rest of us covering space a chain wide to the right and left of him. We saw the water for a stretch of a hundred yards or so glistening, splashing and churning as fresh-startled pigs made out of it to follow those that had already climbed the banks and were scurrying to the prickly-pear scrub over on Pickenjinnie flats. The field of us raced at the creek; then with wild shouts over the edge in twos, threes and fours together! Plunk! Flop! Grunt! Under; up to the surface again; a short swim; then up and over the opposite bank, men and horses wet and slimy, blindly scrambling, the whips going, bumping broadside into one another, clutching for fresh grips of the slippery reins, eyes straining for sight of the darn pigs!"

"Hokey!" the Ryan boys will gasp, while young McCleverty will be too excited to speak.

"When I got over you never saw such a sight. Pigs! There was a mob of them two hundred yards long — black, sandy, piebald, all sizes, all ages and sexes, going like hares for the thickest pear, not more than a quarter of a mile off."

"Christopher!" from the Ryans.

"I wasn't first over. I don't know who was, really. But when I looked across to the right of me there was the city chap, the piebald all slush and looking like a black horse, right on his own, and about a dozen pigs not more than a couple of chains ahead of him."

"*He* was no city bloke!" Mickie Ryan will reaffirm.

"No," you'll agree — "what he didn't know about the Bush wasn't fit to mention.

"Then the fun really started. That mob of blooming pigs, with the lot of us hot of them, spurring and flogging, seemed to fairly fly over the short distance. It soon was a neck and neck go with some of us, though most of the hogs were holding their lead. They had managed to reach the scattered pear — clumps of the cursed stuff that stand out from the thick scrub like sentinels. Those scared hogs scooted in strings and disappeared round clumps, and then hit out in other directions! Ghost, if they didn't turn the hunt into an obstacle-race on us!"

Loud excited mirth from the Ryans.

"Of course we couldn't pull and slew our horses round and in and out of those darn clumps and keep the pace up, too! We had to make hurdles of them; and taking them in our stride turned the hunt into a grand steeplechase. Wars! It was *Over! Over! Over!* keeping your eye on the pig you had marked for your prize all the time. And, my stars! those hurdles kept getting closer and closer, and higher and broader, till the little bay, game as a tiger, blundered in trying to take three in quick succession, and, landing in the middle of the last clump objected to the thorns and prickles, and started bucking his way out, and —"

"And *w-what,* Dick?" young McCleverty will stutter eagerly.

"While I wasn't thinking of him, but watching the darn pig I was after, he dropped me right in the middle of the blanky prickly-pear!"

"Hell!" the others will roar, for they will know all about pear; and taking advantage of the noise, Rover will liberate himself from the weight of your feet, and withdraw to another corner of the room.

"You must have been in a mess, Dick?" Mickie will suggest feelingly.

"I couldn't see out of my eyes for darn prickles," you'll admit with a shudder, "and had them all over my body for weeks, though I stripped off in the creek and was rubbed with sand by the other fellows for about an hour!"

"And how many pigs did they get altogether?" the Ryans will inquire.

"None of them got a darn one," you'll answer grimly — "except the city chap. He stuck to a black sow, in and out, and over everything, till he ran her to a standstill. And when she bailed up she had a snout on her as long as the nose of the smithy's bellows, and she barked at him and everyone else like a retriever dog."

"Cripes!" the Ryans will conclude disappointedly — "that wasn't much to get out of a hunt."

"We mightn't get any more than that if we go after this lot on King's Creek!" young McCleverty, his excitement abating, will suggest.

"Except that, instead of a sow that will bark, you might get a big old boar with tusks a foot long who'll rip your horse up, or take your leg off", you'll conclude.

Chapter 13

After returning from Pilton, where once you had been a stockman, you'll be sitting alone reflecting on the galloping days gone by.

The old station was more like a rising township now than a squatter's headquarters. It had a row of shingle-roofed huts, spacious stables, a carpenter's shop, butcher's shop, store, and blacksmith's forge, where the best horse-shoeing was done for fifty miles around. The "big house" of English architecture, built of red cedar from the ranges, stood in the centre of a glorious garden where grapes, peaches, apricots, oranges, lemons and even bunya pines grew in profusion. The Governor being English an English oak was also growing there. Perhaps the oak was to remind him of home and hearten him under stress of the melancholy of the Australian Bush.

Long-whiskered men, boundary riders, fossickers and shepherds with ruined eyesight astride long, hollow-backed, one-eyed slow-walking horses nodding their grey heads in tune to the strides of them like roosters stepping across a farm paddock on the lookout for grasshoppers, sometimes called at the homestead. The best of stock-horses and hacks were bred on Pilton in your days, and the stockmen were lighthearted, adventurous spirits to whom horses and feats of horsemanship were the great things in life. How to breed ability in horses, how to handle and ride them, how to know the bush, were the problems that occupied their minds — not those of humanity or of government.

"Did y' see them scrubbers that's been comin' out of

Lagoon Creek?" you'll remember a fossicker asked one day.

"Scrubbers?" they echoed in surprise. Had he asked had they seen nuggets of gold lying in the creek he couldn't have surprised them more. For as long as they could remember mobs of wild cattle had inhabited the scrubs of the Great Dividing Range, and from time to time small lots of station beasts missed in the musters would stray off the run to join with the outlaws. In those weird mountain haunts they inbred and increased till no one had any idea as to their numbers. By day they confined their movements to the scrubs, rarely calling to each other, coming out at night to feed on the rank grasses and shrubs in the creek bends and forest valleys. The roaring of the bulls on such occasions would thrill you to the marrow. At long intervals news would be brought to the station of a mob seen in broad day a mile or two from the scrub, perhaps camped boldly in the open valleys. Also that a huge white bullock or a red and white one was among the number.

"Come with us next Saturd'y night and show us where they run", they raptured. "We'll lend you a horse; and camp near the scrub and give them a go for it at daylight in th' mornin'?"

The fossicker said he didn't mind.

Then old Joe, a bullock-driver for thirty hard years, recalled memories:

"There was one o' my bullicks then with th' lagoon scrubbers," he said, "a red an' white one. I wer' workin' him when he went off one night after I unyoked. 'Cocky', he was called in th' team. We was on th' range then haulin' posts for the fence on the plains, ten years ago! Billy Hall seen him over there long after with a mob, and the McCullaghs they seen him. But none o' them couldn't ever run him out; and I believe he wer' a darn lot th' wildest of th' mob. He'd be a fourteen-year-old bullick if he wer' alive now."

*   *   *

Then you'll think of a bright moonlight night in the ranges — a night that softened even the hardest of those lithe, eager-eyed stockmen as they rode in file down the sides of the great range. There were five of us in the party. A light breeze rustled the foliage of the trees. Startled marsupials hopping across our path stopped, and facing us erect, displayed their white breasts like broken signal-posts. Night birds greeted us in their weird haunting notes. Slowly and cautiously we descended into the silent valleys of Lagoon Creek, where the greasy slippery rockbeds shone like layers of silver beneath the moon. There the fossicker took the lead and headed off through the blady green scrub. With true bush craft he rode right on to it. But only a deserted camp was there. All that remained of it were the sapling frame, the ashes of the fireplace, and an empty bag or two.

We unsaddled, hobbled the horses, started a fire, and when the billy was boiled sat around and had supper. Lonely environment. Up the creek the great range rose in grim silence, the moon seeming to rest on it. Below us the big scrub, giving out haunting sounds that crowded our brain with thoughts of a great tomb filled with generations of dead souls and their secret woes. We talked but little, and then only in hushed tones, for this was the wild cattle country, and wild cattle are suspicious things and easily alarmed. After some had smoked a couple of pipes we walked quietly round the horses to see that all was right with them; then rolled ourselves in our blankets and tried to sleep. But our minds were too active — and too filled with visions of what the morning would bring — for slumber. Yet, the night passed rapidly enough.

Soon the dawn would break — we could see it coming with all its tints and streaks of glory. As we stood waiting awhile beside the horses, our arms leaning on the saddles, the big scrub that was dimly outlined began to take shape. The notes and songs and whistles of birds out of number broke out all around us, and what overnight had seemed the silent tomb of dead generations suddenly turned into a concert hall of nature.

"It is only about half a mile across", the fossicker said as he mounted stiffly and led the way again. We followed without talking, but reaching down from force of habit to feel if our girths were right. As we moved across a swelling in the landscape grown over with cherrywood the grey dawn flushed to crimson. The sun was not far off. Down the sloping side, rustling through the cherry-bush, we entered Lagoon Creek, a shallow, pebble-bedded watercourse that cut its way through daisy beds, and hollows, and grassy flats. Running across, and swallowing it up a mile or so down, was the lagoon scrub, looking in the distance as even as a clipped hedge. Wet to the girths with the dew off the grass the horses tossed their heads and sniffed the morning air. Ascending a low bank we suddenly came upon a quantity of cow-dung and cattle tracks. Our hearts went pit-a-pat, and every eye searched the bush around. Still not a word was spoken. On ahead a clump of grass trees and patches of wallaby bush obscured an open valley coated with feathery grass from view. The fossicker threw back a meaning glance, and pointed to the grass and trees. We moved up beside him, taking a shorter grip of our reins — "Look out behind these trees", he said — and then:

"There!" someone cried as the wild mob rose from their camping place, and off! And gad, what a mob — a hundred at least — red, white, black, brindle and blue — cows, bulls, bullocks, heifers and half-grown calves. With their tails on their backs they careered over that open valley for the big vine scrub.

"Head them!" cried Eustace; and out jumped every horse, into the clump of grass trees and out the other side. *"Ride like hell!"* from someone as the way was clear and the mob in full view. So we did; our heels and hands went hard at the horses while the going looked good. Over an embankment, up the slope of a hill rushed the scrubbers close packed, a white beast at the tail of them, a string of black bulls in the lead. Around the black wattles; into the creek again and out of it, plunging and splashing and crashing. Hugging the left side of it they thundered along — the rattle of hoofs in the rear of them coming closer at every stride. Into a wilderness of saplings, bumping them, swaying them, smashing them. Now away from the creek, throwing dust up like the whirl of a windstorm — *"Stick to them!"* came from beside me in a wind-choked voice. Then the rattle of irons and the flapping of heels. As the dingo makes for his lair, the fox for his hole, the 'roo for the ridges, the wild cattle made for the scrub. A few moments more and they were into it. But Burton was catching them, passing them; then around to the head of them went the brown horse. On his heels came the rest of us, the old fossicker trotting along in the rear. The mob were bewildered; they stopped in amazement; we flew through the trees, and in line turned and faced them. The scrub was behind us. A line of wild heads, spear-horned, short-horned, cock-horned, stared hard at us. Streaks and strings of froth hung from the mouths of them.

"Woh! . . . Werp! . . . Woh-h there!" and sharp cracks rang out to distract them. Would they turn and give tail or — Gad, what moments of excitement they were! A black cow, broken-horned and scarred, snorted and went for us. *"Look out! . . . Woh-h!"* But now the whole maddened mob were snorting and charging us. The rest was all shouts, and all bluff and spurring and wheeling and swearing. At the point of the horns they turned us and scattered us. "Ride on, there's a bull right behind you!" But Greygo, caught napping, was gored in both his hindquarters! Then into the scrub on all sides of us they vanished, twisting and jerking their heads to glide the horns through. Two, though, were baffled. Right out from the scrub Burton was racing and shouldering a red and white bullock with horns a yard wide, while Eustace was wheeling and lashing a warrior cow. Uniting our forces we smothered them, hustled them, gave them no chances till we brought them right home and into the yard.

*   *   *

All the station people gathered at the yard to view those scrubbers. And how the captives resented their presence! and they snorted, and shaking their heads pawed at the dust; then charged at the panels.

"You dersen't tell me", said old Joe, "that that's my Cocky?"

The manager endorsed what the brand was.

"Dern me if I don't think so". The dim eyes of the old bullock man strained through the rails. Then lifting his voice he roared — *"Wah Cocky! . . . Woh-h! Come here!"*

The scrubber instantly turned and looked as though he'd heard something that was familiar.

All of us chuckled.

"Gee back, Cocky — you — loafing wild scrub dog!"

Cocky was bewildered. He trotted across the yard, turned and stared again and seemed to understand.

"That's him," old Joe concluded with a joyous chuckle — "but, good lord, ain't he growed?"

Then with a sigh you'll come out of your dreams, and rise to stir the fire.

Chapter 14

It will be a bright moonlight night, almost as bright as day —
brighter than many days — but there'll be no inducement for
you to move out and walk about in it with your concertina,
"making sweet melody and singing many songs".

You've just returned from the city — from Sydney, this time
— where you've spent a full month's holiday, the first real
holiday you had for six years. So you'll be sitting with your
elbow on the table gazing down at Rover scratching himself on
the floor at your feet, and enjoying the holiday over again in
your mind, smiling over some of the incidents — even chuckling
and rousing Rover's interest. He'll suddenly cease pursuing the
fleas and look up at you curiously.

Dave and Joe Rudd, who have been looking forward to your
return, will enter upon you with boisterous greeting, guffawing
and chuckling and passing a friendly word or two to Rover as
one of the family.

"Cripes! Back again, eh, Dick?" Dave dropping into a chair
without bothering to shake hands will drawl, while Joe,
squatting near the ashes of the fireplace, will stutter:

"An' n-not lookin' too bad a-a-after it, neither."

"And blow me," you'll grin, looking happily from one to
the other, "if I wasn't thinking about it, going all over it again
just when y' came in."

"W-w-what was y' th-thinkin' of it, D-Dick," Joe will ask —
"th' shop winders or th' coves s-s-sellin' apples or th' g-girls?"

You'll grin at Joe and answer: "There was no end of shop
windows, as many of them as trees an' logs between here and

heaven knows where. And as for girls, Joe, the flocks of them dressed up like rainbows and with skirts on them about as long as emus' tails that pour out of shops and dens and lanes and holes and corners between five an' six in the evening, after knocking off work, as they call it, and rush for trams an' boats an' trains an' motor-cars — would make you wonder whatever in th' name of the milkcan in the corner there could half o' them find to do, or why they were ever kept after being born!"

"When I was down," Dave will put in grievously, "none of th' blokes ever did anythin' either. There they was in mobs stuck in offices and behind counters doin' nothin' that anyone could see 'cept pinchin' th' girls an' chasin' 'em round tables pullin' at 'em an' askin' who they were out with on Satu'dee, an' did they want anyone with 'em on Sundee? Beehivin' an' sweetheartin' is about what all of 'em do in them places, I reckon."

"I saw plenty of that, too, Dave," you'll agree; "but what I was smiling to myself most for was what I saw of the sort of life they live in flats, as they call them."

"What do y' m-m-mean be f-f-flats, D-Dick — f-f-flat heads?" Joe will ask.

"No — lucen flats, y' goat!" Dave will guffaw at Joe.

"They're the places that thousands of them live in," you'll explain — "instead of houses. Houses some of them were once, but now made into kennels. And you never saw the likes of some of them. What were mansions and halls and swell residences once they've stuck three and four more storeys on to and turned them into these flats — 'self-contained homes', they call some of them."

"W-w-what does that m-m-mean?" Joe will ask — "th-that they t-t-tucker themselves?"

"That I'm not certain about myself; but those that I saw contained a couple of coves or a couple of women, or perhaps a small family. But all divided off into sort of pens."

"Same as we divide th' cowstalls and pigsties?" from Dave.

"You've about struck it, Dave."

"An' quicker than he s-s-struck th' g-g-gold he's b-b-been lookin' for up th' g-g-gully for th' last y-year", Joe will interrupt.

"Alwez puttin' your spoke in where it ain't wanted!" Dave will snap, looking down cynically upon his brother.

"It was McGreen who showed me some of the flats", you'll resume. "He lives in one himself. You chaps will remember him, I suppose. He worked about here years ago doing council jobs."

Dave will have a recollection of him, but Joe will shake his head and thoughtfully drop a fistful of ashes into Rover's ear. The latter will suddenly and vigorously shake *his* head and throw some of the ashes into Dave's eye. Dave, rubbing the optic, will reach for Joe and demand: " 'Ere, what th' 'ell are y' doin'?"

After chuckling at Dave, you'll proceed again:

"He left and went to Sydney when his old man died, and became a land-agent and a flat expert."

"Wh-what's a flat expert, Dick?" from Dave, who'll still be rubbing his eye. "Anything to do with machinery?"

"A expert in f-f-flat-irons or s-s-somethin', I s-s-pose", Joe'll venture.

"Goat!" — from Dave.

Explaining that you scarcely know what it means yourself, you'll go ahead: "Well, Mac took me to this flat of his right at the top of a pile of buildings as high as a mountain; and to get up to his little 'home' we climbed the Lawd knows how many steps and stairs winding and zigzagging like that old cattle-track over the range at Hirst Vale, excepting that you saw no scenery or anything to remind you there was a God or Nature, but all walls, walls with doors in them, shut tight like the doors of the cells of a gaol."

"Oh, 'ell!" — feelingly from Dave.

"And not the habitations of free white people with nothing on their minds. And so, when we reached the top, McGreen, stopping before one of these doors and puffing like a horse, took out his key, flung it open and pointed the way in lordly sort of style for me to enter and sez, 'There you are, Dick — this is our headquarters.' Then he walks round pointing out the furniture to me, and the different apartments, and all the comforts of th' darn caboose."

"Pup-pup-partments?" Joe will query.

"That's what Mac called them", you'll answer. "Two rooms they amounted to — and half of one was the *kitchen!*"

"And where th' diggings did they have their beds?" Dave will interrupt again.

"One bed was in th' 'front room'," you'll grin, "along with the dining-table and the mantelpiece and the chairs and packets of cigarettes and beer bottles and photos of girls high-kicking without a stitch on."

"It m-must have b-b-been as good as goin' to th' pup-pup-picture-show" — mirthfully from Joe.

" 'Cept that you didn't pay anythin', eh, Dick?" Dave will add.

"The other bed, a sort of stretcher, was in the kitchen, where there was more packets of cigarettes and more empty bottles, and a little gas stove with a dirty frying-pan on it, and a toasting-fork and a billy-can of milk (about as big as a tin matchbox, the billy was), and a sink full of cups and saucers and plates waiting to be washed up."

"D-D-Dick, D-Dick," Joe'll object, "you can't s-s-stuff us that McGrGreen is livin' in a place l-l-like that!"

"And thousands of others, Joe, as I've told you."

"Worse'n bloomin' pigs!" Dave will grunt.

"*Pigs!*" you'll exclaim. "Lots of them think they're princes and fairies. And to see some o' them coming out in the mornings — laws! Flash as racehorses."

"And w-wimmen?" from Joe.

"Women *and* girls — 'flappers', 'tarts', 'skirts', 'flames', they call them — and smelling like scented wheat and smut and covered with powder and paint, half an inch thick on some of them. 'The secret of youthfulness', they call it — especially those who are about fifty."

"They ought to be hanged!" — from Dave.

"And the partitions between their flats would make you fellows grin. Between Mac's kitchen and the one in the same 'home', where a couple of tarts lived, was only a light frame of board. A cat or a dog could have knocked it over, and the height of it was about five-foot-six. Hearing some plates rattling and a pan sizzling Mac looked over the top of it and passed the time of evening to his nextdoor neighbour. Of course I had a

look over too" — you'll pause to chuckle, while your listeners
stare in wonderment — "and, ghost! there were women's fancy
things that had been washed hanging across to dry on a string
clothes-line!"

"A clothes-l-l-line in the kuk-kitchen?" Joe'll repeat; and
Dave will guffaw: "Cripes, they're worse than th' blacks!"

"And, 'Hellow, Miss Powdery', said Mac, and of course, I
pulled my head back, seeing a woman there — 'getting ready
for tea?'

" 'Trying to,' Mr. McGreen,' she answered, 'and I'm all on
my own. Mabel's stopping in town to have dinner at th'
Australia with a friend; then off for a motor-car spin.'

"She's got all the luck', says Mac, and winked.

" 'It's with a friend of hers whose up from Adelaide for the
Show.'

" 'Oh, yes, I see', says Mac, and winked back over his
shoulder at me."

"S'pose he reckoned she was tryin' to pull his leg?" Dave
will suggest innocently.

"Mac knew all right", you'll smile. "He told me all about it
afterwards. But to go round the big places in the city where the
eating-shops and lounges, as they call them, are!" You'll break
out in a new vein, and shift the venue. "At about eleven
o'clock in the day, and from five to six when a lot of them
have knocked off work — Hokey! You'll see how a woman
with the new ideas can put away cocktails, as they call 'em,
and gin and cigarettes; and plenty that haven't got any ideas at
all. And their lips — wide-cut lips a lot of them have, too — red
as if they had been brought up eating prickly-pear fruit! There
you'll see them in scores puffing at cigarettes after sampling th'
gin, showing their legs with silk stockings on, crossing them and
recrossing them to attract attention, and with shoes costing two
or three quid with silver buckles and diamonds on them."

"Cripes!" from Dave. "And who pays for 'em?"

"Don't ask me", you'll smile. "I asked Mac that question
myself. But to see them sipping th' gin, then lifting their heads
and puffing out smoke like hens on a hot day drinking water,
was something to think about."

Here you will rise to welcome Ted Williams, telling him to

come in — "there's only Dave and Joe here".

"And w-w-wasn't there any men among them, D-Dick?" Joe will ask.

"Men?" you'll echo, sitting down again at the table. "There were dudes and toffs an' bald-headed old blokes full of money."

"And what would the men be doing, Dick?" Dave will ask.

"Offsiding for th' women," you'll answer — "lighting the cigarettes for them as if it was a favour worth a lot more than you'd think, and beckoning to the white-coated waiters to keep the glasses full."

"Cripes, eh!" from Dave.

"They w-w-would be the leaders of th' m-m-mob", Joe will reckon; then Dave and Ted Williams will join him in mirth.

"And to see them all squatting round bits of tables," you'll conclude — "nothing like this one here o' mine — with their legs coiled round the legs o' them, and around their own legs, and around some of the old blokes' legs, and all of them looking like families of silkworms groping blindly for each other in a tin — well it was all I wanted to see of th' city!"

Chapter 15

An autumn evening in May. After tea you'll short-cut through the grass paddocks on a visit to Don Oberhart, a couple of blocks beyond your little homestead. Rover, accompanying you, will be in his element hunting *en route,* and repeatedly giving useless chase to invisible quarry, returning after each fruitless effort, to pant noisily at your heels.

Your visit to Don will be one of sympathy and encouragement. Having changed his policy and pinned his faith to wheat-growing, he put all his eggs into one basket for several seasons in succession and lost. When you arrive you will find Barney McGee there on the same errand, talking and laughing glibly for Don's benefit.

Neither of you, however, would for worlds let Don know the real purport of your visit; and you'll each lie cheerfully in giving your opinions of the prospective yield and the golden future of wheat-growing generally. You'll reckon the values of wheat lands must in time rise stupendously, and when they do rise those who "hang on" will be on the pig's back. At last Don, who often enough has himself taken a hand in cheering others up, will turn from the fireplace and grunt: "Yes, they'll be on the pig's back right enough, if they're not on their own or in the grave!"

Then you'll make a clumsy attempt to change the subject. But Barney, who has broken more laws and told more lies and got out of more tight places than you probably ever dreamed of, will come to the rescue.

"Do ye know what it was I was thinking of the other day,

Richard?" he'll break in with a broad smile on his sun-flamed face, and shaking his iron-grey head wisely.

You won't know, of course.

"Well, damme if I wasn't thinking of picking up a likely sort of hack somewhere with foot enough to win a handicap or two, and making a few pounds as well as getting some fun out of it."

"Well, why don't you, Barney?" you'll grin.

"I was thinking more than once that that's what I ought to darn well go in for", Oberhart will put in cynically. "I might make more out of race-courses than out of rusty wheat paddocks. Couldn't lose any more, anyway, and it wouldn't be any worse gambling."

"The thing is to pick up the right sort of horse," Barney will emphasise — "one of the kind that Terence McGee bought for a couple of pounds from a drover who was drinking at Ryan's pub."

"Buttonhole?" Oberhart will remember. "You'd go a long way before picking up another like him for the same money, or for a couple of hundred either! He turned out to be a thoroughbred, one of C. B. Fisher's imported horses, sent west to serve some station mares on the Barcoo. I remember him."

"And when Terry put a bushel or two of corn into him and the brushes on him," Barney will enthuse for your benefit, "Gad, but he was the finest looking animal ever ye clapped eyes on, though before that he was just a sleepy old clothes-peg of a sheep-drover's moke."

"Terry could judge a horse in the rough, what a lot of 'em can't do; that was the reason", Don will say, dropping into the armchair he had made for himself out of half a beer-barrel, to smoke thoughtfully, while you reflect on the merits and make of some of the best hacks you knew and rode in bush races.

"He won every race that Terry started him in", Barney will rattle on, smoothing his brow with his rough palm, and fixing his grey roguish old eyes first on you, then on Oberhart. "And after being sold for £500, damme if he didn't win the Brisbane Cup for the fellow who bought him from Terry, and then went south."

You'll think of the meagre monthly cheque you receive from

the factory in return for all your hard constant labour, and sigh enviously.

"What's that long-tailed brown thing you keep running about your place doing nothing?" Oberhart after a silence will ask casually.

"A long-tailed thing? Oh! Miss Maranoa, ye mean." And Barney, breaking into a chuckle, will suspect the other of a joke of some kind. "She's one of the idle rich," he'll add — "lives on the fat of th' farm without doing a hand's turn for her support — like Richard here." And he'll laugh as he fancies he has turned the joke on you.

As though he hadn't heard, Oberhart will continue between puffs from his pipe: "You've had her a long while, Barney. What do you call her Miss Maranoa for? Not a bad cut of a mare. I was watching her trotting along your fence the other day."

"Sure I've had her for five year — since she were a pet foal", Barney suddenly becoming grave will reply. "Her mother, fastest mare that ever wheeled a beast in th' bush, died in th' foaling of her 'way out there in the ranges. And when old Mick Maranoa fell into the hands of the bank and rolled up his swag, which was all he had left out of a couple of thousands, to clear away with, the Devil only knew where to, he left the foal with me to look after till he'd come back, and if he didn't come back I was to reckon it my own for the paddocking of it. 'And', sez he, as he went off, 'handle it at two years, Barney, just to keep it quiet, but don't let anyone ride it at all!' And divil a man has ever been on Miss Maranoa's back but myself."

"Old Mick Maranoa's mare?" you'll suddenly wake up, gaping wonderingly at Barney. "A well-built bay with black points and a beautiful head, was she?"

"She was all that", Barney McGee will affirm, while Don Oberhart, his curiosity aroused, will stare inquisitively at you.

"He won the first handicap held by the squatters at the Plains with her," you'll continue, "and rode her himself with a red swag strapped before him on the saddle."

"Gad!" Barney will laugh, "I believe I've heard him sphake of it, Dick, but I usen't always take a deal of notice of him, for 'twas always horses and races and rumours of races that he liked to talk about. There was no depth in him. But he was the fine horseman — few there were who could ride like him, especially when he had a couple of Ryan's rums on board."

Sitting up straight and eyeing Barney closely you'll ask, "Do you know what that foal was by?"

"You mean the mare, Miss Maranoa, Richard?" from Barney.

"Yes — a mare now."

"How the divil would I know, Richard?" Barney will chuckle. "But do you know yourself?"

"This is getting interesting" — and Don, sitting up, too, will knock the ashes from his pipe.

"Well, yes, I do, since you've told me what you know, and I'm the only person that does know. Old Terry, wherever he is, doesn't know and never did know."

"Why, what's the strong of it, Richard?" Oberhart will ask. "Some horse-planting trick?"

You'll shake your head and answer: "No, but I was working for Jimmie Williams when he rented Greenmount and had Melbourne and Challenger and Kyogle and Italian and Wild Wave sent there for a while, and Jim Edwards, who was managing the place, was allowed to take in a few mares at a high fee to Wild Wave and Challenger, but they had to be pedigreed mares with a certificate."

"By th' powers, there's something behind all this." And Barney, drawing closer, will fix you again with his little grey eyes.

"Old Mick Maranoa brought this mare of his that I've described," you'll continue, "to be mated with Waverley, but Edwards"—

"Do you mean, Richard," Barney will interrupt excitedly, "that Miss Maranoa is got by Waverley? Why, he was one of the greatest thoroughbreds that were ever imported, and won a lot of blue ribbons — sure ye must be dreaming, Richard?"

"Yes, what's the matter with you, Richard?" and Don will gaze dubiously upon you, too.

"I don't say anything of the sort," you'll go on, "for Edwards wouldn't take the mare without a certificate, though he was sure she was at least three-quarter thoroughbred. But," you'll pause to stare alternately into their faces — "but this

mare you have, if she's the foal of Mick Maranoa's mare, was
got by Melbourne — a greater racehorse than ever Waverley
was."

"Melbourne?" Barney will echo in amazement.

"How do you know that, Richard?" from Don.

"Because I had a job at Greenmount under Edwards, I
suppose", you'll answer discreetly.

"But you said he wasn't taking mares without pedigrees?"

"Neither was he to Waverley or Kyogle", you'll repeat.
"Well, there were times when I was in charge of the stud for
half an hour or so, when Edwards was attending to other
things. He was attending to other things on the day when Mick
Maranoa left the stock mare we're talking about; and to tell
you the truth, whether out of kindness or devilment I don't
know, I saw Melbourne enter the yard where she was about five
minutes after Mick had gone. You can guess the rest! Edwards
returned about twenty minutes later, when Melbourne was back
in the stable again. But soon as he saw the old stallion he
suspected, and asked me a lot of awkward questions. And it
was the only time that ever I seriously lied to save my skin or
my job."

"Upon my soul!" and Barney's muscle will twitch with
suppressed excitement.

"If that's the case," Oberhart will suggest calmly, "you've
got a thoroughbred mare in your paddock, Barney, by a
cup-winner and the sire of Archie and Wreatmeat and Yabba!
So what in the name of Erin do you want thinking of picking
up a hack to win a couple of handicaps for? There might be a
goldmine in this Miss Maranoa for all we know."

"Well, I'm certain of this," you'll answer — "that the foal
Mick Maranoa's mare dropped was by Melbourne and no
other."

Then in silence you'll study both their faces as if expecting
them to thank you for having handed them a goldmine.

Suddenly the mood of Barney McGee will change. "Pshaw!"
he'll say. "It mightn't have been the same foal at all, or the
same mare either. And Mick Maranoa knew far too much about
horses to leave a thoroughbred foal in th' keeping of anyone —
not to save his soul, he wouldn't."

"What are you giving us?" Oberhart will interrupt indignantly, while you too will stare wonderingly at Barney.

But Barney will feigh not to understand. "Let's get away home," he'll suggest, "and not be deludin' one another any longer about races and racehorses and th' like. It must be dark outside, I'm thinking." And rising and saying good-night to Oberhart, he'll lead the way out of the door, chuckling.

Arriving home Barney will display a caution and excitement that will seem mysterious even to Mrs. McGee, his faithful companion and drudge for thirty years and more.

"Jamesy!" he will call to his eldest son, who is in bed. "Soon as 'tis light and before you bring the cows in, put Miss Maranoa into th' stable and lock the door, and say never a word to no one that she's there. And Katie" — going to his wife's door — "if anyone calls to ask questions about Miss Maranoa, ye knows nauthin' about her — ye understand?"

Though Mrs. McGee will understand enough, she will ask from under the blankets: "Whatever on earth has come into your head now, Barney, that you're so concerned all at once about old Mick Maranoa's pet foal? Are you afraid that someone is going to steal her from you? Or is Mick himself coming back at last to pay all he owes for the paddocking of her? It would be a blessing if he would."

"Never mind all that," Barney will answer, closing up the house; "but just keep quiet on what I'm telling you in case anyone might come to ask questions about what isn't their business."

That night you'll lie in your bed thinking and recalling those days when you worked at Williams's stud-farm under Edwards, the manager. And in fancy you'll see Mick Maranoa arriving there again, leading his stock mare, and hear him, in the absence of a certificate, pleading in vain for Edwards to mate her with Wild Wave or Challenger. Then, as Mick departs dejectedly but leaving the mare to be called for on his return from town the following days, and Edwards goes off to supervise the stackbuilding, you'll hear again a mighty crash of a stable door, a joyous roar of a stallion, a sudden responsive love squeal; and then you'll see Melbourne, his glossy coat shining in the sun, his eyes afire, his neck arched, bounding across the yard, and Maranoa's stock mare glancing with glad eyes over her shoulder at his approach, and swinging and swaying her flowing tail in assurance of his reception. "Gad!" you'll burst right out, rising from the bed, "this Miss Maranoa, got by Melbourne, could be a cup-winner!"

*   *   *

A glorious Boxing Day 'way back in the 'seventies — the first race-meeting held at Mt. Sibly. "The Mount" consisted of waste country reserved by a Government of squatters for "closer settlement", and bordering this reserved area were mighty stations, such as Headington Hill, Eton Vale, Clifton and Pilton, all lying there within their cheap, pointed sheep fences, like living land sharks.

The race-meeting itself was a squatters' outing. They provided the prizes, shaped the course, marked it out near the foot of the mount. They ran the meet, in fact, all over: took charge of the scales; rang the bell in warning for each race, and "clerked" the course. Also, they provided the performers — rare imported horses, some were, too! The few cockies came along, bringing their families in carts, to look on and spend a shilling or two at the booth if they were lucky enough to have any about them to spend.

But Barney McGee, being a genial, head-wagging Irishman, was an exception. Barney, who was a "sport", turned up leading a bay moke in the rough that he had entered for the Double-rein Bridle. Beside him Jamesy, "th' son", walked proudly, while Maggie, the ten-year-old daughter, trotted breathlessly along on the off-side of the animal.

They came in touch with the crowd, a galaxy of horsemen, buggy-pairs, fours-in-hand, horsemen and horsewomen (these all in belltoppers), families in spring-carts, drays and all the rest, gathered beneath the shade of the wild apple-trees. Their friends, catching view of them, began calling out: "What have you there, Barney? Something imported?"

"Sure, 'tis nothing of a prestige to be imported in this country," he'll laugh while taking a shorter grip of the reins, and nudging the son to keep further away, "for 'tis imported myself I am."

And to "She's only got six thoroughbreds against her", he'll respond: "I wish it were seven, for being thoroughbreds they'd think it's th' Day of Rest, and she'd have it all her own way."

But soon the bell will sound the time to saddle-up for the Double-rein Bridle.

"Are ye ready?" Barney'll ask of the son, as he girths the bay mare tightly. "Shtand ye away, Maggie." Then gripping the son by the bare foot he'll toss him into the saddle and adjust the reins for him.

"Now go your hardest, Jamesy," Maggie will counsel proudly, "and don't let any of them beat you."

"Listen to her!" th' son will grunt, touching Lady McGee lightly with his bare heels and moving her through the staring, laughing, wondering crowd.

Grabbing Maggie by the hand Barney will rush away to take up a position near the winning-post upon Maloney's waggon, that has on it a couple of bales of chaff as an improvised staging.

"Fifty to five you can't pick it in one, Bell?" one purse-proud squatter will call to another.

"What about the bay thing with the bare-footed boy on it?" Bell replies. "What odds it won't win?"

"Twenty to one." And Bell will toss him a sovereign.

"Why, that's my mare ye're backing", Barney will say excitedly to him.

"Well, I've seen worse looking thoroughbreds than her in the rough. Can the boy ride?"

"Phwat! Can Jamesy ride?" Barney will splutter. "Can a duck swim or a business man steal?"

Instantly the crowd, yelling "Off!" will break in, and Barney and Maggie will go perilously near falling from the bales of chaff into the long grass below.

"Good start! Good start!" is all that anyone can hear for several moments. Then: "Young Leopold! Clifton! Brown Hodgson! Rainbow! Rainbow taking the lead."

Another silence.

Suddenly from a throng of throats: "What about the rough thing? Lady McGee! She's gaining on them!"

Shouts of mirth mingled with surprise will rise up. Barney himself will stand stolid. But Maggie, carried away by excitement, will clap her hands and cry, "Go it, Miss Maranoa!" until her parent, pinching her arm, will hiss: "Will ye shut up yer Miss Maranoa and remimber 'tis Lady McGee!" and Maggie will shut up suddenly.

As the field moves up into the straight with the "rough thing" three lengths in the lead and Jamesy in his bare feet sitting her like a rock or a staghorn, the crowd of squatters will be bewildered. But Barney McGee's cocky friends, few though they be, will rush round and cheer him as though another Napoleon had jumped up.

"Your mare's won," they'll shout, "and, by damn, has licked the head off all the imported wonders!"

Though shaking like a leaf, Barney will stand on the waggon watching Lady McGee being led to the scales and the son lifted from the saddle and placed on them. Barney wasn't one of those to count chickens before they were hatched.

But the moment "Weight" is declared, he will grab Maggie by the hand again, and jumping from the waggon will rush to congratulate Jamesy and fondle and pat the restless perspiring mare. Then turning suddenly to Maggie he will shout: "Run home, girrl, quick, an' tell yer mother that Lady McGee have won th' Double-rein Bridle!"

The home is two miles away, but, starting off, Maggie will run like a hare pursued by a hawk.

And while Maggie is running, those who had lost a wager or two will turn to Bell and say: "You knew something about the roughie!"

But Bell will only smile.

*   *   *

Three years or so later.

There'll be much excitement at the cheese factory one morning after New Year, when the papers arrive. The suppliers, some seated in their carts, will be calling to each other: "Miss Maranoa that old Barney McGee and Bell the squatter own between them won the treble yesterday, and is a hot favourite for the Brisbane Cup."

Some will laugh and some will cheer for Barney McGee. But you, biting at your underlip, will keep silence.

A few afternoons following, you and Don Oberhart will be at the railway station unloading your drays and puffing and sweating and feeling dejected, when Barney, wearing a new tailor-cut tweed suit and smoking a cigar, will step from the up-train, and crossing to the goods-shed, will greet you both with a broad smile and a warm handshake.

You'll both respond like a pair of invalids, until he adds:

"She was th' foal that was got by Melbourne from Mick Maranoa's mare all right, as Richard here well knew, and was the only one who did know, and Mick himself died away out back, and Bell the squatter was his trustee. And so, of course — well, I suppose ye understand?"

Chapter 16

A couple of months have passed since Mrs. Juba Lee and Josie King called and collected your sub. to the school treat, but hardly a day has gone by when you haven't been thinking of the time you'll have. The day'll be slow coming; but, when at last the morning of it does arrive, you'll be up and into your pants and boots, and out to put a fire on; and in a minute or two you'll be blowing hard into a pannikin of scalding tea to cool it, looking out at intervals for signs of daylight. Like trains and things when a man's in a tearing hurry, the dawn will be running late. But you'll give it another ten minutes or so, according to your idea of the time. Then if it doesn't start to show over the dark wall of range to the east you won't wait any longer; you'll go on after the cows and horses without it, and let it catch up.

But it doesn't begin to show, and at last you move out into the darkness, groping your way around the yard for the track leading off into the hollow where the stock generally settle when they've had their fill. And Rover, wondering what's the matter, will accompany you. He'll have more confidence in the dark and in himself than you; and, as if making little of you as a superior being, he'll demonstrate how the Creator was more generous in his gifts to a dog than to you, for while you're mooning your way in uncertain fashion he is scampering off into the gloom, racing through trees and brush and fallen timber for the mere joy of it. To cloak your feelings of inferiority you'll descend to the low-down shabby spirit of the human, and "blast" him, and order him away to a place you shouldn't be thinking of on a morning like this. Of course he won't go — he wouldn't desert you, in fact, just now, not if you killed him for it.

So you'll grope along trying to keep to the track, when all at once you'll nearly fall head first over a plough horse that's sound asleep in the long grass. Mighty! Old Nugget'll wake up as if you were someone come to shoot him. He won't be able to find his legs half fast enough; but when he does he'll bound up and stamp round snorting in terror. And when you lift your voice and blast his eyes as you did Rover's he'll gallop off and you'll hear him thundering and blundering over things as if the devil was pursuing him. Next minute you'll hear the rest of the horses whinnying anxiously to one another from different angles, and then the lot of them, taking to their heels, 'll tear recklessly in pursuit of Nugget. You'll stand listening-in — your heart in a flutter lest some will come to grief in a gully or against a tree.

And while following the sounds your attention will be attracted to other noises higher up the ridgeside among the loose stones. You'll turn your ear and catch sounds of cloven hoofs and the cracking of knuckle-bones and joints, accompanied by a mumbling "Moo!" In a second you'll know it's the darn dairy herd, and that they also have taken you for an evil spirit. And when they start running, making an unearthly row, you'll grind your teeth and peer down at your feet and round about in search of Rover. You'll feel that he's the cause of it all, and you'll want to deliver him a square, solid kick in the ribs while the facts are fresh in your mind. And while you're peering blindly around for him, Rover will be sitting on his tail a few yards out of reach, looking at you with love and affection in his eye.

A few minutes more and the grey dawn will start to break in streams of light; the dark, errie objects about you will take shape; Rover in the flesh will appear beside you; not a hundred yards away, the dairy herd will be bunched together, staring back at you; the horses will be at the yard; and the little homestead and its familiar surroundings will all reveal themselves.

It's broad daylight now, and you begin to think it's getting

late; that the morning will be gone before you can get a move
on. So you address a few words of instruction to the cows, and
tail them along to the yard, whistling in imitation of the birds
chorusing across the gully, and wondering if you'll get your
work done in time.

It will be surprising how soon the sun will follow the dawn,
and how high it will be in the sky when you finish up at the
yards, load the milk-cart, attend the horses, pigs and poddies
and fowls; snatch a bit of breakfast and off to the factory.

You won't waste many minutes at the factory, and on the
way back you'll put up a record for a horse and cart over four
miles. You won't wait to close the gate — leaving it open for
once won't matter. So you'll pull the harness off the puffing
horse, pour a can of whey over the heads of the squealing
swine, throw the saddle on your hack and hurry to the house
for a wash and change to your Sunday togs.

Nothing is in your head now but the treat and getting there.
Your laundry will be in fair order, for the Ryan woman ironed
a shirt and collar for you only two or three weeks ago, and
except for being speckled a bit the collar will be white as snow.
Your socks, though, want heeling and toeing; still, when your
boots go over them, they won't be noticed. And if you find
you have to pull your boots off to take part in a high jump or
something got up for adults you'll decide to be careful about it
and pull the socks off along with the boots. Your feet and legs
will need a wash, though; the soil of the cultivation paddock is
clean enough in its way, and different to the germ-laden dust of
the cities; still, it changes the colour of your limbs and makes
you look a skewbald. So you'll get a tub under the tap of the
tank and double yourself up in it before you turn the water on.
Lawd! It's so long since you were under the tap in all your
nakedness that, when you let it flow, it'll fall on your humped
back like a cataract of knives and needles. You'll shudder and
yell, and Rover, who'll be eyeing you sideways all the time, and
forming a dog's opinion of you, in the nude, will gather round
the tub barking at you. But you'll keep on shuddering and
yelling, taking no notice of him until you suddenly feel his two
paws on your shoulders, his hard-worn claws scraping their way
down your bare back, and his joyful bark in your ear; then

you'll howl and roar at him, and in your wrath upset the tub and yourself backwards. And when you kick the empty vessel from you with both feet and rise, you'll cast reflections on Rover's pedigree and chase him two different ways round the home with a missile in your hand.

But you won't take long dressing; and with a last look round, as you lean from the saddle and pull the gate after you, you'll touch the horse with your heels and off! Gee! The feelings that'll be in your head and in your heart will keep lifting you in the stirrups as you rip and rattle along the lanes. And when you come in sight of the picnic-ground there'll be numbers of carts and sulkies and saddle-horses already there. The carts and sulkies will be surrounded by women chattering and calling greetings and questions and suggestions to one another. They'll be the working-bee, and they'll be lifting out baskets of crockery and provender and opening them up; and standing off a piece under some trees will be a circle of old cronies in cropped whiskers, all shaking their heads and expressing surprise at having lived to meet one another again at the same spot on the same day that they met a year before.

As you ride in through the open gate, dragging your hat over your face so that no one will see how self-conscious and uncertain you are of yourself, the local schoolmaster, with a line of boys, will be trailing a rope round looking for a safe tree to erect a swing on. There will be family groups, too, standing about — some of them migrants that were never at a treat before — holding each other by the hand and looking as if they felt uncertain of a welcome. Some more, mostly young couples, will come flying and crushing in behind you on dancing, prancing horses, flashing riding whips as if they were entering a show-ring to pick up prizes for the best hacks.

Putting your horse away in the shade, you'll avoid the women for the present, and make for the old cronies in whiskers. You have more confidence in them and know they'll be easy to pal in with. They'll be telling each other all about the weather; how much rain they got out of the storm that broke over a couple of nights before. Though you'll be standing, listening and smiling for quite a while, they won't notice you've joined them until you mention that scarcely a drop fell at your place. Then they'll turn to you, and shake hands with you, and ask have you, too, taken a day off to come to the treat. And they'll think it strange that you didn't get anything out of that storm! From some of their places it looked as if it was falling in torrents over your way — like wheat coming out of a winnower. But old Haley, who was nearly flooded out, and is proud of being specially favoured by Providence, won't be a little surprised — he will remember that your part of the country, "alez *were* a dry corner".

After a while you'll get restless, and feel a flat tyre. You'll be snatching and blowing at the flies, and looking across from under your hat at the women. And some of them, when your eyes are the other way, will be looking across at you; and then Bill Buck, old Silas King's handyman, in his shirt-sleeves, will drive in with Josie, bareheaded, beside him in a four-wheeler, packed behind with tins and cases of sandwiches and stuff. Without knowing why, you'll begin to feel different. The old cronies will all look up and stare; and when Josie smiles and nods at them as she rolls past like the Duchess of York, they'll feel pleased and will chorus, "Hello, Bill!" Whether Josie saw you standing there and meant those smiles for you you're not quite sure, but her coming just when you were feeling like a flat tyre will seem like an answer to a prayer.

Following the vehicle with their dim eyes and watching it draw up under the trees, where Josie'll jump out and greet their wives and daughters with handshakes, those old cronies will glow with the spirit of equality. And your heart will start beating ahead of time when you hear old Bob Smith come out with, "Now, look you at that! And everyone a'sayin' she were stuck up." But you'll be sliding away from the old cronies, looking as if you're interested in everything but women. You won't feel valiant enough to slay a lion in a pit, but with a clothes-prop you'd take on a dozen old-men 'roos in a paling yard.

"Hello, Dick Gall, you're just in time! We want a good fire made." You'll know it's the voice of Mrs. Juba Lee, and it'll come to you like the Lord wording the Israelite from out the clouds. So you'll try and look surprised as you turn to them, grinning and flushing.

"And we want the tarpaulin put up after you've made the fire, Mr. Gall" — this will come from Josie King, who's in charge of the sandwich section, and she'll have her sleeves rolled above the elbows, and will be trying an apron on, and smiling at you. You'll get confused, the blood will rush to your face, and forgetting about the fire you'll ask where the tarpaulin is.

But Mrs. Lee won't forget, though she'll understand and see through your blushes. "No, you don't", she'll laugh. "We want our fire first, and they can have you all to themselves after."

So, coming to your senses, you'll discard your coat, tossing it away as if you'd finished with it for ever, and there'll be a pile of wood and a fire started quicker than if it had been struck by lightning.

Inspired now with the spirit of achievement, you'll unroll the tarpaulin, and when Josie, who'll leave the others to carry on, will take hold and help to push and drag it over the limb of a fallen tree — when Josie comes close to you, and you feel her breath and the touch of her soft hand against your hard one — you'll get into such a flurry that you'll be pulling and dragging the darn thing the wrong way. And how your heart'll palpitate when at last you find yourself alone with her under the blessed thing for a second! But she won't seem to notice, she'll be concerned only about making a good job of it. At least, that's how it'll impress you.

And just when the job's finished and you're standing surveying it, grinning at her in expectation of the word of praise that'll mean such a lot, long Phil Ryan, a cove your own age, with spurs on his heels and flashing a riding whip, will poke his nose in and say: "Givin' him some work to do, Miss King? He can do with it — no one ever sees him workin' on that farm of his. Can y' give *me* a job? There's a seven-foot snake out on the road that someone killed; would you like me to get it and chop it into sandwiches for the workin'-bee?"

How you will look at him; and when Josie goes off you'll feel you could punch him.

But your feelings will change when the schoolmaster calls out, wanting to know if there's anyone can climb a rope hand over hand and fasten it to the limb to complete the swing, and

Mrs. Juba Lee shouts back that Dick Gall can. You're not sure you can yourself, but you won't let on, so you'll grin cheerfully and roll up your sleeves. It'll seem a pretty stiff climb up that rope when you look at it, and the limb will be rotten! But Mrs. Lee said you can do it, and as no one else is competing you'll squat calmly on the grass beside the dangling hemp, and while a mob gathers round to watch, off will go your boots, leaving your socks on! You won't think of them till you're half-way through with the climb, and while you're straining your arms and gripping with your feet and thinking about the darn limb, you'll hear them laughing under you and the kids calling one another to look at the big hole in your socks, and their mothers telling them to shut up. It'll take a lot of heart out of you; you'll weaken in the arms and for the moment you'll kick and dangle as if you were fighting to defeat the executioner. "Stick to it," the schoolmaster will urge; "you haven't got much farther to go!" To *you* it'll seem a mile, and when you shut your eyes and set your teeth and take fresh grips, and kick your legs getting astride the limb as if you were swimming, one of the socks will leave your foot and float down among the spectators. It will cause a stir. Old McClure will rescue it from the kids and mind it for you till you descend, and when you reach earth you'll be puffing, and in a hurry to put your boots on again.

Your services will be in great demand now — there'll be scarcely anything you won't be asked to take a hand in. But whether you're on the tea buckets or carrying round buns or swinging the girls, your eye will be roaming round in search of Josie. You'll be wanting to keep her in view. She'll be your inspiration and source of enthusiasm. There'll be times, too, when you fancy she's been looking to see where you are. And when big Nellie Ryan, who hasn't spoken to you for eighteen months, finds you are friendly with Josie, whom she doesn't like, she'll forget her coolness towards you and start asking you things, and always running across you by accident and getting more friendly every time. It'll puzzle you a good deal, her following you about; but, of course, you won't be experienced enough to tumble to what it means.

After the kids and most of the adults have been fed several

times on cakes and sandwiches and it's getting near three or four o'clock, a game of rounders for the working-bee will be started, and you and Pat Smith asked to pick sides. That'll be a momentous moment. Hoaky! How you'll be fidgetin' and intriguing in your mind to win the toss so as to make Josie your first pick and have her on your side. Your luck will be in, too; but just when you shout her name as if she was on fire and other girls start shoving her across to you, old Silas King will come driving on to the ground with a flabby swell from the city beside him in the buggy. He doesn't drive a car. The swell has a habit of visiting the Kings whenever there's anything on in the locality.

"Enjoying yourselves — enjoying yourselves! Quite right; quite right!" old Silas will mumble to all of you as he draws up to park the four-wheeler. You won't have seen much of the old gasper since you beat him for your little homestead, and you can't help feeling that you'd sooner go and twist a lion's tail than face him. So, watching his movements out of the corner of your eye as he steps out of the buggy, leaving the swell in it, you'll be consoling yourself by thinking he might have forgotten all about the land matter anyway. So, heading through the crowd, taking no notice of the ball flying past his ear, the old chap'll tell Josie that he has brought Mr. Draper along and wants her to look after him and see he gets a cup of tea and something to eat.

Of course Josie will be too sweet-natured not to seem glad about it, but a colouring of disappointment'll come to her cheeks when she puts down the bat; and, noticing the old chap has left you out of the nods he's given to the others, she'll call his attention to you with — "You know Mr. Gall, Papa?"

A queer feeling will come over you when you hear your name from her! You'll get ready to give him your hand and welcome him to the picnic. But old Silas will only give you a sour look, then ask how you're getting on over there among the bandicoots — have they eaten you out yet?

While you're trying to recover he'll go off with Josie to the buggy; and when you hear the girls whispering near you that he's the ugly bachelor whom old Silas wants Josie to marry because he's got money, you'll get a fit of absent-mindedness and forget which side you are on; and, though you'll be glad when the game is finished, you'll feel disconsolate when you see old Silas mooching off with the schoolmaster and leaving Josie to the other fellow. You can't keep your eyes away from them, and you'd like to know what the city dope's game is.

Later, when you find it's time you were going home to milk your cows, and that city interloper is still laughing and talking to Josie as if he expected to be set to music, you'll feel a desperate urge. You must have a word of some kind with her before you go; so, after telling the others that you are off, and calling "So-long!" you'll get on your horse and ride as close as you can to the buggy, heading for the gate.

"Oh, are you going, Mr. Gall?" Josie'll ask, turning from Draper, and looking up at you with warm blood in her cheeks.

"Yes, must be making tracks now", you'll answer, reining up and feeling you could hop off and strangle the swell with the silk tie he is wearing. Then, holding up her hand to you and smiling, Josie'll hope you enjoyed the day.

My word — you did! And all the way home you'll reckon that everything would have been splendid only for that city swell coming in the buggy.

And next day, and for days and days after, the same thoughts will keep your mind alive; and, unlike the early cloud and the morning dew, the school treat will be a long time passing away.

Chapter 17

You left the ploughing to canter to the railway station to order a wheat truck. You have just returned and it's getting dusk. You've been trying Newchum's paces along the lane, and, warmed up, his eyeballs are dilating and he's looking his noblest. "What did you think of her, old horsey?" you'll question like a big kid, patting him on the neck as you pull the bridle off. "Wouldn't you like to be me — wouldn't you, if you was a man? Don't I know y' would!"

Only the Lord can tell whether the horse understands or not. But as he swings round to roll in the dust he'll nicker as if he did.

Later, seated at table over the steak you've fried, you'll take Rover into your confidence. You'll talk to him while he sits on his tail listening. When you fall into silence he'll whimper and bark. "You ain't met her yet," you'll tell him, "but if you'd been with me this evening you would — you old scoundrel! I met her near th' railway, and I'm going to her place on Sunday. You're not — no matter who's there I'm to go. And I'm not to mind what Papa thinks. How would you like to be me, Rover — wouldn't you sooner be me than the city dope who was trying to mash her at the picnic, looking as if he had just finished a term of epidemics? Cripes, wouldn't *anyone*!"

But proud as you are of yourself, you're feeling shaky and nervous when Sunday arrives. Being favoured by Josie King will be one thing; bracing up to go and see her in her home when you know her old man hasn't a spark of approbation in his make-up for you, and has developed a habit of reading you like a criminal lawyer, will be quite another thing. Still, you're facing it for her. And while you're getting ready, fastening your collar and tie, looking at yourself in the little mirror while your horse is hanging up outside, you'll be building castles in the air, castles in comparison with which Solomon's mansion, built with the help of three score and ten thousand hewing wood for it in the mountains, and three thousand six hundred overseeing, will be only a modest shack. So, closing the door behind you, you'll approach your horse, pulling your hat down in front, pushing it up behind to please your fancy; then into the saddle and off like a despatch-bearer you'll rattle.

It's a wonderful day, the sky pale blue, the air clear, the hills and valleys green; the wild flowers blooming, everything gay and glittering, nothing dull or brown or withering, not even the old rail fences or the dead timber. Full of secret hopes you'll tear along the lanes as if you had all the angels with you.

Coming in sight of "The Meadows" you'll steady the pace and get back to earth again. A procession of thoughts will run through your head that will make you uncomfortable. You'll start asking yourself should you really go or not? Will Josie be home? If you don't see her about what'll you say to *him?*

Drawing nearer the farmyard you'll hear the windmill pumping, and you'll be getting the most out of your eyesight.

To the left, on the wide verandah of the home, there'll be a host of people lounging in squatters' chairs and hammocks. They're visitors; most of them women. How in the name of anyone can you be expected to dismount and mingle with that lot! Josie must have gone mad. You don't know the way to the front of the house — when you worked for old Silas years ago you never got any further than the kitchen. And you don't to go any further now.

They're turning their heads, gawking, wondering who you are. What are you going to do now? Instead of Newchum wheeling and bolting off with you, he keeps stepping out briskly, tossing his head, snatching the bit, showing how glad he feels. You grind your teeth and screw up your courage as you open the gate and enter the yard. A tribe of dogs rush to meet and serenade you.

Being the Sabbath, which old Silas King is careful to see

kept sacred at "The Meadows" since he has become prosperous
and religious, the farm hands will be sitting about in the shade.
You'll pass a cold nod to them; ride on to the stable, ducking
your head under a clothes-line to keep clear of a row of
uninhabited things.

Putting the horse away, you glance round the gravelled path
leading to the front verandah. You'll reproach yourself for
being a darn fool; and you feel that your hour is at hand and
you've been betrayed into the hands of the enemy.

"Unless I'm blind it's Dick Gall." You'll look round and be
confronted by Bill Buck, the handyman of "The Meadows".
He's shuffling solemnly towards you, looking as if he was under
instructions to eject you. But when he asks, "Who is it you
want to see — Mr. King?" and informs you that the Boss never
sees anyone about business on Sunday, you'll start beating
about the bush. And when you've made yourself feel a fraud
and a liar, and Bill can't make head or tail of you, Josie'll come
tripping across the yard looking like a fairy in her white silks,
her hair waving in the wind, to save you.

"Oh, you *did* come, Richard?" She doesn't call you Dick.
And she'll smile with her eyes and lips and teeth. "I was
beginning to wonder if you really would." At that Bill will
touch his hat and make off. And while you're colouring up and
gathering yourself together Josie'll give a little laugh and invite
you to the front verandah.

You go off with her like a big pet stupid sheep being led to
slaughter.

"We've some visitors," she'll tell you, looking up curiously
into your face, "but they're only Mr. and Mrs. Andrew Craig,
Miss Fairfield and her sister and two friends, and Mr. Draper —
a friend of Pa's — and a few others."

"Mr. Draper?" you'll mumble, as if the name was poison,
with the same effect that strychnine would have on you.

"He's talking to Pa," and this time Josie will touch your arm
and look up at you in such a way that, instead of tasting
strychnine, you'll feel you've taken champagne. Gee! you're a
new man in an instant. She's inspired you. Instead of a sheep
you're a lion being led to the wolves by a dove.

You're walking firm, erect, bold; such a feeling never came

over you before. Out of the slough of your humbleness she's exalted you to a pedestal of bravery. You mount the verandah step for step with her; you're laughing with her; you're taking your hat off; smoothing your hair out of your eyes and looking like a party leader taking the platform. Old Silas and Draper and the others are gaping at you. In a voice of gladness Josie introduces you first to one, then to another, as "Mr. Richard Gall". Even to Pa, who, if you had darkened the sun and caused stars and hail to fall on the lawn, couldn't look more surprised. She's determined to make you known. Extending your hand to old Silas, you'll grip his limp fist and shake it heartily, inquiring after his health and expressing pleasure at his robust appearance. You'll greet the swell Draper in the same jovial spirit, recalling that you saw him at the school picnic. Then, displaying all the manners you know (you weren't always a lone, motherless homesteader), you'll bow and smile to the ladies; stoop gracefully to restore to Mrs. Craig a book that has fallen from her lap to the floor, and remain standing till Josie is seated.

Putting you out of his mind, old Silas will sulkily continue the conversation. He'll address his remarks to Draper and the ladies — to everyone but you. You'll listen respectfully to their views, waiting the opportunity to express your own. Catching Josie's eye you'll clear your throat and observe to old Silas: "Just so, Mr. King, but always making the man with the most money top-dog doesn't get the world anywhere. It is the greatest men who should be the servants of the others."

"What!" old Silas will frown on you.

"Servants of the others!" Mr. Draper will sneer, looking meaningly at everyone but you.

"That's what *Christ* was", Josie will say, and beam on you.

"*Christ!* How dare you, girl!" Pa will explode.

"I really think it's time to go", Mr. Draper will rise to his feet.

"We must be moving, too", from the others.

"And Gall, too", Pa will growl towards Josie.

Josie's eyes will flash. "Richard is staying, Pa!" she will say. And you'll look sheepish while the others disperse.

The flush will still be in your cheeks, and in Josie's, too; and she'll be holding out a plate inviting you to a ginger-nut, when old Silas will return. It'll be plain what he's returned for. There's no polish about Silas. He's blunt and proud and ignorant.

"Are you coming here to see my daughter, Gall?" And he'll stare at you with unfriendly eyes.

Seeing you're speechless, Josie will rebuke him with, "Pa!"

"I don't know who you are," Silas will say, ignoring Josie; "you worked for me years ago at odd jobs, like lots of others, but that didn't make you a friend of mine, or of my family's. I don't know you; or where you are from; or anything about you."

With the colour deepening her cheek, and her eyes flashing more and more, Josie will look a picture. And, though you don't feel quite yourself, you're not afraid. But you're thinking hard.

"You might fancy you don't know me, Mr. King", you'll tell him in a quiet way. "But you knew my father once; you worked for him when he owned Borrodale Downs."

"You a son of Donald Gall's? A son of his?"

That's all old Silas will be able to articulate or even think for a second or two, for he'll be on the verge of emotion.

Then, calling to the others to come here, he'll introduce you proudly as "the son of Donald Gall, the squatter, who took up Borrodale Downs in the 'sixties, and was the first to bring Clydesdales to this country. And an old friend of his."

And then you'll know you're set.

Chapter 18

Bringing home a cow with a young calf is different to bringing home a friend to dinner. It's one of the things the Government didn't tell you about when informing you of the richness of the soil, the salubrity of the climate, the heavy rainfall and other happy conditions that would surround your green grey homestead.

But you'll get to know about it all in good time. And one day, when in the middle of the ploughing and you are going for dear life to finish before the ground gets too hard; and when there's a paddock of lucerne waiting to be cut before the leaf falls and a couple of chains of broken fence to be mended, and the roof of the barn to be pitched a couple of feet higher, and the building to be made bigger, and (according to the agricultural experts) a hundred acres of bush-hay to be cut as a stand-by for a rainy day, the Grogan kids will come tearing home from school after losing your newspaper on their way, and a letter you've been waiting for for months with a cheque in it for the sale of pigs, to tell you that Mr. Jerry Moriarty told his boys to tell them to tell you that when he was out on the Commonage he saw a red cow of yours with a white back, and it had a young calf sucking her; and that if you don't go out soon and get her someone else will, and brand the calf.

"A red cow with a white back?" you'll repeat, shaking your head doubtingly. No, you'll be sure he's making a mistake. But the kids were certain that Mr. Moriarty said it was a red cow with a white back, and that she had your brand on, and had a young calf, and was yours. Then you'll think a lot, recalling the colour and image of every beast ever you owned, and letting them pass in procession through your mind as if it was a dip, till at last you'll feel you're being offered a live cow and calf for nothing, and don't like to take them. Yet, somehow you'll get a better opinion of Jerry Moriarty's knowledge of cattle than you had before, and you'll reckon it would be hard for him, who's always riding about the bush and knows everyone's brand, and is more interested in other people's stock than he is in his own, to make an error of that kind.

Also, in your heart you'll feel she can't belong to you, no matter what her brand is. Still, you won't want to convince yourself quite that she's not your property, for if she's not yours, whose can she be? So you'll ponder and reason with yourself until you've finished the milking and the Grogan kids have found the paper and the letter with a cheque in it. But after you've fed the poddies and fallen out with a couple of them for bunting into you as if you were their mother and had teats hanging all round you, you'll get a brain-wave.

You'll remember that when you put your little herd out on the Commonage after buying feed for them all through the last big drought, and went to muster them after the rain came, that some were missing, you reckoned they were dead — you were surprised they weren't all dead — and among them was a little red heifer with a white back, not much larger than a dog, that you had reared on the bucket. "Cripes, that must be her!" you'll chuckle, slapping yourself on the leg. "Grown into a cow, and got a calf!" Then you'll be off, hot-foot, to the house, calling out to the dog, and calling yourself a goat.

There will be no ploughing for you that day. You're on to Newchum after breakfast and off to the Commonage. The plough horses will stand at the fence watching you going with approving eyes. They'd rather meet you in the saddle than between the handles of the plough. Before you're out of sight of the homestead you'll meet Wilkins on his way to the factory, and you'll stop to tell him where you are going. He'll say, "Yairs", and "Y' don't tell me", while filling his pipe from your tobacco and squinting at you through a fly-veil. And when he's lit his pipe and is just going to drive on again he'll say: "Nearly all o' mine died out on that blarsted place; but now, on what you've been tellin' me, p'raps some of them's alive yet, too."

And at the factory he'll spread the news that heifers of yours that died on the Commonage in the big drought have all come to life again, and have got calves, and that you've gone out to bring them all in to milk. Before noon it'll be known all round the country, and talked of round dinner tables; and there'll be some who'll feel pleased to hear that someone's having a bit of luck, even if they are not themselves — and some who won't.

The Commonage, you'll find, isn't laid out like an experimental farm. It's a large area of waste range country hurled over with rocks and fallen timber and precipices, and with a big hell-hole and a little hell-hole occupying most of the area — country that early squatters despised, and so was dedicated by Government to the shire council for the use of small settlers, township people, horse-planters and cattle-duffers. The township people use it when they want firewood, or when they have an old horse or a cow that's likely to die on their hands and run up a bill for being dragged out of the town and burnt; and horse-planters use it all the year round for improving the breed of other people's horses. There will be no gate or sliprails to the Commonage, and the only boundary lines ever it had were surveyors' marks cut into trees, and most of the trees you'll find have been cut down for bees' nests, and slabs, and fencing posts. You'll know it when you're on it by the abundance of bleached bones and scattered horns lying about; and the knee-caps and knuckle-bones shining on the ridge-sides and in all the hollows will look like crops of mushrooms.

It'll be a good season, too, following the drought, and though there'll be little real grass there'll be plenty of vegetation and herbage and green bushes, and the tree-clad ridges will be heavily decked with blossoms and drugged with the drowsy humming of locusts. And, of course, there'll be birds of bright plumage chortling and fluttering in the trees, but as you won't be looking for material to split poetry out of, and won't belong to a Sketch Club or a Nature Study Society, you'll not have much of an eye or an ear for parrots and pee-wees and the like, except maybe wonga pigeons or scrub turkeys, which you could eat — if you had a gun. And you won't be there to collect beetles and bones for the Museum, either; or to see if the kangaroo brings its joey into the world same as cats and cows and realistic artists do, or if it brings it to light through a pouch. So you'll ride ahead over ridges, and in and out of hollows with nothing in your head but a red cow with a white back; and you'll strain for sight of her in places where there'll be no cows of any colour, or bulls or steers either, till your head aches and your eyes feel sore. Your great hope will be to come across her on the tableland, such as it will be, for you'll have no wish to go down into "big hell-hole", or "little hell-hole", in search of her. You've been down in those holes more than once, and prayed to the Almighty for guidance all the time you were trying to get out of them again. And as the search goes on what an imaginative mind you'll have! Every animal that reveals itself to you camped in the undergrowth, or meditating under a tree or scratching itself against a stump, will seem to be a red cow with a white back, and will start your heart jumping till you get right on to it. And those that will be lying down with anything like a red skin, you, of course, will stir up and have a look at their brand. And some of them, lying down chewing th' cud, and dreaming of grass and seasons long gone by, will be hollow-eyed, scaly, whip-marked, old working bullocks that will take a lot of stirring up, too!

You'll work your way round a big mountain to a flat above the springs, where once there was an old station-yard and a slab hut with augur-holes bored in it big enough to hold a gun barrel — a hut used by the squatters when the blacks were said to be bad, and later by horse-planters to camp in when it rained, when you'll catch sight of a mob of cattle through the tree-tops. A track little wider than a plank will take you round the mountain, and the short cuts it will make on the broken sides and stiff climbs will fill you with pride for the bovine as a path-finder. You'll be about to descend the last pinch, your eyes will be bursting and your heart thumping at sight of the mob of all colours, grazing peacefully over on a flat. Suddenly, with a start, Newchum will stop, his ears pricked, and he will stare hard. You'll get a start, too, for a horseman will be scratching and grunting his way up to meet you.

He'll be a grizzly-faced old chap with a bumper of white whiskers, and seemingly born in Solomon's time. And he'll be astride an old brown cob, once a great horse, and still as game as a jumper ant. When the old chap, riding loose as Oxford bags and wearing a spur on one of his heels, and the remains of a cabbage-tree hat on his head, struggles to the top of the pinch where you'll be waiting, he'll want to know things: "Phwat th' devil are y' blockin' the track for? Can't y' get out of th' way of a man's horse? Isn't th' mountain wide enough f'r ye?"

Then you'll grin, and ask him did he see a red cow with a white back anywhere that's got a young calf? "Did I see phwat?" he'll yell, waving a waddy at you that he's carrying in place of a whip. You'll ask him again and he'll grunt: "*Huh* . . . Don't I want all the eyes I have to see me own baists without seein' other people's? . . . Phwat's that back there lookin' up at ye but a red cow with a white back? Are ye a new chum? Gahn wid you!" And on he'll shuffle, scrambling up and up and round that windhaunted old mountain, while you look after him and think of Jim Marsden's Old Dad in "Robbery Under Arms". Then you'll take the track again and corkscrew down off that pinch.

There, looking at you, as the old chap said, will be a red cow with a white back! How your heart will jump and your blood tingle! Gosh! You'll ride round and round her while she'll turn and turn, keeping an eye on you, and wondering what your game is, for cows, like humans, are suspicious of strangers. She'll be a youngish cow, in full milk, and not long been sucked. That must be her, right enough, but you'll want to see the brand, for until you do you'll feel like a cove with a quid on a horse that's half a length in front but has five or six more lengths to go to win. As if to oblige you she'll turn the other way before making off, and there on her milking side, plain as print, will be your brand — "T2D". You'll feel yourself rising right out of the saddle, and for a while you're floating in air. Then you'll remember all about her, and wonder how you ever forgot her. Then, touching Newchum with your heels, you'll shoot out and head her.

She'll stand again, staring indignantly at you, and holding her head a lot higher. Then you'll address words of greeting to her, and like a big kid ask her where her calf is? By inches her tail will go up on the rising tide of excitement; then off she'll go again, this time with a snort. But you won't try to head her again — not just then — you'll be thinking of the calf. You'll know, of course, not being from the city, that a cow with a calf a few days old always puts it to sleep somewhere, after giving it a suck, same as your own mother used to do with yourself; that for a cradle she'll make use of the heads of fallen trees, or undergrowth, or long grass, and that when she sees the offspring curled up snug and comfortable she strolls off to forage a mouthful for herself, and doesn't return to the spot until it's time for refreshments again, or she gets word that the youngster has got out of bed, and is in danger in some way.

So leaving her to herself you'll start hunting round for the calf, riding steadily about, here, there, and everywhere, examining fallen timber, bushes and the rim of the under-growth. You'll shout into places and make all sorts of wild noises and sometimes you'll get off and heave sticks to frighten the little devil out of his sleep, and give himself away. All the time the cow will be feeding, pretending she's not a bit interested in you, until you get "cold" — and right away from the hiding-place. Then she'll lift her head and stare at you as if she's getting afraid you'll find her offspring. But that'll be all bluff. And after a while, when "hot", she won't lift her head at all, but watch you out of the corner of her eye; and she'll stop wagging her ears so as to catch every sound.

And while you're hunting round you'll come across a white cow that's been dead a couple of days. You'll stand looking at her corpse. Poor devil! Her legs will be stiff and pointing to the sun. She's had a calf, too, you can see, and the wild dogs have been at her. But a gentle breeze blowing from her will make even Newchum snort and swing round, and you'll let him go off his own way.

Thinking of the calf again you'll remember old Stopes telling you how he once induced a cow to find its calf by bellowing like one himself. So you'll hang Newchum up somewhere, and putting your hands to your mouth you'll become a lost, lonely calf wanting its mother, until you get hoarse and thirsty. And every time you'll glance round expecting to see the cow making in haste for the spot where her infant is, she'll be feeding in the same old spot, perhaps just going to lie down for a camp. That will try your temper, and feeling you'd like to have old Balaam to swear for you, you'll mount Newchum again and start driving the cow about, anywhere she likes to go, in hopes that she'll take it in her head to go where the calf is. But she'll go everywhere that the calf isn't; and after a while you'll feel nothing but a fool for letting yourself be made an ass of by a cow.

The sun will be getting over a bit now, too, and it will sink pretty early in the Great Divide.

You'll be sitting in the saddle, pulling at Newchum's mane, thinking and looking worried, when suddenly from off the wind away on the rim of the undergrowth will come a couple of bellows with a lot of SOS feeling in them. Then a hell of a moo from the cow; and when you look in her direction she'll be galloping her hardest for the undergrowth, roaring like murder. Then up from the gullies and down off the ridges will come other cattle, bellowing their hardest, too, and kicking up a dust as if they were mobilising for the next war. And while you're staring and wondering what all the hullobaloo is about, a red calf will come bounding blindly out of the undergrowth, bellowing as if the devil had hold of it, and behind it will be a white calf hustled by a couple of dingoes.

Laws! You won't want to know any more. For a furlong or so, you'll work overtime in the saddle, yelling to let the dogs know you're coming; but even before Newchum can cover the distance there'll be a cordon of wild-eyed cattle formed round those calves, some of them with their heads down snorting and charging at the slinking dingoes. The yellow curs will tuck their bushy tails between their legs and side-bound them; and all you will see of them when you arrive on the scene is the whites of their eyes leering back over their shoulders at you as they disappear into the undergrowth.

The commotion won't last long; and the mob will break rank and scatter themselves about. Then you'll make friends with the red cow with the white back, who'll be standing looking grateful, and embracing the red calf, which has also a white back, and will be sucking at her eagerly, and wagging its tail. You won't be sure of its gender at first glance, for at that age, with the woolly hair covering them, it's always hard to tell without handling whether calves are bulls or heifers. But while you'll be admiring the pair, and figuring what the increase will be from them in five years or so, the white calf, who's been wasting time with a couple of old bullocks that he's mistaken for cows, will waddle over to your cow, and claiming her for his mother will start sucking her on the off-side and wagging his tail like one o'clock.

At first you'll be amused, expecting him to get a kick on the jaw that'll knock him silly, but to your surprise, the cow will turn her head to him and start licking and caressing him. "Cripes!" you'll gasp — "it's hers, too! She's got twins!" Yet there's something about that calf that makes it hard for you to believe it's true — the colour, for one thing. Still, there he is, sucking away, and your cow mothering him. You'll look the other cattle over for a cow in milk and a likely mother, but nearly all of them will be old and dry, and shrivelled, and no more likely to have calves than Chinamen. Your doubts about that calf's parentage will start to grow, and while you want to get rich as quick as anyone, knowing that lots got rich and became Js.P. by their cows having two and more calves, you won't want to risk going to gaol.

So you'll sit there in the saddle looking him over and over, and pondering, when all in a second you'll get another brain-wave. Why you didn't get it sooner will be your only wonder. That calf will belong to the dead cow lying in the gully! You'll see nothing in him now but a sure key to quod! So you'll slip between the little beggar and your cow, and "hoosh" him away, and crack the whip at him and race after him for a hundred yards or so, till the poor little brute, the life half scared out of him, will disappear over the head of the gully where his dead mother lies. Then you race back and hustle your cow and her legitimate calf off that flat and up the track leading round the lonesome mountain, at intervals looking back in fear the wretched orphan might be following!

Safe on the top of the first climb you'll spell for a moment to let them get their wind, so as not to knock the calf up too soon. You'll know, of course, that he'll knock up sooner or later, somewhere, before you get home, and that you'll have to carry him in front of you on the saddle. But you want him to walk as far as he can. Then from out of the stillness and the solitude of the gully, away below, will come a plaintive cry from the abandoned motherless thing that will touch you in a soft spot. And when the cow, more humane than you, and less seifish, hears it, she'll lift her head and answer back, and answer back again and again, and will object to going further without him! Laws! What a criminal you feel all the rest of the way home!

Next morning, when you and your dog rise and gather proudly round the new cow and calf, the cries of that helpless little quadruped that you left to starve out there on the Great Divide will still sound in your ears, and you'll wish he had perished with his mother, and that you had never seen him!

Chapter 19

Though it will take you a couple of years to establish a footing at old Silas King's place, and win his consent to your courting Josie, you'll get her all the same, and have a great wedding, too — the greatest ever known in the district, and at old Silas's expense, and in his house.

It will seem as if everything is being taken out of your hands, at first, and that you are no one, especially when he invites nearly all the guests, selecting only those who are friends of his. But you'll soon realise that his arrangements will save you a lot of work as well as worry and expense, which will make up for a lot. Besides, you'll be able to give more time to *her* during the wedding-eve, and everything will go off pleasantly for both of you on the day. Then you'll go off yourselves — go off full of joy and sunshine and plans for the future, after the wedding breakfast, and the kissing and hand-shaking, to spend your honeymoon. You'll spend it at home at your little grey homestead. It will be quieter there, and you'll be left more to yourselves than you would be at a strange place. But you won't decide to spend it there merely because it possesses those virtues and advantages, but more because, having put your heads together a score of times, months before, and thought everything out carefully, you both concluded that unless "Papa" comes good with a hundred or two in cash as a wedding present for all she's done for him in the home, and in the dairy, helping to make him independent, you won't be able to afford a trip anywhere, as you'll want all the money you've scraped together and saved to pay for the furniture and

additions to the house. And though old Silas has got over all
the objections he had to you, personally, and holds the
wedding at his house for you, and tells the guests with tears in
his voice when replying to the toast of the bride's parent, that
he's sure she's selected the right man for her husband — "a
good, industrious, God-fearing dinkum young Aussie" — and
though he's proud to have you for a son-in-law, you won't see
his cheque among the presents displayed on the table . . . In the
excitement of becoming a father-in-law he'll forget all about it.
But you'll feel nothing but good towards him for you'll know
he doesn't mean anything by it — that's it's only a part of his
nature. Lots of well-to-do men, and fathers of families, in these
advanced years, are absent-minded about money and presents.

When at last you're stealing away on the quiet from the
festival with your bride in her travelling dress on your arm, and
all the old women gathering round her, to say the last
good-bye, and whispering hints in her ear, old Silas will be
engaging some of the favoured guests in the parlour where no
flirting and dancing are going on, and he'll be hanging his pious
lip and shaking his head and sighing like a martyr as he tells
them that you ought to be able to afford to take her for a trip
to the Blue Mountains, or somewhere, for your honeymoon, if
you were any sort of a cove at all, especially after all the help
he's been giving you! But as you'll be rolling along the lanes in
the sulky while he's saying it, with your arm round Josie, and
smiling under her hat at her whenever you risk taking your eyes
off the horse, you, of course, won't hear him, and will not be
perturbed by the impression he's giving them of you and the
splendid light he's putting himself in as a benefactor and
helpful parent. So you'll spend your honeymoon in your own
way, and enjoy it perhaps as much as a prince or a millionaire
would. And the little home you'll take Josie to will be as
comfortable as most of the homes that young couples begin
married life in in the bush . . . Besides, being on the spot in
half an hour or so, the time you would otherwise have wasted
travelling long distances by rail or boat, and strolling about
seashores, and streets and parks, you can devote to building a
wash-house, or something, for Josie, or making her a vegetable
garden; and you'll be able to undo a lot of little things you did

on your own account months before, and do them all over
again under her direction and to her liking, and so have the
place looking just as she wants it to look when her young
friends come along to pay their first visits. And a bride's young
friends are always full of eyes and enthusiasm for the place
she's living in when first they visit it — especially the female
section of them. It relieves their depression and gives them hope
of the future.

The first to call, though, will be old Silas, himself. One
afternoon he'll arrive leisurely in his sulky, gazing cynically
about at everything on your little homestead as he approaches.
Of course, you won't be expecting him, and when Josie
excitedly announces that "Papa is coming, Dick! Here's Papa!"
and runs out to meet him, you'll get in a funk, and start
scraping dough from your hands so that he won't see you've
been filling in the honeymoon by showing Josie how you used
to make dampers for yourself when you were "batching".

"Well, please God, I'm glad to see you, my girl, and how are
you getting along in your new home?" Papa will greet her.
"The Lord in his goodness is watching over the two of you, I
hope." Then as he enters the door: "Dick, I suppose is out and
hard at work again?"

Josie, blushing and smiling proudly on your behalf, will
answer that you'll be there in a minute; that neither of you
have done anything yet, "except to milk the cows in the
morning; and it wouldn't do not to milk them".

"No, no, of course" — Silas will agree, taking stock of the
bit of furniture you've started the home with, as he settles
himself on the new sofa — "they'd soon be all ruined if you
didn't."

Meanwhile you've freed the infernal dough from your
fingers, straightened your shirt-sleeves, and, combing your hair
with your hand, you'll come from the kitchen and welcome
your father-in-law in a stammering, uncertain voice, with a face
beaming with fabricated grins. Though it's your honeymoon,
you can't help feeling ashamed of being discovered inside the
house idling the happy hours away, and at an hour, too, when
you know everyone else in the district is out in the fields
working for their lives. And you can't converse freely and get

as near to your father-in-law as you would like to when all the
time you are doubtful how to address him — whether you
should call him "Papa", the same as Josie does, or stick to
"Mister King". Several times it will be on the tip of your
tongue to call him "Papa", but never being brought up to
calling your Old Man by such a polished high-falutin' appellation, the attempt will stick in your throat and nearly choke
you . . .

But after awhile you'll begin to feel more like a relation; and
when at last he asks in an interested way, "Are you going to
plant any barley this year, Dick, or put all your ground under
wheat?" you'll unthinkingly come out with: "Oh, I think I'll
put it all under wheat, Papa" — and soon as you hear what
you've said you'll turn crimson and grin like a criminal. And
when you see Josie trying to keep from laughing, and old Silas
himself staring and biting at his under-lip as if it was your
tongue he had between his teeth, you'll feel sorry you spoke,
and inwardly determine to see him dead before you'll make
such an ass of yourself again!

Still, you'll forget all about it in a minute or two; and you'll
get on so well together that you'll be showing him everything
you've done to make the little home comfortable for Josie, and
detailing the improvements you've made to the farm, and all
that you intend making; to all of which old Silas will nod
approval and appreciation . . . And when Josie in her turn shows
him the wide-end verandah that you added to the house for
her, and explains in raptures that all she wants now to
complete her joy is a small room on the end of it so she can
accommodate an extra visitor any time there might be a rush,
or "where you could sleep, yourself, Papa," she'll enthuse —
"whenever you decide to come and stay for a week with us",
you'll start wondering with a fast-beating heart if old Silas will
open his purse and build the room for you. Just for the
moment a beneficent look on his face will give you the
impression that he might. But it will only be for a moment.
Instead of opening his purse he'll open your eyes.

"There's a room on the verandah of that little old deserted
place on the reserve, Dick", he'll suggest, turning to you. "It
would just suit this verandah if no white ants have got into it."

"Where all the goats camp?" you'll grin in disparagement, and casting a glance of disappointment at Josie.

"But you won't want the *goats!*" he'll bark at you. "And if the timber is still sound you ought to be able to get it as a bargain from the Council; and it wouldn't take you more than a day to pull it down and cart it away while the weather is fine."

You'll look at him as if he was your enemy, and for a while you can't decide what answer to make. But, reading your face like a barometer, Josie will change the subject: "And there is one other thing, though, that Dick has got to get, yet, for me, Papa", she'll say, with a cheerfulness that only a woman can be capable of perpetrating.

"Well, if there's only one, you haven't got a very long list of wants for him to satisfy, my girl" — her parent will interrupt. "You're not like your poor mother was — God rest her in her narrow bed! — when she got married."

And for a moment or two he'll close his eyes in pious reflection.

"And that's a good sulky horse," Josie will conclude. "One I can have to drive whenever I go out without worrying Dick for one that he is working."

"Yes" — old Silas will concur, regarding her thoughtfully with his hollow eyes. And once again you'll get a notion that he means to do something big and generous. You'll know that his grass paddocks are over-run with horses of all descriptions, and your keen mind will run on the familiar forms of several young colts, any one of which would make an ideal sulky horse for a woman.

"A good sulky horse, my girl?" he'll echo in reflection — and you'll reckon your father-in-law is going to come good this time for sure — perhaps make a present of two of those horses, one to each of you. In fact, before he can speak the word you'll be quietly reckoning that to save questions being raised in the future it would be wise to get him to write out a receipt for them right on the spot; also you'll be wondering whether it would be wiser to put your registered brand on them both or wait till Josie applies for a brand of her own to put on hers . . . But when at last old Silas opens his mouth to speak he'll turn to you again and remark: "Well, horses are very cheap just now, Dick, and you oughtn't to have any trouble getting what you want at the sale-yards, on almost any Saturday."

Oh mighty! A sinking feeling will come over you again; but you'll feebly agree with him. Then recovering, you'll reckon the first thing you are going to do when you get back into harness is run into the sale-yards with a few quid in your pocket and see how horses are going. You'll be inclined to let the matter end there, but your father-in-law was always fond of talking about horses, and will wonder that you haven't got a few spare ones running on your farm, "for you never know when you want them", he'll add, as lightly as though acquiring horseflesh is as easy to you with limited means as gathering firewood . . . But when you start coughing instead of answering him, he'll gaze through the window at your yards and cow-sheds and ask: "How many cows are you milking?"

But here, Josie, like the splendid helpmate she promises to be, will come to your rescue again, with: "Dick's been milking ten up to now, Papa; but with me to help him from this on he'll be milking twenty."

"Huh!" old Silas will grunt, "that's not much of a change to get married for, girl. You could get plenty of milking at home when you were single."

"But we'll be milking for ourselves now, Papa", Josie'll laugh, while you'll add a few confirmatory nods and grins.

"Yes — yes; quite so — quite so", from old Silas. Then remembering his time is short; that he only snatched an hour to drive over to see how you were both getting along, and further expressing his gladness at finding you both so well and happy, and in want of nothing, he'll take his departure. But before stepping into the sulky he'll consign Josie again to your care, telling you that "she's in your hands now, and take care of her — take care of her".

Then standing together watching him rolling away down the road you'll turn to Josie, and drawing her to you in the altitude of emotion, your cheek to hers, you'll croon in her ear: "And I am takin' care of you, Josie, ain't I?"

*   *   *

The honeymoon will be fading out now, and you'll be back in harness again. But you're beginning to find you're a different man. Life has become more serious to you; you're an independent person, in your own eyes, and in the eyes of Josie's friends who come to see her. You'll realise how quickly a young wife can raise her husband in the esteem of others, and how he can convince himself that it's all due to his own merits!

So the months go by. You've reaped a good harvest and waved your first sheaf. You're finding it's almost as cheap for two to live as it is for one. Yet, as much as you love each other, and pull evenly together, the same constant, self-contained unvarying society somehow palls. There is something lacking. You don't quite understand what it is . . . Not being an artist, or alleged painter of realism your mind won't dwell on creative effort, or the imitating of nature as a solution. Still, you'll be making the most you can of everything, and doing your best to make life pleasant and prosperous and easy for Josie. She'll be doing her best, too, to help and uplift you – cooking, making, mending, saving and comforting. And she'll become engaged in sewing and cutting out a new sort of clothes and things from patterns lent her by Mrs. Eady and Mrs. Boody on the next homesteads . . . This will seem to be special work she has undertaken which you won't be informed about, until one day she'll startle you by complaining of not being well, and telling you to go at once for her friend, Mrs. Browne. Cripes! You'll nearly be taken ill, too! You'll turn pale. Then you'll think of the horse and sulky, you haven't a car yet, and half bewildered you'll run for the winkers. All the poetry will go out of married life for you as you leave Josie alone and rush up the paddock to catch Snip. As bad luck will have it, there's not an animal within call of the yard – they are all up on the ridge. And just when you locate Snip, after running, blundering and puffing till you're fit to drop, it will suddenly dawn on you that he won't let anyone but Josie, herself, catch him in the paddock. Holy! What are you going to do? And being one of the cunning ones, he won't submit to being yarded on foot! So you'll approach him downheartedly, coaxing, grovelling, crawling to him. But all your efforts will be useless, for he'll calmly look at you, and cocking his tail in disrespect will trot off out of reach. An idea will come to you. You'll run back to the house to put on a dress and hat of Josie's and return to Snip. You've put them on and have come out of the house again, when — salvation! the voice of your father-in-law greets you! You'll stop, surprised. So will he. "What in God's name, man, are you dressed up like that for?" — he will ask — "Are you demented?" But when you gasp out everything to him, he'll become more alarmed and concerned than you.

"For God's sake, here, man —" he will choke, alighting to the ground — "get into my sulky, and go for your life — go for your life! ... You had a right to have your own horse harnessed and ready every night, and every day!"

Next minute you'll be flogging your way along the wide lane at breakneck pace to Mrs. Browne's place, while old Silas will hobble back home on foot, grunting and mumbling grievously at every turn: " 'Twas no place for a man to find himself at such a time — at such a time! ... Young fools ... they will get married ... will get married."

Chapter 20

You'll have a son an' heir, now, as big Mrs. Browne, the nurse, will call your first-born, and a feeling different to anything you ever experienced before will tingle through you — a feeling of pride of parenthood and family responsibility. A determination, too, to work your hardest and make money, and become successful, and provide Josie with a servant and to give the youngster a good education, and make a doctor, or a lawyer, or a Governor of him, and a credit to his country, will take possession of you.

And you'll be glad when the time comes for big Mrs. Browne to roll up her paraphernalia and depart for her home as you were to land her whole and safe at the door of yours a month or so before, after propelling and bumping her in furious fashion over infamous roads in old Silas' sulky that he loaned you. For you'll be able to talk freely to Josie again, and be at liberty to admire and fondle the baby in your own way and say the little things you want to say of it, and to it, and be your real self once more.

And as you drop to your knees in prayerful attitude on the floor to get a close-up of the little, red, drowsy thing that's just dined like a leech, and is resting on its back in its mother's lap she'll smile upon it, and pucking its cheeks tenderly will croon *"Ba-by, ba-by"*; then suddenly she'll call on you to look at it "smiling". Though you're gazing studiously at the helpless brat, even more studiously than you would at a new calf, you won't be sure that you noticed the smile.

"Oh, yes, Dick, it did —" Josie, puckering the pudgy cheeks

some more with fingers and thumb, will proudly affirm:
"There! there, now, again — look, *look* — oh look, Dick!"

"Oh, yes, I saw that time", you'll pleasantly lie, but not
being endowed with the senses of a young mother you can be
forgiven for your blindness and discretion.

But when Josie in her flights of rapture implores you to
"give the dear little darling a kiss", a quivering at the back of
your neck, and feeling of uncertainty as you spread out your
hairy arms to grope for support as you lower your big head will
make you think you're taking a risk of colliding with it and
committing murder! All the same, it will be a new and curious
experience for you, kissing your son an' heir — different in
every way to kissing Josie, herself, for the first time, or for the
fifty-first time. It will seem like starting out to manufacture an
affection, and you won't thrill over it any more than if you
had applied your lips to a protoplasm or blanc-mange.

Next moment, though, as Josie's joy of motherhood
increases, and she adjures you to "kiss the dear little darling
again, Richard, kiss its little legs, they're so sweet", giving the
stumpy, red limbs which she'll expose purposely, a running fire
of them, herself, you'll feel like a criminal that's recalled to
receive a further sentence. When you were courting and made
up your mind to ask her to be your wife, and she agreed to
everything, you certainly didn't foresee that all this sort of
stuff was to be included in the arrangement.

Still, you'll be conscious that, after all, it's only one of the
many duties never numerated — one that comes only with
fatherhood — the finishing touch to man's recreative skill. And
so you'll console yourself in the knowledge that now you're a
family man you must take things as they come, the unpleasant
with the pleasant, and you'll grin through and put up with
them.

"No, no, not 'little Dickie' " — Josie will presently protest.
" 'Richard' we must always call him, dear, not a nick-name like
lots do." Then, bending over the son an' heir, "Oh, you
darling", and she'll push one of its stubby feet into her mouth,
as if it was a lump of toffee.

Starting to share Josie's passion for the bairn your dull eyes
will sparkle, as you wonder "how long it will be before he's

running about and following me down th' paddock?"

"But we mustn't let the little dear walk too soon, Richard", Josie will safeguard, covering the infant's nakedness lest the wind gets at it. "Mrs. Browne says that's why a lot of babies — and she never saw a better-shaped baby than this little darling, Richard, and its the heaviest ever she's brought into the world — why a lot of them, Richard, grow up to be bandy-leg men. Their legs bend under them if they walk too soon, even when they are perfectly formed like this little dear's. And our little Richard —" kissing the youngster again — "musn't have bandy-legs. No, no, no, he mustn't, must he, ducky." And she'll kiss it with greater energy.

"I wonder what he'll really be like, Josie, when he's a *man?*" you'll enthuse, placing a hand lightly and proudly on the brat's head, the skull of which isn't unlike an egg with a soft shell — "looking at him now you would hardly imagine him ever being different, would you?"

"Oh, yes, Richard, *I* can — for he's going to be very tall and awful clever — I'm sure. Mrs. Browne said he has a wonderful forehead for a first baby, no other baby that ever she knew had one like it; and we'll send him to school every day, Richard, and you'll go with him the first day to put his name down and tell the master to take care of him, and see the other boys don't hit him, and perhaps I'll go with him, too, and we'll get him all the best books that he'll want to pass his scholarship to the Grammar — the Toowoomba Grammar, we'll send him to, Richard, it wouldn't be far to go to see him there, or for him to come home in vacation. They marry well who go to the Toowoomba Grammar, so will Richard —" here she'll laugh.

"I'll pick a good pony for him to ride, too," you'll put in — "and make a great horseman of him as well as a scholar. The foal that Bluebell has now will be the one for him — it's going to be a grey, and it'll be at its best as a five-year-old, just when this little nipper —"

"Oh, you mustn't start calling our darling a 'nipper', Richard, or you'll never get out of the way of it!" Josie will interrupt — "always say *Richard.*"

"Richard," you'll repeat — "but hoakey" — you'll excitedly diverge, "did I tell you before, Josie, that they were both born on the same day — he, and Bluebell's foal?"

"No, Richard; were they?"

"They were, and at the same hour."

"Oh, poor little Bluebell! You never told me, and on the same day!"

"The same hour!" you'll gush.

"Then I hope you have been kind to her, Richard", she'll pause to reflect.

"She's doing well, Josie — they both are", you'll assure her. "She's been running on the range, where there's plenty of good grass and water; and if you saw the foal you'd be surprised. A beauty, and races about the ridges out there like a young kangaroo. Gee! I wish this little coney here —" placing your hand lightly again on your offspring's skull — "could race like it." Then removing your hand you'll feel among the folds of its long white robe for a touch of its little red feet.

"But I don't think we'll let Richard have much to do with horses, Richard, so many accidents happen; and look at all the boys, and men also, who have been killed off them! Oh, no, you precious little darling" — showering a fresh consignment of kisses on the son an' heir — "it would never do to let *you* take any risks at all, never! never! never!"

"Well, I don't suppose he'll ever do much milking?" you'll meditate mercenarily.

"Milking?" Josie'll almost choke, "*milking!* What everyone can do! Such a beautiful darling in a dirty old milking yard, among a lot of dirty old cows? Oh, Richard, how could you think of it?"

"I wasn't thinking of it altogether, Josie —" you'll shuffle clumsily, "and I wouldn't have let you help me in the yard, if I could've avoided it; hanged if I would."

"It doesn't matter about me, Richard —" Josie'll assure you bravely, "it's my duty to be where you are. But this little duck" — more kisses — "was given to us for something better than milking. Weren't you, little blue eyes?" and Josie will play with the dimpled cheeks again.

"Well, now what do you reckon he'll be, Josie," you'll ask — "a, what'll I say — *clergyman?*"

"Oh, well," she'll hesitate, "it would be wonderful, of

course, for our Richard to be a clergyman, and for us, too, but
—"

You'll grin meaningly, and wait. "But I'd sooner see the
little duck something different so as he'll have the money and
the position and the will and all that, Richard, to help the poor
clergymen themselves to do what's right, and be a really great
man, which he is going to be Richard."

"To be a shepherd of the shepherds, you mean, Josie?"
you'll grin.

"Well, yes, Richard", she'll agree, uncovering the brat's lower
extremities again and planting fresh kisses on the soles of its
feet, then: "Look, look at the little dear smiling again,
Richard!" And when you'll have looked and nodded obligingly
she'll conclude: "for, of course, we want him to be good as
well as clever; don't we, my beautiful, my precious?"

"But I think a lawyer would be the best to make of him,
Josie," you'll finally decide, rising to your feet from the hard
boards and bending over them both with a wise air, and your
hands behind your back — "*that's* what we'll make him."

"Oh, I think so, too, Richard," Josie'll agree, "but it's a pity
they are so common."

"How grand it'll be to see him standing there in the court,"
you'll enthuse, "a black silk gown hanging round him and a
white curly wig on his head, addressing the old judge and a
jury, perhaps defending *me* in a row like the one I had with
Tim Buckley over that block of land on the range —"

"And winning the case for you, too, Richard — for his
father," Josie'll burst out — "how splendid! It will be lovely!
And I'm sure he will, too."

"Yes, Josie," you'll warm up — "and I can see him, and hear
him addressing them now" — stretching out one of your arms
and placing a foot on the end of the sofa in vain barristerial
pose — "Subject to your Honour's direction on the law relating
to lands leased by the Crown tenants, gentlemen of the jury, I
say, and as sensible men you must agree with me, that the
defendant when he agreed to sublease this land to my client he
knowingly and wilfully —"

Here Josie will interrupt you:

"Richard! Richard!" — she'll cry — "look at baby! — you've

made it sick! He's vom-vomiting! Run for Mrs. Browne, Richard
— *run*!"

But when you've recovered from the fright, you'll see little
Richard, as you had often, as a boy, seen the baby in your own
family — lying on his back, mildly puling. But your mother,
who was hardened, took it calmly. Not being hardened, however, you won't feel as unconcerned over the puling Richard as
your mother would. And in spite of yourself, you'll share
Josie's fears; you'll show it by waving your arms and stamping
your heavy feet and exclaiming: "Oh! poor little bloke! Turn
him over, Josie — *quick!* Turn him 'fore it chokes him!"

Then you'll smile again, and go to work for little Richard,
and be a happy man ever after.

THE END